# The Mammoth
# LOCKED-ROOM MYSTERIES
# AND IMPOSSIBLE CRIMES

The Mammoth Book of

# LOCKED-ROOM MYSTERIES AND IMPOSSIBLE CRIMES

Edited by Mike Ashley

ROBINSON
London

Constable Publishers
3 The Lanchesters
162 Fulham Palace Road
London W6 9ER
www.constablerobinson.com

First published in the UK by Robinson,
an imprint of Constable & Robinson Ltd 2000

Reprinted 2000

A copy of the British Library Cataloguing in
Publication data is available from the British Library

ISBN 1–84119–129–9

Printed and bound in the EU

# CONTENTS

# FOREWORD

*David Renwick*

Life for Alvy Singer in *Annie Hall* can be divided into two categories, the horrible and the miserable. I would add a third: the unbearably tedious. Reality, when it's not simply hideous or depressing, tends to be largely unremarkable – or in other words, real. And if, like Sherlock Holmes and me, you "abhor the dull routine of existence", then books and television shows whose mission is accurately to reflect the world around us will leave you feeling either suicidal or bored witless.

Of course there is a place in detective fiction for the gritty social document, but it's not a place I'd want to go to for a holiday. Personally I like my dramas to be a little improbable and my comedies a little absurd. I like, I suppose, to be taken to the edge: to teeter on the brink of plausibility, where logic lives dangerously yet somehow still manages to survive. For me this is where storytelling becomes exciting: when the writer is prepared to take risks; to bend the limits of invention. And if for Holmes there was respite from the routine in the form of a seven-per-cent solution perhaps the rest of us can at least find solace in a good locked-room mystery.

Although the impossible crime genre has long been well respected in the world of publishing few people in recent times have been so foolish as to try and make it work on television. This is because we are all so highly sophisticated now that heaven forbid a detective series should be *fun*. But in the certain knowledge that *Jonathan Creek* would be branded "preposterous" and "far-fetched" I was cheerfully prepared to have a go, with the quiet conviction that people, not plots, are the key to an audience's acceptance. Providing the characters are real and respond truthfully to whatever you throw at them it is my view that you can take as many liberties with the storylines as you like. (Thus Victor Meldrew's "I don't believe it" in *One Foot in the Grave* is an honest reflection of our own incredulity at the bizarre twists of fate to which he is so often subjected.) Then, as Gideon Fell declares in John Dickson Carr's *The Three Coffins*, "the whole test is, *can* the thing be done? If so, the question of whether it *would* be done does not enter into it." Or as Creek himself points out in *Jack in the Box*, "We mustn't confuse what's impossible with what's implausible. Most of the stuff I cook up for a living relies upon systems that are highly implausible. That's what makes it so difficult to solve. No one ever thinks you'd go to that much trouble to fool your audience."

Of course the problem, as Carr also observed, is that when the effect of a particular crime is magical we expect the cause to be magical also. And when the explanation for our baffling scenario turns out – as it must – to be more prosaic than the events leading up to it we may emerge from the experience feeling cheated. Even the most famous detective story ever written cannot escape this charge: did anyone ever learn that the Hound of the Baskervilles was "bought in London from Ross and Mangles, the dealers in Fulham Road" without a sense of anti-climax? Yet the novel is rightly celebrated because it performs what I believe to be the essential task of any creative work: it pushes the buttons. Within its pages I can think of at least half a dozen classic moments that never fail to send a thrill down the spine; moments that consume and intrigue, that defy you to put the book down. At its very least the "supernatural" mystery has a magnetic power over and above the conventional detective story: when someone appears to have violated the laws of nature we cannot but yearn to know how it was done. At its best it delivers a chillingly clever solution that reverses our whole perspective on events and sends us away with a warm and satisfying glow. When this happens – Carter Dickson's *The Judas Window*, Jacques Futrelle's *The Problem of Cell 13*, Melville Davisson Post's *The Doomdorf Mystery* – then you have a rare treat indeed.

All of which is to argue that a fascination for the impossible crime represents, in all of us, no more or less than a primal thirst for escapism. Like the spectral assailant who has miraculously vanished from the scene of the crime it's comforting occasionally to give reality the slip and retreat into the more fantastical world of our imagination.

# Introduction
# HEY, PRESTO!

*Mike Ashley*

The impossible-crime story is like a good trick. In fact it has to be better than a good trick. Not only must the puzzle fascinate and mystify, but the solution must be just as surprising, yet believable. How often have you had a magician's trick explained and then felt deflated? It almost feels a cheat. Well, these stories had to avoid that. When you read the solution to the crime, you should be able to say, "That was clever. I'd never have thought of that."

That's what I hope we've done in this book. I've endeavoured to bring together a collection of stories that seem utterly baffling and where the solution is equally amazing. Not an easy trick.

Yet despite the impossible crime being such a difficult story to write, it remains at the core of the mystery story. These stories are as much "howdunits" as "whodunits". They're puzzles. They challenge the reader to try and solve the method before the author reveals all.

The whole point about an impossible crime is that when first discovered it must seem as if there was no possible way that the crime could have been committed. The most common approach is the locked-room mystery. In these the victim is found murdered in a room locked from the inside. He's usually alone, and there is no other way into or out of the room. To make it even more fun he may have been shot or stabbed, but there is no murder weapon. There are endless variations on the theme. Other impossible scenarios are bodies found in the snow but with no other footprints beyond his own; property stolen from within a locked safe or room under constant watch; people or things disappearing in full view of an audience. The Golden Rule is that the solution to these crimes must be rational – there should be nothing supernatural or beyond current knowledge and understanding.

You'll have seen a number of these ideas in David Renwick's excellent *Jonathan Creek* television series, and I'm delighted that Mr Renwick has written a special foreword for this book.

You'll find all these ideas and more in this anthology. What I looked for was originality, ingenuity, and a story that did not disappoint. I hope it lives up to both my and your expectations.

For those interested in discovering more about locked-room mysteries and impossible crimes I have provided a capsuled history as an Afterword.

Now, prepare to be baffled.

# WAITING FOR GODSTOW

_Martin Edwards_

_Martin Edwards (b.1955) is a practising solicitor and uses this background for his series of novels featuring Liverpool solicitor Harry Devlin. The series began with_ All the Lonely People _(1991) in which Devlin's wife is found murdered and he becomes the prime suspect. There has been roughly a book a year since then. The following story does not feature Harry Devlin but a new detective, Paul Godstow, who doesn't even realize he has an impossible crime on his hands._

Claire Doherty practised her grief-stricken expression in the mirror. Quivering lip, excellent. Lowered lashes, very suitable. All that she needed to do now was to make sure she kept the glint of triumph out of her eyes and everything would be fine.

She glanced at the living room clock for the thousandth time. Time passed slowly when you were waiting for bad news. The call could not come soon enough, that call which would bring the message that her husband was dead. Then she would have to prepare herself for her new role as a heartbroken widow. It would be a challenge, but she was determined to meet it head on. More than that, she would positively relish playing the part.

If only she didn't have to rely on Zack doing what he had to do. Zack was gorgeous and he did things for her that previously she had only read about in magazines, while having her hair done. But he was young and careless and there was so much that could yet go wrong. No wonder that she kept checking the clock, shaking her watch to see if it had stopped when it seemed that time was standing still. She readily admitted to friends that patience wasn't one of her virtues. Besides, she would add, vices are so much more interesting anyway. Above all, she liked to be in control, hated being dependent on others. It was hard being reduced to counting the minutes until freedom finally came her way.

The phone trilled and she snatched up the receiver. "Yes?" she demanded breathlessly.

"Is that Mrs Doherty?" The voice belonged to a woman. Late twenties, at a guess. She sounded anxious.

"Yes, what is it?" If it was a wrong number, she would scream.

"I'm sorry to bother you, really I am."

"No problem." It was all she could do not to hiss: get off the line, don't you realize I'm waiting for someone to tell me my husband is dead?

"My name is Bailey. Jennifer Bailey from Bradford."

Oh, for God's sake. Karl's latest floosie. Suppressing the urge to give the woman a mouthful, Claire said coldly, "Can I help you?"

"It's just that your husband left a few minutes ago. I'm afraid I kept him longer than expected. He was rather concerned, because he said he would be late home and his mobile didn't seem to be working. So I offered to give you a ring to let you know he is on his way. He said he should be with you in about an hour-and-a-half if the road was clear. You live on the far side of Manchester, I gather?"

"That's right." Claire thought for a moment. "Thank you. It's good of you to let me know."

"My pleasure," Jennifer Bailey said.

She said it as though she meant it. Indeed, she sounded so timid that it was hard to believe that she had probably spent the last couple of hours *in flagrante* with Karl. Perhaps he'd tired of the bimbos and was now taking an interest in the submissive type. Someone as different from herself, Claire thought grimly after she put down the phone, as he could manage to find.

Would the delay have caused a problem? Something else for her to worry about. Zack had refused to tell her precisely how and when he proposed to do what was necessary. He said it was better that way. Claire knew he could never resist a melodramatic flourish. She blamed it on all the videos he watched. It amused her, though, all the same. She'd gathered that he would be keeping his eye on Jennifer Bailey's house, with a view to dealing with Karl when he emerged. So he would have had to wait for a while. Surely that wouldn't have been too much of a challenge. She was having to wait. Was it so much to ask that her lover should also have to bide his time?

The phone rang again. Claire made an effort not to sound too wound-up. "Yes?"

"It's done." Zack sounded pleased with himself, relaxed. He liked to come across as cool, as comfortable with violence as a character from a Tarantino movie. "No worries."

"Wonderful," she said. The tension went out of her; she felt giddy with the sense of release.

"I know I am," he said roguishly.

"How . . .?"

"Hit and run. Stolen Fiesta. No witnesses."

"You're sure about that?"

"Bradford's pretty quiet at night, you know."

"And he's definitely . . .?"

"Believe me," he said with a snigger. "I reversed back the way I'd come, just to make sure. The job's a good 'un."

How could she ever have doubted him? After saying goodbye, she hugged herself with delight. He might only be a boy, but he'd kept his word. He'd promised to free her and that was exactly what he had done. She uttered a silent prayer of thanks that she'd agreed to let him ring her, to prevent the suspense becoming unbearable. He'd said he would nick a mobile from somewhere and call her on it before throwing it away. She'd worried that the call might be traced, but he said the police would never check and, even if they did, so what? She had an alibi and besides, he meant to make sure Karl's death looked like an accident. She should stop fretting and leave it all to him.

She'd gambled on him and her faith had been repaid. She could hardly believe it. Part of her wanted to crack open a bottle of champagne. Never mind waiting for it to be safe for Zack to come here and share in the celebrations. But it wasn't safe. There was no telling when the police might turn up at her door with the tidings of Karl's demise. She made do with a cup of tea. She would need to have all her wits about her, so that no-one would ever suspect there might be more to the death than met the eye.

Poor Karl. She wasn't so heartless as to deny him a thought. At least it had been a quick end. Besides, he didn't have too many grounds for complaint. He had died happy. Jennifer Bailey didn't give the impression of being a ball of fire, but perhaps she'd simply been daunted by the need to speak to her lover's wife on the phone. She'd certainly kept him occupied for most of the evening.

She smiled indulgently, remembering how Karl had down-played his trip to see Jennifer. "I really tried every trick in the book," he'd said. Protesting rather too much, she had thought. "I was desperate to cancel the appointment. I mean, you know what it's like. A one-legger is hopeless, a complete waste of time."

Karl was a salesman. It didn't matter much to him what he sold. Kitchens, carpets, computers. He was good at it. Persuasive. No wonder he had charmed her into marrying him. He could talk for England. Trouble was, he wasn't so hot when it came to performance. But that never seemed to bother him. Currently he was working for a firm that specialized in bespoke loft conversions. The commission was good, provided you made the sale – and that was the rub. No one with any nous ever wanted to bother with a one-legger. The object of a home sales visit was to get the punters to sign up on the dotted line. But people would do anything to avoid making a commitment to buy. When you were dealing with a married couple, it was vital to have them both there, listening to the pitch. If you had to contend with a one-legger, it was too easy for the decision to be dependent on the okay of the absent spouse. If that happened, then nine times out of ten, the sale would never be made. It was all about human nature, as Karl often said. He fancied himself as an amateur psychologist. In fact, Claire thought, he fancied himself, full stop. That was true of Zack too, of course. But with rather more reason.

"She's married, then, this Mrs Bailey?" Claire had asked, a picture of innocence.

"Oh yeah. Husband's away a lot, she says."

*I bet*, Claire thought. "What sort of age is she?"

Karl pursed his lips, considering. "Middle-aged, I'd say. yeah, that's it. Fat, fair and forty."

*Lying bastard.* The woman on the phone had been much younger than that. Oh well. It didn't matter now. Zack had done the necessary. Now all she had to think about was whether she still looked good in black. It was a young colour, she thought, and you needed the figure to carry it off. But she had a few years left in her yet, that was for sure. And with the benefit of the pay-out on Karl's life insurance, she meant to make the most of them.

Suppose it didn't work out with Zack. She dipped into a box of After Eights and told herself she had to be realistic. He was a hunk, and he'd carried out his task more efficiently than she had dared hope, but he wasn't necessarily the ideal lifetime soulmate. No-one so keen on motorbikes and football could be. Not to worry. She could play the field, look around for someone handsome who could help her to get over her tragic loss.

The doorbell sounded. Suddenly her mouth was dry, her stomach churning. This was the test, the moment when she would need to call up all the skills from her days in amateur theatre. She'd tended to be typecast as a dumb blonde, but now she must be shattered by bereavement. She took a deep breath.

The doorbell rang again, long and loud. She checked the mirror. Eyebrows raised, lips slightly parted. Understandable puzzlement at such a late call. A faint touch of apprehension. Perfect.

She remembered to keep the door on the chain. An important detail. These things mattered. The police must not think that she had been expecting them to turn up. In fact, they had moved quickly. Impressive efficiency. She had not thought they would be here so soon.

The door opened and she saw her husband Karl on the step. He was breathing heavily. Yes, despite Zack's claim to have killed him, he was definitely still breathing.

Five minutes later, she was telling herself that it was a good thing that Karl was so obviously – and uncharacteristically – flustered. Flustered and, more typically, self-centred, concerned only with himself. He had not noticed how his arrival had shocked her.

"Here you are." Her hands were trembling as she passed him the tumbler of whisky he had asked for. She poured one for herself. Both of them needed to calm down.

"Thanks, darling." He swallowed the drink in a gulp. "Christ, I needed that."

"Uh-huh." She wasn't going to panic, whatever the tempta-tion. Faced with a husband who had died and achieved resurrec-tion within the space of half-an-hour, the best course was to say as little as possible. He was obviously panic-stricken. And he needed her help. These days he only called her darling when he wanted something.

"Listen," he said hoarsely. His tie was at half mast and his hair, normally immaculate, was a tousled mess. "I have – a bit of a problem."

"What sort of problem?"

"I'm not going to bullshit you," he said, in precisely the sincere tone he adopted when lying to her about his trysts with clients or young girls at work. "I'm in a spot of bother. If any questions are asked, I need you to say that I spent the evening here."

"What?" She was baffled. "Who will be asking questions? Why do you need me to lie for you?"

He caught her wrist, and looked into her eyes, treating her to his soulful expression. "Darling, I'm asking you to trust me."

"But why? I mean, none of this makes sense."

"It – it's not something I can talk about right now. Okay?"

*No*, she wanted to say, *it's bloody well not okay*. But she chose her words with care and spoke more gently than she might have done. "It's just that, if I don't have a clue what has happened, I might just put my foot in it unintentionally. If it's trust we're talking about, don't you think you should trust me enough to tell me what's going on?"

He buried his head in his hands. Claire had never seen him in such a state. If she didn't despise him so much, if she didn't loathe him for not being dead when he was supposed to be, she might almost have felt sorry for him.

"I can't!" It was almost a wail.

"You must," she said, a touch of steel entering her voice.

"But . . ."

She folded her arms. "It's up to you."

He looked up at her. Distressed he might be, but Claire recognized the familiar glint of calculation in his eyes. After a few moments he came to a decision.

"I don't want to say much about it," he said. "But I suppose I do owe you some sort of explanation."

"Yes, you do."

He blinked hard. "It's like this. I had a row with this girl – you know, it's Lynette, who used to work in our office. We were going to go for a drink at this pub in Stockport. Oh, I know it sounds bad, especially after I swore that our little – flirtation – was a thing of the past. But I can explain. Our meeting up was innocent enough, but something happened. There was – an accident. She hit her head. When I tried to bring her round, I realized she was dead."

Claire stared at him, unable to comprehend what he was saying. "You killed Lynette?"

"Oh, don't say it like that. We were in this alleyway near the pub and we started arguing. I gave her a push – a tap, really. She fell over and smashed her head on a jagged stone, simple as that. It was all so sudden. She must have had a thin skull or something. Oh God, I didn't mean this to happen."

"In Stockport, you said? When was this?"

He shrugged, as if irritated by the irrelevance of the question. "Does it matter? Twenty minutes ago, I guess. If that. I broke every speed limit in the book on my way back over here."

"But – your meeting with Jennifer Bailey . . ."

He waved his hand dismissively. "Forget about it. The police mustn't hear about it. I was here at home with you. Watching the box all evening. Okay?"

"I don't understand," she said and it was no more than the truth.

"Oh God," he said again. Tears were trickling down his cheeks. "It just happened. I can't explain any better than that. Not right now."

But he hadn't given any sort of an explanation, so far as Claire was concerned. It wasn't so much the mystery of why he had killed that silly little girl Lynette. Last year's fling had evidently started up again, even though he'd promised he would never see her again after she left the company. No, what Claire could not get her head around was the sheer impossibility of it. How had her husband managed to murder someone in nearby Stockport, when according to Jennifer Bailey he was at one and the same time in Bradford on the other side of the Pennines, and Zack was convinced he'd been run over by a stolen Fiesta?

She wasn't able to contact Zack until the middle of the next morning. Karl didn't work nine-to-five hours and he didn't have any calls to make first thing. But after a night of tossing and turning, he decided to visit the office and file his weekly report. He had managed to regain a semblance of composure and he thought it would be a good idea to be seen to act normally.

On his way out, he kissed her for perhaps the first time in a month. "I just wanted to say – thanks. You've been fantastic. I won't forget that."

Claire gave him a weak smile. It seemed the safest response.

"And you'll remember, won't you? If the police come, we were together all night. You never let me out of your sight for more than a couple of minutes."

"But how do you expect to get away with it?" she asked. "You were with Lynette. Won't someone have seen you?"

He shook his head. "We never made it to the pub. The streets were dead quiet. We both arrived in separate cars. There's nothing to link me with that place. No-one saw us, I'm sure of it."

"I still don't follow," she said. Already she regretted agreeing to help him out. He'd caught her at a bad time the previous night, when she was so shocked by his reappearance that he could have talked her into anything. "I mean, what about Jennifer Bailey? Why not get her to do your dirty work for you?"

His expression was one of genuine horror. "She was a customer. I told you. How could I ask her to give me an alibi? You don't think we were having an affair, do you?"

"Well, I . . ."

"You did! Oh, Claire." He took her hand in his. A romantic gesture; no doubt he employed it with all his conquests. "Listen to me. I realize things haven't been great between us for a while. But we can try again, can't we? I've come to my senses, honestly. You're a wife in a million, I see that now. Will you give me another chance?"

She withdrew her hand. "You're saying you haven't got a thing going with Jennifer Bailey?"

"I told you. She's a middle-aged frump. Last night, I was on my way over to Bradford and I suddenly decided it was a complete waste of time. You know what one-leggers are like. I don't know what got into my head, but I decided to give Lynette a ring. See how she was getting on, for old times' sake, that's all. There was nothing in it. Zilch. She suggested meeting for a quick drink. But when we met, she made it clear she wanted us to get together again. I told her there was nothing doing, that I wanted to make a go of things with you. She became angry, hysterical. I didn't know how to deal with it. She lunged at me and – and that's when I pushed her."

His voice was breaking. He had missed his true vocation, she thought. He was better at acting than she was; he might have made a fortune on the stage. Because he wasn't telling her the truth, of that she was sure. His story didn't begin to explain why his client, the frump, the one-legger, had called her to say that he was on his way home when he was out pubbing with his floosie. She thought about confronting him, telling him about the message from Jennifer Bailey, but decided against it. He obviously knew nothing about the call. She would keep that morsel of information to herself until she had more of a clue as to what he had really been up to.

As she made herself a snack lunch, Claire asked herself if it was possible that the whole story about killing Lynette was some sort of elaborate charade. She wouldn't put it past him. Like most serial adulterers, Karl possessed a vivid imagination and a gift for telling fairy stories that the Brothers Grimm might have envied. Suppose he planned to resume his affair with the girl. The prospect of divorce held no appeal for him, she was well aware of that. Too expensive. Perhaps he had decided to concoct this extraordinary story of killing the girl by accident so that Claire would think she had him in her power and relax. If she thought Lynette was dead, she wouldn't suspect him of continuing to sleep with her, would she?

No. It was too bizarre. Ridiculous, even by Karl's standards of excessively ingenious subterfuge. There had to be some other explanation. She would need to undertake a bit of detective work. But first, she must find out what had gone wrong at Zack's end. She had tried to phone him as soon as Karl had stepped out of the door, but there was no answer on his mobile. She pressed redial, but as the number began to ring, she heard footsteps coming up the path to the front door. Hurrying into the dining room, she saw through the window that a lean young man was standing on the step, pressing the bell. Quickly, she cancelled her call. Zack would have to wait a few minutes.

Her immediate impression when she answered the door was that the young man was almost as gorgeous as Zack. He didn't have the same dark and dangerous eyes, or the muscular shoulders and chest. But he was smart to the point of elegance and his neatly scrubbed face was boyish and appealing. Very nice. Wholesome, you might say. It made a change.

"Mrs Doherty?"

She stared at him with only the slightest nod.

"My name's Godstow. Sergeant Paul Godstow. I'm with the police." He showed her his i.d. "May I come in?"

"Certainly, sergeant." When in doubt, ooze charm. She treated him to a brilliant smile which she hoped would disguise her nervousness. What now? "Can I offer you a drink?"

"Thanks, but no." He followed her into the living room. "You see, Mrs Doherty, it's like this. I just need to ask you one or two questions about last night."

He was checking up on Karl. They had already got wind of her husband's past relationship with Lynette. She swallowed and launched into the tale that she had agreed with her husband. He'd been with her since coming home from a call at half past five. They had eaten together, watched a little television, discussed the need to redecorate the hall and first floor landing. She'd ironed a couple of shirts, he'd done a bit of tidying in the loft. They had retired to bed at about eleven o'clock to sleep, she strongly implied, the sleep of the just.

The policeman frowned. "So you were together all the time?"

"That's right, sergeant." She smiled again. He was dishy, there was no denying it. "Not a very interesting evening, but that's married life for you. The excitement doesn't last."

He looked straight at her. "Depends on who you're married to, I suppose."

"That's true," she murmured. "Will – will that be all?"

"For the moment, Mrs Doherty. It's just possible I may need to come back to ask you one or two more questions."

"Any time, any time at all," she breathed and was secretly entertained when his face turned beetroot red. "Actually, I was preparing lunch when you arrived. Nothing special, just a salad. I don't suppose you'd care to join me?"

"Thanks, but no," he said. "There's a lot to do in connection with the enquiry."

"Oh, well, another time perhaps."

He handed her a card. "This is my number. If anything springs to mind, I'd be glad to hear from you."

"Sorry I haven't been able to help. Perhaps I ought to return the compliment anyway." She found a slip of paper and wrote the number of the house and her own mobile in her flamboyant script. "Don't hesitate to call me."

He considered her carefully. "Thanks, Mrs Doherty."

"Please call me Claire."

"Thanks, Claire. I'm sure we'll talk again."

"Zack? God, I've been trying to get hold of you all day. What went wrong?"

"Nothing," he replied. His voice sounded dreamy, as though he were living out a fantasy. "I went out for a ride on my Harley, that's all. And I felt free as a bird. It's amazing, you know, darling? You can snuff out a life just like that" – she heard him click his fingers – "and guess what? You carry on, same as before. You haven't changed. You're still you. You've murdered someone, but it's not the end of the world. Not for you, at any rate."

"Not for your victim, either," she said grimly.

"What do you mean?"

"Karl's still alive."

She could hear his intake of breath. "This your idea of a joke? Don't tell me you can't cope with what we've done. You told me you were sick of him. I did it for you."

"You didn't do it at all," she said curtly. Rapidly, she told him what had happened. The awestruck silence at the other end was eloquent. "Are you still there?" she demanded.

"I don't get it. There must be some mistake."

"Yes, and it looks like you made it."

"But it all went according to plan."

"Something went wrong with the plan, then."

"No, no, you don't understand."

"That's true, Zack. I don't bloody understand a thing. I suppose it's too much to hope that you can cast any light on this whole God-awful mess?"

"No, I . . ."

He was stammering, sounding like an overgrown schoolkid. He was so much less mature than the sergeant, she thought. Now there was a young man who was going places. Quiet, assured, effective. Everything that Zack was not.

"So tell me what really happened. Did you by any chance run over a bit of sacking that you mistook for my husband? An easy mistake to make in the dark, I suppose. A shop window dummy that seemed to have a bit of life? Or at least more of a brain than you?"

"No, honest. I did the business. He came out of the house, just like you said he would. I mean, I didn't see his face under the streetlight, so it wasn't easy to compare him to that photo you gave me. But he was a big bloke, muscular, walked with a bit of a swagger. It had to be your old man."

Claire groaned. Zack coughed and kept on talking. She thought he was trying to convince himself, rather than her, that he hadn't made the ultimate in fatal errors. "He'd been in there since before I turned up. I couldn't see where he'd parked. I thought it was probably out of sight so the people next door wouldn't twig that something was going on. I was following him down the road and then the pavement came to an end. I'd staked the spot out in the afternoon. Double-checked the address you gave me, the photograph of your old feller. Everything was planned down to the last detail."

"Go on," she said bleakly.

"He was forced to cross over. No choice. And that's when I did it. Put my foot down and went for him. Tossed him up in the air like a pancake and then, when he hit the deck, reversed back over him just to make sure. I'm telling you, no-one could have survived that. I even saw the blood making a pool on the roadside before I drove away. Believe me, he was dead all right. The car was in a right state when I dumped it."

"You're sure about this?"

"I swear to you. On my mother's life."

"There's only one more question, then."

"What's that?" He sounded bewildered. He'd been expecting her undying gratitude and now it had all gone wrong. "Hurry up, there's someone at the door. They're leaning on the buzzer. What's your question?"

"Who exactly was it that you did kill?"

*That was it*, Claire said to herself as she pulled down the ladder that led up to the loft. Zack was finished, as far as she was concerned. She should have remembered her late father's favourite saying. If you want a job done properly, do it yourself. How could she ever have believed that he would do what she wanted without a slip-up? She blamed herself, even though it wasn't her habit. All her life, it seemed, she'd been seduced by men talking big. They always acted small. That nice sergeant would be different, she thought. He hadn't worn a wedding ring: she noticed these things. If only . . .

She reached up to switch on the loft light. It was a large loft, running the length of the house, but so dusty that it made her want to sneeze. Telling the sergeant that Karl had been up here tidying the previous night was probably the biggest lie of all. Her husband thought that life was too short for tidying and he never bothered with their attic. Taking a job with Slickloft had not made the slightest difference. His argument was that if he'd wanted a fourth bedroom he'd have bought a bigger house on day one. Besides, he said that nine out of ten loft conversions were only any use for midgets who liked walking down the middle of a room, and he was six feet three. The loft was, therefore, an admirable hiding place so far as Claire was concerned and she often made good use of it. Amongst the bits and pieces she kept here was the note she had made of Jennifer Bailey's name, address and telephone number: information she had needed for Zack's briefing and which she'd managed to copy surreptitiously from Karl's personal organizer.

In fact, there were two numbers. Home and work, presumably? The codes were different. She recognized one immediately; it was the code for Bradford, she had a cousin who lived there. Next to the other were the initials "AA" and a couple of exclamation marks. Karl had a tedious sense of humour and she could not imagine what had been in his mind. Alcoholics Anonymous? Automobile Association? Agony Aunt? Nothing seemed to make sense at the moment. However, she had more important things to worry about.

She hurried downstairs and dialled the Bradford number, having taken care to withhold her own. "Yes?" The woman sounded subdued, very different from the night before.

"Mrs Bailey? You may not remember, but you rang me last . . ."

"This isn't Mrs Bailey," the woman interrupted. Of course not: she was elderly by the sound of her, probably a pensioner. "My name's Dora Prince, I'm her next door neighbour. I'm sorry, but she's not able to come to the phone right now. I'm afraid she's still in shock. You know what's happened, do you?"

*I wish*, Claire thought. "No . . ."

"It's a terrible tragedy," the woman said, lowering her voice. "Her husband went out last night to pick up some fish and chips and he was run over as he was crossing the road. The driver didn't stop. The policewoman's here now. She hasn't even got round to asking me anything. She's too busy comforting Jennifer, of course. You can imagine."

Yes, Claire could imagine. "Oh dear," she said.

"Awful, isn't it? Such a lovely chap. And a dab hand at do-it-yourself, too. He'll never finish that pergola now, poor fellow. Shall I tell Jennifer you rang?"

"Oh, it's all right. Don't bother. We – we hardly know each other. I don't want to intrude."

As she put the phone down, Claire's heart was pounding. She had solved one mystery, only to be confronted with others. What on earth had possessed Jennifer Bailey to telephone her the previous night? Come to think of it, why had she lied about having seen Karl? And why had Karl said she was a one-legger when her husband – her late husband, thanks to bloody Zack, a real case of collateral damage, poor sod – had apparently been at home with her throughout the evening?

She sighed and looked for Jennifer Bailey's second number, the one which Karl had marked with the initials "AA". The code seemed familiar. Wasn't it Crewe? Curiouser and curiouser. Why would a woman who lived in Bradford have a work number in south Cheshire? Well, it was possible, but it seemed strange. She was seized by the urge to find out what "AA" stood for. She rang the number.

"Hello?" The woman who answered sounded familiar.

"Who is that?"

"Who's calling?" Definitely evasive.

The penny dropped. This was the woman who had rung the

previous evening. Jennifer Bailey. Or rather, someone purporting to be Jennifer Bailey.

"Is that AA?" Claire asked in a hopeful tone.

"Yes." The woman sounded less guarded. "How may I help you?"

"Well, I just wondered . . ."

"You're interested in our services?" The woman seemed to recognize Claire's hesitancy, and to regard it as natural enough.

Claire pondered. Was she calling some kind of brothel? She wouldn't put much past Karl. "Could you give me some details?"

"Of course." The woman became business-like. "It's very simple. The Alibi Agency's name speaks for itself. We provide excuses for people who need them. Most of our business comes by way of word-of-mouth recommendation, but you may have seen that feature article about us in *The Sun*. You want to be in one place when you're supposed to be in another? We can help. Our rates are very reasonable and . . ."

"That's all right, thanks," Claire said faintly. "I've changed my mind."

*Well, well, well.* She made herself a coffee after her evening meal and congratulated herself once again on solving the conundrum. Perhaps she had missed her way in life. She should have been a private detective. It was all so simple. Karl had never intended to visit Jennifer Bailey. She was a blind; he'd mentioned all that stuff about the one-legger simply to throw Claire off the track, lend a touch of verisimilitude to his tall story. He'd arranged to see Lynette and hired the Alibi Agency to impersonate his customer, so that Claire was none the wiser. He knew that their marriage, already on the rocks, could not survive if Claire found out that Lynette was still around. But he'd fallen out with Lynette – perhaps she had wanted him to get a divorce and move in with her and he'd fought shy of making the commitment. Something like that would be typical. Whatever. He'd lost his temper and she'd lost her balance and hit her head on something hard. End of Lynette. Claire smirked to herself. She'd always loathed Lynette.

It occurred to her that she might yet be able to kill two birds with one stone. Suppose she told the police that Karl had threatened her with violence so that she would back up his story? She might say that her conscience would not allow her to live a lie, that she'd decided Karl must pay for his crime. True, she was going to miss out on the life insurance, but she would at least be rid of her husband. And it would serve him right.

She rang the number that the nice sergeant had left with her and was quickly put through.

"This is Claire again. You remember our conversation?" she asked. Just the faintest seductive hint at this stage. Then see how he responded.

"I certainly do," he said. Was it her imagination or was there a faint leer in his voice? She hoped so.

"I won't beat about the bush. I lied to you about my husband. He was out last night, but he threatened what he would do to me if I didn't back him up."

"Ah."

"I hope you won't think too badly of me," she said in her meekest voice. "I felt as though I was under duress."

She told him the story, making no mention of the Alibi Agency. She didn't want to draw attention to the existence of the recently bereaved Mrs Bailey. The policeman listened intently, murmuring his agreement every now and then when she insisted that life with Karl was hellish and that her only wish now was to do the right thing. He was sympathetic, a very good listener.

"I thought," she said tentatively, "that you might like to come back here and take a statement from me. A detailed statement."

"Yes, I'd love to do that."

"You would?"

"Oh yes," he said softly. "And perhaps when we've finished talking about your husband . . ."

"Yes?" she breathed.

". . . I can introduce you to a couple of colleagues of mine from Bradford CID. They've just finished interviewing a young man called Zack Kennedy."

She swallowed. "Oh yes?"

"It's in connection with a death in their patch. A Mr Eric Bailey was killed in a hit and run incident last night. The vehicle was a Fiesta that was later dumped. What's interesting is that they found a photograph in the car. It had slipped between the driver's and passenger's seats. A picture of a man standing proudly next to a Slickloft van, apparently parked outside his own house. Right next to the street name, the name of the street where you live, actually. On the back of the photograph was your husband's name and a brief description. The handwriting is distinctive. As soon as it was shown to me, I recognized it from the note you gave me of your phone number." He paused. "All rather puzzling. Mind you, once it turned out that Mr Kennedy's fingerprints were on the photograph, things started to become clearer. He has a criminal record. Nothing big league, just a few burglaries and car thefts. Possibly you didn't know that?"

Claire made a noise that was half-way between a sigh and a sob.

"No? Ah, well. By the way, the Baileys' neighbour, Mrs Prince, saw the Fiesta yesterday afternoon. The driver was behaving suspiciously, and she gave a description which bears an uncanny resemblance to Mr Kennedy. He's been arrested. The charge will be murder, I guess, but his lack of competence is equally criminal, wouldn't you say? We can chat about it later. I'll be with you in a quarter of an hour."

Slowly, as if in a trance, Claire put the receiver back on the cradle. She couldn't help glancing at the clock. She'd always been impatient, always hated having to hang around. The next fifteen minutes would, she knew, be the longest of her life as she sat helplessly on the sofa and waited for Godstow.

# THE ODOUR OF SANCTITY

*Kate Ellis*

*Kate Ellis (b.1953), who was born in Liverpool but now hails from Cheshire, achieved literary success in 1990 by winning the North-West Playwrights' competition with her play "Clearing Out". More recently she is the author of the fascinating series of West Country crime novels featuring archaeologist Neil Watson and Sergeant Wesley Peterson. The books intriguingly forge connections between modern-day crimes and historical events. The series began with* The Merchant's House *(1998), followed by* The Armada Boy *(1999),* An Unhallowed Grave *(1999) and* The Funeral Boat *(2000). The following story takes Kate Ellis back to her first job as a teacher. "It was inspired by memories of school trips spent herding classes of unpredictable school children around places of historical interest." Well, they certainly inspired a most unusual mystery.*

The brakes hissed with relief as the coach drew up in the car park at the back of Bickby Hall, and Vicky Vine – known as "Miss" on weekdays – climbed out onto the concrete first, clutching a clipboard protectively to her ample chest. Only two girls had been sick on the coach and one boy had bumped his head on the luggage rack. Three casualties: that was good going at this stage.

Vicky did a swift head count as her class emerged from the coach under the disapproving eye of the small, balding car park attendant. All there, every one of them: chattering; pushing; slouching; strutting; blazers shiny and misshapen, ties askew. 8C . . . the flower of Bickby Comprehensive: Vicky looked at them and sighed. She had done the history trip to Bickby Hall so many times: year after year; class after class; the bright and the dull; those interested in history and those who found the Elizabethan mansion, perched incongruously on the edge of a run down housing estate, less appealing than a double maths lesson.

Some girls began to giggle as they spotted their guide. Most of the boys stared, open mouthed, at the apparition.

"Is that the ghost, miss?" one wit asked as the dark haired woman emerged from the Hall's massive oak door in full Elizabethan costume; a huge-skirted creation in faded brocade with big padded sleeves, topped by a limp, yellowed ruff. The woman seemed to glide across the car park towards them, and when she reached Vicky she gave her a nervous smile.

"Hello, Muriel," said Vicky, trying to sound cheerful. "8C today. They shouldn't be much trouble but we'd better search them on the way out. After that unfortunate incident with the penguin on the zoo trip last year, I'm not taking any chances." She lowered her voice. "I was thinking about your Francesca last night. How is she?"

Muriel Pablos managed a weak smile. She looked strained and tired, older than her forty-eight years. "Still the same," she said quietly.

Vicky sighed. "Daughters are such a worry. It was always a pleasure to teach your Francesca . . . unlike some." She looked at her charges whose volume was increasing with their restlessness. It was time to begin the tour before a minor riot broke out. "We'll get started then, Muriel. Ready?"

Muriel watched, straight backed and silent, as Vicky brought some order to 8C. After the din had died down – and all chewing gum had been collected efficiently in a paper bag – she led the way slowly towards the house with a ragged procession of pubescent youth trailing behind.

The excitement began, from 8C's point of view, when they were in the Great Hall. But it wasn't the magnificent hammer-beam roof that grabbed their undivided attention. It was the scream . . . a desperate, primeval cry. It came when Muriel Pablos was in full flow, giving a colourful, fleas and all, description of Elizabethan life. The unearthly sound made her stop in mid-sentence.

"Sounds like someone's being murdered, Miss," a precocious thirteen-year-old girl speculated knowingly.

"Someone's met the ghost, miss," the smallest boy, who looked no more than ten, added with relish.

Then two crop-haired boys skulking by the window turned towards Vicky, their faces ash pale. "We saw him, Miss," said one of them in an awed whisper. "He fell . . . like he was flying. He's there . . . in the courtyard. Do you think he's dead, Miss?"

Vicky and Muriel pushed their way through the crowd of children who were standing, still as startled rabbits. When they reached the leaded window which looked out onto the cobbled courtyard, Muriel knelt up on the window seat and her hand went to her mouth. "It's Jonathan. He was working up in the tower room. I've always said that window was dangerous. I'll have to call an ambulance . . . the police. The nearest phone's in the office upstairs." She scrambled to her feet, preparing for flight.

Vicky took a deep breath as she stood in the doorway watching Muriel hurry away up the great staircase. Then she turned to her class who had fallen uncharacteristically silent. "There's been a terrible accident. As soon as Mrs Pablos gets back from calling the police, I'll go out and see if there's anything I can do. In the meantime can everyone stay away from the window," she added firmly.

Surprisingly, 8C behaved with impeccable restraint until the police arrived.

"Suicide? Chucked himself from that open window up there?" Detective Inspector Anastasia Hardy looked up at the squat, square tower which glowered over the courtyard. "Not much mess, is there . . . considering?" She wrinkled her nose and turned away from the corpse of the fair haired, once handsome, man who lay at her feet in an untidy fashion.

The young doctor who was kneeling on the cobbles examining the body, glanced up at her. "Not suicide," he said casually. "He was already dead when he hit the ground. That's why there's not much blood about." He turned the body over gently. "Here's your cause of death . . . look. Knife wound straight to the heart. And he'd been dead at least half-an-hour before he fell. Sorry to add to your workload, Inspector."

Anastasia Hardy turned to the young uniformed constable standing a few feet away and gave him the benefit of her sweetest smile. She found charm worked wonders with subordinates. She herself had worked for a host of unpleasant superiors on her way up the career ladder and had always vowed never to follow in their footsteps.

"Constable Calthwaite, have you checked that window yet?"

"The door to the tower room's locked, ma'am, and the only key was in the possession of Mr Pleasance . . . er . . . the deceased. I had a look through his pockets before the doc got here and I found it . . . a big old iron thing. With your permission, ma'am, I'd like to try it in the locked door . . . make sure it's the right one," said Joe Calthwaite, eager to make a good impression.

Anastasia nodded. She'd let Constable Calthwaite have his moment of glory . . . or disappointment. He was young and keen; his enthusiasm almost reminded her of her own when she had first joined the force . . . before paperwork and the exhaustion of combining police work with family life had set in.

Calthwaite chatted as he led the way up the winding stairs that led to the tower room. "Someone's already talked to the staff, ma'am. It seems nobody was near the tower when Mr Pleasance fell. And everyone has someone to back up their story. There was a school party in the Great Hall and a couple of the kids actually saw him land in the courtyard. They heard a scream too. A costumed guide was with them . . . a Mrs Muriel Pablos: she called the emergency services. And their teacher, Mrs Vine . . . actually," he said, blushing. "She used to teach me. I was in her class."

"Really?" Anastasia smiled to herself. "So you can vouch for her good character?"

"Oh yes. She's a brilliant history teacher. And I know Mrs Pablos too, but not very well. Her daughter, Francesca and I were in the same class at school. Francesca works at the museum now." A secret smile played on the constable's lips and Anastasia suspected that he'd once had a soft spot for Francesca Pablos.

"I think we'd better talk to the school party first then. They'll be causing a riot if they're shut up in that Great Hall for much longer."

"Actually ma'am, they're looking round the house. Mrs Pablos asked me if she could show them the other wing . . . the parlour, the kitchen and a few of the bedrooms. I didn't think it could do any harm." He looked worried, as though he might have made some dreadful mistake.

"You did the right thing, Constable. As long as they don't go near the murder scene it'll keep them out of mischief."

"Here we are, ma'am . . . top of the tower."

"Good," said Anastasia. The climb had left her breathless. She told herself she should join a health club, take more exercise . . . if she could ever find the time.

PC Joe Calthwaite drew a large iron key from his pocket and placed it in the lock of the ancient door. It turned and the door opened smoothly.

The tower room was larger than Anastasia had expected; a square, spacious chamber lit by a huge window that stretched from floor to ceiling. A section of the window stood open, like a door inviting the unwary to step out into the air.

"Dangerous to leave that window open," Anastasia commented. "Anyone could fall out."

"Someone just has, ma'am."

"And the doctor said he'd been stabbed . . . he'd been dead at least half-an-hour when he fell. Which means somebody threw or pushed the body out . . . not difficult . . . the window reaches to the floor."

"But the door to this room was locked and the only key was in Pleasance's pocket. He was locked in here alone. How does a dead man throw himself from a window in full view of a pair of spotty schoolboys? And he screamed, ma'am. Don't forget they heard a scream."

They stood in the middle of the room, looking round, noting every item, usual and unusual. A massive oak table with sturdy, bulbous legs stood against the wall opposite the window. On it lay piles of leaflets advertising the delights of Bickby Hall and other local attractions. In contrast, a large modern work table stood in the middle of the room. A painting, a portrait of a man in eighteenth-century dress, lay at its centre surrounded by an assortment of trays containing cleaning fluids and materials.

The curator of Bickby Hall had already told one of Calthwaite's colleagues that the dead man cleaned and restored paintings. Jonathan Pleasance had divided his time and skills between the museum in the town centre and the various stately homes and art galleries round about. An evil smelling wad of cotton wool lay, marking the cheap plywood of the table: Pleasance must have been working, removing years of grime from the portrait, just before he died. Calthwaite sniffed the air. The chemical smell was strong. But there was something else as well.

Against the far wall stood a suit of armour, the kind found in stately homes and second rate ghost movies. As Calthwaite stared at it, it seemed to stare back. It leaned on a sword and the young constable's eyes travelled downwards to the tip of the blade. "Ma'am. That stain on the sword. Looks like blood."

Anastasia Hardy had been gazing at the open window. Now she swung round, taking a notebook from her capacious handbag. "So what have we got, Calthwaite? A man falls from a window and there's a scream as he falls. Everyone assumes it's an accident . . . or even suicide. Then the doctor ruins it all by saying he was already dead when he fell, killed by a stab wound. He didn't stagger round the room, injured then tumble out of the open window. He was already well and truly dead. He was alone. The room was locked and the only key was on him when he fell so the killer couldn't have escaped and locked the door behind him. I assume that door is the only way in."

"Apparently, ma'am."

"And the stains on that sword certainly look like blood so that could be our murder weapon. I don't suppose . . ." The inspector and the constable exchanged looks. "The killer might still be in here . . . in the . . ." They both focused their eyes on the suit of armour.

"I'll check, ma'am." Gingerly, PC Calthwaite took the helmet in both hands and lifted it up. It was heavier than he had anticipated but it revealed no guilty face within. The armour was empty. But there was nowhere else to hide in the room. Calthwaite looked round again slowly and sniffed the air. There was a smell, something altogether more homely than the chemicals on the table, more in keeping with the surroundings. It would come to him in time.

A large, faded tapestry hung to the right of the armour, giving relief to the stark white of the walls. Anastasia examined it and lifted the edge carefully, as though she expected it to disintegrate at her touch. "Well, well. Look what I've found." She said triumphantly. Then she dropped the tapestry as though it had become red hot. "There's some kind of room behind here. The killer might still be in there," she mouthed.

"I'll have a look, ma'am," the constable whispered, suddenly nervous. The killer no longer had the murder weapon but Joe Calthwaite didn't relish the thought of coming face to face with a desperate murderer on a dull Wednesday morning.

Happily his fears were groundless. The tiny room concealed by the tapestry contained nothing more alarming than a pile of superfluous publicity material, a few lengths of red silken rope used to keep the public from wandering where they shouldn't, and a trio of wooden signs bearing bossily pointing fingers. But this room hadn't always been used as a storeroom. It had once had another, more dignified, function.

The altar was still there at the far end, draped in a dusty white cloth and topped by an elaborately framed painting of a plump Madonna and Child. Two sturdy, unused candles on high wrought iron stands stood at the side of the room and three more candles with white, unburned wicks had been placed on the altar. It was a small chapel and it had probably been used for its proper purpose in the not-too-distant past. Joe Calthwaite could still smell candles, the waxy odour of sanctity. He had smelt them in the tower room too, mingled with the stench of Jonathan Pleasance's chemical cleaners.

"There's nobody in here, ma'am," he said, turning to Anastasia who was standing behind him, her head bowed as though in prayer.

She looked up. "You'd better make a thorough search in case there's some hidden cupboard or priest hole or something. Dead men don't throw themselves out of windows. Someone or something was up here with him at nine forty when he fell."

Joe Calthwaite nodded. A priest hole, a secret passage: it was obvious. With renewed enthusiasm he began to search; tapping walls, lifting altar covers, looking behind paintings and seeking out suspicious floorboards. However, the priest hole theory rapidly lost its appeal: there was no hiding place either in the tower room or the tiny chapel. And yet the door had been locked and the only key had been found on the body. Joe Calthwaite frowned in concentration as he stared down at the tower room floor. Maybe the killer had escaped through some sort of trap door. But the shiny oak floorboards lay there, mockingly even and undisturbed. Then he spotted a tiny lump of some solid substance on the floor near the middle of the room, interrupting the rich gloss of the wood. He knelt down and touched it with his finger.

"Have you found something?" asked Anastasia, who had been staring out of the window down onto the courtyard in search of inspiration.

"No, ma'am. I don't think so," he replied uncertainly.

He followed her down the narrow stairs. When they reached the point where they met the elaborately carved main staircase, Anastasia turned to him and sighed. "I suppose we'd better ask some questions. Where shall we start?"

It was virtually unanimous. Jonathan Pleasance was a man to avoid. Not that he worked at Bickby Hall full-time: he was only there two mornings each week, which seemed to be more than enough for most of the staff.

The Hall's publicity office had once been an impressive bed chamber. Two people worked there: Jenny was a solemn dark haired young woman dressed in black as though in permanent mourning. Mark, in contrast was an effeminate young man wearing a startling purple shirt. They were reluctant at first to speak ill of the newly dead. But gradually they grew more relaxed in Anastasia's motherly presence and began to voice their true opinions. Jonathan Pleasance was an unpleasant, spiteful man, full of his own importance. He had made barbed comments about Mark's sexual preferences and had made an arrogant pass at Jenny during the staff Christmas party. Mark and Jenny, seemingly united in their contempt for the dead man, provided alibis for each other. They had seen and heard nothing suspicious, and the first they knew of Pleasance's death was when Muriel Pablos had burst in, breathless, to call the police after the schoolboys had seen the body hurtle down into the courtyard. Mark and Jenny displayed no emotion, spouted none of the routine clichés of grief. It was almost as if Jonathan Pleasance's violent death didn't surprise or bother them in the least.

Anastasia decided to question the catering and cleaning staff next. None of them had had much to do with Jonathan Pleasance but the interviews weren't a complete waste of time. The chattiest of the cleaners was only too keen to reveal that the chapel was still used occasionally for special services: the last time had been a fortnight ago when the local vicar had christened the curator's baby son there. Most of the staff had been invited, apart from Jonathan Pleasance who had complained about having to clear his equipment from the tower room for the happy occasion. Joe Calthwaite sat behind the inspector with his notebook on his knee, pondering this interesting snippet of information. Could the aroma of burning church candles linger for a fortnight? He doubted it.

The inspector looked at her watch. It was time to speak to the top man, the curator himself. She liked to see witnesses on their own territory: the more relaxed they were the less they guarded their tongues.

If the curator's secretary, Mrs Barker, had been wearing a starched uniform she would have resembled an old fashioned nanny. As Anastasia and Calthwaite entered her small, well ordered office, she was holding a tiny tape recorder aloft in triumph. "The dictating machine . . . I've been looking for it everywhere, and it's been hidden under the in-tray all the time."

Mrs Barker smiled warmly at the newcomers and appeared to

be enjoying the drama of the situation. "I've never had much to do with Mr Pleasance . . . and I can't say I wanted to. I heard he was one for the ladies," she said meaningfully with a wink which bordered on the cheeky. "In fact," she said almost in a whisper, "he was . . . er . . . friendly with my boss's sister and he let her down rather badly by all accounts. But of course it's terrible that he's dead," she added as a righteous afterthought. "Was it an accident, do you think?"

Anastasia made no comment. "Where were you at nine this morning, Mrs Barker?"

"Mr Samuels and I were in here from half past eight working on an important report. Why?"

Before Anastasia could answer, a man emerged from the inner office. Petroc Samuels, curator of Bickby Hall, was a good looking man in his early forties. His body had lost the slender contours of youth and his dark hair was streaked with grey but his brown eyes sparkled with enthusiasm. He invited Anastasia and Calthwaite into his office and sat back in his swivel chair, relaxed, as the inspector began her questions in a deceptively gentle voice.

"I won't pretend I liked Pleasance. He was good at his job but he wasn't what you'd call a nice man. In fact I discovered what sort of person he was when my sister got involved with him about a year ago. But if we all murdered people we didn't like, the population would halve overnight," Samuels said with a nervous laugh.

"Where were you at nine forty when the body was found?"

"Here with my secretary."

"We think he died about half an hour before that. Where were you then?"

"Here in the office. Mrs Barker and I came in early to work on a report."

"Did you hear the scream when Jonathan Pleasance fell?"

"I heard nothing. I'm rather confused, Inspector. How could he have fallen from the window if he was already dead?"

"That's what we're trying to establish, sir. Did he always lock the tower room door when he was working?"

"Yes. Always. He gets . . . er, got . . . extremely annoyed when he was disturbed. The chapel's used for storage and from time to time people needed to go in there."

"Who stores things in the chapel?"

"Mark and Jenny from publicity; the guides; myself and my secretary. At first he would let people in very grudgingly, but a couple of months ago he decided that he was sick of interruptions so he locked himself in and refused to open the door at all. But as he only worked here two mornings a week it wasn't a major problem."

"Did anyone go up there this morning?"

"If anyone had attempted to knock at that door, Inspector, someone would have heard Pleasance hurling his usual quota of abuse. People learned to steer well clear on the mornings he was in."

"Did Pleasance keep the key to the tower room?"

"No. There's only one key and it's kept in the cupboard by the staff entrance. Pleasance always picked it up on his way in. He'll have been locked in that room alone, Inspector," said Samuels convincingly.

"Pleasance died at around nine o'clock. What time do your staff arrive?"

"Most of them come in at eight forty-five but the guides arrive a little later, about quarter-past nine. All the staff sign in: you can check if you like."

"And Pleasance?"

"He usually came in just before nine o'clock. And before you ask, I didn't see him this morning."

"Was the key in its cupboard when you arrived at eight-thirty?"

"I'm sorry, I've no idea."

Anastasia Hardy stood up and slung her handbag over her shoulder. "Thank you for your help, sir."

After Petroc Samuels had seen them to the door, all co-operation, the good citizen anxious to help the police, Anastasia marched swiftly away from his office and down the magnificent staircase, thinking fleetingly how satisfying it would be to sweep down those stairs in an elegant period costume. She turned to

Calthwaite who was trailing behind, deep in thought. "I think it's time we spoke to those children, Calthwaite. Do you know where they are?"

"They should be back in the Great Hall by now." He hesitated. "Er . . . do you mind if I go and have a word with the car park attendant, ma'am. I noticed him outside when we arrived. It's just an idea I've got."

"In that case I'll have to tackle 8C on my own," she said, hugging her handbag defensively to her chest. "Don't be long will you."

As Anastasia reached the bottom of the stairs, the noise which oozed from the Great Hall sounded like the relentless buzz of bees in a particularly busy hive. She had found 8C.

She took a deep breath before she entered the Hall. She had faced murderers and armed robbers in her time but the prospect of facing thirty exuberant adolescents played havoc with her nerves. As she walked in she could tell that 8C were in high spirits, chattering merrily; the newly broken voices of some of the boys echoing up to the great hammer-beam roof. Anastasia made straight for their teacher who was standing by the massive stone fireplace talking to a middle-aged woman in Elizabethan costume.

"Mrs Vine? I'm so sorry you've had to wait," Anastasia said with a disarming smile. "I'll get one of my constables to take names and addresses then you'll be able to go." Vicky Vine looked relieved as she glanced at her restless charges.

The costumed woman standing beside her fiddled nervously with the jewel which hung around her neck. "Muriel Pablos?" asked Anastasia. The woman nodded. "I'm afraid we need a statement from you. We're interviewing all the staff: it's nothing to worry about."

PC Joe Calthwaite chose that moment to march into the hall and the children fell silent for a few short moments at the sight of a uniformed police officer.

Anastasia watched Vicky Vine greet the constable like an old friend. "Joe. You do look smart," she said, touching his blue serge sleeve. "Enjoying the police force are you? It's what you've always wanted to do isn't it . . . ever since you discovered who started that fire in the school chemistry lab. Joe was one of my prize pupils, Inspector," she told Anastasia with professional pride as the young constable blushed.

Joe grinned modestly and turned to Muriel Pablos. "Hello again Mrs Pablos. I didn't have a chance to ask you earlier. How's Francesca?" Muriel Pablos smiled weakly but didn't answer.

Anastasia's attention began to wander and her sharp eyes spotted a huddle of conspiratorial boys standing near the window. They were up to something. And it wasn't long before she found out what it was.

"Miss," said a whining female voice from the centre of the room. "Darren's got matches, miss . . . and a candle."

"I found them, miss," Darren cried in his defence. "I found them in that window seat. I wasn't going to keep them, miss."

Vicky Vine confiscated the objects of desire with a weary sigh and handed them to Muriel Pablos; a small box of matches and a chubby, half-burned church candle with a blackened wick . . .

Joe leaned towards Anastasia and whispered in her ear. "Ma'am, can I have a quick word outside?"

Watched by thirty pairs of curious eyes, Anastasia followed the constable into the entrance hall, intrigued. "Ma'am," he said as they stood beneath a pair of watching statues. "I've just spoken to the car park attendant . . . he told me something interesting." He paused. "I think I know who killed Jonathan Pleasance. And now I think I know how they did it."

Anastasia stared at him. "Well I'm baffled. A man dies at nine o'clock in a locked room then jumps or falls from the window half an hour later with the only key still in his pocket. But come on, Sherlock. Was the suit of armour computer operated? Or was the murder committed by the resident ghost? Let's hear your brilliant theory."

He looked at Anastasia Hardy and saw a sceptical smile on her lips. "I'll have to ask you to do something for me first, ma'am. Something that would be . . . er . . . better coming from a woman."

"What is it?" she asked, warily.

When Calthwaite told her she raised her eyebrows. "Are you sure that's necessary?"

"Oh yes, ma'am."

"Right, Calthwaite, you lead the way. And let's just hope this doesn't lead to questions being asked in high places."

They re-entered the hall. This time the children seemed quieter, more subdued.

"Mrs Pablos, could we have a word outside in the entrance hall, please?" said Anastasia sweetly. Muriel Pablos glanced at Vicky Vine and followed Anastasia from the room, her long skirts rustling against the stone floor. "If you'd be good enough to lift your skirts up," she said when they were outside.

Muriel looked at her in horror. "This is outrageous . . ."

"I'm not suggesting a strip search, Mrs Pablos. Just lift your skirts up. It'll only take a moment. Constable," she said firmly to Joe. "Stand by the door and make sure no one comes in."

Muriel Pablos looked round in helpless terror. Then she slowly raised her skirts to her knees showing a shapely pair of sun-tanned legs.

"A little higher, please, Mrs Pablos."

Muriel Pablos was about to refuse. Then, as though she knew she was defeated, she lifted the skirts higher to reveal a length of red silken rope, coiled about her body.

"Untie the rope, please Mrs Pablos."

Muriel Pablos slowly uncoiled the rope and it fell to the ground. It was in two sections, each with a burned end. Anastasia summoned PC Joe Calthwaite back and he stood, staring at the rope as though the sight amazed him.

"Well, Constable," said Anastasia. "Are you going to tell us how it was done?"

Calthwaite took his notebook from his top pocket and pulled himself up to his full height. "Well, ma'am, I first became suspicious of Mrs Pablos when the car park attendant told me that her car was already in the visitor's car park when he arrived this morning at eight forty. He said he saw it later in its usual place in the staff car park, and I found that she'd signed in for work as normal at quarter-past nine. We were told by Mr

Samuels, the curator, that Jonathan Pleasance locked himself in
the tower room when he was working and didn't let anyone in, so
then I began to think. If nobody was let in then the killer must
already have been there, probably hidden in the chapel. Pleasance
arrived before nine o'clock so his killer must have been there
earlier, already hidden. The key was only used by Pleasance –
nobody else bothered locking the room – so it was easy. All the
killer had to do was wait, kill Pleasance with the sword, lock the
door as he or she left, drive round into the staff car park and then
arrive for work as normal."

"But the key was found on the body . . ."

"I'll be coming to that, ma'am. Next I tried to work out
exactly how it was done; how it was made to look as though
Jonathan Pleasance had fallen from the window. Then I saw the
lengths of rope stored in the chapel and an odd number of
candles on the altar . . . three . . . so it was possible that one was
missing. I found some candle wax on the floorboards in the
middle of the tower room and I started to think. What if the
body had been held by the open window with a length of rope
secured to, say, that heavy oak side table: then if a lighted candle
was placed under the rope so that it burned through slowly to
give the murderer plenty of time to establish an alibi. Then the
murderer would need some excuse to get away in order to hide
the rope and candle once the body had fallen. That's where the
miniature tape recorder came in. The curator uses one to dictate
letters and his secretary said that she'd mislaid it for a while. I
think the killer borrowed it and recorded a bloodcurdling
scream to be played at the appropriate moment in front of a
full audience to provide the perfect alibi. Nobody else in the
building heard it because the tape was only played in the great
hall. Then the killer ran upstairs to call the police. But first she
made a detour and unlocked the tower room to deal with the
incriminating evidence; she hid the burned candle and matches
in those big padded sleeves where she'd hidden the tape recorder. Then she put them in the window seat until they could
be disposed of properly. It's a pity 8C had to find them and give
the game away isn't it, Mrs Pablos? And the rope . . . well what

better place to hide it than underneath a huge Elizabethan skirt. Am I right so far, Mrs Pablos?"

Muriel Pablos looked at him, pleading. "You knew my Francesca at school, Joe. You know what a lovely girl she is. She met this older man at work in the museum: she was besotted with him, completely infatuated, but she wouldn't tell me his name . . . I never guessed it was Jonathan Pleasance. Then one day he saw me alone and he started to talk about their relationship. The things he said . . . the way he talked about Francesca. He was just using her and he said he intended to end their affair soon because she was getting too possessive . . . too clinging. He said that if she made things awkward for him, he'd make sure she lost her job at the museum: he was going to tell lies about her . . . say she was incompetent. I couldn't just stand by and watch him ruining her career . . . her life. I did it for my daughter."

Anastasia nodded, wondering how she would have felt if such a thing had happened to her own daughter. Then she dismissed the thought and reminded herself of her profession. "Is there anything else you want to say before I arrest you, Mrs Pablos?" she asked sympathetically before reciting the familiar official words.

"I came in at eight this morning and parked in the public car park at the back so none of the staff would see me," Muriel began quietly. "The tower room wasn't locked – only Pleasance ever locked it – so I hid myself in the chapel. When he came in just before nine I killed him. Then I rigged up the rope and the candle, locked the door behind me, got into my car and arrived for work as usual. I had taken pieces of rope home and experimented so that I could time his fall for when I was showing Vicky's class round. When I went upstairs to call the police I made a detour to the tower room like Joe said. I wiped the tape on my way up and put the recorder back on Mrs Barker's desk when I went in to tell her what had happened."

"But the room was locked and the only key was found on the body. According to everyone's statements you never went out into the courtyard . . . never went near the body," said Anastasia, puzzled. Muriel Pablos stood silent. She was saying nothing.

As Muriel was led to a waiting police car, PC Joe Calthwaite walked round to the back of the house where 8C were boarding their coach. He waited patiently until their teacher had counted them on before he spoke to her.

"You were always fond of Francesca weren't you, Mrs Vine," he began gently. "Francesca was brilliant at history, your star pupil. You must have been delighted when she got that job at the museum. I think Mrs Pablos told you about Pleasance and Francesca. I think you helped her. When she came downstairs again you left her looking after your class while you went to check the body for signs of life before the ambulance arrived. I think she'd locked the tower room door behind her and then she passed you the key. While you were bending over the body you put the key in his pocket. Is that right, Mrs Vine?"

Vicky Vine smiled and shook her head. "I couldn't stand by and watch that man hurt Francesca. I had to help somehow." She took a deep breath. "What gave us away?"

"Do you remember when the chemistry lab burned down? I smelled petrol on the culprits' clothes."

"How could I forget."

"Well this time it was candles . . . I kept smelling candles. I've always had a good sense of smell."

As Joe Calthwaite put an arresting hand on her shoulder, his old teacher looked into his eyes and smiled.

# A TRAVELLER'S TALE

*Margaret Frazer*

*Margaret Frazer was originally the alias of two writers, Gail Frazer and Mary Monica Pulver, who between them produced the popular series of novels featuring medieval sleuth, Dame Frevisse. The series began with* The Novice's Tale *(1992). Gail is now continuing the series on her own. The following story, whilst not featuring Dame Frevisse, is also set in the 1400s. It fits into that sub-category of the impossible crime, which is the "locked-carriage" story. Gail told me an interesting aside. "Would you believe that the carriage would not have been called a carriage then? But better a little anachronism, I say, than the major confusion for readers if I'd properly called it a chariot!"*

> When that April with his showers sweet
> The drought of March has pierced to the root . . .
> Then long folk to go on pilgrimages . . .

Damn. He hated that verse.

Not hated, Thomas amended. Was only brutally tired of it, having heard it a few too many times in his life to want it wandering through his head at odd moments. Besides, this wasn't April and he was on no pilgrimage: it was definitely January and he was simply going home after rather too long a time at Westminster, where he'd only gone because he was needed to make a little peace between his cousins Hal and Gloucester, and if ever there was a thankless task in the world, that was it because the only peace either of them wanted was the other one out of his way – forever and in every way, for choice.

Ah, well. He had done what he could for now. They wouldn't kill each other this month, likely, and he'd be home by supper if the weather held and nobody's horse threw a shoe on the ice-set road.

Thomas eyed the grey, lowering sky and judged there was good chance the snow would hold off for the few hours more of riding he needed. January's trouble was that the days were so short. And cold. He huddled his cloak more snugly around his shoulders and was glad of his fur-lined boots and that he had given pairs for New Year's gifts to Giles and Ralph. They were riding behind him now without the displeasure that servants as good as they seemed able to make known without sound or gesture, when they did not approve of whatever their master had dragged them into – such as the long ride from London into Oxfordshire in a cold January with snow threatening – when there was no real need except that Thomas wanted to be home and with his books and family. And although whether those in service to him liked him or not, came second to whether or not they served him well, for choice he preferred to have people around him whom he liked and who, though he could live without it, at least somewhat liked him, too. Hal – otherwise my Lord Bishop of Winchester and son of a royal duke – had been known to tease him that such concern came from his somewhat low-born blood, to which Thomas invariably answered in return that it came from his good common sense and Hal ought to try it some time, thank you very much. Then they would laugh together.

Why was it he could talk and laugh and enjoy Hal's company, and talk and laugh and enjoy Gloucester's company, and all that Hal and Gloucester could do with each other was hate their respective guts? It was tedious of them and more tedious that they needed him to sort them out. Maud would say so over and over when he reached home, until he had given her kisses enough and her present from London – a pretty gold and enameled brooch this time – to make her feel she had been missed while he was gone, and then she would begin to tell him all that had happened the week and a half he'd been away and everything would be back to where it had been before he had left.

The road slacked downward and curved left and he knew that around the curve, beyond this out-thrust of trees, the Chiltern Hills fell steeply away to the lowlands that reached westward for miles upon miles, an open vastness that on a clear summer's day at this hour would be filled with westering sunlight like a bowl full of gold, but today would be all dull shades of lead and grey. But Thomas had seen it from here in every season and weather and loved it every time and way, and besides, from here there were not many miles left to home, though it was further than it seemed because the steep, long drop from the Chilterns had to be managed first and . . .

With a slight sinking of spirits Thomas saw trouble ahead. A carriage stopped right at the crest above the first long downward drop of the road; and by the scurrying of three men around it and the woman standing to one side, wringing her hands and wailing, it was halted for more than the necessary checking of harness and wheels before the start of the treacherous way down.

With wanhope that it was not as bad as it looked, Thomas raised a gloved hand out of the sheltering folds of his cloak and gestured Giles to go forward and ask what the trouble was and if they might be of help, little though he wanted to be; and while Giles heeled his horse into a jog past him, Thomas put his hand back under his cloak, loosened dagger and sword in their sheaths, and then, as he and Ralph drew nearer the carriage, pushed back his cloak to leave his sword-arm free, on the chance this was after all a waylaying rather than simply someone else's trouble.

Just for a moment then the possibility of robbery took stronger hold as Giles, after a brief word with the men there, drew his horse rapidly around and headed back with more haste than a carriage's breakdown warranted, shouting well before he was back to Thomas's side. "There's some people dead here!"

Suddenly not minded to go closer, drawing rein and putting hand to sword-hilt openly, as Ralph moved closer up on his flank, Thomas asked, "I beg your pardon?"

"There's people dead," Giles repeated, stopping beside him. "You know William Shellaston? A merchant from Abingdon?"

"By name." Thomas urged his horse forward. "It's him?"

"And his wife and son, looks like."

"All of them dead? How?"

"There's none of that lot knows. It's only just happened. Or they only just noticed. It's odd, like."

Thomas supposed it was, if three people were dead and their servants had "only just noticed". But he was to them now, clustered beside the carriage, the woman still sobbing for the world to hear.

"I told them who you are," Giles whispered at Thomas's side. "That you're a coroner and all."

"In London," Thomas pointed out, annoyed. For no reason anyone could explain, the office of Chief Butler to the King included the office of Coroner of London, and by that, yes, he was a coroner but, "I've no jurisdiction here."

"They don't need to know that," Giles replied. "What they need is someone to settle them and tell them what to do."

And here he was and had to do it Thomas supposed, and summoned up what he had heard of William Shellaston. A wine merchant whose wines were never of the best, a bad-humoured man, heavy-handed, not given to fair-dealing if he could help it, with a mind to join the landed gentry and the purchase of a manor lately near Henley to help his ambition along. Exactly the sort of man Thomas avoided like the plague because the only interest that sort had in his acquaintance was how much he could do for them.

Well, there wasn't much to be done for him now, if he was dead, Thomas thought, dismounting beside the servants and the carriage that was of the common kind – long-bodied, with low wooden sides, closed in by canvas stretched over metal half-hoops, and high-wheeled to keep it clear of muddy roads. The richer sort were painted, sides and canvas both, but this was all brown wood and bare canvas, nothing to make it remarkable except, Thomas noted, it was solidly built, the only expense spared seeming to have been to decorate it for the eye.

The servants had all begun to talk as soon as his feet were on the ground. "Be quiet," he said, so used to being obeyed it did not surprise him when they fell silent; then said to the man he had singled out as babbling the least at him, "What's in hand here?"

"They're dead. All three of them! We stopped to tell Master Shellaston we were about to start down. He hates to be surprised by the sudden drop and we've orders to always stop to tell him. Only when I called in, no one answered and when I looked in to see why, they were all . . ." He swallowed as if holding down his gorge. ". . . dead."

"That's all you know?"

The man nodded, tight-lipped over apparent gut-sickness.

"That's all any of you know?"

More nods all around.

"No outcry? Nothing? No sign of how they're dead?"

"Nothing," the woman answered, her voice rising shrilly. "They're just dead and it's awful and . . ."

"I'll see for myself," Thomas said curtly, less because he wanted to see anything and more to stop her carrying on. He moved to the carriage's rear, the usual way in. The chain meant to go across the gap to make falling out less easy had been unfastened at one end and looped aside, the last link dropped into the hook on the other side, and the heavy canvas curtain meant to keep draughts out strapped aside, out of the way, giving him a clear view of the long tunnel of the carriage's inside. He stepped up on a chest that had been taken out and set down on the ground for a step – its usual use, to judge by its dried-muddy bottom and the footmarks on its top – and ducked inside. Or as clear a view as the shadows and grey light allowed him; the flaps over the window on each side of the carriage, meant for air and light and a sight of the countryside in better weather, were closed and it took a few moments for his eyes to get used to the gloom.

His sense of smell worked faster. There was a reek to the place that said death, and he pulled a fold of his cloak over his mouth and nose before he ventured further in, able to see well enough now not to tread on . . . anything . . . before he reached the windows. Thomas held his breath while dropping his cloak's fold long enough to roll up and tie the window flaps out of the way to give better light and eventually, he hoped, better air.

In the meanwhile, pressing his cloak over his nose and mouth again, he looked around and saw he had been right: there was nothing here he wanted to see, though it interested him that the inside of the carriage was nothing like its outside. Close-woven green wool lined the canvas cover for colour and comfort, there was well-stuffed padding on the wooden side-walls and woven carpets covered as much of the floor as he could see, for the high-piled cushions of all sizes, meant to make for comfortable sitting against the jounce and lurch of travel, with willow-woven hampers, lidded and strapped to the carriage sides near the entrance, the only other furnishing because anything of wood would be an invitation to bruising in this small carriage.

It was what else the carriage contained he did not want to see, but he looked, God help him, because he was a coroner and there, at the man and woman he presumed were Master and Mistress Shellaston, slumped on their backs among the piled cushions in the middle of the carriage. Their clothing and jewelled rings went finely with the carriage's furnishings and, living, they would probably have claimed they'd rather die than be seen in their present unclean disarray, lying with heads cast back, eyes shut but mouths gaping, arms and legs sprawled, and the place stenching with what their bowels and bladders had loosed in death.

Where was their son?

Stepping carefully, Thomas found him beyond his parents, near the carriage's front. A solid bulk of a child, maybe twelve years old, burrowed into a pile of cushions and curled tightly in on himself like a small hedgehog into its nest. Or he had been tightly curled before his body went slack in – Thomas pressed fingertips against the side of the throat and found, as he expected, no pulse – death.

They were all, as he had been told, dead. Father, mother, son.

How?

As he made his way back to the carriage entrance, Thomas considered the possibilities. Not by a weapon, surely, though the bodies would have to be brought out into better light and looked at to be certain there were no wounds; but if there had been violence of any kind among them, there would have been some sort of struggle, enough to leave some evidence of it, and there was none, nor apparently any outcry the servants riding on either side or behind had heard.

A person could smother on charcoal fumes, always a winter danger, but even if Master Shellaston had dared to have a brazier among so much cloth – and Thomas had noticed none – a canvas-covered carriage with its constant draughts was nowhere anyone was likely to suffocate except by making deliberate effort.

Poison then? A possibility, Thomas granted but doubtfully. From what he'd heard of poisons, most tended to go about their business with a deal of pain, and people did not tend to suffer quietly, so if it had been poison, why, again, had no one cried out?

He ducked thankfully out of the carriage into the open air, stepped down onto the waiting box and from there began giving necessary orders. Since there was now no hope of him reaching home today and no point to staying where they were, growing colder, he said, "There's a village and inn a half mile back. We'll return there and do what needs doing."

No one argued with him and while they went through the awkward business of turning the carriage around, Thomas learned a little more, beginning with the servants' names – Bartel, who claimed to be Master Shellaston's body servant and in charge of the others; Jack, whose size had probably recommended him as a guard on the journey because it surely hadn't been his wits out of which he was presently badly frighted; Godard, the carriage driver who just now had no time for anything but his horses; and Mary, a squawking chicken of a female who seemed more in horror than in grief, saying she was – had been, oh, God save her, what would happen now? – Mistress Shellaston's waiting woman and sobbing harshly to Thomas's question of why she had not been in the carriage, too, "Master Shellaston didn't like to be crowded, didn't like servants breathing down his neck and cluttering his way, he said. He made me always ride pillion behind Bartel and cold it is, too, this time of year and . . ." And probably hard on Bartel, Thomas did not say, dismissing her.

He learned something more from looking at the Shellastons' horses. The servants' mounts were all third-rate beasts of doubtful worth and dull coats, much like the servants themselves, now he thought of it, while the three pulling the carriage tandem, although a plain lot, shaggy with unclipped winter coats and their harness nothing to boast of – no dyed leather, brass trim, or bells to make the journeying more bright – were nonetheless, like the carriage, solid-built and not likely to break down. It seemed Master Shellaston had not been given to show, Thomas thought: he'd spent his money only on his own close-kept comforts and let the world think what it liked.

Did that evidence solid common sense, Thomas wondered. Or merely a contempt for anyone not him?

He was readying to talk to Bartel while watching Godard and Jack work the carriage and its horses around, when the clop of shod hooves on the frozen road warned that more riders were coming. Beside him, Bartel said with what might be disgust or maybe worry, even before the new-comers were in sight, "This'll likely be Master Hugh. Thought he'd be along soon."

"Master Hugh?"

"Master Shellaston's cousin. He's Master Shellaston himself, come to that, but to call him Master Hugh has kept things simpler over the years," Bartel said broodingly and added, as three riders came round the same curve of the road that Thomas had, "Aye, that's him."

He looked to be a man of early middle years, well-wrapped in an ample cloak, riding a shiningly groomed, handsome bay, with two well-turned out servants behind him on lesser but no less well-kept mounts. They all drew rein for the time it took to understand what they were seeing, then Master Hugh came forward at a canter, raising his voice to ask as he came, "Bartel, what's toward?"

There were explanations to be made all over again, Thomas keeping aside, leaving it to the servants, with Master Hugh saying angrily, part way through, "You're making no sense. They can't all be simply dead. I want to see them."

At his order, Godard paused the horses and Master Hugh went

into the carriage as Thomas had, though not for so long, and came out to go aside to the verge and dryly heave before, more pale than he had been, he came back to demand past Bartel to Thomas, "Who are you and what are you doing here?"

"I was on my way home when I overtook all this. I'm Master Thomas Chaucer of Ewelme."

He watched Master Hugh recognize his name and inwardly back off into respect. Doubting he'd have trouble from him now, Thomas asked in his own turn, "How do you come to be here?" peremptory enough that Master Hugh accepted it was no light question.

His look slightly darkening, he answered, "I was following them."

"Why?"

"Because William – my cousin Master Shellaston – told me to. He'd ordered me to come see him at his manor and we'd quarrelled, as always, over a piece of land he'd taken out of an inheritance of mine, and he finally said he wanted to be done with me once and for all, that if I'd go back with him to Abingdon, he'd hand over the deed I wanted and there'd be an end."

"So why weren't you riding with him?"

"Because, as always, my cousin wanted me no more around him than need be. He ordered me to keep well behind him. What business of yours is it to be asking all this?"

"I am a coroner," Thomas said.

Master Hugh's lips moved as if he might have been silently swearing but aloud he only said, jerking his head toward the carriage, fully turned now. "That's your doing, too?"

"We're going back the half-mile to the inn," Thomas said for answer. "You'll of course come with us?" He made it more invitation than order, though he would change that if need be, but Master Hugh merely nodded in agreement.

On his own part, Thomas regretted the need to go back. It would necessitate telling over yet again, to new folk, what was already certain – that the Shellastons were dead – when what he wanted was an answer as to why. He was already hearing among the servants a muttering of, "Devil come for his own", and he knew that once the Devil or "God's will" was brought into a thing folk were too often satisfied not to bother looking further. For himself, profound though his belief in God and the Devil might be, Thomas had never found either one dabbled so directly in the world as this: these deaths were devil's work, right enough, but a man's hand had done it, and as the carriage creaked forward, he rode away from Master Hugh and over beside Godard riding the middle of the three carriage horses, guiding them by reins and voice and a short-tailed whip. The man cast him a shrewd sideways look and said, before Thomas could ask it, "Aye, I'm near as anyone but I didn't hear aught to make me think there was trouble."

"What *did* you hear?"

"Naught but the usual and that was never much once we were under way. They always did their bitch-and-bellow before we started, then settled down to drink themselves into comfort. The lurch and jounce . . ." He twitched his head back to the carriage lumbering behind. ". . . unsettled their stomachs."

"Why didn't they ride, then?"

"Because he'd bought the carriage, damn it, and damn it, they were going to use it, damn it," Godard said without heat, apparently giving Master Shellaston's words and feelings in the matter rather than his own. "Besides, he didn't like to be seen lifting the bottle as much as he did, and a carriage is better than horseback for hiding that."

"He drank then?"

"Then and anytime. And she did, too, come to that, though maybe not so much."

"And the boy?"

"Made him throw up."

"Riding in the carriage?"

"No. The wine they favoured for drink. It made him throw up. Cider, that's what he had to have."

That would have made poisoning them all at once more difficult, with two drinks to deal with rather than one. If it had been poison. Thomas thanked him and swung his horse away and found Giles riding close behind and to his side.

Surprised to find him there, Thomas raised eyebrows at him and Giles said, "The Hugh fellow was looking to ease in and hear what you were saying, so I eased in instead."

Thomas nodded his thanks. "I doubt anything was said he doesn't already know about his cousin, but I'd rather he not know how much I know." Or don't know, he did not add aloud. He and Giles were as alone as they were likely to be this while, riding aside from the carriage, with the three Shellaston servants riding behind the carriage, Master Hugh and his men gone on ahead, and Thomas's Ralph bringing up the rear on Thomas's quiet order to make sure they lost no one along the way, Thomas took the chance of going un-overheard to say, "He looks as likely a possibility as anyone for wanting Master Shellaston dead. But why the woman and boy, too?"

"Because he'll for certain have it all, now they're dead," Giles answered. "There's none others to the family."

"Servant-talk?" Thomas asked, and when Giles had nodded that it was, asked, "How much is all?"

"The business in Abingdon and a good-sized manor Master Shellaston bought a few years back, and the land they'd been quarrelling over these past five years, too, but they'd nearly settled over that anyway, it seems."

"How much does this Master Hugh have on his own?"

"He's not hurting, as they say. He was Master Shellaston's apprentice a while back, with it understood there'd be partnership when all was said and done, but they fell out and he set up on his own in Henley. Looked likely to rival Master Shellaston soon, by what this lot says."

"But no love lost between them?"

"Not a drop."

"Ride here and keep an eye ahead. I'm going back to see what they'll tell me."

"Just about anything you ask," Giles said. "They're starting to warm to the thought they're done with Master Shellaston and his wife."

With that to encourage him, Thomas slowed his horse to the side of the road, letting the carriage lumber on past him, and joined the Shellaston servants. Since he doubted anyone was thinking of anything except what had happened, he forebore subtlety, starting in immediately to them all, with a nod ahead, "So Master Shellaston and his cousin didn't get on together?"

"Not for above the time it takes to spit," Bartel readily agreed.

"Ordered him to ride behind, did he? The way Master Hugh said?"

"Did indeed. You always knew where you stood with Master Shellaston."

"Usually in the bad," said Jack. "Grudged a man the air he breathed and double-grudged Master Hugh any breath at all."

Mary crossed herself. "You shouldn't speak ill of the dead and them not even cold yet."

"They're cold and getting colder and so are we," Bartel said bluntly.

"We should lay them out decently before they stiffen too much," she sniffed. "It's not good, them lying there like that."

She was right, but Thomas wanted someone besides themselves for witness before anything else was done in the carriage, and asked, to divert her, "Had you served Mistress Shellaston long?"

"Three years last Martinmas."

"A good mistress?"

"Not very. Nor not too bad, neither," she hurried to add. "Just . . . a little too quick with her hands sometimes."

"And sharper than ever, now she was childing again," Jack said. "No pleasing her ever."

"She was with child?"

"About five months along," Mary said. "Glad of it, mind you, but it didn't sweeten her any."

Four deaths instead of three then to the credit of whoever had done this thing, Thomas thought grimly, but asked aloud, "Travelling didn't agree with her, from what the driver says."

"Nor did it," Mary said. "She wasn't happy with travelling or happy at Master Shellaston suddenly deciding they'd go back to Abingdon."

"It was sudden?"

"Sudden enough. He and Master Hugh had been yelling at each other off and on since yesterday and then, late this morning, it's up and on the road, let's have this over with, says Master Shellaston, and here we are. Liked keeping folk off balance, he did. Whether he'd have given over the deed once we were home, that's another matter."

"Did Mistress Shellaston quarrel with him over it? The deed or leaving so suddenly?

"Bit snippy at first but nothing untoward."

"They didn't outright quarrel?"

"Nay. They weren't much for quarrelling with each other. Saved all their ire for other folk."

Thomas fell silent, considering what he had and asking nothing more until they had reached the inn yard, and while Master Hugh saw to telling the innkeeper what was the trouble, he went aside to his own men and, first, gave Ralph order to find someone to go to whoever was the coroner for this end of the county and bring him here, and added, seeing his look at the snow-heavy sky. "No need to hurry or risk yourself about it. The weather is cold enough, they'll keep. All I want is to know is he's on his way." And turned to Giles to say, "This place is big enough, there should be an herbwife somewhere. Find her for me."

He would have preferred an apothecary, but a knowledgeable herbwife – and, please God, this one would be – would do as well; and while he waited, he would have preferred to go inside the inn and be comfortable, the way Mary was gone, bustled away on a burst of the innwife's sympathy and curiosity, and Master Hugh whose men and Godard were seeing to the horses while Bartel and Jack were still to hand, kept by a look and gesture from Thomas while he had sent Giles and Ralph about his business, because he had meant to set them as guard on the carriage. But he had also had a hope the cold and ending day would keep people indoors but that was gone along with hope of setting Bartel and Jack to guard. They were already at the centre of a spreading cluster of folk and eagerly telling all they knew – or didn't know, Thomas amended, hearing Bartel saying, "Aye, there they lie, dead as dead and not a mark on them and never a cry. It had to have been the Devil, look you, come for Master Shellaston because he was a hellish master, sure enough."

By tomorrow there'd likely be a band of demons added to the telling, dancing in the road around the carriage with shrieks and the reek of sulphur, Thomas thought and said, "The Devil maybe came for Master Shellaston, but why for his wife and son, too?"

"They were just there," someone among the listeners said, eager to help the story along, "and so Old Nick took 'em, too."

"I've never heard it works that way," Thomas said dryly. "That the Devil can seize innocent souls just because they happen to be nigh a sinner."

"Well," Bartel put in, "she was only half a step not so bad as he was. They were a pair and no mistake."

"But the boy," Thomas said.

"Died of fright," Jack promptly offered.

Bartel, openly enjoying himself, added, full of scorn, "Huh. Likely the Devil decided to save time by coming only once for all of them. They were a matched lot. Young William was shaping to go the same way as his sire and dam and no mistake."

"Here now," Master Hugh protested, come up unnoticed from the inn with a steaming mug of something warm between his hands. "Little Will was a good lad."

"Praying your pardon, sir." Though it was fairly plain Bartel didn't care if he had it or not. "You spoiled him some and got on fine with him because you never crossed him. Some of us weren't so lucky." As if aside but not lowering his voice, he added to Thomas, "And it set Master Shellaston's back up to see how well along they got."

Dragging the talk back to where he needed it to be, Thomas asked, "Today, from the carriage, are you certain there was never any outcry at all?" because he could not believe three people had died without a sound.

"Well . . ." Bartel said.

He and Jack cast quick, doubtful looks at each other, and more forcefully, impatient, Thomas asked, "You heard something. What?"

"We heard . . . I heard and Jack with me, so Mary must have, too, we heard young William give a cry," Bartel admitted unwillingly. "Just once and it wasn't like we hadn't heard such other times. See, Master Shellaston had a heavy hand and was ready with it, especially when he was drinking, which was mostly."

"She could lay one along a man's ear, too, when she wanted, come to that," said Jack bitterly.

"When did you hear this cry?" Thomas asked and added, to their blank looks, "Before or after you passed through here?"

"Ah," said Bartel, understanding. "Before. Wasn't it, Jack?"

"Aye," Jack agreed. "Quite a while before, maybe."

And maybe it had been and maybe it had not, or maybe they were mistook or maybe they were lying – Thomas could think of several reasons, not all guilty ones, why they might be – because the more both men were coming to enjoy this, the less confidence he had in their answers.

"By your leave, sir, she's here," Giles said behind him, and Thomas turned away from the men and their eager listeners to find Giles standing with a firm-built woman, neatly aproned, wimpled and cloaked, her sharply judging eyes meeting his as she curtsyed and said, "Esmayne Wayn at your service, Master Chaucer. I'm herbwife and midwife here. Your man says there's three folk dead and you want me to see."

More happy with her directness than with anything else he'd encountered these past two hours, Thomas said, "Mistress Wayn, thank you for coming. Yes, if you'd be so good as to look and tell me what you think about their deaths . . ."

Master Hugh started what might have been a protest, but a glance from Thomas made him think better of it and he subsided. Meanwhile Bartel at Thomas's nod went to pull the carriage's end curtain aside and tie it back, and Jack hauled out the chest and set it down for a step. "Some better light would help, too," Thomas said to Jack because the day was drawing in toward dark, then he offered Mistress Wayn a hand up.

He felt no need to ready her for what was there. As the village healer and midwife, she had surely seen enough of death in various forms and degrees of unpleasantness for this to be no worse. Besides, the cold was doing its work; the smell was none so bad as it had been, and Mistress Wayn went forward without hesitation, making room for him to follow her as she bent first over Master Shellaston, then over his wife, apparently able to see enough for now by the light from the opened window-flaps. The further jouncing of the carriage seemed not to have moved the bodies, already jostled into settled places between when they had died and when they were found, Thomas supposed. "The child is further on," he said quietly.

Mistress Wayn nodded but took Mistress Shellaston by the chin, moved her head slightly back and forth, then prodded at her stomach and learned close over her face, seemingly sniffing. None of that was anything Thomas would have cared to do and he heard murmurs from the watchers outside and wished the door-curtain could be closed, but Mistress Wayn, ignoring everyone and him, repeated with Master Shellaston what she had done with his wife, before she straightened as much as the low curve of the ceiling allowed her, to look to Thomas and ask, "How long have they been dead?"

"No one is certain. At least three hours at a guess. It's been maybe two since I first saw them and the bodies were cooling by then."

"Best I straighten them, if I may? Much longer and we'll have to wait until they unstiffen again."

"If it will make no difference to what we might learn about how they died . . ."

"You've noted how they're lying and can say so if asked? And that their eyes be closed. Nobody did that, did they?"

Thomas far outranked her in life but she had a greater skill than he at this, and they both accepted the equality that gave them. So her interruption did not matter and he said simply, "I've noted, and no, nobody closed their eyes."

"That's enough then. Cleaning them can come later," and briskly, firmly, she straightened both bodies out of their sprawl, then moved on to young William, still curled into his nest of cushions. "You've noted him, too?" she asked.

"Yes."

"Good." She straightened the boy and rolled him onto his back, moved and prodded and did with him much as she had with his parents, before sitting back on her heels and saying up at Thomas, "His eyes be open, you see. That's the usual way with dead folk that didn't die easy."

"You're saying his parents died easily and he didn't? That they didn't all three die the same way?"

"Aye. Him and her, they died the same as each other, surely." Mistress Wayn nodded to the elder Shellastons. "The boy, he went otherwise. I can smell it on him. He took dwale would be my guess, only I'm not much guessing. It's good for some things, carefully used, but only outwardly. Taken inwardly, it takes not much to kill."

"Poison," Thomas said. "You're saying the boy was poisoned. What about his parents? They had to have been poisoned, too."

"You'd think it," Mistress Wayn said. "It would seem the most likely but they're chancey things, poisons." She sounded almost regretful over it. "What kills one person only makes another sick and there's no way to know beforehand which way it will be. That I can still smell on him –" She nodded at young William. "– tells me he had enough to be almost certain of killing him, being a child. Why he didn't taste it as he started to drink it down, that's a question I don't have answer to. As for his parents and what they drank . . ." She shrugged.

"You don't think it was the same thing?"

"There's no smell of it and it would have to have been more than the amount that killed the boy to kill them quick and quietly. No, whatever they drank down was different, I'd say. I don't know what. It's that they made no outcry and show no sign of suffering I don't understand. Poisons hurt. I'd guess by the way the boy was curled in on himself he was hurting when he died, but with them it's more like they fell to sleep and died without waking up."

"There are potions that do that. Bring on a sleep so deep it turns into death."

"Aye." She still sounded unsatisfied. "But why one kind for them and another for the boy? Why weren't they drinking all the same?"

"Wine made the boy sick," Thomas said absently.

"So two different bottles had to be poisoned." She pushed a half-full, stoppered one lying near young William with her foot. "But still, why two different poisons? And he didn't just fall to sleep, neither," she added with a nod at the boy.

Thomas noticed there was no nonsense about the Devil from her. To her it was plain that poison had killed these three and, like him, she had no doubt that poison was a thing that came from a human hand.

Or poison*s*, it must have been, according to her.

Different poisons by different hands?

Three murders planned – Master and Mistress Shellaston's separate from their son's – by two different people with two different poisons, with it only being chance they happened together?

Or . . .

A sudden, ugly guess rose up in Thomas's mind.

Something of it must have shown in his face because Mistress Wayn asked sharply, "What?"

He shook his head. "I need more questions answered first, before I say."

But at least now he had a better thought of what the questions were.

An hour later, as the day drew in to grey twilight, when he had asked some of those questions and had answers, he gathered in a sideroom of the inn bespoken from the innkeeper for the sake of privacy with Master Hugh, Giles, the other servants, and Mistress Wayn, along with the innkeeper and a few village men for witness. Thomas had not put it that way but had merely asked the innkeeper if there were a few worthy men in the village who might care to join them for hot, spiced cider and talk this cold evening. That he meant to guide the talk he did not say.

After Mistress Wayn had overseen the moving of the bodies respectfully to her house for cleaning and shrouding, he and Giles, without asking Master Hugh's leave – and by his expression he would not have given it if asked – had searched through the carriage, generally seeking, finding specifically, and now asking, "Bartel, the wine Master and Mistress Shellaston were drinking, where did it come from?"

"It was his own. Being a wine merchant, he could lay hands on good stuff when he wanted."

"Was it a new bottle he had . . ."

"Bottles," said Bartel. "Three at least."

That accorded with what Thomas had found in a hamper in the carriage. Safely cushioned among various wrapped food bundles, there had been an empty bottle, a mostly empty bottle, and a full, tightly corked one.

"Could anyone have been at those bottles before they were put into the carriage?"

"Been at them? I filled them from a cask at the manor if that's what you mean, and put them in the hamper and put it into the carriage." Bartel straightened with sudden suspicion. "Hoi, hold up there. You're not saying I put something in them, are you? There were folk around all the time can say I never had chance to."

"Nor do I think you did. I just wanted to know that no one else had chance at them either."

Bartel subsided, not fully happy.

"There was a bottle that had held cider beside young William and then there are these." Thomas held up two pottery vials, slight enough to have fit in a belt pouch. "Do any of you know these?"

No one did, but Bartel's suspicion had been catching. All the Shellaston servants looked wary now and Master Hugh was frowning.

Thomas held one of them higher. "This one held poppy syrup sweetened with sugar, Mistress Wayn tells me. Master Shellaston favoured sweet wine, I gather?" Heads agreed he had, and indeed it had been malmsey in the bottles. Thomas held up the other small bottle. "This one held dwale, otherwise called nightshade, enough of it to kill if drunk straight down. And young William must have, because there was half the cider left in the bottle and no dwale in it."

Thomas regarded the empty vial sadly for a moment, then handed it with the other to Giles to keep. "We found it under young William. The other one was in the bottom of the box used for a step into the carriage. The box that has what's needed to keep the carriage in good order on the road." Spare parts for mending wheels and harness, grease for axles, tools and other odds and ends that might be useful. "It was Mistress Wayn who noticed and showed me the black grease smear on the back of young William's hand that he had mostly wiped off – black grease he could have come by in the carriage nowhere else but in that box. From one of the rags probably, when he hid the other vial there, the one with poppy syrup, after his parents were unconscious. Or after he'd killed them. Before he drank the potion of dwale in the other vial, a potion strong enough it brought him to death almost immediately."

"He killed his parents and then himself?" Master Hugh asked. "Is that what you're saying? He'd have to be off his wits to do any of that!"

"Off his wits or misled," Thomas said levelly. "But to go back to his parents. Let us guess he found a way to put the poppy syrup into one of the bottles of wine. It wouldn't have been hard. They were packed in a hamper with food. He only had to pretend he was taking overlong getting out what he wanted to eat, while pouring the syrup into the wine. After that, he only had to wait until his parents guzzled it down, as it seems was their way with wine. Now, poppy syrup, if you give enough, brings on sleep and if too much is given, it can kill. There was never enough in that vial to kill two people but there was enough to make them both sleep so heavily, helped on by the wine, that they didn't wake even when their son – and it had to have been him, there was no one else there to do it – pressed a pillow over the face of first one of them and then the other. He was a large, solid child, with weight enough to hold a pillow down and smother someone if they were heavily unconscious, the way his mother and father were. And then he closed their dead eyes, to keep them from staring at him."

"But why would he go and do it? Kill them, I mean," protested one of the village men. "It's not natural."

"I'd guess he did it for hatred. From everything I've heard, there was little love lost between him and them. Today, when he cried out in the carriage, probably from the unexpected pain of the dwale working in him, he was heard but no one thought anything about it but that he'd been struck by his mother or father, and that was too usual to take much heed of. Besides, I'd guess he thought – or maybe someone put it in his head – that if he were orphaned, rid of his parents and no one able to say how they died – he'd be given in ward to Master Hugh Shellaston, who got on with him far better than his parents did."

"But then why would he kill himself?" Bartel asked.

"I don't think he did. I think his death was Master Hugh's doing."

Master Hugh jerked up straight in his chair, his stare furious at Thomas before he gathered his thoughts and exclaimed, "That's mad! I was nowhere near any of them when they died. You said yourself my cousin and his bitch-wife were smothered. I was never in the carriage or anywhere near it. And you said the boy drank that poison of his own will and died of it."

"I said he drank it of his own will and died of it, yes. I didn't say he *meant* to die of it. Why bother to hide the vial he'd poisoned his parents with if he was going to kill himself afterwards? He probably thought that what he drank was some light potion that would make him merely sleep and that when he and his dead parents were found he could claim all ignorance of their deaths and simply be weepingly thankful he was spared whatever had killed them. My guess is that you gave him the poppy syrup and dwale, told him the dwale was harmless, maybe even warned him there might be some pain and to keep from being caught he must fight against crying out, which he mostly did. He must have been a brave boy in his way. But he never meant to kill himself. You're the one who's guilty of his death. As guilty as if you'd poured the poison down his throat yourself."

Master Hugh did not give way yet. Instead – with what he probably meant to be the outrage of innocence – he fell back on, "You can't prove any of this!"

"Not at this moment," Thomas said coldly. "But I'll warrant

that if question is made among apothecaries and every herbwife anywhere near where you've been of late, we'll learn of rather many requests for poppy syrup and dwale potion from them."

"No one is going to admit to making him a killing potion," Mistress Wayn said quietly.

"No, and probably none did. But I daresay several will be found who'll admit to making a non-killing potion. Dwale is after all good for some poultices. But put several lots together and they'd kill, yes?" Thomas asked at Master Hugh.

Boldly surly, the man tried, "My shit of a cousin had more enemies than me who'd probably like him dead. And how likely is it I've been wandering around talking to herbwives and apothecaries? I've a life to lead and people who notice where I go and why."

"We'll find out if other enemies had chance to give young William the poisons. We'll see if anyone had as much to gain from their deaths as you do as the only heir. We'll see who's been asking for poppy syrup and dwale, and we'll find, I'll lay odds, that if not you, then some several of your servants have been, sent here and there without knowing what they were doing."

With one of his men already looking at him with widening eyes and dawning alarm. Master Hugh suffused a slow, deep red, rose to his feet and looked around the room for a way out.

"The window is shuttered," Thomas said mildly, "and my man is ordered to stop you going out the door by whatever means are needed. Nor do I think you'll find anyone here, even your own men, ready to help you."

That much Master Hugh had already read in the faces around him; and heavily he dropped back into his chair and said, from the heart, "Damn."

# THE SILVER CURTAIN

## John Dickson Carr

*More than that of any other writer, the name of John Dickson Carr
is indelibly linked with the impossible crime story. For a start, he
wrote more of them than anyone else (though Edward D. Hoch has
overtaken him in the short story stakes), and he explored more
variants on the theme than anyone else, in some cases producing
definitive texts. I've said much about him in my afterword, so I won't
repeat it here. Although his best known detective was Gideon Fell,
Carr wrote several books featuring other detectives, in particular
Henry Merrivale and Colonel March. The following is one of
Colonel March's mysteries and comes from the collection* The
Department of Queer Complaints *(1940).*

The croupier's wrist moved with such fluent ease as to seem
boneless. Over the green baize its snaky activity never hesitated,
never wavered, never was still. His rake, like an enormous butter-
pat, attracted the cards, flicked them up, juggled them, and slid
them in a steady stream through the slot of the table.

No voice was raised in the Casino at La Bandelette. There was
much casualness; hardly any laughter. The tall red curtains and
the padded red floors closed in a sort of idle concentration at a
dozen tables. And out of it, at table number six, the croupier's
monotone droned on.

"*Six mille. Banco? Six mille. Banco? Banco?*"

"*Banco,*" said the young Englishman across the table. The
cards, white and grey, slipped smoothly from the shoe. And the
young man lost again.

The croupier hadn't time to notice much. The people round him, moving in hundreds through the season, were hardly human beings at all. There was a calculating machine inside his head; he heard its clicks, he watched the run of its numbers, and it was all he had time for. Yet so acutely were his senses developed that he could tell almost within a hundred francs how much money the players at his table still retained. The young man opposite was nearly broke.

(Best to be careful. This perhaps means trouble.)

Casually the croupier glanced round his table. There were five players, all English, as was to be expected. There was the fair-haired girl with the elderly man, obviously her father, who had a bald head and looked ill; he breathed behind his hand. There was the very heavy, military-looking man whom someone had addressed as Colonel March. There was the fat, sleek, swarthy young man with the twisty eyebrows (dubious English?), whose complacency had grown with his run of luck and whose wallet stuffed with *mille* notes lay at this elbow. Finally, there was the young man who lost so much.

The young man got up from his chair.

He had no poker face. The atmosphere about him was so desperately embarrassed that the fair-haired girl spoke.

"Leaving, Mr Winton?" she asked.

"Er – yes," said Mr Winton. He seemed grateful for that little help thrown into his disquiet. He seized at it; he smiled back at her. "No luck yet. Time to get a drink and offer up prayers for the next session."

(Look here, thought Jerry Winton, why stand here explaining? It's not serious. You'll get out of it, even if it does mean a nasty bit of trouble. They all know you're broke. Stop standing here laughing like a gawk, and get away from the table. He looked into the eyes of the fair-haired girl, and wished he hadn't been such an ass.)

"Get a drink," he repeated.

He strode away from the table with (imagined) laughter following him. The sleek young man had lifted a moon-face and merely looked at him in a way that roused Jerry Winton's wrath.

Curse La Bandelette and baccarat and everything else.

"There," reflected the croupier, "is a young man who will have trouble with his hotel. *Banco? Six mille. Banco?*"

In the bar, which adjoined the casino-rooms, Jerry Winton crawled up on one of the high stools, called for an Armagnac, and pushed his last hundred-franc note across the counter. His head was full of a row of figures written in the spidery style of France. His hotel-bill for a week would come to – what? Four, five, six thousand francs? It would be presented to-morrow, and all he had was his return ticket to London by plane.

In the big mirror behind the bar a new image emerged from the crowd. It was that of the fat, sleek, oily-faced young man who had cleaned up such a packet at the table, and who was even now fingering his wallet lovingly before he put it away. He climbed up on a stool beside Jerry. He called for mineral water: how shrewd and finicky-crafty these expert gamblers were! He relighted the stump of a cigar in one corner of his mouth.

Then he spoke.

"Broke?" he inquired off-handedly.

Jerry Winton glared at his reflection in the mirror.

"I don't see," Jerry said, with a slow and murderous choosing of words, "that that's anybody's business except mine."

"Oh, that's all right," said the stranger, in the same unpleasantly off-handed tone. He took several puffs at his cigar; he drank a little mineral water. He added: "I expect it's pretty serious, though? Eh?"

"If the matter," said Jerry, turning round, "is of so much interest to you: no, it's not serious. I have plenty of money back home. The trouble is that this is Friday night, and I can't get in touch with the bank until Monday." Though this was quite true, he saw the other's fishy expression grow broader. "It's a damned nuisance, because they don't know me at the hotel. But a nuisance is all it is. If you think I'm liable to go out in the garden and shoot myself, stop thinking it."

The other smiled sadly and fishily, and shook his head.

"You don't say? I can't believe that, now can I?"

"I don't care what you believe."

"You should care," said his companion, unruffled. As Jerry slid down from the stool, he reached out and tapped Jerry on the arm. "Don't be in such a rush. You say you're a boy Croesus. All right: you're a boy Croesus. *I* won't argue with you. But tell me: how's your nerve?"

"My what?"

"Your nerve. Your courage," explained his companion, with something like a sneer.

Jerry Winton looked back at the bland, self-assured face poised above the mineral water. His companion's feet were entangled with the legs of the bar-stool; his short upper lip was lifted with acute self-confidence; and a blank eye jeered down.

"I thought I'd ask," he pursued. "My name is Davos, Ferdie Davos. Everybody knows me." He swept his hand towards the crowd. "How'd you like to make ten thousand francs?"

"I'd like it a whole lot. But I don't know whether I'd like to make it out of any business of yours."

Davos was unruffled. "It's no good trying to be on your dignity with me. It don't impress me and it won't help you. I still ask: how would you like to make ten thousand francs? That would more than cover what you owe or are likely to owe, wouldn't it? I thought so. Do you or don't you want to make ten thousand francs?

"Yes, I do," Jerry snarled back.

"All right. See a doctor."

"*What?*"

"See a doctor," Davos repeated coolly. "A nerve tonic is what you want: pills. No, I'm not wise-cracking." He looked at the clock, whose hands stood at five minutes to eleven. "Go to this address – listen carefully while I tell you – and there'll be ten thousand in it for you. Go to this address in about an hour. No sooner, no later. Do your job properly, and there may be even more than ten thousand in it for you. Number two, Square St Jean, Avenue des Phares, in about an hour. We'll see how your nerve is then."

La Bandelette, "the fillet," that strip of silver beach along the channel, is full of flat-roofed and queerly painted houses which give it the look of a town in a Walt Disney film. But the town itself is of secondary consideration. The English colony, which is of a frantic fashionableness, lies among great trees behind. Close to the Casino de la Forêt are three great hotels, gay with awning and piling sham Gothic turrets into the sky. The air is aromatic; open carriages clop and jingle along broad avenues; and the art of extracting money from guests has become so perfected that we find our hands going to our pockets even in sleep.

This sleep is taken by day. By night, when La Bandelette is sealed up except for the Casino, the beam of the great island lighthouse sweeps the streets. It dazzles and then dies, once every twenty seconds. And, as Jerry Winton strode under the trees towards the Avenue of the Lighthouses, its beam was beginning to be blurred by rain.

Square St Jean, Avenue des Phares. Where? And why?

If Davos had approached him in any other way, Jerry admitted to himself, he would have paid no attention to it. But he was annoyed and curious. Besides, unless there were a trick in it, he could use ten thousand francs. There was probably a trick in it. But who cared?

It was the rain that made him hesitate. He heard it patter in the trees, and deepen to a heavy rustling, as he saw the signboard pointing to the Avenue des Phares. He was without hat or coat. But by this time he meant to see the thing through.

Ahead of him was a street of fashionable villas, lighted by mere sparks of gas. An infernally dark street. Something queer, and more than queer, about this. Total strangers didn't ask you how strong your nerves were, and then offer you ten thousand francs on top of it, for any purpose that would pass the customs. Which was all the more reason why . . .

Then he saw Davos.

Davos did not see him. Davos was ahead of him, walking fast and with little short steps along the dim street. The white beam of the lighthouse shone out overhead, turning the rain to silver; and Jerry could see the gleam of his polished black hair and the light tan topcoat he was now wearing. Pulling up the collar of his dinner-jacket, Jerry followed.

A few yards farther on Davos slackened his pace. He peered round and up. On his left was the entrance to a courtyard, evidently the Square St Jean. But to call it a "square" was noble overstatement; it was only a cul-de-sac some twenty feet wide by forty feet deep.

Two of its three sides were merely tall, blank brick walls. The third side, on the right, was formed of a tall flat house all of whose windows were closely shuttered. But there was at least a sign of life about the house. Over its door burned a dim white globe, showing that there was a doctor's brass name-plate beside the door. A sedate house with blue-painted shutters in the bare cul-de-sac – and Davos was making for it.

All this Jerry saw at a glance. Then he moved back from the cul-de-sac. The rain was sluicing down on him, blurring the dim white globe with shadow and gleam. Davos had almost reached the doctor's door. He had paused as though to consider or look at something; and then . . .

Jerry Winton later swore that he had taken his eyes off Davos only for a second. This was true. Jerry, in fact, had glanced back along the Avenue des Phares behind him and was heartened to see the figure of a policeman some distance away. What made him look quickly back again was a noise from the cul-de-sac, a noise that was something between a cough and a scream, bubbling up horribly under the rain; and afterwards the thud of a body on asphalt.

One moment Davos had been on his feet. The next moment he was lying on his side on the pavement, and kicking.

Overhead the beam of the lighthouse wheeled again. Jerry, reaching Davos in a run of half a dozen long strides, saw the whole scene picked out by that momentary light. Davos's fingers still clutched, or tried to clutch, the well-filled wallet Jerry had last seen at the Casino. His tan topcoat was now dark with rain. His heels scraped on the pavement, for he had been stabbed through the back of the neck with a heavy knife whose polished-metal handle projected four inches. Then the wallet slipped out of his fingers, and splashed into a puddle, for the man died.

\*     \*     \*

Jerry Winton looked, and did not believe his own eyes. Mechanically he reached down and picked up the wallet out of the puddle, shaking it. He backed away as he heard running footfalls pound into the cul-de-sac, and he saw the flying waterproof of a policeman.

"Halt there!" the law shouted in French. The policeman, a dim shape under the waterproof, pulled up short and stared. After seeing what was on the pavement, he made a noise like a man hit in the stomach.

Jerry pulled his wits together and conned over his French for the proper phrases.

"His – this wallet," said Jerry, extending it.

"So I see."

"He is dead."

"That would appear obvious," agreed the other, with a kind of snort. "Well! Give it to me. Quick, quick, quick! His wallet."

The policeman extended his hand, snapping the fingers. He added: "No stupidities, if you please! I am prepared for you."

"But I didn't kill him."

"That remains to be seen."

"Man, you don't think –?"

He broke off. The trouble was that it had happened too rapidly. Jerry's feeling was that of one who meets a super-salesman and under whirlwind tactics is persuaded to buy some huge and useless article before he realizes what the talk is all about.

For here was a minor miracle. He had seen the man Davos stabbed under his eyes. Davos had been stabbed by a straight blow from behind, the heavy knife entering in a straight line sloping a little upwards, as though the blow had been struck from the direction of the pavement. Yet at the same time Davos had been alone in an empty cul-de-sac as bare as a biscuit-box.

"It is not my business to think," said the policeman curtly. "I make my notes and I report to my commissaire. Now!" He withdrew into the shelter of the dim-lit doorway, his wary eye fixed on Jerry, and whipped out his notebook. "Let us have no nonsense. You killed this man and attempted to rob him. I saw you."

"No!"

"You were alone with him in this court. I saw as much myself."

"Yes, that is true."

"Good; he admits it! You saw no one else in the court?"

"No."

"*Justement*. Could any assassin have approached without being seen?"

Jerry, even as he saw the bleak eye grow bleaker, had to admit that this was impossible. On two sides were blank brick walls; on the third side was a house whose door or windows, he could swear, had not opened a crack. In the second's space of time while he looked away, no murderer could have approached, stabbed Davos, and got back to cover again. There was no cover. This was so apparent that Jerry could not even think of a reasonable lie. He merely stuttered.

"I do not know what happened," he insisted. "One minute he was there, and then he fell. I saw nobody." Then a light opened in his mind. "Wait! That knife there – it must have been thrown at him."

Rich and sardonic humour stared at him from the doorway. "Thrown, you say? Thrown from where?"

"I don't know," admitted Jerry. The light went out. Again he stared at blank brick walls, and at the house from whose sealed front no knife could have been thrown.

"Consider," pursued his companion, in an agony of logic, "the position of the knife. This gentleman was walking with his back to you?"

"Yes."

"Good; we progress." He pointed. "The knife enters the back of his neck in a straight line. It enters from the direction where you were standing. Could it have been thrown past you from the entrance to the court?"

"No. Impossible."

"No. That is evident," blared his companion. "I cannot listen to any more stupidities. I indulge you because you are English and we have orders to indulge the English. But this goes beyond reason! You will go with me to the Hôtel de Ville. Look at the note-case in his hand. Does he offer it to you and say: 'Monsieur, honour me by accepting my note-case'?"

"No. He had it in his own hand."

"He had it in his own hand, say you. Why?"

"I don't know."

Jerry broke off, both because the story of his losses at the Casino must now come out with deadly significance, and because they heard the rattle of a door being unlocked. The door of the doctor's house opened; and out stepped the fair-haired girl whom Jerry had last seen at the Casino.

Beside the door the brass name-plate read, "Dr Edouard Hébert," with consulting hours inscribed underneath, and an aggressive, "Speaks English." Behind the girl, craning his neck, stood a bristly middle-aged man of immense dignity. His truculent eyeglasses had a broad black ribbon which seemed to form a kind of electrical circuit with the ends of his brushed-up moustache.

But Jerry Winton was not looking at Dr Hébert. He was looking at the girl. In addition to a light fur coat, she now wore a cream-coloured scarf drawn over her hair; she had in one hand a tiny box, wrapped in white paper. Her smooth, worried face, her long, pale-blue eyes, seemed to reflect the expression of the dead man staring back at her from the pavement. She jerked back, bumping into the policeman. She put her hand on Dr Hébert's arm. With her other hand she pointed sharply to Davos.

"That's the man!" she cried.

M. Goron, prefect of Police, was a comfortable man, a round, cat-like amiable sort of man, famous for his manners. Crime, rare in La Bandelette, distressed him. But he was also an able man. At one o'clock in the morning he sat in his office at the town hall examining his fingernails and creaking back and forth in a squeaky swivel chair whose noise had begun to get on Jerry Winton's nerves.

The girl, who for the tenth time had given her name as Eleanor Hood, was insistent.

"M. Goron!"

"Mademoiselle?" said the prefect politely, and seemed to wake out of a dream.

Eleanor Hood turned round and gave Jerry Winton a despairing look.

"I only wish to know," she urged, in excellent French, "why we are here, Dr Hébert and I. And Mr Winton too, if it comes to that." This time the look she gave Jerry was one of smiling companionship: a human sort of look, which warmed that miscreant. "But as for us – why? It is not as though we were witnesses. I have told you why I was at Dr Hébert's house."

"Mademoiselle's father," murmured M. Goron.

"Yes. He is ill. Dr Hébert has been treating him for several days, and he had another attack at the Casino to-night. Mr Winton will confirm that."

Jerry nodded. The old boy at the table, he reflected, had certainly looked ill.

"I took my father back to our hotel, the Brittany, at half-past eleven," the girl went on, speaking with great intensity. "I tried to communicate with Dr Hébert by telephone. I could not reach him. So I went to his house; it is only a short distance from the hotel. On the way I kept seeing that man – the man you call Davos. I thought he was following me. He seemed to be looking at me from behind every tree. That is why I said, 'That's the man,' when I saw him lying on the pavement with his eyes open. His eyes did not even blink when the rain struck them. It was a horrible sight. I was upset. Do you blame me?"

M. Goron made a sympathetic noise.

"I reached Dr Hébert's house at perhaps twenty minutes to twelve. Dr Hébert had retired, but he consented to go with me. I waited while he dressed. We went out, and on the doorstep we found – what you know. Please believe that is all I know about it."

She had a singularly expressive voice and personality. She was either all anxiety or all persuasiveness, fashioning the clipped syllables. When she turned her wrist, you saw Davos lying in the rain and the searchlight wheeling overhead. Then she added abruptly in English, looking at Jerry:

"He was a nasty little beast; but I don't for a moment believe you killed him."

"Thanks. But why?"

"I don't know," said Eleanor simply. "You just couldn't have."

"Now there is logic!" cried M. Goron, giving his desk an admiring whack.

M. Goron's swivel chair creaked with pleasure. There were many lights in his office, which smelt of creosote. On the desk in front of him lay Davos's sodden wallet and (curiously) the tiny round box, wrapped in a spill of paper, which Eleanor Hood had been carrying. M. Goron never spoke to Jerry, never looked at him; ignored him as completely and blandly as though he were not there.

"But," he continued, growing very sober again, "you will forgive me, mademoiselle, if I pursue this matter further. You say that Dr Hébert has been treating your father?"

"Yes."

M. Goron pointed to the small box on the table.

"With pills, perhaps?"

"Ah, my God!" said Dr Hébert, and slapped his forehead tragically.

For several minutes Jerry had been afraid that the good doctor would have an apoplectic stroke. Dr Hébert had indicated his distinguished position in the community. He had pointed out that physicians do not go out in the middle of the night on errands of mercy, and then get dragged off to police stations; it is bad for business. His truculent eyeglasses and moustache bristling, he left off his stiff pacing of the room only to go and look the prefect in the eye.

"I *will* speak," he said coldly, from deep in his throat.

"As monsieur pleases."

"Well, it is as this lady says! Why are we here? Why? We are not witnesses." He broke off, and slapped at the shoulders of his coat as though to rid himself of insects. "This young man here tells us a story which may or may not be true. If it is true, I do not see why the man Davos should have given him *my* address. I do not see why Davos should have been knifed on my doorstep. I did not know the man Davos, except as a patient of mine."

"Ah!" said the prefect. "You gave him pills, perhaps?"

Dr Hébert sat down.

"Are you mad on the subject of pills?" he inquired, with restraint. "Because this young man" – again he looked with disfavour at Jerry – "tells you that Davos made some drunken mention of 'pills' at the Casino to-night, is that why you pursue the subject?"

"It is possible."

"It is ridiculous," said Dr Hébert. "Do you even question my pills on the desk there? They are for Miss Hood's father. They are ordinary tablets, with digitalin for the heart. Do you think they contain poison? If so, why not test them?"

"It is an idea," conceded M. Goron.

He picked up the box and removed the paper.

The box contained half a dozen sugar-coated pellets. With great seriousness M. Goron put one of the tablets into his mouth, tasted it, bit it, and finally appeared to swallow it.

"No poison?" asked the doctor.

"No poison," agreed M. Goron. The telephone on his desk rang. He picked it up, listened for a moment with a dreamy smile, and replaced it. "Now this is really excellent!" he beamed, rubbing his hands. "My good friend Colonel March, of the English police, has been making investigations. He was sent here when a certain form of activity in La Bandelette became intolerable both to the French and English authorities. You perhaps noticed him at the Casino to-night, all of you?"

"I remember," said Jerry suddenly. "Very large bloke, quiet as sin."

"An apt description," said the prefect.

"But –" began Dr Hébert.

"I said 'all of you,' Dr Hébert," repeated the prefect. "One small question is permitted? I thank you. When mademoiselle telephoned to your house at eleven-thirty to-night, you were not there. You were at the Casino, perhaps?"

Dr Hébert stared at him.

"It is possible. But –"

"You saw M. Davos there, perhaps?"

"It is possible." Still Dr Hébert stared at him with hideous perplexity. "But, M. Goron, will you have the goodness to explain this? You surely do not suspect either mademoiselle or myself of having any concern with this business? You do not think that either mademoiselle or I left the house at the time of the murder?"

"I am certain you did not."

"You do not think either mademoiselle or myself went near a door or window to get at this accursed Davos?"

"I am certain you did not," beamed the prefect.

"Well, then?"

"But there, you see," argued M. Goron, lifting one finger for emphasis, "we encounter a difficulty. We are among thorns. For this would mean that M. Winton must have committed the murder. And that," he added, looking at Jerry, "is absurd. We never for a moment believed that M. Winton had anything to do with this; and my friend Colonel March will tell you why."

Jerry sat back and studied the face of the prefect, wondering if he had heard aright. He felt like an emotional punching-bag. But with great gravity he returned the prefect's nod as a sergent de ville opened the door of the office.

"We will spik English," announced M. Goron, bouncing up. "This is my friend Colonel March."

"'Evening," said the colonel. His large, speckled face was as bland as M. Goron's; his fists were on his hips. He looked first at Eleanor, then at Jerry, then at Dr Hébert. "Sorry you were put to this inconvenience, Miss Hood. But I've seen your father, and it will be all right. As for you, Mr Winton, I hope they have put you out of your misery?"

"Misery?"

"Told you you're not headed for Devil's Island, or anything of the sort? We had three very good reasons for believing you had nothing to do with this. Here is the first reason."

Reaching into the pocket of his dinner-jacket, he produced an article which he held out to them. It was a black leather note-case, exactly like the one already on M. Goron's desk. But whereas the first was stuffed with *mille* notes, this one had only a few hundred francs in it.

"We found this second note-case in Davos's pocket," said Colonel March.

He seemed to wait for a comment, but none came.

"Well, what about it?" Jerry demanded, after a pause.

"Oh, come! Two note-cases! Why was Davos carrying two note-cases? Why should any man carry two note-cases? That is my first reason. Here is my second."

From the inside pocket of his coat, with the air of a conjurer, he drew out the knife with which Davos had been stabbed.

A suggestive sight. Now cleansed of blood, it was a long, thin, heavy blade with a light metal handle and cross-piece. As Colonel March turned it round, glittering in the light, Jerry Winton felt that its glitter struck a chord of familiarity in his mind: that a scene from the past had almost come back to him: that, for a swift and tantalizing second, he had almost grasped the meaning of the whole problem.

"And now we come to my third reason," said Colonel March. "The third reason is Ferdie Davos. Ferdie was a hotel thief. A great deal too clever for us poor policemen. Eh, Goron? Though I always told him he was a bad judge of men. At the height of the summer season, at hotels like the Brittany and the Donjon, he had rich pickings. He specialized in necklaces; particularly in pearl necklaces. Kindly note that."

A growing look of comprehension had come into Eleanor Hood's face. She opened her mouth to speak, and then checked herself.

"His problem," pursued Colonel March, "was how to smuggle the stolen stuff over to England, where he had a market for it. He couldn't carry it himself. In a little place like La Bandelette, Goron would have had him turned inside out if he had as much as taken a step towards Boulogne. So he had to have accomplices. I mean accomplices picked from among the hordes of unattached young men who come here every season. Find some young fool who's just dropped more than he can afford at the tables; and he may grab at the chance to earn a few thousand francs by a little harmless customs bilking. You follow me, Mr Winton?"

"You mean that I was chosen –?"

"Yes."

"But, good lord, how? I couldn't smuggle a pearl necklace through the customs if my life depended on it."

"You could if you needed a tonic," Colonel March pointed out. "Davos told you so. The necklace would first be taken to pieces for you. Each pearl would be given a thick sugar-coating, forming a neat medicinal pill. They would then be poured into a neat bottle or box under the prescription of a well-known doctor. At the height of the tourist rush, the customs can't curry-comb everybody. They would be looking for a pearl-smuggler: not for an obviously respectable young tourist with stomach trouble."

Eleanor Hood, with sudden realization in her face, looked at the box of pills on M. Goron's desk.

"So *that* is why you tasted my pills!" she said to the prefect of police, who made deprecating noises. "And kept me here for so long. And –"

"Mademoiselle, I assure you!" said M. Goron. "We were sure there was nothing wrong with those pills!" He somewhat spoiled the gallant effect of this by adding: "There are not enough of them, for one thing. But, since you received them from Dr Hébert after office hours, you had to be investigated. The trick is neat, hein? I fear the firm of Hébert and Davos have been working it for some time."

They all turned to look at Dr Hébert.

He was sitting bolt upright, his chin drawn into his collar as though he were going to sing. On his face was a look of what can only be called frightened scepticism. Even his mouth was half open with this effect, or with unuttered sounds of ridicule.

"We were also obliged to delay you all," pursued M. Goron, "until my men found Madame Fley's pearls, which were stolen a week ago, hidden in Dr Hébert's surgery. I repeat: it was a neat trick. We might never have seen it if Davos had not incautiously hinted at it to M. Winton. But then Davos was getting a bit above himself." He added: "That, Colonel March thinks, is why Dr Hébert decided to kill him."

Still Dr Hébert said nothing.

It was, in fact, Jerry Winton who spoke. "Sir, I don't hold any brief for this fellow. I should think you were right. But how could he have killed Davos? He couldn't have!"

"You are forgetting," said Colonel March, as cheerfully as though the emotional temperature of the room had not gone up several degrees, "you are forgetting the two note-cases. Why was Davos carrying two note-cases?"

"Well?"

"He wasn't," said Colonel March, with his eye on Hébert.

"Our good doctor here was, of course, the brains of the partnership. He supplied the resources for Ferdie's noble front. When Ferdie played baccarat at the Casino, he was playing with Dr Hébert's money. And, when Dr Hébert saw Ferdie at the Casino to-night, he very prudently took away the large sum you saw in Ferdie's note-case at the tables. When Ferdie came to the doctor's house at midnight, he had only his few hundred francs commission in his own note-case, which was in his pocket.

"You see, Dr Hébert needed that large sum of money in his plan to kill Ferdie. He knew what time Ferdie would call at his house. He knew Mr Winton would be close behind Ferdie. Mr Winton would, in fact, walk into the murder and get the blame. All Dr Hébert had to do was take that packet of *mille* notes, stuff them into another note-case just like Ferdie Davos's, and use it as a trap."

"A trap?" repeated Eleanor.

"A trap," said Colonel March.

"Your presence, Miss Hood," he went on, "gave the doctor an unexpected alibi. He left you downstairs in his house. He went upstairs to 'get dressed.' A few minutes before Davos was due to arrive, he went quietly up to the roof of his house – a flat roof, like most of those in La Bandelette. He looked down over the parapet into that cul-de-sac, forty feet below. He saw his own doorstep with the lamp burning over it. He dropped that note-case over the parapet, so that it landed on the pavement before his own doorstep.

"Well?" continued Colonel March. "What would Davos do? What would *you* do, if you walked along a pavement and saw a note-case bulging with thousand-franc notes lying just in front of you?"

Again Jerry Winton saw that dim cul-de-sac. He heard the rain splashing; he saw it moving and gleaming past the door-lamp, and past the beam of the lighthouse overhead. He saw the jaunty figure of Davos stop short as though to look at something –

"I imagine," Jerry said, "that I'd bend over and pick up the note-case."

"Yes," said Colonel March. "That's the whole sad story. You would bend over so that your body was parallel with the ground. The back of your neck would be a plain target to anybody standing forty feet up above you, with a needle-sharp knife whose blade is much heavier than the handle. The murderer has merely to drop that knife: stretch out his fingers and drop it. Gravity will do the rest.

"My friend, you looked straight at that murder; and you never saw it. You never saw it because a shifting, gleaming wall of rain, a kind of silver curtain, fell across the doorlamp and the beam of the lighthouse. It hid the fall of a thin, long blade made of bright metal. Behind that curtain moved invisibly our ingenious friend Dr Hébert, who, if he can be persuaded to speak –"

Dr Hébert could not be persuaded to speak, even when they took him away. But Eleanor Hood and Jerry Winton walked home through the summer dawn, under a sky coloured with a less evil silver; and they had discovered any number of mutual acquaintances by the time they reached the hotel.

# THE STOLEN SAINT SIMON

*Michael Kurland*

*Michael Kurland (b.1938) first established his name in the science fiction field in the psychedelic sixties, when he wrote several amusing books which turned a number of accepted sf icons on their head, including* Ten Years to Doomsday *(1964), written with Chester Anderson, and* The Unicorn Girl *(1969). Although he has continued to produce novels using sf themes, he has broadened his writing to cover crime and mystery fiction. Sometimes, as in* Star Griffin *(1987), he blends the two. His early book,* A Plague of Spies *(1969), received an Edgar Allan Poe Scroll from the Mystery Writers of America. He has produced several Sherlock Holmes pastiches featuring Moriarty –* The Infernal Device *(1979),* Death by Gaslight *(1982) and* The Great Game *(2001) – and continued the excellent Lord Darcy series started by Randall Garrett,* Ten Little Wizards *(1988), which is chock full of impossible crimes, and* A Study in Sorcery *(1989). The following story gives us not one but two impossible crimes.*

First thing Monday morning Junior called me into his office and told me the tale, leaning back in his battered wooden chair until it looked like only an abiding faith kept it from falling over backwards, with his feet propped up on the well-scarred top of his desk. The front office at Continental Investigations & Security's Los Angeles branch holds a reception area and several interview rooms, all done in well-polished light wood and glass, where our well-groomed lads and lasses listen sympathetically and nod and take notes and impress the hell out of our clients. The "back room" is actually three rooms; one a safe-room for our more confidential files, one with three couches and a small refrigerator and coffee machine for operatives who have to spend the night – or the week – and the third is Junior's office. Abe Wohlstein Junior is older than sin and not at all presentable, but he knows everything there is to know and he runs the place.

After reminding me that Fiduciary Mutual Insurance was one of our larger accounts, and suggesting that I simulate an air of respect while dealing with them, Junior sent me over to Fid Mut's Century City office to see a claims agent named Jamieson.

"It's this old picture," Jamieson said. "It's disappeared. The way they tell it, there's no way it could have gone, and there isn't anyone who could have taken it, but it's gone anyway." A short, narrow, prissy-looking man with a thin black moustache above thin lips, he looked as though he was prepared to disapprove of me at the slightest provocation. But maybe that's just the way he looked.

I lowered myself into the chrome and black chair by his desk. "The way they tell it?"

"Exactly. The way they tell it, it's simply impossible." He smirked. "But we know there's nothing impossible, don't we?"

I told Jamieson that I'd take his word for it, that epistemology wasn't my field, and suggested that he get on with the story. He looked at me with a hurt expression, as though he had just been bitten by a pet guppy.

"The family is named Czeppski," Jamieson said, playing tippity-tap on his computer keyboard and peering at the screen, "Graf Maximilian and Grafin Sylvia." He turned to me. "Graf and grafin – that's Polish for count and countess."

"German," I said.

"Whatever," he said, looking annoyed.

"The Poles use German titles sometimes," I said to mollify him. He didn't look mollified. I stared out the wide picture window. We were on the 37th Floor. I could make out part of Santa Monica through the smog which stretched out in an unbroken layer below me. It was a brown smog day. I understand the green smog is more damaging to your lungs. They say the smog is getting better. They don't say better than what. The sun was somewhere above, and I saw shadows below but no glitter. The smog ate the glitter.

"They've been in the United States for about six months," Jamieson said. "There's also a daughter named Paula. They left the painting in storage in Paris, and it was just shipped over to be auctioned. An old family heirloom that's been buried in a barn for the past sixty years." He scissored a Polaroid from the folder with two well-manicured fingers and handed it to me. It was a medieval-looking painting of a thin man in a dirty white robe with a halo that looked as if it originated in his left nostril and ended in his right ear. His hand was bent at an unnatural angle and pebbles were falling out of it onto a group of emaciated children below. The predominant colours were red, brown and gold.

"Interesting," I said, "but is it art?"

"It should bring at least two million at auction," Jamieson told me. "It is a fourteenth-century depiction of Saint Simon of – ah – someplace – feeding the children."

"Pebbles?" I asked.

"Apparently he threw them stones, which miraculously turned into loaves of bread when they caught them."

"I'll bet he was surprised," I said.

"The painting was authenticated before it left Europe," Jamieson said. "It's insured for one-point-two million. It disappeared last night from the Czeppski apartment. Graf Maximilian wants a cheque. I want to know how it happened – where it went."

"You offering a reward?" I asked. A polite way of asking whether Fiduciary Mutual was willing to buy the painting back from the thieves. They always were unless they thought it was an inside job. Most insurance companies have the ethical standards of rattlesnakes without the rattles. They should be required by law to tie rattles on as a warning when dealing with claimants.

"Not just yet," Jamieson said. "I assume they hid it somewhere. But the police did a thorough search and couldn't find it. That's why I called your office. You find it, then we don't have to cut a cheque."

"Let's see what you've got," I said.

CI&S does most of Fiduciary Mutual's investigative work, so I was familiar with their procedures, even though I'd never worked with Jamieson before. They didn't like hiring detectives, and they only did it when they were convinced that something was wrong. It was then our job to prove that something *was* wrong so they could justify the expense. If we actually found the painting, we'd be in line for a reasonable, but not excessive, bonus.

The folder held about a dozen pages of the sort of paperwork that corporations use to give everyone a feeling that no stone is being unturned. There was a copy of the original insurance application; an international form with all the questions asked in three languages above neat rectangular boxes just too small to write in the answers. The questions had been answered in English, I noticed, in a small, round hand written with a fine point fountain pen. We detectives notice details like that. There were copies of several documents which served to authenticate the picture: a letter from an art expert certifying, I suppose, that the painting was, indeed, art; a formal document on a kind of gridded paper of an odd size that detailed the tests that had been performed on the paint, establishing that it was at least five hundred years old; and a very formal letter from an art historian putting the painting in its proper place in the history of art. The first two documents were in French, the third in English.

The shipping documents showed that the painting had been packed and shipped by a firm picked by the insurance company, one that regularly did the same for entire shows for major art museums. There was a detailed diagram of the shipping crate. There was a document from the shippers certifying that they had turned the painting over to Graf Czeppski in the same condition as they received it. What I assumed was Czeppski's signature was scrawled across the bottom.

I photocopied the three pages in the Czeppski folder that actually told anything about the Czeppskis, along with the four page police report, while Jamieson called the graf for me and made an appointment for three o'clock that afternoon. Then I headed to the Beechwood Café for lunch. It's a piece of the old

Hollywood that hasn't been discovered by the tourists yet, so the locals tend to hang out there. There's something soothing about eating surrounded by old writers and young actors. I studied the information on my photocopies over my natural sandwich with chunk white tuna. If there was anything there to tell me where the St Simon picture was hidden, I didn't see it.

The Czeppskis had lived in Paris for over thirty years, since before daughter Paula was born. They had survived their years of poverty by doing an equestrian act in the *Cirque Montmartre*; horses cantering around the ring, graf and grafin cavorting on and off the horses' backs. A few years ago, while the Soviet empire was busy crumbling, they had gone back to their ancestral estate outside of Szczecinek, a small town in northern Poland which was called Neustettin by the Germans when they thought they owned it. The estate had long since been carved up into pig farms, except for the chateau, which had housed a Soviet Army signals battalion. A little over a mile from the chateau the stable to the Czeppski horse farm, which had once held fifty horses, was still standing. Twenty-seven families lived in it now.

Graf Maximilian dug up what remained of the family fortune from behind the stable, where his father had buried it in 1939 as the Nazis closed in. It consisted of some very valuable jewellery, the tangible result of four centuries of oppressing the serfs; some silver plate used to entertain fellow nobles and royalty when they dropped by; some papers proving the family title to a sizable chunk of southern Poland that the Polish government was not about to give back; and the St Simon. He had immediately taken his family and his heirlooms back to Paris, where he had folded the act, sold the horses and a bit of the jewellery and had the St Simon authenticated.

The image of St Simon stoning the children was painted on a thin cedar board about 86 centimetres high and 62 centimetres wide. Which, for the metrically challenged, is about two feet by three feet. The art experts had decided that it had been painted in Germany in the fourteenth century, probably one panel of a polyptych that formed the altarpiece in a church of St Simon. A painting that might very well be another panel of the polyptych hung in the Valletta art museum on Malta.

The police report told as implausible a story of grand theft as ever I have read. The Czeppskis' apartment was on the eighth floor of a brand new high-rise building at the intersection of Wilshire and Brass, just west of Beverly Hills. All expensive, all elegant, and not at all where I would choose to live in the midst of a major earthquake fault zone. They had left their apartment early evening last night, except for daughter Paula, who didn't leave until a little after eleven. None of them was wearing or carrying anything that could have concealed a two-by-three foot inflexible cedar board. According to the concierge on duty, and I could just picture his grin when he said it, the way Paula was dressed she would have had trouble concealing a toothbrush.

The painting had been there shortly before they left – several reputable citizens had been over for cocktails and could testify to that. It had not been there when Graf and Grafin Czeppski returned from what the reporting officer had written down as "a benefit for indignant actors" at about two in the morning. The only ways downstairs from the Czeppskis' apartment were by the elevator, which wouldn't stop at any floor between the resident's and the lobby, and a staircase which you could enter at any floor but only leave at the lobby floor. There were security cameras in the elevator and at every landing in the staircase. The staff claimed to have seen nothing unusual between when the Czeppskis left and when they returned, and a check of the security camera tapes backed them up on that.

I could see why Fid Mut was suspicious. I had no opinion yet. I hoped to form one within the next few hours.

The doorman admitted me to the lobby, the concierge called upstairs to make sure I was a welcome guest, and then a lobby man walked me to the elevator and punched 8 for me, in case I had forgotten how. He used a key to activate the panel, and then removed it; so even if I had wanted to get off at another floor, the elevator wouldn't have stopped.

Graf Czeppski met me at the door. A tall man with rounded corners wearing a brown suit, a white, button-down shirt with vertical green stripes, and a forest-green tie as wide as his smile, he shook my hand with a hardy, vice-like grip. I managed to pull the hand free before any of the larger bones were broken, and returned his smile.

"You are agent Stanley Baum," he said, "of the insurance company?"

"Yes, sir," I agreed. Not exactly right, but close enough for jazz, as we used to say. I wondered whether I was supposed to call him "your excellency," or "your highness," or something, but then decided not to worry about it. We are all equal here in the Land of the Free, although some are more equal than others. But such inequalities as exist are seldom based on previous patents of nobility.

"Come quite in," he invited. "Look over the house. Question the servitors. This thing is surely a mystery. We are anxious for it to have a solution."

"I'll see what I can do," I told him.

He showed me into the living room. It was a study in chiaroscuro. The walls and drapes were white, the wall-to-wall carpet was black. The drapes which covered the wide picture window hung from a thick black rod and were accented with black cords. There was a long black couch in the shape of an L framing the centre of the room, a large, low black table in front of it, and an easy chair of the same pattern as the couch across from it. They looked modern, but the other pieces in the room – several severe-looking straight-back white chairs, an armoire, and a small desk that had been done in a black stain so that the wood grain showed through – all looked to be of an older European pattern. They might well have been antiques.

His wife and daughter were there, but there wasn't a servitor in evidence. The wife, sitting on one of the straight-back chairs, was thin of body and lip, with a sharp nose. She blended in with the chiaroscuro motif; wearing a straight-line black dress with a touch of white lace around the narrow collar, and had a single strand of pearls the size of walnuts around her neck and a ring with a diamond the size of a major metropolitan area on the ring finger of her right hand. She seemed distinctly annoyed at having to speak to me. I couldn't tell whether it was because I was a detective or because the lapels on my jacket were too narrow.

The daughter, sitting on the couch at the short end of the L, was the woman I had been dreaming about at least once a week since I was seventeen. I won't tell you what sort of dreams they were, but I imagine you can guess. A blue-eyed blonde with sharply chiselled features, she was wearing charcoal grey slacks and a white shirt with the sleeves rolled up, and had that air of quiet elegance that looks so natural and is so difficult and expensive to acquire. She had a lithe, slender, athletic-looking body, and looked to be somewhere around thirty, but I could have been off by a decade in either direction; I'm very bad at guessing women's ages. I'm not much better with men, but I seldom find myself wondering about a man's age.

The graf introduced me and I settled on the corner of the couch away from the daughter, as the chairs looked too fragile to hold me, and pulled out my pocket notebook. Not that I needed it, my memory is trained and practiced, but it gave me that air of authority that I otherwise lack. "If you could tell me what happened," I said to the room at large.

"We've told all that already," Grafin Sylvia said, staring down the edge of her nose at me. "To the police and to that other insurance person. I don't see any need to repeat it for a third time." She was perched on a delicate-looking chair of blackened wood with a white cushioned seat.

Paula shifted in her seat. "In my opinion –" she began.

Grafin Sylvia swivelled to look at her and snapped, "We don't need your opinion!"

Paula's face flushed a deep red, and she took several deep breaths, but then she calmed down and nothing more came of it. A pity. Perhaps later I could take her aside and ask her what she had been going to say.

I stood up, stuck the notebook in my jacket pocket, and buttoned the jacket. "I'm terribly sorry to have bothered you," I said. "I was told that you were anxious to get your cheque for the painting. I'll find my own way out."

"Now, now," the graf said, with a broad smile on his face,

intercepting me on the way to the door. "You'll have to excuse my wife. She is extremely troubled about all this. It has upset her terribly." He glared at his wife and snapped a few words to her in what I assume was Polish.

The grafin allowed a sneer of anxiety to cross her face. "I'm sorry if I gave you the wrong impression, Mr, ah, Baum. This has all been so fatiguing."

"I'm sure losing a two-million dollar painting must be quite tiring," I said, returning to the couch. I took my time settling back onto the cushion and opening my notebook again, and then looked back up at my audience. "Tell me about your household staff."

There was a short pause while they thought this over. "Well, there's Feodore," Paula said, leaning forward. Her teeth, I noticed, gleamed with a whiteness that her toothpaste manufacturer would have approved of, but they looked somehow sharp.

"Feodore?"

"The butler," Paula explained.

"We keep quite a small establishment here," the grafin said. "Only a butler and two maids. But of course the building has a concierge service which supplies many of our needs."

Of course. "Has Feodore been with you long?" I asked.

"About five years," the grafin said. "We brought him with us from Paris. The two maids we acquired here."

"Where are they from?"

"One is from Guatemala. Maria. The other, Estafia, is from Honduras. They are quite bright and capable, and seem completely trustworthy."

"And besides," Graf Czeppski broke in, "they were off yesterday, when the theft happened."

"Could they have snuck in without your knowing it?" I asked.

"They don't have keys," the graf said. "The concierge staff has to let them in."

"Ah," I said, making a random squiggle in my notebook. "Then I guess that lets Maria and Estafia out. What about Feodore?"

"He, also, was away at the time of the theft. He is away for this whole week. Some family matter he had to take care of."

"It was an outside job," Paula said. "Did you not read the police report?"

The police report said no such thing, but I decided not to point that out. "I try to form my own opinion," I told her. "The police and I have different goals."

"Yes," Grafin Sylvia said. "The police are trying to catch the miscreant who took our picture. You are trying to find a way to avoid paying us one million and two hundred thousand dollars."

"I am trying to recover the picture," I said, standing up and putting the notebook in my pocket. "Which will save the insurance company one point two million dollars. But it will also get you back your St Simon; which, I understand, is worth considerably more than that."

The graf shrugged a broad shrug. "I am told it will bring over two million dollars at auction," he said, "but who knows? There is no guarantee. And after the auction house takes its twenty per cent commission – there is little to choose."

"I see," I said.

He took a step toward me, put a finger on the middle button of my shirt, and pushed slightly. "But that is not to say that I would have any reason to arrange for the theft of my own picture," he said in a flat, controlled voice, which was trying to suggest suppressed anger, but seemed overly theatrical. "I know what you people at Fiduciary Mutual are suggesting, but I don't know why you're suggesting it, except in some obscene attempt to refuse to pay the claim. You didn't hesitate to collect the rather substantial premium – and to make me pay for the authentication of the picture and the too-expensive shipping costs."

I stepped forward and he hastily jerked his finger out of the way. "I don't work for Fiduciary Mutual," I told him. "I am a private investigator specializing in cases of fraud and embezzlement. My employer is Continental Investigations & Security." We were nose-to-nose. I hoped my breath was okay; I didn't want to offend. His breath smelled faintly of licorice. "Fiduciary Mutual calls us in when they want to be absolutely sure that there has been no hanky-panky. If I tell them you're clean, then they'll cut you a cheque tomorrow."

"Hanky-panky," the graf said.

"And it is us that they suspect of this hanky-panky?" the grafin asked.

"I don't know that they suspect anyone," I told them, prevaricating perhaps just the smallest bit. "They suspect the situation. It appears to be an impossible crime, but there are no impossible crimes, only misunderstood crimes. They have sent me to see if I can understand it."

There was a prolonged silence as everyone thought this over. Graf Czeppski's belligerent attitude disappeared in a wave of good fellowship, and he smiled a broad smile at me. "Then it is to our interest to help you ascertain what happened, is it not?" he asked.

"It is," I assured him.

"Then ask your questions."

I nodded. "The painting was delivered the day before yesterday. It actually arrived in Los Angeles the day before that, but it was held up in customs. Late last night it was gone. Who, aside from your guests of yesterday evening, knew that the painting was here?"

"The persons from the shipping company," the grafin suggested.

"And?"

"Lasser & Sons, the auction gallery," Graf Czeppski said. "They were to pick it up here today."

That I knew. It was delivered to the Czeppskis instead of directly to the gallery because Lasser & Sons' insurance for this particular auction wouldn't start until today. "Did any of you tell anyone?" I asked. "Among your friends, not connected to the gallery."

Grafin Sylvia lifted her nose higher to stare at me down it. "Are you suggesting that one of our friends might have done this?" she asked in a voice that would chip stone.

"Of course I am," I said. "Tell me which of your friends you could swear wouldn't steal a quarter of a million dollars, and I'll cross him or her off the list."

"A quarter of a million?" Paula asked. "I thought –"

"Thief's wages," I told her. "These days valuable and unique artwork is hard to fence. Whoever took it will be lucky to get that much for it."

After a few more questions I excused myself to prowl around the apartment. The Czeppskis stayed in the living room, trying to ignore the fact that a private detective was poking through their drawers and closets. I tried to think of places that the police might have missed on their search, and I poked and prodded a few possibilities, but nothing came of it. There was a bit of white powder at the bottom of one of the drawers in Paula's bedroom which interested me for a moment, but it proved to be some sort of chalk. The windows in the two bedrooms looked out over a locked courtyard to which the tenants did not have a key, so the painting had probably not been lowered out a window. Unless a confederate was stationed in one of the apartments below. I made a note to check on the tenants in the suspect apartments.

I pulled aside the curtains in the living room. One of the rungs holding the curtains to the oversized curtain rod was not looped over the rod. Paula, who was watching me, did not restrain herself from making comments as I felt along the curtain to make sure a two-by-three foot slab of wood had not been inserted into it somewhere. "Ah!," she exclaimed, "The great detective has found a clue! Not there? Perhaps it has been sewn into the carpet!"

Like Gaul, the large picture window behind the drapes was divided into three parts: an unopenable centre section framed by two smaller casement windows. I cranked open the one on the left and peered out. The window faced West, with a splendid view of the facade of the 1930s apartment building across brass Street. That building only went up ten stories, so the tenants above the tenth floor in this building might have a wonderful view of the tops of buildings in Santa Monica, and maybe even a glimpse of the ocean. Directly below was the black tarred roof of the two-storey parking garage, access to which was available only to workmen, who had to sign out the key. According to building security, the key had not been signed out for three weeks until the police used it this morning. There were a couple of old white five-gallon cans and a coil of black rope visible on the roof, but no painting.

"Perhaps the painting has flown out the window," Paula contributed.

I squinted around at the wall outside the window. There was a hook set in the concrete facing to the right of the window, presumably for the window washers, but no painting dangled from it. A four-inch ledge ran below the window, extending a foot or so past it on either side. There was no painting secured to the ledge.

I surveyed the kitchen and the butler's pantry, areas in which few Czeppskis ever set foot, according to Maria, who was putting various cheeses on a platter when I intruded. The Czeppskis were entertaining that evening, and the concierge was expected to send up food, kitchen staff and waiters momentarily. The plates were stacked in the kitchen, and the silver, freshly shined, much of it sporting what I assumed was the Czeppski crest, was lined up on a table in the butler's pantry. The two rooms were, as far as I could tell, devoid of religious artwork.

I thanked the various Czeppskis for their co-operation and told them someone would be in touch, and rang for the elevator. On the way down, I tried pushing various buttons to see what would happen. Nothing happened until I pushed the stop button, and then the elevator jerked to a stop and a loud alarm went off. Two lobby men and a police detective awaited me on the ground floor when I arrived.

"I don't know what possessed me," I said, stepping out of the elevator. "I just had an irresistible impulse to see what would happen if I pressed that button."

"Don't say anything else until I read you your rights," the detective said. "This time we've got you cold!" His name was Gibson, and we'd worked together on a few cases here and there in the past.

"I confess all," I told him. "I was led astray by evil companions in my youth. Hello, Gibson. You going up to see the graf?"

"Oddly enough I've been waiting down here for you," Gibson

said. "I didn't want to involve the department in whatever horrible falsehoods you were telling the Czeppskis."

Seeing that I neither needed help nor required restraining, the two lobby men returned to their stations. Gibson and I walked over to a couch set in an alcove in the lobby next to the building office. "You have something for me?" I asked. Contrary to the usual notion, public and private detectives actually tend to work fairly closely together when the opportunity presents. They get paid for apprehending the bad guys and we for retrieving the loot, and everybody's happy – as long as we on the private side remember who has the badge.

"Actually I called your office and Wohlstein told me where to find you," Gibson said. "There's something I'd like you to take a look at. A little sort of locked room mystery, just the sort of thing you like. Actually it's right across the street, which is what you call a coincidence."

"I don't believe in coincidences," I told him, "and just because I've been lucky a couple of times –"

Gibson snorted. "Lucky! Listen, if I had your kind of luck I'd be police commissioner. Not that I'd want the job, it's too political. What about the Marsden case? What about the Gallico job? Who but you would have thought he hid the pearls in the butter?"

I sighed. "Okay, let's take a look," I said. "But don't be disappointed if I don't come up with anything.

"I don't expect miracles," he said, but he lied.

The building Gibson took me to was the one across Brass Street that obscured the view from the Czeppskis' window of things westerly. A uniformed officer in the lobby let us in, and we took the ancient elevator up to the ninth floor. "The rental office says the place was rented furnished to a guy named Pedersen about three months ago," Gibson said over his shoulder, leading the way down the corridor. There were eight doors fronting the corridor, by which I deduced that there were eight apartments on the floor. The door to 8-C was open and the crime scene forensic crew was busy inside. An assistant medical examiner was kneeling by the supine body of a white male who looked to be in his forties. The corpse had a couple of holes in his chest. At first glance from ten feet away I would have said he was shot; there wasn't enough blood evident for stab wounds. But snap opinions like that are dangerous, there are too many variables. If the poor guy had been stabbed by an ice pick to the heart, for example, there probably would have been no blood at all.

"It's a one bedroom," Gibson told me. "Nothing special. Looks like all the furniture came with the apartment. Pedersen, if that's who he is, didn't have much of his own. Only some clothing."

"If that's who he is?"

"No identification on the body. We're having the rental agency send over the woman who handled the rental to see if she can identify him."

I nodded. "So what's the mystery?"

Gibson gave a half-nod toward the corpse. "The deceased was seen to enter the building shortly after ten last night. At ten seventeen the nine-one-one operator got the call that three shots had been heard from this apartment. When the first officers arrived at – " Gibson flipped open his notepad "– ten twenty-two, there was a crowd of people gathered around the door. Two of them had been in the hall when the shots were heard. Nobody came out that door. They pounded on the door and yelled for a while, but they very wisely decided not to break in. After all, as far as they knew there was someone with a gun inside." Gibson paused and looked up from his notepad.

"Let me guess," I said. "When the cops broke in there was nobody inside but the recently deceased."

"You've got it in one," Gibson said. "It was locked and bolted from the inside. They had to kick the door down to break in." He gestured at the door, which was splintered and off its hinges, showing the effects of violent entry.

"No other exit?"

"None."

"Windows?"

"In the living room, a picture window that doesn't open flanked by two of those louvre-type windows that open like

Venetian blinds and you'd have to be a cat to get in or out. In the bedroom, a sash window that's locked from the inside and enough dust around it so's it hasn't been opened any time recently."

"Secret passages or trap doors?"

"You're kidding."

"Did you look?"

"Yeah, we looked. If we don't come up with something better, we'll probably send a squad down to take the place apart, but I'm damn sure it'll be a waste of time. I think what we got here is the invisible man. You know – like the Shadow. The guy possesses the power to walk out of rooms without nobody seeing him."

I raised one eyebrow, a gesture I've been trying to perfect since high school. "Life is a glorious cycle of song!" I said. "Two impossible crimes on the same day."

"It's why you private dicks get the big money," Gibson said. "I hear what with overtime and everything you must be clearing pretty close to minimum wage."

"Yeah. And I hear the police department isn't political any more."

He shook his head sadly and I shook my head sadly and I stuck my hands in my pockets and started into the room.

"Wait a second," Gibson said. "We got to put on booties before we go in." He had someone toss him a couple of pair of the white cotton tie-ons that you're supposed to wear over your shoes to make sure you don't track anything into a crime scene, and we put them on. "Keep your hands in your pockets," he told me.

"Yeah," I said. "I know."

I walked slowly around the living room, trying to keep out of the way of the crime scene people, and stared at things. I had no idea what I was looking for. The walls of the living room were landlord green up to waist level, and covered with a fading rose-pattern wallpaper above. There was a beige couch and matching stuffed chair that looked as though they had come into the world during the Eisenhower presidency, a low coffee table well decorated with cigarette burns, and a pair of lamps on end tables that only Southern California landlords don't find funny. A television table sans television set sat across the room from the couch. A floor lamp, one of the sort that was a steel rod with a shaded bulb at one end and four claw feet at the other, was lying on the floor by the window. I peered into the bedroom, which contained a bed and a dresser, and one of those sliding-door closets that stood open and empty.

One wide set of mini-blinds covered the three sections of the living room window. They were pulled up as far as they could go. I looked out of the central picture window, which looked as if it had been cleaned recently except for a couple of greasy-looking circles high on the glass. I rubbed my finger across them and saw that they were on the outside of the glass. The Czeppskis' building loomed at me from across the street. There were a pack of wooden matches, a souvenir of Hollywood key ring devoid of keys, and a small dab of either clay or putty on the window sill, some of the small number of things present that hadn't been supplied by the landlord. I turned back to Gibson. "Bullets?" I asked.

"As far as we can tell, two in the deceased and one in the wall – over there above and to the right of the front door."

"Recent?"

"You thinking he was shot earlier and the sounds they heard in the hall were, maybe, a recording?"

"Just something to eliminate," I said.

"They could smell the gunpowder in the hall, and Dr Gadolfus here says that the deceased bought it right about the time the shots were heard."

The assistant medical examiner looked up. "That's right," he said.

"Did you find the gun?" I asked Gibson.

"It was lying next to the body," he told me. "A Browning.380 automatic. But he didn't shoot himself – that would be too easy. No powder burns. He was shot from at least six feet away."

I shrugged. "The murderer was hiding in the room and mingled with the crowd in the hall when they broke in," I suggested.

"Only the two officers went in," Gibson told me, "and only two officers came out. They say so, and so do the civilian witnesses."

"Just an idea," I said.

"You'll have to do better than that."

"Give me a minute."

"Here's something weird," Dr Gadolfus said, pausing in his labours. In an instant he had five people gathered around him and the body, eager for a view of something weird. "I didn't notice until I turned this work light on," he explained, "because his hands were in shadow. But look at his thumbs."

The body was in something approaching full rigor mortis, and the hands were turned palms down. Dr Gadolfus held a mirror under the right hand so we could see. The ball of the thumb appeared to be dark purple – almost black. "The left thumb is the same," Dr Gadolfus said, "I'd say this man has been finger-printed recently."

"Modern fingerprint fluids don't do that," Gibson said.

"Maybe he was just an old-fashioned sort of guy," I said, but I was thinking of something else. Finally a useful idea had occurred to me. And if I was right, each of these two impossible crimes solved the other. I went slowly around the room, peering at the walls and floor, looking for something – anything – that would fit in with my theory. Finally I spotted it. There was a slight bit of plaster dust – just a touch – in a crack in the floor by the wall, opposite the window.

Gibson came over to see what I was doing. "You ought to get yourself one of them big lenses like Sherlock Holmes used," he said, slapping me on the back.

I straightened up. "You want to make lieutenant?" I asked him.

"What are you talking about?"

"The credit for solving this one won't do me any good," I said. "I'll give it to you."

"You been here for, what, twenty minutes, and already you know who the invisible man is?"

"I know who and how, and about half of why," I told him. "You want it?"

"No joke?"

"No joke."

"Tell me about it."

"Take a couple of uniformed officers and go across the way," I told him, "Up to the Czeppskis' apartment. Read Paula – that's the daughter – her Miranda rights and tell her that Feodore is still alive and he's identified her, or that he wrote her name in blood as he lay dying – something like that. The shock should do it. I'm betting she'll confess."

"Who's Feodore?" Gibson asked.

I pointed to the corpse. "The Czeppskis' butler," I told Gibson. "That's him."

"Where do you get that from?"

"His thumbs. Like you said, that's not fingerprint fluid. That's the colour a butler's thumbs turn when he's been polishing the silver."

"That's a stretch," Gibson said.

"The Czeppskis have a room full of freshly-polished silver," I told him.

"Why the girl?" he asked me. "How'd she do it?"

"You arrest her," I told him, "then we'll talk."

"Even if that is the Czeppskis' butler, I can't just walk in there and arrest this girl on your say so," Gibson said. "Give me something."

I pointed to the floor. "See that white stuff in the crack? It's plaster."

"Yeah, so?"

"Watch!" I said. I prodded at the wall with my forefinger, feeling something rough under the wallpaper as I went. When I had it fairly well located, I turned around. The crime scene crew had all paused what they were doing to watch me. If I was wrong, I was going to feel pretty foolish. But I wasn't wrong. "Lend me a scalpel," I asked Dr Gadolfus.

He fished in his bag and passed me a disposable scalpel, still nicely wrapped in aluminum foil. I peeled it out and ran the blade carefully around the edge of the outline I had mapped out. The rectangle of wallpaper fell away, revealing a two-by-three-foot wood panel that had been carefully inserted into a matching hole cut into the plaster and lathe wall. I gingerly pulled it out and turned it around. "Meet Saint Simon," I said. "He's worth about two million dollars."

Gibson shook his head. "Good enough for me," he said. "You must know something. I'll go pick up the Czeppski girl."

It was close to midnight when I set the St Simon painting down on the floor of Junior's office, leaning it up against the wall. Junior was there, of course. He might have been called back when he heard I was coming in with the painting, but I think he lived there. "Two million dollars on the hoof," I told him. "You'd better put it in the safe 'till morning."

He stared at the painting for a minute, his eyes narrowed, then he turned to me. "Gibson called," he told me. "The girl confessed."

"Yeah," I said. "I thought she would."

"She's not really Czeppski's daughter," Junior said. "She's his mistress. The daughter's still in Paris. Married to a schoolteacher, apparently. Has no intention of leaving."

"So that's it," I said. "So the mistress was planning to skip with the butler and the painting."

"She says the wife was trying to kill her, so she had to get out. They had an agreement, one of these *menages à trois*, but the wife was beginning to feel pushed out, so she was pushing back. The girl was tired of the arrangement, and I suppose the graf, anyway, so she decided to head out and take a little something with her."

I nodded. "It sounds right," I said. "The two ladies didn't seem to be on the best of terms."

"How'd she do it?" Junior asked. "How'd she get the painting out of there? How'd she get out of the room after she shot what's-his-name?"

"Feodore," I said. "Didn't she tell Gibson?"

"She's too busy crying and blaming Feodore for everything. She was in the apartment when he walked in. He was supposed to be in San Francisco waiting for her. She realized that he was planning to take the St Simon himself and split, so they had a big fight and she shot him. In self-defence, she says."

"Could be," I said. "It was a good plan, but it just wasn't her lucky day."

Junior produced a bottle from his desk drawer and put it, and two glasses on the desk. "Fid Mut will be pleased to get that thing back," he said. "Just what was their plan?"

I picked up the bottle to see what he was drinking this month. It was a California pear brandy. I'd never had pear brandy. I tried it. It was good. I poured some more and organized the story in my mind. "Some of this is guesswork," I told him, "but I think most of it will hold."

"Let's hear it," Junior said.

"The apartment Feodore was killed in was their trysting-place," I said. "It may have been picked for its location, or the location might have suggested the scheme, I don't know."

"Just what was the scheme?"

"I'm getting there. Paula and Feodore decided to leave and take the painting with them. Since they would be the obvious suspects, they had to make it look as though it would have been impossible for them to have done it. I would guess that Feodore was supposed to make himself visible in San Francisco when the painting went missing. A couple of days before the theft they ran a string – probably a high-strength monofilament fishing line – between the Czeppskis' front window and the front window in the other apartment. They looped it around the metal rod of a standing lamp, that was pushed up against the louvered window on the left side of the picture window, and took it back across the street. It was probably tied off to a hook outside the Czeppskis' window to make sure it wasn't seen by the Czeppskis. From the street eight floors below it would be completely invisible."

"So they pulled the painting across the street on a string?"

"No. Remember, Feodore wasn't supposed to be there. On the day of the theft Paula waited until ma and pa Czeppski left, and then tied a rope – I'd guess a one-inch braided nylon line from a naval supply store – to one end of the monofilament and pulled it through. It looped around the lamp rod and returned, and she tied both ends off. Then, using the curtain rod from the Czeppskis' apartment for balance, she walked across the rope with the picture strapped to her back. Remember, the Czeppskis had a circus act. What do you want to bet that Paula was a high-wire performer in that circus?"

"Son of a bitch!" Junior remarked.

"She went in through the picture window. The glass pane, I assume, had been previously loosened in its frame. There were two little circles on the glass where she used one of those suction clamps to hold the pane. The old wallpaper on the living room wall had been peeled back, and a hole cut in the plaster and lathe to hold the St Simon. Then she pasted the wallpaper back down. Which, presumably, is when Feodore walked in."

"If he was there to steal the painting and run off by himself, why didn't he wait?" Junior asked.

"He did wait," I told him. "The painting was supposed to have been delivered the day before, but it was held up in customs. So the robbery was scheduled for the day before. He didn't know it had been changed."

"So she shot him and went back out the window."

"Right. Then she put the glass pane back and smeared some putty around the outside to hold it in place – I found a dab of putty on the window sill. She may have even stuck some framing around it or even a nail or two. It must have taken two or three minutes – and all the time a crowd was banging at the front door."

"The lady has good nerves," Junior commented.

"I'd say so. She walked across an eighty-foot length of rope both ways pretty much in the dark. Then when she got back to her apartment she had to put the curtain pole back and rehang the curtains. And in the dark – she couldn't turn the lights on in case someone saw her standing in the window and wondered what she was doing – she missed one of the rungs on the curtain. Then she coiled up the rope and dropped it out the window."

"That's quite a story," Junior said. "Any more to it?"

I shrugged. "I guess that's pretty much it. Then she stripped down to something brief and clinging so the building staff could see she that she wasn't leaving with the St Simon, and went out for a night on the town. If I hadn't picked up on a few little pointers – the curtain rung, the coil of rope on the roof of the garage, the plaster dust – she might have gotten away with it."

Junior mused for a minute. "She probably left fingerprints all over that room," he said. After all, she wasn't planning to kill anybody. But her prints probably aren't on file anywhere here in the 'states, and there wasn't anything to connect the two apartments except proximity. You're right, if Gibson hadn't asked you to look things over, she might have walked away from it. What made you suspect her in the first place?"

"She got a little too talkative and nasty when I was looking out the window. I thought she was trying to distract me by getting me mad, and I wondered just what she was distracting me away from."

Junior drank up his pear brandy and went over to pick up the St Simon. "I'll put this in the safe," he said. "You go home and get some sleep. If Fid Must doesn't find some way to renege on the bonus, I'll see that you get most of it."

"More than I expected," I told him, "but welcome just the same."

# THE PROBLEM OF THE CROWDED CEMETERY

*Edward D. Hoch*

*Edward D. Hoch (b.1930) is a literary phenomenon. He has written over 800 short stories since his debut with "Village of the Dead" in* Famous Detective Stories *for December 1955. This, in an age when the all-fiction magazine has all but curled up and died. He has had a story (sometimes more) in every issue of the prestigious* Ellery Queen's Mystery Magazine *(or EQMM for ease) since May 1973, a record which surely can never be equalled by anyone in any magazine. What is even more amazing about Ed Hoch is his versatility. Despite this awesome level of production his stories still manage to be original and enjoyable. He is able to ring the changes on every idea in the book. Quite a number of his stories have been impossible crimes – more than any other writer's. I mention many of these in my afterword. His best known series of impossible crimes are those narrated by New England doctor Sam Hawthorne, who looks back over his long life and tells the stories of the many strange crimes with which he was involved. The series began with "The Problem of the Covered Bridge"* EQMM, *December 1974) which is set in March 1922. The early stories have been collected as* Diagnosis: Impossible *(1996). I've selected a later story that has not been reprinted since its first outing, and which deals with the most remarkable mystery of how a freshly dead body ends up in a long-buried coffin!*

I used to picnic in Spring Glen Cemetery in my younger days (Dr Sam Hawthorne told his visitor over a suitable libation). That was when the place was more like a park than a cemetery, bisected by a creek that flowed gently through it most of the year. It was only in the spring, with the snow melting on Cobble Mountain, that the creek sometimes overflowed and flooded part of the graveyard.

That was what happened following the especially harsh winter of '36. The flooded creek had so eroded the soil on its banks that several acres of cemetery land had been lost. I was a member of the cemetery's board of trustees at that time and when we met in the spring of 1939 it was obvious something had to be done.

"It's just been getting worse for the past three years," Dalton Swan was saying as he showed us photographs of the damage done by the flooded stream. He was the tall, balding president of the board, a rotating responsibility each of the five members had assumed at one time or another. Swan, a fiftyish bank president, was in the second year of his two-year term.

I shuffled the pictures in my hands before passing them to Virginia Taylor on my right. Aware of the cemetery's shaky financial underpinnings, I asked, "Couldn't this go another year?"

"Look at these pictures, Sam," Dalton Swan argued. "The Brewster family gravesite is almost washed away! Here, you can actually see the corner of a coffin among these tree roots."

"Those coffins need to be dug up and moved," Virginia Taylor agreed. She was a tall, athletic woman in her thirties whom I often glimpsed on the tennis courts around town. The Taylor family had made their money growing tobacco all over the state of Connecticut but all it had earned them was the largest family plot in Spring Glen Cemetery.

We discussed it awhile longer, with Randy Freed, a trustee and the cemetery's legal counsel, suggesting we give it another month. "We simply can't justify this expense if there's another way out."

Dalton Swan scoffed at that. "The only other way is to let the Brewster coffins float down Spring Glen Creek. That what you want?"

Freed bristled, more at Swan's tone of voice than at the words. "Do what you want," he grumbled.

Swan called for a vote on the motion to move the endangered coffins. "I've already spoken with the Brewster family. They'll sign the necessary papers."

Miss Taylor, Swan, and I voted yes, along with Hiram Mullins, a retired real-estate developer who rarely spoke at our meetings. He sat there now with a sad smile on his face, perhaps remembering better days when creeks did not overflow their banks. The only negative vote came from Randy Freed.

"We'll proceed, then, as quickly as possible," Dalton Swan said. "Gunther can have the workmen and equipment here in the morning." Earl Gunther was the cemetery's superintendent, in charge of its day-to-day operation.

"You're making a mistake rushing into it like this," Freed told us. "A truckload of dirt tamped down along the bank of the creek would be a lot easier than relocating those coffins."

"Until it washed away with the next heavy rain," Swan argued. "Be practical, for God's sake!"

It did seem to me that the lawyer was being a bit unreasonable and I wondered why. "If it'll help matters any," I volunteered, "I can be out here in the morning when the workmen arrive, just to make certain nothing is touched but the Brewster plot."

"That would help a great deal, Dr Hawthorne," Virginia Taylor agreed. "We'd all feel better if there was some supervision on this besides Earl Gunther."

The superintendent had not been a special favourite of the trustees since a pair of his day labourers had been found drunk one morning, finishing off a quart of rye whiskey on the back of a toppled tombstone. Sheriff Lens had been called by some horrified mourners and he'd given the two a choice of thirty days in jail or a quick trip out of town. They'd chosen the latter, but the matter had come to the board's attention. Earl Gunther had been warned to stay on top of things if he wanted to keep his job.

After the meeting we sought him out in the house near the cemetery gate. It went with the job, though his office was in the building where we met. Earl's wife Linda ushered us in. "Dear, Dr Hawthorne and Mr Swan are here to see you."

Earl Gunther was a burly man with a black moustache and

thinning hair. He'd been a gravedigger at Spring Glen for years before taking on the job of superintendent. None of the board had been too excited at the prospect, but he seemed to be the best man available. He was newly married to Linda at the time and somehow we felt she might help straighten him out. She had, but not quite enough.

The Spring Glen board of trustees only met quarterly. This April meeting would be our last till the traditional July outing at Dalton Swan's farm. It wasn't something that took a great deal of my time, and until now it had never involved anything other than the perfunctory board meetings. All that was about to change. "Dr Hawthorne will be out in the morning to oversee the disinterment and reburial," Swan told the superintendent. "We don't foresee any problem."

Earl Gunther rubbed his chin. "T'll get a crew lined up, with shovels and a block and tackle. There are six coffins in the Brewster plot. That's gonna be an all-day job."

"It can't be helped. Someone from the family will be here for the reburial, probably with the minister."

"We'll do the best we can," the superintendent informed us.

Dalton Swan nodded. "I'm sure you will."

I drove back to the office where I had a couple of early afternoon appointments. "Any excitement at the meeting?" Mary Best asked, knowing there never was.

"Nothing much. I have to go out there in the morning while they move the Brewster plot. The creek's just eating away at the banks."

She glanced at my appointment book. "Shall I reschedule Mrs Winston for the afternoon?"

"Better make it Friday morning if you can. There's no telling how long I'll be out there."

While I waited for my first patient I glanced at the newspaper headlines. Hitler was insisting on the return of Danzig and a war between Germany and Poland seemed a distinct possibility. Up here in Northmont such concerns were still far away.

Late that afternoon, as I was leaving my office, I saw Virginia

Taylor coming out of the adjoining Pilgrim Memorial Hospital. She paused by her car, waiting till I reached her. "Will you be at Spring Glen in the morning?"

"I'm planning on it."

"That's good. The Brewster family is very concerned that the remains be moved in a dignified manner."

"I'm sure there'll be no problems. Whatever his other faults, Gunther is a good worker."

She nodded and motioned back toward the hospital building. "I do some volunteer work here on Tuesdays. It makes for a full day when there's also a board meeting." She belonged to one of Northmont's older families and spent much of her time with charitable causes. A few years back she'd been engaged to a young lawyer from Providence but they'd broken up, leaving her still unmarried. As often happened with unmarried women, her tennis and travel and volunteer work had managed to fill her life. The family tobacco business had long since been sold to others.

We chatted a while longer and then she went off in the sporty little convertible she drove around town. I'd had a car something like it in my younger days.

In the morning I drove out to the cemetery, arriving before nine. Earl Gunther had a flatbed truck parked by the Brewster plot, its back loaded with shovels and picks, a block and tackle, and a bulky tarpaulin folded into a heap. A half-dozen workmen were just arriving on the scene, walking over from the main gate.

"Good to see you, Doc," Gunther greeted me with a handshake. "I'm using two crews of three men each. One will work on the creek side, digging into the bank. The other will dig in from the top to reach the other coffins. It'll probably take all morning and maybe longer."

I watched the crew by the creek as they shovelled away the soft dirt and cut through some of the tree roots with axes. The tombstones up above told me that the most recent of these graves was over fifteen years old, and a couple dated back to before the turn of the century. As one coffin finally came free an hour later the workmen hoisted it out with the block and tackle, guiding it onto the flatbed truck. After that the pace seemed to pick up.

Before I knew it a second and third coffin had appeared on the flatbed, with a fourth being lifted from its resting place.

I'd wandered around the cemetery while the work was in progress, reading the names off the tombstones, remembering a few old patients whose lives I'd briefly prolonged. Finally, around noon, the last of the six coffins was pulled free of the tough oak roots that encircled it. I walked over to the truck as it was slid into place.

"Good work, Earl," I told him. "It looks like just one or two of the corners were damaged." These burials had been in the days before coffins were enclosed in metal vaults, and the older ones were showing evidence of their decades in the earth, even before the recent ravages of the flooded creek. Still, all six seemed to be reasonably sound. Or at least I thought so before my probing fingers encountered something wet and sticky at the damaged corner of one coffin.

"What's this?" I asked Gunther. My hand had come away moistened by blood and for a moment I thought I'd cut myself.

"You bleeding?"

"I'm not, but this coffin is."

"Coffins don't bleed, Doc, especially after twenty or thirty years."

"I think we better open this one up." The lid was still firmly screwed down and my fingers were useless. "Do you have a tool of some sort?"

"It's just bones," the superintendent argued.

"We'd better have a look."

He sighed and went to get some tools. The lid was unscrewed and easily pried open. I lifted it myself, prepared for the sight of decay. I wasn't prepared for the bloody corpse that confronted me, jammed in on top of the stark white bones.

Impossibly, irrationally, it was the body of Hiram Mullins, who'd sat next to me at the board meeting not twenty-four hours earlier.

It was Sheriff Lens who offered the best commentary when he arrived to view the body less than an hour later. "You've really outdone yourself this time, Doc. How could a man who was alive yesterday end up murdered inside a coffin that's been buried for twenty years?"

"I don't know, Sheriff, but I damn well intend to find out." I'd been questioning Earl Gunther and the workmen while we waited for the sheriff's arrival, but they professed to know nothing. Earl seemed especially upset, nervously wiping the sweat from his brow though the temperature was barely sixty.

"How's the board goin' to react to this, Doc? Will I lose my job?"

"Not if we can show you weren't responsible. But you have to be completely honest with me, Earl. Had any of those graves been dug up during the night?"

"You saw the ground yourself, Doc, before they started digging. It hadn't been touched in years. There's no way a coffin could have been dug up and reburied without leaving traces."

"Did you know Hiram Mullins well?"

"Hardly at all. I saw him when he came to your board meetings, that was it. He seemed like a nice man. Never said much."

That was certainly true, and I used virtually the same words to describe Mullins to the sheriff when he arrived. Sheriff Lens peered distastefully at the body in the coffin and asked, "What do you think caused the wound?"

"Some sharp instrument like a knife, only the blade seems to have been longer and thicker. There's a great deal of chest damage and so much blood that it actually leaked out of this rotted corner of the coffin."

"Good thing it did, or the Brewsters would have been reburied and Mullins along with them." The sheriff had brought a camera with him and was taking some photographs of the crime scene. He'd been doing this recently, following techniques outlined in crime investigation handbooks. He might have been a small-town sheriff but he was willing to learn new things. "What do you know about Mullins?"

I shrugged. "No more than you, I imagine. He was around seventy, I suppose, retired from his own real-estate business. I never saw him except at the cemetery board meetings, every three months."

"His wife is dead and they had no children," the sheriff said. "But how do you think he got into that coffin, Doc?"

"I have no idea."

When I got back to my office I looked through my bookshelves until I found an Ellery Queen mystery I remembered from seven years earlier. It was called *The Greek Coffin Mystery* and it dealt with two bodies discovered in a single coffin. But the second body had been added before the original burial. It didn't help a bit with Hiram Mullins's killing. His body had been added to a coffin already buried for two decades.

Before long my telephone started ringing. The word was getting around. First to call was Randy Freed, the lawyer who served as legal counsel for Spring Glen. "Sam, what's this I hear about old Mullins?"

"It's true. We found his body in one of the coffins Gunther's crew dug up."

"How is that possible?"

"It's not."

"Look here, Sam – you're the last one I'd expect to believe in any sort of supernatural business. Maybe Earl Gunther's crew added the body after they dug up the coffin."

"I was there all the time, Randy, never more than a hundred feet away."

"Do you think Spring Glen could face any sort of liability from the Mullins family?"

"I don't know how much of a family there is, and he was clearly murdered. We just have to figure out how."

"I'll be in touch," Freed told me as he hung up.

The next call came from Dalton Swan, advising me that he was calling an emergency meeting of the cemetery board for the following day. "We have to get to the bottom of this. The board has to issue a statement of some sort and we have to pick someone to fill his place."

The latter didn't seem that urgent to me, since we only met quarterly. "Whatever you say, Dalton. I have some hospital visits in the morning but after that I'm free till afternoon."

"Let's say eleven o'clock, then. I've spoken with Virginia and that time is good for her."

"Fine."

Mary Best came in as I hung up, returning from a late lunch. "What's this business of two bodies in one coffin?" she asked immediately. "Is Spring Glen getting that crowded?"

"I suppose the news is all over town."

She sat down at her reception desk. "All I know is, it's another impossible murder with you right in the centre of things again."

"Believe me, I didn't plan it that way. Until now, being a cemetery trustee was about the easiest position I ever held."

"The creek's the problem there. Maybe they should have gone in with Shinn Corners after all." The nearby town had wanted to develop a new regional cemetery serving both communities, but before anything could be decided the land was sold to a private college now under construction for a September opening.

"I never knew a thing about that till it was over," I admitted. "I don't know that anyone on the board did."

Mary had a way of thinking things through to their basics. "Would Earl Gunther have any reason for killing Mullins?" she asked.

"I can't imagine what it would be. The old man just sat there at the meetings, never said a word about Gunther or anyone else."

"Still, you don't think Gunther could be involved?"

"Maybe. But I don't picture Mullins going out to the cemetery to meet him at the crack of dawn. And even if he did, how would Gunther have gotten the body into a coffin buried six feet deep in firm, undisturbed earth?"

"Let me think about that while I type up the bills," she said. Marry was never one to admit defeat.

I waited around the hospital that afternoon until Doc Prouty completed the autopsy on old Hiram. There were no surprises. "Fully dressed except for collar and tie," he said as he washed up in the autopsy room. "It was a large, deep wound that encompassed the chest and heart. Went in under the rib cage, slanting up."

"What could make a wound like that? A broadsword?"

He chuckled. "Northmont isn't quite that far behind the times. There must be a lot of gardening tools around at the cemetery. I suppose a hedge trimmer could have done it."

"Can you estimate the time of death?"

"He'd eaten breakfast maybe an hour before he died."

"Breakfast?"

"Looks like toast and scrambled eggs."

"I was out there before nine."

A shrug. "People the age of Mullins, living alone, sometimes eat breakfast at four in the morning. I'd say he could have been killed anywhere between five and nine a.m., judging by the body temperature and such."

"Thanks, Doc."

I was halfway out the door when he said, "One more thing."

"What's that?"

"With a wound like this, there's no way the killer could have moved the body without getting blood on his clothes."

I phoned Sheriff Lens with the advance word on the autopsy results. I also told him about the blood. "Didn't notice blood on Gunther or any of his workmen," was his comment.

"Of course not. The killing couldn't have happened while I was there."

"Hiram Mullins drove a fancy Lincoln. Had one long as I can remember. We found it parked in his driveway."

"Well?"

"How'd he get out to the cemetery, Doc? He sure didn't walk at his age. Not in the dark."

It was only a couple of miles, and certainly walkable, but I admitted it was unlikely for someone like Mullins. That meant he'd probably been driven to the spot by his killer. It had been someone he knew and trusted to get him out that early in the morning. Would Earl Gunther have called him? One of the board members?

I finished talking to the sheriff and told Mary she could go home. I stayed awhile longer, puzzling over the life and death of a man I'd barely known, a silent man I'd seen four times a year and barely nodded to. I wondered if that ignorance was his fault or mine.

"Dr Hawthorne?"

I looked up at the sound of my name and saw a young woman standing in the doorway. The light from the hall was at her back and it took me an instant to recognize Linda Gunther, Earl's wife. "Can I help you?" I asked, certain the reason for her visit must be medical.

"I just wanted to speak with you about Earl, and about what happened this morning. I hear there's a meeting—"

"Sit down. I was just closing for the day."

"I know my husband has been in trouble with the cemetery board before. He was worried about losing his job. Now, with what happened this morning, he's afraid of being arrested."

"We have no reason to believe Earl is implicated in the killing. I was there the whole time the coffins were being disinterred. If he'd done anything unusual, I'd have noticed."

"But some of the others have never liked him."

"I don't know that that's true. He's always done his job."

"Is there anything I can do to help him?"

"Just tell the truth if Sheriff Lens has any questions. Did anything unusual happen this morning, for instance?"

"Nothing. Earl got up around seven and I fixed him breakfast. Then he walked over to the Brewster gravesite."

"What did you two have for breakfast?"

"Juice, cereal, toast, coffee. He has the same thing every morning."

"No eggs?"

"No. Why do you ask?"

"Just wondered. You didn't hear any unusual noises during the night or early morning?"

"No. Should I have?"

"If Hiram Mullins was murdered in the cemetery he might have screamed or cried out."

"We didn't hear anything."

I remembered what Doc Prouty had said about the blood. "What was your husband wearing when he went out?"

"His work overalls, like always."

"Did he have more than one pair?"

"He keeps an extra down at the tool shed."

I tried to reassure her. "Don't worry, Mrs Gunther. We're having a special meeting of the cemetery board in the morning, but it's not to take any action against your husband. We'll be talking about a replacement for Mullins."

"And Earl—?"

"—has nothing to worry about if he isn't involved in the killing. He won't be blamed just because it happened in the cemetery."

Linda Gunther allowed herself a cautious smile. "Thank you, Dr Hawthorne. I appreciate that."

After she'd gone I decided for the first time that she was a fairly attractive woman. Surely she could have done better than Earl Gunther for a husband, but then the ways of love and marriage are sometimes strange.

I had two hospital patients to visit in the morning, both recovering nicely from mild heart attacks. Then I checked in with Mary at the office and told her I'd be driving out to the cemetery for the board meeting. "I thought that wasn't till eleven o'clock," she said.

"I want to get there early and nose around, especially in the tool shed."

"Do you know how it was done?"

"Pure magic," I told her with a grin.

When I arrived at Spring Glen the morning sun was filtering through the spring leaves, bathing the place in a soft, inviting glow. I was an hour early for the meeting and I was surprised to find I wasn't the first to arrive. Virginia Taylor's sporty convertible occupied one of the parking spaces, though she was nowhere in sight.

I avoided the red-brick superintendent's house where Gunther and his wife lived and headed down the gently curving road toward the tool shed. Off in the distance I could see a couple of workmen removing some limbs from a tree ravaged by winter storms. The shed was unlocked, as it usually was when there were workmen about. I searched around among the tools for Earl's extra pair of overalls but found nothing.

Just as I was about to give up my search I spotted a large pair of hedge trimmers that seemed to be hiding behind a piece of canvas. I pulled them out, not thinking about fingerprints, and examined the blades for bloodstains. They appeared to have been wiped clean, but near the juncture of the blades were rust-colored spots that would be worth examining. I wrapped them in an oily cloth, trying not to damage fingerprints any more than I already had.

I was leaving the shed with my find when I saw Virginia Taylor walking toward me. "What have you got there?"

"Hedge trimmers. Could be the murder weapon."

"I always forget that you're something of a detective."

"Just an amateur."

"I wanted to see the spot where Hiram's body was found," she explained. "They seem to have removed all the Brewster coffins now."

"Did you know Hiram well? I only saw him at the meetings."

"He handled some real-estate transactions for my family years ago. He was good at making deals."

"A man of few words."

She smiled. "He could keep his mouth shut. Sometimes that's a valuable asset."

"Did he still work?"

She shook her head. "He's been retired for a year or so, ever since he put together the parcels of land for the new college in Shinn Corners."

"He was probably an interesting man. I'm sorry I never got to know him better. I remember last summer's party at Swan's place. Even out there I never saw him without a stiff collar and tie." It was still the era of highly starched detachable collars and men like Mullins and Swan wore them regularly. I preferred a shirt with an attached collar, as did younger men like Randy Freed.

We strolled back toward the small office building where the

board held its meetings. A part-time secretary helped Gunther with the bookwork when she was needed, but most days he was there alone unless he was supervising a work crew. Today, as always, he gathered up his papers to leave us in privacy.

"Stay a few minutes, Earl," I suggested. "We'll want to talk with you about what happened."

"Sure, whatever you say." He stayed at his desk rather than join us at the board table. Almost at once two more cars pulled up outside and I saw that Swan and Freed were arriving.

The lawyer was first through the door, all business. "We've got a serious problem here, Gunther. I'm worried about the cemetery's liability."

Dalton Swan took his seat at the head of the table, running a hand through his thinning hair. "We'll get to that later, Randy. Let's everyone sit down and go over what we know. Have you been able to learn anything, Sam?"

"Not much," I admitted. I ran through the autopsy report for them and then turned to Gunther. "Earl, you usually keep a clean set of overalls in the tool shed, don't you?"

"That's right."

"I was just looking for them. They're not to be found. I did find this hedge trimmer, though, with what looks like traces of blood."

Virginia Taylor made a face. "Sam thinks it could be the murder weapon."

"It's possible."

Dalton Swan now shifted his gaze to the cemetery super-intendent. "Isn't that tool shed kept locked, Earl?"

"Sure, most of the time."

"Was it locked night before last?"

"Well—" Gunther looked uneasy. "See, we had all this work to do in the morning, digging up those coffins for reburial. I thought some of the workmen might arrive early so I left the shed unlocked for them. Nobody dug up the graves before we got there, though. Doc saw that for himself."

"That's right," I agreed reluctantly. "The coffins were still underground when I got there."

"Do you have any idea how Mullins's body could have gotten in there?" Swan asked.

"None. It's like a miracle."

"All right." Swan waved him away. "Leave us alone for a few minutes."

Earl left the office and walked across the driveway to his house.

"Who do you have in mind as Hiram's replacement?" Virginia asked.

It was Randy Freed who answered. "I spoke to Dalton on the phone and made a suggestion. Milton Doyle is—"

"Not another lawyer!" Virginia exploded. "Cemeteries are about families, not lawsuits, for God's sake! How about another woman?"

"We have a woman," Swan answered quietly.

"Then how about *two* women? You men could still outvote us."

"It's worth considering," I agreed. "I suggest we adjourn until after the funeral. In the meantime maybe we can come up with some good women nominees."

Virginia Taylor gave me a smile of thanks and Swan agreed to adjourn until the following Monday. As we were leaving, Freed said, "It doesn't seem the same without old Mullins."

"He never said anything."

"But he was there, right in that chair! With those popping eyes and that bull neck he always looked as if his collar was strangling him."

Something occurred to me. "Randy, where would the records of real-estate transactions for the new college be kept?"

"Shinn Corners. At the courthouse."

It was just a hunch, but it was worth a drive to Shinn Corners. On the way over I started putting the pieces together in my mind. There was a way it could have been done. I saw it clearly now. Sometimes killers set out to create impossible situations but that hadn't been the case here. The killer had only wanted a safe way to dispose of the body, a way that would keep it hidden for another twenty years.

The courthouse was a big old building dating from the turn of the century with a stone fence already grown dark and weathered. In a big room I found maps and deeds, records stretching back a hundred years and longer. A girl in her late teens, a part-time clerk, came to my assistance at once. "The new college? We're very excited about it. I'm already enrolled for September."

"That's great," I said, meaning it. "I need to see the deeds on the various pieces of property that make up the college land. Would that be difficult?"

"No, not at all. It's a matter of public record."

There were so many individual parcels of land involved that the task seemed hopeless at first. Then I spotted Hiram Mullins's name and started concentrating on the deals he'd handled. I turned over the page of one deed and found the name I'd been seeking. After that it was easy.

I phoned Mary at the office and told her to postpone my afternoon appointments till the following day. "That's easy," she said. "There's only the Kane boy, and his mother says he's feeling fine now. The spots are all gone."

"Tell her to keep him out of school the rest of the week. He can go back on Monday."

"Sheriff Lens has been looking for you."

"I'll call him."

A moment later I had the sheriff's familiar voice on the other end of the line. "Where are you, Doc?"

"Over in Shinn Corners, checking the real-estate transactions regarding the new college."

"Why the college?" he wondered.

"It was the last deal Hiram Mullins worked on before his full retirement."

"Find anything?"

"A motive, I think."

"We've got something too. My deputies came up with a pair of bloodstained overalls. Earl Gunther admits they're his. Had his initials inside."

"Where were they found?"

"On the bank of the creek. Looks like Earl rolled them up and tossed them into the water, only they fell about a foot short.

There's a collar and tie with bloodstains, too. Remember, they were missing from Hiram's body."

"I remember. What are you going to do now?"

"Arrest Earl Gunther for the murder, of course. Those overalls are the proof we need."

"Look, Sheriff, you can bring him in for questioning but don't charge him yet. I'll be at your office in an hour."

I covered the back country roads in record time and arrived at the sheriff's office just as he was starting to question the cemetery superintendent. Linda Gunther was outside in the waiting room, looking nervous, and I tried to comfort her.

"Earl's in trouble, isn't he?"

"Yes, but he could be in lots worse trouble. Try to relax until we finish talking to him."

Inside the office Sheriff Lens was talking with Gunther while a deputy made notes. "I never wore those overalls to kill Mullins," the superintendent was saying. "Someone found them in the tool shed."

"Come on, Earl – you expect us to believe that?"

"I'm innocent!" He turned to me for help. "You believe me, don't you, Dr Hawthorne?"

I sat down across the table and chose my words carefully. "You didn't kill Mullins, but you're hardly innocent, Earl. You'd better tell us the whole truth if you expect to get out of this with your hide."

"What do you mean?"

"You know how the body got into the Brewster coffin."

"I—"

"What you gettin' at, Doc?" the sheriff asked.

"We've been saying all along that the ground over those coffins was solid and undisturbed, and that's perfectly true. But the ground on the creek side was a different story. The coffins were being moved, remember, because the waters of the flooded creek had so eroded the banks of the creek that some coffins were actually visible, held only by the tree roots that enveloped them. The morning of the murder I watched your crews shovel away the soft dirt and chop out those roots."

"Then you saw that I didn't—"

"I saw what you wanted me to see, Earl. That dirt was soft because it had been removed and replaced the night before. You went down there and saw one coffin virtually free of the earth, its corner badly damaged. You were afraid I, or one of the other trustees, would raise a fuss if we saw that, so you removed it yourself, using the block and tackle on your flatbed truck. You placed the coffin on the truck, carefully hiding it beneath a bulky folded tarpaulin and some tools. You had two crews digging, concentrating on their own efforts, not paying much attention to each other. At some point when I'd strolled off examining tombstones it was easy enough for you to yank off the tarp and reveal one more coffin. I remember thinking that the second and third coffins appeared on the truck before I knew it."

"If he pulled that trick he must have killed Mullins," the sheriff argued.

"Not at all. Earl had been in trouble with the trustees before and he was afraid we'd fire him for sure if we saw how bad he'd allowed that Brewster plot to get. He was only worried about his job. He had no way of knowing a murderer would find the coffin in the early morning hours and decide it was the perfect place to hide a body."

Sheriff Lens was still sceptical. "Who'd have a motive for killing the old guy?"

"Someone who'd used him to assemble parcels of land for the new college. Someone in a position to hear the talk about a possible new community cemetery with Shinn Corners and use that information to buy up property, then derail that project and sell the land to the private college for a huge profit."

"You talkin' about one of the trustees, Doc?"

"Exactly. No one else would have had the knowledge and the position to bring it off. No one else could have enlisted Mullins's help when he was in virtual retirement. I found the name I expected on those deeds over in Shinn Corners this afternoon. Mullins must have threatened to talk, or maybe tried a little blackmail. It's doubtful that anyone but another board member could have lured him to the cemetery early that morning, probably on the pretext of checking the erosion, and then killed him. The killer had to know about the tool shed, and the extra overalls, to protect his clothing from bloodstains. The killer might even have had a key, in case the shed was locked. The trustee put on the overalls, picked up the hedge trimmers, and went out to meet Mullins when he arrived. A quick thrust beneath the rib cage and it was over. The coffin lid was unscrewed and Mullins was added to those long-dead bones. Only there was too much blood, and a damaged coffin that allowed it to seep through and be seen."

"Which one, Doc?"

"Even without the name on those courthouse records I would have known. The overalls covered everything except the killer's collar and the top of the tie. Why were the dead man's collar and tie missing? Certainly he'd worn them. Mullins even wore them to summer picnics. No, the blood didn't get on the victim's collar and tie but on the killer's! A few drops splattered above the protective overalls. So the killer discarded his and replaced them with the victim's. The bull-necked Mullins would have had a collar big enough to fit any of the other trustees."

"Which one, Doc?" Sheriff Lens asked again.

"There was only one possibility. Miss Taylor is a woman, after all, with no need for male attire. Randy Freed and I wear shirts with attached collars. Only the dead man and Dalton Swan still wore the detachable collars. Dalton Swan, president of the board of trustees, whose term began before the land deal was closed, who was in the best position to hush up any proposal for a community cemetery and buy the land for himself, who could have gotten Mullins to front for him with the college people, who knew about the tool shed and could have killed Mullins and hidden the body without difficulty, who would have needed to replace his own bloodstained collar and tie before appearing that morning at his bank. The collar and tie you found can be traced to Swan. That and the land deal should be all the evidence you need."

"Dalton Swan . . ."

"That's your killer. Go get him, Sheriff."

# DEATH RIDES
# THE ELEVATOR

*Lois H. Gresh & Robert Weinberg*

*Lois H. Gresh (b.1956) works in the computer industry as a programmer and systems analyst and has written hundreds of technical manuals. She has written many short science fiction and horror stories and her first novel,* The Termination Node *(1999), an ingenious computer technothriller, was co-written with Robert Weinberg. Weinberg (b.1946) is an American author, bookdealer and editor who has written several novels of fantastic fiction, including a series featuring occult detective Alex Warner, starting with* The Devil's Auction *(1988).*

*Dedicated to the "other" Roger Whitaker*

It's fortunate that Will Rogers never met Cyrus Calhoun. Otherwise, Rogers' view of his fellow man might have changed forever. Calhoun was a prime example of a self-centred, obnoxious, cold-hearted banker with no redeeming graces. He liked to brag that he didn't care one bit about his fellow man – just his client's money. As the controlling stockholder of Manhattan National Trust, the nation's fifth largest Savings and Loan, Calhoun made more enemies in a week then most men made in a lifetime. Not that it mattered to the multi-millionaire. He treated ordinary people like peasants. Or worse, like ants to be stepped on. Until one fine day when he learned that stepping into the wrong place at the wrong time can get anyone, rich or poor, into a lot of trouble.

An odd twist of serendipity crossed my path with Calhoun's on his day of reckoning. My boss, Penelope Peters, relied on Manhattan National for all of her banking needs. Which means, since Penelope never left her home on Manhattan's West Side, every Friday I drove to the bank's main office and deposited the week's earnings. Some weeks were better than others, but rarely was our deposit less than ten thousand dollars.

Penelope Peters is a genius and she knows it. She charges her clients accordingly. They pay her fees without complaining because by the time they reach Penelope, there's no other choice left. She's the final resort, and despite her astronomical fees, her schedule is booked months in advance.

While Penelope does the thinking, I do the chores. My name's Sean O'Brien and I serve as Penelope's connection with the outside world. I do most of the household shopping – except for food, which is handled by the boss's chef, Julian Scapaletto – as well as keeping the books, paying the bills, and just about anything else Penelope requires. I'm thirty-five, stand six feet two, and weigh two forty. I have a degree in accounting, a private detective's badge, and a black belt in karate. Sherlock Holmes has his Dr Watson, Nero Wolfe his Archie Goodwin, Timmy has Lassie. Penelope Peters has me. It's strictly a business arrangement and I'm not complaining. Working for Penelope Peters is always interesting. Plus, she pays me a hell of a salary, more even than I think I'm worth.

My first and only encounter with Cyrus Calhoun occurred on Friday, August 20, 1999. I was standing patiently in line to make the weekly deposit. It had been a good week and there were cheques worth fifteen thousand dollars in my attache case. I was wearing a dark grey, double-breasted pinstripe suit, white shirt, and grey and black tie decorated with pictures of Bogart and Bergman from *Casablanca*. No tie without a picture was my motto. It was a Christmas gift from my boss.

Around the house, if I'm not working, I dress in casual slacks and a polo shirt. On business, I always wear a suit and tie. Since I represent Penelope everywhere outside her home, she insists I project a prosperous image. God forbid anyone should think she wasn't rich. Her explanation was short and simple. "Rich people who never leave their houses under any circumstances are merely eccentric. Poor people who act the same way are thought to be insane. Considering the choices, I prefer eccentric."

Anyway, waiting for a teller, I was reviewing the latest video releases in my mind. Friday nights Penelope preferred watching a movie on the large screen TV in the parlour. We'd been exceptionally busy during the past few months so had not seen anything since early summer. Since the boss likes mystery or spy flicks, I was debating the relative merits of *Ronin* versus *The Negotiator*. *Ronin* starred De Niro and Jean Reno, both of whom I liked. *The Negotiator* had Samuel L. Jackson and Kevin Spacey. Penelope liked Jackson from *Pulp Fiction*, which I thought was overrated. So, I stood there, lost in thought, weighing the pros and cons of which film to rent, when suddenly a woman's shriek broke the normal hush of the bank's lobby.

A shriek is different from a scream. Take it from someone who served two years as an MP in Germany. A scream blends loud and distressed. A shriek combines horror and fright. Screams are bad, shrieks are much worse.

Tucking my case under one arm, I leapt over the guide rope and sprinted in the general direction of the shrieks. The location wasn't far, around a twenty-foot long wall of fine marble. I skidded to a stop five feet from the spot. A young woman, dark hair, dressed in a bank uniform, was frozen solid in front of an elevator door. Her hands covered her eyes while her mouth continued to howl like a police siren. One of the bank's security guards, an old geezer with white hair, had his arms around the woman, trying to calm her down. Another five or six people, all dressed in business clothes, surrounded the elevator door. More were arriving every second. White faces were changing to vomit green. A man about my age, dressed in a three-piece suit that cost my salary for a year, stumbled hurriedly out of the crowd. He looked ready to heave up his breakfast. Wordlessly, I pointed to the nearest bathroom. Then, using my considerable weight and muscle, I shouldered my way through the growing crowd to see what had caused the ruckus.

The elevator was a fancy one. There were no mirrors like in most elevators. The rich prefer not to look at their wrinkles. Instead, the walls were decorated with fine mahogany panelling, highlighted with gold leaf. A large dropped light fixture on the ceiling provided bright white illumination. The thick green carpet seemed to be an expensive weave. A wall plate indicated that the elevator was for the private use of Cyrus Calhoun, the bank's CEO.

As to Mr Calhoun, he was the cause of the woman's shrieks. Or to be precise, his two parts were the cause of her distress. The body of the millionaire was sprawled in the rear right corner of the elevator, shoulders wedged tight against the walls. They were able to make such close contact because there was nothing between them to serve as a barrier. Calhoun's head, a limp, bloody ball, rested on the green carpet in the middle of the car. The banker's eyes were wide open, as if curious about the stir his appearance had caused.

Obviously, the decapitation had taken place in the elevator car. The walls, ceiling, and floor were covered with blood. Blood still trickled down his chest in a small but steady stream. I'm no doctor but I knew enough about killing to know Calhoun hadn't been dead more than a few minutes. The scene was one of the most striking sights I've encountered in all my life. A man's head and body, chopped apart, in what essentially was a locked room. From what I could gather from the babbling of the shrieker, she had been walking past the private elevator when the doors opened and she saw the corpse. One point she made perfectly clear. No one else had been in the elevator when it came to rest. The corpse had been all alone.

Sensing a mystery and perhaps some money, I flipped out my pocket phone and dialled home. Penelope answered on the fourth ring.

"Hello," she said in that odd way of hers, making the word into a statement, not a question.

"No time for pleasantries," I said. "I'm at the bank. Cyrus Calhoun, in two separate pieces, just arrived by his private elevator to the first floor. Head's on one side of the car, body's on the other. A witness who saw the door open claims nobody else was inside. Sound interesting?"

"Possibly," said Penelope. "Manhattan National Trust can't afford a long, drawn-out mystery. Notoriety is bad business, especially for banks. If there's no rational explanation found, call me back when possible. Give my regards, as always, to Inspector Norton. I'm sure he'll be there shortly."

"Speak of the devil," I said, as I switched off the phone and snapped it closed. Give bank security an *A* for effort. They had New York's top homicide cop, flanked by an entire team of specialists, here quicker than dialing 911. He glared at me with his usual "what the hell are you doing here, O'Brien?" stare but didn't bother to stop and say hello. Once he spotted me, Norton always concluded I was at the scene of the crime for a reason. More often than not, he was right. I work for Penelope Peters, and her job is solving problems. Including such problems as murder, robbery, arson, and kidnapping. Penelope hates crime like any good, upstanding citizen. Only in her case, she makes it pay.

"What a mess," declared the good Inspector, looking inside the elevator. His voice sounded like a truck driving over gravel. A big-boned man, he stood six feet four and weighed a hundred and sixty pounds. Entirely bald, with sunken cheeks and a beak-like nose, Norton looked like a walking skeleton. A bout with lung cancer five years ago had nearly killed him. No more cigars for the Inspector. Unable to function properly without something in his mouth, he constantly chewed gum. "What a stinkin' bloody mess."

His hawk-like gaze swept the crowd of onlookers like a vulture sizing up possible meals. "Nobody leaves. I want statements from everybody in this hall." His brows curled into a deep frown when he looked at me. "Especially you, O'Brien. I want to know exactly how you're involved in this disaster."

Immediately, everyone near me moved two steps back, as if they'd suddenly discovered a rabid dog in their midst. Norton knows how to make a guy feel two feet tall. That's one of his more endearing talents.

He waved his team of experts forward. "Find me some answers," he said. "The sooner the better."

The interrogations lasted about an hour. The Inspector handled some, his assistant Stanley Dryer the rest. Nobody had much to tell. Norton, of course, left me for last. He was about to give me the third degree when three middle-aged men dressed in thousand-bucks-a-pop suits emerged from an elevator across the hall. They headed in a beeline for Norton. Following them, dressed in a green-grey uniform was a short, stocky man with a confused expression on his face. The name-tag on his outfit identified him as Roger Stern, building engineer.

Standing only a few feet from Norton, I tried valiantly to blend in with the scenery. Fortunately, nobody paid much attention to me. At my weight and size, remaining unnoticed is not one of my greatest talents.

"I'm Garrett Calhoun," said the tallest of the men. Lines of grey streaked his black hair and his lips were thin and bloodless. "Cyrus is my brother. A terrible tragedy, Inspector. Terrible, terrible. Any clues about how it happened? Was his death an accident?"

Norton snorted. His tongue emerged, wrapped in gum, then retreated. "Accident? Unlikely when a man's been decapitated. Not the usual method to commit suicide. Sorry, Mr Calhoun, but your brother was murdered."

"Impossible," interjected the second suit. Shorter than Cyrus Calhoun's brother Garrett, this one was plump, wore thick brown plastic glasses, and had a trace of black moustache. "All three of us saw Cyrus enter the elevator alone. It's his private car. He only rides it between the fortieth floor and the lobby. Entire journey takes less than a minute. You're not suggesting someone climbed into the elevator somehow, chopped off my father-in-law's head in one minute, and then disappeared? That's absurd."

"I don't believe I caught your name?" said Norton.

"Tom Vance," said the guy with the glasses. "I'm married to Grace Calhoun, Cyrus Calhoun's daughter and Garrett's niece."

"Well, thanks for the info, Mr Vance," said Norton, ever calm and polite. He could have been discussing the weather instead of a brutal murder. There was no outrage left in Norton. He'd seen too many dead bodies to get angry. To him, solving crime was a job, not a crusade.

The Inspector turned to the third member of the group. "Ralston Calhoun, right?" Norton asked. "I believe we met once or twice at the Mayor's Spring Fundraiser."

The man, tall and slender, with light brown hair and light brown eyes, nodded. Of the three, he was the youngest by a dozen years or more. "Your prime suspect," said Ralston, with a slight twist of a smile. "Cyrus was my stepfather. With him dead, I stand to inherit a hefty fortune."

"Nah," said Norton. "Department furnished me details about the corporation. You make a great suspect, but so do your two relatives. As the three surviving stockholders in the company, you'll all do quite well with Calhoun dead. None of you has to worry about begging on the street. It's common knowledge you've been asking the old man to step down from the Board of Directors for years, and that he's constantly refused. Dry those big crocodile tears. Everybody hated the old bastard. After I get statements from all of you, you're free to go and get yourself smashing drunk. I know that's what I'd do if I owned shares in this bank. From what Mr Calhoun senior stated, I assume you all alibi each other?"

"Exactly," said Vance. "None of us could have had anything to do with the crime. It was right after our weekly board meeting. We were all upstairs in the reception lobby of the fortieth floor, saying goodbye to old Cyrus when the elevator door closed. We didn't know anything unusual had taken place until we got a phone message from the front desk."

"Didn't exactly rush down here," said Norton. "Talking to your lawyers first, I expect. Give your statements to my assistant, then you're free to go. Good luck with the press."

He frowned, rubbed his eyes. The usual signs he was getting a headache. I couldn't blame him. Murders in rooms locked from the inside were bad enough. But a murder in an elevator riding down forty stories?

Around that time, Norton noticed me trying to make like a potted plant. Surprisingly, he didn't say a word. Perhaps he was already thinking about Penelope. Not that I could blame him. More than once she'd solved seemingly impossible crimes. Though I had to admit, I was at a loss to explain how she'd figure out this hatchet job. Especially since she never, no matter what the circumstances, left her house.

Norton was talking again, this time to Roger Stern, the short stocky guy who was the building engineer. "I understand you were up on the fortieth floor of the building this morning," said Norton. "Any special reason?"

"Mr Calhoun was complaining about the air conditioning in his private quarters. Normally, I let one of the engineers handle such complaints, but when it comes from the boss, I do the job myself."

"Then you were present when Calhoun left the office and stepped into the private elevator?"

"Yes, sir," said Stern. He spread his hands wide. "Don't look to me for explanations. Once the door closed, I went back to work. Everything Mr Vance said about the elevator is true. Impossible for anyone to climb inside and chop off Mr Calhoun's head. Or get out afterward."

"Any chance the elevator stopping at another floor?" asked Norton. "Murderer jumps in, kills Calhoun with a machete, and jumps out all in the span of few seconds."

"Sounds like something out of James Bond." Stern shook his head. "This elevator was built according to Mr Calhoun's specifications. For his use only. Operates by key. It runs from the fortieth floor to the lobby and back up again. No stops in-between. Once the boss got into the car, it descended straight as an arrow to this foyer."

"Forget the machete angle," called Andy Jackson, one of Norton's team, from inside the elevator. "Wound's a clean slice. No chop-chop stuff here. More like a guillotine than a butcher knife."

"Terrific," said Norton, frustration evident in his voice. "Just terrific." He looked into the elevator where his crew was working. "Anything else you gentlemen can add to the discussion? A clue, perhaps?"

"Found a dozen slivers of wood on the carpet," said Mel Thomas. He held one up. It was the size and shape of a large toothpick. It was red with blood. "Scattered all over."

"There's a door in the ceiling, right?" said Norton. "Maybe the killer shook the wood loose when he moved the light fixture coming in from above?"

"Building code requires a trap door on top of every elevator," replied Stern. "It's kept bolted. I'll need to lower the elevator to the basement to inspect it."

"Do it," said Norton. There was a resigned look on his face, as if knowing what to expect in advance. "Okay if my men stay on board?"

"No problem," said Stern, pulling out a huge set of keys. "It'll just take me a minute or so."

I decided to use that minute to report to my boss. Over the years, I've learned how to deliver a concise but complete outline of a criminal investigation. Penelope didn't say a word during my entire recital.

"Wood fragments," she said, when I finished. "How interesting. Has the elevator been lowered yet?"

"It's down," I replied, glancing over my shoulder. "Norton's examining the trap door right now. He has that disgusted look on his face. There's a thin layer of dust everywhere. Not a chance anyone entered the car from the roof."

"Of course not," said Penelope. "Ask the good Inspector to let you look at the corner of the roof above where the body was found. I mean the roof of the elevator, on the outside of it. Search for spots in the dust. Then call me back."

"Spots in the dust on top of the elevator?" I muttered, closing the phone. "Sure, why not. Who am I to question a genius?"

Getting permission from Norton to examine the top of the car was easier than I expected. The Inspector was in a foul mood, but he was no fool. He'd seen my quick phone call and knew who had really made the request. Norton preferred solving crimes on his own. But he never refused Penelope's help. Especially since she made sure he always got all the credit. Penelope shunned publicity. She sleuthed strictly for the cash.

No surprise. I found three small blotches in the dust exactly where Penelope said to look. After telling Norton about my discovery, I called my boss. She answered on the first ring.

"Well?"

"Three spots," I replied. "Norton's crew is examining them now."

"Drops of Mr Calhoun's blood," said Penelope. "Please put Mr Norton on the line."

"Hey, Inspector," I said. "Call for you."

Norton took the phone from me and listened. The conversation didn't last long. It never does. He nodded a few times, said "Nine is fine," and snapped the phone closed.

"Get going," he said to me. "Your boss wants you back at her office, I'll arrive there at nine tonight. With guests."

"We'll be waiting," I replied. "I'll put out some of those Belgian chocolates you like so much."

He grunted, which is about the nearest thing to thanks I ever get from the Inspector.

Leaving the crime scene, I checked and found the bank tellers were still working. Business never stops, even for death. I made my deposit, then headed for home, wondering how Penelope knew about the blood spots dotting the dust on the roof of the elevator.

I didn't find out until nine that evening. As soon as I returned home, Penny had me draw a detailed picture of the elevator and the position of the torso and head. She stared at it for five minutes, while I waited in breathless anticipation for some profound remark. I should have known better.

"Neatly done," she declared, handing me back the picture. "A simple problem that should net us ten thousand dollars." She waved a slender hand at me in dismissal. "Help Julian in the kitchen. We'll be serving coffee and cake for our guests this evening. He could use your help."

"Serving them coffee before or after you expose the killer?" I asked, knowing the answer.

"After, of course. It would be uncivilized to break bread with a murderer in my house. Now stop delaying and get going. I'm not saying another word about the crime until tonight."

Mumbling to myself about secretive women, I wandered into the kitchen, leaving Penelope in her study. She picked up the copy of *Intensity* she'd been reading when I entered. Unable to go outside, my boss likes to read thrillers for vicarious fun. Though she has plenty of problems of her own, she likes reading about other people who have even worse problems.

The smell of fine coffee and even finer chocolate filled the house when Inspector Norris, with Detective Dryer in tow, arrived on our doorstep at exactly nine pm. Standing behind the two cops were the three Calhoun heirs and the building engineer, Roger Stern. No lawyers, which was a good sign. Lawyers can drag out a twenty minute meeting into an all-night marathon.

"Welcome, gentlemen," I said. "You too, Inspector. Ms Peters is waiting for you in her study."

Norton, who knew the way, led the others to the office. It was a magnificent room, with the back wall lined by bookshelves stretching from floor to ceiling. Penelope's library contained books on everything from anthropology to zoology. She had read them all. A hand-woven Moroccan rug covered the floor. Souvenirs from all over the world dotted the other walls. Penelope had many grateful clients across the globe. The only things missing from the study were windows. There were no windows in any of the rooms Penelope used.

In the exact centre of the room stood the boss's ebony desk. It glistened black in the recessed white lights. The only thing on top of the desk was a phone-intercom system and a pad of white paper. Penelope disliked clutter. Behind the wood behemoth was a tall chair covered with black leather. In front of the desk were six heavy wooden chairs with red cushions. When Penelope spoke, I preferred to stand.

"Please be seated," I said. "Ms Peters will be here in a moment."

Norton dropped into his usual position, the end chair on the right. Dryer, who also knew the routine, took the chair on the far left. Our four visitors from the bank took the seats in the middle.

Penelope, of course, observed everyone from a peephole in the door leading to the kitchen. She preferred that people be seated before she entered a room. A minute after our guests were in their positions, she pushed open the door and briskly walked to the desk. Sitting on the black leather chair, she smiled and nodded to her audience. Being men, they all smiled back.

At five seven and a hundred and ten pounds, Penelope Peters looks like an overweight model. She has thin facial bones, a small nose, and rosebud lips. She's slender but shapely, and she knows how to dress to impress.

This evening, she was wearing a sleeveless green dress with a white shawl draped over her shoulders. Her earrings were a matched set of sparkling emeralds, the same bright green as her eyes. Her brown hair was cut short and fell in a soft wave to the top of her shoulders. Her intense gaze and intelligence, coupled with an air of innocence, often made me think that she would have made a fine Joan of Arc.

"Gentlemen," she said in her soft, mellow voice, "thank you for coming here tonight on such short notice. I appreciate your co-operation."

"What I don't understand is why we couldn't have held the meeting in our board room tomorrow morning," said Tom Vance. "It's late and I'm exhausted. Answering questions all day for the cops isn't easy."

"Agreed," said Penelope. She leaned forward, resting her head in her hands, elbows pressed to the desk. "Two reasons. First, I only conduct business from this office. I suffer from an extreme case of agoraphobia, brought on by a genetic problem. If I make the slightest attempt to go outside, my body is overwhelmed by a panic-anxiety attack. The symptoms, I assure you, are quite unpleasant. So, until physicians find some cure for my phobia, I am bound by the confines of my house."

"So, you're a virtual prisoner in your own home," said Vance. "Seems like a pretty dreadful way to live."

Penelope shrugged. "The condition developed when I was a teenager and grew progressively worse as I aged. Fortunately, by the time I found I could no longer leave my house, my business was established and my income was more than satisfactory. Compared to many other disabled people, I feel quite fortunate."

"You said two reasons," declared Garrett Calhoun. Drumming his fingers on the side of his armchair, he was obviously anxious to be gone. "What's the second?"

"You have a serious problem," said Penelope. "The president of your bank was murdered this morning in a rather spectacular fashion. Knowing the Press, the story will continue to make headlines for weeks, especially if the killer isn't apprehended. Your internal security will be judged insufficient, considering it couldn't even protect the bank's largest shareholder. TV and radio thrive on unsolved mysteries. The negative publicity will cost your bank many thousands, perhaps millions of dollars in withdrawn funds or closed accounts. Do you agree?"

"Well—" began Garrett.

"We agree," said Vance. "What's it to you?"

"I run a consulting business," said Penelope. "I solve problems. Mostly I work for major companies, oftentimes governments. Even businessmen when necessary. Perhaps in some sort of cosmic balancing act for my bizarre phobia, I have an IQ that can't be measured by any standardized test. I provide answers, gentlemen. If you agree to pay me ten thousand dollars, I'll solve your crime *tonight*. Squashing the story before it has a chance to grow out of control.

"As the majority stockholders in the bank, you have the authority to make such a transaction. I have a standard contract drawn up," and Penelope reached into the top drawer of her desk and drew out the papers, "and Inspector Norton can serve as witness."

"And – And – if we don't agree to this outrageous demand?" sputtered Garrett Calhoun.

"Then you can depend on the good Inspector and New York's finest to find the criminal. No matter how long it takes. If ever."

"Well, I find this whole charade ridiculous" said Garrett, rising from his chair.

"Oh, shut up and sit down, Garrett," said Tom Vance. He stared at Penelope. "If we sign this document, you'll guarantee to name the killer and explain how the murder was committed before we leave tonight? We won't be stuck in one of those ongoing O.J. Simpson nightmares?"

"Sign the document and I'll do so immediately," said Penelope. "Ask Inspector Norton if you like. I've helped him on a number of occasions in the past. Have I ever failed, Inspector, to deliver on my promises?"

"Ms Peters has assisted my department more than once," said Norton. He hated being put on the spot but Penelope was a precious asset he couldn't afford to lose. "If she says she'll deliver, she will. She always does."

"Good enough for me," said Vance. Grabbing a pen from the desk, he signed the contract in bold letters. "Go ahead, you two. Unless you're afraid of the truth."

"Nonsense," said Garrett Calhoun. Still, he read the entire document carefully before finally signing.

Ralston didn't bother to look. He merely shrugged and signed. "I'm not guilty," he said. "Why should I worry?"

"Murderers are always so self assured," said Penelope with a slight smile. "They assume no one is smarter than they are. Inspector, all we require now is your signature."

Norton signed, as he had done more than a dozen times before. Dryer peered at me. I shrugged. I had absolutely no idea which of the three shareholders was the killer.

Norton handed Penelope the contract. She scanned it quickly then dropped it back into the desk drawer.

"You were on the fortieth floor when Mr Calhoun was murdered, were you not, Mr Stern?"

"Yes, miss," said Stern. "Fixing the air conditioning vent in the boss's office. Just as I told the police."

"You also told them that it was impossible for the elevator to stop on any floor other than the ground level?"

"Yes, miss," said Stern. He sounded puzzled, not sure why Penelope was asking.

"The trap door on the top of the elevator was sealed to your satisfaction?"

"Yes, miss. It hasn't been used for at least two months."

"Two months," repeated Penelope. "I assume that's when you looped the wire noose around the outside of the light fixture and made sure the wire was held securely in place with those wooden sticks. Then you punched a small hole in the corner of the ceiling where you proceeded to wind the rest of the wire to the elevator cables."

Stern's face was white. "I have no idea what you're talking about, miss. No idea at all."

"Yes, you do, Mr Stern. But in case you've forgotten the details, I'll state them all for you.

"For some reason, you wanted to kill Mr Calhoun. From what I've heard about him, he was not a likeable man. I'm sure Inspector Norton's men will discover your motive in due course. However, like most killers, you preferred not to pay the penalty for your crime."

Stern was staring at Penelope as if hypnotized. Dryer and Norton were both on their feet. I had taken a position a few feet behind him. That's one of the reasons I don't like to be seated when Penelope's solving a case.

"The actual execution of the scheme was quite simple for a man of your talents. Two months ago, you took a long roll of steel wire, probably 24 gauge that is so thin it's hardly noticeable, and made a loop – a noose – out of it. Opening the noose wide, you put it around the top of the light fixture. To make sure it wouldn't slide off, you steadied it with tiny wooden dowels. You took the end of the wire and slipped it through a tiny hole you made in the top corner of the elevator. I assume you measured off around ten feet or so and tied the wire to a sturdy steel claw. Then you just threaded the rest of the wire among the hoist ropes, so it ran with them whenever the elevator moved."

"This – this –" began Stern, then his voice faltered and drifted off into nothingness.

"The elevator, with the invisible steel wire, continued to function perfectly. It was a trap waiting to be sprung. That opportunity arose when you were called to the fortieth floor to fix the air conditioning. When Mr Calhoun walked to the elevator, you used your keys and quickly entered the machine room directly above the hoistway. There's an opening through the floor for the driving machine. Using a grappling pole, you latched onto the metal claw, tugged it loose from the hoist ropes and hooked it onto the deflector shield. That's just below the machine room and solid as a rock. Then locking the door again, you left the machine room and went back to fixing the air conditioner."

"Lies," muttered Stern. "All lies."

"I don't think so," said Penelope. "When the elevator door closed, the car started moving downward. With the 24 gauge wire fastened by the hook to the immovable shield, the noose immediately tightened. The pressure yanked off the pins holding it in place and the wire circle fell like a lasso over Calhoun. He didn't have time to make a sound. An elevator drops *fast*. Continuing to constrict, the slip-knot noose zipped up his body until it caught beneath his chin, circling his neck like a garrotte. In an instant, the wire circle jerked him off his feet, up to the top of the elevator. Something had to give. The dropping elevator probably didn't even shudder when the rapidly contracting noose sliced his head right off his shoulders. A moment later, the wire disappeared through the hole in the ceiling, leaving no clue as to how the beheading was accomplished. A near perfect crime."

"Damn," said Detective Dryer. "I've heard of men being strangled to death by a wire noose but never beheaded."

"A falling elevator's a great deal stronger than any human, Mr Dryer," said Penelope. "If you search the hoistway directly above the fortieth floor, I suspect you'll find the wire used to commit the crime. With all the excitement due to the murder, I doubt if Mr Stern had a chance to remove it."

Stern shook his head. His voice quivered as he spoke. "It's still there. Things happened just like you said. Doesn't matter that you figured it out. Old bastard's dead. He tried to rape my daughter, then threatened to blackball me if she went to the police. That's when I decided to kill him."

"Tell it to the jury," said Penelope. "Considering Calhoun's reputation in Manhattan, you'll probably get off with five years probation and a contract servicing the elevators in City Hall."

Norton and Dryer left a few minutes later, Stern between

them. Ushering the Inspector to the door, I managed to slip him a handful of Belgian chocolates before he exited.

Back in her office, Penelope was explaining to the three Calhouns how she figured out the crime without examining the scene. Julian was serving coffee and chocolate cake. My boss might be confined to her house, but she knows how to live well.

"Since it was clear no one could have entered the car and killed Mr Calhoun, I eliminated that possibility immediately. The pieces of wood found on the floor were covered with blood, indicating they had fallen before the murder. This meant that something had happened within the elevator when it started moving, something that made the wooden fragments splinter and fall to the carpet. I theorized a noose tightening. All that remained was to check if there were bloodstains from the wire on the outside roof of the elevator. Mr O'Brien confirmed that. The solution was merely an exercise in simple logic."

"You *are* a genius," said Ralston Calhoun.

"The world is filled with mysteries," said Penelope. She drank no coffee nor ate any chocolate. Caffeine aggravated her agoraphobia. "Many very intelligent people work solving them. My skill lies in making that talent pay."

Penelope always sounds modest after solving crimes. Especially after she's just relieved her clients of ten thousand dollars. Now that takes real genius.

# THE BURGLAR WHO
# SMELLED SMOKE

*Lynne Wood Block & Lawrence Block*

*Lawrence Block (b.1938) is one of the most highly respected writers of crime and mystery fiction. He was made a Grand Master by the Mystery Writers of America in 1994 and several of his stories and novels have won literary awards. His name first appeared with the short story "You Can't Lose" (Manhunt, February 1958) but over the next two years a lot of material appeared pseudonymously until* Death Pulls a Double Cross *was published in 1961. His recent books usually feature one of two main characters. There's the alcoholic ex-policeman, Matt Scudder, who first appeared in,* In the Midst of Death *(1976) and whose cases include the Edgar Award winning* A Dance at the Slaughterhouse *(1991) and the tour-de-force* When the Sacred Ginmill Closes *(1986). And then there's the bookstore owner and compulsive thief Bernie Rhodenbarr whose books, after the first two, are always recognizable by the title beginning* The Burglar Who . . . *The first book,* Burglars Can't Be Choosers *(1977), involves an impossible crime. And so does the following, one of the rare Rhodenbarr short stories, written with his wife, Lynne.*

I was gearing up to poke the bell a second time when the door opened. I'd been expecting Karl Bellermann, and instead I found myself facing a woman with soft blond hair framing an otherwise severe, high-cheekboned face. She looked as if she'd been repeatedly disappointed in life but was damned if she would let it get to her.

I gave my name and she nodded in recognition. "Yes, Mr Rhodenbarr," she said. "Karl is expecting you. I can't disturb him now as he's in the library with his books. If you'll come into the sitting room I'll bring you some coffee, and Karl will be with you in –" she consulted her watch "– in just twelve minutes."

In twelve minutes it would be noon, which was when Karl had told me to arrive. I'd taken a train from New York and a cab from the train station, and good connections had got me there twelve minutes early, and evidently I could damn well cool my heels for all twelve of those minutes.

I was faintly miffed, but I wasn't much surprised. Karl Bellermann, arguably the country's leading collector of crime fiction, had taken a cue from one of the genre's greatest creations, Rex Stout's incomparable Nero Wolfe. Wolfe, an orchid fancier, spent an inviolate two hours in the morning and two hours in the afternoon with his plants, and would brook no disturbance at such times. Bellermann, no more flexible in real life than Wolfe was in fiction, scheduled even longer sessions with his books, and would neither greet visitors nor take phone calls while communing with them.

The sitting room where the blond woman led me was nicely appointed, and the chair where she planted me was comfortable enough. The coffee she poured was superb, rich and dark and winey. I picked up the latest issue of *Ellery Queen* and was halfway through a new Peter Lovesey story and just finishing my second cup of coffee when the door opened and Karl Bellermann strode in.

"Bernie," he said. "Bernie Rhodenbarr."

"Karl."

"So good of you to come. You had no trouble finding us?"

"I took a taxi from the train station. The driver knew the house."

He laughed. "I'll bet he did. And I'll bet I know what he called it. 'Bellermann's Folly,' yes?"

"Well," I said.

"Please, don't spare my feelings. That's what all the local rustics call it. They hold in contempt that which they fail to understand. To their eyes, the architecture is overly ornate, and too much a mixture of styles, at once a Rhenish castle and an alpine chalet.

And the library dwarfs the rest of the house, like the tail that wags the dog. Your driver is very likely a man who owns a single book, the Bible given to him for Confirmation and unopened ever since. That a man might choose to devote to his books the greater portion of his house – and, indeed, the greater portion of his life – could not fail to strike him as an instance of remarkable eccentricity." His eyes twinkled. "Although he might phrase it differently."

Indeed he had. "The guy's a nut case," the driver had reported confidently. "One look at his house and you'll see for yourself. He's only eating with one chopstick."

A few minutes later I sat down to lunch with Karl Bellermann, and there were no chopsticks in evidence. He ate with a fork, and he was every bit as agile with it as the fictional orchid fancier. Our meal consisted of a crown loin of pork with roasted potatoes and braised cauliflower, and Bellermann put away a second helping of everything.

I don't know where he put it. He was a long lean gentleman in his mid-fifties, with a full head of iron-grey hair and a moustache a little darker than the hair on his head. He'd dressed rather elaborately for a day at home with his books – a tie, a vest, a Donegal tweed jacket – and I didn't flatter myself that it was on my account. I had a feeling he chose a similar get-up seven days a week, and I wouldn't have been surprised to learn he put on a black tie every night for dinner.

He carried most of the lunchtime conversation, talking about books he'd read, arguing the relative merits of Hammett and Chandler, musing on the likelihood that female private eyes in fiction had come to out-number their real-life counterparts. I didn't feel called upon to contribute much, and Mrs Bellermann never uttered a word except to offer dessert (*apfelküchen*, lighter than air and sweeter than revenge) and coffee (the mixture as before but a fresh pot of it, and seemingly richer and darker and stronger and winier this time around). Karl and I both turned down a second piece of the cake and said yes to a second cup of coffee, and then Karl turned significantly to his wife and gave her a formal nod.

"Thank you, Eva," he said. And she rose, all but curtseyed, and left the room.

"She leaves us to our brandy and cigars," he said, "but it's too early in the day for spirits, and no one smokes in Schloss Bellermann."

"Schloss Bellermann?"

"A joke of mine. If the world calls it Bellermann's Folly, why shouldn't Bellermann call it his castle? Eh?"

"Why not?"

He looked at his watch. "But let me show you my library," he said, "and then you can show me what you've brought me."

Diagonal mullions divided the library door into a few dozen diamond-shaped sections, each set with a mirrored pane of glass. The effect was unusual, and I asked if they were one-way mirrors.

"Like the ones in police stations?" He raised an eyebrow. "Your past is showing, eh, Bernie? But no, it is even more of a trick than the police play on criminals. On the other side of the mirror –" he clicked a fingernail against a pane "– is solid steel an inch and a half thick. The library walls themselves are reinforced with steel sheeting. The exterior walls are concrete, reinforced with steel rods. And look at this lock."

It was a Poulard, its mechanism intricate beyond description, its key one that not a locksmith in ten thousand could duplicate.

"Pickproof," he said. "They guarantee it."

"So I understand."

He slipped the irreproducible key into the impregnable lock and opened the unbreachable door. Inside was a room two full stories tall, with a system of ladders leading to the upper levels. The library, as tall as the house itself, had an eighteen-foot ceiling panelled in light and dark wood in a sunburst pattern. Wall-to-wall carpet covered the floor, and oriental rugs in turn covered most of the broadloom. The walls, predictably enough, were given over to floor-to-ceiling bookshelves, with the shelves themselves devoted entirely to books. There were no paintings, no Chinese ginger jars, no bronze animals, no sets of armour, no cigar humidors, no framed photographs of family members, no hand-coloured engravings of

Victoria Falls, no hunting trophies, no Lalique figurines, no Limoges boxes. Nothing but books, sometimes embraced by bronze bookends, but mostly extending without interruption from one end of a section of shelving to the other.

"Books," he said reverently – and, I thought, unnecessarily. I own a bookstore, I can recognize books when I see them.

"Books," I affirmed.

"I believe they are happy."

"Happy?"

"You are surprised? Why should objects lack feelings, especially objects of such a sensitive nature as books? And, if a book can have feelings, these books ought to be happy. They are owned and tended by a man who cares deeply for them. And they are housed in a room perfectly designed for their safety and comfort."

"It certainly looks that way."

He nodded. "Two windows only, on the north wall, of course, so that no direct sunlight ever enters the room. Sunlight fades book spines, bleaches the ink of a dust jacket. It is a book's enemy, and it cannot gain entry here."

"That's good," I said. "My store faces south, and the building across the street blocks some of the sunlight, but a little gets through. I have to make sure I don't keep any of the better volumes where the light can get at them."

"You should paint the windows black," he said, "or hang thick curtains. Or both."

"Well, I like to keep an eye on the street," I said. "And my cat likes to sleep in the sunlit window."

He made a face. "A cat? In a room full of books?"

"He'd be safe," I said, "even in a room full of rocking chairs. He's a Manx. And he's an honest working cat. I used to have mice damaging the books, and that stopped the day he moved in."

"No mice can get in here," Bellermann said, "and neither can cats, with their hair and their odour. Mould cannot attack my books, or mildew. You feel the air?"

"The air?"

"A constant sixty-four degrees Fahrenheit," he said. "On the cool side, but perfect for my books. I put on a jacket and I am perfectly comfortable. And, as you can see, most of them are already wearing their jackets. Dust jackets! Ha ha!"

"Ha ha," I agreed.

"The humidity is sixty per cent," he went on. "It never varies. Too dry and the glue dries out. Too damp and the pages rot. Neither can happen here."

"That's reassuring."

"I would say so. The air is filtered regularly, with not only air conditioning but special filters to remove pollutants that are truly microscopic. No book could ask for a safer or more comfortable environment."

I sniffed the air. It was cool, and neither too moist nor too dry, and as immaculate as modern science could make it. My nose wrinkled, and I picked up a whiff of something.

"What about fire?" I wondered.

"Steel walls, steel doors, triple-glazed windows with heat-resistant bulletproof glass. Special insulation in the walls and ceiling and floor. The whole house could burn to the ground, Bernie, and this room and its contents would remain unaffected. It is one enormous fire-safe."

"But if the fire broke out in here . . ."

"How? I don't smoke, or play with matches. There are no cupboards holding piles of oily rags, no bales of mouldering hay to burst into spontaneous combustion."

"No, but—"

"And even if there were a fire," he said, "it would be extinguished almost before it had begun." He gestured and I looked up and saw round metal gadgets spotted here and there in the walls and ceiling.

I said, "A sprinkler system? Somebody tried to sell me one at the store once and I threw him out on his ear. Fire's rough on books, but water's sheer disaster. And those things are like smoke alarms, they can go off for no good reason, and then where are you? Karl, I can't believe—"

"Please," he said, holding up a hand. "Do you take me for an idiot?"

"No, but—"

"Do you honestly think I would use water to forestall fire? Credit me with a little sense, my friend."

"I do, but—"

"There will be no fire here, and no flood, either. A book in my library will be, ah, what is the expression? Snug as a slug in a rug."

"A bug," I said.

"I beg your pardon?"

"A bug in a rug," I said. "I think that's the expression."

His response was a shrug, the sort you'd get, I suppose, from a slug in a rug. "But we have no time for language lessons," he said. "From two to six I must be in the library with my books, and it is already one-fifty."

"You're already in the library."

"Alone," he said. "With only my books for company. So. What have you brought me?"

I opened my briefcase, withdrew the padded mailer, reached into that like Little Jack Horner and brought forth a plum indeed. I looked up in time to catch an unguarded glimpse of Bellermann's face, and it was a study. How often do you get to see a man salivate less than an hour after a big lunch?

He extended his hands and I placed the book in them. "*Fer-de-Lance*," he said reverently. "Nero Wolfe's debut, the rarest and most desirable book in the entire canon. Hardly the best of the novels, I wouldn't say. It took Stout several books fully to refine the character of Wolfe and to hone the narrative edge of Archie Goodwin. But the brilliance was present from the beginning, and the book is a prize."

He turned the volume over in his hands, inspected the dust jacket fore and aft. "Of course I own a copy," he said. "A first edition in dust wrapper. This dust wrapper is nicer than the one I have."

"It's pretty cherry," I said.

"Pristine," he allowed, "or very nearly so. Mine has a couple of chips and an unfortunate tear mended quite expertly with tape. This does look virtually perfect."

"Yes."

"But the jacket's the least of it, is it not? This is a special copy."

"It is."

He opened it, and his large hands could not have been gentler had he been repotting orchids. He found the title page and read, "'For Franklin Roosevelt, with the earnest hope of a brighter tomorrow. Best regards from Rex Todhunter Stout.'" He ran his forefinger over the inscription. "It's Stout's writing," he announced. "He didn't inscribe many books, but I have enough signed copies to know his hand. And this is the ultimate association copy, isn't it?"

"You could say that."

"I just did. Stout was a liberal Democrat, ultimately a World Federalist. FDR, like the present incumbent, was a great fan of detective stories. It always seems to be the Democratic presidents who relish a good mystery. Eisenhower preferred Westerns, Nixon liked history and biography, and I don't know that Reagan read at all."

He sighed and closed the book. "Mr Gulbenkian must regret the loss of this copy," he said.

"I suppose he must."

"A year ago," he said, "when I learned he'd been burglarized and some of his best volumes stolen, I wondered what sort of burglar could possibly know what books to take. And of course I thought of you."

I didn't say anything.

"Tell me your price again, Bernie. Refresh my memory."

I named a figure.

"It's high," he said.

"The book's unique," I pointed out.

"I know that. I know, too, that I can never show it off. I cannot tell anyone I have it. You and I alone will know that it is in my possession."

"It'll be our little secret, Karl."

"Our little secret. I can't even insure it. At least Gulbenkian was insured, eh? But he can never replace the book. Why didn't you sell it back to him?"

"I might," I said, "if you decide you don't want it."

"But of course I want it!" He might have said more but a glance at his watch reminded him of the time. "Two o'clock," he said, motioning me toward the door. "Eva will have my afternoon coffee ready. And you will excuse me, I am sure, while I spend the afternoon with my books, including this latest specimen."

"Be careful with it," I said.

"Bernie! I'm not going to *read* it. I have plenty of reading copies, should I care to renew my acquaintance with *Fer-de-Lance*. I want to hold it, to be with it. And then at six o'clock we will conclude our business, and I will give you a dinner every bit as good as the lunch you just had. And then you can return to the city."

He ushered me out, and moments later he disappeared into the library again, carrying a tray with coffee in one of those silver pots they used to give you on trains. There was a cup on the tray as well, and a sugar bowl and creamer, along with a plate of short-bread cookies. I stood in the hall and watched the library door swing shut, heard the lock turn and the bolt slide home. Then I turned, and there was Karl's wife, Eva.

"I guess he's really going to spend the next four hours in there," I said.

"He always does."

"I'd go for a drive," I said, "but I don't have a car. I suppose I could go for a walk. It's a beautiful day, bright and sunny. Of course your husband doesn't allow sunlight into the library, but I suppose he lets it go where it wants in the rest of the neighbourhood."

That drew a smile from her.

"If I'd thought ahead," I said, "I'd have brought something to read. Not that there aren't a few thousand books in the house, but they're all locked away with Karl."

"Not all of them," she said. "My husband's collection is limited to books published before 1975, along with the more recent work of a few of his very favourite authors. But he buys other contemporary crime novels as well, and keeps them here and there around the house. The bookcase in the guest room is well stocked."

"That's good news. As far as that goes, I was in the middle of a magazine story."

"In *Ellery Queen*, wasn't it? Come with me, Mr Rhodenbarr, and I'll—"

"Bernie."

"Bernie," she said, and coloured slightly, those dangerous cheekbones turning from ivory to the ink you find inside a seashell. "I'll show you where the guest room is, Bernie, and then I'll bring you your magazine."

The guest room was on the second floor, and its glassed-in bookcase was indeed jam-packed with recent crime fiction. I was just getting drawn into the opening of one of Jeremiah Healy's Cuddy novels when Eva Bellermann knocked on the half-open door and came in with a tray quite like the one she'd brought her husband. Coffee in a silver pot, a gold-rimmed bone china cup and saucer, a matching plate holding shortbread cookies. And, keeping them company, the issue of *EQMM* I'd been reading earlier.

"This is awfully nice of you," I said. "But you should have brought a second cup so you could join me."

"I've had too much coffee already," she said. "But I could keep you company for a few minutes if you don't mind."

"I'd like that."

"So would I," she said, skirting my chair and sitting on the edge of the narrow captain's bed. "I don't get much company. The people in the village keep their distance. And Karl has his books."

"And he's locked away with them . . ."

"Three hours in the morning and four in the afternoon. Then in the evening he deals with correspondence and returns phone calls. He's retired, as you know, but he has investment decisions to make and business matters to deal with. And books, of course. He's always buying more of them." She sighed. "I'm afraid he doesn't have much time left for me."

"It must be difficult for you."

"It's lonely," she said.

"I can imagine."

"We have so little in common," she said. "I sometimes wonder why he married me. The books are his whole life."

"And they don't interest you at all?"

She shook her head. "I haven't the brain for it," she said. "Clues and timetables and elaborate murder methods. It is like working a crossword puzzle without a pencil. Or worse – like assembling a jigsaw puzzle in the dark."

"With gloves on," I suggested.

"Oh, that's funny!" She laughed more than the line warranted and laid a hand on my arm. "But I should not make jokes about the books. You are a bookseller yourself. Perhaps books are your whole life, too."

"Not my whole life," I said.

"Oh? What else interests you?"

"Beautiful women," I said recklessly.

"Beautiful women?"

"Like you," I said.

Believe me, I hadn't planned on any of this. I'd figured on finishing the Lovesey story, then curling up with the Healy book until Karl Bellermann emerged from his lair, saw his shadow, and paid me a lot of money for the book he thought I had stolen.

In point of fact, the *Fer-de-Lance* I'd brought him was legitimately mine to sell – or very nearly so. I would never have entertained the notion of breaking into Nizar Gulbenkian's fieldstone house in Riverdale. Gulbenkian was a friend as well as a valued customer, and I'd rushed to call him when I learned of his loss. I would keep an ear cocked and an eye open, I assured him, and I would let him know if any of his treasures turned up on the grey or black market.

"That's kind of you, Bernie," he'd said. "We will have to talk of this one day."

And, months later, we talked – and I learned there had been no burglary. Gulbenkian had gouged his own front door with a chisel, looted his own well-insured library of its greatest treasures, and tucked them out of sight (if not out of mind) before reporting the offence – and pocketing the payoff from the insurance company.

He'd needed money, of course, and this had seemed a good way to get it without parting with his precious volumes. But now he needed more money, as one so often does, and he had a carton full of books he no longer legally owned and could not even show off to his friends, let alone display to the public. He couldn't offer them for sale, either, but someone else could. Someone who might be presumed to have stolen them. Someone rather like me.

"It will be the simplest thing in the world for you, Bernie," old Nizar said. "You won't to do any breaking or entering. You won't even have to come to Riverdale. All you'll do is sell the books, and I will gladly pay you ten per cent of the proceeds."

"Half," I said.

We settled on a third, after protracted negotiations, and later over drinks he allowed that he'd have gone as high as forty per cent, while I admitted I'd have taken twenty. He brought me the books, and I knew which one to offer first, and to whom.

The FDR *Fer-de-Lance* was the prize of the lot, and the most readily identifiable. Karl Bellermann was likely to pay the highest price for it, and to be most sanguine about its unorthodox provenance.

You hear it said of a man now and then that he'd rather steal a dollar than earn ten. (It's been said, not entirely without justification, of me.) Karl Bellermann was a man who'd rather buy a stolen book for a thousand dollars than pay half that through legitimate channels. I'd sold him things in the past, some stolen, some not, and it was the volume with a dubious history that really got him going.

So, as far as he was concerned, I'd lifted *Fer-de-Lance* from its rightful owner, who would turn purple if he knew where it was. But I knew better – Gulbenkian would cheerfully pocket two-thirds of whatever I pried out of Bellermann, and would know exactly where the book had wound up and just how it got there.

In a sense, then, I was putting one over on Karl Bellermann, but that didn't constitute a breach of my admittedly elastic moral code. It was something else entirely, though, to abuse the man's hospitality by putting the moves on his gorgeous young wife.

Well, what can I say? Nobody's perfect.

*   *   *

Afterward I lay back with my head on a pillow and tried to figure out what would make a man choose a leather chair and room full of books over a comfortable bed with a hot blonde in it. I marvelled at the vagaries of human nature, and Eva stroked my chest and urged a cup of coffee on me.

It was great coffee, and no less welcome after our little interlude. The cookies were good, too. Eva took one, but passed on the coffee. If she drank it after lunchtime, she said, she had trouble sleeping nights.

"It never keeps me awake," I said. "In fact, this stuff seems to be having just the opposite effect. The more I drink, the sleepier I get."

"Maybe it is I who have made you sleepy."

"Could be."

She snuggled close, letting interesting parts of her body press against mine. "Perhaps we should close our eyes for a few minutes," she said.

The next thing I knew she had a hand on my shoulder and was shaking me awake. "Bernie," she said. "We fell asleep!"

"We did?"

"And look at the time! It is almost six o'clock. Karl will be coming out of the library any minute."

"Uh-oh."

She was out of bed, diving into her clothes. "I'll go downstairs," she said. "You can take your time dressing, as long as we are not together." And, before I could say anything, she swept out of the room.

I had the urge to close my eyes and drift right off again. Instead I forced myself out of bed, took a quick shower to clear the cobwebs, then got dressed. I stood for a moment at the head of the stairs, listening for conversation and hoping I wouldn't hear any voices raised in anger. I didn't hear any voices, angry or otherwise, or anything else.

*It's quiet out there*, I thought, like so many supporting characters in so many Westerns. And the thought came back, as it had from so many heroes in those same Westerns: *Yeah . . . too quiet*.

I descended the flight of stairs, turned a corner and bumped into Eva. "He hasn't come out," she said. "Bernie, I'm worried."

"Maybe he lost track of the time."

"Never. He's like a Swiss watch, and he *has* a Swiss watch and checks it constantly. He comes out every day at six on the dot. It is ten minutes past the hour and where is he?"

"Maybe he came out and—"

"Yes?"

"I don't know. Drove into town to buy a paper."

"He never does that. And the car is in the garage."

"He could have gone for a walk."

"He hates to walk. Bernie, he is still in there."

"Well, I suppose he's got the right. They're his rooms and his books. If he wants to hang around—"

"I'm afraid something has happened to him. Bernie, I knocked on the door. I knocked loud. Perhaps you heard the sound upstairs?"

"No, but I probably wouldn't. I was all the way upstairs, and I had the shower on for a while there. I take it he didn't answer."

"No."

"Well, I gather it's pretty well soundproofed in there. Maybe he didn't hear you."

"I have knocked before. And he has heard me before."

"Maybe he heard you this time and decided to ignore you." Why was I raising so many objections? Perhaps because I didn't want to let myself think there was any great cause for alarm.

"Bernie," she said, "what if he is ill? What if he has had a heart attack?"

"I suppose it's possible, but—"

"I think I should call the police."

I suppose it's my special perspective, but I almost never think that's a great idea. I wasn't mad about it now, either, being in the possession of stolen property and a criminal record, not to mention the guilty conscience that I'd earned a couple of hours ago in the upstairs guest room.

"Not the police," I said. "Not yet. First let's make sure he's not just taking a nap, or all caught up in his reading."

"But how? The door is locked."

"Isn't there an extra key?"

"If there is, he's never told me where he keeps it. He's the only one with access to his precious books."

"The window," I said.

"It can't be opened. It is this triple pane of bulletproof glass, and—"

"And you couldn't budge it with a battering ram," I said. "He told me all about it. You can still see through it, though, can't you?"

"He's in there," I announced. "At least his feet are."

"His feet?"

"There's a big leather chair with its back to the window," I said, "and he's sitting in it. I can't see the rest of him, but I can see his feet."

"What are they doing?"

"They're sticking out in front of the chair," I said, "and they're wearing shoes, and that's about it. Feet aren't terribly expressive, are they?"

I made a fist and reached up to bang on the window. I don't know what I expected the feet to do in response, but they stayed right where they were.

"The police," Eva said. "I'd better call them."

"Not just yet," I said.

The Poulard is a terrific lock, no question about it. State-of-the-art and all that. But I don't know where they get off calling it pickproof. When I first came across the word in one of their ads I knew how Alexander felt when he heard about the Gordian knot. Pickproof, eh? We'll see about that!

The lock on the library door put up a good fight, but I'd brought the little set of picks and probes I never leave home without, and I put them (and my God-given talent) to the task.

And opened the door.

"Bernie," Eva said, gaping. "Where did you learn how to do that?"

"In the Boy Scouts," I said. "They give you a merit badge for it if you apply yourself. Karl? Karl, are you all right?"

He was in his chair, and now we could see more than his well-shod feet. His hands were in his lap, holding a book by William Campbell Gault. His head was back, his eyes closed. He looked for all the world like a man who'd dozed off over a book.

We stood looking at him, and I took a moment to sniff the air. I'd smelled something on my first visit to this remarkable room, but I couldn't catch a whiff of it now.

"Bernie—"

I looked down, scanned the floor, running my eyes over the maroon broadloom and the carpets that covered most of it. I dropped to one knee alongside one small Persian – a Tabriz, if I had to guess, but I know less than a good burglar should about the subject. I took a close look at this one and Eva asked me what I was doing.

"Just helping out," I said. "Didn't you drop a contact lens?"

"I don't wear contact lenses."

"My mistake," I said, and got to my feet. I went over to the big leather chair and went through the formality of laying a hand on Karl Bellermann's brow. It was predictably cool to the touch.

"Is he—"

I nodded. "You'd better call the cops," I said.

Elmer Crittenden, the officer in charge, was a stocky fellow in a khaki windbreaker. He kept glancing warily at the walls of books, as if he feared being called upon to sit down and read them one after the other. My guess is that he'd had less experience with them than with dead bodies.

"Most likely turn out to be his heart," he said of the deceased. "Usually is when they go like this. He complain any of chest pains? Shooting pains up and down his left arm? Any of that?"

Eva said he hadn't.

"Might have had 'em without saying anything," Crittenden said. "Or it could be he didn't get any advance warning. Way he's sitting and all, I'd say it was quick. Could be he closed his eyes for a little nap and died in his sleep."

"Just so he didn't suffer," Eva said.

Crittenden lifted Karl's eyelid, squinted, touched the corpse here and there. "What it almost looks like," he said, "is that he was smothered, but I don't suppose some great speckled bird flew in a window and held a pillow over his face. It'll turn out to be a heart attack, unless I miss my guess."

Could I just let it go? I looked at Crittenden, at Eva, at the sunburst pattern on the high ceiling up above, at the putative Tabriz carpet below. Then I looked at Karl, the consummate bibliophile, with FDR's *Fer-de-Lance* on the table beside his chair. He was my customer, and he'd died within arm's reach of the book I'd brought him. Should I let him *requiescat* in relative *pace*? Or did I have an active role to play?

"I think you were right," I told Crittenden. "I think he was smothered."

"What would make you say that, sir? You didn't even get a good look at his eyeballs."

"I'll trust your eyeballs," I said. "And I don't think it was a great speckled bird that did it, either."

"Oh?"

"It's classic," I said, "and it would have appealed to Karl, given his passion for crime fiction. If he had to die, he'd probably have wanted it to happen in a locked room. And not just any locked room, either, but one secured by a pickproof Poulard, with steel-lined walls and windows that don't open."

"He was locked up tighter than Fort Knox," Crittenden said.

"He was," I said. "And, all the same, he was murdered."

"Smothered," I said. "When the lab checks him out, tell them to look for Halon gas. I think it'll show up, but not unless they're looking for it."

"I never heard of it," Crittenden said.

"Most people haven't," I said. "'It was in the news a while ago when they installed it in subway toll booths. There'd been a few incendiary attacks on booth attendants – a spritz of something flammable and they got turned into crispy critters. The Halon gas was there to smother a fire before it got started."

"How's it work?"

"It displaces the oxygen in the room," I said. "I'm not enough of a scientist to know how it manages it, but the net effect is about the same as that great speckled bird you were talking about. The one with the pillows."

"That'd be consistent with the physical evidence," Crittenden said. "But how would you get this Halon in here?"

"It was already here," I said. I pointed to the jets on the walls and ceiling. "When I first saw them, I thought Bellermann had put in a conventional sprinkler system, and I couldn't believe it. Water's harder than fire on rare books, and a lot of libraries have been totalled when a sprinkler system went off by accident. I said something to that effect to Karl, and he just about bit my head off, making it clear he wouldn't expose his precious treasures to water damage.

"So I got the picture. The jets were designed to deliver gas, not liquid, and it went without saying that the gas would be Halon. I understand they're equipping the better research libraries with it these days, although Karl's the only person I know of who installed it in his personal library."

Crittenden was halfway up a ladder, having a look at one of the outlets. "Just like a sprinkler head," he said, "which is what I took it for. How's it know when to go off? Heat sensor?"

"That's right."

"You said murder. That'd mean somebody set it off."

"Yes."

"By starting a fire in here? Be a neater trick than sending in the great speckled bird."

"All you'd have to do," I said, "is heat the sensor enough to trigger the response."

"How?"

"When I was in here earlier," I said, "I caught a whiff of smoke. It was faint, but it was absolutely there. I think that's what made me ask Karl about fire in the first place."

"And?"

"When Mrs Bellermann and I came in and discovered the body, the smell was gone. But there was a discoloured spot on the carpet that I'd noticed before, and I bent down for a closer look at it." I pointed to the Tabriz (which, now that I think about it, may very well have been an Isfahan). "Right there," I said.

Crittenden knelt where I pointed, rubbed two fingers on the spot, brought them to his nose. "Scorched," he reported. "But just the least bit. Take a whole lot more than that to set off a sensor way up there."

"I know. That was a test."

"A test?"

"Of the murder method. How do you raise the temperature of a room you can't enter? You can't unlock the door and you can't open the window. How can you get enough heat in to set off the gas?"

"How?"

I turned to Eva. "Tell him how you did it," I said.

"I don't know what you're talking about," she said. "You must be crazy."

"You wouldn't need a fire," I said. "You wouldn't even need a whole lot of heat. All you'd have to do is deliver enough heat directly to the sensor to trigger a response. If you could manage that in a highly localized fashion, you wouldn't even raise the overall room temperature appreciably."

"Keep talking," Crittenden said.

I picked up an ivory-handled magnifier, one of several placed strategically around the room. "When I was a Boy Scout," I said, "they didn't really teach me how to open locks. But they were big on starting fires. Flint and steel, fire by friction – and that old standby, focusing the sun's rays though a magnifying glass and delivering a concentrated pinpoint of intense heat onto something with a low kindling point."

"The window," Crittenden said.

I nodded. "It faces north," I said, "so the sun never comes in on its own. But you can stand a few feet from the window and catch the sunlight with a mirror, and you can tilt the mirror so the light is reflected through your magnifying glass and on through the window. And you can beam it onto an object in the room."

"The heat sensor, that'd be."

"Eventually," I said. "First, though, you'd want to make sure it would work. You couldn't try it out ahead of time on the sensor, because you wouldn't know it was working until you set it off.

Until then, you couldn't be sure the thickness of the window glass wasn't disrupting the process. So you'd want to test it."

"That explains the scorched rug, doesn't it?" Crittenden stooped for another look at it, then glanced up at the window. "Soon as you saw a wisp of smoke or a trace of scorching, you'd know it was working. And you'd have an idea how long it would take to raise the temperature enough. If you could make it hot enough to scorch wool, you could set off a heat-sensitive alarm."

"My God," Eva cried, adjusting quickly to new realities. "I thought you must be crazy, but now I can see how it was done. But who could have done such a thing?"

"Oh, I don't know," I said. "I suppose it would have to be somebody who lived here, somebody who was familiar with the library and knew about the Halon, somebody who stood to gain financially by Karl Bellermann's death. Somebody, say, who felt neglected by a husband who treated her like a housekeeper, somebody who might see poetic justice in killing him while he was locked away with his precious books."

"You can't mean me, Bernie."

"Well, now that you mention it . . ."

"But I was with you! Karl was with us at lunch. Then he went into the library and I showed you to the guest room."

"You showed me, all right."

"And we were together," she said, lowering her eyes modestly. "It shames me to say it with my husband tragically dead, but we were in bed together until almost six o'clock, when we came down here to discover the body. You can testify to that, can't you, Bernie?"

"I can swear we went to bed together," I said, "And I can swear that *I* was there until six, unless I went sleepwalking. But I was out cold, Eva."

"So was I."

"I don't think so," I said. "You stayed away from the coffee, saying how it kept you awake. Well, it sure didn't keep *me* awake. I think there was something in it to make me sleep, and that's why you didn't want any. I think there was more of the same in the pot you gave Karl to bring in here with him, so he'd be dozing peacefully while you set off the Halon. You waited until I was asleep, went outside with a mirror and a magnifier, heated the sensor and set off the gas, and then came back to bed. The Halon would do its work in minutes, and without warning even if Karl wasn't sleeping all that soundly. Halon's odourless and colourless, and the air cleaning system would whisk it all away in less than an hour. But I think there'll be traces in his system, along with traces of the same sedative they'll find in the residue in both the coffee pots. And I think that'll be enough to put you away."

Crittenden thought so, too.

When I got back to the city there was a message on the machine to call Nizar Gulbenkian. It was late, but it sounded urgent.

"Bad news," I told him. "I had the book just about sold. Then he locked himself in his library to commune with the ghosts of Rex Stout and Franklin Delano Roosevelt, and next thing he knew they were all hanging out together."

"You don't mean he died?"

"His wife killed him," I said, and I went on to tell him the whole story. "So that's the bad news, though it's not as bad for us as it is for the Bellermanns. I've got the book back, and I'm sure I can find a customer for it."

"Ah," he said. "Well, Bernie, I'm sorry about Bellermann. He was a true bookman."

"He was that, all right."

"But otherwise your bad news is good news."

"It is?"

"Yes. Because I changed my mind about the book."

"You don't want to sell it?"

"I *can't* sell it," he said. "It would be like tearing out my soul. And now, thank God, I don't have to sell it."

"Oh?"

"More good news," he said. "A business transaction, a long shot with a handsome return. I won't bore you with the details, but the outcome was very good indeed. If you'd been successful in selling the book, I'd now be begging you to buy it back."

"I see."

"Bernie," he said, "I'm a collector, as passionate about the pursuit as poor Bellermann. I don't ever want to sell. I want to add to my holdings. "He let out a sigh, clearly pleased at the prospect. "So I'll want the book back. But of course I'll pay you your commission all the same."

"I couldn't accept it."

"So you had all that work for nothing?"

"Not exactly," I said.

"Oh?"

"I guess Bellermann's library will go on the auction block eventually," I said. "Eva can't inherit, but there'll be some niece or nephew to wind up with a nice piece of change. And there'll be some wonderful books in that sale."

"There certainly will."

"But a few of the most desirable items won't be included," I said, "because they somehow found their way into my briefcase, along with *Fer-de-Lance*."

"You managed that, Bernie? With a dead body in the room, and a murderer in custody, and a cop right there on the scene?"

"Bellermann had shown me his choicest treasures," I said, "so I knew just what to grab and where to find it. And Crittenden didn't care what I did with the books. I told him I needed something to read on the train and he waited patiently while I picked out eight or ten volumes. Well, it's a long train ride, and I guess he must think I'm a fast reader."

"Bring them over," he said. "Now."

"Nizar, I'm bushed," I said, "and you're all the way up in Riverdale. First thing in the morning, okay? And while I'm there you can teach me how to tell a Tabriz from an Isfahan."

"They're not at all alike, Bernie. How could anyone confuse them?"

"You'll clear it up for me tomorrow. Okay?"

"Well, all right," he said. "But I hate to wait."

Collectors! Don't you just love them?

# NO WAY OUT

## Michael Collins

*Michael Collins is the best known alias of prolific American mystery writer Dennis Lynds (b.1924). He has written books as William Arden, Mark Sadler, and John Crowe. He also also written stories featuring such famous detectives as The Shadow, Nick Carter and Charlie Chan. But most people will know him for his books featuring the one-armed private eye Dan Fortune who first appeared in* Act of Fear *(1967). Collins has also written at least one locked-room mystery with Dan Fortune, "No One Likes to Be Played for a Sucker" (EQMM, July 1969). In addition to the following story, Collins also wrote "The Bizarre Case Expert" (EQMM, June 1970, as William Arden), about a murder in a room under constant observation.*

Next to wine, women, and whisky, Slot-Machine Kelly's favourite kick was reading those real puzzle-type mysteries. You know, the kind where the victim gets his on top of a flagpole and they can't find the weapon because it was an icicle and melted away.

"There was this one I liked special," Slot-Machine said to Joe Harris. "Guy was knocked off in an attic room. The guy was alone; there was a cop right outside the door; and another cop was down in the street watching the one window. The guy got shot twice – once from far, once from real close. Oh, yes – and there were powder burns on him. The cops got into the room in one second flat, and there was no one there except the stiff. How about that baby?"

"I'm crazy with suspense," Joe said as he mopped the bar with his specially dirty rag.

"Simple," Slot explained. "The killer shot from another attic across the street; that was the first shot. Then he tossed the gun across, through the window, and it hit the floor. It had a hair trigger, and it just happened to hit the victim again!"

"You're kidding," Joe said. "You mean someone wants you to believe odds like that?"

"It's possible," Slot said.

"So's snow in July," Joe said. "The guy who wrote that one drinks cheaper booze than you do."

"Don't just promise, pour," Slot-Machine said.

Slot-Machine liked these wild stories because things like that never happened in his world. When he got a murder it was 99 per cent sure to be something about as exotic as a drunk belting his broad with a beer bottle in front of forty-two talkative witnesses at high noon.

"Did you know that 90 per cent of all murders are committed by guys with criminal records?" Slot went on informatively. "The victim usually has a record, too, and they usually know each other. A lot of them take place in bars. It's near midnight, and both guys are swinging on the gargle."

"And the bartender gets hauled in for serving whisky to drunks," Joe said.

"Life is dull," Slot sighed.

Which was why this time Slot-Machine Kelly was not even aware that he had a puzzler until it happened. Things like this just didn't happen in Slot-Machine's world. When they did there had to be a logical explanation and a reason. In the real world a man has to figure the odds and forget about guns with improbable hair triggers. Only no matter how you sliced it, there was no reason for the guard to be dead, no way the rubies could have been stolen, and no way out of that tenth-storey room. It was 100 per cent impossible. But it had happened.

It all started with the usual routine. Mr Jason Moomer, of Moomer, Moomer & McNamara, Jewel Merchants, came to Slot's dusty office one bright morning with a job offer. The morning was bright, but Slot-Machine wasn't. He was nursing a fine hangover from a bottle of Lafite-Rothschild '53 he had found in Nussbaum's Liquor Store. The price had been right, and Slot had killed the bottle happily over a plebeian steak.

"It was the brandy afterward," Slot explained to Moomer. "Speak soft; my skull's wide open."

"For this job you stay sober," Moomer said.

"Don't ask for miracles," Slot said.

"You did a good job for us before," Moomer said. "My partners think you're not reliable, but I vouched for you."

"You're a brave man," Slot said.

"You know the setup," Moomer said. "We're displaying the rubies in a suite at the North American Hotel. They're on display all day for three days, and they're locked in the safe at night. Twenty-four-hour watch on all doors, at the safe, with the jewels when they're out. We're hiring three shifts of Burns guards, five men to a shift to cover the three doors, the safe, and the elevators, just in case. We're hiring a private detective to work with each shift, to keep his eyes and ears open."

"You got more protection than a South American dictator," Slot-Machine said.

"There are five rubies, a matched set. They're worth perhaps a quarter of a million dollars."

"Maybe you need the Army," Slot-Machine said.

"You'll change shifts each day," Moomer went on. "I'm hiring Ed Green and Manny Lewis for the other shifts. You'll all wear uniforms, so you'll look like ordinary guards."

"A tight setup," Slot said.

Slot-Machine disliked regular work, and he particularly disliked uniformed-guard work. But, as usual, his bank account looked like a tip for a hashhouse waitress, and Joe's current employer was already beginning to count the shots in the Irish-whisky bottle every time Slot appeared in Joe's bar.

"You got a deal," Slot said. "I have a little free time. You're lucky."

"Well," Moomer said, "if you're so busy, you won't need any money in advance."

"You're dreaming again," Slot said.

Moomer grinned, paid $50 in advance, and left. Slot counted

the money four times. He sighed unhappily. It always came out to $50. He hated clients who could count. At least, he decided, it would be easy work except for the wear and tear on his feet.

He was wrong. Before it was over, he had a dead man, five missing rubies, a very unfriendly Jason Moomer, a suspicious Captain Gazzo, and a room from which there was no way out except for a bird.

For two days all the trouble Slot-Machine had was tired feet. The suite in the North American was crowded with ruby-lovers, and jewellery dealers who loved only money, for the whole two days. The uniformed guards, and the three private detectives, earned their pay.

During the day the guard at the elevator checked credentials. Slot-Machine knew that this was necessary, but it was not a very valuable precaution. Moomer, Moomer & McNamara wanted to see their rubies sold, and almost anyone could get an invitation.

There were three doors to the suite. Two were locked on both sides, but a uniformed guard was stationed at each door anyway, as an additional security measure. The third door was the only entrance and exit to the suite. The Burns man there kept his pistol in plain sight. There was no need for guards on the windows. The suite was ten floors up without a fire escape.

The fifth Burns guard stood like an eagle-eyed statue right behind the display case. It would have taken an invisible man with wings to steal the rubies during the day. Which did not stop the Messrs. Moomer and McNamara from prowling like frightened hyenas.

"If you see anything suspicious, get to the alarm fast," Jason Moomer explained to the guard at the display case. "The alarm is wired into the case itself, but there's the extra switch just in case."

"You're in charge of your shift, Kelly," Maximilian Moomer said. "Just stay sober!"

Old Maximilian did not like Slot-Machine. That came from the fee Slot had charged for finding a stolen diamond tiara a few years ago. Maximilian was a skinflint, and he had always suspected Slot of stealing the tiara and returning it for the handsome fee. Slot hadn't, but he had thought it a good idea.

"Bringing in detectives is ridiculous anyway," Maximilian Moomer said. "The uniformed guards are enough."

"I think we should have had the showing in our own strong room," Angus McNamara said. The tall Scotsman seemed the most nervous of the three owners.

But nothing happened for the first two days, and at night everything was quiet. The Burns men remained on guard at all the doors; the elevator remained under watch; and the man inside the suite camped in front of the safe.

Day or night, Slot-Machine Kelly, Ed Green, and Manny Lewis kept a roving eye on everything as they wandered through the rooms and halls in their uniforms. The detectives could not be told from the other Burns guards. For two days Slot-Machine cat-footed through the four rooms, eyeing the rubies and the guests and sneaking some of the free liquor when no one was looking. The only incident occurred on the second day when Slot was off duty.

Ed Green was on duty at the time. It happened just as the dayshift was going off. The swingshift guards had taken their stations, and Ed Green was talking to Manny Lewis outside the room, when the alarm went off like a scared air-raid siren.

People started to mill and shout. Manny Lewis ran to check the other doors. Ed Green and the uniformed guards poured into the main room and surrounded the display case. The guard at the case already had his gun out.

"What is it!" Green had snapped.

A very nervous and embarrassed young woman stood near the alarm switch. "I turned it," she said. "I'm sorry. I thought it was for the waiter."

Green swore angrily, and the Moomer brothers insisted that the attractive offender be taken to the police. The young woman did not seem to mind too much. She checked out nice and clean; she was the legitimate secretary of a small merchant named Julius Honder.

"The dame was just curious," Green said to Slot-Machine. "At least we got sort of a drill."

The guard system had worked fine. No one on the doors had left his post, and the Moomers and McNamara seemed happier. The final precaution, the electronic scanner that was set up to cover the elevators during the day and the single exit from the lobby of the hotel at night, was working perfectly.

"It's a vacation with pay," Slot told Joe before he went on duty on the third day. "A cockroach couldn't get into that room, and a germ couldn't get out."

It happened on the third day.

Slot-Machine had the lobster shift on the third day – midnight to eight o'clock in the weary morning. He had stopped for a couple of quick whiskies at Joe's tavern, and when he arrived he had to hurry into his uniform. The five Burns men of his shift were ready and waiting.

Ed Green greeted Slot-Machine. After the shift had been changed and Slot's men were in their places at the locked doors and in front of the safe, Green and Slot had a cigarette just outside the main door to the suite. The Burns men of Green's shift relaxed in the hallway.

The two shots exploded the silence a second or two before the alarm went off.

The shots were inside the suite. The alarm clanged like a wounded elephant.

"Come on!" Green shouted.

The Burns guards poured into the suite. They all rushed into the room where the safe was.

"Stay alert!" Slot snapped to his Burns man who was on the front door.

He watched his man pull his gun and stand alert, and then he hurried inside the suite and into the room where the safe was. The first thing he saw was the open safe. The second thing he saw was the body of the guard lying in front of the safe with Ed Green bending over it.

"Twice, right through the heart!" Green said.

"Search the place!" Slot snapped. "Tear it apart."

Slot-Machine and Green checked the safe. It was clean as a

whistle. It had been neatly and expertly burned open. The torch was still on the floor. The safe was a small one, and it had not taken much burning.

Ed Green called the police. Slot-Machine called the Burns men on the single night exit from the hotel downstairs, and told them to start the scanner and let no one out of the hotel without checking them. By this time all the Burns guards had torn the apartment apart and had found nothing at all.

By the time Captain Gazzo of Homicide arrived, in company with Sergeant Jonas and Lieutenant Mingo of Safe and Loft, the Moomers and McNamara were also there. Maximilian Moomer was almost hysterical.

"Search them all! Search Kelly! No one could have gotten in or out of this room!" Maximilian wailed.

"He's got a point," Captain Gazzo said to Slot-Machine.

"Green and I were together," Slot said.

"I wouldn't trust Green too far, either," Sergeant Jonas said.

Lieutenant Mingo had finished his examination of the suite. Now he broke in on the hysterical owners of the rubies.

"Here it is, Captain. Safe was torched – an easy job. All windows are locked inside. A caterpillar couldn't have come up or down those walls outside anyway. The torch is still here. We searched all the guards, nothing on them. The Burns men on the doors never left their posts."

Gazzo turned to the Burns man who had remained at the front door of the suite the whole time.

"No one came out?"

"No, sir," the Burns man said. "I never budged. The guy at the elevators never moved, and no one came out except Green, Kelly, and the other guards."

"In other words," Gazzo said. "No one went in, no one came out. Only – we've got a dead man and we don't have five rubies worth a quarter of a million in real cold money."

In the room everyone looked at everyone else. The Moomers and McNamara were ready to cry like babies.

\*     \*     \*

It was an hour later, and Gazzo and Mingo had been over and over the situation fifty times with Slot-Machine Kelly and Ed Green. The morgue wagon had come, and the white-suited attendants were packing the body in its final basket.

"The Burns boys from my shift want to go home," Green said. "We've searched every part of them except their appendix."

"OK," Gazzo said. "But you'd better check them through that scanner downstairs, just in case."

"That's some machine," Lieutenant Mingo said admiringly. "You just dab the rubies with a little radioactive material, and the scanner spots them forty feet away."

"It also spots radium watch dials and false teeth," Gazzo pointed out. "Let's get back to our little puzzle, OK? First, how did anyone get into the room?"

Everyone looked blank. Slot-Machine rubbed the stump of his missing arm. It was an old habit he had when he was thinking.

"It's impossible," Slot-Machine said, "so there has to be an answer. Look at the odds. It's a million to one against the guy being invisible. It's two million to one against him having wings. It's a couple of hundred to one against that guard having shot himself."

"Very funny, Kelly," Gazzo said.

"Wait," Slot-Machine said. "I'm serious. We got to rule out science fiction, weird tales, and magic. So how did he get *into* the room past all of Green's guards? Be simple. There's only one way – he was already in the room."

"Kelly's shootin' the vein again," Jonas said.

Even the morgue attendants turned to look at Slot-Machine. They had the body by head and feet, and they paused with it in mid-air, their mouths open. Gazzo looked disgusted. But Ed Green and Lieutenant Mingo did not.

"He's right," Ed Green said. "We never searched, never thought of it."

"It's not an uncommon MO," Lieutenant Mingo agreed. "Now that I think of it, the suite is full of closets piled with junk. It wouldn't have been hard as long as the guy knew the guards didn't search."

Captain Gazzo morosely watched the morgue attendants close their basket and carry it out. The captain did not seem very pleased about the whole matter.

"Which means the joint was cased," Gazzo said. "OK, it figures. Our ghost has to be a pro. He got in by hiding here for about five hours. Now, how did he get out?"

"Yeah," Sergeant Jonas said. "You guys didn't search the place because a snake couldn't have sneaked out of this suite."

"You had twelve guards around and in the suite, damn it," Gazzo said. "Twelve! A worm couldn't have crawled out!"

Slot-Machine seemed to be watching something very interesting in the centre of the far wall. His one good hand was busily rubbing away at the stump of his left arm. Now he began to talk without taking his eyes away from the blank wall.

"Let's talk it out," Slot said. "He didn't fly out, he didn't crawl out, he didn't dig out, he . . ."

"Trap door?" Sergeant Jonas said.

Lieutenant Mingo shook his head.

"First thing I checked. The floors are solid. Checked the rooms below, too," Mingo added.

"Secret doors in the walls?" Gazzo suggested.

"Hell, Captain," Ed Green said, "we know a little about our work. We went over the walls with a microscope."

Slot rubbed his stump and nodded. "Keep it up; we're ruling out. Look, the guy was a pro; he was in the room; he had to have his plan to get out. It had to be workable. It had to be simple."

"Maybe he's still inside the room," Green said.

"Negative," Mingo replied. "I combed the place."

"What do we have?" Slot-Machine said. "He's in here, and there are eleven guards outside and one inside with him. He shoots the guard, torches the safe, and . . . Hold on! That's not right. He burned that safe fast, but not fast enough to do it between the time of the shots and all of us busting in.

"So he must have torched the safe *first* – then shot the guard and set off the alarm! He couldn't have torched the safe with the guard still awake, so it follows that he must have knocked the guard out. But why did he kill the guard later? He knew the shots would bring us running. He must have *wanted* the shots to bring us in just when it happened. Why did he pull the job at the exact moment when there were twelve guards instead of six? He timed it for the shift change."

There was a long silence in the room. Sergeant Jonas looked blank. Ed Green was obviously trying to think. Mingo shook his head. Only Gazzo seemed to see what Slot-Machine was seeing on the blank wall.

"No one came out," Gazzo said softly. "There was no way out. Only a killer got out with five rubies. So, like Kelly says, we rule out magic, and somehow a guy walked out."

Gazzo turned to the Burns guard who had been on the main door.

"Do you know *all* the guards who work with you?" Gazzo asked.

"Sure, Captain," the Burns man said. "Well, I mean, I know most of them to look at. I know the boys in my shift, and—"

"Yeah," Gazzo cut him short. "There it is. So damned simple. He just walked out in the confusion. Right, Kelly? He was probably behind the front door waiting. He probably even helped search the suite with all of you. He was just . . ."

"Wearing a Burns uniform," Slot-Machine said. "He simply mingled in with us. That's why he timed it for two shifts to be here. He mingled with us, and walked out through the front door."

The swearing in the room would have done credit to a Foreign Legion barrack. Everyone began to move at once. Mingo called in to alert the Safe and Loft Squad to start watching all fences in the city. Ed Green went to check with the guard on the elevator. Jonas called downstairs to the single exit door. Gazzo just swore. Ed Green came back.

"Burns man on the elevator says he did see a Burns man go for the stairs," Green said. "God, he was lucky! How could he know we wouldn't search him? I mean, we searched all the guards mighty quick. He couldn't be sure he could get away so fast. He took a hell of a risk."

Sergeant Jonas hung up the telephone in anger.

"Green's shift of Burns men passed out twenty minutes ago," Jonas said, "and they were all clean. That scanner didn't find anything on them."

"How many men?" Gazzo said.

"Six," Jonas said.

Gazzo cursed. "He's out!"

"But the rubies aren't," Green said. "He must have stashed them somewhere inside. That means he plans to come back for them."

Slot-Machine shook his head. "I don't know. He planned this mighty careful. We could have searched him right here in the room like Green says."

"All right, genius," Gazzo said. "You've figured how he got into the suite and how he got out. Now tell us how he plans to get the stones out if he didn't stash them. No one's gone out of this hotel since it happened except through that front door where the scanner is."

"He just had to know about the scanner," Slot-Machine said. "This was a foolproof plan. So he must have figured a way around that scanner."

"Great," Gazzo said. "Only, no one got out of here without being checked."

Slot-Machine stood up suddenly.

"One person did! Gazzo, come on!"

Slot-Machine led them all from the suite in a fast dash for the first elevator.


The night was dark on the city. The streets were bare and cold in the night. Traffic moved in small tight groups down Sixth Avenue as the lights changed. The late night revellers staggered their weary way home. In the all-night delicatessens the clerks yawned behind their counters.

In Gazzo's unmarked car the five sat alert and waiting. Gazzo swore softly, and Ed Green smoked hard on his cigarette. Slot-Machine leaned forward tensely and watched the car-exit below the towering glass and steel of the North American Hotel. Suddenly Slot leaned over and touched Jonas, who was behind the wheel.

The morgue wagon came out from under the hotel and turned left down Sixth Avenue. Jonas eased the car away from the curb and followed the morgue wagon.

They drove down Sixth Avenue, turned across town toward the west, and the morgue wagon moved steadily on its way a half a block away. The silent procession turned again on Ninth Avenue and continued on downtown toward the morgue.

Suddenly, as the morgue wagon slowed at a traffic light, the back door of the wagon opened. A man jumped out. The man hit the pavement, stumbled, and then began to run fast toward the west.

The man wore the uniform of a Burns guard.

The morgue wagon continued on its grim journey. Jonas swung the police car in a squealing turn and gunned the motor down the side street. The running man was forty feet ahead. Jonas roared after him. The man heard the motor, looked back, and then dashed toward a fence. In a flash he was over the fence, and gone.

Slot-Machine and Gazzo were out of the police car before Jonas had brought it to a halt. Mingo and Green were close behind them. Slot-Machine was the first of the three over the fence with a powerful pull of his single arm.

The man in the Burns uniform was scrambling over a second fence just ahead.

The chase went on down the rows of back yards and fences in the silent darkness of the night. At each fence Slot-Machine gained on the uniformed runner. As he went over the last fence before a looming dark building ended the row of back yards, the uniformed man turned and shot.

Slot-Machine ducked but didn't stop. He went over the last fence in a mad leap and dive. Another shot hit just below him, and wood splinters cut his cheek. In the next second, Slot-Machine was on the uniformed man who was trying frantically to get off one more shot.

The man in uniform never made it. Slot-Machine drove him back against the brick wall of the building with the force of his rush. His pivoting body slammed into the wall, his gun went flying, and he came off the wall like a rebounding cue ball on a lively pool table.

Slot's one good hand caught the uniformed man across the throat. He collapsed with a single choking squawk like the dying gurgle of a beheaded chicken.

By the time Gazzo, Green, and Mingo had caught up with Slot and his victim, Slot was holding the rubies in his hand. In the beam of light from Mingo's flashlight, the deep red stones shone like wet blood.

Slot-Machine handed the pistol to Gazzo.

"This'll be the murder weapon," he said. "It's a regulation Burns pistol; he was a meticulous type."

Mingo was bending over the supine man, who had not even begun to wake up. The lieutenant looked up at Gazzo and shook his head.

"No one I recognize," Mingo said. "Chances are, he's not a known jewel thief."

"That figures," Slot said. "I think you'll find his name is Julius Honder, a legitimate jewel merchant."

"Why Honder?" Ed Green said.

"He had to have cased the job," Slot said. "He knew we'd all go running into the suite. Remember that woman? The one who thought the alarm was a waiter's button? She was Honder's secretary. I expect we'll find her waiting at Honder's office for the boss to bring home the loot."

From the dark, Sergeant Jonas came up. The Homicide sergeant looked down at the sleeping killer and thief.

"So he made another change," Jonas said, "and played one of the morgue boys?"

Slot-Machine shook his head.

"Too risky," Slot-Machine said. "Gazzo said no one had gotten out of the building through the front door. You don't take a stiff out the front way, right? He knew that. The stiff went out through the basement. What tipped me was what I said myself – why did he kill the guard *after* he'd opened the safe and got the stones? To get us into the room, I said.

"Only the *alarm* alone would have done that. There had to be another reason. All at once it came to me. He killed the guard just to have a way of hiding the stones on the body and getting them out!"

They all looked down at the uniformed man who was just beginning to groan as he came awake. There was a certain admiration in the eyes of the police.

"He knew we wouldn't search the dead man until you got him to the morgue," Slot-Machine said. "So he had to get the stones from the body before it reached the slab. It was quite simple. He just hid in the wagon. Who would think to look for him there?"

Later, in the tavern where Joe Harris was working, Ed Green leaned on the bar beside Slot-Machine Kelly and bought Slot a fourth expensive Irish whisky. Green was still admiring Slot.

"You just got to think logical," Slot-Machine explained. "Figure the odds. Miracles are out, so there has to be a simple explanation. The more complicated it looks in real life, the simpler it has to be when you figure it out."

"You make it sound easy," Green said. "Have another shot."

"Twist his arm," Joe said as he poured. "The thinker. So it turned out it was Julius Honder, right?"

"Yeah," Slot said as he tasted his Irish whisky happily. "He needed cash. Too bad he needed a corpse. He'll fry crisp as bacon."

# OFF THE FACE
# OF THE EARTH

*Clayton Rawson*

*Clayton Rawson (1906–71) was one of the masters of the impossible crime story. He was by profession a stage magician, or more properly an illusionist, and he subsequently wrote a series of novels and short stories featuring The Great Merlini as the magician expert called in by the police to solve the latest unusual crime. The first book,* Death from a Top Hat *(1938), which dealt with a series of crimes involving magicians, was filmed as* Miracles for Sale *(1939) and established Rawson with a second career as an author and editor. Rawson and John Dickson Carr used to love setting each other challenges for stories. The following story arose when Carr challenged Rawson to write a story in which someone walks into a telephone booth and vanishes. See if you can work out how it's done.*

The lettering in neat gilt script on the door read: *Miracles For Sale*, and beneath it was the familiar rabbit-from-a-hat trademark. Inside, behind the glass showcase counter, in which was displayed as unlikely an assortment of objects as could be got together in one spot, stood The Great Merlini.

He was wrapping up half a dozen billiard balls, several bouquets of feather flowers, a dove pan, a Talking Skull, and a dozen decks of cards for a customer who snapped his fingers and nonchalantly produced the needed number of five-dollar bills from thin air. Merlini rang up the sale, took half a carrot from the cash drawer, and gave it to the large white rabbit who watched proceedings with a pink sceptical eye from the top of a nearby escape trunk. Then he turned to me.

"Clairvoyance, mind-reading, extrasensory perception," he said. "We stock only the best grade. And it tells me that you came to pick up the two Annie Oakleys I promised to get you for that new hit musical. I have them right here."

But his occult powers slipped a bit. He looked in all his coat pockets one after another, found an egg, a three-foot length of rope, several brightly-coloured silk handkerchiefs, and a crumpled telegram reading: NEED INVISIBLE MAN AT ONCE. SHIP UNIONTOWN BY MONDAY. – NEMO THE ENIGMA. Then he gave a surprised blink and scowled darkly at a sealed envelope that he had fished out of his inside breast pocket.

"That," I commented a bit sarcastically, "doesn't look like a pair of theatre tickets."

He shook his head sadly. "No. It's a letter my wife asked me to mail a week ago."

I took it from him. "There's a mail chute by the elevators about fifteen feet outside your door. I'm no magician, but I can remember to put this in it on my way out." I indicated the telegram that lay on the counter. "Since when have you stocked a supply of invisible men? That I would like to see."

Merlini frowned at the framed slogan: *Nothing Is Impossible* which hung above the cash register. "You want real miracles, don't you? We guarantee that our invisible man can't be seen. But if you'd like to see how impossible it is to see him, step right this way."

In the back, beyond his office, there is a larger room that serves as workshop, shipping department and, on occasion, as a theatre. I stood there a moment later and watched Merlini step into an upright coffin-shaped box in the centre of the small stage. He faced me, smiled, and snapped his fingers. Two copper electrodes in the side walls of the cabinet spat flame, and a fat, green, electric spark jumped the gap just above his head, hissing and writhing. He lifted his arms; the angry stream of energy bent, split in two, fastened on his fingertips, and then disappeared as he grasped the gleaming spherical electrodes, one with each hand.

For a moment nothing happened; then, slowly, his body began to fade into transparency as the cabinet's back wall became increasingly visible through it. Clothes and flesh melted until only the bony skeletal structure remained. Suddenly, the jawbone moved and its grinning white teeth clicked as Merlini's voice said:

"You must try this, Ross. On a hot day like today, it's most comfortable."

As it spoke, the skeleton also wavered and grew dim. A moment later it was gone and the cabinet was, or seemed to be, empty. If Merlini still stood there, he was certainly invisible.

"Okay, Gypsy Rose Lee," I said. "I have now seen the last word in strip-tease performances." Behind me I heard the office door open and I looked over my shoulder to see Inspector Gavigan giving me a fishy stare. "You'd better get dressed again," I added. "We have company."

The Inspector looked around the room and at the empty stage, then at me again, cautiously this time. "If you said what I think you did—"

He stopped abruptly as Merlini's voice, issuing from nowhere, chuckled and said, "Don't jump to conclusions, Inspector. Appearances are deceptive. It's not an indecent performance, nor has Ross gone off his rocker and started talking to himself. I'm right here. On the stage."

Gavigan looked and saw the skeleton shape taking form within the cabinet. He closed his eyes, shook his head, then looked again. That didn't help. The grisly spectre was still there and twice as substantial. Then, wraithlike, Merlini's body began to form around it and, finally, grew opaque and solid. The magician grinned broadly, took his hands from the electrodes, and bowed as the spitting, green discharge of energy crackled once more above him. Then the stage curtains closed.

"You should be glad that's only an illusion," I told Gavigan. "If it were the McCoy and the underworld ever found out how it was done, you'd face an unparalleled crime wave and you'd never solve a single case."

"It's the Pepper's Ghost illusion brought up to date," Merlini said as he stepped out between the curtains and came toward us.

"I've got more orders than I can fill. It's a sure-fire carnival draw." He frowned at Gavigan. "But *you* don't look very entertained."

"I'm not," the Inspector answered gloomily. "Vanishing into thin air may amuse some people. Not me. Especially when it really happens. Off stage in broad daylight. In Central Park."

"Oh," Merlini said. "I see. So that's what's eating you. Helen Hope, the chorus girl who went for a walk last week and never came back. She's still missing then, and there are still no clues?"

Gavigan nodded. "It's the Dorothy Arnold case all over again. Except for one thing we haven't let the newspapers know about – Bela Zyyzk."

"Bela what?" I asked.

Gavigan spelled it.

"Impossible," I said. "He must be a typographical error. A close relative of Etoain Shrdlu."

The Inspector wasn't amused. "Relatives," he growled. "I wish I could find some. He not only claims he doesn't have any – he swears he never has had any! And so far we haven't been able to prove different."

"Where does he come from?" Merlini asked. "Or won't he say?"

"Oh, he talks all right," Gavigan said disgustedly. "Too much. And none of it makes any sense. He says he's a momentary visitor to this planet – from the dark cloud of Antares. I've seen some high, wide, and fancy screwballs in my time, but this one takes the cake – candles and all."

"Helen Hope," Merlini said, "vanishes off the face of the earth. And Zyyzk does just the opposite. This gets interesting. What else does he have to do with her disappearance?"

"Plenty," Gavigan replied. "A week ago Tuesday night she went to a Park Avenue party at Mrs James Dewitt-Smith's. She's another candidate for Bellevue. Collects Tibetan statuary, medieval relics, and crackpots like Zyyzk. He was there that night – reading minds."

"A visitor from outer space," Merlini said, "and a mindreader to boot. I won't be happy until I've had a talk with that gentleman."

"I have talked with him," the Inspector growled. "And I've had indigestion ever since. He does something worse than read minds. He makes predictions." Gavigan scowled at Merlini. "I thought fortune tellers always kept their customers happy by predicting good luck?"

Merlini nodded. "That's usually standard operating procedure. Zyyzk does something else?"

"He certainly does. He's full of doom and disaster. A dozen witnesses testify that he told Helen Hope she'd vanish off the face of the earth. And three days later that's exactly what she does do."

"I can see," Merlini said, "why you view him with suspicion. So you pulled him in for questioning and got a lot of answers that weren't very helpful?"

"Helpful!" Gavigan jerked several typewritten pages from his pocket and shook them angrily. "Listen to this. He's asked: 'What's your age?' and we get: 'According to which time – solar, sidereal, galactic, or universal?' Murphy of Missing Persons, who was questioning him, says: 'Any kind. Just tell us how old you are.' And Zyyzk replies: 'I can't answer that. The question, in that form, has no meaning.'" The Inspector threw the papers down disgustedly.

Merlini picked them up, riffled through them, then read some of the transcript aloud. "Question: How did you know that Miss Hope would disappear? Answer: Do you understand the basic theory of the fifth law of interdimensional reaction? Murphy: Huh? Zyyzk: Explanations are useless. You obviously have no conception of what I am talking about."

"He was right about that," Gavigan muttered. "Nobody does."

Merlini continued. "Question: Where is Miss Hope now? Answer: Beyond recall. She was summoned by the Lords of the Outer Darkness." Merlini looked up from the papers. "After that, I suppose, you sent him over to Bellevue?"

The Inspector nodded. "They had him under observation a

week. And they turned in a report full of eight-syllable jaw-breakers all meaning he's crazy as a bedbug – but harmless. I don't believe it. Anybody who predicts in a loud voice that somebody will disappear into thin air at twenty minutes after four on a Tuesday afternoon, just before it actually happens, knows plenty about it!"

Merlini is a hard man to surprise, but even he blinked at that. "Do you mean to say that he foretold the exact time, too?"

"Right on the nose," Gavigan answered. "The doorman of her apartment house saw her walk across the street and into Central Park at four-eighteen. We haven't been able to find anyone who has seen her since. And don't tell me his prediction was a long shot that paid off."

"I won't," Merlini agreed. "Whatever it is, it's not coincidence. Where's Zyyzk now? Could you hold him after that psychiatric report?"

"The D A," Gavigan replied, "took him into General Sessions before Judge Keeler and asked that he be held as a material witness." The Inspector looked unhappier than ever. "It would have to be Keeler."

"What did he do?" I asked. "Deny the request?"

"No. He granted it. That's when Zyyzk made his second prediction. Just as they start to take him out and throw him back in the can, he makes some funny motions with his hands and announces, in that confident manner he's got, that the Outer Darkness is going to swallow Judge Keeler up, too!"

"And what," Merlini wanted to know, "is wrong with that? Knowing how you've always felt about Francis X. Keeler, I should think that prospect would please you."

Gavigan exploded. "Look, blast it! I have wished dozens of times that Judge Keeler would vanish into thin air, but that's exactly what I don't want to happen right now. We've known at headquarters that he's been taking fix money from the Castelli mob ever since the day he was appointed to the bench. But we couldn't do a thing. Politically he was dynamite. One move in his direction and there'd be a new Commissioner the next morning, with demotions all down the line. But three weeks ago the Big

Guy and Keeler had a scrap, and we get a tip straight from the feed box that Keeler is fair game. So we start working over-time collecting the evidence that will send him up the river for what I hope is a ninety-nine-year stretch. We've been afraid he might tumble and try to pull another 'Judge Crater.' And now, just when we're almost, but not quite, ready to nail him and make it stick, this has to happen."

"Your friend, Zyyzk," Merlini said, "becomes more interesting by the minute. Keeler is being tailed, of course?"

"Twenty-four hours a day, ever since we got the word that there'd be no kick-back." The phone on Merlini's desk rang as Gavigan was speaking. "I get hourly reports on his movements. Chances are that's for me now."

It was. In the office, we both watched him as he took the call. He listened a moment, then said, "Okay. Double the number of men on him immediately. And report back every fifteen minutes. If he shows any sign of going anywhere near a railroad station or airport, notify me at once."

Gavigan hung up and turned to us. "Keeler made a stop at the First National and spent fifteen minutes in the safety-deposit vaults. He's carrying a suitcase, and you can have one guess as to what's in it now. This looks like the payoff."

"I take it," Merlini said, "that, this time, the Zyyzk forecast did not include the exact hour and minute when the Outer Darkness would swallow up the Judge?"

"Yeah. He sidestepped that. All he'll say is that it'll happen before the week is out."

"And today," Merlini said, "is Friday. Tell me this. The Judge seems to have good reasons for wanting to disappear which Zyyzk may or may not know about. Did Miss Hope also have reasons?"

"She had one," Gavigan replied. "But I don't see how Zyyzk could have known it. We can't find a thing that shows he ever set eyes on her before the night of that party. And her reason is one that few people knew about." The phone rang again and Gavigan reached for it. "Helen Hope is the girlfriend Judge Keeler visits the nights he doesn't go home to his wife!"

Merlini and I both tried to assimilate that and take in what

Gavigan was telling the telephone at the same time. "Okay, I'm coming. And grab him the minute he tries to go through a gate." He slammed the receiver down and started for the door.

"Keeler," he said over his shoulder, "is in Grand Central. There's room in my car if you want to come."

He didn't need to issue that invitation twice. On the way down in the elevator Merlini made one not very helpful comment.

"You know," he said thoughtfully, "if the judge does have a reservation on the extra-terrestial express – destination: the Outer Darkness – we don't know what gate that train leaves from."

We found out soon enough. The Judge stepped through it just two minutes before we hurried into the station and found Lieutenant Malloy exhibiting all the symptoms of having been hit over the head with a sledge hammer. He was bewildered and dazed, and had difficulty talking coherently.

Sergeant Hicks, a beefy, unimaginative, elderly detective who had also seen the thing happen looked equally groggy.

Usually, Malloy's reports were as dispassionate, precise, and factual as a logarithmic table. But not today. His first paragraph bore a much closer resemblance to a first-person account of a dope-addict's dream.

"Malloy," Gavigan broke in icily. "Are you tight?"

The Lieutenant shook his head sadly. "No, but the minute I go off duty, I'm going to get so plas—"

Gavigan cut in again. "Are all the exits to this place covered?"

Hicks replied, "If they aren't, somebody is sure going to catch it."

Gavigan turned to the detective who had accompanied us in the inspector's car. "Make the rounds and double-check that, Brady. And tell headquarters to get more men over here fast."

"They're on the way now," Hicks said. "I phoned right after it happened. First thing I did."

Gavigan turned to Malloy. "All right. Take it easy. One thing at a time – and in order."

"It don't make sense that way either," Malloy said hopelessly. "Keeler took a cab from the bank and came straight here. Hicks and I were right on his tail. He comes down to the lower level and goes into the Oyster Bar and orders a double brandy. While he's working on that, Hicks phones in for reinforcements with orders to cover every exit. They had time to get here, too; Keeler had a second brandy. Then, when he starts to come out, I move out to the centre of the station floor by the information booth so I'm ahead of him and all set to make the pinch no matter which gate he heads for. Hicks stands pat, ready to tail him if he heads upstairs again.

"At first, that's where I think he's going because he starts up the ramp. But he stops here by this line of phone booths, looks in a directory and then goes into a booth halfway down the line. And as soon as he closes the door, Hicks moves up and goes into the next booth to the left of Keeler's." Malloy pointed. "The one with the Out-of-Order sign on it."

Gavigan turned to the Sergeant. "All right. You take it."

Hicks scowled at the phone booth as he spoke. "The door was closed and somebody had written 'Out of Order' on a card and stuck it in the edge of the glass. I lifted the card so nobody'd wonder why I was trying to use a dead phone, went in, closed the door and tried to get a load of what the Judge was saying. But it's no good. He was talking, but so low I couldn't get it. I came out again, stuck the card back in the door and walked back toward the Oyster Bar so I'd be set to follow him either way when he came out. And I took a gander into the Judge's booth as I went past. He was talking with his mouth up close to the phone."

"And then," Malloy continued, "we wait. And we wait. He went into that booth at five ten. At five twenty I get itchy feet. I begin to think maybe he's passed out or died of suffocation or something. Nobody in his right mind stays in a phone booth for ten minutes when the temperature is ninety like today. So I start to move in just as Hicks gets the same idea. He's closer than I am, so I stay put.

"Hicks stops just in front of the booth and lights a cigarette, which gives him a chance to take another look inside. Then I figure I must be right about the Judge having passed out. I see the match Hicks is holding drop, still lighted, and he turns quick and plasters his face against the glass. I don't wait. I'm already on my way when he turns and motions for me."

Malloy hesitated briefly. Then, slowly and very precisely, he let us have it. "I don't care if the Commissioner himself has me up on the carpet, one thing I'm sure of – *I hadn't taken my eyes off that phone booth for one single split second since the Judge walked into it.*"

"And neither," Hicks said with equal emphasis, "did I. Not for one single second."

"I did some fancy open-field running through the commuters," Malloy went on, "skidded to a stop behind Hicks and looked over his shoulder."

Gavigan stepped forward to the closed door of the booth and looked in.

"And what you see," Malloy finished, "is just what I saw. You can ship me down to Bellevue for observation, too. It's impossible. It doesn't make sense. I don't believe it. But that's exactly what happened."

For a moment Gavigan didn't move. Then, slowly, he pulled the door open.

The booth was empty.

The phone receiver dangled off the hook, and on the floor there was a pair of horn-rimmed spectacles, one lens smashed.

"Keeler's glasses," Hicks said. "He went into that booth and I had my eyes on it every second. He never came out. And he's not in it."

"And that," Malloy added in a tone of utter dejection, "isn't the half of it. I stepped inside, picked up the phone receiver Keeler had been using, and said, 'Hello' into the mouthpiece. There was a chance the party he'd been talking to might still be on the other end." Malloy came to a full stop.

"Well?" Gavigan prodded him. "Let's have it. Somebody answered?"

"Yes. Somebody said: '*This is the end of the trail, Lieutenant.*' Then – hung up."

"You didn't recognize the voice?"

"Yeah, I recognized it. That's the trouble. It was – *Judge Keeler*!"

Silence.

Then, quietly, Merlini asked, "You are quite certain that it was his voice, Malloy?"

The Lieutenant exploded. "I'm not sure of anything any more. But if you've ever heard Keeler – he sounds like a bullfrog with a cold – you'd know it couldn't be anyone else."

Gavigan's voice, or rather, a hollow imitation of it, cut in. "Merlini. Either Malloy and Hicks have both gone completely off their chumps or this is the one phone booth in the world that has two exits. The back wall is sheet metal backed by solid marble, but if there's a loose panel in one of the side walls, Keeler could have moved over into the empty booth that is supposed to be out of order . . ."

"Is supposed to be . . ." Malloy repeated. "So that's it! The sign's a phony. That phone isn't on the blink, and his voice –" Malloy took two swift steps into the booth. He lifted the receiver, dropped a nickel, and waited for the dial tone. He scowled. He jiggled the receiver. He repeated the whole operation.

This specimen of Mr Bell's invention was definitely not working.

A moment or two later Merlini reported another flaw in the Inspector's theory. "There are," he stated after a quick but thorough inspection of both booths, "no sliding panels, hinged panels, removable sections, trapdoors, or any other form of secret exit. The sidewalls are single sheets of metal, thin but intact. The back wall is even more solid. There is one exit and one only – the door though which our vanishing man entered."

"He didn't come out," Sergeant Hicks insisted again, sounding like a cracked phonograph record endlessly repeating itself. "I was watching that door every single second. Even if he turned himself into an invisible man like in a movie I saw once, he'd still have had to open the door. And the door didn't budge. I was watching it every single—"

"And that," Merlini said thoughtfully, "leaves us with an invisible man who can also walk through closed doors. In short

– a ghost. Which brings up another point. Have any of you noticed that there are a few spots of something on those smashed glasses that look very much like – blood?"

Malloy growled. "Yeah, but don't make any cracks about there being another guy in that booth who sapped Keeler – that'd mean *two* invisible men . . ."

"If there can be one invisible man," Merlini pointed out, "then there can be two."

Gavigan said, "Merlini, that vanishing gadget you were demonstrating when I arrived . . . It's just about the size and shape of this phone booth. I want to know—"

The magician shook his head. "Sorry, Inspector. That method wouldn't work here under these conditions. It's not the same trick. Keeler's miracle, in some respects, is even better. He should have been a magician; he's been wasting his time on the bench. Or has he? I wonder how much cash he carried into limbo with him in that suitcase?" He paused, then added, "More than enough, probably, to serve as a motive for murder."

And there, on that ominous note, the investigation stuck. It was as dead an end as I ever saw. And it got deader by the minute. Brady, returning a few minutes later, reported that all station exits had been covered by the time Keeler left the Oyster Bar and that none of the detectives had seen hide nor hair of him since.

"Those men stay there until further notice," Gavigan ordered. "Get more men – as many as you need – and start searching this place. I want every last inch of it covered. And every phone booth, too. If it was Keeler's voice Malloy heard, then he was in one of them, and—"

"You know, Inspector," Merlini interrupted, "this case not only takes the cake but the marbles, all the blue ribbons, and a truck load of loving cups too. That is another impossibility."

"What is?"

"The voice on the telephone. Look at it. If Keeler left the receiver in this booth off as Malloy and Hicks found it, vanished, then reappeared in another booth and tried to call this number, he'd get a busy signal. He couldn't have made a connection. And if he left the receiver on the hook, he could have called this number, but someone would have had to be here to lift the receiver and leave it off as it was found. It keeps adding up to two invisible men no matter how you look at it."

"I wish," Malloy said acidly, "that you'd disappear, too."

Merlini protested. "Don't. You sound like Zyyzk."

"That guy," Gavigan predicted darkly, "is going to wish he never heard of Judge Keeler."

Gavigan's batting average as a prophet was zero. When Zyyzk, whom the Inspector ordered brought to the scene and who was delivered by squad car twenty minutes later, discovered that Judge Keeler had vanished, he was as pleased as punch.

An interstellar visitor from outer space should have three eyes, or at least green hair. Zyyzk, in that respect, was a disappointment. He was a pudgy little man in a wrinkled grey suit. His eyes, two only, were a pale, washed-out blue behind gold-rimmed bifocals, and his hair, the colour of weak tea, failed miserably in its attempt to cover the top of his head.

His manner, however, was charged with an abundant and vital confidence, and there was a haughty, imperious quality in his high, thin voice which hinted that there was much more to Mr Zyyzk than met the eye.

"I issued distinct orders," he told Gavigan in an icy tone, "that I was never, under any circumstances, to be disturbed between the sidereal hours of five and seven post-meridian. You know that quite well, Inspector. Explain why these idiots have disobeyed. At once!"

If there is any quicker way of bringing an inspector of police to a boil, I don't know what it is. The look Gavigan gave the little man would have wrecked a Geiger counter. He opened his mouth. But the searing blast of flame which I expected didn't issue forth. He closed his mouth and swallowed. The Inspector was speechless.

Zyyzk calmly threw more fuel on the fire. "Well," he said impatiently tapping his foot. "I'm waiting."

A subterranean rumble began deep in Gavigan's interior and then, a split second before he blew his top, Merlini said quietly, "I understand, Mr Zyyzk, that you read minds?"

Zyyzk, still the Imperial Roman Emperor, gave Merlini a scathing look. "I do," he said. "And what of it?"

"For a mind-reader," Merlini told him, "you ask a lot of questions. I should think you'd know why you've been brought here."

That didn't bother the visitor from Outer Space. He stared intently at Merlini for a second, glanced once at Gavigan, then closed his eyes. The fingertips of one white hand pressed against his brow. Then he smiled.

"I see. Judge Keeler."

"Keeler?" Gavigan pretended surprise. "What about him?"

Zyyzk wasn't fooled. He shook his head. "Don't try to deceive me, Inspector. It's childish. The Judge has vanished. Into the Outer Darkness – as I foretold." He grinned broadly. "You will, of course, release me now."

"I'll – I'll *what*?"

Zyyzk spread his hands. "You have no choice. Not unless you want to admit that I could sit in a police cell surrounded on all sides by steel bars and cause Judge Keeler to vanish off the face of the earth by will power alone. Since that, to your limited, earthly intelligence, is impossible, I have an impregnable alibi. Good day, Inspector."

The little man actually started to walk off. The detectives who stood on either side were so dazed by his treatment of the Inspector that Zyyzk had gone six feet before they came to life again and grabbed him.

Whether the strange powers he claimed were real or not, his ability to render Gavigan speechless was certainly uncanny. The Inspector's mouth opened, but again nothing came out.

Merlini said, "You admit then that you are responsible for the Judge's disappearance?"

Zyyzk, still grinning, shook his head. "I predicted it. Beyond that I admit nothing."

"But you know how he vanished?"

The little man shrugged. "In the usual way, naturally. Only an adept of the seventh order would understand."

Merlini suddenly snapped his fingers and plucked a shiny

silver dollar from thin air. He dropped it into his left hand, closed his fingers over it and held his fist out toward Zyyzk. "Perhaps Judge Keeler vanished – like this." Slowly he opened his fingers. The coin was gone.

For the first time a faint crack appeared in the polished surface of Zyyzk's composure. He blinked. "Who," he asked slowly, "are you?"

"An adept," Merlini said solemnly, "of the eighth order. One who is not yet satisfied that you are what you claim to be." He snapped his fingers again, almost under Zyyzk's nose, and the silver dollar reappeared. He offered it to Zyyzk. "A test," he said. "Let me see you send that back into the Outer Darkness from which I summoned it."

Zyyzk no longer grinned. He scowled and his eyes were hard. "It will go," he said, lifting his hand and rapidly tracing a cabalistic figure in the air. "And you with it!"

"Soon?" Merlini asked.

"Very soon. Before the hour of nine strikes again you will appear before the Lords of the Outer Darkness in far Antares. And there—"

Gavigan had had enough. He passed a miracle of his own. He pointed a cabalistic but slightly shaking finger at the little man and roared an incantation that had instant effect.

"*Get him out of here!*"

In the small space of time that it took them to hurry down the corridor and around a corner, Zyyzk and the two detectives who held him both vanished.

Gavigan turned on Merlini. "Isn't one lunatic enough without you acting like one, too?"

The magician grinned. "Keep your eyes on me, Inspector. If I vanish, as predicted, you may see how Keeler did it. If I don't, Zyyzk is on the spot and he may begin to make more sense."

"That," Gavigan growled, "is impossible."

Zyyzk, as far as I was concerned, wasn't the only thing that made no sense. The Inspector's men turned Grand Central station inside out and the only trace of Judge Keeler to be found were the smashed spectacles on the floor of that phone booth.

Gavigan was so completely at a loss that he could think of nothing else to do but order the search made again.

Merlini, as far as I could tell, didn't seem to have any better ideas. He leaned against the wall opposite the phone booth and scowled darkly at its empty interior. Malloy and Hicks looked so tired and dispirited that Gavigan told them both to go home and sleep it off. An hour later, when the second search had proved as fruitless as the first, Gavigan suddenly told Lieutenant Doran to take over, turned, and started to march off.

Then Merlini woke up. "Inspector," he asked, "where are you going?"

Gavigan turned, scowling. "Anywhere," he said, "where I don't have to look at telephone booths. Do you have any suggestions?"

Merlini moved forward. "One, yes. Let's eat."

Gavigan didn't look as if he could keep anything in his stomach stronger than weak chicken broth, but he nodded absently. We got into Gavigan's car and Brady drove us crosstown, stopping, at Merlini's direction, in front of the Williston building.

The Inspector objected, "There aren't any decent restaurants in this neighbourhood. Why—"

"Don't argue," Merlini said as he got out. "If Zyyzk's latest prediction comes off, this will be my last meal on earth. I want to eat here. Come on." He crossed the pavement toward a flashing green and purple neon sign that blinked: *Johnson's Cafeteria. Open All Night.*

Merlini was suddenly acting almost as strangely as Zyyzk. I knew very well that this wasn't the sort of place he'd pick for his last meal and, although he claimed to be hungry, I noticed that all he put on his tray was crackers and a bowl of soup. Pea soup at that – something he heartily disliked.

Then, instead of going to a table off in a corner where we could talk, he chose one right in the centre of the room. He even selected our places for us. "You sit there, Inspector. You there, Ross. And excuse me a moment. I'll be right back." With that he turned, crossed to the street door through which we had come, and vanished through it.

"I think," I told Gavigan, "that he's got a bee in his bonnet."

The Inspector grunted. "You mean bats. In his belfry." He gave the veal cutlet on his plate a glum look.

Merlini was gone perhaps five minutes. When he returned, he made no move to sit down. He leaned over the table and asked, "Either of you got a nickel?"

I found one and handed it to him. Suspiciously, Gavigan said, "I thought you wanted to eat?"

"I must make a phone call first," the magician answered. "And with Zyyzk's prediction hanging over me, I'd just as soon you both watched me do it. Look out the window behind me, watch that empty booth – the second from the right. And keep your eyes on it every second." He glanced at his wrist watch. "If I'm not back here in exactly three minutes, you'd better investigate."

I didn't like the sound of that. Neither did Gavigan. He started to object. "Now, wait a minute. You're not going—"

But Merlini had already gone. He moved with long strides toward the street door, and the Inspector half rose from his chair as if to go after him. Then, when Gavigan saw what lay beyond the window, he stopped. The window we both faced was in a side wall at right angles to the street, and it opened, not to the outside, but into the arcade that runs through the Williston building.

Through the glass we could see a twenty-foot stretch of the arcade's opposite wall and against it, running from side to side, was a row of half a dozen phone booths.

I took a quick look at the clock on the wall above the window just as Merlini vanished through the street door. He reappeared at once in the arcade beyond the window, went directly to the second booth from the right, and went inside. The door closed.

"I don't like this," I said. "In three minutes the time will be exactly—"

"Quiet!" Gavigan commanded.

"—exactly nine o'clock," I finished. "Zyyzk's deadline!"

"He's not going to pull this off," Gavigan said. "You keep your eyes on that booth. I'm going outside and watch it from the street entrance. When the time's up, join me."

I heard his chair scrape across the floor as he got up, but I kept my eyes glued to the scene beyond the window – more precisely to one section of it – the booth into which Merlini had gone. I could see the whole face of the door from top to bottom and the dim luminescence of the light inside.

Nothing happened.

The second hand on the wall clock moved steadily, but much too slowly. At five seconds to the hour I found myself on my feet. And when the hand hit twelve I moved fast. I went through the door, turned left, and found Gavigan just inside the arcade entrance, his eyes fixed on the booth.

"Okay," he said without turning his head. "Come on."

We hurried forward together. The Inspector jerked the door of the second booth open. The light inside blinked out.

Inside, the telephone receiver dangled, still swaying, by its cord.

The booth was empty.

Except for one thing. I bent down and picked it up off the floor – Merlini's shiny silver dollar.

Gavigan swore. Then he pushed me aside, stepped into the booth and lifted the receiver. His voice was none too steady. He said one word into the phone.

"Hello?"

Leaning in behind him, I heard the voice that replied – Merlini's voice making a statement that was twice as impossible as anything that had happened yet.

"Listen carefully," it said. "And don't ask questions now. I'm at 1462–12 Astoria Avenue, the Bronx. Got that? 1462–12 Astoria. Keeler's here – and a murderer! *Hurry!*"

The tense urgency of that last command sent a cold shiver down my spine. Then I heard the click as the connection was broken.

Gavigan stood motionless for a second, holding the dead phone. Then the surging flood of his emotions spilled over. He jiggled the receiver frantically and swore again.

"Blast it! This phone is dead!"

I pulled myself out of a mental tailspin, found a nickel, and dropped it in the slot. Gavigan's verbal fireworks died to a mutter as he heard the dial tone and he jabbed savagely at the dial.

A moment later the Telegraph Bureau was broadcasting a bowdlerized version of Gavigan's orders to the prowl cars in the Astoria Avenue neighbourhood. And Gavigan and I were running for the street and his own car. Brady saw us coming, gunned his motor, and the instant we were aboard, took off as though jet-powered. He made a banked turn into Fifth Avenue against a red light, and we raced uptown, siren screaming.

If Zyyzk had been there beside us, handing out dire predictions that we were headed straight for the Pearly Gates, I wouldn't have doubted him for a moment. We came within inches of that destination half a dozen times as we roared swerving through the crosstown traffic.

The Astoria address wasn't hard to find. There were three prowl cars parked in front of it and two uniformed cops on the front porch. One sat on the floor, his back to the wall, holding a limp arm whose sleeve was stained with blood. There were two round bullet holes in the glass of the door above him. As we ran up the walk, the sound of gun fire came from the rear of the house and the second cop lifted his foot, kicked in a front window, and crawled in through the opening, gun in hand.

The wounded man made a brief report as we passed him. "Nobody answered the door," he said. "But when we tried to crash the joint, somebody started shooting."

Somebody was still shooting. Gavigan, Brady, and I went through the window and toward the sound. The officer who had preceded us was in the kitchen, firing around the jamb of the back door. An answering gun blazed in the dark outside and the cop fired at the flash.

"Got him, I think," the cop said. Then he slipped out through the door, moved quickly across the porch and down the steps. Brady followed him.

Gavigan's pocket-flash suddenly sent out a thin beam of light. It started a circuit of the kitchen, stopped for a moment as it picked up movement just outside the door, and we saw a third uniformed man pull himself to a sitting position on the porch floor, look at the bloodstain on his trouser leg, and swear.

Then the Inspector's flash found the open cellar door.

And down there, beside the beginning of a grave, we found Judge Keeler.

His head had been battered in.

But he couldn't find Merlini anywhere in the house. It wasn't until five minutes later, when we were opening Keeler's suitcase, that Merlini walked in.

He looked at the cash and negotiable securities that tumbled out. "You got here," he said, "before that vanished, too, I see."

Gavigan looked up at him. "But you just arrived this minute. I heard a cab out front."

Merlini nodded. "My driver refused to ignore the stop lights the way yours did. Did you find the Judge?"

"Yes, we found him. And I want to know how of all the addresses in Greater New York, you managed to pick this one out of your hat?"

Merlini's dark eyes twinkled. "That was the easy part. Keeler's disappearance, as I said once before, added up to *two* invisible men. As soon as I knew who the second one must be, I simply looked the name up in the phone book."

"And when you vanished," I asked, "was that done with two invisible men?"

Merlini grinned. "No. I improved on the Judge's miracle a bit. I made it a one-man operation."

Gavigan had had all the riddles he could digest. "We found Keeler's body," he growled ominously, "beside an open grave. And if *you* don't stop—"

"Sorry," Merlini said, as a lighted cigarette appeared mysteriously between his fingers. "As a magician I hate to have to blow the gaff on such a neatly contrived bit of hocus pocus as The Great Phone Booth Trick. But if I must – well, it began when Keeler realized he was going to have to take a runout powder. He knew he was being watched. It was obvious that if he and Helen Hope tried to leave town by any of the usual methods, they'd both be picked up at once. Their only chance was to vanish as abruptly and completely as Judge Crater and Dorothy Arnold once did. I suspect it was Zyyzk's first prediction that Miss Hope would disappear that gave Keeler the idea. At any rate, that was what set the wheels in motion."

"I thought so," Gavigan said. "Zyyzk was in on it."

Merlini shook his head. "I'm afraid you can't charge him with a thing. He was in on it – but he didn't know it. One of the subtlest deceptive devices a magician uses is known as 'the principle of the impromptu stooge.' He so manages things that an unrehearsed spectator acts as a confederate, often without ever realizing it. That's how Keeler used Zyyzk. He built his vanishing trick on Zyyzk's predictions and used them as misdirection. But Zyyzk never knew that he was playing the part of a red herring."

"He's a fraud though," Gavigan insisted. "And he does know it."

Merlini contradicted that, too. "No. Oddly enough he's the one thing in this whole case that is on the level. As you, yourself, pointed out, no fake prophet would give such precisely detailed predictions. He actually does believe that Helen Hope and Judge Keeler vanished into the Outer Darkness."

"A loony," Gavigan muttered.

"And," Merlini added, "a real problem, at this point, for any psychiatrist. He's seen two of his prophecies come true with such complete and startling accuracy that he'll never believe what really happened. I egged him into predicting my disappearance in order to show him that he wasn't infallible. If he never discovers that I did vanish right on time, it may shake his belief in his occult powers. But if he does, the therapy will backfire; he'll be convinced when he sees me, that I'm a doppelganger or an astral double the police have conjured up to discredit him."

"If you don't stop trying to psychoanalyze Zyyzk," Gavigan growled impatiently, "the police are going to conjure up a charge of withholding information in a murder case. Get on with it. Helen Hope wasn't being tailed, so her disappearance was a cinch. She simply walked out, without even taking her toothbrush – to make Zyyzk's prediction look good – and grabbed a plane for Montana or Mexico or some such place where Keeler was to meet her later. But how did Keeler evaporate? And don't you give me any nonsense about two invisible men."

Merlini grinned. "Then we'd better take my disappearance

first. That used only one invisible man – and, of course, too many phone booths."

Then, quickly, as Gavigan started to explode, Merlini stopped being cryptic. "In that restaurant you and Ross sat at a table and in the seats that I selected. You saw me, through the window, enter what I had been careful to refer to as the second booth from the right. Seen through the window, that is what it was. But the line of phone booths extended on either side beyond the window and your field of vision. Viewed from outside, there were nine – not six – booths, and the one I entered was actually the third in line."

"Do you mean," Gavigan said menacingly, "that when I was outside watching the second booth, Ross, inside, was watching the third – and we both thought we were watching the same one?"

"Yes. It isn't necessary to deceive the senses if the mind can be misdirected. You saw what you saw, but it wasn't what you thought you saw. And that—"

Then Gavigan did explode, in a muffled sort of way. "Are you saying that we searched the *wrong* phone booth? And that you were right there all the time, sitting in the next one?"

Merlini didn't need to answer. That was obviously just what he did mean.

"Then your silver dollar," I began, "and the phone receiver—"

"Were," Merlini grinned, "what confidence men call 'the convincer' – concocted evidence which seemed to prove that you had the right booth, prevented any sceptical second thoughts, and kept you from examining the other booths just to make sure you had the right one."

I got it then. "That first time you left the restaurant, before you came back with that phoney request for the loan of a nickel – that's when you left the dollar in the second booth."

Merlini nodded. "I made a call, too. I dialed the number of the second booth. And when the phone rang, I stepped into the second booth, took the receiver off the hook, dropped the silver dollar on the floor, then hurried back to your table. Both receivers were off and the line was open."

"And when we looked into the second booth, you were sitting right next door, three feet away, telling Gavigan via the phone that you were in the Bronx?"

Merlini nodded. "And I came out after you had gone. It's a standard conjuring principle. The audience doesn't see the coin, the rabbit, or the girl vanish because they actually disappear either before or after the magician pretends to conjure them into thin air. The audience is watching most carefully at the wrong time."

"Now wait a minute," the Inspector objected. "That's just exactly the way you said Keeler couldn't have handled the phone business. What's more he couldn't. Ross and I weren't watching you the first time you left the restaurant. But we'd been watching Keeler for a week."

"And," I added, "Malloy and Hicks couldn't have miscounted the booths at the station and searched the wrong one. They could see both ends of that line of booths the whole time."

"They didn't miscount," Merlini said. "They just didn't count. The booth we examined was the fifth from the right end of the line, but neither Malloy nor Hicks ever referred to it in that way."

Gavigan scowled. "They said Keeler went into the booth '*to the right of the one that was out of order*.' And the phone in the next booth *was* out of order."

"I know, but Keeler didn't enter the booth next to the one we found out of order. He went into a booth next to one that was marked: Out of Order. That's not quite the same."

Gavigan and I both said the same thing at the same time: "The sign had been moved!"

"Twice," Merlini said, nodding. "First, when Keeler was in the Oyster Bar. The second invisible man – invisible because no one was watching him – moved it one booth to the right. And when Keeler, a few minutes later, entered the booth to the right of the one bearing the sign, he was actually in the second booth from the one whose phone didn't work.

"And then our second invisible man went into action again. He walked into the booth marked out of order, smashed a duplicate pair of blood-smeared glasses on the floor, and dialed the Judge's phone. When Keeler answered, he walked out again, leaving the receiver off the hook. It was as neat a piece of mis-direction as I've seen in a long time. Who would suspect him of putting through a call from a phone booth that was plainly labelled out of order?"

Cautiously, as if afraid the answer would blow up in his face, the Inspector asked, "He did all this with Malloy and Hicks both watching? And he wasn't seen – because he was invisible?"

"No, that's not quite right. He was invisible – because he wasn't suspected."

I still didn't see it. "But," I objected, "the only person who went anywhere near the booth next to the one Keeler was in—"

Heavy footsteps sounded on the back porch and then Brady's voice from the doorway said, "We found him, Inspector. Behind some bushes the other side of the wall. Dead. And do you know who—"

"I do now," Gavigan cut in. "Sergeant Hicks."

Brady nodded.

Gavigan turned to Merlini. "Okay, so Hicks was a crooked cop and a liar. But not Malloy. He says he was watching that phone booth every second. How did Hicks switch that Out-of-Order sign back to the original booth again without being seen?"

"He did it when Malloy wasn't watching quite so closely – *after* Malloy thought Keeler had vanished. Malloy saw Hicks look into the booth, act surprised, then beckon hurriedly. Those actions, together with Hicks's later statement that the booth was already empty, made Malloy think the judge had vanished sooner than he really did. Actually Keeler was still right there, sitting in the booth into which Hicks stared. It's the same deception as to time that I used."

"Will you," Gavigan growled, "stop lecturing on the theory of deception and just explain when Hicks moved that sign."

"All right. Remember what Malloy did next? He was near the information booth in the center of the floor and he ran across toward the phones. Malloy said, 'I did some fancy open-field running through the commuters.' Of course he did. At five-twenty the station is full of them and he was in a hell of a hurry. He couldn't run fast and keep his eyes glued to Hicks and that phone booth every step of the way; he'd have had half a dozen head-on collisions. But he didn't think the fact that he had had to use his eyes to steer a course rather than continue to watch the booth was important. He thought the dirty work – Keeler's disappearance – had taken place.

"As Malloy ran toward him through the crowd, Hicks simply took two steps sideways to the left and stared into the phone booth that was tagged with the Out-of-Order card. And, behind his body, his left hand shifted the sign one booth to the left – back to the booth that was genuinely out of order. Both actions took no more than a second or two. When Malloy arrived, 'the booth next to the one that was out of order' was empty. Keeler had vanished into Zyyzk's Outer Darkness *by simply sitting still and not moving at all!*"

"And he really vanished," Gavigan said, finally convinced, "by walking out of the next booth as soon as he had spoken his piece to Molloy on the phone."

"While Malloy," Merlini added, "was still staring goggle-eyed at the phone. Even if he had turned to look out of the door, all he'd have seen was the beefy Hicks standing smack in front of him carefully blocking the view. And then Keeler walked right out of the station. Every exit was guarded – except one. An exit big enough to drive half a dozen trains through!"

"Okay," the Inspector growled. "You don't have to put it in words of one syllable. He went out through one of the train gates which Malloy himself had been covering, boarded a train a moment before it pulled out, and ten minutes later he was getting off again up at 125th Street."

"Which," Merlini added, "isn't far from Hick's home where we are now and where Keeler intended to hide out until the cops, baffled by the dead-end he'd left, relaxed their vigilance a bit. The judge was full of cute angles. Who'd ever think of looking for him in the home of one of the cops who was supposed to be hunting him?"

"After which," I added, "he'd change the cut of his whiskers or trim them off altogether, go to join Miss Hope, and they'd live happily ever after on his ill-gotten gains. Fadeout."

"That was the way the script read," Merlini said. "But Judge Keeler forgot one or two little things. He forgot that a man who has just vanished off the face of the earth, leaving a deadend trail, is a perfect prospective murder victim. And he forgot that a suitcase full of folding money is a temptation one should never set before a crooked cop."

"Forgetfulness seems to be dangerous," I said. "I'm glad I've got a good memory."

"I have a hunch that somebody is going to have both our scalps," Merlini said ominously. "I've just remembered that when we left the shop—"

He was right. I hadn't mailed Mrs Merlini's letter.

# MURDER STRIPS OFF

*Amy Myers*

*I should have expected it! When I first contacted authors in the hope they'd be interested in contributing to this anthology I was delighted with the diversity and originality of ideas that were suggested. And yes, I should have expected it. After all, what could be more impossible than a murder committed in full view of an audience when the only possible suspects are the strippers on the stage! And it's very clear that they had no weapons to hand! Amy Myers (b.1938) is the author of the popular series featuring August Didier, the Victorian/Edwardian chef/detective. The following story delightfully introduces Nick Didier, following in his great-grandfather's footsteps.*

"Never again." Hamish Scott scrabbled into his clothes for dear life. "Those hyenas are going to tear it off one of these days. Count me out."

"If I had a prick like yours, mate," Paul Duncan sniggered, eyeing the weedy former schoolteacher from top to toe, "I'd feel the same." He squared his footballer's shoulders, and admired himself in the cracked mirror of the scruffy room allotted to them at the pub.

"I'm with you, Hamish." Jason Knight saw where his best interests lay, but the redundant salesman in him sought to smooth things over. "None of us can quit, can we, Greta?" They couldn't – she'd made sure of that.

"Glad you remembered which side your privates are buttered." Tony Hobbs (ex-colonel) heaved himself up ostentatiously with the aid of his stick, banged it on the floor to emphasize his authority, and limped to the piano to place an affectionate hand on his wife's shoulder. "I've worked my ass off managing you lot, and so's Greta."

The three men kept silent as they bitterly recalled just how darling Greta had worked her ass off on their account.

"If only my boys would try to get along better," Greta purred reproachfully, but the small black eyes in the solid face flickered malevolently. "You all dance to my tunes so admirably it seems a pity to break the trio up. Perhaps I'll try a new routine. How would that be?"

Even Tony danced to Greta's tune, but tonight Hamish had reached breaking point. "I won't do it. I won't even do Wednesday." His voice rose to a shriek. "I want out *now!*"

"Oh, you will mate," Paul said viciously. Wednesday meant serious money, even the vastly reduced amount that dribbled down to them, and no replacement could learn the routines in two days. "Face it, Hamish. She's got us by the short and curlies."

"Sweet of you, my great big cuddly teddy bear. *Tonight's* teddy bear?" Greta suggested lightly, while her husband listened impassively.

Paul fell suddenly silent, and Justin saw his chance.

"Come on, Hamish. One more show won't kill you."

"All right, but Wednesday's the last." Hamish hurled his defiance at their trainer, pianist and de facto boss.

Greta grinned. "Over my dead body."

How did he land up in this hole? It was Nick Didier's philosophy that a job was a job and even the most repellent had something to offer if you could stand back a few paces and think of something worse. Spider-catching in Antarctica, for instance. He hated the cold, he hated spiders, and compared with these horrors catering for Women's Only Night at a steamy club looked tolerable, even if they were gathered to watch male strippers. This trio, The Bubbling Berties, hardly lived up to their name – they looked dead miserable.

"Fancy 'em, do you?"

Les leered over Nick's shoulder, as he watched the trio from the doorway of the kitchen at the side of the hall. Les's Crappy Catering Company (as Nick termed it) had finished its own role for the evening, and two hundred or so women were gearing up to scream their loudest, having drunk enough to dull their indigestion pains.

"I'd sooner fancy your food, mate," Nick replied amiably.

Les only laughed. His only concession to haute cuisine was the names he gave the muck. Turkish Salsa, Thai Salad of Minty Prawns, and Cajun Chicken à l'Orange turned out to be yoghurt flavoured with almond essence, pink slop prawn cocktail (with a parsley leaf as garnish if it wasn't too expensive) capped by your old friend fried chicken with a tired orange segment. With the right names the ladies would love roasted cowpats, Les maintained, only he didn't call them cowpats.

Four weeks in the food trade had convinced Nick this career was not for him. Apparently his great-grandfather had been a master chef. Good luck to the old codger. Then Dad had changed his mind and said he was a detective. Yeah, great, Nick had thought jealously. The Case of the Stolen Spotted Dick maybe. Detection was *his* thing, he didn't want to tread in family footprints.

Les seemed to have a point about the cowpats, judging by the approving noise level as dinner was served. And now it was being raised even higher, as the Bubbling Berties, seated at a bar across the rear of the stage with their backs to the audience, went into action:

"*Oh, what a bubbling gent I am . . .*"

The three top-hatted, tuxedo-clad men burst into song as they whizzed round on their barstools, raising glasses of something that sparkled, whether champagne or not. The glasses were twirled, and raised again as the Berties simultaneously (or almost) drank a toast to the audience.

Directly in front of Nick, an upright piano on floor level by the low stage was being pounded by a middle-aged woman in a tight black evening dress she'd outgrown several sizes earlier. That must be Greta Hobbs, he decided. She was some sort of cousin of

Les's, and apparently it was she who had persuaded the misguided owner of the club into making use of Les's services. Greta picked up a glass standing on the piano top, to swig champagne in a toast to her troupe, and as the bubbles in it sparkled in the brightness of the spotlight above her, the Berties awarded her a toast in return.

Nick's mind began to fantasize. Suppose inside that piano there was a gun rigged up ready to shoot the pianist, as in Ngaio Marsh's novel? Or even a poisoned dart? That way suspicion would fall on someone on stage, but because everyone was watching, no one could possibly have done it. It would be the impossible murder. *Yes*! He liked it.

Somewhat reluctantly, it seemed to him, the Berties were launching themselves into an inefficient dance routine, as various items of outer clothing and then shirts were discarded, and the audience began to rehearse their war whoops. The top hats, however, remained firmly on the Berties' heads.

On retiring to their stools, a skinny individual who didn't look as if he gained much work satisfaction wove his way in a double shuffle, glass once more in hand, to the corner where the piano top provided a convenient resting place for it as he proceeded to remove his trousers. He tossed them into the wings, crooning his solo verse:

"*I bubble every evening and I bubble every day . . .*"

Nick decided the loud roars of enthusiasm could only be anticipation for future revelations when the scarlet bikini briefs disappeared. The elderly gent sitting at the end of the front row behind her was already waving his stick in excitement.

"What's that old geezer doing amongst all these women?" he asked Les.

"That old geezer, son, is Colonel Tony Hobbs, retired, Greta's ever-adoring husband and the Bubbling Berties' manager." Les cast a scornful look at the Bertie currently bubbling in the limelight. "And *that's* Hamish Scott. Greta took pity on him when he cracked up –" Les was a fair man, so he added, "– if you can call it that. She fancied a bit of intellect, she said, even though he's not much better than Tony in the how's your father department."

With obvious relief, and abandoning his glass, Hamish wriggled his way back to the bar to join his colleagues for the next chorus. The solo routine was then repeated, first by the beefy white-briefed Bertie ("Paul Duncan", Les sniggered. "All three of them are her ex-lovers, but in Paul's case not so much of the 'ex'.") and then by the younger one sporting natty bright blue bikini briefs. Les obliged again. "Jason Knight, replaced at work by a computer. Greta offered him the job no computer can do."

All three Bubbling Berties were back at the bar for the last chorus, displaying their patriotically-clad lower limbs. Their three glasses remained with Greta's on the piano-top, but *still* they hung on to their top hats. It gave a remarkably seedy, almost obscene effect, and those hats began to exert a fascination over Nick. When – if ever – would *they* come off?

Not yet. The removal of the briefs was discreetly managed behind the stools, and as the music changed to the traditional stripper music the audience was treated to the sight of three G-stringed Berties standing at the bar, first Paul on stage left, then Hamish in the middle, then Justin, and drinking from a second set of champagne-filled glasses. Smoke and audience noise reached a crescendo, as the be-thonged trio, hands on hips, legs apart, faced their increasingly appreciative audience.

Nick gulped. The whole affair was repulsive. Perhaps women viewed it differently, although none of his girlfriends had ever been into this kind of thing. It occurred to him uneasily they were hardly likely to tell him, even if they were.

The music crashed out towards its finale, with all eyes glued to the thongs. At last they were whipped away and the Bubbling Berties displayed all their glory to a now hysterical audience. (Nick must have been the only spectator looking at those terrible top hats.) Some women were climbing on their seats, others seemed ready to rush the stage.

In a crowning act of bravado the Berties marched to the piano, and reclaimed their abandoned glasses. At long last the hats were discarded, tossed to a waiting hand from the wings, as they toasted their pianist once again. Greta rose to her feet, toasted them, and resumed her seat to continue the triumphant musical finale.

"Amazing, ain't it?" Les seemed admiring of this ghastly performance. "You'd never think they loathed each other – and that they hate old Greta even more."

"I thought you said they were her lovers."

"She blackmailed them into starting this game by saying she'd tell their wives. She's a sexy old thing is Greta, and her husband's useless. Now she won't let them leave."

"They've got minds of their own, haven't they?"

"If they had once, Greta brainwashed them with dreams of fame and fortune in Hollywood, and by pointing out how upset their wives would be to miss out on the Oscars and the Tony. *And* how much their wives wouldn't like to hear their housekeeping cash comes from other women screaming at their husbands' pride and joys. Someone will do the old bag in one day," he added casually.

"Murder? You're not serious, Les?"

A harsh jangle rang out from the piano, as Greta's fingers slipped from the keys, her face convulsed. Her body first slumped, then took the stool with it as it crashed to the floor.

It was his knowledge of first aid that sent Nick unwillingly to the Greta's side. It was one thing to fantasize on poisoned darts, quite another to face a possibly dead body. Her husband was hobbling around in shock waving his stick at all and sundry, but that was a fat lot of use.

First aid looked redundant, and if Nick's suspicions about its being some sort of cyanide poisoning were right, he had to act quickly. She might not be dead, and if she were, there might be evidence lying around. Poisoned darts? Standing tall to every one of his 5 foot 4 inches, he croaked to the club owner: "Call the police as well as the ambulance, and keep the audience here. No one should touch *anything*. Not even—" he yelled, seeing Paul halfway into his thong, "*that*".

"Listen, mate," Paul said viciously, "I ain't proposing to stand here like a limp chili pod waiting for the fuzz just because old Greta's had a drop too much."

Nick summoned up his courage. "She may have been murdered."

That stopped all three Berties, thongs or no thongs, and a red-faced Tony Hobbs came charging onto the stage, yelling, "It was one of you, wasn't it? You bastards, you murdered my wife. Which one of you did it?"

"I said *may*," Nick shouted. "But I can't see how. It would have been impossible, except by a poisoned dart – unless –"

"Impossible's enough for me," Paul interrupted. "I'm putting my thong on. Want to make anything of it, nipper?"

Nick didn't, and the other two Berties quickly followed Paul's lead.

"Aren't we the little hero, then?" Les was torn between his usual sneer and reluctant admiration. "The club won't be offering you any medals for *inviting* the fuzz, though, they come all too often without asking."

"Tough." Nick still felt shaky at his own daring.

The ambulance arrived at the same time as the patrol car, and it became clear that Nick's diagnosis of unnatural death might be correct.

"How do you know so much about it, anyway?" Les averted his eyes from his cousin's corpse, lying by the piano by itself, awaiting the arrival of higher police authority. It looked lonely, and Nick felt protective of the late Greta Hobbs.

"She smelt like your Turkish Salsa gone wrong, that's why. And she'd blue lips and thrown up." It didn't seem right talking about it.

"Maybe that was the chicken," Les said uneasily. He'd sent some food to the group before the show began.

Sherlock Holmes used to be treated with more respect, Nick reflected bitterly, as he retired to a corner with Les. He was an aficionado of crime fiction from Poe through Conan Doyle, Dorothy Sayers, Christie, right up to Peter and Phil Lovesey, Chaz Brenchley and anything he could lay his hands on. He was addicted, whether it be hard-boiled realism or soft-boiled cosy, and irrespective of whether great-grandad used to dabble with a magnifying glass in deepest Muckshire. Tonight Nick's nose had twitched just as it had in protest at Les putting dried parsley in the prawns. Something hadn't been *right*.

When higher police authority arrived, Nick had visions of Jack Frost clapping him on the back, or Inspector Morse reluctantly congratulating him. Unfortunately Detective Superintendent Bishop wasn't like either of them. His amiable smile gave him the look of everybody's ideal family doctor. While the police doctor was examining the corpse and most of the audience were filing out under the guidance of a sergeant, he was ambling around the taped-off areas of stage and auditorium like a lazy trout, but Nick couldn't help noticing his eyes darted everywhere like a particularly hungry piranha fish. They fell on Nick and Les.

"Who might you be? Two more strippers?"

"Catering staff," Les growled. "We done the supper."

Nick nudged him, seeing pitfalls ahead, but the piranha spotted him.

"I don't wonder you're worried, sir," he said soothingly to Nick. "We won't know for sure this is poison till the PM's done, but you'll have a few questions to answer if it is. You won't mind that, I'm sure."

"I was the one who said you should be called in," Nick yelped.

Bishop shook his head sadly. "The last fellow who tried that double bluff on me is doing life."

"If it was cyanide," Nick said desperately, "it must have been on a poisoned dart unless—" An eyebrow was raised, and he continued hastily, "Our dinner was over by nine o'clock and she didn't die till ten-twenty." Too late, he realized poisoned darts were out, for he wouldn't have smelled almonds then.

"Fancy you knowing what poison it might have been, sir. Washed everything up, have you?"

"Yes," Les answered bleakly.

"Don't worry about a thing, sir. We'll find something," Bishop assured him cheerily. "If there's anything to find," he added as a throwaway.

"Did any of the glasses on the piano smell of almonds?" Nick asked hopefully.

Bishop's smile became even more genial. "Why? Didn't drop anything in, did you?"

"No." It came out as a bleat.

"Just joking, lad. You'll get used to my merry sense of humour. Why do you think the poison was in a glass?"

"I don't, because although she had just drunk from one—"

"Who filled it?"

"I don't know, but she couldn't have died that way." Nick could wait no longer to produce his ace. "She'd drunk from it earlier without ill-effect, and the Berties had all drunk from the other three glasses on the piano. Suicide is out because she couldn't have added anything to the glass between the two toasts. So unless the poison was added intentionally by someone on stage, murder would be impossible."

A silence, then Bishop said: "Impossible isn't a word I like." He beckoned to the three Berties, still sitting miserably on stage in their thongs, resentful of the scene of crime's photographers' ill-concealed smirks.

Bishop saw Nick's struggles to control an insane desire to laugh. "Shock, lad. Seen many corpses, have you?"

"No."

"I have, and thank God I never get over it. When you do, that's the time to quit."

Tony Hobbs was sitting in the first row of seats outside the tape, declaring at intervals that he was used to shock, making it sound as if his wife got murdered every day. He was ashen-faced, though, and in Nick's opinion looked about to pass out as the Berties joined him.

"Our street clothes are over there," Hamish told Bishop hopefully, pointing to the "wings" – an all-purpose room at the side of the stage where the lighting and curtain controls were.

"Now bagged up and the temporary property of Her Majesty's Police Force, sir."

A stunned silence. "You expect us to bloody well go home like this?" Justin screeched.

"No, we'll need those thongs too."

Hamish began to weep, and Bishop relented. "The sergeant

will organize something. Can't have you frightening the horses. Now, gentlemen, I want you to repeat *exactly* what you did this evening. And you," he jabbed a finger at Nick, "keep out of it."

Tony Hobbs elected to fill Bishop in on the background. "These three gentlemen worked to my wife's choreography. At the beginning six glasses were put on the bar, two each for the men, and a seventh on the piano for my wife, and just before the show Greta filled them all herself. Any poison would have had to be added after that, I suppose," he added forlornly, "since everyone drank from the same bottle."

"Who," Bishop enquired, "put the glasses in position before the show?"

"Hamish," said his two colleagues gleefully.

"But we *all* drank from them earlier," Hamish reminded Bishop anxiously as they began the routine, miming the strip-tease, and using seven glasses from the kitchen. "Murder's impossible, just like the kid said."

"Where did you get the glasses from?" Bishop asked.

"We bring them with us," Hamish replied miserably. "I got them out of their case."

Hamish couldn't have doctored one beforehand, Nick realized happily; he was right. The poison could only have been added on stage.

As Hamish took his glass to the piano to begin the final stages of the striptease, Bishop interrupted. "Is that exactly where you placed your glass tonight?"

"I can't remember."

"Try," Bishop suggested in his best family doctor manner.

Hamish slowly inched it somewhat nearer to the one representing Greta's, which was on far stage left of the piano top, to be accessible for her right hand. When his turn came, Paul placed his just to the right of Hamish's, leaving the three glasses in a row.

"It wasn't there, mate," Justin pointed out. "Yours was dead behind Greta's, as it usually is. I saw you put it down, both times, and I put mine behind Hamish's."

"Maybe. I've other things on my mind," Paul said sullenly.

"She told me Paul was going to be her blue-eyed boy tonight," Les whispered to Nick.

"What did her husband think of that?"

"Doubt if he thought much of it, but he was used to it. Anyway, he thought she was the greatest thing since whisky."

It seemed strange to Nick, but then what made one marriage work and another not was a mystery anyway. What he did know was that husbands were the natural suspect in the case of a murdered wife.

As if on cue, Tony returned to the attack. "I repeat, which one of you bastards did it?" he asked quietly. "It had to be one of you three and you all hated her. None of you appreciated her."

"Tell me more," Bishop suggested politely, as the trio remained silent.

It was Hamish who threw the first stone. "Why couldn't *someone* have crept up from behind her? They could have added the poison, when Greta was watching us. She wouldn't have noticed."

"How about you, Tony?" Paul chimed in viciously. "You were nearest."

Justin leapt on this convenient bandwagon. "Find out Paul was still hard at it, did you, Tony?"

Tony stared at them reproachfully. "Even if," he said heavily, "I had any reason to wish harm to Greta, gentlemen, I was a good three feet away from the piano, I am a tall man, and I would have been visible in the light of the spot above her had I moved to poison my poor wife's drink." He sat down again, shaking with emotion. It looked genuine enough to Nick, and the facts were on Tony's side.

"I would have seen you for a start," Nick volunteered.

"You don't think," Bishop suggested mildly, "one of the two hundred ladies in the audience would have noticed too? Not one of them did."

"Perhaps it was at the psychological moment." Nick was suddenly inspired.

"What the hell's that?" Paul grunted.

"When we showed our willies." Hamish displayed his intellect.

"Everyone's eyes were riveted on us then. They wouldn't have noticed anything else."

"Ever taken an eye test?" Bishop smiled regretfully. "Most people have a field of vision that would be aware of *some* movement to the right or left, no matter what was going on. No murderer could take the risk of showing himself, spotlight or not. I fear the evidence so far suggests Mr Didier is right, that suicide is ruled out, and the poison could only have been added on stage."

"Cheers, Nick," Les said gratefully but prematurely.

"However," Bishop beamed, "there is something none of you gentlemen seem to have considered, even you, Mr Didier." Nick waited for the jaws to snap. "Poison isn't a murderer's manna, descending from the heavens. It has to come *in* something, whether it be a bottle for liquid or as in the case of cyanide, some form of box or wrapping for crystals." Bishop sighed as he saw the blank faces around him.

"May I point out," he continued softly, "that all three of you on stage ended up mother naked at the piano? Just how did one of you manage to both carry the poison there, and dispose of the container?"

A stunned silence, and then a united howl of relief from the Berties: "We didn't!"

Nick thought this through. Be blowed if he was going to be eaten alive by Bishop. "They could have poisoned their own glass after they'd drunk from it the first time, taken it to the piano and then switched glasses with Greta's."

"Very good, lad," Bishop said briskly. "But they'd still need to secrete the wrapping somewhere." He turned to the Berties. "Did any of you gentlemen notice anything unusual about the placing of the glasses?"

No one had. The relative positions had been as normal. Although, in the haste of the routine, the spacing between each glass changed, the order of the four did not.

"And you, Mr Duncan – you were on stage left in the line-up by the bar, and at the piano finale, did you sense or see any movement to the rear of the piano? No dark-cloaked villains?"

Paul reluctantly shook his head.

"Well, then, gentlemen, it seems you're in the clear." A pause. "Unless your full body searches reveal anything."

"You're not bloody serious, are you?" Paul moaned.

"Oh, I am, Mr Duncan, believe me. The sergeant here is very gentle though – usually."

Gentle or not, the sergeant found nothing.

"Wouldn't body cavities be a dangerous place to conceal cyanide?" Nick had become absorbed in the problem.

"Remarkable the way you cooks know so much about poison," Bishop said admiringly. "We're taking samples from all your food and kitchen utensils, of course."

Les howled. "How am I supposed to make a living?"

"It's what made a death we're here to find out. Every scrap of paper, clothing, food and glasses will be bagged up for forensics to check, and every millimetre of stage and kitchen will be searched."

"The hats!" Nick cried desperately. "They kept them on almost to the end. The poison must have been concealed in one of them."

"Who *is* that bloody little squirt?" Paul cast his eyes up to an unmerciful heaven.

"If so, we'll find traces," Bishop assured him. "The way we're going at the moment, however, it looks as if we can rule out Greta Hobbs' death by murder. Much as I dislike the word, it does look impossible." He grinned at the now visibly rejoicing Berties. "Mind you, you'd be surprised how often we think that at this stage."

The sight of a huge mobile caravan drawn up in the side street next to the club, obviously, from Nick's careful study, an incident room, was unnerving and confirmation enough that it had been murder. That made his summons back here with Les all the more daunting. Curiosity fought with fear of the "fix it on anyone" approach so beloved by the police in his reading material. Even spider-catching in Antarctica suddenly seemed preferable.

"Ah, our young detective." Bishop greeted him from one

corner of the kitchen made available for a table and chairs. "You'll be pleased to hear you can go."

"But that's a scene of crimes' van outside, isn't it?" Nick was taken aback.

"Must be the CIA."

Nick lingered as Les hastily cleared up and left. "You mean she wasn't poisoned?" He tried not to sound disappointed.

"She was, but we've cleared your food."

"So it was the drink?"

"It was. Forensic had a sleepless night. Nothing in the bottle, nothing in any of the glasses – save the one nearest to the lady, which was bung full of cyanide. And before you say suicide, forensic have found no traces of crystals in her clothing or handbag."

Nick bade a silent last farewell to poisoned darts. "Suppose one of the strippers poisoned one of the *extra* three glasses on the bar and took that with him over to the piano, instead of the one he'd first drunk from?"

"Ashamed of you, lad. Where did he keep the crystals? And there'd be a fifth glass on the piano."

"The hat?" Nick asked without much hope.

"Forget about hats. They were clean, too. What is it every self-respecting amateur detective pounces on?"

Nick didn't like being mocked. "Fingerprints."

"Right. And that's why Mr Paul Duncan is at the station helping with enquiries."

"All the glasses would have Hamish Scott's prints on." Nick was thinking it through. "So if he were the murderer he wouldn't need to worry about his prints being on Greta's glass, but the others would."

"Greta's glass had Duncan's prints on it as well as her own and Scott's. If we could find how he transported the poison, we could wrap this up. Now, you've quite a name at Scotland Yard, so you think about it."

"I've never even had a caution." What the hell was this?

"I went there to the Black Museum a while ago. Back in the dark ages there was an Auguste Didier who helped Rose of the

Yard in a few cases, generally those with fancy touches in them. Any relation?"

"Great-grandfather," Nick muttered reluctantly. Too much eagerness to claim kinship might not go down too well, and in any case he wasn't sure the news was welcome. True, an amateur detective in deepest Muckshire as a rival was way outclassed by one working with Scotland Yard. Maybe he'd check into it sometime.

"Just in case you have plans to follow in great-grandad's footsteps, I solve my own cases. Plain *and* fancy. Right?"

"Right," Nick hastily agreed.

"I don't see how Paul Duncan can be guilty," Nick proclaimed. Thinking of the impossible murder took his mind off his surroundings. Les's kitchen in the rented industrial unit lurched its way through every food inspection, surviving more by luck of timing than merit.

"I told you to make that with huss." Les peered peevishly at Nick's work.

"For a monkfish kebab?"

"Who's going to notice? It all gets charred to a cinder on the barbi."

"All the Berties hated her, but they all stayed."

"Ah, well, it was a living of some sort, even if Greta and good old Tony kept sixty per cent of it, and went on deluding them that they were building up a fund so that they could finance a launch into the big time. Not nice of Greta. It's cheating," Les added virtuously. He removed a chunk of fish from the end of each kebab. "Give 'em room to breathe," he explained casually.

"No one came up from the rear, but what about from that side room on stage? The owner and his lighting chap were there. Of course, they still had to get the poison onto the stage."

Les decided to be helpful. "You said it had to have been added between the two guzzling bouts. How about just stretching out from the wings?"

"Someone would have noticed a five-foot arm," Nick retorted scathingly.

Les expired with a final shot. "Maybe it dropped from the ceiling. Now, could you condescend to earn some of that fortune I pay you?"

Nick did not reply. Les had set off a train of thought. He remembered Sherlock Holmes and the snake gliding down the bellrope; he remembered Dorothy Sayers, and an ingenious contraption; he even remembered poisoned darts . . .

"You again? Solved it yet?"

"I wondered if you'd checked the wings," Nick blurted out, none too sure of his ground once faced with Bishop.

An amiable, if sardonic, smile. "Be my guest. Check 'em yourself. Let me know if I've missed anything. And let me tell you, Commander Bond, we've checked the spotlights and curtains half a dozen times. No cyanide crystals were showered down by guided missile, and no curtain rods left their moorings to deposit any either. *Nor* did anyone shoot a dart at her and poison the glass as a blind, *or* paint cyanide onto the piano keys so it would get absorbed into her fingers – but you didn't think of that one."

"No," Nick admitted. "But the hats—"

Bishop smote his forehead. "Of course!" he cried. "Whyever didn't you mention hats before?"

Nick ploughed doggedly on. "When the Berties stood at the piano nude, the last thing to go was the hats. Suppose the poison was held inside the brim and the murderer simply waved the hat low over the glass, released the poison somehow, then threw the hat offstage where it was switched for an identical unadulterated one."

"Collusion? The owner *will* be pleased. You go and practise releasing cyanide crystals from a secret compartment on your head, as you jig up and down starkers. When you've succeeded, I'll take you seriously."

Nick subsided, crestfallen.

"If you can tell me how Paul Duncan did it – and I'm sure he did – I'll stick a testimonial to you in the Black Museum," Bishop said more kindly, "next to your ancestor. Remember, all these weird and wonderful ways you've doubtless read about in fiction didn't have to pass the scrutiny of a couple of hundred screaming women – not to mention Mr Nick Didier's. However glued they were to the attractions of the Berties' persons, *someone* was going to see if poison shot down from the spotlights, just as they'd have noticed if any of the trio went fishing around in their fancy togs for a few cyanide crystals. Paul Duncan claims that he picked up Greta's glass by accident; if he's right, how did the poison get into *his* glass? I may be eating my own words, but perhaps this really is an impossible murder."

"And I'll eat my hat if it is," Nick vowed silently.

If you eliminate the impossible, the improbable must be true, Nick told himself. It was an old-established principle in detective fiction. Only what *was* the improbable? If it was impossible for anyone on the stage to have carried out the murder, and the wings and ceiling had been ruled out, that left the audience – which had also been ruled out. Anyone walking up to her would have been noticed, and her husband who was closest was devoted to her. Even if that were a sham, Nick would undoubtedly have seen him, even at the critical moment of the strip, since he was tall enough for the full spotlight on the piano to pick him up if he approached his wife, and surely the women next to him and behind him would have noticed if he'd moved, even in the darkness.

So it was back to the Bubbling Berties, who had motive and opportunity, if not means of transporting the poison. Nick stared gloomily at Les's Baked Alaska, composed more like traditional concrete than traditional meringue and ice-cream. Les's inadequacies had driven Nick to look up a cookery book last night to see how these dishes *should* be made. There were critical moments in cooking a Baked Alaska. Extreme heat applied to extreme cold. Alaska was as cold as Antarctica, and cooking the baked version was as risky as spider-catching . . .

"If this is a wild goose chase, friend Didier, you'll find you've cooked your own," Bishop had threatened genially. But it wasn't, and geniality had vanished by the time Bishop called him in again three days later. Bishop glared at him. "Are you expecting me to say I was wrong and you were right?"

"No, sir, I'm not expecting that."

Bishop eyed him sharply. "And I don't take to being mocked." A pause. "What gave you the idea, incidentally?"

"My spider-catcher, sir," Nick confessed shamefacedly. "It's a handy gadget with a wire running from the handle; when it's pulled, the trap at the end opens up. I thought something similar might suit our murderer's purpose. A walking stick with a wire cut into it, and a removable tip to release the poison, would work very well, if he kept it at shoulder height to avoid the full spotlight on his wife, and chose his moment. I didn't imagine he would keep the stick afterwards, of course, but I reasoned a blackmailer might make it his business to get hold of it. I doubt if your evidence bagging would go so far as to deprive a disabled man of his stick."

"We did find it, and it was where you'd said it would be. Tony Hobbs is still denying he killed his wife, but you've helped me prove it," Bishop generously admitted.

"No, I didn't, sir. I don't believe Tony did murder his wife. I don't know whether or not he loved her, but he didn't like her carrying on with other men, which she enjoyed flaunting. She underestimated his resentment, particularly when he found it was still going on. I think he knew he'd get nowhere by an outright challenge, so he chose this method. Unfortunately his *intended* victim, prancing around at the back of the stage as the Berties whipped off their thongs, spotted Tony doctoring his glass which was placed as usual behind Greta's. He probably couldn't believe his luck, when he cottoned on to what might be happening. If it was innocent, no problem. If it wasn't, he could choose between denouncing Tony or seizing his own opportunity for a double hit: ridding himself of Greta and milking Tony dry.

"He chose, all right. When he returned to the piano, he picked up Greta's glass, not his own, to drink from, probably using his left hand, and masking the extra stretch with his right arm from the other two. Then he replaced Greta's glass behind his own, making sure the others *did* see him do so, and stole the stick at the first opportunity so that he could blackmail Tony into giving back all the money he'd pinched from them. He needed the stick because he couldn't come forward later and suddenly claim to remember seeing Tony doctoring the glass, but he could 'find' the stick and allow it to 'jog his memory'. And so it was Paul Duncan deliberately murdered Greta, not the Colonel."

Nick grinned, as he added: "There was no reason for me to mock you. Two murders at half-cock don't add up to one full monty. The murder of Greta Hobbs by Paul Duncan *was* impossible – just as you thought, sir."

# OUT OF HIS HEAD

*Thomas Bailey Aldrich*

*This story and the next three are a little group of early impossible crime stories to give a flavour of the past. In fact this story is one of the very earliest, the second only after Poe's "The Murders in the Rue Morgue", to feature an amateur detective seeking to solve a locked-room murder. The story is a self-contained episode in the rather rambling novel* Out of His Head *(1862). Thomas Bailey Aldrich (1836–1907) was an American poet, author and editor – he edited the* Atlantic Monthly *from 1881 to 1890. He wrote a number of stylish and idiosyncratic novels and stories of which the most popular in his day was "Marjorie Daw" (1873) about a man who falls in love with a girl he later discovers never existed. In* The Stillwater Tragedy *(1880), Aldrich introduced a private detective some years before Doyle created Sherlock Holmes. Although the following is the oldest story in this anthology, it remains remarkably fresh today, a testament to Aldrich's skills and inventiveness.*

## I

I am about to lift the veil of mystery which, for nearly seven years, has shrouded the story of Mary Ware; and though I lay bare my own weakness, or folly, or what you will, I do not shrink from the unveiling.

No hand but mine can now perform the task. There was, indeed, a man who might have done this better than I. But he went his way in silence. I like a man who can hold his tongue.

On the corner of Clarke and Crandall Streets, in New York, stands a dingy brown frame-house. It is a very old house, as its obsolete style of structure would tell you. It has a morose, unhappy look, though once it must have been a blythe mansion. I think that houses, like human beings, ultimately become dejected or cheerful, according to their experience. The very air of some front-doors tells their history.

This house, I repeat, has a morose, unhappy look, at present, and is tenanted by an incalculable number of Irish families, while a picturesque junk-shop is in full blast in the basement; but at the time of which I write, it was a second-rate boarding-place, of the more respectable sort, and rather largely patronized by poor, but honest, literary men, tragic-actors, members of the chorus, and such like gilt people.

My apartments on Crandall Street were opposite this building, to which my attention was directed soon after taking possession of the rooms, by the discovery of the following facts:

First, that a charming lady lodged on the second-floor front, and sang like a canary every morning.

Second, that her name was Mary Ware

Third, that Mary Ware was a danseuse, and had two lovers – only two.

Mary Ware was the leading lady at The Olympic. Night after night found me in the parquette. I can think of nothing with which to compare the airiness and utter abandon of her dancing. She seemed a part of the music. She was one of beauty's best thoughts, then. Her glossy gold hair reached down to her waist, shading one of those mobile faces which remind you of Guido's picture of Beatrix Cenci – there was something so fresh and enchanting in the mouth. Her luminous, almond eyes, looking out winningly from under their drooping fringes, were at once the delight and misery of young men.

Ah! you were distracting in your nights of triumph, when the bouquets nestled about your elastic ankles, and the kissing of your castanets made the pulses leap; but I remember when you lay on your cheerless bed, in the blank day-light, with the glory faded from your brow, and "none so poor as to do you reverence."

Then I stooped down and kissed you – but not till then.

Mary Ware was to me a finer study than her lovers. She had two, as I have said. One of them was commonplace enough – well-made, well-dressed, shallow, flaccid. Nature, when she gets out of patience with her best works, throws off such things by the gross, instead of swearing. He was a lieutenant, in the Navy I think. The gilt button has charms to soothe the savage breast.

The other was a man of different mould, and interested me in a manner for which I could not then account. The first time I saw him did not seem like the first time. But this, perhaps, is an after-impression.

Every line of his countenance denoted character; a certain capability, I mean, but whether for good or evil was not so plain. I should have called him handsome, but for a noticeable scar which ran at right angles across his mouth, giving him a sardonic expression when he smiled.

His frame might have set an anatomist wild with delight – six feet two, deep-chested, knitted with tendons of steel. Not at all a fellow to amble on plush carpets.

"Some day," thought I, as I saw him stride by the house, "he will throw the little Lieutenant out of that second-story window."

I cannot tell, to this hour, which of those two men Mary Ware loved most – for I think she loved them both. A woman's heart was the insolvable charade with which the Sphinx nipt the Egyptians. I was never good at puzzles.

The flirtation, however, was food enough for the whole neighbourhood. But faintly did the gossips dream of the strange drama that was being shaped out, as compactly as a tragedy of Sophocles, under their noses.

They were very industrious in tearing Mary Ware's good name to pieces. Some laughed at the gay Lieutenant, and some at Julius Kenneth; but they all amiably united in condemning Mary Ware.

This state of affairs had continued for five or six months, when it was reported that Julius Kenneth and Mary Ware were affianced. The Lieutenant was less frequently seen in Crandall Street, and Julius waited upon Mary's footsteps with the fidelity of a shadow.

Yet – though Mary went to the Sunday concerts with Julius
Kenneth, she still wore the Lieutenant's roses in her bosom.


## II


One drizzly November morning – how well I remember it! – I
was awakened by a series of nervous raps on my bed-room door.
The noise startled me from an unpleasant dream.

"O, sir!" cried the chambermaid on the landing. "There's been
a dreadful time across the street. They've gone and killed Mary
Ware!"

"Ah!"

That was all I could say. Cold drops of perspiration stood on
my forehead.

I looked at my watch; it was eleven o'clock; I had over-slept
myself, having sat up late the previous night.

I dressed hastily, and, without waiting for breakfast, pushed
my way through the murky crowd that had collected in front of
the house opposite, and passed up stairs, unquestioned.

When I entered the room, there were six people present: a
thick-set gentleman, in black, with a bland professional air, a
physician; two policemen; Adelaide Woods, an actress; Mrs
Marston, the landlady; and Julius Kenneth.

In the centre of the chamber, on the bed, lay the body of Mary
Ware – as pale as Seneca's wife.

I shall never forget it. The corpse haunted me for years
afterwards, the dark streaks under the eyes, and the wavy hair
streaming over the pillow – the dead gold hair. I stood by her for a
moment, and turned down the counterpane, which was drawn up
closely to the chin.


"There was that across her throat
Which you had hardly cared to see."


At the head of the bed sat Julius Kenneth, bending over the icy
hand which he held in his own. He was kissing it.

The gentleman in black was conversing in undertones with

Mrs Marston, who every now and then glanced furtively toward Mary Ware.

The two policemen were examining the doors, closets and windows of the apartment with, obviously, little success.

There was no fire in the air-tight stove, but the place was suffocatingly close. I opened a window, and leaned against the casement to get a breath of fresh air.

The physician approached me. I muttered something to him indistinctly, for I was partly sick with the peculiar mouldy smell that pervaded the room.

"Yes," he began, scrutinizing me, "the affair looks very perplexing, as you remark. Professional man, sir? No? Bless me! – beg pardon. Never in my life saw anything that looked so exceedingly like nothing. Thought, at first, 'twas a clear case of suicide – door locked, key on the inside, place undisturbed; but then we find no instrument with which the subject could have inflicted that wound on the neck. Queer. Party must have escaped up chimney. But how? Don't know. The windows are at least thirty feet from the ground. It would be impossible for a person to jump that far, even if he could clear the iron railing below. Which he couldn't. Disagreeable things to jump on, those spikes, sir. Must have been done with a sharp knife. Queer, very. Party meant to make sure work of it. The carotid neatly severed, upon my word."

The medical gentleman went on in this monologuic style for fifteen minutes, during which time Kenneth did not raise his lips from Mary's fingers.

Approaching the bed, I spoke to him; but he only shook his head in reply.

I understood his grief.

After regaining my chamber, I sat listlessly for three or four hours, gazing into the grate. The twilight flitted in from the street; but I did not heed it. A face among the coals fascinated me. It came and went and came. Now I saw a cavern hung with lurid stalactites; now a small Vesuvius vomiting smoke and flame; now a bridge spanning some tartarean gulf; then these crumbled, each in its turn, and from out the heated fragments peered the one inevitable face.

★      ★      ★

The *Evening Mirror*, of that day, gave the following detailed report of the inquest:

"This morning, at eight o'clock, Mary Ware, the celebrated danseuse, was found dead in her chamber, at her late residence on the corner of Clarke and Crandall Streets. The perfect order of the room, and the fact that the door was locked on the inside, have induced many to believe that the poor girl was the victim of her own rashness. But we cannot think so. That the door was fastened on the inner side, proves nothing except, indeed, that the murderer was hidden in the apartment. That the room gave no evidence of a struggle having taken place, is also an insignificant point. Two men, or even one, grappling suddenly with the deceased, who was a slight woman, would have prevented any great resistance. The deceased was dressed in a ballet-costume, and was, as we conjecture, murdered directly after her return from the theatre. On a chair near the bed, lay several fresh bouquets, and a water-proof cloak which she was in the habit of wearing over her dancing-dress, on coming home from the theatre at night. No weapon whatever was found on the premises. We give below all the material testimony elicited by the coroner. It explains little.

"*Josephine Marston* deposes: I keep a boarding house at No. 131 Crandall Street. Miss Ware has boarded with me for the past two years. Has always borne a good character as far as I know. I do not think she had many visitors; certainly no male visitors, excepting a Lieutenant King, and Mr Kenneth to whom she was engaged. I do not know when King was last at the house; not within three days. I am confident. Deceased told me that he had gone away. I did not see her last night when she came home. The hall-door is never locked; each of the boarders has a latchkey. The last time I saw Miss Ware was just before she went to the theatre, when she asked me to call her at eight o'clock (this morning) as she had promised to walk with 'Jules,' meaning Mr Kenneth. I knocked at the door nine or ten times, but received no answer. Then I grew frightened and called one of the lady boarders, Miss Woods, who helped me to force the lock. The key fell on the floor inside as we pushed against the door. Mary Ware was lying on the bed, dressed. Some matches were scattered under the gas-burner by the bureau. The room presented the same appearance it does now.

"*Adelaide Woods* deposes: I am an actress by profession. I occupy the room next to that of the deceased. Have known her twelve months. It was half-past eleven when she came home; she stopped in my chamber for perhaps three-quarters of an hour. The call-boy of The Olympic usually accompanies her home from the theatre when she is alone. I let her in. Deceased had misplaced her night-key. The partition between our rooms is of brick; but I do not sleep soundly, and should have heard any unusual noise. Two weeks ago, Miss Ware told me she was to be married to Mr Kenneth in January next. The last time I saw them together was the day before yesterday. I assisted Mrs Marston in breaking open the door. (Describes the position of the body, etc., etc.)

"Here the call-boy was summoned, and testified to accompanying the deceased home the night before. He came as far as the steps with her. The door was opened by a woman; could not swear it was Miss Woods, though he knows her by sight. The night was dark, and there was no lamp burning in the entry.

"*Julius Kenneth* deposes: I am a master-machinist. Reside at No.—Forsythe street. Miss Ware was my cousin. We were engaged to be married next—(Here the witness' voice failed him.) The last time I saw her was on Wednesday morning, on which occasion we walked out together. I did not leave my room last evening: was confined by a severe cold. A Lieutenant King used to visit my cousin frequently: it created considerable talk in the neighbourhood: I did not like it, and requested her to break the acquaintance. She informed me, Wednesday, that King had been ordered to some foreign station, and would trouble me no more. Was excited at the time, hinted at being tired of living; then laughed, and was gayer than she had been for weeks. Deceased was subject to fits of depression. She had engaged to walk with me this morning at eight. When I reached Clark Street I learned that she—(Here the witness, overcome by emotion, was allowed to retire.)

"*Dr Wren* deposes: (This gentleman was very learned and voluble, and had to be suppressed several times by the coroner. We furnish a brief synopsis of his testimony.) I was called in to view the body of the deceased. A deep incision on the throat, two inches below the left ear, severing the left common carotid and the internal jugular vein, had been inflicted with some sharp instrument. Such a wound would, in my opinion, produce death almost instantaneously. The body bore no other signs of violence. A slight mark, almost indistinguishable, in fact, extended from the upper lip toward the right nostril – some hurt, I suppose, received in infancy. Deceased must have been dead a number of hours, the rigor mortis having already supervened, etc., etc.

"*Dr Ceccarini* corroborated the above testimony.

"The night-watchman and seven other persons were then placed on the stand; but their statements threw no fresh light on the case.

"The situation of Julius Kenneth, the lover of the ill-fated girl, draws forth the deepest commiseration. Miss Ware was twenty-four years of age.

"Who the criminal is, and what could have led to the perpetration of the cruel act, are questions which, at present, threaten to baffle the sagacity of the police. If such deeds can be committed with impunity in a crowded city, like this, who is safe from the assassin's steel?"

### III

I could but smile on reading all this serious nonsense.

After breakfast, the next morning, I made my toilet with extreme care, and presented myself at the sheriff's office.

Two gentlemen who were sitting at a table, busy with papers, started nervously to their feet, as I announced myself. I bowed very calmly to the sheriff, and said, "*I am the person who murdered Mary Ware!*"

Of course I was instantly arrested; and that evening, in jail, I had the equivocal pleasure of reading these paragraphs among the police items of the *Mirror*:

"The individual who murdered the ballet-girl, in the night of the third inst., in a house on Crandall Street, surrendered himself to the sheriff this forenoon.

"He gave his name as Paul Lynde, and resides opposite the place where the tragedy was enacted. He is a man of medium stature, has restless grey eyes, chestnut hair, and a supernaturally pale countenance. He seems a person of excellent address, is said to be wealthy, and nearly connected with an influential New England family. Notwithstanding his gentlemanly manner, there is that about him which would lead one to select him from out a thousand, as a man of cool and desperate character.

"My Lynde's voluntary surrender is not the least astonishing feature of this affair; for, had he preserved silence he would, beyond a doubt, have escaped even suspicion. The murder was planned and executed with such deliberate skill, that there is little or no evidence to complicate him. In truth, there is *no* evidence against him, excepting his own confession, which is meagre and confusing enough. He freely acknowledges the crime, but stubbornly refuses to enter into any details. He expresses a desire to be hanged immediately!

"How Mr Lynde entered the chamber, and by what means he left it, after committing the deed, and why he cruelly killed a lady with whom he had had (as we gather from the testimony) no previous acquaintance – are enigmas which still perplex the public mind, and will not let curiosity sleep. These facts, however, will probably be brought to light during the impending trial. In the meantime, we await the dénouement with interest."

## IV

On the afternoon following this disclosure, the door of my cell turned on its hinges, and Julius Kenneth entered.

In *his* presence I ought to have trembled; but I was calm and collected. He, feverish and dangerous.

"You received my note?"

"Yes; and have come here, as you requested." I waved him to a chair, which he refused to take. Stood leaning on the back of it.

"You of course know, Mr Kenneth, that I have refused to reveal the circumstances connected with the death of Mary Ware? I wished to make the confession to you alone."

He regarded me for a moment from beneath his shaggy eyebrows.

"Well?"

"But even to you I will assign no reason for the course I pursued. It was necessary that Mary Ware should die."

"Well?"

"I decided that she should die in her chamber, and to that end I purloined her night-key."

Julius Kenneth looked through and through me, as I spoke.

"On Friday night after she had gone to the theatre, I entered the hall-door by means of the key, and stole unobserved to her room, where I secreted myself under the bed, or in that small clothes-press near the stove – I forget which. Sometime between eleven and twelve o'clock, Mary Ware returned. While she was in the act of lighting the gas, I pressed a handkerchief, saturated with chloroform, over her mouth. You know the effect of chloroform? I will, at this point spare you further detail, merely remarking that I threw my gloves and the handkerchief in the stove; but I'm afraid there was not fire enough to consume them."

Kenneth walked up and down the cell greatly agitated; then seated himself on the foot of the bed.

"Curse you!"

"Are you listening to me, Mr Kenneth?"

"Yes!"

"I extinguished the light, and proceeded to make my escape from the room, which I did in a manner so simple that the detectives, through their desire to ferret out wonderful things, will never discover it, unless, indeed, *you* betray me. The night, you will recollect, was foggy; it was impossible to discern an object at four yards distance – this was fortunate for me. I raised the window-sash and let myself out cautiously, holding on by the sill, until my feet touched on the moulding which caps the window below. I then drew down the sash. By standing on the extreme left of the cornice, I was able to reach the tin water-spout of the adjacent building, and by that I descended to the sidewalk."

The man glowered at me like a tiger, his eyes green and golden with excitement: I have since wondered that he did not tear me to pieces.

"On gaining the street," I continued coolly, "I found that I had brought the knife with me. It should have been left in the chamber – it would have given the whole thing the aspect of suicide. It was too late to repair the blunder, so I threw the knife—"

"Into the river!" exclaimed Kenneth, involuntarily.

And then I smiled.

"How did you know it was I!" he shrieked.

"Hush! they will overhear you in the corridor. It was as plain as day. I knew it before I had been five minutes in the room. First, because you shrank instinctively from the corpse, though you seemed to be caressing it. Secondly, when I looked into the stove, I saw a glove and handkerchief, partly consumed; and then I instantly accounted for the faint close smell which had affected me before the room was ventilated. It was chloroform. Thirdly, when I went to open the window. I noticed that the paint was scraped off the brackets which held the spout to the next house. This conduit had been newly painted two days previously – I watched the man at work; the paint on the brackets was thicker than anywhere else, and had not dried. On looking at your feet, which I did critically, while speaking to you, I saw that the leather on the inner side of each boot was slightly chafed, paint-marked. It is a way of mine to put this and that together!"

"If you intend to betray me—"

"O, no, but I don't or I should not be here – alone with you. I am, as you may allow, not quite a fool."

"Indeed, sir, you are as subtle as—"

"Yes, I wouldn't mention him."

"Who?"

"The devil."

Kenneth mused.

"May I ask, Mr Lynde, what you intend to do?"

"Certainly – remain here."

"I don't understand you," said Kenneth with an air of perplexity.

"If you will listen patiently, you shall learn why *I* have acknowledged this deed, why *I* would bear the penalty. I believe there are vast, intense sensations from which we are excluded, by the conventional fear of a certain kind of death. Now, this pleasure, this ecstasy, this something, I don't know what, which I have striven for all my days, is known only to a privileged few – innocent men, who, through some oversight of the law, are *hanged by the neck!* How rich is Nature in compensations! Some men are born to be hung, some have hanging thrust upon them, and some (as I hope to do) achieve hanging. It appears ages since I commenced watching for an opportunity like this. Worlds could not tempt me to divulge your guilt, nor could worlds have tempted me to commit your crime, for a man's conscience should be at ease to enjoy, to the utmost, this delicious death! Our interview is at an end, Mr Kenneth. I held it my duty to say this much to you."

And I turned my back on him.

"One word, Mr Lynde."

Kenneth came to my side, and laid a heavy hand on my shoulder, that red right hand, which all the tears of the angels cannot make white again.

"Did you send this to me last month?" asked Kenneth, holding up a slip of paper on which was scrawled, *Watch them* – in my handwriting.

"Yes," I answered.

Then it struck me that these few thoughtless words, which some sinister spirit had impelled me to write, were the indirect cause of the whole catastrophe.

"Thank you," he said hurriedly. "I watched them!" Then, after a pause, "I shall go far from here. I can not, I *will* not die yet. Mary was to have been my wife, so she would have hidden her shame – O cruel! she, my own cousin, and we the last two of our race! Life is not sweet to me, it is bitter, bitter; but I shall live until I stand front to front with *him*. And you? They will not harm you – *you* are a madman?"

Julius Kenneth was gone before I could reply.

The cell door shut him out forever – shut him out in the flesh. His spirit was not so easily exorcised.

After all, it was a wretched fiasco. Two officious friends of mine, who had played chess with me, at my lodgings, on the night of the 3rd, proved an alibi; and I was literally turned out of the Tombs; for I insisted on being executed.

Then it was maddening to have the newspapers call me a monomaniac.

*I* a monomaniac?

What was Pythagoras, Newton, Fulton? Have not the great original lights of every age, been regarded as madmen? Science, like religion, has its martyrs.

# THE DOOMDORF MYSTERY

*Melville Davisson Post*

*In Uncle Abner, Melville Davisson Post (1871–1930) created one of the great unforgettable early American detectives. The stories are set in Virginia in the early days of the nineteenth century where Abner is a severe but just upholder of the law. Post was by profession a lawyer, out of which came the idea for his stories about the unscrupulous legal genius Randolph Mason, in* The Strange Cases of Randolph Mason *(1896). Uncle Abner did not appear until 1911 with the stories collected as* Uncle Abner, Master of Mysteries *(1918). Abner had a near puritanical belief in divine justice, which is only too apparent in the following story, perhaps the most inventive of the whole series.*

The pioneer was not the only man in the great mountains behind Virginia. Strange aliens drifted in after the Colonial wars. All foreign armies are sprinkled with a cockle of adventurers that take root and remain. They were with Braddock and La Salle, and they rode north out of Mexico after her many empires went to pieces.

I think Doomdorf crossed the seas with Iturbide when that ill-starred adventurer returned to be shot against a wall; but there was no Southern blood in him. He came from some European race remote and barbaric. The evidences were all about him. He was a huge figure of a man, with a black spade beard, broad, thick hands, and square, flat fingers.

He had found a wedge of land between the Crown's grant to Daniel Davisson and a Washington survey. It was an uncovered triangle not worth the running of the lines; and so, no doubt, was left out, a sheer rock standing up out of the river for a base, and a peak of the mountain rising northward behind it for an apex.

Doomdorf squatted on the rock. He must have brought a belt of gold pieces when he took to his horse, for he hired old Robert Steuart's slaves and built a stone house on the rock, and he brought the furnishings overland from a frigate in the Chesapeake; and then in the handfuls of earth, wherever a root would hold, he planted the mountain behind his house with peach trees. The gold gave out; but the devil is fertile in resources. Doomdorf built a log still and turned the first fruits of the garden into a hell-brew. The idle and the vicious came with their stone jugs, and violence and riot flowed out.

The government of Virginia was remote and its arm short and feeble; but the men who held the lands west of the mountains against the savages under grants from George, and after that held them against George himself, were efficient and expeditious. They had long patience, but when that failed they went up from their fields and drove the thing before them out of the land, like a scourge of God.

There came a day, then, when my Uncle Abner and Squire Randolph rode through the gap of the mountains to have the thing out with Doomdorf. The work of this brew, which had the odours of Eden and the impulses of the devil in it, could be borne no longer. The drunken Negroes had shot old Duncan's cattle and burned his haystacks, and the land was on its feet.

They rode alone, but they were worth an army of little men. Randolph was vain and pompous and given over to extravagance of words, but he was a gentleman beneath it, and fear was an alien and a stranger to him. And Abner was the right hand of the land.

It was a day in early summer and the sun lay hot. They crossed through the broken spine of the mountains and trailed along the river in the shade of the great chestnut trees. The road was only a path and the horses went one before the other. It left the river when the rock began to rise and, making a detour through the grove of peach trees, reached the house on the mountain side. Randolph and Abner got down, unsaddled their horses and turned them out to graze, for their business with Doomdorf would not be over in an hour. Then they took a steep path that brought them out on the mountain side of the house.

A man sat on a big red-roan horse in the paved court before the door. He was a gaunt old man. He sat bare-headed, the palms of his hands resting on the pommel of his saddle, his chin sunk in his black stock, his face in retrospection, the wind moving gently his great shock of voluminous white hair. Under him the huge red horse stood with his legs spread out like a horse of stone.

There was no sound. The door to the house was closed; insects moved in the sun; a shadow crept out from the motionless figure, and swarms of yellow butterflies maneuvered like an army.

Abner and Randolph stopped. They knew the tragic figure – a circuit rider of the hills who preached the invective of Isaiah as though he were the mouthpiece of a militant and avenging overlord; as though the government of Virginia were the awful theocracy of the Book of Kings. The horse was dripping with sweat and the man bore the dust and the evidences of a journey on him.

"Bronson," said Abner, "where is Doomdorf?"

The old man lifted his head and looked down at Abner over the pommel of the saddle.

" 'Surely,' " he said, " 'he covereth his feet in his summer chamber.' "

Abner went over and knocked on the closed door, and presently the white, frightened face of a woman looked out at him. She was a little, faded woman, with fair hair, a broad foreign face, but with the delicate evidences of gentle blood.

Abner repeated his question.

"Where is Doomdorf?"

"Oh, sir," she answered with a queer lisping accent, "he went to lie down in his south room after his midday meal, as his custom is; and I went to the orchard to gather any fruit that might be ripened." She hesitated and her voice lisped into a whisper: "He is not come out and I cannot wake him."

The two men followed her through the hall and up the stairway to the door.

"It is always bolted," she said, "when he goes to lie down."
And she knocked feebly with the tips of her fingers.

There was no answer and Randolph rattled the doorknob.

"Come out, Doomdorf!" he called in his big, bellowing voice.

There was only silence and the echoes of the words among the
rafters. Then Randolph set his shoulder to the door and burst it
open.

They went in. The room was flooded with sun from the tall
south windows. Doomdorf lay on a couch in a little offset of the
room, a great scarlet patch on his bosom and a pool of scarlet on
the floor.

The woman stood for a moment staring; then she cried out:

"At last I have killed him!" And she ran like a frightened hare.

The two men closed the door and went over to the couch.
Doomdorf had been shot to death. There was a great ragged hole
in his waistcoat. They began to look about for the weapon with
which the deed had been accomplished, and in a moment found it
– a fowling piece lying in two dogwood forks against the wall. The
gun had just been fired; there was a freshly exploded paper cap
under the hammer.

There was little else in the room – a loom-woven rag carpet on
the floor; wooden shutters flung back from the windows; a great
oak table, and on it a big, round, glass water bottle, filled to its
glass stopper with raw liquor from the still. The stuff was limpid
and clear as spring water; and, but for its pungent odor, one
would have taken it for God's brew instead of Doomdorf's. The
sun lay on it and against the wall where hung the weapon that had
ejected the dead man out of life.

"Abner," said Randolf, "this is murder! The woman took that
gun down from the wall and shot Doomdorf while he slept."

Abner was standing by the table, his fingers round his chin.

"Randolph," he replied, "what brought Bronson here?"

"The same outrages that brought us," said Randolph. "The
mad old circuit rider has been preaching a crusade against
Doomdorf far and wide in the hills."

Abner answered, without taking his fingers from about his
chin:

"You think this woman killed Doomdorf? Well, let us go and ask Bronson who killed him."

They closed the door, leaving the dead man on his couch, and went down into the court.

The old circuit rider had put away his horse and got an ax. He had taken off his coat and pushed his shirtsleeves up over his long elbows. He was on his way to the still to destroy the barrels of liquor. He stopped when the two men came out, and Abner called to him.

"Bronson," he said, "who killed Doomdorf?"

"I killed him," replied the old man, and went on toward the still.

Randolph swore under his breath. "By the Almighty," he said, "everybody couldn't kill him!"

"Who can tell how many had a hand in it?" replied Abner.

"Two have confessed!" cried Randolph. "Was there perhaps a third? Did you kill him, Abner? And I too? Man, the thing is impossible!"

"The impossible," replied Abner, "looks here like the truth. Come with me, Randolph, and I will show you a thing more impossible than this."

They returned through the house and up the stairs to the room. Abner closed the door behind them.

"Look at this bolt," he said; "it is on the inside and not connected with the lock. How did the one who killed Doomdorf get into this room, since the door was bolted?"

"Through the windows," replied Randolph.

There were but two windows, facing the south, through which the sun entered. Abner led Randolph to them.

"Look!" he said. "The wall of the house is plumb with the sheer face of the rock. It is a hundred feet to the river and the rock is as smooth as a sheet of glass. But that is not all. Look at these window frames; they are cemented into their casement with dust and they are bound along their edges with cobwebs. These windows have not been opened. How did the assassin enter?"

"The answer is evident," said Randolph: "The one who killed Doomdorf hid in the room until he was asleep; then he shot him and went out."

"The explanation is excellent but for one thing," replied Abner: "How did the assassin bolt the door behind him on the inside of this room after he had gone out?"

Randolph flung out his arms with a hopeless gesture.

"Who knows?" he cried. "Maybe Doomdorf killed himself."

Abner laughed.

"And after firing a handful of shot into his heart he got up and put the gun back carefully into the forks against the wall!"

"Well," cried Randolph, "there is one open road out of this mystery. Bronson and this woman say they killed Doomdorf, and if they killed him they surely know how they did it. Let us go down and ask them."

"In the law court," replied Abner, "that procedure would be considered sound sense; but we are in God's court and things are managed there in a somewhat stranger way. Before we go let us find out, if we can, at what hour it was that Doomdorf died."

He went over and took a big silver watch out of the dead man's pocket. It was broken by a shot and the hands lay at one hour after noon. He stood for a moment fingering his chin.

"At one o'clock," he said. "Bronson, I think, was on the road to this place, and the woman was on the mountain among the peach trees."

Randolph threw back his shoulders.

"Why waste time in a speculation about it, Abner?" he said. "We know who did this thing. Let us go and get the story of it out of their own mouths. Doomdorf died by the hands of either Bronson or this woman."

"I could better believe it," replied Abner, "but for the running of a certain awful law."

"What law?" said Randolph. "Is it a statute of Virginia?"

"It is a statute," replied Abner, "of an authority somewhat higher. Mark the language of it: 'He that killeth with the sword must be killed with the sword.'"

He came over and took Randolph by the arm.

"Must! Randolph, did you mark particularly the word 'must'? It is a mandatory law. There is no room in it for the vicissitudes of chance or fortune. There is no way round that word. Thus, we reap what we sow and nothing else; thus, we receive what we give and nothing else. It is the weapon in our own hands that finally destroys us. You are looking at it now." And he turned him about so that the table and the weapon and the dead man were before him. " 'He that killeth with the sword must be killed with the sword.' And now," he said, "let us go and try the method of the law courts. Your faith is in the wisdom of their ways."

They found the old circuit rider at work in the still, staving in Doomdorf's liquor casks, splitting the oak heads with his ax.

"Bronson," said Randolph, "how did you kill Doomdorf?"

The old man stopped and stood leaning on his ax.

"I killed him," replied the old man, "as Elijah killed the captains of Ahaziah and their fifties. But not by the hand of any man did I pray the Lord God to destroy Doomdorf, but with fire from heaven to destroy him."

He stood up and extended his arms.

"His hands were full of blood," he said. "With his abomination from these groves of Baal he stirred up the people to contention, to strife and murder. The widow and the orphan cried to heaven against him. 'I will surely hear their cry,' is the promise written in the Book. The land was weary of him; and I prayed the Lord God to destroy him with fire from heaven, as he destroyed the Princes of Gomorrah in their palaces!"

Randolph made a gesture as of one who dismisses the impossible, but Abner's face took on a deep, strange look.

"With fire from heaven!" he repeated slowly to himself. Then he asked a question. "A little while ago," he said, "when we came, I asked you where Doomdorf was, and you answered me in the language of the third chapter of the Book of Judges. Why did you answer me like that, Bronson? – 'Surely he covereth his feet in his summer chamber.' "

"The woman told me that he had not come down from the room where he had gone up to sleep," replied the old man, "and that the door was locked. And then I knew that he was dead in his summer chamber like Eglon, King of Moab."

He extended his arm toward the south.

"I came here from the Great Valley," he said, "to cut down

these groves of Baal and to empty out this abomination; but I did not know that the Lord had heard my prayer and visited His wrath on Doomdorf until I was come up into these mountains to his door. When the woman spoke I knew it." And he went away to his horse, leaving the ax among the ruined barrels.

Randolph interrupted.

"Come, Abner," he said; "this is wasted time. Bronson did not kill Doomdorf."

Abner answered slowly in his deep, level voice:

"Do you realize, Randolph, how Doomdorf died?"

"Not by fire from heaven, at any rate," said Randolph.

"Randolph," replied Abner, "are you sure?"

"Abner," cried Randolph, "you are pleased to jest, but I am in deadly earnest. A crime has been done here against the state. I am an officer of justice and I propose to discover the assassin if I can."

He walked away toward the house and Abner followed, his hands behind him and his great shoulders thrown loosely forward, with a grim smile about his mouth.

"It is no use to talk with the mad old preacher," Randolph went on. "Let him empty out the liquor and ride away. I won't issue a warrant against him. Prayer may be a handy implement to do a murder with, Abner, but it is not a deadly weapon under the statutes of Virginia. Doomdorf was dead when old Bronson got here with his Scriptural jargon. This woman killed Doomdorf. I shall put her to an inquisition."

"As you like," replied Abner. "Your faith remains in the methods of the law courts."

"Do you know of any better methods?" said Randolph.

"Perhaps," replied Abner, "when you have finished."

Night had entered the valley. The two men went into the house and set about preparing the corpse for burial. They got candles, and made a coffin, and put Doomdorf in it, and straightened out his limbs, and folded his arms across his shot-out heart. Then they set the coffin on benches in the hall.

They kindled a fire in the dining room and sat down before it, with the door open and the red firelight shining through on the dead man's narrow, everlasting house. The woman had put some cold meat, a golden cheese and a loaf on the table. They did not see her, but they heard her moving about the house; and finally, on the gravel court outside, her step and the whinny of a horse. Then she came in, dressed as for a journey. Randolph sprang up.

"Where are you going?" he said.

"To the sea and a ship," replied the woman. Then she indicated the hall with a gesture. "He is dead and I am free."

There was a sudden illumination in her face. Randolph took a step toward her. His voice was big and harsh.

"Who killed Doomdorf?" he cried.

"I killed him," replied the woman. "It was fair!"

"Fair!" echoed the justice. "What do you mean by that?"

The woman shrugged her shoulders and put out her hands with a foreign gesture.

"I remember an old, old man sitting against a sunny wall, and a little girl, and one who came and talked a long time with the old man, while the little girl plucked yellow flowers out of the grass and put them into her hair. Then finally the stranger gave the old man a gold chain and took the little girl away." She flung out her hands. "Oh, it was fair to kill him!" She looked up with a queer, pathetic smile.

"The old man will be gone by now," she said; "but I shall perhaps find the wall there, with the sun on it, and the yellow flowers in the grass. And now, may I go?"

It is a law of the story-teller's art that he does not tell a story. It is the listener who tells it. The story-teller does but provide him with the stimuli.

Randolph got up and walked about the floor. He was a justice of the peace in a day when that office was filled only by the landed gentry, after the English fashion; and the obligations of the law were strong on him. If he should take liberties with the letter of it, how could the weak and the evil be made to hold it in respect? Here was this woman before him a confessed assassin. Could he let her go?

Abner sat unmoving by the hearth, his elbow on the arm of his chair, his palm propping up his jaw, his face clouded in deep lines. Randolph was consumed with vanity and the weakness of ostentation, but he shouldered his duties for himself. Presently he stopped and looked at the woman, wan, faded like some prisoner of legend escaped out of fabled dungeons into the sun.

The firelight flickered past her to the box on the benches in the hall, and the vast, inscrutable justice of heaven entered and overcame him.

"Yes," he said. "Go! There is no jury in Virginia that would hold a woman for shooting a beast like that." And he thrust out his arm, with the fingers extended toward the dead man.

The woman made a little awkward curtsy.

"I thank you, sir." Then she hesitated and lisped, "But I have not shoot him."

"Not shoot him!" cried Randolph. "Why, the man's heart is riddled!"

"Yes, sir," she said simply, like a child. "I kill him, but have not shoot him."

Randolph took two long strides toward the woman.

"Not shoot him!" he repeated. "How then, in the name of heaven, did you kill Doomdorf?" And his big voice filled the empty places of the room.

"I will show you, sir," she said.

She turned and went away into the house. Presently she returned with something folded up in a linen towel. She put it on the table between the loaf of bread and the yellow cheese.

Randolph stood over the table, and the woman's deft fingers undid the towel from round its deadly contents; and presently the thing lay there uncovered.

It was a little crude model of a human figure done in wax with a needle thrust through the bosom.

Randolph stood up with a great intake of the breath.

"Magic! By the eternal!"

"Yes, sir," the woman explained, in her voice and manner of a child. "I have try to kill him many times – oh, very many times! – with witch words which I have remember; but always they fail. Then, at last, I make him in wax, and I put a needle through his heart; and I kill him very quickly."

It was as clear as daylight, even to Randolph, that the woman was innocent. Her little harmless magic was the pathetic effort of a child to kill a dragon. He hesitated a moment before he spoke, and then he decided like the gentleman he was. If it helped the child to believe that her enchanted straw had slain the monster – well, he would let her believe it.

"And now, sir, may I go?"

Randolph looked at the woman in a sort of wonder.

"Are you not afraid," he said, "of the night and the mountains, and the long road?"

"Oh no, sir," she replied simply. "The good God will be everywhere now."

It was an awful commentary on the dead man – that this strange half-child believed that all the evil in the world had gone out with him; that now that he was dead, the sunlight of heaven would fill every nook and corner.

It was not a faith that either of the two men wished to shatter, and they let her go. It would be daylight presently and the road through the mountains to the Chesapeake was open.

Randolph came back to the fireside after he had helped her into the saddle, and sat down. He tapped on the hearth for some time idly with the iron poker; and then finally he spoke.

"This is the strangest thing that ever happened," he said. "Here's a mad old preacher who thinks that he killed Doomdorf with fire from Heaven, like Elijah the Tishbite; and here is a simple child of a woman who thinks she killed him with a piece of magic of the Middle Ages – each as innocent of his death as I am. And, yet, by the eternal, the beast is dead!"

He drummed on the hearth with the poker, lifting it up and letting it drop through the hollow of his fingers.

"Somebody shot Doomdorf. But who? And how did he get into and out of that shut-up room? The assassin that killed Doomdorf must have gotten into the room to kill him. Now, how did he get in?" He spoke as to himself; but my uncle sitting across the hearth replied:

"Through the window."

"Through the window!" echoed Randolph. "Why, man, you

yourself showed me that the window had not been opened, and
the precipice below it a fly could hardly climb. Do you tell me
now that the window was opened?"

"No," said Abner, "it was never opened."

Randolph got on his feet.

"Abner," he cried, "are you saying that the one who killed
Doomdorf climbed the sheer wall and got in through a closed
window, without disturbing the dust or the cobwebs on the
window frame?"

My uncle looked Randolph in the face.

"The murderer of Doomdorf did even more," he said. "That
assassin not only climbed the face of that precipice and got in
through the closed window, but he shot Doomdorf to death and
got out again through the closed window without leaving a single
track or trace behind, and without disturbing a grain of dust or a
thread of a cobweb."

Randolph swore a great oath.

"The thing is impossible!" he cried. "Men are not killed today
in Virginia by black art or a curse of God."

"By black art, no," replied Abner; "but by the curse of God,
yes. I think they are."

Randolph drove his clenched right hand into the palm of his
left.

"By the eternal!" he cried. "I would like to see the assassin who
could do a murder like this, whether he be an imp from the pit or
an angel out of Heaven."

"Very well," replied Abner, undisturbed. "When he comes
back tomorrow I will show you the assassin who killed Doomdorf."

When day broke they dug a grave and buried the dead man
against the mountain among his peach trees. It was noon when
that work was ended. Abner threw down his spade and looked up
at the sun.

"Randolph," he said, "let us go and lay an ambush for this
assassin. He is on the way here."

And it was a strange ambush that he laid. When they were
come again into the chamber where Doomdorf died he bolted the

door; then he loaded the fowling piece and put it carefully back on its rack against the wall. After that he did another curious thing: He took the blood-stained coat, which they had stripped off the dead man when they had prepared his body for the earth, put a pillow in it and laid it on the couch precisely where Doomdorf had slept. And while he did these things Randolph stood in wonder and Abner talked:

"Look you, Randolph . . . We will trick the murderer . . . We will catch him in the act."

Then he went over and took the puzzled justice by the arm.

"Watch!" he said. "The assassin is coming along the wall!"

But Randolph heard nothing, saw nothing. Only the sun entered. Abner's hand tightened on his arm.

"It is here! Look!" And he pointed to the wall.

Randolph, following the extended finger, saw a tiny brilliant disk of light moving slowly up the wall toward the lock of the fowling piece. Abner's hand became a vice and his voice rang as over metal.

"'He that killeth with the sword must be killed with the sword.' It is the water bottle, full of Doomdorf's liquid, focusing the sun . . . And look, Randolph, how Bronson's prayer was answered!"

The tiny disk of light travelled on the plate of the lock.

"It is fire from heaven!"

The words rang above the roar of the fowling piece, and Randolph saw the dead man's coat leap up on the couch, riddled by the shot. The gun, in its natural position on the rack, pointed to the couch standing at the end of the chamber, beyond the offset of the wall, and the focused sun had exploded the percussion cap.

Randolph made a great gesture, with his arm extended.

"It is a world," he said, "filled with the mysterious joinder of accident!"

"It is a world," replied Abner, "filled with the mysterious justice of God!"

# THE ADVENTURE OF THE JACOBEAN HOUSE

*C.N. & A.M. Williamson*

*Early "impossible crime" stories sometimes used gimmicks that were later outlawed as unfair by aficionados of the miracle mystery. The obvious one was the secret panel, which was popular in Victorian mystery novels. Although the following story does include a secret panel, it is not directly related to the solution of the mystery, and although the device used is another one of those later abandoned by authors, its use here is both ingenious and fascinating. Charles Williamson (1859–1920) was an English journalist who married American writer Alice Livingston (1869–1933) in 1895. They began collaborating in 1902, when they hit on the idea of a novel based on a series of accounts of a man who is acting as a chauffeur, driving an American heiress around Europe. The book, The Lightning Conductor (1902), was so popular that they produced a whole series of books based on car journeys. The title of The Scarlet Runner (1908) refers to the car by which detective Christopher Race travels to solve his next mystery. It shows just how romantic the car was perceived in its early days. The book enjoyed some success and was even adapted into a silent film in 1916. The following is one of the more baffling episodes.*

The day after Christopher Race came back to London from his tour with the man of the "Missing Chapter" he found on his table a queer telegram. It said: "Please come at once with your car and try solve mystery at old house now used as hotel patronized by motorists. Same rate paid per day for necessary time as for automobile tour.—SIDNEY CHESTER, Wood House, New Forest. References, London and Scottish Bank." And the message was dated two days back.

Christopher did not see why he should be applied to as a solver of mysteries. However, the telegram sounded interesting. He liked old houses, and his desire to accept the offer was whetted by the fact that it had been made several days ago, and might have been passed on to someone else by this time.

At all events, he thought he would answer the wire, and he did so before washing away the dust of travel which he had accumulated at the rate of thirty miles an hour.

"Just back from journey. Found telegram," he wired. "Am I still wanted? If so, can come."

When an answer arrived he had Scarlet Runner ready for another start.

"Yes, urgently wanted," ran the reply. "Hope you can start this afternoon. But don't come to Wood House. Will meet you at the Sandboy and Owl, within mile of Ringhurst as you come from London. Please let me know probable hour of arrival. – CHESTER."

Christopher wired again, "Hope to reach you about seven." And his hope was justified, as it usually was when he had to depend upon Scarlet Runner. He had often passed the Sandboy and Owl, and remembered the roadside inn for its picturesqueness, so that he lost no time in finding the way.

"I have come to see a Mr Chester, who will be here in ten or fifteen minutes," Race said to the landlord, who looked as if he might have had a meritorious past as a coachman in some aristocratic household.

The sporting eye of the old man suddenly twinkled. "I think, sir," he answered, "that the person you expect has arrived, and is waiting in my private parlour, which I have given up for the – for the purpose."

The landlord's manner and slight hesitation, as if in search of the right word, struck Christopher as odd; but it was too late to catechize the old man in regard to Mr Chester, no matter how diplomatically.

The dusk of autumn draped the oak-beamed hall with shadow, and one lamp only made darkness seem more visible. The landlord opened a door at the end of a dim corridor, and said respectfully to someone out of sight, "The gentleman with the motor has arrived." Then he backed out of the way, and Christopher stepped over the threshold. He saw a girl rise up from a chair, crumpling a telegram which she had been reading by the light of a shaded lamp.

She wore a riding habit, and a neat hat on sleek hair the colour of ripening wheat. She was charmingly pretty, in a flowerlike way. Her great eyes, which now appeared black, would be blue by daylight, and her figure was perfect in the well-cut habit; but she was either pale and anxious-looking, or else the lamplight gave that effect.

"I beg your pardon," exclaimed Christopher. "I've come from London to see a Mr Sidney Chester, and was told I should find him here, but—"

"I'm Sidney Chester," said the girl. "It was I who telegraphed for you to come and help us."

Christopher was surprised, but he kept his countenance, and pretended to take this revelation as a matter of course.

"Sidney is a woman's name as well as a man's," she went on, "and there was no use explaining in a telegram. Please sit down, and I'll – no, I can't promise to make you understand, for the thing's beyond understanding; but I'll tell you about it. First, though, I'd better explain why I sent for you. I don't mean to flatter you, but if there's any chance of the mystery being solved, it can only be done by a man of your sort – clever and quick of resource, as well as an accomplished motorist. That's my reason; now for my story. But perhaps you've heard of Wood House and the strange happenings there? We've tried to keep the talk out of the papers, but it was impossible; and there've been paragraphs in most of them for the last fortnight."

"I've been touring for a fortnight," replied Christopher, "and hav'n't paid much attention to the papers."

"I'm glad," answered the girl, "because you'll listen to what I have to tell you with an unbiased mind. You don't even know about Wood House itself?"

Christopher had to admit ignorance, though he guessed from the girl's tone that the place must be famous, apart from its mysterious reputation.

"It's a beautiful old house," she went on, the harassed expression of her face softening into tenderness. "There are pictures and accounts of it in books about the county. We've got the loveliest oak panelling in nearly all the rooms, and wonderful furniture. Of course, we love it dearly – my mother and I, the only ones of the family who are left – but we're disgustingly poor; our branch of the Chesters have been growing poorer for generations. We had to see everything going to pieces, and there was no money for repairs. There were other troubles, too – oh, I may as well tell you, since you ought to know everything concerning us if you're to do any good. I was silly enough to fall in love with a man who ought to marry an heiress, for he's poor, too, and has a title, which makes poverty harder and more grinding. He's let his house – a show place – and because he won't give me up and look for a rich girl (he wouldn't have to look far or long), he's trying to get a fortune out of a ranch in Colorado. That made me feel as if I *must* do something, and we couldn't let Wood House, because there's a clause in father's will against our doing so. We're obliged to live there, or forfeit it to the person who would have inherited it if the place had been entailed and had had to go to a male heir.

"But no such thought came to poor father as that mother and I would dream of making the house into an hotel, so it didn't occur to him to provide against such a contingency. It was I who had the idea – because I was desperate for money; and I heard how people like old houses in these days – Americans and others who aren't used to things that are antique. At last I summoned up courage to propose to mother that we should advertise to entertain motorists and other travellers.

"Every penny we could spare, and a lot we couldn't, we spent on advertising, when she'd consented, and two months ago we opened the house as an hotel. Our old servants were good about helping, and we got in several new ones. We began to make the most astonishing success, and I was delighted. I thought if all went on well I need have nothing to do with managing the place after this year. I might marry if I liked, and there would be the income rolling in; so you see, after these dreams, what it is to find ruin staring us in the face. That sounds melodramatic, but it's the truth."

"The truth often is melodramatic," said Christopher. "I've discovered that lately. Things happen in real life that would be sneered at by the critics as preposterous."

"This thing that is happening to us is preposterous," said Miss Chester. "People come to our house, perhaps for dinner or lunch, or perhaps for several days. But which ever it may be, during one of the meals – always the last if they're having more than one – every piece of jewellery they may be wearing, and all the money in their pockets and purses – except small silver and copper – disappear mysteriously."

"Perhaps not mysteriously," suggested Christopher. "You mentioned having engaged new servants. One of them may be an expert thief."

"Of course, that was our first idea," said the girl. "But it would be impossible for the most expert thief, even a conjurer, to pull ladies' rings from their fingers, unfasten clasps of pearl dog-collars, take off brooches and bracelets or belts with gold buckles, and remove studs from shirt-fronts or sleeve-links from cuffs, without the knowledge of the persons wearing the things."

"Yes, that would be impossible," Christopher admitted.

"Well, that is what happens at Wood House every day, and has been happening for the last fortnight. People sit at the table, and apparently everything goes on in the most orderly way; yet at the end of the meal their valuables are gone."

"It sounds like a fairy story," said Christopher.

"Or a ghost story," amended Sidney Chester.

Christopher did not smile, for the girl's childish face looked so distressed that to make light of what was tragedy to her would have been cruel. The ghost theory, however, he was not ready to entertain.

"I think the explanation will turn out to be more prosaic," he said. "It would be difficult for ghosts to make jewellery and money invisible as well as themselves."

"Yes," replied Miss Chester, seriously.

"So we must turn our attention elsewhere."

"Ah, but where?"

"I suppose that's what you want me to find out?"

"Exactly. And I wouldn't let you come to Wood House until I'd told you the story. Whatever It is that works the mischief there mustn't know that you are different from any other tourist. You're prepared now. I want you to watch, to set your wits to work to find out the mystery. Of course, you must leave your valuables in care of the landlord here. You'll motor over this evening, won't you, and say you wish to have a room?"

"With pleasure," said Christopher. "And I'll do my best to help."

"Thanks for taking an interest. Then I'll go now. I shall just be able to ride home in time for dinner."

"But there are questions still which I'd better ask you," said Christopher; "as we're not to have any private communication at Wood House. How many indoor servants have you?"

"Three housemaids, one dear old thing who has been with us for years, and two young girls lately got in – one from London, one from our own neighbourhood; a butler we've had since I can remember, two new footmen from London, and an old cook-housekeeper, who has had two assistants since we opened as an hotel. That's all, except a stray creature or two about the kitchen. I must tell you, too, that with the new servants we had the best of references. They've been with us for two months now, and the mystery only began, as I said, a fortnight ago. The first thing that happened was when a rich American family, doing a motor tour round England, came to stop for a night, and were so delighted with the place that they made up their minds to stay from Saturday to Monday. On Sunday night at dinner the two girls and their mother lost jewellery worth thousands, and Mr Van Rensalaer, the father, was robbed of five hundred pounds in notes – all he had with him except his letter of credit, which wasn't taken. You can imagine how they felt – and how we felt. Of course, we sent for a detective, but he could discover nothing. He said it was the queerest affair he ever heard of. Not a jewel, not a penny has ever been recovered; and at least twenty people who have come to us since have suffered in the same way."

"Still, they come. You haven't lost your clients?" said Christopher.

"Not yet; for though most of those who arrive have read about the mystery in the papers (if they haven't, we feel obliged to warn them) they don't believe the stories. They think the thing must have been planned to work up a sensation, and they're so certain things stolen will come back, though they're enchanted with the house at first, before the Thing happens. Just now we're getting crowds who come to try and ferret out the mystery, or because they've made bets that *they* won't lose anything. But soon the sort of people we want will stop away, and we shall get only vulgar curiosity-mongers; then, when we cease to be a nine days' wonder, there'll be nobody, and we shall have to give up. That's what I look forward to, and it will break my heart."

"Something will have to be done," said Christopher – puzzled, but anxious to be encouraging. "Have you no guest who has been with you several weeks?"

"One," the girl returned, half reluctantly, as if she guessed his reason for putting this question. "It's – a man."

"A young man?"

"Yes, a young man."

"How long has he been in the house?"

"Several weeks. He's painting a picture, using the King's room, as we call it, for a background – the room Charles II had when an ancestor of ours was hiding him, and would dart down into a secret place underneath whenever a dangerous visitor arrived."

"Oh, an artist?"

"Not a professional. He—".

"Can't you remember how long he has been with you?"

"Between three weeks and a fortnight." The girl blushed, her white face lovely in its sudden flush of colour. "I see what's in your mind. But there's nothing in that, I assure you. The merest coincidence. You don't look as if you were ready to believe me, but you will when I tell you that it's Sir Walter Raven, the man I'm engaged to marry. When I wrote him about our scheme he didn't like the idea, but soon I let him know what a success it was proving. I even hinted that I might think over the resolution I'd made not to marry him for years, because, after all, I mightn't have to be a burden. He was so excited over the letter that he left his ranch in charge of his partner and came over at once. It was a great surprise to see him, but – it was a very agreeable one. He's been my one comfort – except, of course, our dear cousins – since the evil days began."

"He hasn't been able to throw any light on the problem?"

"No, though he's tried in every way."

"Does he know you've sent for me?"

"I haven't told him, because it would seem as if I couldn't trust him to get to the bottom of the mystery. You see, though he's tremendously clever, he isn't that sort of man. He's been in the Army, and used to drift along, amusing himself as he could, until he met me, and decided to go to work. He's different from you."

"Not so different as she thinks," Christopher said to himself; only he had been driven from amusement to work by a reason less romantic, and, unlike Sir Walter Raven, had not met the right woman yet, but he expected to find her some day.

"When you've got hold of a clue, as I feel you will," Sidney Chester went on, "then I'll tell Sir Walter, and he'll be delighted. Till then, though, you shall be for him, as for everybody else except myself, a guest in the house, like other guests. Luckily, we can give you a place to keep that famous car of yours. We've had part of the stables made into a garage. Now, have you asked me everything?"

"Not yet," answered Christopher, selfishly less sorry to detain her than he would have been had she been middle-aged and plain. "I want to know what servants are in the rooms where these robberies occur?"

"The butler, Nelson, in the dining-hall, or one of the footmen if the meal is being served in a private sitting-room."

"Only those, except the guests?"

"Since the mystery began I've sometimes been there to watch and superintend, and one of my cousins, either Morley or his wife. And in the dining-hall Sir Walter Raven is kind enough to keep an eye on what goes on, while appearing to be engaged with his luncheon or dinner."

"Yet the robberies take place just the same under your very eyes?"

"Yes. That is the mysterious part. The whole thing is like a dream. But you will see for yourself. Only, as I said, take care not to have anything about you which They – whoever, whatever They are – can steal."

"I don't think I shall trouble to put away my valuables," said Christopher. "It wouldn't break me if I lost them, and I can't feel that such a thing will happen to me."

"Ah, others have felt that, and regretted their confidence."

"I sha'n't regret mine," laughed the young man. "And I never carry much money."

"Remember, I've warned you!" cried the girl.

"My blood be on my own head," he smiled, in return, and at last announced that the catechism was finished. She gave him her hand, and he shook it reassuringly; then, it being understood that, as it was late, he would dine at the inn and arrive at Wood House after nine, she left him. Five minutes later, standing at the window, he saw her ride off on a fine hunter.

As he ate chops and drank a glass of ale Christopher considered what he had heard of the mystery, and did not know what to think of it.

He could not believe that things happened as Miss Chester described. He thought that a sensitive imagination, rendered more vivid by singular events, must have led her into exaggeration. However, he was keenly interested, and the fact that Sir Walter Raven had been in the house since the strange happenings began added to the piquancy of the situation. He admired the girl so much that he would regret disillusionment for her; yet her *fiancé's* presence for precisely that length of time was an odd coincidence. He might be anxious to force her to abandon the scheme which he appeared to approve, and – he might have hit upon a peculiar way of doing it. How he could have gone about accomplishing such an object in such a manner Christopher could not see; yet his attention focused on Sir Walter Raven as a central figure in the mystery.

The road from the Sandboy and Owl, through Ringhurst and on to Wood House, was beautiful. Christopher had passed over it before, and, coming to the gateway and lodge of the place he sought, he remembered having remarked both, though he had not then known the name of the estate.

He steered Scarlet Runner between tall stone gate-posts topped with stone lions supporting shields, acknowledged a salutation from an elderly man at the door of the old black and white lodge, and drove up a winding avenue under beeches and oaks.

Suddenly, rounding a turn, he came in sight of the house, standing in the midst of a lawn cleared of trees, in a forest-like park.

It was a long, low building of irregular shape, the many windows with tiny lozenge-panes brightly-lit behind their curtains. In the moonlight the projecting upper storeys with gabled roofs and ivy-draped chimneys, the walls chequered in black and white, with wondrous diapering of trefoils, quatrefoils, and chevrons, were clearly defined against a wooded background. The house could have few peers in picturesqueness if one searched all England. Christopher was not surprised that the plan of turning it into an hotel had attracted many motorists and other tourists.

He was received by a mild, old, white-haired butler, and a footman in neat livery was sent to show him the way to the garage. Scarlet Runner disposed of for the night, he returned to the house and entered a square hall, where a fire of logs in a huge fireplace sent red lights flickering over the carved ceiling, the fine antique cabinets stored with rare china, the gate-legged tables, and high-backed chairs.

His name was announced as if he had been an invited guest arriving at a country house, and from a group near the fireplace came forward to welcome him a young man with a delightful face.

Glancing past him for an instant, as he advanced, Christopher saw Sidney Chester in evening dress; a dainty old lady whom he took to be her mother; a rather timid-looking little woman, whose pretty features seemed almost plain in contrast with Miss Chester's; a handsome, darkly sunburnt young man, with a soldierly, somewhat arrogant air; also seven or eight strangers, divided into different parties scattered about the hall.

"How do you do? Is it possible we're to have the pleasure of entertaining the famous Mr Race?" said the young man who came to greet Christopher. "My name is Morley Chester, and I play host for my cousins, Mrs Chester and her daughter."

Christopher disclaimed the adjective bestowed upon him, but admitted that he was the person who had had a certain adventure in Dalvania, and one or two others that had somehow got into the papers. Then Mr Chester introduced him to the two cousins, mother and daughter (he meeting the girl as if for the first time), to the pretty, quiet young woman who was, it appeared, Mrs Morley Chester, and added an informal word or two which made Sir Walter Raven and Mr Christopher Race known to each other.

Sidney Chester's *fiancé* was, after all, very pleasant and frank in manner, his haughty air being the effect, perhaps, of a kind of proud reserve. Christopher could not help feeling slightly drawn to the young man, as he usually was to handsome people; but there was no doubt in his mind that Mr Morley Chester was an agreeable person. He was not fine-looking, but his way of speaking was so individual and engaging that Christopher did not wonder at Miss Chester for referring to him as her dear cousin.

Assuredly he was the right man for this trying position. His tact and graciousness must put the shyest stranger at ease, and he struck the happy mean between the professional and amateur host, necessary in a country house where paying guests were taken.

He went with Christopher to show two or three rooms which were free, and the new arrival having selected one, and settled about the price, Morley Chester said, half laughingly, half ruefully, "I suppose you've heard about our mystery?"

Christopher confessed that rumours had reached him.

"We think it right to warn everyone who comes," said his host. "Not that our warnings have much effect. People think nothing will happen to *them* – that *they* won't be caught napping; or it amuses them to lose their things, as one gives up one's watch or rings to a conjurer to see what he will do. At worst, though, you're safe for some time.

"The ghostly thief – as we've begun to believe him – lets our visitors alone until just before they're leaving. He always seems to know their intentions. It's a new way of 'speeding the parting guest.' But, if I make light of our troubles, we feel them seriously enough in reality."

Christopher was offered supper, but refused, as he had lately dined; and he did not go downstairs again until after the ladies had gone to bed. Then he joined the men in the smoking-room, and observed with veiled interest not only the guests, but the servants who brought in whisky and soda. There was not a face of which he could say to himself that the expression was sly or repellent.

Before Mr Chester and Sir Walter Raven no one mentioned the trouble in the house; but next morning, sitting in the hall which was the favourite gathering-place, he caught scraps of gossip. No one present had yet been robbed, but everyone had heard something queer from others who had left the place, and as a rich brewer, lately knighted, intended to go away in his motor after luncheon that day, he was being chaffed by his acquaintances.

"I suppose you'll give your watch and money to your chauffeur before you sit down for the last meal?" laughed an American girl who had arrived some days before in her motor-car.

"No, I sha'n't," replied Sir Henry Smithson, valiantly. "I don't believe in this nonsense. I'll show you what I have got on me, and as I am now so shall I be when I go into the dining-hall."

With this he displayed a gorgeous repeater, with his monogram and crest in brilliants; indicated a black pearl scarf-pin, turned a sapphire and diamond ring set in aluminium on a fat finger, and jingled a store of coins his pocket, which he announced to be gold, amounting to fifty pounds. "I've a few notes, too," said he, "and

I expect to have them just the same when I finish my lunch as when I go in."

"Well, we shall all lunch at the same time, and watch," remarked the American girl.

The paying guests at Wood House either breakfasted in their own rooms or in a cheerful morning room, more modern than most parts of the quaint old house; therefore, Christopher Race had not seen the dining-hall of which Miss Chester had spoken. He did not join in the conversation with the brewer; nevertheless, when he saw that gentleman swaggering to luncheon, he followed at a distance, everybody else moving in the same direction at the same time.

It was, indeed, a beautiful room, this dining-hall which Sidney Chester had praised. It was wainscoted to the ceiling in old oak carved in the exquisite linen fold pattern, and though it was worm-eaten and showed signs of excessive age, Christopher, who called himself a judge of antiquities, thought the panelling would be almost worth its weight in gold.

The tables for guests were arranged somewhat oddly, probably, Christopher supposed, with a view to showing off the room and its furniture to advantage. The tables were small, of a size to accommodate parties of from two to eight persons, and ranged along two sides of the dining-hall, placed against one of the walls. In the middle of the room stood a huge old refectory table, with carved sides and legs, and leaves to draw out, a splendid specimen of the Tudor period; but no plates were laid upon this. It was used as a serving table; and against the wall on the right of the door, as one entered from the great hall, was a magnificent oak sideboard, loaded with handsome pieces of ancient silver.

Christopher had a table to himself at the end of the long room, and Sir Henry Smithson sat at a larger one not far away. He had invited the American girl, her chaperon, and Sir Walter Raven to share with him his farewell meal, and much champagne flowed. There was a good deal of talk and laughter at that and other tables, but the luncheon was served by the butler and two footmen in ceremonious style, Mr Morley Chester unostentatiously superintending behind a screen which hid the door used by the servants. Not one of the three ladies of the Chester family was in the room.

All went on in the most orderly manner, and the food was good, as well as nicely served, though it struck Christopher that it was rather long between courses. He ate with good appetite until the meal was drawing to an end, when he began to realize that he was tired, and would be glad to get into the garden and smoke a cigarette. He liked the smell of the old oak which came to him from the panelled wall, yet he thought that the fresh air would be pleasant.

Suddenly, as Christopher was beginning upon biscuits and cheese, Sir Henry Smithson sprang up in his chair, exclaiming, "By Jove!"

Then came a clatter of voices at his table, both ladies there crying out in consternation.

"What has happened?" asked Morley Chester, coming out from behind the screen, while Sir Walter Raven sat looking pale and concerned, and the mild-faced butler saved himself from dropping a bottle of port.

"Everything has gone!" ejaculated Miss Reese, the American. "His watch and chain – his ring – his scarf-pin – and –"

"And my money," finished Sir Henry Smithson.

"I'm dreadfully sorry," stammered Mr Chester. "I begged you to be careful."

"Oh, I've got myself to blame, I suppose," broke in the brewer. He gave a rough laugh, but it did not sound genuine. "Who on earth would have thought such things could be? Well, seeing's believing. This is the queerest house I was ever in. It's bewitched."

"So we are beginning to think," said Chester, deeply mortified. "I can't begin to express my regret –"

"My own fault," said Sir Henry. "I'll say no more about it – for the present. But I wouldn't be sorry to see that repeater of mine again. If you don't mind I'll send a detective down on this business."

Chester assured him that he would like nothing better, and that he only hoped the detective might be more successful than others they had already had at their own expense. People left their tables and crowded round Sir Henry, who was, indeed, shorn of the jewellery he had displayed before luncheon. No one seemed to doubt his word that it had disappeared during the meal without his knowledge, but Christopher made a mental note to write up to town for information concerning the brewer's character. He was a responsible man by reputation, but he might have eccentricities. He might wish to draw attention to himself by pretending to be a victim of the mystery.

Presently, after the dining-hall had been searched in vain for trace of the lost treasures, Sir Henry Smithson went off in his motor, a sadder and a wiser man.

After this, whenever any guest was about to leave the house, history repeated itself, except in one or two instances where precaution had been considered the better part of valour, and no jewellery or money brought into the dining-hall for the last meal.

Meanwhile Christopher had had a look into the two private sitting-rooms, which were separated from the dining-hall only by one long, narrow room used of late as a kind of office. He even ordered dinner in one of them, but nothing happened during the meal.

"I believe people do it themselves when nobody is looking," Christopher thought that night, meditating in his own room. "Can it be that there is some supernatural influence in this old house which puts people into an hysterical state, hypnotizes them, so to speak, and makes them do abnormal things?"

Certain it was that he had grown nervous and, as he expressed it, "jumpy." He suffered from headache, an ailment he had scarcely known before; slept fitfully, starting awake, often with the fancy that he heard a sound in his bedroom. When he dreamed, it was always of old oak and the smell of oak. He felt dull and disinclined to think for long on any subject. In the mornings when he got up there were lines under his eyes, and he had little appetite. Either he imagined it, or the Morley Chesters and their cousin Sidney also looked ill. Perhaps this was not surprising, as the mystery in the house caused them constant anxiety, but Sir Walter Raven was losing his sunburnt tint, and it seemed to Christopher more or less the same with the butler and footman, and all the guests who remained longer than three or four days at Wood House. He was the last man to dwell on ghostly fancies, yet after he remained for a week at the place without being able to earn a penny of the money Miss Chester had offered, he was half ready to credit the idea that the house was haunted.

"If anybody had been doing conjuring tricks I should have had the wit to discover it by this time," he reflected. But if there was anything material to discover, professionals were no more successful than the amateur. There was a new footman in the dining-room, and Morley Chester whispered to Christopher one day that he was a detective in the employ of Sir Henry Smithson.

Race had almost abandoned his suspicions of Sir Walter Raven, whom he liked more and more, when, on his eighth night at Wood House, a sound startled him from a dream of linen fold patterned panelling. Usually, when he waked thus, it was to find all silent, and he would turn over and fall asleep once more, telling himself that the noise had been part of his dream. But this time it continued. There was a queer creaking behind the wainscot.

Of course, it might be rats. Rats could make any sort of sound in the night; and yet he did not think that rats had made this sound. It was too like a foot treading on a loose board, and then stepping on it a second time.

Christopher struck a match and looked at his watch. It was two o'clock. He determined to stop awake the next night and listen for the same thing again. He did so; and it came, at almost exactly the same hour. That day, and the day before, a mysterious disappearance of jewellery had taken place.

In the morning Christopher asked the servant who brought his morning tea who occupied the adjoining room. "Sir Walter Raven," was the answer. Race was angry with himself for not having learned earlier who his neighbour was; but during the day, as he passed, and saw the door of the next room ajar, he glanced in. It seemed to him that there was an inexplicable distance between this door and his. The rooms were supposed to adjoin each other. His own door was near the dividing wall, and so was Sir Walter's, yet there was a wide space between.

Through the open door of Sir Walter Raven's room he could see a low window, with a cushioned seat in the embrasure. In his room there was one of the same size and shape. To prevent mistake he propped a book against the lozenge-panes of his own window, and went out to walk round the rambling house and reconnoitre.

Yes, there was the book; and there was Sir Walter's window farther on towards the left. But there was something between which did not puzzle Christopher as much as it would had he not noticed the distance separating the doors of the two adjoining rooms. Half-way between the two low windows was a tiny one, so overgrown with ivy that it was all but invisible, even to an observant eye.

"Sir Walter Raven must have a cupboard in his wall, lit by that little window," Christopher decided, "or else there's a secret 'hidie hole' between his room and mine."

As Sir Walter's door stood open, Christopher could peer into the room, by pausing as he passed through the corridor, and discover for himself whether there was a cupboard door in the wall. If anyone saw him looking in, it would be simple to explain that he had absent-mindedly mistaken the room for his own, farther on. But he was not seen and had plenty of time, lingering on the threshold, to make certain that no cupboard door was visible in the oak wainscot of the wall. If there were a door it was a secret one.

Christopher was sure now that some place of concealment existed between his room and Sir Walter Raven's, and he was sure, too, that someone entered there at night. What was that someone's errand, and had it any connection with the mystery? This was a question which Christopher considered it his business to find out as soon as possible.

To begin with, he tapped the wainscoting in his own room, and was interested to discover that his knock gave out a hollow sound. He believed that there was but the one thickness of oak between him and the secret, whatever it might be, which lay beyond.

The panelling here was simple, without any elaboration of carving. The wainscot, which reached from floor to ceiling, was divided into large squares framed in a kind of fluting. Having examined each of these squares on the wall nearest Sir Walter Raven's he gave up the hope that there was any hidden door or sliding panel.

"I could saw out a square, though," he thought, "and look at what's on the other side; or I could squeeze through if it seemed worth while. A panel behind the curtain of my bed would do; and I could stick it in again, so that if anybody suspected there was something up they would hardly be able to see what I'd been doing."

Apparently no one ever entered the hiding-place except in the night, about two o'clock. The noises behind the wainscoting continued for a few minutes only, and after that all was silence.

In the afternoon Christopher motored into Ringhurst to buy a small saw, and a bull's-eye lantern such as policemen use. On the way back he overtook Sir Walter with Sidney, and they accepted his offer to give them a lift back to Wood House. "Queer thing, I'm used to tramping about the whole day, and don't turn a hair after a twenty-five-mile walk; but lately I feel done up after eight," said the young man, who was looking pale and heavy-eyed. "I suppose it must be that the climate's relaxing."

Christopher was pricked with a guilty pang. He was engaged by Miss Chester to act as a detective, and yet he felt ashamed of suspecting and plotting against the man she loved. He liked Raven, too. Altogether, keen as he was to fathom the mystery, he wished that he had never come to Wood House.

They talked about the robberies as Christopher drove the car home, Sidney sitting beside him, Sir Walter leaning forward in the tonneau. "After all, it will end in our going away from the dear old place," sighed Sidney, with tears in her eyes. "The strain is wearing mother out; and, you know, if neither of us continues living in the house it will go, as I told you, to the man who would have been the heir had the entail not been broken."

"You'll both come out with me to Colorado and forget your

troubles. Let the chap have the place, and be thankful it's off your hands," said Raven.

He spoke with the sincerity of a lover, not like a schemer who would force a woman to his will by foul means if fair ones proved not strong enough.

"I feel a beast spying on him and working against him," thought Christopher. "Suppose he knows nothing about the secret place next his room? Suppose the noises are made by rats? And what if, after all, the people who think they have been robbed never have been robbed? I'll give Raven the benefit of the doubt until I've tried one more experiment."

Tea was going on in the hall when Scarlet Runner arrived at Wood House. There were letters for Christopher, and he announced in the hearing of everyone, including the servants, that unless he should get a telegram advising him to the contrary he must leave Wood House, where he had spent such an enjoyable fortnight, immediately after breakfast the next morning.

"You'll not come back to us?" asked Sidney, with veiled meaning in her voice.

Christopher pretended not to notice the meaning. "I'm sorry to say I shan't be able to," he answered. "Already I've been here longer than I expected."

He did not mean to take any money from the girl, but though she could not be aware of this resolution, she seemed really sorry to have him go, failure as he had been – thus far.

Christopher took longer over dressing for dinner that night than usual. He hesitated whether to wear the studs and sleeve-links he liked best, or others which he did not care about. Also he was half minded to lock his watch up in his suit-case. Finally, however, he resolved to make his experiment bravely. "I'm not hysterical," he said to himself, "though I might get to be if I stopped here much longer. *I* shan't steal my own things and hide them, if that's what other people do."

Throughout his stay at Wood House he had taken his meals at the same small table, except once or twice when he had been asked to join new-made acquaintances for dinner. But to-night he invited Sir Walter Raven to dine with him, "as it was his last evening." The young man accepted, and they talked of Colorado. Sir Walter was inviting him to come out to his ranch some day, when suddenly the expression of the once healthy, sunburnt, now slightly haggard face changed.

"By Jove!" exclaimed Raven, the blood mounting to his forehead.

"What's the matter?" asked Christopher.

"I'm not a particularly observant chap, but I suppose I would have noticed if you'd come in without your shirt-studs. You didn't by any chance forget to put them in, did you?"

"No; I had them in, right enough," said Race. Looking down he saw that the white expanse of his evening shirt lacked the finish of the two pearl studs he had worn when he came into the room. His cuffs hung loose, empty of his favourite pair of links. Hastily touching his watch-pocket, he found it limp and flat.

"Well, yes, it *is* 'by Jove,'" he remarked, grimly.

"Shall we call Morley Chester and tell him what's happened?" asked Raven.

"No," said Christopher, who sat with his back turned towards the other occupants of the room, his table being at the end by a window, and he having given his usual seat to his guest; "I'd rather not make a fuss. I shall sit till the others have gone, and no one will be the wiser. I'm sick of sensations, and don't want to pose as the hero of one if I can help it."

"Some people seem to like it," said Raven.

"So I've thought," replied Christopher. But his theory was upset. He could not believe in any ghostly influence strong enough to impose illusions upon his mind. A queer thrill went through him. He was struck with horror by the mystery, which had never impressed itself so vividly upon him before.

It was a relief when the rest of the diners left the room, and he was free to slip away without making statements or answering questions. Luckily for him – if unluckily for the Chesters – there were few guests in the house. Those who were there – with the exception of Sir Walter Raven – were new arrivals, and strangers to Christopher. For this reason he escaped the fire of curiosity which raged round most departing visitors at Wood House. He went to his room, locked the door, and, having listened with his ear at the wainscoting, presently began as noiselessly as possible to saw out a selected square from the oak panelling behind his curtained four-poster bed. The saw was sharp, and he worked as energetically as if he had an injury to avenge. In an hour he had the panel ready to come out of its frame. But he did not venture to take it out and commence his explorations until the house was still for the night.

Not once while he worked had there been the faintest sound on the other side. Removing the square of wainscoting at last as if it had been a pane in a window (odd, the oak here hadn't half that strong, subtle fragrance of rich old wood that it had downstairs in the dining-hall and the two private sitting-rooms!), Christopher turned on the light of his lantern and peered into the obscurity on the other side.

There was a hollow space between this wall and the next – a space rather more than two feet wide. Christopher had moved his bed, and cut into a panel so low down that to peer into the opening he had to kneel. The square aperture he had made was so large that by squeezing he could thrust his shoulders through as well as his head. So far as he could see, there was no door on the opposite side, nor was there furniture of any sort in the secret place the stream of light lit up. But at the far corner there was something low and long, and blacker than the darkness. It might be a heavy beam, he thought, against a wall, or it might be a box.

Withdrawing his head, he looked at the quaint grandfather clock which stood in a corner of his room. It was never right within half an hour, but he had now no watch to consult. According to the old timepiece it wanted twenty minutes to two. Perhaps it was later, perhaps earlier; but, in any case, Christopher had time to make researches before the nightly footfalls were due.

It was difficult to wriggle through the square hole in the wainscoting, but he did it, after ridding himself of coat and waistcoat. Now he stood in a long, narrow space between the walls of his own room and Sir Walter Raven's. He had slipped off his pumps, and in stockinged feet began cautious explorations, the lantern making a pathway of light. The thing he had seen at the far end was not a beam. It was a box – two boxes – three boxes – of common wood, such as come into every household from the stores. They had lids, but the lids were not nailed down. Christopher lifted one. The box was filled with jewellery, heaped up in neat piles, according to its kind, on some dark garment folded underneath. There were a pile of bracelets, a pile of brooches, a pile of rings, and a collection of watches like glittering gold eggs in a nest. The second box had the same description of contents, though there were more miscellaneous articles – gold or jewelled belt-buckles, hatpins, a diamond dog-collar or two, and several strings of pearls. In the third box, much smaller than the other two, were purses, some of leather, some of gold or silver netting; cigarette-cases with jewelled monograms; and, weighted down by a lump of gold chains, lay a quantity of bank-notes.

The ghost of Wood House did his work in a business-like manner!

Of gold coins there were none. Even the most prudent ghost might venture to put these to use without delay, when a sharp and practised eye had found them not to be marked suspiciously.

"What a haul it has been," Christopher said to himself. His valuables did not appear to have been added to the collection, but he shrewdly suspected that they would be put into place that night. He had only to wait and see who came to put them there; or should he go farther in this adventure first?

Behind the row of wooden boxes was a square hole, black as the heart of night. Christopher's lantern showed him that from the top of this opening descended a narrow staircase, winding round upon itself like a corkscrew. He set his foot on the first step, and it squeaked. Then he knew what it was that had waked him every night – a foot treading upon that stair – perhaps other stairs below.

"I'll see what's at the bottom," thought Christopher; and was in the act of stepping over the low barrier of boxes when he heard a distant sound.

It was faint, yet it made Christopher pause. He withdrew his foot from the top step of the stairway, and, covering the light, lay

on his side behind the boxes which would, until a person
advancing had risen to a level higher than the wooden lids, form
a screen to hide him.

The sound continued, growing gradually more distinct. Someone was tip-toeing towards the stairs. Someone was on the stairs.
Someone was coming up. There was a wavering glimmer of light,
a little light, like that of a candle.

Christopher lay very still. He hardly even breathed.

The light was moving up the dark wall, and throwing a strange
black shadow, which might be the shadow of a head. A stair
creaked. Another stair. That clock must have been slow, or else
the ghost was before its time. Now there was a long-drawn, tired
breath, like a sigh, and in the advancing light gleamed something
white and small. For a moment it hung in the midst of shadow,
then it descended on the lid of the middle box. It was a woman's
hand.

Quick as thought Christopher seized and held it tightly, at the
same instant rising up and flashing his lantern.

There was a stifled gasp; the hand struggled vainly; he pulled it
towards him, though its owner stumbled and nearly fell, and
Christopher found himself face to face with Mrs Morley Chester.

"Let me go!" she panted. "Oh, I implore you!"

"I'll not let you go," said Christopher, in a voice as low as hers,
but mercilessly determined. "This game is up. You shall tell me
everything, or I swear I'll alarm the house, send for the police,
and have you arrested, you and your husband."

"Not my husband!" faltered the "dear little cousin," the
pretty, timid creature who had always seemed to Christopher
pathetic in her gentle self-effacement, her desire to help Cousin
Sidney. "He – he has nothing to do with this. I—"

"Oh, yes, he has; everything to do with it," insisted Christopher, brutally, meaning to frighten her. "You couldn't have
managed this yourself. I'm not an ordinary guest. I'm here as
a detective, and I've been working up the case for a fortnight.
Now, I want your confession. Be quick, please, or you'll regret
it."

"How cruel you are!" sobbed the woman.

Christopher laughed. "How cruel you have both been to those who trusted you – and to others likely to be suspected in your stead."

"I would do anything for Morley," said Morley's wife.

Still holding her wrist, he pulled her gently, but firmly, up to the top of the steps, and did not loosen his grasp until he stood between her and the stairway.

"If you wish to save him you know what to do," the young man said.

"You won't send us to prison if I tell you the whole story?"

"I'll do my best for you, if you make a clean breast of it; but the contents of these boxes must be restored to their owners, for your cousin's sake if nothing else. I promise to shut my eyes to your escaping with your husband, before any public revelation is made, provided I'm satisfied that you tell me the whole truth now."

"I will, oh, I will! You know, Morley would have had this place if common justice had been done – if the entail hadn't been broken."

"Ah, *he* is the heir of whom Miss Chester spoke!"

"Of course, who else could be? He's the only one left in the male line. And think what it was for him to find out through an expert, whose word he couldn't doubt, that there's coal enough under the park to make him an immensely rich man, if only he hadn't been robbed of his rights."

"He didn't tell Miss Chester of this discovery?"

"Naturally not. If she or her mother gave up living here the estate would come to him after all. He hoped for that. And when he heard of her plan to open a kind of hotel he helped her get a licence and offered to manage the business. That was because he had an idea, which he hoped he could work. His father, who died when Morley was a boy, was a professor of chemistry, and made some clever inventions and discoveries, but they never brought in money. There was one thing he found after spending a year in Persia for his health. He discovered that out of a plant there – a plant no one had ever thought of importance before – an extract could be produced which would make people unconscious, at the same time causing their muscles to remain so rigid that if they were standing they would remain on their feet, or would not drop what they might be holding in their hands. When they came to themselves again they would not feel ill, would not even know they had lost consciousness for a moment.

"Morley's father was much excited about this preparation and hoped it would be as important as curare, if not chloroform. He named the stuff arenoform, as nearly as possible after the plant, and published his discovery to the medical profession. But then came a dreadful blow. After many experiments to change and improve it, nothing could be done to prolong unconsciousness enough to make arenoform really useful to doctors and surgeons. The effect wouldn't last longer than five or six minutes, and the patients were terribly exhausted next day, so that the stuff would not do even for dentists in extracting teeth, as it was more depressing than gas. One of the most wonderful things about it was that a lot of people could be made unconscious at once, even in a big room, by a spray of arenoform floating in the air. But though that was curious and interesting, it was not of practical use, so arenoform was a failure.

"The disappointment was so great that Morley's father was never the same again. He always hoped that some experiment would make the thing a success, and, instead of gaining the fortune he'd expected, he spent more money than he could spare from his family in importing quantities of the plant from Persia, and manufacturing the extract in his own laboratory. Then he died, and there were hundreds and hundreds of the bottles in the house, of no use to anybody; but Morley had promised his dying father not to let them be destroyed. Everyone forgot the discovery of arenoform, for you see Dr Chester has been dead twenty years. Only Morley didn't forget; and it was the existence of that quantity of arenoform in the house left him by his father which put the idea of coming here into his head. He experimented with the stuff on a dog, and found it was as powerful as on the day it was made. Then he told me, and I promised to help in any way I could.

"Next to the dining-hall on one side, and separating it from the two rooms used as private sitting-rooms for guests, is a long, rather ugly room which Morley asked Sidney to give him as a private office. Night after night he worked there before the house was opened to the public, and afterwards too, perfecting his scheme. He perforated the walls, so that, by means of a little movable machine which I could work, a spray of arenoform could be showered through the oak wainscoting either into the dining-hall on one side or the two sitting-rooms on the other. Then he had the tables ranged along the wall; and as one peculiarity of arenoform is that it smells like wood – wonderfully like old oak – no detective could have suspected anything by coming to sniff about the place afterwards. Besides, the perforations in the wainscoting are so small that they seem no different from the worm-holes which are slowly spoiling the old oak.

"When Morley was in the dining-hall or one of the sitting-rooms – which ever place we planned to have something happen – I would be in the locked office, and at a signal which he would give me when most of the servants were out of the room waiting to bring in a new course, I would turn on the spray. He always kept at the very farthest end of the room, behind the screen, and put his face to an open window there. Then, when everybody in the room was under the influence, which they were in a minute or two, he would take whatever he wanted from some unconscious man or woman, or even several persons, before anyone woke up. We've had no one to help us except an assistant of the cook, whom I bribed to make it as long between courses as possible. When I was ready to have the servants go in with the next dish I would touch a little electric bell in the office which Morley had arranged to communicate with the kitchen. The cook's assistant knows nothing, though, except that for some reason it was convenient to me not to have the meals hurried, and to be able to regulate exactly the moment when the different courses should go in.

"Of course, the horrid stuff has affected our health – Morley's and mine – as well as that of everybody else, who has been near when the machine was worked, or lived in the house for any length of time. But we hoped that Sidney and her mother would soon give up. Then the place would be Morley's, and we would be repaid for everything. While if they held on we should at least have the jewels.

"When Morley was working at the walls he discovered the way into this secret place out of our office – not the only 'hidie hole' in the house – but neither Sidney nor her mother knows of its existence. We thought it would be useful to get things out of the way, for fear of detectives searching our boxes, and so it has been. Morley has always sent me up, because I am so light and small and don't make as much noise on the creaking stairs as a man would. Now you know the whole story. And if you have any sense of justice you'll admit that Morley isn't to blame, when the place should have been his, and not Sidney's or her mother's."

Long before dawn Mr and Mrs Morley Chester left Wood House. Next day Christopher told Sidney and Sir Walter Raven the tale as it had been told to him. Also, he mentioned the coal. Also, he showed them the store of jewels and bank-notes.

Where the Morley Chesters went Christopher and others did not know, and did not want to know; but when an advertisement was put into all the most important papers that the mysterious thief at Wood House had been discovered, and that everybody who had lost anything could have it returned by claiming it, the enlightened police were unable to get upon the track of the missing ones.

Christopher would not accept any payment from Sidney Chester. But he would like to have a piece of her wedding-cake to "dream on." He did not think that it would cause him to dream of old oak.

# THE MOTOR BOAT

## Jacques Futrelle

*One of the many tragedies linked with the sinking of the* Titanic *was the death of author Jacques Futrelle (1875–1912). Futrelle was the creator of Professor S.F.X. Van Dusen, better known as "The Thinking Machine" because of his remarkable grasp of logic and deduction in solving apparently impossible crimes. Van Dusen came to prominence in one of the best known of all locked-room mysteries, "The Problem of Cell 13", serialised in* The Boston American *in 1905. Dusen claimed that he could escape from a locked cell in the strongest prison kept under constant watch. The story was run as a contest to see if anyone could come up with the solution. The way in which Futrelle achieves his escape is perhaps the most ingenious in all fiction. I have not selected that story here, partly because it is almost constantly in print in some book or another, but mostly because it is not a crime story, but an extremely clever challenge. After this story Dusen is consulted, usually by newspaper reporter Hutchinson Hatch, on all manner of bizarre and seemingly impossible crimes. The following story, which first appeared in the* Sunday Magazine *(9 September 1906) is much less well known, though it is wonderfully bizarre.*

Captain Hank Barber, master mariner, gripped the bow-rail of the *Liddy Ann* and peered off through the semi-fog of the early morning at a dark streak slashing along through the grey-green waters. It was a motor boat of long, graceful lines; and a single figure, that of a man, sat upright at her helm staring uncompromisingly ahead. She nosed through a roller, staggered a little, righted herself and sped on as a sheet of spray swept over her.

The helmsman sat motionless, heedless of the stinging splash of wind-driven water in his face.

"She sure is a-goin' some," remarked Captain Hank, reflectively. "By Ginger! If she keeps it up into Boston Harbor, she won't stop this side o' the Public Gardens."

Captain Hank watched the boat curiously until she was swallowed up, lost in the mist, then turned to his own affairs. He was a couple of miles out of Boston Harbor, going in; it was six o'clock of a grey morning. A few minutes after the disappearance of the motor boat Captain Hank's attention was attracted by the hoarse shriek of a whistle two hundred yards away. He dimly traced through the mist the gigantic lines of a great vessel – it seemed to be a ship of war.

It was only a few minutes after Captain Hank lost sight of the motor boat that she was again sighted, this time as she flashed into Boston Harbor at full speed. She fled past, almost under the prow of a pilot boat, going out, and was hailed. At the mess table later the pilot's man on watch made a remark about her.

"Goin'! Well, wasn't she though! Never saw one thing pass so close to another in my life without scrubbin' the paint offen it. She was so close up I could spit in her, and when I spoke the feller didn't even look up – just kept a-goin'. I told *him* a few things that was good for his soul."

Inside Boston Harbor the motor boat performed a miracle. Pursuing a course which was singularly erratic and at a speed more than dangerous she reeled on through the surge of the sea regardless alike of fog, the proximity of other vessels and the heavy wash from larger craft. Here she narrowly missed a tug; there she skimmed by a slow-moving tramp and a warning shout was raised; a fisherman swore at her as only a fisherman can. And finally when she passed into a clear space, seemingly headed for a dock at top speed, she was the most unanimously damned craft that ever came into Boston Harbor.

"Guess that's a through boat," remarked an aged salt, facetiously as he gazed at her from a dock. "If that durned fool don't take some o' the speed offen her she'll go through all right – wharf an' all."

Still the man in the boat made no motion; the whizz of her
motor, plainly heard in a sudden silence, was undiminished.
Suddenly the tumult of warning was renewed. Only a chance
would prevent a smash. Then Big John Dawson appeared on the
string piece of the dock. Big John had a voice that was noted from
Newfoundland to Norfolk for its depth and width, and possessed
objurgatory powers which were at once the awe and admiration of
the fishing fleet.

"You ijit!" he bellowed at the impassive helmsman. "Shut off
that power an' throw yer hellum."

There was no response; the boat came on directly toward the
dock where Big John and his fellows were gathered. The fishermen and loungers saw that a crash was coming and scattered
from the string piece.

"The *durned* fool," said Big John, resignedly.

Then came the crash, the rending of timbers, and silence save
for the grinding whir of the motor. Big John ran to the end of the
wharf and peered down. The speed of the motor had driven the
boat half way upon a float which careened perilously. The man
had been thrown forward and lay huddled up face downward and
motionless on the float. The dirty water lapped at him greedily.

Big John was the first man on the float. He crept cautiously to
the huddled figure and turned it face upward. He gazed for an
instant into wide staring eyes then turned to the curious ones
peering down from the dock.

"No wonder he didn't stop," he said in an awed tone. "The
durned fool is dead."

Willing hands gave aid and after a minute the lifeless figure
lay on the dock. It was that of a man in uniform – the uniform
of a foreign navy. He was apparently forty-five years old, large
and powerful of frame with the sun-browned face of a seaman.
The jet black of moustache and goatee was startling against the
dead colour of the face. The hair was tinged with grey; and on
the back of the left hand was a single letter – "D" – tattooed in
blue.

"He's French," said Big John authoritatively, "an' that's the
uniform of a Cap'n in the French Navy." He looked puzzled a

moment as he stared at the figure. "An' they ain't been a French man-o'-war in Boston Harbor for six months."

After awhile the police came and with them Detective Mallory, the big man of the Bureau of Criminal Investigation; and finally Dr Clough, Medical Examiner. While the detective questioned the fishermen and those who had witnessed the crash, Dr Clough examined the body.

"An autopsy will be necessary," he announced as he arose.

"How long has he been dead?" asked the detective.

"Eight or ten hours, I should say. The cause of death doesn't appear. There is no shot or knife wound so far as I can see."

Detective Mallory closely examined the dead man's clothing. There was no name or tailor mark; the linen was new; the name of the maker of the shoes had been ripped out with a knife. There was nothing in the pockets, not a piece of paper or even a vagrant coin.

Then Detective Mallory turned his attention to the boat. Both hull and motor were of French manufacture. Long, deep scratches on each side showed how the name had been removed. Inside the boat the detective saw something white and picked it up. It was a handkerchief – a woman's handkerchief, with the initials "E.M.B." in a corner.

"Ah, a woman's in it!" he soliloquized.

Then the body was removed and carefully secluded from the prying eyes of the press. Thus no picture of the dead man appeared. Hutchinson Hatch, reporter, and others asked many questions. Detective Mallory hinted vaguely at international questions – the dead man was a French officer, he said, and there might be something back of it.

"I can't tell you all of it," he said wisely, "but my theory is complete. It is murder. The victim was captain of a French man-of-war. His body was placed in a motor boat, possibly a part of the fittings of the warship and the boat set adrift. I can say no more."

"Your theory is complete then," Hatch remarked casually, "except the name of the man, the manner of death, the motive, the name of his ship, the presence of the handkerchief and the precise reason why the body should be disposed of in this fashion instead of being cast into the sea.''

The detective snorted. Hatch went away to make some inquiries on his own account. Within half a dozen hours he had satisfied himself by telegraph that no French was craft had been within five hundred miles of Boston for six months. Thus the mystery grew deeper; a thousand questions to which there seemed no answer arose.

At this point, the day following the events related, the problem of the motor boat came to the attention of Professor Augustus S.F.X. Van Dusen, The Thinking Machine. The scientist listened closely but petulantly to the story Hatch told.

"Has there been an autopsy yet?" he asked at last.

"It is set for eleven o'clock today," replied the reporter. "It is now after ten."

"I shall attend it," said the scientist.

Medical Examiner Clough welcomed the eminent Professor Van Dusen's proffer of assistance in his capacity of MD, while Hatch and other reporters impatiently cooled their toes on the curb. In two hours the autopsy had been completed. The Thinking Machine amused himself by studying the insignia on the dead man's uniform, leaving it to Dr Clough to make a startling statement to the press. The man had not been murdered; he had died of heart failure. There was no poison in the stomach, nor was there a knife or pistol wound.

Then the inquisitive press poured in a flood of questions. Who had scratched off the name of the boat? Dr Clough didn't know. Why had it been scratched off? Still he didn't know. How did it happen that the name of the maker of the shoes had been ripped out? He shrugged his shoulders. What did the handkerchief have to do with it? Really he couldn't conjecture. Was there any inkling of the dead man's identity? Not so far as he knew. Any scar on the body which might lead to identification? No.

Hatch made a few mental comments on officials in general and skilfully steered The Thinking Machine away from the other reporters.

"Did that man die of heart failure?" he asked, flatly.

"He did not," was the curt reply. "It was poison."

"But the Medical Examiner specifically stated that there was no poison in the stomach," persisted the reporter.

The scientist did not reply. Hatch struggled with and suppressed a desire to ask more questions. On reaching home the scientist's first act was to consult an encyclopedia. After several minutes he turned to the reporter with an inscrutable face.

"Of course the idea of a natural death in this case is absurd," he said, shortly. "Every fact is against it. Now, Mr Hatch, please get for me all the local and New York newspapers of the day the body was found – not the day after. Send or bring them to me, then come again at five this afternoon."

"But – but –" Hatch blurted.

"I can say nothing until I know all the facts," interrupted The Thinking Machine.

Hatch personally delivered the specified newspapers into the hands of The Thinking Machine – this man who never read newspapers – and went away. It was an afternoon of agony; an agony of impatience. Promptly at five o'clock he was ushered into Professor Van Dusen's laboratory. The scientist sat half smothered in newspapers, and popped up out of the heap aggressively.

"It was murder, Mr Hatch," he exclaimed, suddenly. "Murder by an extraordinary method."

"Who – who is the man? How was he killed?" asked Hatch.

"His name is—" the scientist began, then paused. "I presume your office has the book *Who's Who In America*? Please 'phone and ask them to give you the record of Langham Dudley."

"Is he the dead man?" Hatch demanded quickly.

"I don't know," was the reply.

Hatch went to the telephone. Ten minutes later he returned to find The Thinking Machine dressed to go out.

"Langham Dudley is a ship owner, fifty-one years old," the reporter read from notes he had taken. "He was once a sailor before the mast and later became a ship owner in a small way. He was successful in his small undertakings and for fifteen years has been a millionaire. He has a certain social position, partly through his wife whom he married a year and a half ago. She was Edith

Marston Belding, a daughter of the famous Belding family. He has an estate on the North Shore."

"Very good," commented the scientist. "Now we will find out something about how this man was killed."

At North Station they took train for a small place on the North Shore, thirty-five miles from Boston. There The Thinking Machine made some inquiries and finally they entered a lumbersome carry-all. After a drive of half an hour through the dark they saw the lights of what seemed to be a pretentious country place. Somewhere off to the right Hatch heard the roar of the restless ocean.

"Wait for us," commanded The Thinking Machine as the carry-all stopped.

The Thinking Machine ascended the steps, followed by Hatch, and rang. After a minute or so the door was opened and the light flooded out. Standing before them was a Japanese – a man of indeterminate age with the graven face of his race.

"Is Mr Dudley in?" asked The Thinking Machine.

"He has not that pleasure," replied the Japanese, and Hatch smiled at the queerly turned phrase.

"Mrs Dudley?" asked the scientist.

"Mrs Dudley is attiring herself in clothing," replied the Japanese. "If you will be pleased to enter."

The Thinking Machine handed him a card and was shown into a reception room. The Japanese placed chairs for them with courteous precision and disappeared. After a short pause there was a rustle of silken skirts on the stairs, and a woman – Mrs Dudley – entered. She was not pretty; she was stunning rather, tall, of superb figure and crowned with a glory of black hair.

"Mr Van Dusen?" she asked as she glanced at the card.

The Thinking Machine bowed low, albeit awkwardly. Mrs Dudley sank down on a couch and the two men resumed their seats. There was a little pause; Mr Dudley broke the silence at last.

"Well, Mr Van Dusen, if you –" she began.

"You have not seen a newspaper for several days?" asked The Thinking Machine, abruptly.

"No," she replied, wonderingly, almost smiling. "Why?"

"Can you tell me just where your husband is?"

The Thinking Machine squinted at her in that aggressive way which was habitual. A quick flush crept into her face, and grew deeper at the sharp scrutiny. Inquiry lay in her eyes.

"I don't know," she replied at last. "In Boston, I presume."

"You haven't seen him since the night of the ball?"

"No. I think it was half past one o'clock that night."

"Is his motor boat here?"

"Really, I don't know. I presume it is. May I ask the purpose of this questioning?"

The Thinking Machine squinted hard at her for half a minute. Hatch was uncomfortable, half resentful even, at the agitation of the woman and the sharp, cold tone of his companion.

"On the night of the ball," the scientist went on, passing the question, "Mr Dudley cut his left arm just above the wrist. It was only a slight wound. A piece of court plaster was put on it. Do you know if he put it on himself? If not, who did?"

"I put it on," replied Mrs Dudley, unhesitatingly, wonderingly.

"And whose court plaster was it?"

"Mine – some I had in my dressing room. Why?"

The scientist arose and paced across the floor, glancing once out the hall door. Mrs Dudley looked at Hatch inquiringly and was about to speak when The Thinking Machine stopped beside her and placed his slim fingers on her wrist. She did not resent the action; was only curious if one might judge from her eyes.

"Are you prepared for a shock?" the scientist asked.

"What is it?" she demanded in sudden terror. "This suspense—"

"Your husband is dead – murdered – poisoned!" said the scientist with sudden brutality. His fingers still lay on her pulse. "The court plaster which you put on his arm and which came from your room was covered with a virulent poison which was instantly transfused into his blood."

Mrs. Dudley did not start or scream. Instead she stared up at The Thinking Machine a moment, her face became pallid, a little shiver passed over her. Then she fell back on the couch in a dead faint.

"Good!" remarked The Thinking Machine complacently. And then as Hatch started up suddenly: "Shut that door," he commanded.

The reporter did so. When he turned back, his companion was leaning over the unconscious woman. After a moment he left her and went to a window where he stood looking out. As Hatch watched he saw the color coming back into Mrs Dudley's face. At last she opened her eyes.

"Don't get hysterical," The Thinking Machine directed calmly. "I know you had nothing whatever to do with your husband's death. I want only a little assistance to find out who killed him."

"Oh, my God!" exclaimed Mrs Dudley. "Dead! Dead!"

Suddenly tears leaped from her eyes and for several minutes the two men respected her grief. When at last she raised her face her eyes were red, but there was a rigid expression about the mouth.

"If I can be of any service—" she began.

"Is this the boat house I see from this window?" asked The Thinking Machine. "That long, low building with the light over the door?"

"Yes," replied Mrs Dudley.

"You say you don't know if the motor boat is there now?"

"No, I don't."

"Will you ask your Japanese servant, and if he doesn't know, let him go see, please?"

Mrs Dudley arose and touched an electric button. After a moment the Japanese appeared at the door.

"Osaka, do you know if Mr Dudley's motor boat is in the boat house?" she asked.

"No, honourable lady."

"Will you go yourself and see?"

Osaka bowed low and left the room, closing the door gently behind him. The Thinking Machine again crossed to the window and sat down staring out into the night. Mrs Dudley asked questions, scores of them, and he answered them in order until she knew the details of the finding of her husband's body – that is, the details the public knew. She was interrupted by the reappearance of Osaka.

"I do not find the motor boat in the house, honourable lady."

"That is all," said the scientist.

Again Osaka bowed and retired.

"Now, Mrs Dudley," resumed The Thinking Machine almost gently, "we know your husband wore a French naval costume at the masked ball. May I ask what you wore?"

"It was a Queen Elizabeth costume," replied Mrs Dudley, "very heavy with a long train."

"And if you could give me a photograph of Mr Dudley?"

Mrs Dudley left the room an instant and returned with a cabinet photograph. Hatch and the scientist looked at it together; it was unmistakably the man in the motor boat.

"You can do nothing yourself," said The Thinking Machine at last, and he moved as if to go. "Within a few hours we will have the guilty person. You may rest assured that your name will be in no way brought into the matter unpleasantly."

Hatch glanced at his companion; he thought he detected a sinister note in the soothing voice, but the face expressed nothing. Mrs Dudley ushered them into the hall; Osaka stood at the front door. They passed out and the door closed behind them.

Hatch started down the steps but The Thinking Machine stopped at the door and tramped up and down. The reporter turned back in astonishment. In the dim reflected light he saw the scientist's finger raised, enjoining silence, then saw him lean forward suddenly with his ear pressed to the door. After a little he rapped gently. The door was opened by Osaka, who obeyed a beckoning motion of the scientist's hand and came out. Silently he was led off the veranda into the yard; he appeared in no way surprised.

"Your master, Mr Dudley, has been murdered," declared The Thinking Machine quietly, to Osaka. "We know that Mrs Dudley killed him," he went on as Hatch stared, "but I have told her she is not suspected. We are not officers and cannot arrest her.

Can you go with us to Boston, without the knowledge of anyone here and tell what you know of the quarrel between husband and wife to the police?"

Osaka looked placidly into the eager face.

"I had the honour to believe that the circumstances would not be recognized," he said finally. "Since you know, I will go."

"We will drive down a little way and wait for you."

The Japanese disappeared into the house again. Hatch was too astounded to speak, but followed The Thinking Machine into the carry-all. It drove away a hundred yards and stopped. After a few minutes an impalpable shadow came toward them through the night. The scientist peered out as it came up.

"Osaka?" he asked softly.

"Yes."

An hour later the three men were on a train, Boston bound. Once comfortably settled the scientist turned to the Japanese.

"Now if you will please tell me just what happened the night of the ball?" he asked, "and the incidents leading up to the disagreement between Mr and Mrs Dudley?"

"He drank elaborately," Osaka explained reluctantly, in his quaint English, "and when drinking he was brutal to the honourable lady. Twice with my own eyes I saw him strike her – once in Japan where I entered his service while they were on a wedding journey, and once here. On the night of the ball he was immeasurably intoxicated, and when he danced, he fell down to the floor. The honourable lady was chagrined and angry – she had been angry before. There was some quarrel which I am not comprehensive of. They had been widely divergent for several months. It was, of course, not prominent in the presence of others."

"And the cut on his arm where the court plaster was applied?" asked the scientist. "Just how did he get that?"

"It was when he fell down," continued the Japanese. "He reached to embrace a carved chair and the carved wood cut his arm. I assisted him to his feet and the honourable lady sent me to her room to get court plaster. I acquired it from her dressing table and she placed it on the cut."

"That makes the evidence against her absolutely conclusive," remarked The Thinking Machine, as if finally. There was a little pause, and then: "Do you happen to know just how Mrs Dudley placed the body in the boat?"

"I have not that honour," said Osaka. "Indeed I am not comprehensive of anything that happened after the court plaster was put on except that Mr Dudley was affected some way and went out of the house. Mrs Dudley, too, was not in the ball room for ten minutes or so afterwards."

Hutchinson Hatch stared frankly into the face of The Thinking Machine; there was nothing to be read there. Still deeply thoughtful Hatch heard the brakeman bawl "Boston" and mechanically followed the scientist and Osaka out of the station into a cab. They were driven immediately to Police Headquarters. Detective Mallory was just about to go home when they entered his office.

"It may enlighten you, Mr Mallory," announced the scientist coldly, "to know that the man in the motor boat was not a French naval officer who died of natural causes – he was Langham Dudley, a millionaire ship owner. He was murdered. It just happens that I know the person who did it."

The detective arose in astonishment and stared at the slight figure before him inquiringly; he knew the man too well to dispute any assertion he might make.

"Who is the murderer?" he asked.

The Thinking Machine closed the door and the spring lock clicked.

"That man there," he remarked calmly, turning on Osaka.

For one brief moment there was a pause and silence; then the detective advanced upon the Japanese with hand outstretched. The agile Osaka leapt suddenly, as a snake strikes; there was a quick, fierce struggle and Detective Mallory sprawled on the floor. There had been just a twist of the wrist – a trick of jiu jitsu – and Osaka had flung himself at the locked door. As he fumbled there, Hatch, deliberately and without compunction, raised a chair and brought it down on his head. Osaka sank down without a sound.

It was an hour before they brought him around again. Meanwhile the detective had patted and petted half a dozen suddenly acquired bruises, and had then searched Osaka. He found nothing to interest him save a small bottle. He uncorked it and started to smell it when The Thinking Machine snatched it away.

"You fool, that'll kill you!" he exclaimed.

Osaka sat, lashed hand and foot to a chair, in Detective Mallory's office – so placed by the detective for safe keeping. His face was no longer expressionless; there were fear and treachery and cunning there. So he listened, perforce, to the statement of the case by The Thinking Machine who leaned back in his chair, squinting steadily upward and with his long, slender fingers pressed together.

"Two and two make four, not *some*times but *all* the time," he began at last as if disputing some previous assertion. "As the figure 'two,' wholly disconnected from any other, gives small indication of a result, so is an isolated fact of little consequence. Yet that fact added to another, and the resulting fact added to a third, and so on, will give a final result. That result, if every fact is considered, *must* be correct. Thus any problem may be solved by logic; logic is inevitable.

"In this case the facts, considered singly, might have been compatible with either a natural death, suicide or murder – considered together they proved murder. The climax of this proof was the removal of the maker's name from the dead man's shoes, and a fact strongly contributory was the attempt to destroy the identity of the boat. A subtle mind lay back of it all."

"I so regarded it," said Detective Mallory. "I was confident of murder until the Medical Examiner—"

"We prove a murder," The Thinking Machine went on serenely. "The method? I was with Dr Clough at the autopsy. There was no shot, or knife wound, no poison in the stomach. Knowing there was murder I sought further. Then I found the method in a slight, jagged wound on the left arm. It had been covered with court plaster. The heart showed constriction without apparent cause, and while Dr Clough examined it I took off this court plaster. Its odour, an unusual one, told me that poison had been transfused into the blood through the wound. So two and two had made four.

"Then – what poison? A knowledge of botany aided me. I recognized faintly the trace of an odour of an herb which is not only indigenous to, but grows exclusively in Japan. Thus a Japanese poison. Analysis later in my laboratory proved it was a Japanese poison, virulent, and necessarily slow to act unless it is placed directly in an artery. The poison on the court plaster and that you took from Osaka is identical."

The scientist uncorked the bottle and permitted a single drop of a green liquid to fall on his handkerchief. He allowed a minute or more for evaporation then handed it to Detective Mallory who sniffed at it from a respectful distance. Then The Thinking Machine produced the bit of court plaster he had taken from the dead man's arm, and again the detective sniffed.

"The same," the scientist resumed as he touched a lighted match to the handkerchief and watched it crumble to ashes, "and so powerful that in its pure state mere inhalation is fatal. I permitted Dr Clough to make public his opinion – heart failure – after the autopsy for obvious reasons. It would reassure the murderer for instance if he saw it printed, and besides Dudley did die from heart failure; the poison caused it.

"Next came identification. Mr Hatch learned that no French warship had been within hundreds of miles of Boston for months. The one seen by Captain Barber might have been one of our own. This man was supposed to be a French naval officer, and had been dead less than eight hours. Obviously he did not come from a ship of his own country. Then from where?

"I know nothing of uniforms, yet I examined the insignia on the arms and shoulders closely after which I consulted my encyclopedia. I learned that while the uniform was more French than anything else, it was really the uniform of *no country*, because it was not correct. The insignia were mixed.

"Then what? There were several possibilities, among them a fancy dress ball was probable. Absolute accuracy would not be essential there. Where had there been a fancy dress ball? I trusted to the newspapers to tell me that. They did. A short dispatch from a place on the North Shore stated that on the night before the man was found dead there had been a fancy dress ball at the Langham Dudley estate.

"Now it is as necessary to remember *every* fact in solving a problem as it is to consider every figure in arithmetic. Dudley! Here was the 'D' tattooed on the dead man's hand. *Who's Who* showed that Langham Dudley married Edith Marston Belding. Here was the 'E.M.B.' on the handkerchief in the boat. Langham Dudley was a ship owner had been a sailor, was a millionaire. Possibly this was his own boat built in France."

Detective Mallory was staring into the eyes of The Thinking Machine in frank admiration; Osaka to whom the narrative had thus far been impersonal, gazed, gazed as if fascinated. Hutchinson Hatch, reporter, was drinking in every word greedily.

"We went to the Dudley place," the scientist resumed after a moment. "This Japanese opened the door. Japanese poison! Two and two were still making four. But I was first interested in Mrs Dudley. She showed no agitation and told me frankly that she placed the court plaster on her husband's arm, and that it came from her room. There was instantly a doubt as to her connection with the murder; her immediate frankness aroused it.

"Finally, with my hand on her pulse – which was normal – I told her as brutally as I could that her husband had been murdered. Her pulse jumped frightfully and as I told her the cause of death it wavered, weakened and she fainted. Now if she had known her husband was dead – even if she had killed him – a mere statement of his death would not have caused that pulse. Further I doubt if she could have disposed of her husband's body in the motor boat. He was a large man and the manner of her dress even, was against this. Therefore she was innocent.

"And then? The Japanese, Osaka, here. I could see the door of the boat house from the room where we were. Mrs Dudley asked Osaka if Mr Dudley's boat were in the house. He said he didn't know. Then she sent him to see. He returned and said the boat was not there, *yet he had not gone to the boat house at all*. Ergo, he knew the boat was not there. He may have learned it from another servant, still it was a point against him."

Again the scientist paused and squinted at the Japanese. For a moment Osaka withstood the gaze, then his eyes shifted and he moved uncomfortably.

"I tricked Osaka into coming here by a ludicrously simple expedient," The Thinking Machine went on steadily. "On the train I asked if he knew just how Mrs Dudley got the body of her husband into the boat. Remember at this point he was not supposed to know that the body had been in a boat at all. He said he didn't know and by that very answer admitted that he knew the body had been placed in the boat. He knew because he put it there himself. He didn't merely throw it in the water because he had sense enough to know if the tide didn't take it out, it would rise, and possibly be found.

"After the slight injury Mr Dudley evidently wandered out toward the boat house. The poison was working, and perhaps he fell. Then this man removed all identifying marks, even to the name in the shoes, put the body in the boat and turned on full power. He had a right to assume that the boat would be lost, or that the dead man would be thrown out. Wind and tide and a loose rudder brought it into Boston Harbor. I do not attempt to account for the presence of Mrs Dudley's handkerchief in the boat. It might have gotten there in one of a hundred ways."

"How did you know husband and wife had quarrelled?" asked Hatch.

"Surmise to account for her not knowing where he was," replied The Thinking Machine. "If they had had a violent disagreement it was possible that he would have gone away without telling her, and she would not have been particularly worried, at least up to the time we saw her. As it was, she presumed he was in Boston; perhaps Osaka here gave her that impression?"

The Thinking Machine turned and stared at the Japanese curiously.

"Is that correct?" he asked.

Osaka did not answer.

"And the motive?" asked Detective Mallory, at last.

"Will you tell us just why you killed Mr Dudley?" asked The Thinking Machine of the Japanese.

"I will not," exclaimed Osaka, suddenly. It was the first time he had spoken.

"It probably had to do with a girl in Japan," explained The Thinking Machine, easily. "The murder had been a long cherished project, such a one as revenge through love would have inspired."

It was a day or so later that Hutchinson Hatch called to inform The Thinking Machine that Osaka had confessed and had given the motive for the murder. It was not a nice story.

"One of the most astonishing things to me," Hatch added, "is the complete case of circumstantial evidence against Mrs Dudley, beginning with the quarrel and leading to the application of the poison with her own hands. I believe she would have been convicted on the actual circumstantial evidence had you not shown conclusively that Osaka did it."

"Circumstantial fiddlesticks!" snapped The Thinking Machine. "I wouldn't convict a dog of stealing jam on circumstantial evidence alone, even if he had jam all over his nose." He squinted truculently at Hatch for a moment. "In the first place well behaved dogs don't eat jam," he added more mildly.

# MURDER IN THE AIR

## Peter Tremayne

*We return from our trip through the past to a brand new story, which is certainly up to date. And how much more impossible can you get than a murder in a locked toilet in an aircraft at 30,000 feet! Peter Tremayne (b.1943) is the author of a number of novels of the supernatural and bizarre as, well as a highly acclaimed historical mystery series set in the seventh century featuring the Irish advocate Sister Fidelma. The first in the series was* Absolution by Murder *(1994).*

Chief Steward Jeff Ryder noticed the worried expression on the face of Stewardess Sally Beech the moment that she entered the premier class galley of the Global Airways 747, Flight GA 162. He was surprised for a moment as he had never seen the senior stewardess looking so perturbed before.

"What's up, Sal?" he greeted, in an attempt to bring back her usual impish smile. "Is there a wolf among our first class passengers causing you grief?"

She shook her head without a change of her pensive expression.

"I think one of the passengers is locked in the toilet," she began.

Jeff Ryder's smile broadened and he was about to make some ribald remark.

"No," she interrupted as if she had interpreted his intention. "I am serious. I think that something might have happened. He has been in there for some time and the person with whom he was travelling asked me to check on him. I knocked on the door but there was no reply."

Ryder suppressed a sigh. A passenger locked in the toilet was uncommon but not unknown. He had once had to extricate a eighteen stone Texan from an aircraft toilet once. It was not an experience that he wanted to remember.

"Who is this unfortunate passenger?"

"He's down on the list as Henry Kinloch Gray."

Ryder gave an audible groan.

"If a toilet door is stuck on this aircraft, then it just had to be Kinloch Gray who gets stuck with it. Do you know who he is? He's the chairman of Kinloch Gray & Brodie, the big multi-national media company. He has a reputation for eating company directors alive but as for the likes of you and me, poor minnows in the great sea of life . . ." He rolled his eyes expressively. "Oh Lord! I'd better see to it."

With Sally trailing in his wake, Ryder made his way to the premier class toilets. There was no one about and he saw immediately which door was flagged as "engaged". He went to it and called softly: "Mister Kinloch Gray? Is everything all right, sir?" He waited and then knocked respectfully on the door.

There was still no response.

Ryder glanced at Sally.

"Do we know roughly how long he has been in there?"

"His travelling companion said he went to the toilets about half-an-hour ago."

Ryder raised an eyebrow and turned back to the door. His voice rose an octave.

"Sir; Mister Kinloch Gray, sir; we are presuming that you are in some trouble in there. I am going to break the lock. If you can, please stand back from the door."

He leant back, raised a foot and sent it crashing against the door by the lock. The flimsy cubicle lock dragged out its attaching screws and swung inwards a fraction.

"Sir . . .?" Ryder pressed against the door. He had difficulty pushing it, something was causing an obstruction. With some force, he managed to open it enough to insert his head into the cubicle and then only for a moment. He withdrew it rapidly, his features had paled. He stared at Sally not speaking for a moment or two. Finally he formed some words. "I think he has been shot," he whispered.

The toilets had been curtained off and the captain of the aircraft, Moss Evans, one of Global Airway's senior pilots, had been sent for having been told briefly what the problem was. The silver haired, sturdily built pilot, had hid his concerns as he made his way from the flight deck through the premier class section, smiling and nodding affably to passengers. His main emotion was one of irritation, for it had only been a few moments since the aircraft had passed its midpoint, the "point of no return", half-way into its flight. Another four hours to go and he did not like the prospect of diverting to another airport now and delaying the flight for heaven knew how long. He had an important date waiting for him.

Ryder had just finished making an announcement to premier class passengers with the feeble excuse that there was a mechanical malfunction with the forward premier class toilets, and directing passengers to the mid-section toilets for their safety and comfort. It was typical airline jargon. Now he was waiting with Sally Beech for the captain. Evans knew Ryder well for, Jeff had been flying with him for two years. Ryder's usually good humour was clearly absent. The girl also looked extremely pale and shaken.

Evans glanced sympathetically at her; then turned to the shattered lock of the cubicle door.

"Is that the toilet?"

"It is."

Evans had to throw his weight against the door and managed to get his head inside the tiny cubicle.

The body was sprawled on the toilet seat, fully dressed. The arms dangled at the sides, the legs were splayed out, thus preventing the door from fully opening. The balance of the inert body was precarious. From the mouth to the chest was a bloody mess. Bits of torn flesh hung from the cheeks. Blood had splayed on the side walls of the cubicle. Evans felt the nausea well up in him but suppressed it.

As Ryder had warned him, it looked as though the man had been shot in the mouth. Automatically, Evans peered down not knowing what he was looking for until he realized that he should be looking for a gun. He was surprised when he did not see one. He peered around again. The hands dangling at the sides of the body held nothing. The floor of the cubicle to which any gun must have fallen showed no sign of it. Evans frowned and withdrew. Something in the back of his mind told him that something was wrong about what he had seen but he could not identify it.

"This is a new one for the company's air emergency manual," muttered Ryder, trying to introduce some humour into the situation.

"I see that you have moved passengers back from this section," Evans observed.

"Yes. I've moved all first class passengers from this section and we are rigging a curtain. I presume the next task is to get the body out of there?"

"Has his colleague been told? The person he was travelling with?"

"He has been told that there has been an accident. No details."

"Very well. I gather our man was head of some big corporation?"

"Kinloch Gray. He was Henry Kinloch Gray."

Evans pursed his lips together in a silent whistle.

"So we are talking about an influence backed by megabucks, eh?"

"They don't come any richer."

"Have you checked the passenger list for a doctor? It looks like our man chose a hell of a time and place to commit suicide. But I think we'll need someone to look at him before we move anything. I'll proceed on company guidelines of a medical emergency routine. We'll notify head office."

Ryder nodded an affirmative.

"I've already had Sally check if there are any doctors on board. As luck would have it, we have two in the premier class. They are both seated together. C One and C Two."

"Right. Get Sally to bring one of them up here. Oh, and where is Mister Gray's colleague?"

"Seated B 3. His name is Frank Tilley and I understand he is Gray's personal secretary."

"I'm afraid he'll have to stand by to do a formal identification. We'll have to play this strictly by the company rule book," he added again as if seeking reassurance.

Sally Beech approached the two men in seats C One and Two. They were both of the same age, mid-forties; one was casually dressed with a mop of fiery red hair, looking very unlike the stereotype idea of a doctor. The other appeared neat and more smartly attired. She halted and bent down.

"Doctor Fane?" It was the first of the two names which she had memorized.

The smartly dressed man glanced up with a smile of inquiry.

"I'm Gerry Fane. What can I do for you, miss?"

"Doctor, I am afraid that we have a medical emergency with one of the passengers. The captain extends his compliments and would greatly appreciate it if you could come and take a look."

It sounded like a well repeated formula. In fact, it was a formula out of the company manual. Sally did not know how else to deliver it but in the deadpan way that she had been trained to do.

The man grimaced wryly.

"I am afraid my doctorate is a Ph.D in criminology, miss. Not much help to you. I think that you will need my companion, Hector Ross. He's a medical doctor."

The girl glanced apologetically to the red haired man in the next seat and was glad to see that he was already rising so that she did not have to repeat the same formula.

"Don't worry, lass. I'll have a look but I am not carrying my medical bag. I'm actually a pathologist returning from a conference, you understand? Not a GP."

"We have some emergency equipment on board, doctor, but I don't think that you will need it."

Ross glanced at her with a puzzled frown but she had turned and was leading the way along the aisle.

Hector Ross backed out of the toilet cubicle and faced Captain Evans and Jeff Ryder. He glanced at his watch.

"I am pronouncing death at thirteen-fifteen hours, captain."

Evans stirred uneasily.

"And the cause?"

Ross bit his lip.

"I'd rather have the body brought out where I can make a full inspection." He hesitated again. "Before I do, I would like my colleague, Doctor Fane, to have a look. Doctor Fane is a criminal psychologist and I have great respect for his opinion."

Evans stared at the doctor, trying to read some deeper meaning behind his words.

"How would a criminal psychologist be able to help in this matter unless . . .?"

"I'd appreciate it all the same, captain. If he could just take a look?" Ross's tone rose persuasively.

Moments later, Gerry Fane was backing out of the same toilet door and regarding his travelling companion with some seriousness.

"Curious," he observed. The word was slowly and deliberately uttered.

"Well?" demanded Captain Evans impatiently. "What is that supposed to mean?"

Fane shrugged eloquently in the confined space.

"It means that it's not well at all, captain," he said with just a hint of sarcasm. "I think we should extricate the body so that my colleague here can ascertain the cause of death and then we can determine how this man came by that death."

Evans sniffed, trying to hide his annoyance.

"I have my company's chairman waiting on the radio, doctor. I would like to be able to tell him something more positive. I think you will understand when I tell you that he happens to know Mister Gray. Same golf club or something."

Fane was ironic.

"*Knew*, I'm afraid. Past tense. Well, you can tell your chairman that it rather looks as though his golfing partner was murdered."

Evans was clearly shocked.

"That's impossible. It must have been suicide."

Hector Ross cleared his throat and looked uneasily at his friend.

"Should you go that far, old laddie?" he muttered. "After all . . ."

Fane was unperturbed and interrupted him in a calm decisive tone.

"Whatever the precise method of inflicting the fatal wound, I would think that you would agree that it looked pretty instantaneous. The front parts of the head, below the eyes and nose are almost blown away. Nasty. Looks like a gunshot wound to the mouth."

Evans had recovered the power of speech. Now, as he thought about it, he realized the very point that had been puzzling him. It was his turn to be sarcastic.

"If a gun was fired in there, even one of low calibre with a body to cushion the impact of the bullet, it would have had the force to pierce the side of the aircraft causing decompression. Do you know what a bullet can do if it pierces an aircraft fuselage at thirty-six thousand feet?"

"I did not say for certain that it was a gun," Fane maintained his gentle smile. "I said that it looked like a gunshot."

"Even if it were a gunshot which killed him, why could it not have been a suicide?" the chief steward interrupted. "He was in a locked toilet for Chrissake! It was locked on the inside."

Fane eyed him indulgently.

"I made a point about the instantaneous nature of the wound. I have never known a corpse to be able to get up and hide a weapon after a successful suicide bid. The man is sprawled in there dead, with a nasty mortal wound that was pretty instantaneous in causing death . . . and no sign of any weapon. Curious, isn't it?"

Evans stared at him in disbelief.

"That's ridiculous . . ." There was no conviction in his voice.

"You can't be serious? The weapon must be hidden behind the door or somewhere."

Fane did not bother to reply.

"But," Evans plunged on desperately, knowing that Fane had articulated the very thing that had been worrying him; the missing weapon. "Are you saying that Gray was killed and then placed in the toilet?"

Fane shook his head firmly.

"More complicated than that, I'm afraid. Judging from the blood splayed out from the wound, staining the walls of the cubicle, he was already in the toilet when he was killed and with the door locked from the inside, according to your chief steward there."

Jeff Ryder stirred uncomfortably.

"The door *was* locked from the inside," he confirmed, defensively.

"Then how . . .?" began Evans.

"That is something we must figure out. Captain, I have no wish to usurp any authority but, if I might make a suggestion . . .?"

Evans did not answer. He was still contemplating the impossibility of what Fane had suggested.

"Captain . . .?"

"Yes? Sorry, what did you say?"

"If I might make a suggestion? While Hector does a preliminary examination to see if we can discover the cause of death, will you allow me to question Gray's colleague and then we might discover the why as well as the how?"

Evans lips compressed thoughtfully.

"I don't feel that I have the authority. I'll have to speak to the chairman of the company."

"As soon as possible, captain. We'll wait here," Fane replied calmly. "While we are waiting, Doctor Ross and I will get the body out of the toilet."

Hardly any time passed before Moss Evans returned. By then Ross and Fane had been able to remove the body of Kinloch Gray from the toilet and lay it in the area between the bulkhead and front row of the premier class seats. Evans cleared his throat awkwardly.

"Doctor Fane. My chairman has given you full permission to act as you see fit in this matter . . . until the aircraft lands, that is. Then, of course, you must hand over matters to the local police authority." He shrugged and added, as if some explanation were necessary: "It seems that my chairman has heard of your reputation as a . . . a criminologist? He is happy to leave the matter in the hands of Doctor Ross and yourself."

Fane inclined his head gravely.

"Will you be diverting the aircraft?" he asked.

"My chairman has ordered us to continue to our point of destination, doctor. As the man is dead, it is pointless to divert in search of any medical assistance."

"Good. Then we have over three hours to sort this out. Can your steward provide me with a corner where I can speak with Gray's colleague? She tells me that he is his personal secretary. I want a word without causing alarm to other passengers?"

"See to it, Jeff," Captain Evans ordered the chief steward. He glanced at Fane. "Don't they say that murder is usually committed by someone known to the victim? Doesn't that make this secretary the prime suspect? Or will every passenger have to be checked out to see if they have some connection with Gray?"

Fane smiled broadly.

"I often find that you cannot make general rules in these matters."

Evans shrugged.

"If it helps, I could put out an address asking all passengers to return to their seats and put on their seat belts. I could say that we are expecting turbulence. It would save any curious souls from trying to enter this area."

"That would be most helpful, captain," Hector Ross assured him, looking up from his position by the corpse.

Evans hesitated a moment more.

"I am going back to the flight deck. Keep me informed of any developments."

Within a few minutes of Evans leaving, there came the sound of raised voices. Fane looked up to see the stewardess, Sally Beech, trying her best to prevent a young man from moving forward towards them. The young man was very determined.

"I tell you that I work for him." His voice was raised in protest. "I have a right to be here."

"You are in tourist class sir. You have no right to be here in premier class."

"If something has happened to Mister Gray then I demand . . ."

Fane moved quickly forward. The young man was tall, well-spoken, and, Fane observed, his handsome looks were aided by a tan which came from a lamp rather than the sun. He was immaculately dressed. He sported a gold signet ring on his slim tapering fingers. Fane had a habit of noticing hands. He felt much could be told about a person from their hands and how they kept their fingernails. This young man obviously paid a great deal of attention to maintaining well manicured nails.

"Is this Mister Gray's secretary?" he asked Sally.

The stewardess shook her head.

"No, doctor. This is a passenger from tourist class. He claims to have worked for Mister Gray."

"And your name is?" queried Fane swiftly, his sharp eyes on the young man's handsome features.

"Oscar Elgee. I was Mister Gray's manservant." The young man spoke with a modulated voice that clearly betrayed his public school background. "Check with Frank Tilley, in premier class. He is Mister Gray's personal secretary. He will tell you who I am."

Fane smiled encouragingly at Sally Beech.

"Would you do that for me, Miss Beech, and also tell Mister Tilley that I would like to see him here when convenient?" When she hurried away, Fane turned back to the new arrival. "Now, Mister Elgee, how did you hear that there had been an . . . an accident?"

"I heard one of the stewardesses mentioning it to another back in the tourist class," Elgee said. "If Mister Gray has been hurt . . ."

"Mister Gray is dead."

Oscar Elgee stared at him for a moment.

"A heart attack?"

"Not exactly. Since you are here, you might formally identify your late employer. We need an identification for Doctor Ross's record."

He stood aside and allowed the young man to move forward to where the body had been laid out ready for Ross's examination. Ross moved to allow the young man to examine the face. Elgee halted over the body and gazed down for a moment.

"*Terra es, terram ibis*," he muttered. Then his face broke in anguish. "How could this have happened? Why is there blood on his face? What sort of accident happened here?"

"That's exactly what we are attempting to find out," Ross told him. "I take it that you formally identify this man as Henry Kinloch Gray?"

The young man nodded briefly, turning away. Fane halted him beyond the curtained area.

"How long did you work for him, Mister Elgee?"

"Two years."

"What exactly was your job with him?"

"I was his manservant. Everything. Chauffeur, butler, cook, valet, handyman. His *factotum*."

"And he took you on his trips abroad?"

"Of course."

"But I see he was a stickler for the social order, eh?" smiled Fane.

The young man flushed.

"I don't understand."

"You are travelling tourist class."

"It would not be seemly for a manservant to travel first class."

"Quite so. Yet, judging from your reactions to his death, you felt a deep attachment to your employer?"

The young man's chin raised defiantly and a colour came to his cheeks.

"Mister Gray was an exemplary employer. A tough businessman, true. But he was a fair man. We never had a cross word. He was a good man to work for. A great man."

"I see. And you looked after him? Took care of his domestic

needs. If I recall the newspaper stories, Harry Gray was always described as an eligible bachelor."

Fane saw a subtle change of expression on the young man's face.

"If he had been married then he would hardly have needed my services, would he? I did everything for him. Even repairing his music centre or his refrigerator. No; he was not married."

"Just so," smiled Fane, glancing again at Elgee's hands. "Repairing a music centre requires a delicate touch. Unusual for a handyman to be able to do that sort of thing."

"My hobby is model making. Working models." There was a boastful note in his voice.

"I see. Tell me, as you would be in the best position to know, did your employer have any enemies?"

The young man actually winced.

"A businessman like Harry Gray is surrounded by enemies." He looked up and saw Sally Beech ushering a bespectacled man into the compartment. "Some enemies work with him and pretended to be his confidants," he added with a sharp note. He paused and frowned as the thought seemed to occur to him. "Are you saying that his death was . . . was suspicious?"

Fane noticed, with approval, that Sally had motioned her new charge to sit down and did not come forward to interrupt him. He turned to the young man.

"That we will have to find out. Now, Mister Elgee, perhaps you would return to your seat? We will keep you informed of the situation."

The young man turned and went out, hardly bothering to acknowledge the new arrival who, in turn, seemed to drop his eyes to avoid contact with the personable young man. There was obviously no love lost between the manservant and secretary.

Leaving Hector Ross to continue his examination with the aid of the aircraft's emergency medical kit, Fane went up to where the newcomer had been seated. Sally Beech, waiting with her charge, gave him a nervous smile.

"This is Mister Francis Tilley. He was travelling with Mister Gray."

Frank Tilley was a thin and very unattractive man in his mid-thirties. His skin was pale, and his jaw showed a permanent blue shadow which no amount of shaving would erase. He wore thick, horn rimmed spectacles which seemed totally unsuited to his features. His hair was thin and receding and there was a nervous twitch at the corner of his mouth.

Fane motioned the stewardess to stand near the door to prevent any other person entering the premier class compartment, and turned to Tilley.

"He's dead, eh?" Tilley's voice was almost a falsetto. He giggled nervously. "Well, I suppose it had to happen sometime, even to the so-called great and the good."

Fane frowned at the tone in the man's voice.

"Are you saying that Mr Gray was ill?" he asked.

Tilley raised a hand and let it fall as if he were about to make a point and changed his mind. Fane automatically registered the shaky hand, the thick trembling fingers, stained with nicotine, and the raggedly cut nails.

"He was prone to asthma, that's all. Purely a stress condition."

"Then, why . . .?"

Tilley looked slightly embarrassed.

"I suppose that I was being flippant."

"You do not seem unduly upset by the death of your colleague?"

Tilley sniffed disparagingly.

"Colleague? He was my boss. He never let anyone who worked for him forget that he was the boss, that he was the arbiter of their fate in the company. Whether the man was a doorman or his senior vice-president, Harry Kinloch Gray was a "hands on" chairman and his word was law. If he took a dislike to you, then you were out immediately, no matter how long you had worked with the company. He was the archetypical Victorian self-made businessman. Autocratic, mean and spiteful. He should have had no place in the modern business world."

Fane sat back and listened to the bitterness in the man's voice.

"Was he the sort of man who had several enemies then?"

Tilley actually smiled at the humour.

"He was the sort of man who did not have any friends."

"How long have you worked for him?"

"I've spent ten years in the company. I was his personal secretary for the last five of those years."

"Rather a long time to spend with someone you don't like? You must have been doing something right for him not to take a dislike to you and sack you, if, as you say, that was his usual method of dealing with employees."

Tilley shifted uneasily at Fane's sarcasm.

"What has this to do with Mister Gray's death?" he suddenly countered.

"Just seeking some background."

"What happened?" Tilley went on. "I presume that he had some sort of heart attack?"

"Did he have a heart condition then?"

"Not so far as I know. He was overweight and ate like a pig. With all the stress he carried about with him, it wouldn't surprise me to know that that was the cause."

"Was this journey a particularly stressful one?"

"No more than usual. We were on our way to a meeting of the executives of the American subsidiaries."

"And so far as you noticed, Mr Gray was behaving in his usual manner?"

Tilley actually giggled. It was an unpleasant noise.

"He was his usual belligerent, bullying, and arrogant self. He had half-a-dozen people to sack and he wanted to do it in a public ritual to give them the maximum embarrassment. It gave him a buzz. And then . . ."

Tilley hesitated and a thoughtful look came into his eyes.

"He was going through some documents from his case. One of them seemed to fascinate him and after a moment or two he started to have one of his attacks . . ."

"Attacks? I thought that you said that he had no health problems . . .?"

"What I actually said was that he was prone to asthma. He did have these stress-related asthma attacks."

"So you did. So he began to have an asthma attack? Did he take anything for it?"

"He carried one of those inhalers around with him. He was vain and thought that none of us knew about it. The great chairman did not like to confess to a physical weakness. So when he had his attacks he would disappear to treat himself with the inhaler. It was so obvious. Ironic that he had a favourite quotation from *Ecclesiastes*, '*Vanitas vanitatum, omnis vanitas*'!"

"So are you saying that he went to the toilet to take his inhaler?"

"That is what I am saying. After a considerable time had passed, I did get concerned."

"Concerned?" Fane smiled thinly. "From what you are telling me, concern about your boss's well-being was not exactly a priority with you."

Tilley lips thinned in a sneer.

"Personal feelings do not enter into it. I was not like Elgee who puts his all into the job. I was being paid to do a job and I did it with integrity and with professionalism. I did not have to like Harry Gray. It was no concern of mine what Harry Gray did or did not do outside of the job he paid me to do. It did not concern me who his lover was nor who his mortal enemies were."

"Very well. So he went to the toilet and did not come back?"

"As I said, after a while, I called the stewardess and she went to check on him. That was no more nor less the concern of my position as his secretary."

"Wait there a moment, Mister Tilley."

Fane moved to where Sally Beech was standing, still pale and slightly nervous, and said quietly:

"Do you think you could go to Mister Gray's seat and find his attaché case? I'd like you to bring it here."

She returned in a short while with a small brown leather case.

Fane took it to show to Frank Tilley.

"Do you identify this as Gray's case?"

The man nodded reluctantly. "I don't think you should do that," he protested as Fane snapped open the clasps.

"Why not?"

"Confidential company property."

"I think an investigation into a possible homicide will override that objection."

Frank Tilley was surprised.

"Homicide . . .? But that means . . . murder. No one said anything about murder."

Fane was too busy shifting through the papers to respond.

He pulled out a sheet and showed it to Tilley.

"Was this what he was looking at just before he began to have breathing difficulties?"

"I don't know. Perhaps. It was a piece of paper like it, that's all I can say."

The sheet was a tear sheet from a computer printout. It had two short sentences on it.

"You will die before this aircraft lands. *Memento, 'homo', quia pulvis es et in pulverem revertis.*"

Fane sat back with a casual smile. He held out the paper to the secretary.

"You are a Latin scholar, Mister Tilley. How would you translate the phrase given here?"

Tilley frowned.

"What makes you say that I am a Latin scholar?"

"A few moments ago you trotted out a Latin phrase. I presumed that you knew its meaning."

"My Latin is almost non-existent. Mister Gray was fond of Latin tags and phrases so I tried to keep up by memorizing some of those he used frequently."

"I see. So you don't know what this one means?"

Tilley looked at the printed note. He shook his head.

"*Memento* means remember, doesn't it?"

"Have you ever heard the phrase *memento mori*? That would be a more popular version of what is written here."

Tilley shook his head.

"Remember something, I suppose?"

"Why do you think the Latin word for 'man' has quotation marks around it?"

"I don't know what it means. I do not know Latin."

"What this says roughly is – Remember, man, that you are dust and to dust you will return. It was obviously written on a computer, a word processor. Do you recognize the type?"

Tilley shook his head.

"It could be any one of hundreds of company standards. I hope you are not implying that I wrote Mister Gray a death threat?"

"How would this have made its way into his attaché case?" Fane said, ignoring the comment.

"I presume someone put it there."

"Who would have such access to it?"

"I suppose that you are still accusing me? I hated him. But not so that I would cut my own throat. He was a bastard but he was the goose who laid the golden egg. There was no point in being rid of him."

"Just so," muttered Fane, thoughtfully. His eye caught sight of a note pad in the case and he flicked through its pages while Frank Tilley sat looking on in discomfort. Fane found a list of initials with the head, "immediate dismissal" and that day's date.

"A list of half-a-dozen people that he was about to sack?" Fane observed.

"I told you that he was going to enjoy a public purge of his executives and mentioned some names to me."

"The list contains only initials and starts with O.T.E." He glanced at Tilley with a raised eyebrow. "Oscar Elgee?"

"Hardly," Tilley replied with a patronising smile. "It means Otis T. Elliott, the general manager of our US database subsidiary."

"I see. Let's see if we can identify the others."

He ran through the other initials to which Tilley added names. The next four were also executives of Gray's companies. The last initials were written as "Ft".

"F.T. is underscored three times with the words 'no pay off!' written against it. Who's "F.T.?"

"You know that F.T. are my initials," Tilley observed quietly. His features were white and suddenly very grave. "I swear that he never said anything to me about sacking me when we discussed those he had on his list. He never mentioned it."

"Well, was there anyone else in the company that the initials F.T. could apply to?"

Tilley frowned, trying to recall but finally shook his head and gave a resigned shrug.

"No. It could only be me. The bastard! He never told me what he was planning. Some nice little public humiliation, I suppose."

Hector Ross emerged from the curtained section and motioned Fane to join him.

"I think I can tell you how it was done," he announced with satisfaction.

Fane grinned at his friend.

"So can I. Tell me if I am wrong. Gray went into the toilet to use his inhaler to relieve an attack of asthma. He placed the inhaler in his mouth, depressed it in the normal way and . . ."

He ended with a shrug.

Ross looked shocked.

"How did you . . .?" He glanced over Fane's shoulder to where Frank Tilley was still sitting, twitching nervously. "Did he confess that he set it up?"

Fane shook his head.

"No. But was I right?"

"It is a good hypothesis but needs a laboratory to confirm it. I found tiny particles of aluminium in the mouth, and some plastic. Something certainly exploded with force, sending a tiny steel projectile into the back roof of the mouth with such force that it entered the brain and death was instantaneous, as you initially surmised. Whatever had triggered the projectile disintegrated with the force. Hence there were only small fragments embedded in his mouth and cheeks. There were some when I searched carefully, around the cubicle. Diabolical."

"This was arranged by someone who knew that friend Gray had a weakness and banked on it. Gray didn't like to take his inhaler in public and would find a quiet corner. The plan worked out very well and nearly presented an impossible crime, an almost insolvable crime. Initially it appeared that the victim had been shot in the mouth in a locked toilet."

Hector Ross smiled indulgently at his colleague.

"You imply that you already have the solution?"

"Oh yes. Remember the song that we used to sing at school?

"Life is real! Life is earnest!
And the grave is not its goal;
Dust thou art, to dust returnest,
Was not spoken of the soul."

Hector Ross nodded.

"It's many a day since I last sang that, laddie. Something by Longfellow, wasn't it?"

Fane grinned.

"It was, indeed. Based on some lines from the *Book of Genesis* – '*terra es, terram ibis* – dust thou art, to dust thou shalt return'. Get Captain Evans here, please." He made the request to the Chief Steward, Jeff Ryder, who had been waiting attendance on Ross. When he had departed, Fane glanced back to his friend. "There is something to be said for Latin scholarship."

"I don't follow, laddie."

"Our murderer was too fond of the Latin in-jokes he shared with his boss."

"You mean his secretary?" He glanced at Frank Tilley.

"Tilley claims that he couldn't even translated *memento mori*."

"Remember death?"

Fane regarded his friend in disapproval.

"It actually means 'remember *to* die' and a *memento mori* is usually applied to a human skull or some other objection which reminds us of our mortality."

Captain Evans arrived and looked from Fane to Ross in expectation.

"Well, what news?"

"To save any unpleasant scene on the aircraft, captain, I suggest you radio ahead and have the police waiting to arrest one of your passengers on a charge of murder. No need to make any move until we land. The man can't go far."

"Which man?" demanded Evans, his grim faced.

"He is listed as Oscar Elgee in the tourist class."

"How could he . . .?"

"Simple. Elgee was not only Gray's manservant but I think you'll find, from the broad hints Mister Tilley gave me, that he was also his lover. Elgee seems to confirm it by a death note with a Latin phrase in which he emphasized the word *homo*, meaning man, but, we also know it was often used as a slang term in my generation for 'homosexual'."

"How would you know that Elgee was capable of understanding puns in Latin?" asked Ross.

"The moment he saw Gray's body, young Elgee muttered the very words. *Terra es, terram ibis* – dust you are, to dust you will return."

"A quarrel between lovers?" asked Ross. "Love to hatred turned – and all that, as Billy Shakespeare succinctly put it?"

Fane nodded.

"Gray was giving Elgee the push, both as lover and employee, and so Elgee decided to end his lover's career in mid-flight, so to speak. There is a note in his attaché case that Elgee was to be sacked immediately without compensation."

Tilley, who had been sitting quietly, shook his head vehemently.

"No there isn't," he interrupted. "We went through the list. I told you that the initials O.T.E. referred to Otis Elliott. I had faxed that dismissal through before we boarded the plane."

Fane smiled softly.

"You have forgotten F.T."

"But that's my . . ."

"You didn't share your boss's passion for Latin tags, did you? It was the F.T. that confused me. I should have trusted that a person with Gray's reputation would not have written *F* followed by a lower case *t* if he meant two initials F.T. I missed the point. It was not your initials at all, Mister Tilley. It was Ft meant as an abbreviation. Specifically, *fac*, from *facere*: to do; and *totum*: all things. *Factotum*. And who was Gray's *factotum*?"

There was a silence.

"I think we will find that this murder was planned for a week or two at least. Once I began to realize what the mechanism was which killed Gray, all I had to do was look for the person capable of devising that mechanism as well as having motive and opportunity. Hold out your hands, Mister Tilley."

Reluctantly the secretary did so.

"You can't seriously see those hands constructing a delicate mechanism, can you?" Fane said. "No, Elgee, the model maker and handyman, doctored one of Gray's inhalers so that when it was depressed it would explode with an impact into the mouth, shooting a needle into the brain. Simple but effective. He knew that Gray did not like to be seen using the inhaler in public. The rest was left to chance and it was a good chance. It almost turned out to be the ultimate impossible crime. It might have worked had not our victim and his murderer been too fond of their Latin in-jokes."

# THE PULP CONNECTION

*Bill Pronzini*

*Bill Pronzini (b.1943) is a prolific writer of mystery stories, westerns and science fiction, and also a fine anthologist, selecting material from his enviable collection of pulp and digest magazines. Indeed the old pulps are crucial to solving the following story. In the mystery fiction field, Pronzini is probably best known for his stories and novels featuring the Nameless Detective, which began with* The Snatch *(1971) and include two story collections:* Casefile *(1983) and* Spadework *(1996). Quite a few of the stories are impossible crimes.*

The address Eberhardt had given me on the phone was a corner lot in St Francis Wood, halfway up the western slope of Mt Davidson. The house there looked like a baronial Spanish villa – a massive two-story stucco affair with black iron trimming, flanked on two sides by evergreens and eucalyptus. It sat on a notch in the slope forty feet above street level, and it commanded an impressive view of Lake Merced and the Pacific Ocean beyond. Even by St Francis Wood standards – the area is one of San Francisco's moneyed residential sections – it was some place, probably worth half a million dollars or more.

At four o'clock on an overcast weekday afternoon this kind of neighbourhood is usually quiet and semi-deserted; today it was teeming with people and traffic. Cars were parked bumper to bumper on both fronting streets, among them half a dozen police cruisers and unmarked sedans and a television camera truck. Thirty or forty citizens were grouped along the sidewalks, gawking, and I saw four uniformed cops standing watch in front of the gate and on the stairs that led up to the house.

I didn't know what to make of all this as I drove past and tried to find a place to park. Eberhardt had not said much on the phone, just that he wanted to see me immediately on a police matter at this address. The way it looked, a crime of no small consequence had taken place here today – but why summon me to the scene? I had no idea who lived in the house; I had no rich clients or any clients at all except for an appliance outfit that had hired me to do a skip-trace on one of its deadbeat customers.

Frowning, I wedged my car between two others a block away and walked back down to the corner. The uniformed cop on the gate gave me a sharp look as I came up to him, but when I told him my name his manner changed and he said, "Oh, right, Lieutenant Eberhardt's expecting you. Go on up."

So I climbed the stairs under a stone arch and past a terraced rock garden to the porch. Another patrolman stationed there took my name and then led me through an archway and inside.

The interior of the house was dark, and quiet except for the muted sound of voices coming from somewhere in the rear. The foyer and the living room and the hallway we went down were each ordinary enough, furnished in a baroque Spanish style, but the large room the cop ushered me into was anything but ordinary for a place like this. It contained an overstuffed leather chair, a reading lamp, an antique trestle desk-and-chair and no other furniture except for floor-to-ceiling bookshelves that covered every available inch of wall space; there were even library-type stacks along one side. And all the shelves were jammed with paperbacks, some new and some which seemed to date back to the 1940s. As far as I could tell, every one of them was genre – mysteries, Westerns and science fiction.

Standing in the middle of the room were two men – Eberhardt and an inspector I recognized named Jordan. Eberhardt was puffing away on one of his battered black briars; the air in the room was blue with smoke. Eighteen months ago, when I owned a two-pack-a-day cigarette habit, the smoke would have started me coughing but also made me hungry for a weed. But I'd gone to a doctor about the cough around that time, and he had found what he was afraid might be a malignant lesion on one lung. I'd had a bad scare for a while; if the lesion *had* turned out to be malignant, which it hadn't, I would probably be dead or dying by now. There's nothing like a cancer scare and facing your own imminent mortality to make you give up cigarettes for good. I hadn't had one in all those eighteen months, and I would never have one again.

Both Eberhardt and Jordan turned when I came in. Eb said something to the inspector, who nodded and started out. He gave me a nod on his way past that conveyed uncertainty about whether or not I ought to be there. Which made two of us.

Eberhardt was wearing a rumpled blue suit and his usual sour look; but the look seemed tempered a little today with something that might have been embarrassment. And that was odd, too, because I had never known him to be embarrassed by anything while he was on the job.

"You took your time getting here, hotshot," he said.

"Come on, Eb, it's only been half an hour since you called. You can't drive out here from downtown in much less than that." I glanced around at the bookshelves again. "What's all this?"

"The Paperback Room," he said.

"How's that?"

"You heard me. The Paperback Room. There's also a Hardcover Room, a Radio and Television Room, a Movie Room, a Pulp Room, a Comic Art Room and two or three others I can't remember."

I just looked at him.

"This place belongs to Thomas Murray," he said. "Name mean anything to you?"

"Not offhand."

"Media's done features on him in the past – the King of the Popular Culture Collectors."

The name clicked then in my memory; I had read an article on Murray in one of the Sunday supplements about a year ago. He was a retired manufacturer of electronic components, worth a couple of million dollars, who spent all his time accumulating popular culture – genre books and magazines, prints of television and theatrical films, old radio shows on tape, comic books and strips, original artwork, Sherlockiana and other such items. He was reputed to be one of the foremost experts in the country on these subjects, and regularly provided material and copies of material to other collectors, students and historians for nominal fees.

I said, "Okay, I know who he is. But I—"

"Was," Eberhardt said.

"What?"

"Who he *was*. He's dead – murdered."

"So that's it."

"Yeah, that's it." His mouth turned down at the corners in a sardonic scowl. "He was found here by his niece shortly before one o'clock. In a locked room."

"Locked room?"

"Something the matter with your hearing today?" Eberhardt said irritably. "Yes, a damned locked room. We had to break down the door because it was locked from the inside, and we found Murray lying in his own blood on the carpet. Stabbed under the breastbone with a razor-sharp piece of thin steel, like a splinter." He paused, watching me. I kept my expression stoic and attentive. "We also found what looks like a kind of dying message, if you want to call it that."

"What sort of message?"

"You'll see for yourself pretty soon."

"Me? Look, Eb, just why did you get me out here?"

"Because I want your help, damn it. And if you say anything cute about this being a big switch, the cops calling in a private eye for help on a murder case, I won't like it much."

So that was the reason he seemed a little embarrassed. I said, "I wasn't going to make any wisecracks; you know me better than that. If I can help you I'll do it gladly – but I don't know how."

"You collect pulp magazines yourself, don't you?"

"Sure. But what does that have to do with—"

"The homicide took place in the Pulp Room," he said. "And the dying message involves pulp magazines. Okay?"

I was surprised, and twice as curious now, but I said only, "Okay." Eberhardt is not a man you can prod.

He said, "Before we go in there, you'd better know a little of the background. Murray lived here alone except for the niece, Paula Thurman, and a housekeeper named Edith Keeler. His wife died a few years ago, and they didn't have any children. Two other people have keys to the house – a cousin, Walter Cox, and Murray's brother David. We managed to round up all four of those people, and we've got them in a room at the rear of the house.

"None of them claims to know anything about the murder. The housekeeper was out all day; this is the day she does her shopping. The niece is a would-be artist, and she was taking a class at San Francisco State. The cousin was having a long lunch with a girl friend downtown, and the brother was at Tanforan with another horseplayer. In other words, three of them have got alibis for the probable time of Murray's death, but none of the alibis is what you could call unshakable.

"And all of them, with the possible exception of the house-keeper, have strong motives. Murray was worth around three million, and he wasn't exactly generous with his money where his relatives are concerned; he doled out allowances to each of them, but he spent most of his ready cash on his popular-culture collection. They're all in his will – they freely admit that – and each of them stands to inherit a potful now that he's dead.

"They also freely admit, all of them, that they could use the inheritance. Paula Thurman is a nice-looking blonde, around twenty-five, and she wants to go to Europe and pursue an art career. David Murray is about the same age as his brother, late fifties; if the broken veins in his nose are any indication he's a boozer as well as a horseplayer – a literal loser and going downhill fast. Walter Cox is a mousy little guy who wears glasses about six inches thick; he fancies himself an investments expert but doesn't have the cash to make himself rich – he says – in the stock market. Edith Keeler is around sixty, not too bright, and stands to inherit a token five thousand dollars in Murray's will; that's why she's what your pulp detectives call 'the least likely suspect.'"

He paused again. "Lot of details there, but I figured you'd better know as much as possible. You with me so far?"

I nodded.

"Okay. Now, Murray was one of these regimented types – did everything the same way day after day. Or at least he did when he wasn't off on buying trips or attending popular-culture conventions. He spent two hours every day in each of his Rooms, starting with the Paperback Room at eight am. His time in the Pulp Room was from noon until two pm. While he was in each of these Rooms he would read or watch films or listen to tapes, and he would also answer correspondence pertaining to whatever that Room contained – pulps, paperbacks, TV and radio shows, and so on. Did all his own secretarial work – and kept all his correspondence segregated by Rooms."

I remembered these eccentricities of Murray's being mentioned in the article I had read about him. It had seemed to me then, judging from his quoted comments, that they were calculated in order to enhance his image as King of the Popular Culture Collectors. But if so, it no longer mattered; all that mattered now was that he was dead.

Eberhardt went on, "Three days ago Murray started acting a little strange. He seemed worried about something, but he wouldn't discuss it with anybody; he did tell the housekeeper that he was trying to work out 'a problem.' According to both the niece and the housekeeper, he refused to see either his cousin or his brother during that time; and he also took to locking himself into each of his Rooms during the day and in his bedroom at night, something he had never done before.

"You can figure that as well as I can: he suspected that somebody wanted him dead, and he didn't know how to cope with it. He was probably trying to buy time until he could figure out a way to deal with the situation."

"Only time ran out on him," I said.

"Yeah. What happened as far as we know it is this: the niece came home at twelve forty-five, went to talk to Murray about getting an advance on her allowance and didn't get any answer when she knocked on the door to the Pulp Room. She got worried, she says, went outside and around back, looked in through the window and saw him lying on the floor. She called us right away.

"When we got here and broke down the door, we found Murray lying right where she told us. Like I said before, he'd been stabbed with a splinterlike piece of steel several inches long; the outer two inches had been wrapped with adhesive tape – a kind of handle grip, possibly. The weapon was still in the wound, buried around three inches deep."

I said, "That's not much penetration for a fatal wound."

"No, but it was enough in Murray's case. He was a scrawny man with a concave chest; there wasn't any fat to help protect his vital organs. The weapon penetrated at an upward angle, and the point of it pierced his heart."

I nodded and waited for him to go on.

"We didn't find anything useful when we searched the room," Eberhardt said. "There are two windows, but both of them are nailed shut because Murray was afraid somebody would open one of them, and the damp air off the ocean would damage the magazines; the windows hadn't been tampered with. The door hadn't been tampered with either. And there aren't any secret panels or fireplaces with big chimneys or crap like that. Just a dead man alone in a locked room."

"I'm beginning to see what you're up against."

"You've got a lot more to see yet," he said. "Come on."

He led me out into the hallway and down to the rear. I could still hear the sound of muted voices; otherwise the house was unnaturally still – or maybe my imagination made it seem that way.

"The coroner's people have already taken the body," Eberhardt said. "And the lab crew finished up half an hour ago. We'll have the room to ourselves."

We turned a corner into another corridor, and I saw a uniformed patrolman standing in front of a door that was a foot or so ajar; he moved aside silently as we approached. The door was a heavy oak job with a large, old-fashioned keyhole lock; the wood on the jamb where the bolt slides into a locking plate was splintered as a result of the forced entry. I let Eberhardt push the door inward and then followed him inside.

The room was large, rectangular – and virtually overflowing with plastic-bagged pulp and digest-sized magazines. Brightly coloured spines filled four walls of floor-to-ceiling bookshelves and two rows of library stacks. I had over 6,000 issues of detective and mystery pulps in my Pacific Heights flat, but the collection in this room made mine seem meager in comparison. There must have been at least 15,000 issues here, of every conceivable type of pulp and digest, arranged by category but in no other particular order: detective, mystery, horror, weird menace, adventure, Western, science fiction, air-war, hero, love. Then and later I saw what appeared to be complete runs of *Black Mask*, *Dime Detective*, *Weird Tales*, *The Shadow* and *Western Story*; of *Ellery Queen's Mystery Magazine* and *Alfred Hitchcock's Mystery Magazine* and *Manhunt*; and of titles I had never even heard of.

It was an awesome collection, and for a moment it captured all my attention. A collector like me doesn't often see anything this overwhelming; in spite of the circumstances it presented a certain immediate distraction. Or it did until I focused on the wide stain of dried blood on the carpet near the back-wall shelves, and the chalk outline of a body which enclosed it.

An odd, queasy feeling came into my stomach; rooms where people have died violently have that effect on me. I looked away from the blood and tried to concentrate on the rest of the room. Like the Paperback Room we had been in previously, it contained nothing more in the way of furniture than an overstuffed chair, a reading lamp, a brass-trimmed rolltop desk set beneath one of the two windows and a desk chair that had been overturned. Between the chalk outline and the back-wall shelves there was a scattering of magazines which had evidently been pulled or knocked loose from three of the shelves; others were askew in place, tilted forward or backward, as if someone had stumbled or fallen against them.

And on the opposite side of the chalk outline, in a loosely arranged row, were two pulps and a digest, the digest sandwiched between the larger issues.

Eberhardt said, "Take a look at that row of three magazines over there."

I crossed the room, noticing as I did so that all the scattered and shelves periodicals at the back wall were detective and mystery; the pulps were on the upper shelves and the digests on the lower ones. I stopped to one side of the three laid-out magazines and bent over to peer at them.

The first pulp was a 1930s and 1940s crime monthly called *Clues*. The digest was a short-lived title from the 1960s, *Keyhole Mystery Magazine*. And the second pulp was an issue of one of my particular favorites, *Private Detective*.

"Is this what you meant by a dying message?"

"That's it," he said. "And that's why you're here."

I looked around again at the scattered magazines, the disarrayed shelves, the overturned chair. "How do you figure this part of it, Eb?"

"The same way you're figuring it. Murray was stabbed somewhere on this side of the room. He reeled into that desk chair, knocked it over, then staggered away to those shelves. He must have known he was dying, that he didn't have enough time or strength to get to the phone or to find paper and pencil to write out a message. But he had enough presence of mind to want to point *some* kind of finger at his killer. So while he was falling or after he fell he was able to drag those three magazines off their shelves; and before he died he managed to lay them out the way you see them. The question is, why those three particular magazines?"

"It seems obvious why the copy of *Clues*," I said.

"Sure. But what clues was he trying to leave us with *Keyhole Mystery Magazine* and *Private Detective*? Was he trying to tell us how he was killed or who killed him? Or both? Or something else altogether?"

I sat on my heels, putting my back to the chalk outline and the dried blood, and peered more closely at the magazines. The issue of *Clues* was dated November 1937, featured a Violet McDade story by Cleve F. Adams and had three other, unfamiliar authors' names on the cover. The illustration depicted four people shooting each other.

I looked at *Keyhole Mystery Magazine*. It carried a June 1960 date and headlined stories by Norman Daniels and John Collier; there were several other writers' names in a bottom strip, a couple of which I recognized. Its cover drawing showed a frightened girl in the foreground, fleeing a dark, menacing figure in the background.

The issue of *Private Detective* was dated March, no year, and below the title were the words, "Intimate Revelations of Private Investigators." Yeah, sure. The illustration showed a private eye dragging a half-naked girl into a building. Yeah, sure. Down in the lower right-hand corner in big red letters was the issue's feature story: "Dead Man's Knock," by Roger Torrey.

I thought about it, searching for connections between what I had seen in here and what Eberhardt had told me. Was there anything in any of the illustrations, some sort of parallel situation? No. Did any of the primary suspects have names which matched those of writers listed on any of the three magazine covers? No. Was there any well-known fictional private eye named Murray or Cox or Thurman or Keeler? No.

I decided I was trying too hard, looking for too specific a connection where none existed. The plain fact was, Murray had been dying when he thought to leave these magazine clues; he would not have had time to hunt through dozens of magazines to find particular issues with particular authors or illustrations on the cover. All he had been able to do was to reach for specific copies close at hand; it was the titles of the magazines that carried whatever message he meant to leave.

So assuming *Clues* meant just that, clues, *Keyhole* and *Private Detective* were the sum total of those clues. I tried putting them together. Well, there was the obvious association: the stereotype of a private investigator is that of a snooper, a keyhole peeper. But I could not see how that would have anything to do with Murray's death. If there had been a private detective involved, Eberhardt would have figured the connection immediately and I wouldn't be here.

Take them separately then. *Keyhole Mystery Magazine*. Keyhole. That big old-fashioned keyhole in the door?

Eberhardt said, "Well? You got any ideas?" He had been standing near me, watching me think, but patience had never been his long suit.

I straightened up, explained to him what I had been ruminating about and watched him nod: he had come to the same conclusions long before I got here. Then I said, "Eb, what about the door keyhole? Could there be some connection there, something to explain the locked-room angle?"

"I already thought of that," he said. "But go ahead, have a look for yourself."

I walked over to the door, and when I got there I saw for the first time that there was a key in the latch on the inside. Eberhardt had said the lab crew had come and gone; I caught hold of the key and tugged at it, but it had been turned in the lock and it was firmly in place.

"Was this key in the latch when you broke the door down?" I asked him.

"It was. What were you thinking? That the killer stood out in the hallway and stabbed Murray through the keyhole?"

"Well, it was an idea."

"Not a very good one. It's too fancy, even if it was possible."

"I guess you're right."

"I don't think we're dealing with a mastermind here," he said. "I've talked to the suspects and there's not one of them with an IQ over a hundred and twenty."

I turned away from the door. "Is it all right if I prowl around in here, look things over for myself?"

"I don't care what you do," he said, "if you end up giving me something useful."

I wandered over and looked at one of the two windows. It had been nailed shut, all right, and the nails had been painted over some time ago. The window looked out on an overgrown rear yard – eucalyptus trees, undergrowth and scrub brush. Wisps of fog had begun to blow in off the ocean; the day had turned dark and misty. And my mood was beginning to match it. I had no particular stake in this case, and yet because Eberhardt had called me into it I felt a certain commitment. For that reason, and because puzzles of any kind prey on my mind until I know the solution, I was feeling a little frustrated.

I went to the desk beneath the second of the windows, glanced through the cubbyholes: correspondence, writing paper, envelopes, a packet of blank cheques. The centre drawer contained pens and pencils, various-sized paper clips and rubber bands, a tube of glue, a booklet of stamps. The three side drawers were full of letter carbons and folders jammed with facts and figures about pulp magazines and pulp writers.

From there I crossed to the overstuffed chair and the reading lamp and peered at each of them in turn. Then I looked at some of the bookshelves and went down the aisles between the library stacks. And finally I came back to the chalk outline and stood staring down again at the issues of *Clues*, *Keyhole Mystery Magazine* and *Private Detective*.

Eberhardt said impatiently, "Are you getting anywhere or just stalling?"

"I'm trying to think," I said. "Look, Eb, you told me Murray was stabbed with a splinterlike piece of steel. How thick was it?"

"About the thickness of a pipe cleaner. Most of the 'blade' part had been honed to a fine edge and the point was needle-sharp."

"And the other end was wrapped with adhesive tape?"

"That's right. A grip, maybe."

"Seems an odd sort of weapon, don't you think? I mean, why not just use a knife?"

"People have stabbed other people with weapons a hell of a lot stranger," he said. "You know that."

"Sure. But I'm wondering if the choice of weapon here has anything to do with the locked-room angle."

"If it does I don't see how."

"Could it have been *thrown* into Murray's stomach from a distance, instead of driven there at close range?"

"I suppose it could have been. But from where? Not outside this room, not with that door locked on the inside and the windows nailed down."

Musingly I said, "What if the killer wasn't in this room when Murray died?"

Eberhardt's expression turned even more sour. "I know what you're leading up to with that," he said. "The murderer rigged some kind of fancy crossbow arrangement, operated by a tripwire or by remote control. Well, you can forget it. The lab boys searched every inch of this room. Desk, chairs, bookshelves, reading lamp, ceiling fixtures – everything. There's nothing like that here; you've been over the room, you can tell that for yourself. There's nothing at all out of the ordinary or out of place except those magazines."

Sharpening frustration made me get down on on knee and stare once more at the copies of *Keyhole* and *Private Detective*. They had to mean something, separately or in conjunction. But what? What?

"Lieutenant?"

The voice belonged to Inspector Jordan; when I looked up he was standing in the doorway, gesturing to Eberhardt. I watched Eb go over to him and the two of them hold a brief, soft-voiced conference. At length Eberhardt turned to look at me again.

"I'll be back in a minute," he said. "I've got to go talk to the family. Keep working on it."

"Sure. What else?"

He and Jordan went away and left me alone. I kept staring at the magazines, and I kept coming up empty.

*Keyhole Mystery Magazine.*

*Private Detective.*

Nothing.

I stood up and prowled around some more, looking here and there. That went on for a couple of minutes – until all of a sudden I became aware of something Eberhardt and I should have noticed before, should have considered before. Something that was at once obvious and completely unobtrusive, like the purloined letter in the Poe story.

I came to a standstill, frowning, and my mind began to crank out an idea. I did some careful checking then, and the idea took on more weight, and at the end of another couple of minutes I had convinced myself I was right.

I knew how Thomas Murray had been murdered in a locked

room. Once I had that, the rest of it came together pretty quick. My mind works that way; when I have something solid to build on, a kind of chain reaction takes place. I put together things Eberhardt had told me and things I knew about Murray, and there it was in a nice ironic package: the significance of *Private Detective* and the name of Murray's killer.

When Eberhardt came back into the room I was going over it all for the third time, making sure of my logic. He still had the black briar clamped between his teeth and there were more scowl wrinkles in his forehead. He said, "My suspects are getting restless; if we don't come up with an answer pretty soon, I've got to let them go on their way. And you, too."

"I may have the answer for you right now," I said.

That brought him up short. He gave me a penetrating look, then said, "Give."

"All right. What Murray was trying to tell us, as best he could with the magazines close at hand, was how he was stabbed and who his murderer is. I think *Keyhole Mystery Magazine* indicates how and *Private Detective* indicates who. It's hardly conclusive proof in either case, but it might be enough for you to pry loose an admission of guilt."

"You just leave that part of it to me. Get on with your explanation."

"Well, let's take the 'how' first," I said. "The locked-room angle. I doubt if the murderer set out to create that kind of situation; his method was clever enough, but as you pointed out we're not dealing with a mastermind here. He probably didn't even know that Murray had taken to locking himself inside this room every day. I think he must have been as surprised as everyone else when the murder turned into a locked-room thing.

"So it was supposed to be a simple stabbing done by person or persons unknown while Murray was alone in the house. But it wasn't a stabbing at all, in the strict sense of the word; the killer wasn't anywhere near here when Murray died."

"He wasn't, huh?"

"No. That's why the adhesive tape on the murder weapon – misdirection, to make it look like Murray was stabbed with a homemade knife in a close confrontation. I'd say he worked it the way he did for two reasons: one, he didn't have enough courage to kill Murray face to face; and two, he wanted to establish an alibi for himself."

Eberhardt puffed up another great cloud of acrid smoke from his pipe. "So tell me how the hell you put a steel splinter into a man's stomach when you're miles away from the scene."

"You rig up a death trap," I said, "using a keyhole."

"Now, look, we went over all that before. The key was inside the keyhole when we broke in, I told you that, and I won't believe the killer used some kind of tricky gimmick that the lab crew overlooked."

"That's not what happened at all. What hung both of us up is a natural inclination to associate the word 'keyhole' with a keyhole in a door. But the fact is, there are *five other keyholes* in this room."

"What?"

"The desk, Eb. The rolltop desk over there."

He swung his head around and looked at the desk beneath the window. It contained five keyholes, all right – one in the rolltop, one in the centre drawer and one each in the three side drawers. Like those on most antique rolltop desks, they were meant to take large, old-fashioned keys and therefore had good-sized openings. But they were also half-hidden in scrolled brass frames with decorative handle pulls; and no one really notices them anyway, any more than you notice individual cubbyholes or the design of the brass trimming. When you look at a desk you see it as an entity: you see a *desk*.

Eberhardt put his eyes on me again. "Okay," he said, "I see what you mean. But I searched that desk myself, and so did the lab boys. There's nothing on it or in it that could be used to stab a man through a keyhole."

"Yes, there is." I led him over to the desk. "Only one of these keyholes could have been used, Eb. It isn't the one in the rolltop because the top is pushed all the way up; it isn't any of the ones in the side drawers because of where Murray was stabbed – he would have had to lean over at an awkward angle, on his own initiative, in order to catch that steel splinter in the stomach. It has to be the centre drawer then, because when a man sits down at a desk like this, that drawer – and that keyhole – are about on a level with the area under his breastbone."

He didn't argue with the logic of that. Instead, he reached out, jerked open the centre drawer by its handle pull and stared inside at the pens and pencils, paper clips, rubber bands and other writing paraphernalia. Then, after a moment, I saw his eyes change and understanding come into them.

"Rubber band," he said.

"Right." I picked up the largest one; it was about a quarter-inch wide, thick and strong – not unlike the kind kids use to make slingshots. "This one, no doubt."

"Keep talking."

"Take a look at the keyhole frame on the inside of the centre drawer. The top doesn't quite fit snug with the wood; there's enough room to slip the edge of this band into the crack. All you'd have to do then is stretch the band out around the steel splinter, ease the point of the weapon through the keyhole and anchor it against the metal on the inside rim of the hole. It would take time to get the balance right and close the drawer without releasing the band, but it could be done by someone with patience and a steady hand. And what you'd have then is a death trap – a cocked and powerful slingshot."

Eberhardt nodded slowly.

"When Murray sat down at the desk," I said, "all it took was for him to pull open the drawer with the jerking motion people always use. The point of the weapon slipped free, the rubber band released like a spring, and the splinter shot through and sliced into Murray's stomach. The shock and impact drove him and the chair backward, and he must have stood up convulsively at the same time, knocking over the chair. That's when he staggered into those bookshelves. And meanwhile the rubber band flopped loose from around the keyhole frame, so that everything looked completely ordinary inside the drawer."

"I'll buy it," Eberhardt said. "It's just simple enough and

logical enough to be the answer." He gave me a sidewise look. "You're pretty good at this kind of thing, once you get going."

"It's just that the pulp connection got my juices flowing."

"Yeah, the pulp connection. Now, what about *Private Detective* and the name of the killer?"

"The clue Murray left us there is a little more roundabout," I said. "But you've got to remember that he was dying and that he only had time to grab those magazines that were handy. He couldn't tell us more directly who he believed was responsible."

"Go on," he said, "I'm listening."

"Murray collected pulp magazines, and he obviously also read them. So he knew that private detectives as a group are known by all sorts of names – shamus, op, eye, snooper." I allowed myself a small, wry smile. "And one more, just as common."

"Which is?"

"Peeper," I said.

He considered that. "So?"

"Eb, Murray also collected every other kind of popular culture. One of those kinds is prints of old television shows. And one of your suspects is a small, mousy guy who wears thick glasses; you told me that yourself. I'd be willing to bet that some time ago Murray made a certain obvious comparison between this relative of his and an old TV show character from back in the fifties, and that he referred to the relative by that character's name."

"*What* character?"

"Mr Peepers," I said. "And you remember who played Mr Peepers, don't you?"

"Well, I'll be damned," he said. "Wally Cox."

"Sure. Mr Peepers – the cousin, Walter Cox."

At eight o'clock that night, while I was working on a beer and reading a 1935 issue of *Dime Detective*, Eberhardt rang up my apartment. "Just thought you'd like to know," he said. "We got a full confession out of Walter Cox about an hour ago. I hate to admit it – I don't want you to get a swelled head – but you were right all the way down to the Mr Peepers angle. I checked with the housekeeper and the niece before I talked to Cox, and they both told me Murray called him by that name all the time."

"What was Cox's motive?" I asked.

"Greed, what else? He had a chance to get in on a big investment deal in South America, and Murray wouldn't give him the cash. They argued about it in private for some time, and three days ago Cox threatened to kill him. Murray took the threat seriously, which is why he started locking himself in his Rooms while he tried to figure out what to do about it."

"Where did Cox get the piece of steel?"

"Friend of his has a basement workshop, builds things out of wood and metal. Cox borrowed the workshop on a pretext and used a grinder to hone the weapon. He rigged up the slingshot this morning – let himself into the house with his key while the others were out and Murray was locked in one of the Rooms."

"Well, I'm glad you got it wrapped up and glad I could help."

"You're going to be even gladder when the niece talks to you tomorrow. She says she wants to give you some kind of reward."

"Hell, that's not necessary."

"Don't look a gift horse in the mouth – to coin a phrase. Listen, I owe you something myself. You want to come over tomorrow night for a home-cooked dinner and some beer?"

"As long as it's Dana who does the home cooking," I said.

After we rang off I thought about the reward from Murray's niece. Well, if she wanted to give me money I was hardly in a financial position to turn it down. But if she left it up to me to name my own reward, I decided I would not ask for money at all; I would ask for something a little more fitting instead.

What I really wanted was Thomas Murray's run of *Private Detective*.

# STAG NIGHT

### Marilyn Todd

*Marilyn Todd worked as a PA before setting up her own secretarial agency, but these days she writes full time. She is the author of the audaciously delightful series of mysteries set in ancient Rome, in the early days of the Empire. The first was I, Claudia (1995), and the series currently runs to six volumes. This is her second Claudia short story, but the first "impossible" murder.*

Fat and replete against the trunk of an ancient oak tree, the old boar suddenly snorted awake. What was that? Hairy ears pricked forward, straining, craning – but through the dappled shade they discerned only the liquid trill of a flycatcher, the rustle of foraging beetles. Unconvinced, he lifted his snout and sniffed the sultry air. Ripe woodland raspberries. Chanterelles. The musk of a badger who'd passed through last night. Familiar scents, which should have reassured a seasoned tusker – yet the bristles down his back refused to be pacified. Obedient to a million years of instinct, the old boar lumbered to his feet.

Then he smelled it.

*Dog!* Dog and . . . and – He was halfway up the bank before he placed the memory.

Man.

Dog and *man*, and as he shambled towards the brow of the hill, the glade behind him filled with alien sounds. The clash of steel. Shouts. Baying. And the sickening scratch and slither as frantic claws sought a purchase on the slippery leaf litter . . .

Only once did the old boar glance back. The hunt was gaining. One man was way out in front now, the sunlight off the hunter's long spear blinding the boar's button eyes. This was not his first brush with the enemy. Last time, when he'd stupidly allowed himself to be cornered, he escaped only by goring two dogs to death and leaving one human male badly gashed. Even then, someone shot an arrowhead into his haunch, but he'd been lucky. The barb dropped out as he ran and the wound quickly healed. Nevertheless, it was a lesson learned the hard way and today the stakes were higher than ever.

The first litter of the year had been raised, this was the mating season again. The old tusker had sows and his territory to protect . . .

And so it was, crashing through the undergrowth, with the smell of sweat and metal closing fast, that the wily boar prepared his defence—

## II

"Disappeared?" A little worm wriggled in Claudia's stomach, leaving behind an icy cold trail. "Cypassis, grown men don't vanish in broad daylight in front of a dozen other men."

But her tone did not match the strength of her argument – goddammit, the hunt was turning into a nightmare! First her bodyguard, Junius, was stretchered home, bloodied and unconscious, having lost his footing up on the ridge. Then two more men returned, wounded and weak. And now we hear that another member of the party's come a cropper . . .

"Exactly how is Soni supposed to have performed this feat of magic?" she asked. Dear me, the lengths men go to for a few yellowed tusks and some antlers to hang on the wall! "Taken wings, like Pegasus?"

"I know it sounds ridiculous," said her ashen-faced maid. "But apparently Soni was leading the hunt one minute and – pfft! gone the next. There was talk of a boar – perhaps that distracted him, maybe he took off alone, but the point is, he hasn't come home – and – and—" Cypassis spread her large hands in a gesture of helplessness. "And the worrying part is, no-one really cares that he's missing."

Yes, well, Claudia thought. They wouldn't be the first rich bastards not to give a toss about their slaves. "Have you questioned the bearers?" she asked. Surely they'd care that one of their number might lie at the mercy of ferocious wild beasts?

"That lot!" Cypassis sneered. "Within ten minutes of returning, they were too drunk to string two words together!"

"And Junius?" Claudia ventured. "I suppose he can't shed light on the matter?"

"Still no change in the poor boy's coma," Cypassis said sadly, and a nail drove itself in to Claudia's heart.

It was her fault Junius was on the ferry landing, poised to cross the River Styx. A lump formed in her throat and refused to subside. The trouble was, the young Gaul had been so *eager* to join this morning's hunt! She paced her bedroom floor and put the stinging in her eyes down to the brilliance of the setting sun. Max, the hunt's organizer had been against it from the start – Junius being a rank amateur and all that – but Claudia had prevailed, pleading her bodyguard's case that the last time he'd been hunting had been as a ten-year-old lad with his father, long before he'd become a slave through the wars.

Also, she wanted to give Junius a treat.

Max's hunts were famed the length and breadth of Italy – rich businessmen handed over small fortunes for the privilege of being one of the few – and if her bodyguard was to go hunting, dammit, he might as well go with the best! And now look. Waxy and pale, barely breathing, they'd scraped him up from the foot of a gully and carried him home on a stretcher.

"He'll be fine," she assured Cypassis. "I've seen these head wounds before, it's simply a question of time."

Liar. She'd never seen one in her life, had no idea whether Junius would pull through or not, but there was no point in both of them worrying themselves to a frazzle.

"And you can stop fretting about Soni. He was the star of today's show and, trust me, heroes don't pop like bubbles." Sweet Minerva's magic, to hear them talk, you'd think the boy was a god in the making, not simply another bearer Max had trained up!

"They said he led the hunt from the *start*," Cypassis said breathlessly. "Ran like a hare, according to one. Even uphill. Even weighed down with his javelin and arrows!"

Remembering his bunched muscles and stomach harder than permafrost, it was easy to see why Cypassis had been so eager to fulfil her errand of seeking out the young slave. Claudia glanced at the girl's bosom, bouncing and generous like puppies in hay, and knew that no man alive had yet rejected charms given so freely and yet totally without obligation. Cypassis loved 'em and left 'em, usually with dazed grins on their faces and memories warm enough to last them a lifetime, and Soni – red-blooded hunk that he was – would be putty in those broad Thessalian hands. If Wonderboy was missing, it was certainly not because he was hiding!

With Claudia's bodyguard out of action, who better, she'd thought, than Soni for a replacement? His skill, his courage, his cunning had been praised from the rafters, and let's not forget his strength and his stamina. Thus, Cypassis had been despatched to fetch him with a view to sounding him out, but that had been over two hours ago . . .

Across the atrium, where cedar-scented oil lamps hung from every pillar, where water cascaded down five circular tiers of a fountain and where marble athletes wrestled, boxed or weighed up the discus, an orchestra suddenly struck up, making her jump. Every note from the horns and the cymbals, the trumpets and drums dripped testosterone.

"Oh, no! The banquet!" Cypassis clapped her hands over her mouth. "I didn't realize it was so late!" She scurried across to Claudia's jewel box and rooted out a handful of ivory pins. "There's your hair to pin up, your shoes need a buff—"

"You concentrate on finding Soni," Claudia said. Any fool can give their sandals a rub on the back of her calves, and as for her curls – well, they'd simply have to get on with it. "Unless," she grinned, "you'd rather I approached someone else?"

Deep dimples appeared in Cypassis' cheeks, and some of the

colour returned. "I'll settle for Soni," she grinned back. "I hear he holds his women as tight as his liquor!"

Masculine voices boomed out in the hall, laughing, recounting, reliving, as they made their way to the banquet and Claudia clipped on earstuds shaped like a bee. Gold – naturally. A present from Max. She buffed up her armband, inlaid with carnelian and pearls, another gift, and fixed a filigree silver tiara into her hair. The tiara had been the first in this generous line, along with alabaster pots containing precious Arabian perfumes, intricate onyx figurines and rare spices all the way from the Orient.

Despite knives scraping against plate, silver platters being cleared and replaced, despite music and voices growing louder and louder, as though each had to compete with the other, Claudia made no move to join the men in the banqueting hall. Instead she leaned her elbows on the warm windowsill. The setting sun had sponged the enveloping hills a warm heather pink and the mew of the peacocks strutting on the lawn cut through the rasp of the crickets and the low-pitched croon of the hoopoe. Far in the distance, a wagon clattered over the cobbles, bringing home the last of the harvest. Down in the fertile lowlands of the Tiber, the wheat would have been threshed and winnowed a whole month before and would already be piled in granaries guarded by tomcats. But this was Aspreta, hilly and wooded, deep in the Umbrian hills.

This was the land of the huntsman.

Of one man in particular, Max – who had tamed the wild woods around his sumptuous villa to create vast landscaped gardens awash with artificial lakes, temples and grottoes. With watercourses rippling their way down the hillsides. With fishponds and porticoes and foaming white fountains, which the dying sun had transmuted into molten copper. A skein of ducks flew overhead, and the air was rich with the smell of freshly scythed grass and the merest hint of ripe apples. It was surely impossible for anything sinister to have occurred in this Umbrian idyll. There would, Claudia felt certain, be a perfectly simple explanation for Soni's disappearance . . .

She poured herself a glass of chilled Thracian wine and sipped slowly. Dear me, Max's lands were so vast, a girl had to positively squint to even *see* the hunting grounds from the villa. A smile twisted one side of her mouth. Oh, yes. This was definitely the right decision, accepting his invitation to stay . . .

She pictured her host, tanned and blond, lean and muscular, and knew that the sight of him in an open-shouldered hunting tunic cut high above the knee had fluttered many a female heart in its time—

Max. She rolled the name around on her tongue. Max. Ducatius Lepidus Glabrio Maximus to be precise, but known (for obvious reasons) as Max. And this fabulous estate was his. Or more accurately, was his and *his alone*. No wife – Max divorced wives like most men shuck peas – but more importantly, no heirs either. Claudia sighed happily. That's right. No little Max's running around, waiting to inherit the pile. Idly she wondered how quickly a girl might conceive, to redress this obvious imbalance . . .

The sun sank below the hilltops, swamping the valley in its garnet embrace, as swallows made their final parabolas over the lake. A perfect night for seduction, she reflected. A perfect night for—

A gentle tap on the door cut through her reverie. "Claudia?"

Many a fair-skinned man will suffer for a day outdoors in the sun, but the hunt had had the opposite effect on Claudia's host. It had deepened his tan, lightened his hair, and set off the white of his linen tunic to Greek god perfection.

"Are we too raucous for you, darling?" Aegean blue eyes ranged over the arch of her breasts, her exquisite jewels, the rich tangle of curls piled high on her head. "Is that why you haven't joined us?"

"Are you sure you want me?" she countered, as the door closed softly behind him. "I am, after all, the only female guest and . . . well, boys will be boys and all that."

"Janus, how could I not want you?" His eyes were smoky, his voice a rasp. "Claudia—" He opened his clenched fist to reveal a shining sapphire ring. "It's a betrothal ring."

Oh, Max. How predictable you men are!

"Oh, Max, this is so unexpected!"

For a minute he said nothing, and she watched the rise and fall of his magnificent chest. Then, as he was about to speak, the moment was broken when, emitting a cry not unlike a strangled cat, one of the peacocks on the lawn shook its tailfeathers then spread them in a brilliant display of iridescence to a pair of peahens who continued to strut with total indifference.

"Isn't it risky, allowing such precious birds to roam free?" Claudia asked, as he advanced towards her, his soft leather sandals making no sound on the dolphin mosaic. He smelled faintly – very faintly – of almonds. "Suppose your wild beasts fancied a nibble? They'd surely be the easiest of targets."

"In my business," Max whispered, his hand slipping round the curve of her waist, "a man can leave nothing to chance."

For a beat of six, Claudia watched as the drab peahens flapped in to the branch of a walnut tree, to settle down for the night. Then she gently removed his hand. The peacock's fantail fell limp.

"Over that hill –" Max swept the rejected arm towards a spot far on the horizon as though that had been its original intention "– runs a high perimeter fence with some pretty ferocious spikes on the top." He laughed. It was a melodious, gentle, masculine laugh, pitched seductively low. "The only threat to these beautiful birds is my cook. He claims their roasted flesh is delicious!"

And when searching blue eyes bored deep into her own, Claudia saw a man who was very much pleased with himself. Not smug, not self-satisfied. Just quietly confident, like a man who's achieved something special. Any other time and she'd have put that down to his counting all those lovely gold pieces that he'd fleeced off the men who were so noisily swilling his wine – had it not been for that little matter of the sapphire ring.

"That perimeter fence," he continued, "was erected not only to keep my hunting beasts in, but also to keep other animals out. Since I breed my own stock," he whispered, and she felt his breath on her cheek, "I can't risk weakening the strain by letting them loose with the native population. My bears, for instance, are particularly belligerent, and it's touches like these that give my hunts their – shall we say, *competitive* edge."

Claudia knew what he meant. Only last year, the scion of one of Rome's leading tribunes had died of wounds received whilst tangling with one of Max's famous wild wolves – an incident which, far from deterring others, had in fact doubled the hunter's trade. The greater the danger, apparently, the more men wanted a slice – especially rich men, who had never seen action in war. It was a pretty bizarre consequence for two decades of peace, but man's compulsion to dance with Death had made Max wealthy in the extreme. Who was Claudia Seferius to decry a system that worked?

"Somehow we seem to have drifted away," he said quietly, "from the subject of this little trinket . . ."

The drifting was not accidental. "Max, this isn't the time." Claudia kept her gaze on the horizon. "With the banquet in full swing, you should be there for your guests."

He lifted the back of her hand to his lips and kissed it lightly. "Beauty. Intelligence. And impeccable manners, as well. Darling, you and I will forge a brilliant alliance."

Claudia said nothing, and it was only when she was alone once more in her bedroom that she realized that, somewhere along the line, Max had pressed the betrothal ring into the palm of her hand. She slipped it on to her finger and watched the light reflect off its facets.

Hot damn, this was working out well.

### III

"To Claudia!"

"Hurrah for the lady!"

"A toast to Claudia Seferius!"

One cheer after another ran round the banqueting hall, drowning the flutes in the background. All this, she thought, because I was the one who put Max on to Soni at the slave auction – what *would* they have been like, had she suggested he purchase a whole string! Goblets chinked, roasts were carved, and plates of salmon and oysters and hazel hens were passed round as slaves continuously topped up the wine. *Except*. Claudia coaxed a scallop out of its shell. Except Max had only bought the one slave, and what a magnificent specimen he was, this Soni from Gaul.

As a Greek balladeer recounted Jason's triumphant lifting of the Golden Fleece, Claudia leaned against the arm of her couch and thought back to her first meeting with Max. Was it really only three weeks ago? So much had changed in that short space of time. She popped the scallop into her mouth and reflected that, without that chance meeting at the slave auction, she would not be here tonight as . . . well, as "guest of honour", shall we say, of the man on whom Rome's wealthiest citizens descended with greater regularity than a double dose of prunes, and where small fortunes changed hands for the gamble of turning wives into widows . . .

"See this?" A portly marble merchant on the couch opposite lifted the hem of his tunic to show his fellow diners a livid red scar. "The puncture wound was so bloody deep, I'm left with a permanent limp, but he was a plucky bugger, I tell you. Game to the end."

"Call that a scar?" The magistrate beside him yanked at his neckline to expose a long and jagged line, barely healed. "Compared to mine, yours is a scratch."

Much to the balladeer's confusion, all eight then began dismantling expensive clothing in a bid to compare injuries, each insisting theirs was the worst while swearing at the same time that their quarry was the bravest, the toughest, possessing by far the most guile – *ever*. The singer's words became drowned in the melee and Max shot a slow, but happy wink at Claudia. He had noticed, then, the ring which she wore on her finger . . .

Perhaps not as rich as Midas, hunts which were famed the length and breadth of Italy had enabled Max to not only purchase this fabulous villa stuffed with antiques and fine art, but lands that stretched to every horizon. No, sir. Claudia impaled a prawn on her knife. Without that chance meeting in Rome, Claudia Seferius would not be sitting here tonight with the man around whom Great Plans revolved . . .

Sometimes, she reflected, the gods on Olympus *do* smile down on mortals. Her mind drifted back. She'd been crossing the

Forum from the east and another man had been crossing the Forum from the west. Marcus Cornelius Orbilio, to be precise, but— But dammit the man's name was not important! What mattered was that the sweetest of all goddesses, Fortune (may her name live for ever), Fortune arranged for the slave auction to be held smack in the middle of their crossing paths. And Marcus Cornelius, god bless him, knew Max . . .

Marcus.

Marcus Cornelius.

Marcus Cornelius Orbilio.

Something skittered inside her when she pictured his face and she gulped at her wine to settle the jitters. Pfft! So what if he was tall and dark and – all right – not exactly bad looking? Who cared that his hair was wavy, except where it sometimes fell over his forehead, and that he wore the long tunic of a patrician? Marcus Whatsisname Thingy meant nothing to her. Nothing whatsoever. Less than zilch. In fact, the only reason her pulse raced now was owing to the lack of legality of certain scrapes she'd been in, seeing as how Supersnoop was attached to the Security Police.

In fact, that's what she'd been doing in the Forum, returning from some rather dodgy dealings, but hell, what other option is there, when merchants conspire to freeze a young widow out of the wine trade that she'd been thrust into after inheriting her late husband's business? Goddammit she'd married the old goat for his money, the least others could do is allow her to spend it. But no. Supersnoop's always there, sticking his investigative snout in her business, hoping to catch her red-handed. One day he'd cotton on that she was too damned smart for him, but in the meantime Marcus God-but-I'm-handsome Orbilio had, for once in his miserable life, come up trumps.

Until then, Claudia was stuck with relying on moneylenders, con-tricks and bluff to keep the creditors at bay, but Fortune was favouring more than the brave that day. She was favouring Claudia Seferius. It was obvious, from their frosty introductions, that the two men weren't exactly bosom buddies and chances are the meeting would have come to nothing – had Max not then excused himself, saying he needed to purchase a slave from the block.

"Just the one?" Claudia had asked. Normally people picked up quite a number. "One is hardly worth coming to Rome for."

Suddenly the opening was there for the blond hunter to score points over his aristocratic rival. "My lovely Claudia," Max had rasped, his eyes stroking her curves. "For me, one person is *always* enough." Arched eyebrows indicated the auction block. "Which of those slaves would you recommend?"

"It depends on what qualities you're looking for," she'd purred back, with barely a glance in Marcus' direction.

"In men," Max replied huskily, "it has *got* to be staying power. Don't you agree?"

"I wouldn't settle for anything less." From the corner of her eye, she saw the flush rise on Marcus' face and, noticing Junius jabbering away in his native tongue to a fellow Gaul beside the auction block, she found it delectably easy to add, "Personally, I've always found Gauls to have extremely strong backs . . ."

Marcus by that time was glaring daggers and Max, capitalizing on this sexual undercurrent, instantly bid for the Gaul, whose name, it transpired, was Soni. The same Soni who had done the hunt so proud today.

All in all, Claudia thought, things were going exceedingly well . . .

Especially that exquisite moment when, swallowing his pride, Orbilio enquired whether he might attend Max's forthcoming hunt. Knowing these were extravaganzas to die for, Claudia watched his face turn to thunder when Max oh-so-politely informed him that, alas, he only ever took ten men on a hunt and, he was so very sorry, but the next was fully booked . . .

As it happened, Claudia had been in the courtyard this morning when the hunt had set off. And there were eight men present, not ten. Dear me, she really must remember to mention that numbers thing to Marcus next time she saw him—

*If* she saw him again. The chances were, now he knew she was ensconced here with Max, he'd stop pestering her and stick his nose into someone else's illegal wranglings.

". . . I parried to the left, made a feint, dodged back to the right, but he was too smart for me . . ."

". . . I was impaled once, right here." More linen was bunched up to expose violated flesh. "Tossed me right on to my shoulder, he did . . ."

*He!* A wave of disgust washed over Claudia. They talk about boars, bears and wolves as though they were the hunter's equals, yet how often do you see stags armed with a slingshot, or running with their own pack of dogs? She looked round the banqueting hall, at watery red eyes, fists thumping on tables, where words were already slurring, and wondered how these cloistered, over-weight city-types would fare in one-to-one combat. With no bearers carrying their spears or their arrows. With no dogs at their side to hound wild creatures into panic. Just them out there, with only their wits to keep them alive . . .

"Having fun, darling?"

"Absolutely."

And what would it be like, living with a constant succession of drunken braggarts, day in and day out? Max coped admirably, but then the post-hunt entertainment – this orgy of showing off afterwards – was part and parcel of the package he sold. He was, she decided, a magician. An illusionist. A man who – *abracada-bra!* – turns fat slobs into young bucks, and should they look in the mirror back in Rome and see who they really are, then hey presto! All they need do is hand over more coins and suddenly they're heroes again. The "war" wounds were not only worth the pain and aggravation. They were fundamental to the whole process.

She recalled their return this afternoon, whooping and holler-ing in the courtyard amid carcasses of slaughtered beasts and a welter of blood-caked spears, concerned only with the glory of their own achievements and not a single thought for the wounded. Or a lowly slave, who hadn't come home . . .

"Is our hero not invited to join the celebrations?"

For perhaps a count of ten you could have heard the proverbial pin drop following Claudia's question, then everyone clamoured at once, most of them bursting into raucous, drunken, astonished laughter.

"You mean *Soni?*"

"Not in here, love!"

"Soni? Join *us?* Now that's rich!"

Claudia felt a tug on her elbow as Max gently steered her away from the couch. "That," he said, speaking through his forced smile, "was extremely embarrassing, darling. My guests comprise merchants, politicians – the cream of Roman society." He paused. "They do not take their dinners with slaves."

"They take their dinners with dogs."

"Cyclone and Thunderbolt are exceptions," he said, and his blue eyes were steel. "The other dogs remain in the kennels, and never, ever do *any* of the bearers join in the banquet."

"No matter how competent?"

"No matter how competent." She felt his whole body unstiffen. "I admire your liberated ideas about slaves and equality," Max said, winding one of her curls around his little finger. "But it's my job to give these men what they want, and believe me, they don't pay several thousand sesterces to dine with common slaves. Ah! The desserts."

Platters of melons and cherries, quinces in honey, almond cakes and dates stuffed with apple passed by in mouth-watering succession.

"Come sit by me while we eat, it gives me an excuse to slip my arm round your lovely smooth shoulder."

"Shortly," Claudia promised. "There's something I must attend to first."

"Of course." Max gently released the ringlet. "Hurry back, darling," he whispered, rubbing the sapphire ring on her finger. "Your beauty is all that makes the evening tolerable. Oh, and Claudia—"

"Yes?" She turned in the doorway.

"Betrothal rings go on the left hand, my love."


# IV

The room in which Junius lay was lit only by a single lamp of cheap oil, whose stuttering flame cast staccato shadows against the far wall. No mosaics covered his floor, no painted scenes brought bare plaster to life. Even the welter of bandages which swaddled his head seemed uncared for.

"You blockhead," Claudia whispered, wiping a bead of sweat from his cheek. "What did you have to go and get yourself beaned for?"

Dust motes danced in the wavering flame, and the scent of her spicy Judaean perfume blocked out the smell of caked blood. He was lucky, according to Max's physician, that no bones were broken, he'd taken one helluva tumble, but watching the shallow breathing and the waxy texture of his skin, lucky was not the first word which came to Claudia's mind. Her hands bunched into fists. Dammit, Max knew the terrain up on the ridge like the back of his hand, he should have warned Junius that shale was dangerous. The stretcher-bearers told her what happened – how he'd lost his footing under the weight of the weaponry he was carrying – but the fact that the accident happened at all was the problem. She should not have allowed Junius to go. Max knew he was inexperienced, dammit he should have insisted the boy stayed behind – but since he hadn't, then he should bloody well have taken better care of his charge!

She opened the shutter, allowing a small breeze to sport with the flame. From here, there was only a view of the cowshed, plus a hint of the moon through the oaks. Far away, a fox barked and she felt, rather than heard, the door open behind her.

"How is he?"

Claudia's heart flipped a somersault. It can't be. Sweet Janus, this isn't possible – She waited until her pulse settled down. "Lazy as ever," she said, not turning round. "But that's servants for you these days. Not a thought for anyone but themselves."

The baritone chucked softly, and her heart began to spin like a top.

"I've just come from the banqueting hall," Marcus said. "And I think it's a reasonable prediction to say there'll be some jolly sore heads in the morning."

Claudia did not smile. "Orbilio, what the hell are you doing here?"

"Oh." He rubbed a hand over his chin. "Just passing."

"On your way where, exactly?"

"Home."

She took in the long patrician tunic, the high patrician boots, the firm patrician jaw. And wondered why it was that little pulse always beat at the side of his neck when they were alone. "Isn't this something of a detour for you? Say, of some one hundred miles?"

His teeth showed white in the darkness and she could smell his sandalwood unguent, even through the pongs from the cowshed. Then the grin disengaged and his voice, when he spoke, was a rasp. "Claudia, you must leave, it's dangerous here."

She closed the shutter, and the flame straightened up. "It's the Emperor's fault," she told the comatose bodyguard. "He will keep subsidising theatrical productions, some of the drama's bound to rub off. Or could it be, Junius, that this aristocrat's simply jealous of Max?"

"This has nothing to do with—*Is that a betrothal ring on your finger?*"

"See what I mean?" she asked the welter of bloodstained bandages.

"It is! It's a betrothal ring! Claudia, you can't marry that man, he's worn out five wives already."

"Six has always been my lucky number."

"Fine!" He threw his hands in the air. "Fine. Do what you like, only for gods' sake, let's discuss this back in Rome. I have horses outside, we—"

Claudia spun round to face him. "Who the bloody hell do you think you are? My guardian? My husband? I'm not one of your flunkies."

"You've got me wrong—"

"I haven't got you at all, and that's the root of it. You're jealous as hell that I'm here with Max, and moreover, I intend to stay here, Orbilio. I have Great Plans for my future—"

"As Soni had Great Plans for his!"

Claudia felt the ground shift underfoot. "Soni?"

"Dammit, he was one of our best undercover agents." Orbilio slammed a fist into the palm of his hand. "When he failed to report back, I came looking – only I can't find him anywhere."

The floorboards became marsh, and Claudia slumped down on Junius' narrow pallet bed. "Soni's a *policeman*?"

"Of sorts," Marcus said. "Why?" She saw him stiffen. "Do you know anything about his disappearance?"

Claudia rubbed at her forehead. "Yes . . . No . . ." The room was spinning around her. Umbrian idylls crumbled to dust as she explained how Soni hadn't come home from the hunt.

"Shit." Orbilio sank on to the bed beside her, and buried his head in his hands. "That means someone rumbled his cover and took the opportunity of this morning's excitement to kill him."

But how? When? Obviously suspicious, Soni's idea of life insurance was to keep himself in full view of the hunt. How could he possibly have been eliminated without witnesses? What was it the head bearer had said? *Now you see him, now you don't*—

"What—" Claudia could not bring herself to say "who". "What are you investigating?"

Orbilio spiked his hands through his hair, and when he spoke, his voice was weary. "Max," he said slowly, "makes too much money for my liking. I mean, look at this place, Claudia. A man doesn't make legitimate millions from stag hunts and bears! So I started making some enquiries and . . ."

"And what?"

For a long time, the only sound in the room was the shallow breath of the unconscious bodyguard. Then: "I couldn't be certain – after all, the top echelon of Rome are visitors here. I had to tread softly. So I set up that business at the slave auction—"

Soni was a plant?

"Goddammit, Orbilio, you set me up, too!"

That was no accidental meeting, that day in the Forum – Supersnoop had been waiting for her! He knew where she'd been, she knew where she was going, and on top of it all, he damn well knew Max would be there. Both of them, plums for the picking!

"I needed you to add authenticity," Marcus said. "That way,

Max would suspect nothing and I'd have an undercover agent to sound out my theory." He scrubbed his eyeballs with his thumbs. "What the hell am I supposed to say to his mother?"

Several more minutes ticked past, and the candle guttered and spat.

"I think it's fair to say that, having rumbled Soni," Marcus said quietly, "they feared Junius was also a spy."

Nausea clogged Claudia's throat as she studied the comatose form on the bed. "His injuries aren't accidental?"

"Don't you think it's strange he has only head wounds? For a chap who supposedly tumbled down a ravine, it seems odd no bones were broken." He paused, before adding, "I'm sure they believed they were bringing his corpse home to you."

Tears scalded Claudia's eyes. Sweet Jupiter, that might yet be the case . . .

"What hunch were you working on?" Claudia asked, but her words were cut short as the door to the sickroom burst open, spilling bright orange light on to the floor.

"Seize him!"

Half a dozen men rushed into the room, grabbing a kicking, struggling, protesting Marcus and hauling him in to the corridor. Claudia shot after them, but there were too many and Orbilio was quickly bundled down the slave wing, watched by a blond huntsman with Aegean blue eyes.

"Where are you taking him?" Claudia demanded, but a strong arm shot out to restrain her.

"Stay out of this," Max growled. He needed both hands to contain his struggling fireball. "This is between Orbilio and me." To his men, he said, "Get a horse, tie him to it, then escort this *gentleman* to Rome."

"This is outrageous," Claudia hissed.

"I know," Max admitted. By the gods, she could squirm! "But I can't allow people to go around slandering me, particularly well-connected patrician policemen."

"He says—"

"I know what he says, and perhaps he genuinely believes I'm up to my ears in extortion or blackmail, but Jupiter's balls, I'm no gangster. I won't have the slur bandied about. Now, Orbilio's pride might be hurt, riding home hogtied, but it *will* only be pride."

He released her at last, leaving them both panting and red from exertion.

"What of his claim that Junius' injuries aren't consistent with a fall?" she spat, and to her astonishment, Max burst out laughing.

"Have you seen the bruises on that poor bugger's body? Junius hit his head on a rock, Claudia. Knocked himself out – and you know yourself what happens when drunks roll about. The body goes limp."

Actually, that was true . . .

"Orbilio's problem," Max chuckled, "is not that I might be a gangster, not even that I make more money than Midas by ripping off rich bastards hand over fist. His problem is, I have *you!*"

Claudia slipped off the armband, the one set with carnelians and pearls, and ran it round and round in her hand. "Like you have Soni, you mean?"

Aegean blue eyes flickered briefly. "Soni," he said, "is a slave. Yes, I own slaves. Yes, unlike you, I don't treat them as equals. And yes, I've been married five times, if that's what you're driving at, but I never think of women as chattels." He drew a deep breath. "Whether you believe me or not is another matter," he added.

"Whether I believe you," she said slowly, "rests on my seeing Soni, face to face, right this minute."

An astonished expression crossed Max's face. "Are you serious?"

"Is there a problem?"

"No. No, of course not," he stuttered. "It's just that . . . It's just that I'm jealous, my love. I know I can't compete with a stripling half my age and whose pecs are solid steel, but . . . well, I'm not in bad shape and, unlike a slave, I can give you wealth unimaginable—"

Not unimaginable, Max. I've imagined it many times.

"I want to buy Soni," she snapped, "not sleep with the boy."

If everything was above board, then there would be no obstacle. Max had denied her nothing so far.

"Ah." For a moment, he faltered, then the old seductive laugh returned as he led her back through the lofty atrium, rich with its cedarwood oils. "In that case, darling, you must accept him as a gift, with my compliments. May he serve you as well as he's served me."

Claudia felt a tidal wave of relief wash over her. For once, Supersnoop was wide of the mark. Junius *had* simply cracked his head on a rock before falling down that ravine! But what of Soni?

Suppose, she thought, trailing her hand in the fountain as she passed, Max had decided to satisfy himself that Soni was all that he'd seemed? Soni's refusal to comply with a criminal act would have blown his cover right out of the water, and suddenly Claudia was extremely keen to meet the man who had staged his own disappearance in broad daylight without arousing suspicion and yet had returned with a convincing explanation!

Glancing at Max, suave and easy, Claudia found no problem in picturing him up to his ears in racketeering, using the hunts as a front, both to make deals at the highest of levels and also to enforce any threats. He led her in to his office and clapped his hands. Immediately, a negro slave answered the call.

"Fetch Soni here, will you?"

"Master?" the old man's face creased in a frown.

"Stop dithering, man. Just fetch him. Shoo!"

Strong hands poured two goblets of rich honey mead, hesitating a fraction before handing Claudia hers. "You— You aren't going to marry me, are you?" Max asked quietly.

"No," she admitted. "I'm not."

His gifts were welcome, of course – the tiaras, the earstuds. But the Great Plan had been to ingratiate herself with his wealthy clientele and sign them up for hefty consignments of Seferius wine. Well-oiled (thanks to Max) they'd be pushovers for good, vintage wine and would be in no mood to worry about loaded prices. Especially when the alternative was this sickly concoction. Yuk. Two parts thunderbolt, one part bile, it was watered down with three ladlefuls of the River Styx. No wonder they had to add honey!

"Claudia –"

His voice came from down a dark tunnel, and the tunnel was closing in all around.

"Claudia?"

The voice echoed like stones in a barrel and her vision grew cloudy. Bloody mead! Filthy stuff.

"Is everything all right, darling?"

"Perfectly."

But everything was not all right.

Jellified knees gave way. Lights went dim. And Claudia collapsed in a heap on the floor.

## V

Was she dead? Was this blackness Stygian gloom? There were no three-headed dogs about, but there was barking. Claudia tried to lift her head, and found it had been glued to the floor. When she finally raised it, she wanted to hold it with both hands to prevent it rolling into the corner.

Except . . . Except her hands had been glued down, as well. She couldn't lift them. Ignoring the hammering inside her head, she tried harder. *And found not hangover lethargy, but ropes binding her tight.*

"I'm sorry it ended like this," said a familiar voice from the corner. The chair creaked when he stood up. "But you would keep pressing the subject of Soni. Oh, Claudia. If only you'd let it go."

Primeval creatures slithered down Claudia's spine. And how strange. High summer, yet her teeth were chattering . . . She struggled, but the knots were professional and her skin chafed itself raw.

"You know." When he knelt down, she could smell the leather of his boots. "You really are very lovely." He ran a hand gently down the length of her cheek. "Had your brain been full of feathers, we could have had a wonderful marriage and raised some damned good looking kids." He sighed at what was not to be. "Unfortunately, though, dawn is breaking. Time to leave."

Cold. So very cold. "People will come looking for me," she gabbled. "Marcus, for one, won't let it drop—"

"Ah, but this is terrible country for bandits. So many tragic accidents can befall a beautiful woman." Either Max had thought it out carefully during the night, or else he'd done this before. "Oh, don't look like that." He dragged her to her feet and propelled her to the door. "I'm not so hard-hearted that I won't pay for a lavish funeral tribute and endow the most magnificent of marble tombs you could imagine in a prominent position along the Appian Way."

"You spoil me."

The door cranked open and two hefty bearers pushed her into the pale pink dawn light. The barking escalated, and some of the dogs started baying. The sound, she realized with a chill, was caused by impatience. Their desire to get underway.

"Max?" Surely he wouldn't kill her? Not Max.

But Max clicked his fingers, and the bearers manhandled her into the courtyard, where eight fat city men in short tunics milled around. None looked in Claudia's direction. Terror gripped at her throat.

"Please—" She could hardly breathe. "Help me. For gods' sake, one of you, help me!"

Last night, these men were her friends. Business colleagues. They'd laughed at her jokes, given her contracts for rich, vintage wine.

A vice tightened round her ribcage. Oh, sweet Juno in heaven. It's not that they can't hear me. It's not that they imagine I'm drunk. They're not helping, for the simple reason they're busy. Checking spears and arrows and slings . . . And when they do glance around, it's not a terrified girl that they're seeing. *They're simply assessing the strength of their prey.*

The true horror of Max's hunting parties slammed into her, filleting every bone from her body. Finally she understood what had happened to Soni.

Why he was way out in front of the others.

*The slave, goddammit, was the quarry.*

That's why Max only wanted the one. Only ever the one . . .

"You'll never get away with it," she cried, as the cart bumped over the lawns. Past the peacocks. Past the watercourses. Past the shimmering man-made lakes rimmed with reeds.

"Wrong," Max replied, as they approached the wooded hunting grounds. Behind, the bearers loped along at a steady rhythm, their dogs straining at the leash. "All over the Empire, you'll find men bored with a quarter century's peace. Sons of warriors who've only ever heard about the clash of weapons, the bittersweet fear of hand-to-hand combat. And since they've never ridden into battle themselves, they hunt boar, they hunt stag, they hunt bear for their thrills and to affirm their manhood. Unfortunately, with some, that's not enough." Slowly, he reined in the horses. "Some seek a further dimension."

Aegean blue eyes scanned her face.

"Can you imagine how much these men are prepared to pay to hunt humans? Thousands, Claudia. Thousands upon thousands, and you know the best part? There's an unlimited market out there. Oh, I know you're going to tell me your clever friend, Marcus is on to me. He's suspected me for some time, but what can he prove? Nothing! Not one bloody thing."

Drawing a broad hunting knife, he cut through her bonds in a businesslike fashion. For how many others, she wondered, had he done this?

"You have intelligence, cunning and resilience, Claudia Seferius, you will be a worthy adversary." Max took her trembling chin between his thumb and forefinger. "Your tomb will do you credit, I promise."

Claudia spat in his face. "Go to hell."

"I probably shall," he agreed. "Now then. We always give the quarry a chance. Here's a slingshot, a javelin and a short stabbing dagger. Try," he whispered, glancing at the businessmen, "to take at least one of them with you."

Breath was too precious to waste on this son-of-a-bitch, her mind whirled like a cap in the wind. The estate was fenced in; the gates closed behind them; guards were posted; and ferocious spikes topped the perimeter fence. What the hell chance did she have?

"We normally give a count of a hundred," he said, "but seeing as how you're a woman, I think two hundred is fair—"

Though she had weapons in her hands Claudia made no effort to kill him. He'd be prepared, would only injure her, consigning her to a lingering death. She had no choice. She set off – a victim of the very men on whom, only last night, she had wished this particular fate.

Behind her, she could hear Max counting aloud. "Sixteen. Seventeen."

Father Mars. Mighty Jupiter. Can you hear me up on Olympus? Can you help?

"Twenty-two. Twenty-three."

*"Nobody move, you're surrounded."*

For a second, Claudia's heart stopped beating.

*"Drop your weapons, put your hands in the air."*

Then the breath shot out of her lungs. That was no Olympian deity. That baritone was quite unmistakable, even through the shell he used as his loudspeaker—

As one, fifty archers stepped out from the bushes, their arrowtips aimed at the group. Almost before the daggers and javelins had crashed to the ground, eight men began babbling. Explaining. Exonerating. Bribing.

"You all right?"

Claudia hadn't realized she had collapsed, until a strong hand pulled her up. Even then, her knees were so weak, the only way to stay upright was with his arm tight round her waist.

"Nothing better than a run in the country," she said, and it was odd, but her teeth were still chattering.

Orbilio grinned, and brushed the hair from her eyes with his thumb.

"I thought they'd run you out of town," she said.

"I was expecting some form of trouble," he replied. "Which is why I brought back-up." He paused. "It took a little persuading, but eventually one of Max's heavies told us of Max's plans for you. Hence the trap we were able to lay overnight."

Behind him, pleading, protesting, terrified merchants were rounded up – men of substance, yet men of no substance at all – while the bearers tried to explain how they were under duress to obey, that they got drunk to blot out the horror, that if they didn't participate, they would become the next quarry. For many years afterwards Claudia was able to recall, with bloodcurdling clarity, everyone's clamouring at once. *While not one word of remorse fell from their lips.*

"You know this won't come to trial?" Orbilio said, steadying her with his grip. "Senior politicians and influential businessmen on slave hunts? The scandal would de-stabilize the Empire in no time, Augustus wouldn't risk it."

"They'll get off?" The prospect of these scum swaggering free was almost too much to bear.

"No, no!" Orbilio was certain of that. "It's suicide for these boys," he said, leaving unspoken the fact that, in at least two cases, the exit would require a certain assistance.

The soldiers, meanwhile, were being none too gentle with their captives, yet throughout the whole ignominious defeat, one man had said nothing. Outmanned and outnumbered, Max surrendered at once, quietly and without fuss, and stood, hands bound in front of him, as his rich clientele and his poor bullied bearers were kicked in to the cart.

His passive acceptance alone should have alerted them.

"Shit!" shouted the captain of the archers. "After him!"

Sprinting through territory as familiar as his own back terrace, Max hurdled tree roots and obstacles with the grace and ease of a gazelle, heading deeper and deeper into the woods.

"Wait." Orbilio's voice was calm. His authority stopped the men in his tracks. "This is his ground, we can't hope to either catch or outwit him. Soldier!"

A burly archer stepped up. "Sir."

Orbilio relieved him of his dark yew bow and weighted it in his hands. Carefully, he plucked an arrow from the quiver. Sweet Janus, the white tunic was now barely a dot!

"Marcus," breathed Claudia. "Leave this to the archer." So many trees in between, it needed an expert!

"This," said Orbilio, notching the arrow into his bow, "is for Soni."

Claudia felt her heart thump. "I'm just as much to blame as you are," she said. "I know you put him up as a plant, but it was my urging that bought him his grave."

The bow lifted.

"This," he repeated, "is personal."

With a hiss, the arrow departed. Silence descended on the clearing – the men in the cart, the soldiers, Claudia, Marcus – watching as one as the arrow took flight. No-one breathed.

In front of them, the white dot grew smaller. Then, with a cry, Max fell forward. No-one spoke. Not even when Max hauled himself to his knees, then his feet, and then began running again . . .

The colour drained from Orbilio's face. "I winged him," he gasped. "Only winged him."

The arrow, they could see now, was lodged in his shoulder. Painful. But hardly life-threatening.

Orbilio wiped his hand over his face, as though the gesture might turn back time. Give him one more chance to make good.

Then—"Look!" Claudia pointed. Marcus followed her finger.

In the distance, a huge bristly boar came charging out of the undergrowth, tusks lowered. His furious snorting could be heard in the clearing. As though in slow motion, they watched as he lunged at the figure in white. They watched, too, as Max tried to duck, turn away, but the wily old boar had been there before.

This was the mating season, remember.

He had sows and a territory to protect . . .

# MR STRANG
# ACCEPTS A CHALLENGE

*William Brittain*

*William Brittain (b.1930), now retired but for many years a high school teacher, has been writing mystery stories for over thirty years, starting with "Joshua" (Alfred Hitchcock's Mystery Magazine, October 1964). He then began a series of delightful tales in* Ellery Queen's Mystery Magazine *which explored mysteries in the styles of various authors, starting with "The Man Who Read John Dickson Carr" (December 1965), itself a locked-room murder, and covering Ellery Queen, Rex Stout, Agatha Christie and Arthur Conan Doyle. By then he had published his first story featuring Mr Strang, a high school teacher with a gift for unravelling the unusual. The first was "Mr Strang Gives a Lecture" (EQMM, March 1967). By my count there have been over thirty Mr Strang stories since then, several of them impossible crimes, but unaccountably none have been collected into book form. Here's one of the most intriguing.*

*MONDAY: THE CHALLENGE* The 29 students in Mr Strang's classroom gravely considered the two sentences scrawled across the freshly washed blackboard:

> *All A's are C's.*
> *All B's are C's.*

"The apparent conclusion – that all A's are B's – does have a certain allure, a kind of appealing logic."

Mr Strang blinked myopically, his wrinkled face resembling that of a good-natured troll. Then he whirled, and his chalk drew a large screeching X through both sentences.

"Of course," he snapped, "it's also dead wrong. Its error can easily be verified by substituting 'teenager' for A, 'ostrich' for B, and 'two-legged' for C in the original premises. Thus, all teenagers are two-legged, all ostriches are two-legged, and therefore all teenagers are ostriches. I doubt you'd accept that conclusion."

"I dunno," guffawed a voice from the rear of the room. "Melvin's a teenager, and he looks like an ostrich."

Laughter, in which Mr Strang joined. The student's comment hadn't been spiteful, simply an attempt to inject humour into a period of intense mental activity.

Mr Strang's elective class in Logic and Scientific Method was one of the most popular courses in Aldershot High School. It was also one of the most difficult in which to enroll. Those students finally accepted – invariably seniors – had risen to the top of the academic ranks like cream in fresh milk. With these students, a teacher could pull out all the stops, being not so much an instructor as a participant in a free give-and-take of theories and ideas.

The politeness of the members of the class was tempered by their scepticism. They were willing to weigh and consider the most heretical hypotheses, mercilessly rejecting what they believed to be sham, hypocrisy, or incompetence. After each period Mr. Strang felt exhausted, yet exhilarated – somewhat like a runner who has just broken the four-minute mile. In teachers' heaven all classes would be like this one.

"Let us, then, consider the logical fallacy of undistributed middle," he went on. He drew a large circle on the blackboard with two smaller circles like staring eyes inside it. "If the large circle represents category C, and the smaller ones are A and B—"

He paused. In the far corner of the room three students had their heads together and were whispering earnestly. "We seem to have a rump session meeting over there," said the teacher. "Mr Cornish, Miss Doyle, Mr Lockley – what is it?"

There was a moment of embarrassed silence. "I yield to the

gentleman in the maroon sweater," Mr Strang said. "What's going on, Jerry?"

Jerome Lockley was tall, black, and beautiful. As he slowly uncoiled from his seat it seemed as if he wouldn't stop until his head hit the ceiling. Looking down from a height of over six and a half feet, he bestowed a sly grin on the old science teacher.

"Well, Mr Strang," Jerry began. "You understand we all dig the way you teach this class. I mean, you keep us hopping, but it's kind of fun. Like basketball drills. And you're a right guy personally. If somebody gets in a little trouble, you try to help out instead of just dropping the dime on him. So I wouldn't want you to take anything I say the wrong way."

"Take what the wrong way?" asked the teacher.

"Since we've been in this class we've hypothesized, syllogized, and organized. We've deduced, induced, inferred, and referred. Right?"

"Right, Jerry. That's what the class is all about."

"Yeah, but the first day you told us that all this logic stuff would help us in the real world." He jerked a thumb toward the window. "Out there, where it's all at. But so far all we've seen are little X's that are all Y's, and stuff about ostriches and diagrams like that one on the board."

"But there's still nearly seven weeks to go—"

Jerry shook his head. "Not good enough, Mr Strang." He pointed toward the boy and girl with whom he had been whispering. "Richie and Alice and me, we'd like to know right now if what we've been learning is really gonna help us, or are we just spinning our wheels in here. How about it? Did you mean what you said that first day, or were you just jiving us?"

"The last quarter of the semester is devoted to practical applications. But until you've learned the basic theories—"

"Right on, Mr. Strang. We dig that. But *you* know all those theories, don't you? I mean you could put 'em to use if you had to?"

"I hope so, Jerry. Although I must say that often emotion tends to—"

"Okay, Mr. Strang. Then prove it. Prove this logic of yours really works."

Mr Strang chuckled, but in his mind there was a twinge of foreboding. "And just what did you have in mind?"

The others in the class looked up expectantly at the tall boy. Jerry thrust his head forward, daring the old teacher.

"We want you to figure out how Simon Winkler was wasted."

Mr Strang reacted as if a bucket of cold water had been thrown over him. For long seconds he gazed at Jerry, speechless. "But that happened last summer," he said finally. "And even the police haven't been able to – I mean, there's no evidence really, that he was – uh – 'wasted.' I assume you mean murdered?"

Jerry shrugged. "Come on, man. Them two ladies was standing right there, weren't they? And the priest. As for the fuzz, what do they know? They never took this class, did they?"

In a daze Mr Strang shook his head. In the far corner Richie Cornish tugged at Jerry's sweater. "Sit down. He's not gonna try it."

"Sure he will!" argued Jerry. "Mr Strang's my main man. And he'll figure it out too."

"Half a dollar?"

"It's a bet."

Jerry turned back to the teacher. "Now you got this deduction scam down pat. And it's not like you've got no facts to go on. That case was on the front page in all the papers for weeks, and we all know you got a few connections with the local cops."

"But I can't just barge in and reopen a police investigation that—"

Jerry cocked his head to one side. "You can't, Mr Strang?" he asked cynically. "Or you won't?"

So there it was. The gauntlet had been flung down, the challenge had been hurled. All 29 students waited for Mr Strang's answer. The old teacher took a deep breath and then sat on his high stool, a foolish grin on his face.

"Very well, Jerry," he said slowly. "I don't guarantee any results, but I can try."

"Right on, man!" Jerry extended an arm rigidly, his fist clenched.

As the bell rang, the students left, the sound of their excited whisperings buzzing in the old teacher's ears. He slumped over the demonstration table, cradling his head in his hands.

"Vorticella!" he said harshly. "Leonard Strang, you are an old fool!"

TUESDAY: THE CASE Detective Sergeant Paul Roberts stood at the front of the classroom, looking about warily. The kids had been decent enough so far, but who could tell what they might be plotting? Who in hell ever knew what was going on inside kids' heads these days?

The only reason he was here was because he hadn't been alert enough to think of a plausible excuse when Mr Strang had called him yesterday evening to ask him to come to the classroom and discuss the Winkler case. Oh, sure, he did owe the old teacher a favour – many of them, in fact. But standing here in front of this group of sharp-eyed youngsters . . . Roberts envied Mr Strang his classroom cool.

The old boy had done his homework right enough. There was Father Raymond Penn over in the corner, the case's only un-biased witness. The young cleric's unkempt hair and bushy beard made him look more like a hippie than a priest, in spite of the black suit and collar. Roberts was glad he'd stopped by the precinct's records section to get the still-open file on the Winkler case. It wouldn't do to annoy Mr Strang by coming in unpre-pared. He cleared his throat loudly.

"Last July twenty-first," he began, "over in the Bay Ridge section of Aldershot, Simon Winkler died. The cause of death was a blow on the head – a fantastically powerful blow, since not only was the skull shattered, but two of the cervical vertebrae were crushed.

"Now Simon's aunts, Agnes and Lucille Winkler, were within a few feet of him when he died. Furthermore, they both had every reason to want him dead. And yet it's impossible that either of them struck him down. The police even investigated the possi-bility that the whole thing was an accident. But that was just as impossible. You see, we not only can't find out how the blow was landed, but also, whatever object struck Simon Winkler seems to have disappeared."

The students leaned forward like bloodhounds on the scent. "I don't have to worry about withholding information," the detective went on, "because there's nothing to withhold. By the time we're through here today, you'll know as much about the case as I do, and I was the man in charge of it. But the police are really stumped by this one. I guess the newspapers are too. All over the state they headlined it *The Weird Winkler Death*."

"That's all right," Jerry Lockley drawled. "Mr Strang'll figure out what really happened, with logic and all that jazz."

Roberts made a wry grin. "Just a word of warning," he said. "Although Lucille Winkler died last month of a stroke at the age of eighty, her older sister Agnes – an invalid in a wheelchair – is still alive, in a nursing home. So no rash accusations, okay? The laws concerning slander and defamation of character apply here just as well as anywhere else."

"Paul," said Mr Strang ingenuously. "We merely intend to examine the evidence and see where it leads."

"Oh, sure, Mr Strang. Just like you always do." A loud guffaw from the rear, and Roberts turned back to the class. "I'll just start things off by saying that at the time Simon Winkler came to call on his aunts, he was in the process of trying to take their house away from them by some kind of sharp legal ploy. The two old women hated his guts. They made no bones during the entire investigation about how much they despised their nephew. So Simon Winkler's visit to his aunts was hardly a social call."

He motioned to the priest. "Now I'd like to introduce the man who was actually present in the house at the time of Simon Winkler's death. Want to step up here, Father Penn, please?"

Father Raymond Penn came to the front of the classroom, where he used a finger to hook the white collar tab out of his shirt and undo the top button. To most of the boys the young priest seemed like a "right buy"; many of the girls found him adorable. He jammed his hands into his pants pockets and looked out at the class as if puzzled and bewildered by the human condition.

"By the time Lucille Winkler got in touch with me, Simon had already phoned her several times," he began. "Lucille had put him off with one excuse or another, but when it became clear that eventually she'd have to see him about who really owned the house, she set a date and asked me to be there. She wanted a witness present, you see.

"When I arrived at the Winkler house that afternoon, the weather was about as wet as it could be. Rain had been pouring down for the past few days and nights, and the weatherman had predicted more of the same. I banged the knocker on the front door and heard Lucille fumbling with the lock, but by the time it opened, my hat was just a mass of soaked cloth.

"Lucille took my hat and raincoat to dry them off at the stove in the kitchen. Since she also had to tend to Agnes in the wheelchair, she left me alone in the living room for quite some time."

He shrugged. "Matter of fact, I read three chapters in a book on fishing that was on the coffee table. I was just deciding whether I'd spent my next vacation catching bass in Canada or fishing for blue marlin off Mexico when she came back, wheeling Agnes in front of her. Gone about half an hour, I'd say."

Roberts looked significantly at Mr Strang. Puckishly the teacher wiggled his fingers.

"We chatted for a while," Penn went on. "Mostly about the weather. Lucille prattled on a lot about spending most of the previous dry week dragging the lawn sprinklers around that big back yard of theirs, and now here they had so much water it was like living under a faucet.

"Finally Agnes looked out the window. 'I think Simon has arrived, Lucille,' she said. 'We must have some tea.'

"Outside, Simon Winkler was getting out of a cab. From what I could see, he was about fifty or fifty-five years old."

"Fifty-four," interrupted Roberts.

The priest nodded. "But then I glanced back and noticed Lucille," he went on. "She was giving her sister the oddest look. Then she said, 'I'll put the water on.' She went out to the kitchen, but she was only gone for a minute or so."

Penn took a deep breath, and his eyes grew wide. "Now we come to the part the newspapers called weird. Me, I say it's downright eerie. You see, just as Lucille came back, there was a loud knocking at the front door, and Simon Winkler was shouting through it for someone to hurry and open up. 'Soaked to the skin!' I heard him yell. I felt sorry for him because I'd been through the same thing just an hour before. Lucille was fumbling with the bolt – she had arthritis in both hands – and I was wishing there were a window in the door so I could at least make a sign to him that we were opening the door as fast as we could, when" – the priest's voice grew low and sonorous – "when there was the sound of a dull thump from outside. That was followed by another sound – like something heavy sliding down the length of the door."

The students looked at him in rapt silence. This was what they had been waiting for.

"Seconds later we got the door open. And the rain poured in on us, because something was propping open the outer storm door." Penn pulled out a handkerchief and mopped his brow.

"The thing holding open the storm door," he continued, "was the body of Simon Winkler. He was lying on the front stoop with blood gushing from his head. There were some gardening implements on the stoop – a bushel basket and some other things – and the blood had stained them all red, even in the rain. I was numb. Didn't know what to think or do. Finally I felt for a pulse. There was none. Winkler was dead."

A pencil falling to the floor sounded like a cannon shot in the classroom.

"Well," said Penn, "I tried to get the women back into the house. But they just stood in the doorway, staring at the body. Finally I told Lucille to go inside and call the police. Agnes and I remained in the doorway looking down at the body. The rain was coming in, but it seemed almost obscene just to leave the body there without anyone – I mean—"

He swallowed loudly, mopped at his face with the handkerchief, and sagged into a chair.

"What hit him?" asked Richie Cornish.

Roberts got to his feet. "That's what we'd like to know too, young fella," he said. "It was at this point the police entered the case. The first patrol car that pulled up found Father Penn and Agnes Winkler looking down at the body at the doorway. A sheet was put around the body and the sheet immediately soaked through with rain and blood."

Roberts drew out a report form from the file folder he was holding and consulted it, speaking in a low voice: "I arrived on the scene at four thirty-five pm. We ran a grease pencil outline of the body on the stoop and then had the body taken to the morgue. By that time the door was closed again, but before knocking I looked around a little. There, on one side of the stoop, was a bushel basket with a handful of weeds in it, and a metal sprinkling can lying on its side. On the other side of the stoop was a shiny new pair of grass shears and a little trowel. And that was all."

The detective's expression was grim, and he stared almost belligerently at the class. "Each of those things weighed a pound or two at most," he snapped. "Sure, some of 'em could give a man a headache or even knock him out if he was hit with enough force. And the grass shears would have made a perfect stabbing weapon, except that Winkler wasn't stabbed. His skull was crushed like an eggshell. And dammit – excuse me, Mr Strang – there just was nothing around heavy enough to do it. We checked the stoop and walk for loose cement or to see whether a part of the wrought-iron railing might have been pulled away. Nothing."

He spread his hands. "There you have it. Oh, sure, we went inside and questioned Lucille, Agnes, and Father Penn. And we got the same story you heard just now. I even had the house searched. Neat as a pin, everything in its place. And absolutely no indication that someone besides the two women might have been living there, or hiding there, who could have done it.

"And now," he said, "let's take a look at the scene of the crime." The detective nodded at two boys at the rear of the room. One lowered the window shades and the other pressed the switch of a slide projector. A shaft of light lanced across the room, and on the screen at the front appeared a picture of an incredibly ugly house surrounded by what seemed to be acres of badly kept lawns and gardens.

"The Winkler house. It's off by itself on a private lane. Hipped roof, with three gables evenly spaced out along its upper section, well back from the eaves. Front door in the center, with a window on either side of it. Two more windows on the second floor. No fancy woodwork. Just a completely functional house."

"Looks like a big old barn," commented a student.

"It should," Roberts replied. "When Andrew Winkler – Lucille and Agnes' grandfather – had the house built, he used the plans of a barn. Andrew was as rich as Midas, but he was too cheap to hire an architect. In fact, the records show that he pulled some kind of financial gimmick so he didn't have to pay the builder more than half of what the job was worth."

Somewhere a student chuckled.

"When Andrew died," Roberts continued, "his son Jacob got the house. He added those three gables. According to the stories, Jake was something of a character. He showed his patriotism by flying a huge American flag he hung from that big pole sticking out from the centre gable there, and at the same time increased the family fortune by robbing the government blind back in Roosevelt's day."

"Oh?" said a boy brightly. "Was that Franklin D.?"

"No," replied Roberts. "Teddy. Anyway, Jacob Winkler had three children. Lucille and Agnes, and then much later, a boy who later became Simon's father. When Jacob died, he left the house and grounds to the two women."

He paused. "Are you getting all this straight?"

"Yeah, we're right with you," said Jerry Lockley. "But enough of this history jazz. Let's get back to the good stuff."

"Just a little more background. It seems that about a year ago Simon Winkler discovered a flaw in his aunts' title to the house and property. By that time the women had gone through nearly all their money. They lost a bundle in the stock market crash of '29. The house was about all they had left. But Simon saw an opportunity to get the house for himself, leaving Lucille and Agnes with nothing. A cruel, heartless attitude, of course, but in my business we come across that sort of thing all the time. Anyway, he wrote to his aunts outlining his position and indicating that within a short time he'd be fully prepared to take them to court over the ownership of the place unless they could reach some kind of settlement with him."

"And that's what the meeting last July was all about?" asked Alice Doyle.

"That was it. So you see, the women make perfect suspects as far as motive is concerned. But means and opportunity? No way."

The detective shook his head. "So there you have it. The death of Simon Winkler. Was it a perfect crime? Was it an accident? We just don't know. Frankly, this case seems immune to any logical approach. But I'd be very happy if Mr Strang could shed any light on it. I don't like cases that remain in the Open File." He chuckled. "And neither does the lieutenant."

Silence. Twenty-nine pairs of eyes looked expectantly at Mr. Strang who was staring off into space.

"Any questions?" asked Roberts finally.

Jerry Lockley's hand shot up. Roberts nodded in his direction.

"I been thinking, you know," said Jerry. "Couldn't those ladies have tossed something out of the window of that centre gable – something heavy? Whammo! Down it comes on ol' Simon's head. What about that, Mr Roberts?"

The detective shook his head. "First of all, both women were old and weak. They could hardly have lifted a heavy object, much less toss it out a window. And even if one of them managed it, the gable is set back from the roof's edge. The distance down from the gable to the eaves is about eight feet. So the object would have either made a hole in the shingles or stayed on the roof or rolled off the edge, smashing the gutter. Our investigation showed everything intact and nothing was found on the roof. And remember, both Agnes and Lucille were at the front door with Father Penn at the exact moment of death. Finally, any object heavy enough to smash Winkler's skull couldn't have landed very far from the body. But we found nothing."

Jerry sank back into his seat.

"What if a guy hit Winkler and ran away fast?" someone called.

"Uh, uh. A man – especially one carrying a heavy object – would have left tracks in the soft earth unless he went straight down the front walk. And that walk's long enough so that even an Olympic runner couldn't have gotten away before the door was opened and he'd be seen."

Silence.

"Anything more?" Roberts asked.

"Just one thing, Paul," said Mr Strang softly.

"What's that?"

"Was there a laundry room anywhere on the ground floor?"

Roberts screwed up his face, puzzled. "Yeah," he said finally. "Right next to the kitchen. A little room with an automatic washer at least fifteen years old. Why?"

"Did the laundry room have an outside window?"

Roberts consulted his folder. "A little one, yeah. But—"

"Thank you, Paul," said the teacher. "Thank you very much."

"Hey, you mean you've got a handle on this case?"

The teacher nodded.

"Well, give!"

Before Mr Strang could reply, the bell rang.

Over the excited humming of the students as they shoved their way toward the door, Jerry Lockley's voice rang out loudly.

"Well, all *RIGHT!*"

*WEDNESDAY: THE CONCLUSION* "Glad to see you back, Paul," Mr Strang began. "I'm just sorry Father Penn couldn't make it." He turned to address the class.

"The murder of Simon Winkler—"

"Wait a minute!" Paul Roberts called out. "I told you yesterday, without proof you can't accuse—"

"Oh, to be sure, but Winkler *was* murdered. By his aunts, of course, The problem is *how* they did it. And I hope to explain that today."

He pressed his fingers together thoughtfully. "Lucille and Agnes Winkler," he said. "Represented to us yesterday as a pair of sweet, frightened, rather doddering old octogenarians. And yet their grandfather did a builder out of his just payment, their father swindled money from the government, and their nephew was preparing to take the roof from over their heads through legal chicanery. From one generation to the next the Winkler family has not only been devious but completely without scruples. If only from the standpoint of heredity, can we expect less from the ladies?

"I say no! The method of murder was not only heartless, as all murders are, it was also devilishly clever – as might be expected from the descendants of Andrew and Jacob Winkler."

"Hardly proof, Mr Strang," said Roberts. "What about the weapon?"

"Ah, yes, the weapon. I was struck, Paul, by your description of the gardening tools at the front door. Would women who kept the house as neat as a pin – your words, Paul – have left those objects lying about? I doubt it. Furthermore, you mentioned a *shiny* new pair of grass shears. Shiny, after three days and nights of wet weather? No rust? Oh, come now.

"No, the tools were put there, probably just before Father Penn arrived, for just one purpose – to camouflage the murder weapon.

"Now what are the requirements for such a weapon? Basically it must be heavy – massive, in fact. Therefore we eliminate the basket, the trowel, and the shears. All too light."

He bent down behind the demonstration table and brought up an object that bonged as it hit the table's hard surface.

"A sprinkling can," he said simply. "Borrowed from my landlady and similar, I daresay, to the one you found, Paul. Weight, perhaps a pound or two. But—"

He moved the can underneath the curved faucet at one end of the table and turned the water on full. In a few seconds the can was brimming. Mr Strang hooked a spring scale to the handle and lifted.

"Fourteen pounds," he announced. "A massive club indeed. A weapon fit for a Samson. That's what struck down Simon Winkler. So heavy and deadly when full" – he emptied the water into the sink and tossed the can into the air – "and so light and harmless when empty."

"But—" Roberts began.

"How was the blow delivered? Jerry Lockley's theory of yesterday was close to the mark."

Jerry tapped his brow, but Roberts shook his head. "Mr Strang, neither of those ladies could toss something that heavy eight feet from the second floor onto—"

"No, Paul." The teachers finger traced a diagonal in the air. "It was eight feet from the gable to the eaves. But that's on a diagonal, down a sloping roof. The actual horizontal distance couldn't have been much more than four feet, maybe less."

"Even so, a can full of water being heaved four feet? By two old women who weren't even on the same floor? What are you trying to give me?"

"You're forgetting something. On that centre gable there was a means to suspend the can beyond the edge of the roof. Think, Paul. All of you. Think back to Jacob Winkler. Remember what—"

"The flagpole!" cried Jerry Lockley. "Hey, yeah. A can attached to the rope on that flagpole and pulleyed out to clear the roof."

"And since the pole was for a large flag, it would be fairly sturdy," nodded the teacher.

Then Jerry shook his head. "No way, Mr Strang."

"Why, Jerry?"

"Look, the can is hanging there, right? Maybe getting full of water from the rain. But you want us to believe it just happened to break loose at exactly the right time? I ain't buying that."

"Of course not. You see, when the can was hauled out to the end of the flagpole, it was empty. And the rain was simply a cover for what really happened."

"Huh?"

"What did Lucille Winkler tell Father Penn she'd been doing the week before the rain?"

"Moving lawn sprinklers. So what?"

"Hoses," said the teacher. "Think of the lengths of hose required to water that huge yard. Put together they'd make an incredible length."

Jerry's finger moved upward and then horizontally, making an inverted L in the air. Then a broad grin split his face. "That's why you asked about the laundry room, ain't it, Mr Strang?"

"You mean—" Roberts began.

Mr Strang nodded. "Imagine a length of hose attached to a faucet in the laundry room – a faucet which had to be threaded to accommodate the washing machine and to which a garden hose could therefore be attached. Imagine that hose leading out the laundry window, up the rear of the house, through the upper hallway to the middle gable in front. Think of it snaking out along the flagpole with its open end directly over a sprinkling can hanging there."

"I see what you mean," said the detective. "But you still haven't answered the boy's question. How could the can be made to break loose at exactly the right time?"

"As I said earlier, the gardening tools were out of place, considering the weather," Mr Strang answered. "But there's another incongruous element here, Paul. Do you recall what Father Penn was reading while waiting for Lucille in the living room?"

"Yeah, a book on fishing. So?"

"In a house inhabited by two aged spinsters? Highly unlikely reading material, wouldn't you say? No, that book was in the house for a specific purpose."

"What purpose?"

"Research. On fishing line."

"Huh?"

"Fishing line," Mr Strang repeated. "It's the one type of string or cord that's made to extremely close breaking tolerances. That's so those who catch fish on lighter lines will receive more credit for the skill than those who use heavier tackle. And there's a line which breaks at a strain of twelve pounds. The breaking strain is precise to within an ounce or so. I verified that yesterday with a call to Morey's Sport Shop."

Mr Strang preened, brushing at the wrinkled lapels of his jacket as if he were wearing regal finery. "In summary, class – Paul – here's how the murder must have been accomplished. The

Winkler women invited Simon to call on a day when heavy rain was a certainty. That morning Lucille lowered a long length of hose from an upstairs rear window to the window in the laundry room and attached one end of the hose to the tap in the laundry room. The other end was led to the front center gable, where both hose and sprinkling can were tied to the flagpole rope by the same piece of twelve-pound-test fishing line. This apparatus was hauled out to a point directly above the front stoop. The sheer wall of the house, which left neither Father Penn nor Simon Winkler protected from the pelting rain, also had nothing to divert the can in its fall. Oh, I'm sure Lucille tested the rig several times in previous weeks to get the trajectory exactly right. Just as I'm sure she tested the amount of time it took the can to fill to a point where the line would break.

"On the appointed day the sisters invite Father Penn to visit – the perfect, incorruptible, unimpeachable witness. Finally the three of them see Simon arriving. At that point Agnes suggests tea. Why? As an excuse for her sister to leave the room, of course. Then the sisters had their private little joke."

"What joke?" asked Roberts.

"You'll recall that as Simon was getting out of the taxi, Father Penn noticed a strange look which passed between the ladies. And then, what did Lucille say to Agnes?"

"Why—" Roberts's eyes widened. "It was '*I'll put the water on*'."

There was a collective gasp from the students.

"I see you catch my meaning," said the teacher. "On her way to the kitchen Lucille enters the laundry room and turns on the tap to a degree determined by earlier practise. As Simon arrives at the door, the can above his head is filling."

"Wouldn't he have seen it hanging there?" asked Roberts.

"Unlikely. In a rainstorm the tendency is to lower the head into the collar of the coat." Mr Strang proceeded to demonstrate. "Inside the front door Lucille fumbles with the bolt. After all, the timing may not be absolutely perfect. She must wait for the can to drop.

"At length it does, smashing into Simon's skull with almost the force of a cannonball. The can drops to one side, spilling its contents onto the already soaked earth, and lands innocently among the strategically placed gardening tools. The hose above snaps back to the roof, and its stream of water sluices across the shingles and into the gutters, joining the torrent gushing down the leaders."

"But weren't those two taking a big chance?" Roberts asked. "I mean, what if Simon had moved just a little bit to one side or the other?"

"Not too big a chance," was the reply. "You see, Simon had to open the storm door to get at the knocker. Now when he heard Lucille fumbling with the lock inside, it would be instinctive for him to hold the storm door open so he could get inside in a hurry. And at that point his position would be as predictable as the phases of the moon."

"But wouldn't we have seen that hose draped through the house when we came to investigate?" asked the detective.

"Probably – if it had been left in place. But Lucille went back into the house to call the police. I suspect that it was then she turned off the water in the laundry room and disconnected the hose. Then she slipped upstairs and dragged the rest of the hosing through the house and pushed it out the rear window. Once it fell to the ground out in back, it became just an innocent length of rubber tubing."

The old teacher made a stiff but elegant bow to his class. "Alpha and omega," he said, grinning. "Do any of you have any questions?"

There was a clinking of coins followed by Jerry Lockely's whisper: "Pay up, Richie. I told you he'd come through."

For several moments Roberts considered Mr Strang's solution. "It hangs together, I'll say that for it," he announced finally. "Weird, like the papers said, but that had to be how it was done. Only—"

"Only what, Paul?"

"How do we go about proving it?"

"Is that really necessary?" Mr Strang caressed the briar pipe in his jacket pocket. "I mean with Lucille already dead and Agnes in a nursing home with little time left—"

"Oh, I wouldn't take any official action. I'd just like to know for my own satisfaction. And to be able to close out this case."

"Perhaps you might begin by checking the local sporting and camping stores. Lucille must have purchased that fishing line somewhere."

The detective patted the teacher on the back with a massive hand. "Mr. Strang, you're something else. I don't suppose you'd ever consider taking up police work on a full-time basis."

"Sorry, Paul. My class and I have an appointment with the fallacy of undistributed middle." The teacher drew a large circle on the board with two smaller circles inside it. "And we're three days late as it is."

# THE LEGS THAT WALKED

## H.R.F. Keating

*H.R.F. Keating (b.1926), known to his friends as Harry, is best known for his novels featuring the Bombay detective Ganesh Ghote. The very first of this series,* The Perfect Murder *(1964), which won an Edgar Award as that year's best first novel, included an impossible crime involving the disappearance of a one-rupee note, though* Go West, Inspector Ghote *(1981), set in Los Angeles, involves a much more gory impossible death. Keating is also a well-read student of crime fiction and has written several reference books about the genre, such as* The Bedside Companion to Crime *(1989), and he knows his way around the impossible crime field. His books and stories have an irrepressible sense of humour, which is much evident in the following story, which I'd classify as a "locked-tent" mystery!*

The Deputy Commissioner looked at Inspector Ghote standing at alert attention in front of his wide semi-circular desk with its piles of papers, each held down under the breeze of the overhead fan by a round silvery paperweight bearing his initials.

"You're a man who admires our Indian classical music, Ghote?" he said.

Ghote experienced a washing-over wave of absolute puzzlement.

"No, sir, no, not at all," he answered with the truth almost before he had gathered himself together.

The Deputy Commissioner continued to look at him, blank-faced.

"You are a first-class connoisseur of same, isn't it?" he asked again, each word heavy with meaning.

And now Ghote ceased to be puzzled.

"Yes, sir, yes," he replied. "Yes, I am."

"Good man. Right, I am sending you to the Annual Festival of the Indian Music Society this evening, out at Chembur. Just keep an eye on things, yes?"

Puzzlement returned.

"Sir, what sort of things it is?"

The Deputy Commissioner frowned.

"Just go there, Ghote, and— And – And keep your eyes open."

"Yes, sir."

Should I leave now, Ghote asked himself. Should I just only click heels to Deputy Commissioner sahib, turn smartly and march from his cabin?

But, he thought then, if I am going out to this festival and fail to see whatever I am meant to be keeping my eye on, then that will be worse than seeming not to understand here and now.

"Sir," he said, "can you be telling anything more?"

The Deputy Commissioner brought his lips hard together in a puff of barely suppressed fury.

"Very well, very well," he snapped. "So, listen. It has just come to my attention – never mind how – that Gulshan Singh, our damned Number One ganglord, believes something which the police should take note of will happen out at the festival this evening."

"What sort of *something*, sir?" Ghote asked, before he realized that the Deputy Commissioner had already said more than he wanted to.

"Something, Ghote. Something. Do I have to dot every *i*, cross every *t*?" A glower at the twirling fan above. "Well, I suppose it may be relevant that tonight's singer is, as it happens, the daughter of Vasudev Kalgutkar, otherwise known as plain Va-subhai."

"The Number One ganglord?" Ghote could not help exclaiming, acutely aware of the contrast between the high-class culture event he was being sent to and the murky world of the city's gangs. And then in another heart-sinking moment he realized that the Deputy Commissioner had already given the Number One title to Gulshan Singh.

"Yes, yes. Vasubhai," the Deputy Commissioner answered, mercifully unaware, it seemed, of Ghote's unwitting rival claim. "And Vasubhai, let me tell you, had the damn cheek a couple of weeks ago to send me – myself, Deputy Commissioner, Crime Branch – an invitation to the recital, or whatever it is, some damn daughter of his is giving tonight. So I am sending you there, Ghote. To keep your damned eyes open. Yes?"

"Yes, sir."

Nevertheless out at the recreation ground at Chembur that evening, shortly before the swift onset of darkness, Ghote was still conscious of not knowing much more about what to keep his eye on than he had done in the Deputy Commissioner's cabin. Yes, most probably the place to watch was the gaily coloured tented shamiana under which *The Beauteous Bhakti*, as according to the posters Vasubhai's daughter was called, was to sing. At no doubt interminable length. Whatever it was that had caused Vasubhai's deadly rival, Gulshan Singh, to hint that a police presence would be needed was most likely to happen there. So far, so good.

Ghote had already taken every sensible precaution that occurred to him. Two tough constables had been posted at the entrance to the fenced-off audience area with its rows of slatted wooden chairs. Along each one of those rows he had marched himself, looking for anything that might possibly be suspicious. He had trodden over every inch of the luxurious carpet, supplied no doubt by Ganglord Vasubhai, on which Bhakti was to sing. But he had made no discoveries at all. He had even traced the thick black cable supplying the lighting for the evening's performance all the way back to the generator gently throbbing on a truck in the road outside. But, again, there was no sign of anything untoward. Only, at the far side of the deserted recreation ground a mali was urging on a bullock pulling an ancient lawn-mower. Peace under the still light, cloudless sky.

The beauteous Bhakti was to put on her costume in a small dressing-room forming the back part of the shamiana. Going into its darkened shade, Ghote saw the room was as bare as it could possibly be. Its floor was no different from the rest of the neatly mown grass all round. Its walls were the canvas of the shamiana, supported at their corners by thin poles. A number of these, apparently unneeded, protruded indeed from a small green tarpaulin in one corner. But, besides this, the little room contained nothing but a bare trestle table, a single little gilt chair and, on a stand, a full-length mirror in which Bhakti could make sure she was truly beauteous before coming out from its single doorway to sing.

Satisfied, Ghote as a last precaution made a careful inspection of the rear of the whole shamiana. All the lower edges of its colourful canvas, he found, were well pegged into the ground. Its roof was firmly sewn down. Beyond any doubt no one could creep in that way so as to – Was this what Gulshan planned? – attack the beauteous Bhakti. Of course, when eventually Bhakti stepped out someone could perhaps shoot her from a distance. But, if this was what was to happen and not something else altogether, bar looking out for any places where a marksman could hide, there was nothing sensible to be done.

Ghote had hardly sat himself down to wait and wonder at the end of one of the rows of wooden chairs when a big all-white Contessa came motoring fast across the grass and up to the entrance gate. Its driver brought it to a fine screeching halt, and from it stepped none other than Ganglord Vasubhai, a somehow impressively powerful figure, despite his short, almost squat frame made all the more arrogant by the brick-red safari suit he was wearing. He was hastily followed by one of his bodyguards carrying a small suitcase, his flapping kurta barely concealing a pistol holster.

Ghote jumped to his feet and ushered the ganglord past his two solid constables.

"Vasubhai sahib," he greeted him. "You are remembering myself, Inspector Ghote, Crime Branch?"

The ganglord confronted him, contriving to look down at him although in fact he was a little the shorter.

"Yes, yes. Ghote. Once, when I was very young, you took my knife from me. My best and sharpest knife. Forgiven now. That was long ago, and I have had many others since. But why is Deputy Commissioner sahib not here? I was sending invitation, full-colour picture of my Bhakti, plenty-plenty gold lettering, red silk string also."

"Deputy Commissioner is sending myself in advance," Ghote lied. "To be making sure everything is hundred per cent in order."

"Fine, fine. And he is coming himself? In good time also?"

Ghote thought it wisest to avoid a direct answer.

"But, excuse me, Vasubhai sahib," he said quickly. "If I am to be doing my duty to my level best, I must be asking to see inside that case your bodyguard is carrying."

He feared that the ganglord would be too conscious of his own dignity to agree. But he need not have worried.

"Good, good. Maxi precautions. One very fine dancer is to perform here, each and every thing must be fully pukka."

The surly, silent bodyguard planked the suitcase on the ground and opened its catches. A magnificent green Kanchivaram sari was revealed.

"Yes, I may take inside?" the ganglord asked, picking up the case the bodyguard had snapped closed.

"Certainly, certainly."

Ghote waited at the edge of the big carpet, the bodyguard a stony pillar beside him. He decided to take the opportunity to give the whole area one more careful scrutiny. Was it Vasubhai that Gulshan Singh was planning to kill here? Was that what was going to happen? But, he thought, it is not very likely. There are rules to their game. Neither top gangster would get rid of his rival directly: doing so would bring instant and equal reprisal. Only gang members at the bottom of the heap were expendable.

So, what was to happen after all? Seemingly nothing.

There followed a terrible thought. Had the Deputy Commissioner become alarmed for no good reason? And how would he tell him, if it was so, that he had been tricked?

Minutes passed. Ghote began to wish that Vasubhai would

come out of the dressing-room. It would be something if he could be sure where the ganglord actually was. But no doubt the beauteous Bhakti's doting father was taking his time to arrange that Kanchivaram sari to its best effect, draping it perhaps first across the bare wooden table and then over the little gilt chair. And next changing his mind and doing it the other way round. He even might be holding it up against his ugly brick-red safari suit and looking at himself in the tall mirror.

"Vasubhai must be very-very proud of his daughter," he said to the hulking, silent bodyguard.

The fellow simply grunted by way of answer.

Ghote took another look all round. A few early comers were making their way across the neatly mown grass towards the entrance gate, the women in their best, bright glowing saris, the men less colourful in smart shirts and trousers. Behind them the musicians had also arrived, a drummer with his pair of tablas, a woman who would pluck the droning accompaniment from her tall-necked, deep-bowled instrument, a big fat man lugging his heavy, much decorated harmonium.

Then, bursting out from between the canvas flaps of the dressing-room entrance like a bull released from its stall – or a bullet from a gun even, Ghote thought – Ganglord Vasubhai took two striding paces out on to the big carpet and stopped dead.

"Inspector, Inspector. Something you must be seeing."

There was such a note of urgency in his voice that Ghote could not stop himself running across.

"Inside, inside," Vasubhai yelled at him, voice hoarse with emotion.

Ghote, going past him towards the dressing-room, found himself recording that a thick sheen of sweat had sprung up all over the ganglord's formidable face.

The moment he broke through the entrance curtain behind him he understood why Vasubhai had been so alarmed. Evidently for some reason or other he must have flicked back the green tarpaulin on the bundle of unused tent poles. And he had revealed that more than tent poles were tucked away there out of sight. He had revealed a body.

Ghote had immediately smelt blood.

But, going closer, he saw that the corpse had, in fact, been strangled. The mark left by the cord was unmistakable. The dead man was small and utterly nondescript in appearance. His face, Ghote thought with a quick flick of pity, could be that of a hundred, of a thousand, other people. Not a single distinguishing mark. Nor was what he was wearing any more an indication of who he might be, just a simple, much-stained white banian vest and a pair of equally dirty khaki half-pants. But, blotting out everything else, was the monstrous fact that, right up close to the bottom of those greasy old khaki shorts, both the man's legs had been cut off.

It was from the two hacked-off stumps, Ghote realized, that the smell of blood must be coming. But in that case – the thought came crashing in – it must have been Vasubhai himself, inside the little room for longer than expected, who was responsible. Certainly, if the dead man's legs had been cut off before Vasubhai had gone into the dressing-room he himself would have smelt blood when he had taken a glancing look at the heap of tent poles under the tarpaulin.

Why, why, he cursed himself, had he not done what Vasubhai must have done and lifted the tarpaulin to make sure nothing suspicious was under it? But he had not. There had not seemed to be any reason to lift up the sheet when the ends of the poles were projecting from it, though now it was plain there had been many fewer of those than it had seemed. The ones scattered now on the grass must have been carefully arranged round the body of the small man whose corpse had been put in the dressing-room. For some reason? For what reason?

And why had this man been strangled, this scrawny little figure, who might be any one of a thousand, no, of ten or twenty thousand other almost anonymous people going about the city scraping out some sort of a living? Certainly his murder was not going to be a case for the elite Crime Branch. The local police would have to carry out some sort of an investigation, though there was almost no chance that the murder of such an almost faceless victim could be tied down to some equally anonymous killer.

Unless . . . Unless the killer could possibly be Vasubhai, there for so long in the little darkened dressing-room? But, no. No, that little insignificant corpse must have been put under that green tarpaulin long before Vasubhai had entered.

But Vasubhai, did he still carry the sort of knife he always had so long ago? Very likely, though if so it was well concealed now. So, demand to search him? Not all that easy a thing to do. Vasubhai, ganglord though he is, is definitely a man of influence in this crime-dominated city of ours. Politicians by the dozen in his pocket. Offend him and I could find myself posted to the Armed Police in some distant, distant part of the State. All right, if it was plain he had committed a murder, I would arrest the fellow here and now. But it is not, not at all.

In any case, if he was busy in here hacking off the poor blank-faced victim's legs, why should he have done such a thing? And, more to the point, much more, where on earth are those legs now? Or, rather, where in this little room are those legs?

Ghote took a deep breath and gave the whole small canvas-walled place a careful inspection. But, even before he had begun, he had been all but certain he would find nothing. There was nowhere at all under the canvas roof where any objects as evident as two human legs could be kept out of sight. Not under the bare table. Not behind the solitary standing tall mirror. Not beneath the little gilt chair. Nor among the litter of tent poles beside the body. There was not the least sign either that, somehow, the well-pegged edges of the canvas had been prised up enough for Vasubhai to have thrust the legs outside, or even any knife he might have had.

Close inspection will be necessary fully to confirm that. But, peer as I may at the pegs and the grass beside them, I am damn sure I will find no signs of disturbance.

He took another good look at Vasubhai, still standing just inside the entrance. One thing was patently evident: the fellow was certainly not holding two such bloody objects as those legs. Nor, after rushing out of the dressing-room, had he had any opportunity whatsoever to have hurled them one after another anywhere out of sight. And nowhere in that brick-red safari suit could he possibly have concealed anything as bulky as two human legs, however short in stature their owner.

Wait. That suitcase. But surely it must be altogether too small?

He strode across to where it had been put on the bare table and flicked it open. And there was the gorgeous Kanchivaram sari, just as he had seen it before. He even plunged his hand in, for all that logic told him it was a ridiculous act, to see if the legs were inside, shallow though the case was. But, if there were no legs, there was something else. There was a long-bladed knife.

But it was, as far as a single hard look told, unstained by any blood. And, of course, it could have been in there untouched the whole time.

Ghote cursed himself. Why didn't I make a thorough search of this case when I was first been shown its contents? But there was no reason why I should have done. I was not at all knowing there was a body inside the room here, or that somebody was going to cut off that anonymous fellow's legs? If they had? If Vasubhai has? But, if, if, if he did, where are the legs? Where?

All right, make one final, final check.

Calling to one of the constables by the entrance gate, Ghote quietly told him to keep a strict watch on the waiting ganglord. Then a quick race round the whole exterior of the shamiana.

But it served only to confirm beyond any possibility of doubt that the dead man's legs had not been somehow pushed out into the open.

Ghote gave a great sigh.

Only one thing to do now. From his back trouser pocket he pulled his mobile and swiftly tapped out a number.

"Deputy Commissioner sahib? Ghote here, sir. At the music festival. And, sir, there has been a murder. Sir, with one most hard to explain circumstance. Sir, you must come."

The Deputy Commissioner came. But not alone. When over the air Ghote had answered all his questions he had plainly come to the conclusion that the extraordinary circumstances required extraordinary measures. So, there was the Crime Branch-trained search team, and the Branch dogs, Akbar, Moti and Caesar, with their handlers. There was Sergeant Moos, in charge of Head-quarters Fingerprint Section. There was even someone Ghote had seen only once before, the Deputy Commissioner's wife's favourite guru, Swami Mayananda, believed to have mystic powers far beyond the everyday.

Snapping out commands, the Deputy Commissioner rapidly put everyone to work. Each square inch of the grass floor of the dressing-room was examined by the hands-and-knees searchers. The carpet outside was equally subjected to a comprehensive patting examination. Akbar, Moti and Caesar were set to tugging their handlers here, there and everywhere, sniffing and sniffing. At the entrance gate the handful of early arrivals were each subjected to questioning, even though Ghote had assured the Deputy Commissioner that none of them had penetrated the fenced-off audience area. The musicians were body-searched from head to foot, although they, too, had never come beyond the surrounding fence. Sergeant Moos, crouching and kneeling, stretching and peering, spread clouds of his dark and light dusting powders over every surface he could find, likely and unlikely. Everywhere there was buzzing activity. Only the swami, who ignoring the Deputy Commissioner, had sat himself down cross-legged beside the neglected body of the nondescript victim and had entered into a trance, provided a small aura of stillness.

But no results of any sort emerged.

"Damn it," the Deputy Commissioner shouted eventually. "That man's legs are somewhere. Somewhere. Find them, find them. The damn things can't have just walked."

Then he realized the dreadful pun his fury had caused him to perpetrate, and, for want of a better person to vent his rage upon, directed a glare of unrestrained ferocity towards Ghote, who, after having on the Deputy Commissioner's own orders escorted the Beauteous Bhakti's father to wait in his car, had placed himself on one of the audience chairs in the back row. Solitary and ignored, he had sat there waiting, feeling all he could do was to keep an eye on the two constables keeping their eyes on the brick-suited ganglord.

At last Vasubhai rolled down a window in the big Contessa, its engine softly running in order to operate the air-conditioner; driver and bodyguard two stone-still presences in the front seats.

"Deputy Commissioner sahib," he called out. "My daughter would be coming at any minute. She is late already. What to do?"

The Deputy Commissioner shot him a glance, still sparking with fury.

"Oh, take her back home, man," he shouted. "Take her back home. You are not thinking she will be giving her recital now, are you?"

"No, no, Deputy Commissioner. Out of question, a singer of my Bhakti's status. So I will be saying goodbye itself."

A tap on the shoulder of the Contessa's driver and the engine was revved up.

And then Ghote jumped from his chair. With a wildly launched leap he vaulted the fence behind him. And, as the ganglord's big car began to move off, he flung himself into its path.

"Stop," he shouted. "Stop. Police orders."

From inside the car Vasubhai yelled to his driver "Go on, man, go on."

But Ghote stood his ground. And, with the car's gleaming chrome bumper actually touching his legs, the driver brought it to a halt.

The Deputy Commissioner came striding up.

"What the hell is going on?" he demanded.

"Sir," Ghote said. "Sir, I have just only realized how the legs of the murdered man were coming to disappear."

"Nonsense, man, nonsense. Legs cannot just disappear. They are here somewhere, I tell you. They are somewhere inside that shamiana. They must be."

Ghote drew in a breath.

"Sir, no," he said.

"What the hell do you mean *No*, Inspector? Have you gone out of your head?"

"Sir, it is simple. Sir, I am believing this is where we were going wrong. Not looking, sir, for one obvious answer."

Rapidly he corrected himself.

"Sir, it is where I myself was going wrong when I was telephoning yourself, sir."

"You were going wrong? That I can believe. So, how was it you were making the mistake of calling out the whole of Crime Branch?" Eh, man? How? How?"

"Sir, as I was saying, sir. It is altogether most simple. Sir, I am realizing now who that fellow dead inside there must be. Sir, he would be someone Vasubhai here was planting in the gang of his rival, Gulshan Singh. A spy, sir. A jasoos. And, sir, Gulshan Singh must have discovered same. That is why he was sending some message to yourself, sir, saying there was something at this festival now that would interest police. He was wanting us, and whole world also, to see what happens to anyone who tries and attempts to infiltrate his gang."

"Ha. Well, I dare say you could be right there, Inspector. I thought something on those lines might be in the air. That's why I sent you here to keep an eye on things. And what did you do? You let that jasoos be murdered right under your own eyes."

"No, sir."

"No? Are you contradicting me, Ghote? To my face?"

"Sir, answer is simple. Sir, this spy was not strangled here in that dressing-room and his legs cut off. If they had been, sir, I would have smelt blood as soon as I was entering to carry out inspection. But, sir, I was not. I was smelling blood just only later when Vasubhai was calling to me to go in there."

"Now, what the hell are you saying?"

"Sir, just that the jasoos was strangled and his body put under that tarpaulin before even I was coming here. He must have been murdered by Gulshan Singh at his own place and then brought here so that, when time was ripe, he would be found and Vasubhai would be losing very much of respect with each and every member of his own gang."

"Inspector, how the hell can you have the face to say that a body that was found by you yourself, with the mutilated stumps of its legs still bleeding, was put here before you were even coming?"

"Sir, quite simple. The fellow was never having any legs."

He paused a moment in the hope that what he had brought himself to say would penetrate to the Deputy Commissioner in time.

"Sir," he went on, gulping a little, "that man must have been one of the legless beggars that are everywhere in the city, sir, going here-there on their little wheeled platforms. And only if Vasubhai's gang members were seeing a legless beggar, would it be plain to them that the hundred per cent nondescript spy put into Gulshan Singh's gang had been found out, sir. Sir, because of that man having no distinguishing feature except for not having any legs, what was it Vasubhai had to do when he was find his body? Sir, he must at each and every cost make it look as if the body was not that of his jasoos. He must make it look, sir, as if it was the body of a man who was having as many legs as any other person. Then there would be no rumour or gup, sir, about a legless beggar having been murdered. You must be well knowing, sir, what I was remembering: in cases of asphyxia, such as death by strangling, blood clotting is by no means immediate. Sir, you will find, I am thinking, those cut-off layers of flesh in the pockets of Vasubhai's safari suit, or, if they are now inside his car itself, there may be some blood stains on the inside of the pockets."

And find the two layers of flesh they did, and some bloodstains. But who took all the credit? The Deputy Commissioner, of course.

# THE NEXT BIG THING

*Peter T. Garratt*

*Peter Garratt (b.1949) is a clinical psychologist who has written scores of stories of fantasy and science fiction since his first sale "If the Driver Vanishes . . ." (1985). His mystery stories have also appeared in my anthologies* Shakespearean Whodunnits *and* Shakespearean Detectives.

"This Morrigan May's husband is *here*! I think you'd better see him." Monique said. She's the *de facto* head of our partnership, often said to be the best Clinical Psychologist in the UK, not just the best paid. She's as good a boss as I'm ever likely to get, but does have a thing about bad publicity. It was Friday, the week's paperwork was heaped up, and a cancellation had offered a mirage of a chance to shut myself in my office and clear it. But an angry widower arriving with news of a dead client, a possible suicide, couldn't be kept out by a plastic "Engaged" sign.

Still, I sat hesitated, making sure I remembered all I could. Megan May . . . Morrigan was her writing name . . . hadn't come to see me to talk about suicidal feelings. She'd digressed a lot onto aspects of her unusual career, but didn't make it sound suicidally bad, and I hadn't bothered with a full history. I feared my notes had been scrappy, and hoped profoundly that she hadn't hidden some dark pocket of depression which her husband would know about and expect me to have uncovered and in some way dealt with.

Monique led the way to her consulting room. She likes our

suite to look respectable but glamorous, her own image. The carpets are blue and the walls white, with pictures of Phraxos and other Greek islands, including one of Monique, dark-haired and tanned, leading a group at the Phraxos Personal Growth Centre.

I flicked my hair and straightened my tie, then realized that wasn't necessary. The man in Monique's room was about thirty-five, with long brown hair in a pony-tail, a short beard like stubble gone just beyond designer, and a battered leather jacket over a black T-shirt with part of a lurid red pattern just visible. Monique said: "Mr May, this is Owen GlenMorgan. He did see your late wife once, but only once."

I extended my hand and said: "I was very sorry to hear about your wife." I was trying to sound sympathetic, but as in our one meeting Morrigan May had said nothing suggestive of suicide, I felt as much puzzled and alarmed.

"Edwin May. In theory we were separated but . . ."

"It was a bolt from the blue?" Monique enquired solicitously.

"I knew those bastards at BattleSpear were putting her under a lot of pressure, but . . . I wouldn't even put it past them to . . . no, mustn't get paranoid!"

As I was trying to remember who the bastards at BattleSpear were, he blinked back tears, reached into a black shoulderbag marked "WORLD SCIENCE FANTASY CONVENTION – BRIGHTON", and pulled out a book. "This was her."

It was a hardback called *The Merlinus* with a battered dust-jacket. The front showed a boy in Druid garb beside a ruin. He was surrounded by warriors and was trying to face down their leader. Edwin May fumbled out the back flap. It had a full-colour picture of Morrigan. I remembered her more clearly now. Like me, she was Welsh but marooned long-term in London. She had a very distinctive hairstyle, bobbed and dyed red near the roots, then a wide blonde band, with the tips a luminous green, so her head resembled a traffic light switched to "Go". She wore a little black leatherette top and a lot of silver jewellery. I remembered that in our one interview she had touched on her appearance and its relationship to her career: "I've been the Next Big Thing in British SF for ten years now. That's rather a long time to be next.

Image helps. If I look like a mixture of punk, pagan and technogoth I sell a few extra copies. I get far enough past the break-even point to stay in print."

She had made a little knowing smile at that point, and though there was a slight air of sadness about her . . . she wore a dark outfit even though it wasn't revealing or leathery . . . she had a vibrancy which was brittle but real. I liked working with people like Megan, or Morrigan. She'd become epileptic after an accident, and then for some reason dropped out of an academic career to become a writer. She didn't explain that in detail, because she hadn't regretted the decision. Like so many creative people, her life had become a constant struggle to do what she wanted and postpone the day when she'd have to appease her bank manager by looking through Sits Vac for a job selling replacement kitchens. She'd put it off for ten years and had sounded pleased with her progress. It was shocking to think she was dead. I said to Edwin May: "Just exactly what happened?"

"It was a week ago. Friday. A day or two earlier, I suppose. I went round on Friday with Dai . . . our son . . . Megan was supposed to have him for the weekend. My sister gets him to school, Megan never could get up in the morning. We went round on Friday and rang and there was no answer. Dai had a key and he said it would be OK to let ourselves in and wait. It was about half four. We went into the flat and I put the kettle on and looked at some letters that had arrived. I didn't open them at that stage, but I was her agent, still am I suppose, there were a lot of letters on the mat and I was looking for publishers' logos on . . . there was something I didn't like about the flat that day. Not the way she kept it . . . full of BattleSpear crap . . . the place stank of joss and piss. That wasn't like Megan . . . she hated the smell of joss, said it made her feel she was going to fit, and if she did fit, well, she usually did piss herself, but she always cleaned up. She was disciplined like that."

Megan's main reason for coming to see me had been to discuss the medicine she'd been taking for her epilepsy. As a non-medical psychologist, I could only give her general advice about that, so I'd referred her on to a neurologist, Professor Vron. Edwin went on: "Dai called me to the bedroom. I hadn't been in there since we split, but . . . the whole thing was so *unlike* Megan.

"There wasn't any doubt . . . she was cold as . . . I'd never seen anyone dead before . . . and for our *son* to find her!"

Monique offered him a box of tissues, and he grabbed a thick wad and wept into it for a long time. I didn't know why they had split up, but it didn't sound to have been an irreparable breach. A hint of jealousy, but more to do with differences in lifestyle and writing policy, she'd said in passing: mainly him differing loudly from her. Now he was crying as though he'd realized for the first time that maybe marriage was about not dying alone because there's no one to pop in and ask if you want a cup of tea and *notice* you're dying.

Megan had been on phenobarbitone, an old fashioned anti-convulsant which had once doubled as a tranquilliser. Its use had long been restricted to a few cases of epilepsy which responded to it best, because people could get too tolerant to it. Eventually, to get an effect a person needed a potentially lethal dose, and if misused, as it often had been in the past, it could be more dangerous than heroin. Morrigan May had insisted that safer and more modern anti-convulsants had less impact on her fits. If she was going to take pills, they had to be phenobarbs, though she would prefer to take none.

He started to calm down and dry his eyes, and I said: "I suppose she must have inadvertently taken an overdose of the phenobarb. I'm surprised she was still on it . . . I did send her to a neurologist who should have tried to get her onto something safer. In the old days there were lots of phenobarb ODs, and most of them were accidental."

He stared at me blankly. "She didn't mention all the strain . . . all the hassles she was getting from BattleSpear?"

"No." I added cautiously: "Just who is BattleSpear?"

He didn't answer but pulled a document out of his bag. "Just look at that!"

The letterhead had a logo of a Conan-like figure hurling an enormous spear. It was a critique of a book, presumably one of Morrigan's. It was full of comments like: "*P3 par 1: Do your homework! Trulls are quite distinct from Urks, the latter being able to use but not service a stun laser, while stupid Trulls are quite unable to comprehend that such a small and shiny item could be a weapon!*

*P3 par 2: Rubbish! Trulls have enhanced Night Vision, but that does not mean they suffer from snow blindness in good light!"*

and in the same vein for seven pages.

"I don't know why BattleSpear went into publishing! They're just toy makers, not even games really, toys with rules for playing, ripped off from sensible people. How could a writer, a sensitive artist like her, be expected to tolerate that! They're men playing in a child's world and nerds in a grown-up's! I'm sueing them! They're responsible for her death, and I need you to help prove it!"

The flat was in Wandsworth, above a shop in a small parade opposite the Common, in an area where the Victorian streets had been ramped and chicaned against speeding motorists by gentrifiers who nevertheless all owned cars. I had once briefly been a police officer, and it felt as if Monique and I were staking the place out, as we waited for Edwin May after our regular day's work had finished. We were in my reconditioned Morris Minor, rear wheels on a double and the front sharing a Residents Only bay with a Honda Goldwing. Monique had decided against using her Merc . . . she thought that if he saw it, May might decide to sue us rather than BattleSpear. She said: "Let's formulate this case before he gets here."

"We have a writer, published but not especially successful."

"I'd never heard of her."

"I did a search on the Internet. Alta Vista found her. She began with a series of eco-SF novels . . . the *Deep Green* trilogy. She got rave reviews from small magazines, got nominated for awards no one's ever heard of. Then she switched to the fantasy historical stuff he showed us, Dark Age, Celtic, slightly more sellable, but not a real breakthrough. Her husband is her agent. He drifts off, perhaps because she signs with a down-market teen-games firm."

"He really hated them!" Monique said with feeling. "Did she say anything to you, to suggest this firm BattleSpear somehow drove her to suicide?"

"Not exactly. She said they were stressful to work for, but that was why she wanted to come off the phenobarbs, thought she was using them for the wrong reasons. She said she was getting preoccupied with long-term health, holistic approaches to health . . . even writing a book about holistic health."

"Doesn't sound suicidal at all. Isn't that him? Edwin May?"

Across the street, a man was pushing the bell of Morrigan's flat. He wore an old leather jacket, brown, and though it was August and a fine late afternoon, the collar was turned up. He looked a bit like Edwin May: I couldn't see if he had the trade-mark pony-tail because of the collar, but when he stepped back from the door I saw it wasn't him. The pale, bony face looked similar, but this man had stubble rather than beard and he wore a collar and tie. He looked up at the flat, at the greengrocer's below which seemed to have closed, walked slowly away. I said:

"It's not him. This guy's ringing, not unlocking."

"OK! You agree it doesn't sound like suicide?"

"I think she cut the tablets down too quickly, had a fit, then put them back up too quickly. So the fact that working for Battle-Spear was not a paradise, and her hubby seems to have had a better deal lined up which has now gone down the drain, is just unlucky coincidence."

"Here he comes. We'd better handle him carefully, Owen. He's got all her problems and his own, and he thinks she was Marilyn. In his paranoid moments, he even plays with the idea some BattleSpear conspirator killed her."

We got out and crossed the road. Edwin May came to a halt in front of the narrow entrance to the flat. He looked at that chipped green door with its tarnished brass knocker as if his whole life lay behind it, and that life was over. He said: "I can't put it off any more. I haven't been in since . . . all that ghastly nonsense with the police." He pulled out a Yale key and made a stab for the lock, hitting the metal surround and pushing it in with a scrape.

Inside the door was a heap of letters, bills, and free papers. He said: "You know, the contract must have come through this door while she was . . . lying there."

"Which contract, sorry?" I asked.

"The one I told you about. The joint contract with Robinson's and Meridian TV. A novel, 'The Healer', a TV series, and a factual show and a factual book about faith healing to go with it. Lots of TV personals for her. The whole thing well into six figures. After all her work, she'd really arrived, and then . . ."

We followed him cautiously up a dark stairway. I said: "Mr May, did I hear you say Morrigan was working on a factual book about faith healing, or just a novel?"

"Both. She did a hell of a lot of research on it. Let's see." A bright light flicked above, and I realized the stairs led to a big open-plan lounge. "I think there's a picture here . . ."

The room was full of odd pieces of furniture, none very new, which looked to have been bought separately for price rather than style or even function. The only expensive items were the TV and video, though there was a fairly new games console in another corner. The walls were stacked with books, mostly not in cases, almost to eye-height: above them the room was decorated with a wide variety of artwork: bookjackets . . . I recognized the one from *The Merlinus* . . . photographs, and a number of large framed or blockmounted oil paintings on fantasy themes. It was the kind of room my own circle of friends were only just starting to settle out of; though it had a distinct and unpleasant smell of urine, as though an unhousetrained cat lived there. If there was also a hint that joss sticks had been burned there, it was very faint, perhaps because there was a draught.

Edwin had gone to an area of snapshot photos. "Here's one of Megan at Lourdes with Lionel Fanthorpe."

I said: "Did she appear on 'Fortean TV'?"

"A couple of times. She was more of a sceptic than Lionel, though not with a 'K' like some of her old uni pals. She was *so* looking forward to getting her own show, putting over her particular point of view."

Monique had been looking round the room impassively. Someone who only knew her from the office might have assumed she disapproved, though I happened to know her private life was just as Bohemian as Morrigan's had been. She said: "I gather you're implying she believed in faith healing, Mr May."

He said hurriedly: "Well, she didn't call it belief, because she'd done a science degree, and unlike a lot of SF writers, she kept up with as much real science as she could. She had a collection of cases where some kind of Healing seemed to have worked, not necessarily Christian or religious, she was looking for ways of assembling some kind of control group when . . . Oh God! Excuse me a minute!"

He abruptly stopped, as though he had seen something even more terrible than the ubiquitous reminders of his wife's life and death, and hurried out of the large room, through a door decorated with a seaside cartoon of a girl in a bath. I heard flushing almost at once, and the ugly thought came to me that he was disposing of something . . . other than some female item which embarrassed him.

I wondered if he could have been overcome with other emotions than grief. In our session, Morrigan had almost dismissed him, an ineffectual old pal she had grown apart from. It had been he who had persuaded her to write fiction and not do postgrad studies, a move which had scarcely justified itself financially after ten years. And the breakdown of their marriage wasn't only over lifestyle and the BattleSpear situation: "We married for Dai, really. It was meant to be an open marriage, friends co-operating over a son. His idea, but he didn't like the way it turned out. I went on the pull about once a year, and usually succeeded. He tried it all the time, and hardly ever got anywhere. He didn't like that."

He might not have liked her exhibition of art. She'd been a model for most of the oil paintings, originals of book-covers I'd seen on racks, not her own. Usually, model-Morrigan wore something to cover her hair, not much more over the rest of her body, waving a weapon or other fantasy item. The faces were clearly her, though some of the bodies must have been modelled by someone more buxom.

I doubt I'd have suspected Edwin of committing a murder if he hadn't kept hinting that someone had done so. Megan said that exhibitionistic self-promotion kept her afloat, and he'd have known and lived with that. And he could hardly have killed her for money. She'd died before he knew about the contract. He hoped for it perhaps, but didn't *know*. I wasn't arrogant enough to suppose a man could murder a goose which hadn't yet laid any golden eggs, then rely on my post-mortem Psychological profile to get the gold from the unlikely mine of BattleSpear.

The bathroom led directly off the lounge: next to it on the same side was the open door to a kitchen. In the opposite wall were two more doors, to bedrooms I supposed, one open, one closed. I went to the open one in search of the source of the draught I'd noticed. I wondered if someone could have broken in that way, looked inside, and found a child's room. A small casement window was open a crack but locked in position, the main window double-locked shut. I was just examining an oddity, an incense-boat on the ledge of the child's window, when a doorbell rang loudly. May called from the bathroom: "Could you see who that is?"

I went downstairs and got to the door just as the bell rang again. I opened it to find the man we had seen earlier, while we were waiting. He did look like Edwin May, though the resemblance was increased because both were pale and red-eyed. May wore a short beard, but this man had just shaved rarely and carelessly, with little more than a day's growth around his lips, but much more in the awkward corners of his face. He glared at me and snarled: "Who the devil are you?"

"I . . . we are here with Mr May." Introducing oneself in such situations is never easy. People are funny about being seen around psychologists. He moved to go in past me and I said: "While we're on introductions, just who are you?"

An awkward thought struck me, and I said: "Mr May's in the bathroom. You're not the late Mrs May's boyfriend, are you?"

"No," he said, taking advantage of my uncertainty to push past me and on up the stairs. "She never mentioned a boyfriend. I'm a very old friend. Dr Alan Glade. I was Megan's tutor at LSS . . . London School of Science."

I followed him up, feeling out of place. What authority did I have to stop him, a stranger myself in the home of a one-session dead client? Luckily, Edwin emerged from the bathroom as we reached the top of the stairs. His face was dead white and covered in sweat. He saw Glade in a double-take and said: "What are you doing here?"

"I left . . ." Glade checked, then, seemed to compose himself. "I know I've left it a bit late to offer condolences, but I'd like to. I . . . never quite knew how things stood between you two."

"How they stand is, I'm a totally unprepared single parent. I've not been emotionally able to set foot in this place . . . now I'm here with two shrinks in tow . . . this is Owen GlenMorgan . . . Megan saw him . . . and Monique de Macaque. I've gotta sort out a million things. You . . . why couldn't you write? Or e-mail?"

"Well, I lent Megan some research papers and oddments, the *Skep Tactics* book on so-called healing and some other stuff, and I need to reclaim them for . . ."

"*Nothing* is going out of here till I've done . . . what you do. Make an inventory, I suppose. E-mail me a list. I have to go through all her stuff with the shrinks . . . not stuff that'd interest you . . . Battle-Spear stuff. I have to find out what made her do it."

Being in the death flat had taken the oddly aggressive drive out of Alan Glade. He looked as deflated as a reveller who had gate-crashed a party, and discovered it was a wake . . . which was more or less what he was. He said: 'Well, yes, sorry again, I knew it and you obviously knew it, she should never have got involved with those battleSpear people. I'll . . . yes, I'll e-mail you."

He went quietly down the stairs and let himself out. Edwin began to explain. "I just saw that, and it was too much for me." He pointed at a large open shopping bag full of clothes. "Her washing machine had packed up, she never got round to getting it fixed, and she used to get a bag ready for my sister Ann to do . . . Ann never minds being helpful that way, but this sort of thing, she can't handle at all!"

He looked about to make another dash for the toilet. Monique intervened: "That's odd! I looked in the kitchen, and saw an 'on' light on the washing machine." She added: "It's the same make as mine!" in a tone which said expensive Harley Street shrinks wouldn't otherwise know much about kitchen equipment.

"That should *not* be on!" Edwin snapped, rushing to the kitchen.

"Could anyone else have been in here?" I asked.

"No, No! Not even BattleSpear, let's be realistic! Police at least checked that, though they didn't look into anything else!"

Which might have been their job, but wasn't mine. "You're saying this is a suspicious death, and the police have obviously been here. What did they find?"

"What they looked for, which was nothing! Two constables checked for signs of a break-in, labelled her a hippy who popped pills. That was all they knew, and they decided it was all they needed to know. If she'd been lying there with a bloody great spear stuck through her, they'd have said it was a syringe!"

Monique nodded. "But you feel her death resulted from a kind of negligence?"

"BattleSpear negligence! That's a good word! I went to the station and asked for someone in charge. I wanted to explain that they'd harassed her till she flipped and gave up and muddled her pills. Harassment's a crime isn't it? All I got was some sergeant who'd tried to turn his memoirs into a novel, and he said that if they locked up all the rude, grasping, shortchanging publishers in London, they'd have no cells left for other kinds of crime. But I managed to get the inquest adjourned and if you can do me a profile of how they upset her frame of mind, treating an artist like a shopgirl, I might get a sensible verdict!"

I had my doubts. I glanced at Monique. She was listening with the interested, compassionate, otherwise expressionless poker face she uses for all awkward clients. I'm told I use it too. Edwin turned back to the kitchen. "What's in here!" He opened the washing machine and let out an incredibly vile smell of old urine.

"That's *terrible!*" I said, hastily adding: "What *is* in there?" before he could back away and make me investigate myself.

He held his nose and looked inside. "Just her jeans and panties. She must have had a fit and forgotten it was bust. The fits affected her memory, you see. That must be why the place smelled bad."

"Not entirely." Monique said. "I think the smell we noticed

earlier came from this couch." She went into the living room and pointed at a black, leather-look settee which faced the TV.

"So she had a fit watching TV. She must have remembered to try and wash her clothes, but forgotten to clean that up. God! If only *someone* had been here!"

He again looked ready to rush for the toilet. To distract him, I said: "Did you say there was also a smell of joss incense? I think I've found out why."

I indicated the open bedroom. It had a single bed, made, and was decorated with childish posters, mostly of fantasy adventures and carrying the BattleSpear logo. There was a large table on which a game based on such scenes had been set out with metal figures and toy scenery. I expected Edwin to complain at this invasion of his son's room, but he refrained: presumably it was allowable for children to enjoy BattleSpear. I indicated the incense boat on the window ledge. Two joss sticks had burned right down. Edwin said: "Beats me! It's unbelievable. Megan hated the smell of joss, ever since her accident. She never used it."

I knew the smell of joss sometimes came as an aura before her fits. "This accident. Did it have anything to do with her epilepsy?"

"It did. Megan did a hard course, Joint honours, no bloody puns, Envo' Sci' and Biochemistry. She was told . . . Glade told her . . . she was heading for a First on the strength of a project. She went out to celebrate with some of her course, got slewed, went to someone's room, rolled up and lit up. Lots of joss but not much dope, I heard. I wasn't there, myself, that time." He stopped abruptly, I suppose numbering the times in Megan's life when he *wasn't there*. "So they ran out of dope and Megan set out on a bike to get some more. No one knows exactly what happened. She was found by the road. When she came to, she couldn't remember.

"Not long after that she started getting the joss . . . aura, they call it . . . and then getting fits. Totally buggered her exams. Memory was a sieve made of Swiss cheese. Oddly enough she was better on those pills. Most of the time. She'd oversleep and couldn't get up to do a job, so she started writing seriously. Didn't totally swear off dope, just bicycles. And joss, more to the point."

"Did anyone but your son use this room?" I wasn't that interested in joss sticks. I wanted to access and assess his jealousy.

"I suppose so. Not lately. She was so into researching the bloody BattleSpear game . . . she used to play it by e-mail, for Christ's sake . . . at least she didn't let the nerds get up here!"

Monique asked: "How about that character who was here just now? The old friend . . . ex-tutor?"

"Doubt it. He was even more anti-joss than she was. Spent all his time trying to keep her away from what he called hippies. Me, mostly. I suppose you'd better see where I found her."

He went back to the living-room, then stopped abruptly. "Of course Glade felt she had to be an academic like him. Kept telling her to get a medical cert and sue the uni if they wouldn't let her do a Ph.D. I don't know if that's relevant."

I doubted it. I sensed he was stalling, not wanting to go back into that room. He went on: "Luckily, she got a break almost at once. She got a story in *Interzone* . . . top SF zine . . . and that led to her getting a novel contract. Pissed *Doctor* Glade off . . . we didn't see him for ages. Anyway, he . . ."

Monique took charge. "Were you going to show us where you found her?"

"Yes." He took a deep breath.

I felt desperately sorry for him. "Look, I know this isn't easy."

He opened the door to the last room. The curtains were open, but not the windows, which had ventilating fans set into two panes. It was dominated by a large double bed, with the covers thrown back. There was a computer, another games table, even some BattleSpear posters, though these had adult . . . or at least teenboy . . . themes, women warriors in leather or rubber armour. Most of these weren't modelled by Morrigan, but over the bed was a large painting on glass. It showed her underwater, appearing to rise through the sea toward the sunrise . . . or sunset, I realized. The picture was so positioned that the light of the setting sun through the window might sometimes reach it.

Morrigan's hair was uncovered, the green ends blending with the water, the red and yellow with the sunset. It was the only picture I saw in the flat in which she appeared to be entirely naked, though it was hard to be certain, as seaweed and fish were floating strategically.

He caught the direction of my gaze. "The original cover painting from the Morrigan May special issue from *Interzone*. It's by Sexton, the top fantasy artist."

While not exactly provocative, I felt the nude image would remind anyone who entered the room that it held potential for other games than BattleSpear. I said: "I never quite understood what caused the two of you to split up."

"Nothing!" he shouted. "Oh, odd differences over this and that, not even real quarrels. We never stopped getting on, helping each other . . ."

Monique said quickly: "So! It's dramatic and ironic . . . you found her lying like Marilyn Monroe, dead from barbiturates."

"Not exactly. There was no last call . . . I swear it! Not to me, anyway. Maybe to someone dodgy . . . no. No!" He blinked, then said: "But there is another odd thing. What was it . . . '*all the morning papers said, was that Marilyn, was found in the nude!*'? Well Megan used to like sleeping nude, in fact she always did in summer, unless she thought she might fit, in which case she'd wear a thick pair of panties.

"This was different. She was naked below the waist, even though she'd probably just fitted, but she had on a sweatshirt and even a bra. She *never* normally wore a bra to sleep."

"OK, OK, this was an odd situation," I said. I'd liked Megan, and nothing I'd seen in the flat suggested she was a person who would kill herself deliberately and leave her body for her son to find. I thought Edwin disliked that idea as much as I did, but he was afraid of the more logical formulation of an accident. If Megan's faith in healing had led her to prematurely abandon her drugs, then lose track of the safe dose and overdo them, her life's work was in vain. His continual flirting with the idea of an impossible murder told me this was a safer theory for his peace of mind. Unfortunately, publishers tend to prefer their authors alive. Once they're famous they can die and someone will keep on writing their books, but no one would ghost-write and publish Megan's healing theories under these circumstances. So I added with feeling: "And a tragic one! But how do you know it wasn't just unusual? She wasn't expecting you . . . do you know exactly when . . ."

"No. Like I said, she didn't phone . . . post-mortem suggests . . . late Wednesday or early Thursday."

"Did she call anyone at all?"

"I don't know . . . hold on . . . wasn't there a phone bill in that heap I just brought up? That'll be itemized!"

He went to get it. I tried to imagine the scene in that room: above, the peaceful image of Morrigan floating up toward the sunrise, unsuspecting as the nude in *Jaws*; below the real Megan, troubled in ways I could not analyze, sinking far too deep into the sea of sleep.

"It is a phone bill . . . that's good, it's itemized right up to last Friday, when . . . no, those look like the calls I made . . . nothing for Thursday and not much Wednesday either . . . wait a minute . . . there's one some hours after the rest."

He stopped and shuddered. "Sounds like that last call."

I said: "Do you recognize the number?"

"No. Do you think we should try it?"

"Why not?" I didn't want Megan to have made a last, despairing call to someone who failed to help; but my reputation, and therefore my living, depended on being prepared to ignore what I wanted to believe and find out what really happened. I got Edwin to show me the phone in the lounge and the number to dial. It rang twice, then an automated voice began: "The Department of Clinical Biochemistry of St Dunstan's University Hospital is closed. Please leave a message after the tone. If you need to make urgent contact, the following staff members have mobiles: Dr Alan Glade, Senior Lecturer and Director of the . . ."

"Our *old friend* Dr Glade. Let's just get this mobile number. Shall I ring it?" Edwin nodded, and I dialled the number. It was another answering service. I left him a message to contact us, then looked back at the phone bill.

"Apart from the Glade call in the late afternoon, we only have three calls, all to one number, all late morning."

Edwin May looked over my shoulder. "I think that's her Internet Service Provider. She'd have been logging on. That's it . . . why didn't I think of it! Her last message must have been an e-mail."

"They were some time before the call to Dr Gla . . ." I petered out, as Edwin hurried to the bedroom and started booting up the PC. I followed, wondering uneasily what he would find. If she had died by her own hand, I cursed my incompetence in not adequately evaluating the risk. She just hadn't seemed like a danger to herself. Could someone have somehow fed her extra pills? I had suspected Edwin May himself, but it was a far-fetched theory, inspired by his own odd idea that BattleSpear could have been directly not indirectly responsible. But May seemed far more excited by her professional than her sexual life. He found something on the computer and said: "Look at this: '*It's a real downer that everything I write for BS has to be redone so often. I do have other projects and the stress is undermining my health*'"

"What e-mail is this?" I asked. "Is it dated?"

"It's to her friend Molly Brown, another top pro writer, someone who'd understand!" he said in a tone which implied a mere psychologist had no hope of understanding any writer. "It's quite recent. Not Wednesday. One pm Monday. Oh, God, listen to this, they were really upsetting her! '*Things have been a lot worse since 20K got going! Everything has to be redone twenty thousand times!*'"

"What's TwentyK?" Monique asked. "Some kind of Millennium project?"

"No, futuristic BattleSpear. Really, it's just the usual Trulls and Urks with ray-guns. But some of it is seriously pervy, not really pre-teen stuff. The ironic thing is, Megan rather threw herself into BS, till they started hassling her. She joined SLOBS . . . that's the Super League of BattleSpear, watched their videos . . . I think she's still got the latest crud in the video now! You need to see this!"

He jumped up and hurried back to the lounge. On the shelf between TV and VCR, there was an open cassette case, depicting the usual leatherette-clad woman in conflict with some humanoid monstrosity, both armed with futuristic weapons. "Let's see."

He remoted the set and it rapidly flickered to life. Flickered was the word. The picture on the screen flashed on and off like a strobe as heavy nightclub music thumped through the flat. Edwin could just be heard above it: "That's crap! They've really done it now! How can BS have sent her something like this! Strobe lights brought on her fits like crusties give you nits!"

I was starting to make out the picture from the brief flashes of moving image. It didn't look like a futuristic battle scene. A girl was dancing wildly, dressed only in a red and green bikini with gold tassels and matching gloves. Behind her, other girls danced in similar outfits without the gloves, around a muscular black youth with multi-coloured dreadlocks. They appeared to be on the stage of a club.

Monique said: "Isn't that the Glove Girl?"

I nodded, pleased she'd spoken first. "The Glove Girl and Clive" is one of those nocturnal shows respectable psychologist types seldom admit to being up late enough to know about.

Suddenly the music stopped and the Glove Girl was shown mopping the sweat off her face and starting to interview one of the dancers. Just as suddenly the screen went grey and snowy, then another flickering began, not strobe-like this time, but the usual damage one gets on a tape which has been partially over-recorded. This settled to show figures armed with rayguns against a crude graphic of spaceships landing.

Monique asked: "Could she have surfed onto the show with the strobe, had a fit, then accidentally pressed 'record'?"

I wondered. Someone had stopped recording "The Glove Girl" when the strobe ended. Before I could comment, the doorbell rang. Edwin was so stressed he didn't move at first. I said: "I'll deal with it."

The caller was Alan Glade. The sight of him filled me with irritation and suspicion, though as he wasn't suspected of anything, and in fact had lost his earlier belligerent manner, politely waving his mobile and saying: "This thing's bust. I keep meaning to get it fixed. It takes messages but I can't ring out. So, when I saw you wanted to contact me and I was still in the area . . ."

Uncertainly, I invited him up, explaining that Megan's last call had been to his lab. He said: "Actually, that was me," then paused, looking alarmed, and went on: "She was sort of OK when I left, though I was worried about the way she mucked about with her medication. She'd been totally taken in by this healing crap and got out of her depth. That's why I stayed so long."

Edwin said anxiously: "You mean she *didn't* make a last phone call? After she'd taken the overdose?"

"Not to me. I don't think she had the lab number. As for overdose, well, I think it was more an accident than something planned.

"We'd been meeting to talk about this bloody faith healing book. Frankly, she'd got the emphasis all wrong. She talked about a control group, but she didn't have one. She was just collecting cases, isolated one-offs. I went round, it would have been the Tuesday, to show her some real evidence and talk it over.

"Megan was in an odd mood. She wouldn't listen to reason. She'd been using faith healing and other quack techniques to control her fits, and it hadn't worked. She'd gone back on anticonvulsants, too many as far as I could see, her system wasn't used to the dose she'd gone back to.

"I was so worried, I stayed over on Tuesday night." He glanced anxiously at May. "Not in the bedroom. I dozed off in here on the couch. Megan slept very late in the morning . . . it was hard to wake her. I decided to take the day off work. When she woke up, I went and did some shopping for her, then spent some time trying to get her to see someone to get the medication changed. She said it was only stress, she was trying to write two books at once, the healing book . . ." he indicated a blue folder on a low desk in one corner, ". . . and the next BattleSpear book. Well, at least that one was meant to be sci-fi. She said she'd soon have it sorted out. Actually, she was looking a bit better when I got a call on this." He held up the defective mobile. "It doesn't ring out . . . can be handy sometimes, but that time, there was a serious problem at the lab. I had to get over there."

I glanced at Monique. Reason told me we should make an excuse and leave. No note, no last call, no last e-mail.

But I didn't like Glade, and I especially didn't like the way he was obsessively trashing those of his dead ex-student's beliefs which he hadn't drilled into her. I didn't necessarily disagree that faith healing was a kind of placebo: but if some people could direct the placebo, what harm could they do?

I opened the blue file. The top document was headed: **MY OWN CASE**. It began: *"Twice now, I have succeeded in going for six months without having epileptic fits or taking damaging medication. I attribute this partly to meditation and holistic techniques, but also to the power of Healing . . . not explicitly religious, but a power science cannot yet explain, but should start trying to explore."*

Next to the folder was a lurid paperback. It was called *The Warrior*. The cover had a BattleSpear logo and showed the usual black-suited and helmeted figure, brandishing a laser-sword and charging down the gangplank of a spacecraft. Unlike the other Morrigan May books, it was one I had seen in shops . . . indeed, indeed, huge displays of them. I was about to say that it must have been a stress on a writer to work on two so contrasting projects, when Glade went on: "Y'know, the tragic thing was, she was never the same after her accident." He indicated the area of wall with her personal photos. "Back then," pointing to shots of a slightly younger Megan in obvious fancy dress, Vampirella, Magenta from "Rocky Horror", "She dressed up, but she knew it was a game. Later, this . . . madness!"

He was indicating a group photograph, Megan in the centre of smiling thirty-somethings clustered round a motorcycle. All wore bike-gang gear, but the black leather had been replaced by white. May said defensively: "White Riders. Well, Megan was obviously a pillion rider. They wanted to get magic and spirituality away from the Satan-idiots on one side, and the china teacup set on the other."

Glade ploughed on: "It's as if the real Megan died in the

accident. As if her damaged brain wasn't her real self. The real Megan did not believe in Magic."

The words came into my mind then, like a strobeflash, that if her mind was dead, he had only killed her body. That hadn't been the part of her he needed, or not officially.

Intuition wasn't something I liked to rely on, but I've learned that sometimes it's all one has. I realized that when the thought came, when Glade spoke, I had been looking at a *Radio Times*, which was on the table by the couch, open to Tuesday night late. The item I was looking for was there, and with a cold feeling of disgust I realized it had been underlined.

I said: "Well, at least something can be salvaged. Just think of the publicity: 'Healer Author met mysterious, Marilyn-like death.'" I looked at Glade and tapped the blue file. "I'm sure the publishers can edit her book up from these notes. And the TV, there'll be out-takes from other shows she did, all these stills. She didn't *live* for nothing!"

"But that's madness! Publish the ravings of a demented, brain-damaged . . ." He strode toward the desk as if meaning to grab the blue file and run with it. I held it up and said: "You'd like to destroy this, wouldn't you! I should think that's why you came back! To destroy it, that and the tape!"

He made a grab at it, but I was bigger than him, and held it over my head. I feared he would have a go at me, and I might need to bring it down sharply as a weapon, but he just stood there breathing heavily and shaking with anger. May was staring, totally bewildered: I noticed Monique slide silently to the phone. I said: "You remind me of an Evangelical Christian I once treated." He opened his mouth and I cut him off: "He wouldn't learn Yoga or anything similar because it was Hindu, Pagan, Unchristian, and therefore of the Devil!"

"There's no Devil!" he said. "There's no Christ. There's no proof of any of the things she was asserting in that bloody book!"

"That's what you told her on Tuesday, but she wouldn't listen. Brain-damaged. That was what she'd been, since she had her accident and stopped being your student."

"She was my best ever student! She should have been a scientist . . . not this! The real Megan would never have . . ."

"That's what you thought, when she wouldn't listen to you on Tuesday and crashed out on her pills. You lay down on the couch. You tried to sleep, but you were just thinking, watching TV. Looking through the *Radio Times*. You saw a warning that a show was due to come on with dancing to strobe light.

"Then it came to you. You grabbed the remote and recorded the strobe, recording it over whatever was in the video. Maybe you didn't know then if you were going to do it. But the next day she was still ignoring what you said. She wasn't your student any more, *your* scientist. It was her life's work or yours, and yours was more important. You rang off work, and went shopping. You bought some joss sticks and lighted them in the spare room." I thought I saw him nod then, but he stiffened and began to disagree. I spoke over him: "Megan began to panic. She thought she was having the aura for a fit. You said, 'Don't worry, take your pills, maybe have one extra' . . . of course you didn't remind her, she'd have had some already, she was taking too many. You said, 'Sit down, take you pills, let's watch a video.' And as soon as she'd taken them, before they could take effect, you put on the tape with the strobe, and it must have worked and given her a fit.

"I don't suppose it made it more difficult, watching her convulsing, wetting herself, brain-damaged and no longer a scientist. You turned off the video, and as soon as she came to, you said: 'You've had a fit, you must have forgotten your pills!' Of course, by then she'd forgotten she *had* taken them!

"You began to clean up. You got her out of her jeans and pants and put them in the washing machine. You didn't know it was broken.

"You got Megan into bed. You didn't take her top off. I don't know if you realized she usually slept nude . . . it was one detail that wouldn't have mattered if you hadn't had the call from work. You made the mistake of calling back from here. Something important, was it?"

He stood silent for a second. I guessed he wasn't used to lying about killing, or to killing itself for that matter. In the end he said:

"It was a serious problem. Contamination caused by a spillage. One of my students had made a total lash-up."

"Even your students make lash-ups. Now it was your turn to panic. You had to get back to the lab and not say where you'd been. You rushed off and the door locked behind you. Later, you realized you'd left the doctored tape in the machine, other odds and ends like the joss sticks. You came back saying it was for your notes. My guess is you came back several times when no one was here."

He looked terrified. I can only say, he didn't look like an innocent man. All he could say was a cliche, especially for him. He said: "You can't prove any of this . . ." but as he said it, not actually denying his guilt, Edwin May charged at him, sending him flying. He crashed into the desk, smashing it and knocking the *Warrior* book to the floor. But they were not warriors, and I found it relatively easy to separate them while Monique phoned the police.

All he would say later was repeat: "There's no proof." I thought it ironic, as well as sad. Morrigan May had gone from a world in which proof, or at least disproof, was considered possible. She had dared to go into a world where there was no proof of anything. And he had followed her.

# THE SECOND DRUG

*Richard A. Lupoff*

*Richard A. Lupoff (b.1935) first established his reputation as a writer of uncategorizable science fiction and fantasy, influenced by but clearly not imitating the early pulp adventure writers like Edgar Rice Burroughs and Doc Smith. However, no one reading* One Million Centuries *(1967) or* Into the Aether *(1974) would regard the stories as looking backward, and others, like* Sword of the Demon *(1978) and* Lovecraft's Book *(1985) establish their own niches. More recently Lupoff has turned to writing crime novels featuring San Franciscan insurance investigator Hobart Lindsey. The first was* The Comic Book Killer *(1988). The following story features a new detective, Abel Chase, and hopefully will be the first of a series.*

The great Bosendorfer piano responded eagerly to Abel Chase's practised hands, its crashing notes echoing from the high, raftered ceiling of the music room. Beyond the tall, westward-facing windows, the January night was dark and wind-swept. The warm lights of the college town of Berkeley sparkled below, and beyond the black face of the bay the more garish illumination of San Francisco shimmered seductively.

The sweet tones of the Guarnarius violin bowed by Chase's confidante and associate, Claire Delacroix, dashed intricately among the piano chords. Clad in shimmering silver, Claire offered a dramatic contrast to Chase's drab appearance. Her platinum hair, worn in the soft style of an earlier age, cascaded across the gracefully rounded shoulders that emerged from her silvery, bias-cut gown. A single diamond, suspended from a delicate silver chain, glittered in the hollow of her throat. Her deep-set eyes, a blue so dark as at times to appear almost purple, shone with a rare intelligence.

Abel Chase's hair was as dark as Claire's was pale, save for the patches of snow which appeared at the temples. Chase wore a neatly-trimmed black moustache in which only a few light-coloured hairs were interspersed. He was clad in a pale, soft-collared shirt and a tie striped with the colours of his *alma mater*, a silken dressing gown and the trousers of his customary mid-night blue suit. His expression was saturnine.

"Enough, Delacroix." He ceased to play, and she lowered her bow and instrument. "Stravinsky has outdone himself," Chase allowed. "A few corrections and suggestions, notably to the second *eclogue*, and his manuscript will be ready for return. His *cantilène* and *gigue* are most affecting, while the *dithyrambe* is a delight. After his more ambitious orchestral pieces of recent years, it is fascinating to see him working on so small a canvas."

Chase had risen from the piano bench and taken two long strides toward the window when the room's freshly restored silence was shattered by the shrilling of a telephone bell. Chase whirled and started toward the machine, but his associate had lifted the delicate French-styled instrument from its cradle. She murmured into it, paused, then added a few words and held the instrument silently toward her companion.

"Yes." He held the instrument, his eyes glittering with inter-est. He raised his free hand and brushed a fingertip along the edge of his moustache. After a time he murmured, "Definitely dead? Very well. Yes, you were right to re-seal the room. I shall come over shortly. Now, quickly, the address." He continued to hold the telephone handset to his ear, listening and nodding, then grunted and returned it to its cradle.

"Delacroix, I am going to the city. Please fetch your wrap, I shall need you to drive me to the dock. And perhaps you would care to assist me. In that case, I urge you to dress warmly, as a light snowfall has been falling for several hours – a most unusual event for San Francisco." Without waiting for a response he strode to his own room, hung his dressing gown carefully in a cedar-lined closet and donned his suit coat.

Claire Delacroix awaited him in the flagstone-floored foyer. She had slipped into a sable jacket and carried an elegant purse woven of silvery metal links so fine as to suggest cloth. Chase removed an overcoat from a rack beside the door, slipped into its warm confines, and lifted hat and walking stick from their places.

Shortly a powerful Hispano-Suiza snaked its way through the winding, darkened roads of the Berkeley hills, Claire Delacroix behind the wheel, Abel Chase seated beside her, a lap robe warming him against the wintry chill.

"I suppose you'd like to know what this is about," Chase offered.

"Only as much as you wish to tell me," Claire Delacroix replied.

"That was Captain Baxter on the telephone," Chase told her.

"I knew as much. I recognized his gruff voice, for all that Baxter dislikes to speak to women."

"You misjudge him, Delacroix. That's merely his manner. He has a wife and five daughters to whom he is devoted."

"You may be right. Perhaps he has his fill of women at home. I suppose he's got another juicy murder for you, Abel."

Chase's moustache twitched when Claire Delacroix called him by his familiar name. He was well aware that it would have been futile to ask her to address him by his given name, Akhenaton, and Claire Delacroix knew him far too intimately to refer to him as Doctor Chase. Still, "Abel" was a name few men were permitted to use in conversation with him, and no woman save for Claire Delacroix.

"The man is distraught. He seems to think that a vampire has struck in San Francisco, draining the blood of a victim and leaving him for dead."

Claire Delacroix laughed, the silvery sound snatched away on the wind. "And will the victim then rise and walk, a new recruit to the army of the undead?"

"You scoff," Chase commented.

"I do."

There was a momentary pause, then Chase said, "As do I. Baxter is at the site. He has studied the circumstances of the crime and concluded that it is impossible, by any normal means. Therefore and *ipso facto*, the solution must be supernatural,"

"You of course disagree."

"Indeed. The very term *supernatural* contradicts itself. The natural universe encompasses all objects and events. If a thing has occurred, it is necessarily not supernatural. If it is supernatural, it cannot occur."

"Then we are confronted with an impossible crime," Claire Delacroix stated.

Abel Chase shook his head in annoyance. "Again, Delacroix, a contradiction in terms. That which is impossible cannot happen. That which happens is therefore, by definition, possible. No," he snorted, "this crime is neither supernatural nor impossible, no matter that it may seem to be either – or both. I intend to unravel this tangled skein. Remain at my side if you will, and be instructed!"

The dark, winding road had debouched by now into the town's downtown district. On a Saturday night during the academic year warmly clad undergraduates stood in line to purchase tickets for talkies. The young intellectuals in their cosmopolitanism chose among the sensuality of Marlene Dietrich in *The Blue Angel*, the collaborative work of the geniuses Dali and Buñuel in *L'Age d'Or*, the polemics of the Ukrainian Dovzhenko's *Zemlya*, and the simmering rage of Edward G. Robinson in *Little Caesar*.

Young celebrants gestured and exclaimed at the unusual sight of snowflakes falling from the January sky. Their sportier (or wealthier) brethren cruised the streets in Bearcats and Auburns. The Depression might have spread fear and want throughout the land, but the college set remained bent on the pursuit of loud jazz and illicit booze.

Claire Delacroix powered the big, closed car down the sloping avenue that led to the city's waterfront, where Abel Chase's power boat rode at dock, lifting and falling with each swell of the bay's cold, brackish water.

Climbing from the car, Chase carefully folded his lap robe and placed it on the seat. He turned up the collar of his warm overcoat, drew a pair of heavy gloves from a pocket and donned them. Together, he and Claire Delacroix crossed to a wooden shed built out over the bay. Chase drew keys from his trouser pocket, opened a heavy lock, and permitted Claire to enter before him. They descended into a powerful motor boat. Chase started the engine and they roared from the shed, heading toward the San Francisco Embarcadero. The ferries had stopped running for the night. Tramp steamers and great commercial freighters stood at anchor in the bay. The powerboat wove among them trailing an icy, greenish-white wake.

Steering the boat with firm assurance, Chase gave his assistant a few more details. "Baxter is at the Salamanca Theatre on Geary. There's a touring company doing a revival of some Broadway melodrama of a few years back. Apparently the leading man failed to emerge from his dressing room for the third act, and the manager called the police."

Claire Delacroix shook her head, puzzled. She had drawn a silken scarf over her platinum hair, and its tips were whipped by the night wind as their boat sped across the bay. "Sounds to me like a medical problem more than a crime. Or maybe he's just being temperamental. You know those people in the arts."

Chase held his silence briefly, then grunted. "So thought the manager until the door was removed from its hinges. The actor was seated before his mirror, stone dead." There was a note of irony in his soft voice.

"And is that why we are ploughing through a pitch black night in the middle of winter?" she persisted.

"The death of Count Hunyadi is not a normal one, Delacroix."

Now Claire Delacroix smiled. It was one of Abel Chase's habits to drop bits of information into conversations in this manner. If the listener was sufficiently alert she would pick them up. Otherwise, they would pass unnoted.

"Imre Hunyadi, the Hungarian matinee idol?"

"Or the Hungarian ham," Chase furnished wryly. "Impoverished petty nobility are a dime a dozen nowadays. If he was ever a count to start with."

"This begins to sound more interesting, Abel. But what is this about a vampire that makes this a case for no less than the great

Akhenaton Beelzebub Chase rather than the San Francisco Police Department?"

"Ah, your question is as ever to the point. Aside from the seemingly supernatural nature of Count Hunyadi's demise, of course. The manager of the Salamanca Theatre states that Hunyadi has received a series of threats. He relayed this information to Captain Baxter, and Baxter to me."

"Notes?"

"Notes – and worse. Captain Baxter states that a dead rodent was placed on his dressing table two nights ago. And finally a copy of his obituary."

"Why didn't he call the police and ask for protection?"

"We shall ask our questions when we reach the scene of the crime, Delacroix."

Chase pulled the powerboat alongside a private wharf flanking the San Francisco Ferry Building. A uniformed police officer waited to catch the line when Chase tossed it to him. The darkly-garbed Chase and the silver-clad Claire Delacroix climbed to the planking and thence into a closed police cruiser. A few snowflakes had settled upon their shoulders. Gong sounding, the cruiser pulled away and headed up Market Street, thence to Geary and the Salamanca Theatre, where Chase and Delacroix alighted.

They were confronted by a mob of well-dressed San Franciscans bustling from the theatre. The play had ended and, as with the younger crowd in Berkeley, the theatregoers grinned and exclaimed in surprise at the falling flakes. Few of the men and women, discussing their evening's entertainment, hailing passing cabs or heading to nearby restaurants for post-theatrical suppers, took note of the two so-late arrivers.

A uniformed patrolman saluted Abel Chase and invited him and Claire Delacroix into the Salamanca. "Captain Baxter sends his compliments, Doctor."

"Nice to see you, Officer Murray. How are your twins? No problems with croup this winter?"

Flustered, the officer managed to stammer, "No, sir, no problems this year. But how did you—?"

Before Murray could finish his question he was interrupted by a stocky, ruddy-complexioned individual in the elaborate uniform of a high-ranking police officer. The Captain strode forward, visibly favouring one leg. He was accompanied by a sallow-faced individual wearing a black tuxedo of almost new appearance.

"Major Chase," the uniformed police official saluted.

Chase smiled and extended his own hand, which the Captain shook. "Clel. You know Miss Delacroix, of course."

Claire Delacroix extended her hand and Captain Cleland Baxter shook it, lightly and briefly.

"And this is Mr Quince. Mr Walter Quince, wasn't it, sir?"

Walter Quince extended his own hand to Chase, tilting his torso at a slight angle as he did so. The movement brought his hatless, brilliantined head close to Chase, who detected a cloying cosmetic scent. He shook Quince's hand, then addressed himself to Baxter.

"Take me to the scene of the incident."

Baxter led the Chase and Delacroix through the now-darkened Salamanca Theatre. Quince ran ahead and held aside a dark-coloured velvet curtain, opening the way for them into a narrow, dingy corridor. Abel Chase and Claire Delacroix followed Baxter into the passage, followed by Quince.

Shortly they stood outside a plain door. Another police officer, this one with sergeant's chevrons on his uniform sleeve, stood guard.

"Hello, Costello," Chase said. "How are your daughter and her husband doing these days?"

"Doctor." The uniformed sergeant lifted a finger to the bill of his uniform cap. "They've moved in with the missus and me. Times are hard, sir."

Chase nodded sympathetically.

"This is Count Hunyadi's dressing room," Quince explained, indicating the doorway behind Costello.

Chase asked, "I see that the door was removed from its hinges, and that Captain Baxter's men have sealed the room. That is good. But why was it necessary to remove the hinges to open the door?"

"Locked, sir."

"Don't you have a key, man?"

"Count Hunyadi insisted on placing a padlock inside his dressing room. He was very emphatic about his privacy. No one was allowed in, even to clean, except under his direct supervision."

Abel Chase consulted a gold-framed hexagonal wristwatch. "What time was the third act to start?"

"At 10:15, sir."

"And when was Hunyadi called?"

"He got a give-minute and a two-minute call. He didn't respond to either. I personally tried to summon him at curtain time but there was no response."

Abel Chase frowned. "Did you then cancel the rest of the performance?"

"No, sir. Elbert Garrison, the director, ordered Mr Hunyadi's understudy to take over the role."

"And who was that fortunate individual?"

"Mr Winkle. Joseph Winkle. He plays the madman, Renfield, And Philo Jenkins, who plays a guard at the madhouse, became Renfield. It was my duty to take the stage and announce the changes. I made no mention of Count Hunyadi's – illness. I merely gave the names of the understudies."

"Very well. Before we proceed to examine the victim and his surroundings, I will need to see these so-called threatening notes."

Captain Cleland Baxter cleared his throat. "Looks as if the Count was pretty upset by the notes. Everybody says he destroyed 'em all. He complained every time he got one but then he'd set a match to it."

An angry expression swept across Chase's features.

Baxter held up a hand placatingly. "But the latest – looks like the Count just received it tonight, Major – looks like he got riled up and crumpled the thing and threw it in the corner."

Baxter reached into his uniform pocket and extracted a creased rectangle of cheap newsprint. "Here it is, sir."

Chase accepted the paper, studied it while the others stood silently, then returned it to the uniformed captain with an admonition to preserve it as potentially important evidence.

Next, he removed the police seal from the entrance to the

dressing room and stepped inside, followed by Claire Delacroix, Captain Baxter, and the theatre manager, Walter Quince.

Chase stood over the still form of Imre Hunyadi, for the moment touching nothing. The victim sat on a low stool, his back to the room. The head was slumped forward and to one side, the forehead pressed against a rectangular mirror surrounded by small electrical bulbs. His hands rested against the mirror as well, one to either side of his head, his elbows propped on the table.

"We observe," Chase stated, "that the victim is fully dressed in formal theatrical costume, complete with collar and gloves."

"And ye'll note that he's deathly pale, Major," the police Captain put in. "Deathly pale. Drained by the bite of a vampire, I say."

Chase pursed his lips and stroked his dark moustache. "I would not be so quick to infer as much, Captain," he warned. "The victim's face is indeed deathly pale. That may be stage makeup, however."

Chase lifted an emery board from the dressing table and carefully removed a speck of makeup from Hunyadi's cheek. "Remarkable," he commented. "You see—" He turned and exhibited the emery board to the room. "It is indeed pale makeup, appropriate, of course, to the Count's stage persona. But now, we observe the flesh beneath."

He bent to peer at the skin he had exposed. "Remarkable," he said again. "As white as death."

"Just so!" exclaimed the Captain of homicide.

"But now I let us examine the victim's hands."

With great care he peeled back one of Hunyadi's gloves. "Yet again remarkable," the Abel Chase commented. "The hands are also white and bloodless. Well indeed, there remains yet one more cursory examination to be made."

Carefully tugging his trousers to avoid bagging the knees of his woollen suit, he knelt beside Count Hunyadi. He lifted Hunyadi's trouser cuff and peeled down a silken lisle stocking. Then he sprang back to his full height.

"Behold!"

The Count's ankle was purple and swollen.

"Perhaps Miss Delacroix – Doctor Delacroix, I should say – will have an explanation."

Claire Delacroix knelt, examined the dead man's ankles, then rose to her own feet and stated, "Simple. And natural. This man died where he sits. His body was upright, even his hands were raised. His blood drained to the lower parts of his body, causing the swelling and discoloration of the ankles and feet. There is nothing supernatural about post-mortem lividity."

Chase nodded. "Thank you."

He turned from the body and pointed a carefully manicured finger at Quince. "Is there any other means of access to Hunyadi's dressing room?"

"Just the window, sir."

"Just the window, sir?" Abel Chase's eyes grew wide. "Just the window? Baxter—" He turned to the Captain of police. "Have you ordered that checked?"

Flustered, Baxter admitted that he had not.

"Quickly, then. Quince, lead the way!"

The manager led them farther along the dingy corridor. It was dimly illumined by yellow electrical bulbs. They exited through the stage door and found themselves gazing upon a narrow alley flanked by dark walls of ageing, grime-encrusted brick. To their right, the alley opened onto the normally busy sidewalk, now free of pedestrians as San Franciscans sought cover from the chill and moisture of the night. To the left, the alley abutted a brick wall, featureless save for the accumulated grime of decades.

"There it is, sir."

Chase raised his hand warningly. "Before we proceed, let us first examine the alley itself," Chase instructed. Using electric torches for illumination, they scanned the thin coating of snow that covered the litter-strewn surface of the alley. "You will notice," Chase announced, "that the snow is undisturbed. Nature herself has become our ally in this work."

Chase then stepped carefully forward and turned, surveying the window. "Fetch me a ladder," he ordered. When the implement arrived he climbed it carefully, having donned his gloves once again. He stood peering through a narrow opening, perhaps fourteen inches wide by six inches in height. A pane of pebbled glass, mounted on a horizontal hinge in such a manner as to divide the opening in half, was tilted at a slight angle. Through it, Chase peered into the room in which he and the others had stood moments earlier.

From his elevated position he scanned the room meticulously, dividing it into a geometrical grid and studying each segment in turn. When satisfied, he returned to the ground.

Walter Quince, incongruous in his evening costume, folded the ladder. "But you see, sir, the window is much too small for a man to pass through."

"Or even a child," Chase added.

There was a moment of silence, during which a wisp of San Francisco's legendary fog descended icily from the winter sky. The rare snowfall, the city's first in decades, had ended. Then a modulated feminine voice broke the stillness of the tableau. "Not too small for a bat."

They returned to the theatre. Once again inside the building, Chase doffed his warm outer coat and gloves, then made his way to the late Count Hunyadi's dressing room, where the cadaver of the emigré actor remained, slowly stiffening, before the glaring lights and reflective face of his makeup mirror. Irony tingeing his voice, Chase purred, "You will note that the late Count casts a distinct reflection in his looking glass. Hardly proper conduct for one of the undead." He bent to examine the cadaver once more, peering first at one side of Hunyadi's neck, then at the other.

Chase whirled. "Was he left-handed?"

Walter Quince, standing uneasily in the doorway, swallowed audibly. "I – I think so. He, ah, remarked something about it, I recall."

Abel Chase placed the heels of his hands on the sides of Hunyadi's head and moved it carefully to an upright position. He made a self-satisfied sound. "There is some stiffness here, but as yet very little. He is recently dead. Delacroix, look at this. Clel, you also."

As they obeyed he lowered Hunyadi's head carefully to his right shoulder, exposing the left side of his neck to view above the high, stiff collar of his costume shirt.

"What do you see?" Chase demanded.

"Two red marks." Captain Cleland Baxter, having moved forward in his rolling, uneven gait, now leaned over to study the unmoving Hunyadi's neck. "He played a vampire," the police captain muttered, "and he carries the marks of the vampire. Good God! In this Year of Our Lord 1931 – it's impossible."

"No, my friend. Not impossible," Chase responded. "Supernatural? That I doubt. But impossible? No." He shook his head.

Claire Delacroix scanned the dressing room, her dark, intelligent eyes flashing from object to object. Sensing that the attention of the theatre manager was concentrated on her, she turned her gaze on him. "Mr Quince, the programme for to-night's performance includes a biography of each actor, is that not correct?" When Quince nodded in the affirmative, she requested a copy and received it.

She scanned the pages, touching Abel Chase lightly on the elbow and bringing to his attention several items in the glossy booklet. Chase's dark head and Claire Delacroix's platinum tresses nearly touched as they conferred.

Chase frowned at Walter Quince. "This biography of Mr Hunyadi makes no mention of a wife."

"Imre Hunyadi is – was – unmarried at the time of . . ." He inclined his own head toward the body.

"Yes, his demise," Chase furnished.

Quince resumed. "Theatrical biographies seldom mention former spouses."

"But gossip is common within the theatrical community, is it not?"

"Yes." There was an uncomfortable pause. Then Quince added, "I believe he was married twice. The first time in his native Hungary. To one Elena Kadar."

"Yes, I have heard of her," Chase furnished. "A brilliant woman, sometimes called the Hungarian Madame Curie. She was engaged for some years in medical research, in the field of anesthesiology. I've read several of her papers. Apparently she treated Habsburg soldiers who had been wounded in the Great War and was greatly moved by their suffering. Hence the direction of her experiments. She ended her life a suicide. A tragic loss."

"Ach, Major, Major, you know everything, don't you?" Captain Baxter exclaimed.

"Not quite," Chase demurred. Then, "Under what circumstances, Quince, was the Hunyadi marriage dissolved?"

The theatre manager reddened, indicating with a minute nod of his head toward Claire Delacroix that he was reluctant to speak of the matter in the presence of a female.

"Really," Claire Delacroix said, "I know something of the world, Mr Quince. Speak freely, please."

"Very well." The manager took a moment to compose himself. Then he said, "Some years before the Great War, Mr Hunyadi travelled to America as a member of a theatrical troupe. *Magyar Arte*, I believe they were called. They performed plays in their native language for audiences of immigrants. While touring, Hunyadi took up with his Hungarian leading lady. A few years later they moved to Hollywood to pursue careers in motion pictures. The woman's name was—" He looked around furtively, then mentioned the name of a popular film actress.

"They had one of those glittering Hollywood weddings," he added.

"With no thought of a wife still in Hungary?" Claire Delacroix inquired.

Quince shook his head. "None. Count Hunyadi made several successful silents, but when talkies came in, well, his accent, you see . . . There are just so many roles for European noblemen. Word within our community was that he had become a dope fiend for a time. He was hospitalized, then released, and was hoping to revive his career with a successful stage tour."

"Yes, there were rumours of his drug habit," Captain Baxter put in. "We were alerted down at the Hall of Justice."

Abel Chase looked around. "What of—" He named the actress who had been Imre Hunyadi's second wife.

"When her earnings exceeded his own, Count Hunyadi spent her fortune on high living, fast companions and powerful motor cars. When she cut him off and demanded that he look for other work, he brought a lawsuit against her, which failed, but which led to a nasty divorce."

"Tell me about the other members of the cast."

"You're thinking that his understudy might have done him in?" Baxter asked. "That Winkle fellow?"

"Entirely possible," Chase admitted. "But a premature inference, Clel. Who are the others?"

"Timothy Rodgers, Philo Jenkins," Quince supplied. "Estelle Miller and Jeanette Stallings, the two female leads – Lucy and Mina. And of course Samuel Pollard – Van Helsing."

"Yes." Abel Chase stroked his moustache thoughtfully as he examined the printed programme. "Captain Baxter, I noticed that Sergeant Costello is here tonight. A good man. Have him conduct a search of this room. And have Officer Murray assist him. And see to it that the rest of the theatre is searched as well. I shall require a thorough examination of the premises. While your men perform those tasks I shall question the male cast members. Miss Delacroix will examine the females."

Baxter said, "Yes, Major. And – is it all right to phone for the dead wagon? Count Hunyadi has to get to the morgue, don't you know, sir."

"Not yet, Clel. Miss Delacroix is the possessor of a medical education. Although she seldom uses the honourific, she is entitled to be called doctor. I wish her to examine the remains before they are removed."

"As you wish, Major."

Chase nodded, pursing his lips. "Delacroix, have a look before you question the women of the cast, will you. And, Quince, gather these persons, Rodgers, Pollard, Winkle, and Jennings for me. And you'd better include the director, as well, Garrison."

Claire Delacroix conscientiously checked Hunyadi for tell-tale signs, seeking to determine the cause of the Hungarian's death. She conducted herself with a professional calm. At length she looked up from the remains and nodded. "It is clear that the immediate cause of Count Hunyadi's death is heart failure." She looked from one to another of the men in the dressing room. "The puzzle is, for what reason did his heart fail? I can find no overt cause. The death might have been natural, of course. But I will wish to examine the marks on his neck. Definitely, I will wish to examine those marks."

"I think they're a mere theatrical affectation," Walter Quince offered.

"That may be the case," Claire Delacroix conceded, "but I would not take that for granted. Then –" she addressed herself to Captain Baxter "– I would urge you to summon the coroner's ambulance and have the remains removed for an autopsy at the earliest possible moment."

"You can rest assured of that," Captain Baxter promised. "Nolan Young, the county coroner, is an old comrade of mine."

Shortly the men Chase had named found themselves back on the stage of the Salamanca Theatre. The setting held ever the ominous, musty gloom of a darkened Transylvanian crypt. All had changed from their costumes to street outfits, their dark suits blending with the dull grey of canvas flats painted to simulate funereal stone.

A further macabre note was struck by their posture, as they were seated on the prop caskets that added atmosphere to the sepulchral stage setting.

Rather than a dearth, Abel Chase found that he was confronted by a surfeit of suspects. Each actor had spent part of the evening on-stage; that was not unexpected. As the hapless Jonathan Harker, Timothy Rodgers had won the sympathy of the audience, and Abel Chase found him a pleasant enough young man, albeit shaken and withdrawn as a result of this night's tragedy.

Joseph Winkle, accustomed to playing the depraved madman Renfield, tonight had transformed himself into the elegant monster for the play's final act. Philo Jenkins, the shuffling, blustering orderly, had stepped into Winkle's shoes as Renfield. It had been a promotion for each.

Yet, Abel Chase meditated, despite Captain Baxter's earlier suggestion that Winkle might be a suspect, he would in all likelihood be too clever to place himself under suspicion by committing so obvious a crime. Philo Jenkins was the more interesting possibility. He would have known that by murdering Hunyadi he would set in motion the sequence of events that led to his own advancement into Winkle's part as Renfield. At the bottom of the evening's billing, he had the most to gain by his promotion.

And Rodgers, it was revealed, was a local youth, an aspiring thespian in his first significant role. It appeared unlikely that he would imperil the production with no discernible advantage to himself.

The director, Garrison, would have had the best opportunity to commit the crime. Unlike the other cast members, who would be in their own dressing rooms – or, for such lesser lights as Rodgers, Winkle and Jenkins, a common dressing room – between the acts of the play, Garrison might well be anywhere, conferring with cast members or the theatre staff, giving performance notes, keeping tabs, in particular, on a star known to have had a problem with drugs.

"Garrison." Abel Chase whirled on the director. "Had Hunyadi relapsed into his old ways?"

The director, sandy-haired and tanned, wearing a brown suit and hand-painted necktie, moaned. "I was trying to keep him off the dope, but he always managed to find something. But I think he was off it tonight. I've seen plenty of dope fiends in my time. Too many, Doctor Chase. Haven't you come across them in your own practice?"

"My degree is not in medicine," Chase informed him. "While Miss Delacroix holds such a degree, my own fields of expertise are by nature far more esoteric than the mundane study of organs and bones."

"My mistake," Garrison apologized. "For some reason, powder bouncers seem to gravitate to the acting profession as vipers do to music. Or maybe there's something about being an actor that makes 'em take wing. They start off sniffing gin and graduate to the needle. I could tell, Mister Chase, and I think Hunyadi was OK tonight."

Chase fixed Garrison with a calculatedly bland expression. Unlike the actors Winkle and Jenkins, the director lacked any obvious motive for wishing Hunyadi dead. In fact, to keep the production running successfully he would want Hunyadi functional. Still, what motive unconnected to the production might Garrison have had?

And there was Samuel Pollard. As Van Helsing, Chase knew, Pollard would have appeared with the lined face and grey locks of an aged savant, a man of five decades or even six. To Chase's surprise, the actor appeared every bit as old as the character he portrayed. His face showed the crags and scars of a sexagenarian, and his thin fringe of hair was the colour of old iron.

In response to Chase's questions, Pollard revealed that he had spent the second intermission in the company of the young actress who had appeared as the character Mina, Jeanette Stallings.

"Is that so?" Chase asked blandly.

"We have – a relationship," Pollard muttered.

Chase stared at the grizzled actor, pensively fingering his moustache. He restrained himself from echoing John Heywood's dictum that there is no fool like an old fool, instead inquiring neutrally as to the nature of the relationship between Pollard and the actress.

"It is of a personal nature." Pollard's tone was grudging.

"Mr Pollard, as you are probably aware, I am not a police officer, nor am I affiliated with the municipal authorities in any formal capacity. Captain Baxter merely calls upon me from time to time, when faced with a puzzle of special complexity. If you choose to withhold information from me, I cannot compel you to do otherwise – but if you decline to assist me, you will shortly be obliged to answer to the police or the district attorney. Now I ask you again, what is the nature of your relationship with Miss Stallings?"

Pollard clasped and unclasped his age-gnarled hands as he debated with himself. Finally he bowed his head in surrender and said, "Very well. Doctor Chase, you are obviously too young to remember the great era of the theatre, when Samuel Pollard was a name to conjure with. You never saw me as Laertes, I am certain, nor as Macbeth. I was as famous as a Barrymore or a Booth in my day. Now I am reduced to playing a European vampire hunter."

He blew out his breath as if to dispel the mischievous imps of age.

"Like many another player in such circumstances, I have been willing to share my knowledge of the trade with eager young talents. That is the nature of my relationship with Miss Stallings."

"In exchange for which services you received what, Mister Pollard?"

"The satisfaction of aiding a promising young performer, Doctor Chase." And, after a period of silence, "Plus an honorarium of very modest proportions. Even an artist, I am sure you will understand, must meet his obligations."

Chase pondered, then asked his final question of Pollard. "What, specifically, have you and Miss Stallings worked upon?"

"Her diction, Doctor Chase. There is none like the Bard to develop one's proper enunciation. Miss Stallings is of European origin, and it was in the subtle rhythms and emphases of the English language that I instructed her."

With this exchange Abel Chase completed his interrogation of Rodgers, Winkle, Jenkins, Pollard, and Garrison. He dismissed them, first warning them that none was absolved of suspicion, and that all were to remain in readiness to provide further assistance should it be demanded of them.

He then sought out Claire Delacroix. She was found in the office of the theatre manager, Walter Quince. With her were Estelle Miller and Jeanette Stallings. Chase rapped sharply on the somewhat grimy door and admitted himself to Quince's sanctum.

The room, he noted, was cluttered with the kipple of a typical business establishment. The dominant item was a huge desk. Its scarred wooden surface was all but invisible beneath an array of folders, envelopes, scraps and piles of paper. A heavy black telephone stood near at hand. A wooden filing cabinet, obviously a stranger to the cleaner's cloth no less than to oil or polish, stood in one corner. An upright typewriter of uncertain age and origin rested upon a rickety stand of suspect condition.

Claire Delacroix sat perched on the edge of the desk, occupying one of the few spots not covered by Quince's belongings. One knee was crossed over the other, offering a glimpse of silk through a slit in the silvery material of her skirt.

She looked up as Abel Chase entered the room. Chase nodded. Claire introduced him to her companions. "Miss Miller, Miss Stallings, Doctor Akhenaton Beelzebub Chase."

Chase nodded to the actresses. Before another word was uttered the atmosphere of the room was pierced by the shrill clatter of the telephone on Walter Quince's desk. Claire Delacroix lifted the receiver to her ear and held the mouthpiece before her lips, murmuring into it. She listened briefly, then spoke again. At length she thanked the caller and lowered the receiver to its cradle.

"That was Nolan Young, the coroner," she said to Chase. "I think we had best speak in private, Abel."

Chase dismissed the two actresses, asking them to remain on the premises for the time being. He then asked Claire Delacroix what she had learned from the county coroner.

Claire clasped her hands over her knee and studied Abel Chase's countenance before responding. Perhaps she sought a sign there of his success – or lack thereof – in his own interrogations. When she spoke, it was to paraphrase closely what Nolan Young had told her.

"The coroner's office has performed a quick and cursory post-mortem examination of Imre Hunyadi. There was no visible cause of death. Nolan Young sustains my preliminary attribution of heart failure. But of course, that tells us nothing. There was no damage to the heart itself, no sign of embolism, thrombosis, or abrasion. What, then, caused Hunyadi's heart to stop beating?"

Abel Chase waited for her to continue.

"The condition of Hunyadi's irises suggests that he was using some narcotic drug, most likely cocaine."

"Such was his history." Chase put in. "Nevertheless, Elbert Garrison observed Hunyadi closely and believes that he was not under the influence."

"Perhaps not," Claire acceded. "An analysis of his blood-stream will tell us that. But the two marks on his neck suggest otherwise, Abel."

Chase glanced at her sharply. He was a man of typical stature, and she a woman of more than average height. As he stood facing her and she sat perched on the edge of Walter Quince's desk, they were eye to eye.

"Study of the two marks with an enlarging glass shows each as the locus of a series of needle-pricks. I had observed as much, myself, during my own examination of the body. Most of them are old and well healed, but the most recent, Nolan Young informs, is fresh. It had apparently been inflicted only moments before Hunyadi's death. If those marks were the sign of a vampire's teeth, then the creature more likely administered cocaine to his victims than extracted blood from them."

"You are aware, Delacroix, I do not believe in the super-natural."

"Not all vampires are of the supernatural variety," she replied.

Abel Chase ran a finger pensively beneath his moustache. "What is your professional opinion, then? Are you suggesting that Hunyadi died of erythroxylon alkaloid intoxication?"

"I think not," frowned Claire Delacroix. "If that were the case, I would have expected Nolan Young to report damage to the heart, and none was apparent. Further, the condition of the needle-pricks is most intriguing. They suggest that Hunyadi had received no injections for some time, then resumed his destructive habit just tonight. I suspect that a second substance was added to the victim's customary injection of cocaine. The first drug, while elevating his spirits to a momentarily euphoric state, would have, paradoxically, lulled him into a false sense of security while the second killed him."

"And what do you suppose that fatal second drug to have been?"

"That I do not know, Abel. But I have a very strong suspicion, based on my conversation with the ladies of the company – and on your own comments earlier this night."

"Very well," Chase growled, not pleased. He knew that when Claire Delacroix chose to unveil her theory she would do so, and not a moment sooner. He changed the subject "What did you learn from the Misses Miller and Stallings?"

"Miss Miller is a local girl. She was born in the Hayes Valley section of San Francisco, attended the University of California in

Los Angeles, and returned home to pursue a career in drama. She still lives with her parents, attends church regularly, and has a devoted boyfriend."

"What's she doing in a national touring company of the vampire play, then? She would have had to audition in New York and travel from there."

"Theatre people are an itinerant lot, Abel."

He digested that for a moment, apparently willing to accept Claire Delacroix's judgment of the ingenue. "Her paramour would almost certainly be Timothy Rodgers, then."

"Indeed. I am impressed."

"Rodgers did not strike me as a likely suspect," Chase stated.

"Nor Miss Miller, me."

"What about Miss Stallings?" he queried.

"A very different story, there. First of all, her name isn't really Jeanette Stallings."

"The *nom de theatre* is a commonplace, Delacroix. Continue."

"Nor was she born in this country."

"That, too, I had already learned. That was why Pollard was coaching her in diction. Where was Miss Stallings born, Delacroix, and what is her real name?"

It was the habit of neither Abel Chase nor Claire Delacroix to use a notebook in their interrogations. Both prided themselves on their ability to retain everything said in their presence. Without hesitation Claire stated, "She was born in Szeged, Hungary. The name under which she entered the United States was Mitzi Kadar."

"Mitzi Kadar! Imre Hunyadi's Hungarian wife was Elena Kadar."

"And Mitzi's mother was Elena Kadar."

"Great glowing Geryon!" It was as close to an expletive as Abel Chase was known to come in everyday speech. "Was Jeanette Stallings Imre Hunyadi's daughter? There was no mention of a child in any biographical material on Hunyadi."

"Such is my suspicion," Claire Delacroix asserted.

"You did not have the advantage of reading the threatening note that Captain Baxter found in Hunyadi's dressing room, Delacroix."

"No," she conceded. "I am sure you will illuminate me as to its content."

"It was made up to look like a newspaper clipping," Chase informed. "But I turned it over and found that the obverse was blank. It appeared, thus, to be a printer's proof rather than an actual cutting. Every newspaper maintains obituaries of prominent figures, ready for use in case of their demise. When the time comes, they need merely fill in the date and details of death, and they're ready to go to press. But I don't think this was a real newspaper proof. There was no identification of the paper – was it the *Call* or the *Bulletin* the *Tribune* or the *Gazette*? The proof should indicate."

Abel Chase paused to run a finger beneath his moustache before resuming. "The typographic styles of our local dailies differ from one another in subtle but significant detail. The *faux* obituary came from none of them. It was a hoax, created by a malefactor and executed by a local job printer. It was cleverly intended as a psychological attack on Hunyadi, just as was the dead rodent that was found in his dressing room."

"And for what purpose was this hoax perpetrated?" Delacroix prompted.

"It did not read like a normal newspaper obituary," Abel Chase responded. "There is none of the usual respectful tone. It stated, instead, that Hunyadi abandoned his wife in Hungary when she was heavy with child."

"An act of treachery, do you not agree?" Claire put in.

"And that his wife continued her career as a medical researcher while raising her fatherless child until, the child having reached her majority, the mother, despondent, took her own life."

"Raising the child was an act of courage and of strength, was it not? But the crime of suicide – to have carried her grief and rage for two decades, only to yield in the end to despair – who was more guilty, the self-killer or the foul husband who abandoned her?"

Chase rubbed his moustache with the knuckles of one finger. "We need to speak with Miss Stallings."

"First, perhaps we had best talk with Captain Baxter and his men. We should determine what Sergeant Costello and Officer Murray have found in their examination of the premises."

"Not a bad idea," Chase assented, "although I expect they would have notified me if anything significant had been found."

Together they sought the uniformed police captain and sergeant. Costello's statement was less than helpful. He had examined the inner sill opening upon the window through which Abel Chase had peered approximately an hour before. It was heavily laden with dust, he reported, indicating that even had a contortionist been able to squeeze through its narrow opening, no one had actually done so.

"But a bat might have flown through that window, sir, without disturbing the dust," the credulous Costello concluded.

Murray had gone over the rest of the backstage area, and the two policemen had examined the auditorium and lobby together, without finding any useful clues.

"We are now faced with a dilemma," Abel Chase announced, raising his forefinger for emphasis. "Count Hunyadi was found dead in his dressing room, the door securely locked from the inside. It is true that he died of heart failure, but what caused his heart to fail? My assistant, Doctor Delacroix, suggests a mysterious drug administered along with a dose of cocaine, through one of the marks on the victim's neck." He pressed two fingers dramatically into the side of his own neck, simulating Hunyadi's stigmata.

"The problem with this is that no hypodermic syringe was found in the dressing room. Hunyadi might have thrown a syringe through the small open window letting upon the alley. But we searched the alley and it was not found. It might have been retrieved by a confederate, but the lack of footprints in the so-unusual snow eliminates that possibility. A simpler explanation must be sought."

Abel Chase paused to look around the room at the others, then resumed. "We might accept Sergeant Costello's notion that a vampire entered the room unobtrusively, in human form. He administered the fatal drug, then exited by flying through the window, first having taken the form of a bat. It might be possible for the flying mammal to carry an empty hypodermic syringe in its mouth. This not only solves the problem of the window's narrow opening, but that of the undisturbed dust on the sill and the untrampled snow in the alley. But while I try to keep an open mind at all times, I fear it would take a lot of convincing to get me to believe in a creature endowed with such fantastic abilities."

Accompanied by Claire Delacroix, Chase next met with Jeanette Stallings, the Mina of the vampire play. Jeanette Stallings, born Mitzi Kadar, was the opposite of Claire Delacroix in colouration and in manner. Claire was tall, blonde, pale of complexion and cool of manner, and garbed in silver. Jeanette – or Mitzi – sported raven tresses surrounding a face of olive complexion, flashing black eyes, and crimson lips matched in hue by a daringly modish frock.

Even her makeup case, an everyday accoutrement for a member of her profession, and which she held tucked beneath one arm in lieu of a purse, was stylishly designed in the modern mode.

"Yes, my mother was the great Elena Kadar," she was quick to admit. In her agitation, the nearly flawless English diction she had learned with the assistance of Samuel Pollard became more heavily marked by a European accent. "And that pseudo-Count Hunyadi was my father. I was raised to hate and despise him, and my mother taught me well. I celebrate his death!"

Abel Chase's visage was marked with melancholy. "Miss Stallings, your feelings are your own, but they do not justify murder. I fear – I fear that you will pay a severe penalty for your deed. The traditional reluctance of the State to inflict capital punishment upon women will in all likelihood save you from the noose, but a life behind bars would not be pleasant."

"That remains to be seen," Jeanette Stallings uttered defiantly. "But even if I am convicted, I will have no regrets."

A small sigh escaped Chase's lips. "You might have a chance after all. From what I've heard of the late Count Hunyadi, there will be little sympathy for the deceased or outrage at his murder. And if you were taught from the cradle to regard him with such hatred, a good lawyer might play upon a jury's sympathies and win you a lesser conviction and a suspended sentence, if not an outright acquittal."

"I told you," Jeanette Stallings replied, "I don't care. He didn't know I was his daughter. He pursued the female members of the company like a bull turned loose in a pasture full of heifers. He was an uncaring beast. The world is better off without him."

At this, Chase nodded sympathetically. At the same time, however, he remained puzzled regarding the cause of Hunyadi's heart failure and the means by which it had been brought about. He began to utter a peroration on this twin puzzle.

At this moment Claire Delacroix saw fit to extract a compact from her own metallic purse. To the surprise of Abel Chase, for until now she had seemed absorbed in the investigation at hand, she appeared to lose all interest in the proceedings. Instead she turned her back on Chase and Jeanette Stallings and addressed her attention to examining the condition of her flawlessly arranged hair, her lightly rouged cheeks and pale mouth. She removed a lipstick from her purse and proceeded to perfect the colouring of her lips.

To Abel Chase's further consternation, she turned back to face the others, pressing the soft, waxy lipstick clumsily to her mouth. The stick of waxy pigment broke, smearing her cheek and creating a long false scar across her pale cheek.

With a cry of grief and rage she flung the offending lipstick across the room. "Now look what I've done!" she exclaimed. "You'll lend me yours, Mitzi, I know it. As woman to woman, you can't let me down!"

Before Jeanette Stallings could react, Claire Delacroix had seized the actress's makeup case and yanked it from her grasp.

Jeanette Stallings leaped to retrieve the case, but Abel Chase caught her from behind and held her, struggling, by both her elbows. The woman writhed futilely, attempting to escape Chase's grasp, screeching curses all the while in her native tongue.

Claire Delacroix tossed aside her own purse and with competent fingers opened Jeanette Stallings' makeup case. She removed from it a small kit and opened this to reveal a hypodermic syringe and a row of fluid-filled ampoules. All were of a uniform size and configuration, and the contents of each was a clear, watery-looking liquid, save for one. This container was smaller than the others, oblong in shape, and of an opaque composition.

She held the syringe upright and pressed its lever, raising a single drop of slightly yellowish liquid from its point.

"A powerful solution of cocaine, I would suggest," Claire ground between clenched teeth. "So Imre Hunyadi behaved toward the women of the company as would a bull in a pasture? And I suppose you ministered to his needs with this syringe, eh? A quick way of getting the drug into his bloodstream. But what is in this other ampoule, Miss Kadar?"

The Hungarian-born actress laughed bitterly. "You'll never know. You can send it to a laboratory and they'll have no chance whatever to analyze the compound."

"You're probably right in that regard," Claire conceded. "But there will be no need for that. Anyone who knows your mother's pioneering work in anesthesiology would be aware that she was studying the so-called spinal anesthetic. It is years from practical usage, but in experiments it has succeeded in temporarily deadening all nerve activity in the body below the point in the spinal cord where it is administered."

Jeanette Stallings snarled.

"The danger lies in the careful placement of the needle," Claire Delacroix continued calmly. "For the chemical that blocks all sensation of pain from rising to the brain, also cancels commands from the brain to the body. If the anesthetic is administered to the spinal cord above the heart and lungs, they shortly cease to function. There is no damage to the organs – they simply come to a halt. The anesthetic can be administered in larger or smaller doses, of course. Mixed with a solution of cocaine, it might take several minutes to work."

To Abel Chase she said, "In a moment, I will fetch Captain Baxter and tell him that you are holding the killer for his disposition."

Then she said, "You visited your father in his dressing room between the second and third acts of the vampire play. You offered him cocaine. You knew of his habit and you even volunteered to administer the dose for him. He would not have recognized you as his daughter as he had never met you other than as Jeanette Stallings. You injected the drug and left the room. Before the spinal anesthetic could work its deadly affects, Count Hunyadi locked the door behind you. He then sat at his dressing table and quietly expired."

Still holding the hypodermic syringe before her, Claire Delacroix started for the door. Before she had taken two steps, Jeanette Stallings tore loose from the grasp of Abel Chase and threw herself bodily at the other woman.

Claire Delacroix flinched away, holding the needle beyond Jeanette Stallings' outstretched hands. Abel Chase clutched Stallings to his chest.

"Don't be a fool," he hissed. "Delacroix, quickly, fetch Baxter and his men while I detain this misguided child."

Once his associate had departed, Abel Chase released Mitzi Kadar, stationing himself with his back to the room's sole exit.

Her eyes blazing, the Hungarian-born actress hissed, "Kill me now, if you must. Else let me have my needle and chemicals for one moment and I will end my life, myself!"

Without awaiting an answer, she hurled herself at Abel Chase, fingernails extended liked the claws of an angry tigress to rip the eyes from his head.

"No," Chase negatived, catching her once again by both wrists. He had made a lightning-like assessment of the young woman, and formed his decision. "Listen to me, Mitzi. Your deed is not forgivable but it is understandable, a fine but vital distinction. You can be saved. You had better have me as a friend than an enemy."

As suddenly as she had lunged at the amateur sleuth, Mitzi Kadar collapsed in a heap at his feet, her hands slipping from his grasp, her supple frame wracked with sobs. "I lived that he might die," she gasped. "I do not care what happens to me now."

Abel Chase placed a hand gently on her dark hair. "Poor child," he murmured, "poor, poor child. I will do what I can to help you. I will do all that I can."

# ICE ELATION

## *Susanna Gregory*

*Susanna Gregory (b.1958) is the author of the historical mystery novels about Matthew Bartholomew, a teacher in medicine at Michaelhouse in Cambridge, in the fourteenth century. The series began with* A Plague on Both Your Houses *(1996). Previously she had worked in a coroner's office, which gave invaluable insight into criminal behaviour. By profession she is a biologist with a special interest in Antarctic research, spending every winter (or summer in the southern hemisphere) in the Antarctic. And what better place for an impossible mystery, than a scientific station with no one else for miles around. Miss Gregory provides her own background to the story.*

The point on the Antarctic Continent that is farthest from the coast in all directions is called the Pole of Inaccessibility. Since 1957, a Russian base has operated from near this remote spot, where scientists have been drilling through the 3,700 metre-thick ice – partly to reach the bedrock that lies below, and partly because the gasses contained in the compacted layers of ice that are excavated provide valuable information about past climate.

In 1995, a startling discovery was made. The ice does not lie directly on top of the bedrock at Vostok; instead, surveys have detected a body of water about the size of Lake Ontario, which has been sealed between ice and rock for at least half a million years, and possibly a lot longer. The scientists were faced with a dilemma: should they stop drilling, so that this "sterile" lake remains uncontaminated, or should they continue to dig and risk damaging a unique environment – and possibly risk it harming us? In September 1999, the decision was made to continue, using the Russian base and funds from American sources.

It will be some time before we know the secrets of Lake Vostok, and until then we can only speculate about what has laid undisturbed for aeons. This story does just that, and starts on one short, bleak day in late autumn, just as a team of eight scientists are about to break into the lake with a drill that is on its last legs . . .

"Hurry up," ordered Paxton, shivering in the sharp wind that gusted across the ice cap. "I'm freezing."

"I'm trying," replied Hall, tugging furiously at the door to the drill-house. "But something's jamming this closed."

Paxton sighed, stamping his feet and rubbing his hands together in a futile attempt to keep warm in the sub-zero temperatures. Even in the dim daylight of a late-autumn morning, Vostok Station was a frigid place: the coldest temperature ever recorded on Earth had been at Vostok.

In all directions, he could see nothing but ice. It was hard, flat, and featureless, except for the occasional ridge or trough where the wind had shaped it. For hundreds of miles, from the Pole of Inaccessibility to the sea, the ice lay across the Antarctic Continent like a thick blanket. Under the immense pressure of its own weight, it inched towards to the coast, where it formed floating shelves that eventually shattered into flat-topped icebergs the size of countries.

Vostok Station was a ramshackle collection of buildings; a deep layer of snow covered the roofs, so heavy that they buckled in places. The largest hut contained the cramped cubicles that comprised the scientists' sleeping quarters; the smallest was the kitchen. There were also two labs – one for examining the ice samples that the drill produced, and the other filled with meteorological equipment. And finally, there was the drill-house.

Because the storms that regularly screamed through the base destroyed anything that stood in their way, the drill that ate through the ice towards Lake Vostok had to be protected. It stood in a hangar, twenty feet high, and was a hissing, rattling, roaring machine that provided the focus of all activity at the station. Seven of the team of eight scientists, who had been detailed to remain at Vostok until the drill reached the lake, stood outside the drill-house now, waiting for Hall to open the door and let them in.

"Tanya must've locked it," said Hall, still hauling on the handle. "She was on drill duty this afternoon."

"Why would she do that?" asked Paxton. He gestured at the empty expanse that surrounded them. "It's not like we need to worry about burglars."

Paxton had three Americans, three Russians, and a fellow Britisher under his command. Of them all, he found the bellicose Texan, Hall the most difficult to like.

Hall shrugged. "We've almost reached the lake. Maybe Tanya wants to be alone when the drill reaches it – claim the glory for herself. After all, who knows what might be down there?"

"Our readings say we won't break through 'til tomorrow," said Paxton, forcing himself to ignore Hall's unpleasant snipe at the affable Russian.

"*If* we break through," mumbled the morose Russian Pavel Senko gloomily. "The drill's just about had it and we're lucky to have got this far."

"But the drill isn't running," said Hall truculently, although none of his colleagues needed him to point that out. The sudden and ominous silence as the drill had stopped was what had brought them from their work in the first place. "We won't break through tomorrow unless we drill today, and Tanya's switched the thing off."

Senko's compatriot, an affable bear of a man called Ivan Bannikov, dismissed Hall's concerns. "Tomorrow we'll break new grounds in science," he said with a grin, taking a hip-flask from his pocket and grimacing as he swallowed some of its fiery contents. "We'll take samples from a lake that's been sealed from the rest of the world for hundreds of thousands of years. What'll we find, d'you think?"

"Microscopic creatures, plants, and perhaps even fish that've evolved in complete isolation," replied Senko immediately. It was not the first time the scientists had aired this debate, and all had their own ideas about what was waiting for them. "We'll discover new species that no one's ever seen before."

"Right," agreed British-born Julie Franklin, her blue eyes gleaming with excitement. "But we'll have to be careful – they may be toxic to us. Who knows whether their environment and ours are still compatible?"

"I think we'll just find water," said Paxton, sceptical of their fanciful hopes for exotic discoveries. "We won't find any life."

"I hope you're wrong," said Hall fervently. "I want to take home something a bit more exciting than a bottle of water – assuming Tanya hasn't stolen the results for herself, that is."

Senko glared at him. "If you're accusing us Russians—"

"No one's accusing anyone of anything," interrupted Paxton hastily, not wanting the Russian and the American to argue. He hammered on the door. "Tanya? Are you in there? Open the door."

"Of course she's in there," snapped Hall. "She's not in her room, the labs, or the kitchen. The only place she *can* be is here."

"She may be ill," said Julie, frowning anxiously. She liked the quiet, intelligent Tanya.

Paxton elbowed Hall out of the way and hit the door with his shoulder as hard as he could. With a sharp, splintering sound of tearing wood, it flew inwards.

"She isn't here," said Senko, when a quick glance around the single-roomed building revealed that it was empty. "It wasn't her who locked the door."

Paxton studied the door in puzzlement. "Well, someone did; it was locked from the inside. You can see where the bolt's still in place."

Hall leaned down to inspect it. "No wonder I couldn't get it open. Tanya must've done it."

"But she isn't here," repeated Senko. "This building's nothing but four walls, a roof, and a floor that's four kilometres of solid ice. There's nowhere to hide; she isn't here."

"But the door was locked from the inside," insisted Hall.

"That means someone *in here* locked it. And since the rest of us were together in the labs, and we know there isn't another living soul within nine hundred miles of us, Tanya's the only one who could've done it."

"This is really odd," said Julie nervously. "The only place Tanya could be is here, but we can all see she isn't. So where is she?"

An exhaustive search of the camp did not reveal the whereabouts of Tanya. She had last been seen at lunch time, when the others had teased her because it was her turn to do "drill duty". The drill was temperamental, and needed constant attention while it ran. Monitoring it in the frigid drill-house, to ensure its pumps were clear and that it was well lubricated, was not popular with the scientists, who would rather be in the heated labs doing their own work.

Tanya had dressed in her warmest clothes, and the team had heard the drill start up. And no one had seen her since. There was a limited number of places anyone could be at Vostok: she was not under the beds, in the tiny cupboards in which belongings were stored, or among the stacks of supply crates. The only possible explanation for her absence was that she had gone for a walk.

"She wouldn't do that," objected Senko. "There's nowhere to go, and she'd never abandon the drill."

Paxton knew that was true. Tanya, like all of them, was reliable and conscientious. She would never shirk her duties, especially given that they were so close to reaching the lake.

"We should look for her," said Julie, worried. "She may've fallen and hurt herself."

"The drill-house is the tallest building," said Paxton. "We can climb on its roof and see if we can spot her."

"I'll go," offered Julie. "The weight of the snow's already made it buckle, and I'm lighter than the rest of you. We don't want it to collapse and damage the drill – not now."

She quickly scaled a ladder, and then stepped cautiously onto the snow-laden roof. Taking a pair of powerful binoculars, she scanned the expanse of ice slowly and carefully. But there was nothing to see. When her fingers began to ache from the cold, and the tears from her watering eyes froze on her cheeks, she descended again.

"The weather's clear today," she said. "I could see thirty miles easy. If Tanya were out there, I'd have spotted her. You know how colour stands out on the ice."

"We saw her less than three hours ago, anyway," said Senko. "She couldn't have walked that far."

"So, she isn't on the ice and she isn't in the base," said Hall, puzzled. "Where is she?"

No one could answer him.

"We could look for footprints," suggested Wilkes, a soft-spoken Virginian who always sported a cowboy-like necktie as part of his cold-weather clothing. "They'd lead us to her."

"The ice is too hard for footprints," said Paxton. "And even if we did find some, they won't necessarily be hers. We all wander outside the camp from time to time."

For the rest of the day, until it became too dark and too cold, they inspected every crack and crevice at the station, and scoured the featureless ice outside. Julie reported Tanya's disappearance to the American base at McMurdo, and when Paxton stumbled into the kitchen late that night, cold and weary after his fruitless search, she told him that McMurdo was fog-bound, and that no plane would be available to help them for several days.

"We've got to do something," said Senko, as members of the team gathered to discuss what to do next. "Tanya's missing. We can't go about our business like nothing's happened."

"What d'you suggest?" asked Hall tiredly. "We've looked everywhere. What else can we do?"

Senko shook his head helplessly. "There must be something. Perhaps she climbed inside an empty fuel can."

"We checked them," said Julie. "And every empty crate. She isn't here."

"I can think of one solution to this," said Hall quietly. "The stress of not knowing whether the drill will make it to Lake Vostok became too much for her. So she walked out onto the ice, dug a hole, and buried herself."

"The ice is too hard," said Senko, dismissive of the American he did not like. "And how could she've done it with none of us seeing? Even if she walked ten miles – unlikely in three hours – she'd still be visible from here."

"And she wasn't suicidal at lunch time," added Paxton. "Normally, she hated drill duty, but she was okay today, because we're so close to breaking through."

"But she shut the thing down, and we've wasted the whole day searching for her," said Hall bitterly. "Now we might never reach the lake."

"We will," said Paxton. "I'm on first watch tomorrow – I'll start early, and we'll continue 'til we reach it; then we'll tell McMurdo to evacuate us. We've been here six months, and by tomorrow, we'll have done all we came to do."

"I only hope the drill lasts," said Julie anxiously.

"All we need is one sample," said Hall. "More would be better, obviously, but one sample will at least tell us whether there's life down there."

"Where are Wilkes and Bannikov?" asked Senko, noting that two of the remaining seven were missing. "Still searching?"

Paxton shook his head. "I saw Bannikov ten minutes ago. He said they'll join us when they've changed."

The words were barely out of his mouth when Bannikov burst into the room, bringing with him a flurry of tiny flakes, more like ice dust than snow.

"I can't find Wilkes," he said breathlessly. "I've looked everywhere. He's not in the camp."

Stomach churning, Paxton raced outside to look in the huts and the labs, ignoring the burly Russian's protestations that he'd already checked them. Bannikov was right: Wilkes was not on the base.

"What happened?" Paxton demanded, while the others clustered around in alarm. "You said both of you were back."

"We *were* both back," insisted Bannikov, his usually florid face pale. He took the hip-flask from his pocket and raised it to his lips with unsteady hands. "He wanted to look in the drill-house one last time before giving up for the night; I went to change. After a few minutes, I went to the drill-house to make sure he was alright. I couldn't find him."

"That makes two," said Hall, glancing around him fearfully. "What's happening here?"

"More to the point," said Senko in a nervous whisper. "Who's going to be next?"

A more thorough search of the base revealed nothing: there was no sign of Wilkes, just as there had been no sign of Tanya. The two scientists seemed to have disappeared into thin air. Paxton found the cowboy-style necktie, twisted and frozen, in the drill-house, but it gave no clue as to what had happened to its owner.

"This is impossible," he said, gazing down at the material. "People don't just disappear."

Hall turned to Senko. "The Russians didn't put secret tunnels here, did they? This base was built during the Cold War, and so it's possible they did something like that. Wilkes and Tanya may've fallen down one."

Senko shook his head. "They only built what you can see – no hidden rooms or passages. And even if there were, they'd have collapsed under the weight of the snow by now."

"Then maybe someone else is here," said Hall. He gave Senko and Bannikov an unpleasant look. "We announce our progress every night on the radio, and so the whole of Antarctica knows we're on the verge of tapping into Lake Vostok. Maybe not everyone wants us to be successful."

"We're at the Pole of Inaccessibility," Paxton pointed out, determined that the Texan should not start to blame the Russians. "A rival band of scientists can't simply fly in, snatch our samples, and leave."

"Why not?" demanded Hall.

Paxton sighed. "First, only specially adapted planes can land here; and second, any unauthorized craft would be detected on radar and stopped. Plus there's the fact that we'd have heard the engines."

"Then maybe they came by land," pressed Hall. "It wouldn't be easy, but it's not impossible."

"It is," said Julie. "You can't cross Antarctica with a backpack, you know. It'd be a huge undertaking, needing a lot of logistical support. Such an expedition would be detected in no time."

"And we'd have seen anyone approaching on foot," added Paxton.

"Even if someone did come by land, it doesn't explain why Tanya and Wilkes are missing," said Bannikov reasonably. "We've searched all around the base. If someone else were here, we'd have found evidence of it – and we didn't."

"So, what're we going to do?" asked Hall, fear stark in his eyes. "Do we wait here until we disappear, one by one?"

"There are six of us: we'll stay in pairs," said Paxton, not liking the way Hall's panic was beginning to spread to the others. "And we'll radio McMurdo for an immediate evacuation."

"Maybe it's something to do with the lake," said Julie, casting a nervous glance towards the drill-house. "Tanya went missing when she was supposed to be drilling, and Wilkes disappeared when he went there to look for her."

"Such as what?" asked Paxton incredulously. "D'you think a monster from the untapped deep has wriggled its way up the drill shaft and is doing away with our friends?"

Julie's expression indicated that she did not consider his mocking suggestion so improbable. "I always said we'd find something dangerous down there. I assumed it'd be a microbe that might cause some deadly disease, but maybe there's something bigger."

"Are you serious?" demanded Paxton, scarcely believing his ears. "You're a scientist, Julie! All we'll find down there is water."

"Perhaps she's right," said Hall, swallowing hard. "We don't know what might've happened in a body of water that's been sealed for thousands of years."

That Hall was willing to believe some mysterious creature had slithered up the drill shaft was not a surprise to Paxton – the Texan watched a lot of science fiction videos, and his gullibility had provided the Russians with a good deal of entertainment during the long Antarctic evenings – but Paxton was astonished that such an idea should have come from the practical, rational Julie Franklin.

"We should contact McMurdo," he said, pushing the idiotic notion from his mind and heading for the radio in the kitchen. "Tell them about Wilkes."

"We should tell them about the lake, too," said Julie, running to catch up with him. "We should warn them."

"Warn them about what?" asked Paxton. "You've no evidence that whatever happened to Tanya and Wilkes has anything to do with the lake. There'll be some perfectly rational explanation—"

"But there isn't, is there?" demanded Julie angrily. "Two people've disappeared without trace from a place that – quite literally – has no way out. There isn't a rational explanation."

"Maybe we shouldn't tell them what we think," said Hall, following them into the kitchen. "If my government think we've unearthed some weird creature, they'll put us in quarantine and we'll never get out of here."

Bannikov and Senko exchanged an amused glance with the shy American called Morris who was their radio expert. Paxton was relieved to see that at least three of his team had not taken leave of their senses, even if Julie and Hall had.

"It's not funny!" snapped Julie, angered by their smiles. She glowered at them until they left, and then turned to Paxton. "Tell McMurdo now."

"I'll do no such thing," said Paxton firmly. "They'll think we've gone stark raving mad. I'll report Wilkes' disappearance and that's it."

The sleepy voice of the radio operator at McMurdo snapped into wakefulness when Paxton informed him that a second member of the expedition was missing. Just as Paxton was about to break the connection, Hall made a lunge for the transmitter and snatched it from his hand. Paxton tried to grab it back again before Hall made a total fool of himself, but tiredness made him slow, and the Texan had informed the startled operator about Julie's theory and signed off before Paxton could stop him.

"You've been watching too many movies," Paxton said in disgust. "I'm going to bed."

"I'm coming with you," said Hall, following him outside to where Morris, Bannikov and Senko stood in an uncertain group in the darkness, reluctant to leave the halo of light thrown out by the kitchen. "I'm not walking alone around here."

"Good thinking," said Bannikov. He retrieved his hip-flask from his pocket and took a swig. "I'll take one last look in the labs and the drill-house, and then I'm turning in, too. Morris can come with me. Julie should stay with Senko."

Senko slapped Hall on the back and gave him a wicked grin. "Watch out for gigantic ice worms."

Julie glared at him. "Laugh all you like. You'll see."

Paxton slept badly that night, and was awake well before dawn the following morning. He walked to the kitchen, and found Julie, Hall, and Senko already there, drinking coffee from over-sized plastic mugs. He accepted the cup Julie offered him, then struggled into his thick outdoors clothing in preparation for a chilly spell in the drill-house.

Hall helped him start the engine – always a tricky business after a cold night – while Senko and Julie watched. They held their breath as the machine chugged reluctantly into life. With a screech of metal, and a furious hiss of water, the drill began to revolve, faster and faster until the noise of it filled the small room, and its choking fumes made the scientists cough.

Perhaps because the engine had been shut down earlier than usual the previous day, the drill sounded different that morning. It ran more smoothly, and the labouring, wheezing noises usually associated with its early starts were absent. They exchanged hopeful glances: perhaps they'd be successful after all.

The drill was like a giant mosquito, sending a long probe of diamond-hard teeth through the ice, although at a depth nearing four kilometres it was becoming unreliable. However, after a while, the cylinder that carried the ice-cores to the surface began to emerge.

"That's not ice!" yelled Senko suddenly, making everyone jump. "That's water! We're through!"

Paxton saw the Russian was right, and they all clustered around to inspect the container, where tell-tale bubbles indicated that water, not ice, was being sampled.

"Lake Vostok," said Hall in an awed voice. He tapped the cylinder with his forefinger. "No one's ever set eyes on this before. We've done it!"

Senko gave a whoop of delight, and then grabbed Hall in a bear hug that had the American gasping for breath. Julie joined them, dancing around the chilly hut like an excited child. Paxton watched them, smiling.

"Put your masks on," he instructed, when their euphoria was spent. "We need to be careful."

"Why?" asked Julie immediately. "D'you agree that there might be something dangerous down there?"

"No," said Paxton shortly. "It's because I don't want the sample contaminated by our breath."

Carefully, he began to transfer the water into a screw-topped sterile container that would be shipped home for study. After all the waiting and anticipation, the brownish liquid that the drill produced was an anticlimax. It wasn't even clear, although Paxton knew that the drill's lubricants were largely responsible for that. Later, the contaminants would be removed, and the water studied in its clean state.

While he worked, the others fired up the drill again. There was a tearing, screeching sound, and the engine revved furiously. Paxton ducked instinctively as a sharp crack like a gunshot indicated that the probe had sheared. White smoke filled the drill-house, and the engine spluttered into silence.

"That was it," said Senko, crouching to examine it. "Ice pressure's finally distorted the borehole to the point where the drill can't work. We were just in time."

Hall nodded at the canister that held the murky water. "That'll be enough. In a few years, someone'll sink another hole and get more, but until then, this'll do."

Senko shook his head over the drill. "I'll fetch a new bit and try again, but I doubt it'll work."

When he had gone, Julie edged towards Paxton, leaning over

his shoulder and speaking in a low whisper so that Hall would not hear.

"The drill sounded different from the moment it started this morning. Did you notice?"

Paxton nodded absently, concentrating on his work. "It ran more smoothly than normal."

"Quite. You know what that means, don't you?"

Paxton gazed at her when the implications dawned on him. He cursed himself for not being more alert. He had listened to the drill chewing its way through ice for six months and should have realized that the difference in sound that day was significant.

"The drill wasn't cutting ice," he said. "It was already in the water when we started it."

Julie nodded. "The lake must've been tapped yesterday, while Tanya was working on it. Perhaps the ice is less dense near the water, and she made better time than our instruments said she would. But it seems Tanya reached the lake first."

Paxton nodded. "We'll credit her with its discovery in our reports."

Julie sighed irritably. "That's not what I meant. My point is that Tanya broke into the lake and then went missing. Wilkes came here to look for her, and he's missing, too."

"Not this again," began Paxton tiredly. "I don't—"

He was interrupted by Senko, who burst into the drill-house so abruptly that he almost ripped the damaged door from its hinges.

"They've gone! Both of them!" he gasped. "I've checked the kitchen and the labs. They're not here; they've gone the same way as Tanya and Wilkes."

"Who?" asked Hall stupidly, an expression of puzzlement on his heavy features. "What are you talking about?"

"Morris and Bannikov!" yelled Senko in exasperation. "I went to tell them that we'd broken through. They're not here. They've gone!"

Julie regarded Paxton steadily. "And where did they say they were going, before they went to bed last night?" she asked quietly.

"To check the labs," said Hall. He swallowed hard. "And the drill-house."

"Yes," said Julie softly. "The drill-house."

Paxton remained convinced that Julie's explanation was impossible, but was unable to provide her with an alternative one. He radioed McMurdo, and was too disheartened to object when Hall took the microphone to add that the disappearances of Tanya, Wilkes, Morris, and Bannikov were somehow connected to drilling into the lake. Julie nodded agreement, while Senko sighed and indicated with a forefinger tapping his temple that he thought they were both insane.

With the others in tow, Paxton went to inspect Morris and Wilkes' sleeping quarters. Neither were neat in their habits, and it was difficult to say whether they had slept in their beds the previous night. Therefore, it was not possible to prove or disprove Julie's suspicion that the last thing they had done was visit the drill-house for one final look for their missing colleagues.

"Their rooms are the two nearest the exit," said Paxton, frowning. "I never hear them coming or going anyway, because the heating makes too much noise."

"I think I heard Morris," said Senko, whose room was next door. "I didn't sleep well last night, and I heard him moving about, moaning."

"What do you mean, 'moaning'?" demanded Paxton. "Why didn't you mention this before?"

"Because I assumed he was distressed over Tanya and Wilkes, and it didn't seem right to tell you about it. But I may be wrong: the heaters mask sounds, as you just said yourself."

Julie stared at her feet. "Tanya and I were good friends and I was upset last night. It was probably me you heard."

"It may've been," said Senko, shrugging. "I tried not to listen."

Paxton sighed. "Well, there's a rational explanation for these disappearances, and I'm going to find out what it is. People simply don't vanish."

Hall backed away from him. "Count me out. I'm not going anywhere near that drill-house."

"Good," said Paxton. "All of you can stay here. There's safety in numbers."

"There wasn't for Morris and Bannikov," Senko pointed out. "They were together, but they still went."

"Stay here anyway," said Paxton. "You can keep an eye on each other."

"What do you mean?" demanded Julie, regarding him warily.

"I mean that it's possible one of us is responsible. If the three of you are together, then nothing untoward's going to happen."

"Unless the culprit's you," said Julie softly.

"In that case, you'll be safe with Hall and Senko," said Paxton shortly. "I'm going to look around the drill-house, since that's where people go missing. I'll find out what's going on if I have to tear it apart plank by plank."

"Wait," said Julie, running after him. "I'm coming with you. You said we should we stay in pairs, and you're right. Hall can stay with Senko."

They reached the drill-house, and Paxton dropped to his hands and knees to begin an intricate inspection of the floor. Julie watched.

"What are you looking for?"

Paxton shrugged. "I'll know when I find it. Four people don't disappear and leave no trace. Maybe I'll find a spot of blood, or something that suggests foul play."

Julie looked unconvinced, but knelt next to him and poked about with the sturdy penknife she always carried. It was cold, miserable work, and after about an hour, she stood, closing the knife with a snap.

"This is hopeless. There's nothing here. I'm going back to the others."

Paxton did not blame her. As the door closed, he moved to a new area, beginning to feel that she was right and that he was wasting his time. He was stiff from kneeling on the ice, and the prospect of a hot drink in the kitchen was an attractive proposition. He was about to give in to it, when a spot of colour caught his eye. It was a fragment of wood, and attached to it were a few hairs – long, dark hairs, like Tanya's.

He studied them thoughtfully. He had found what seemed to be a clue, but had no idea what its significance could be. Had the hairs been in the drill-house for some time – before Tanya had disappeared – or had they been pulled from her head during some kind of struggle? He realized that there was no way to know.

Placing his find in a sample bag, he began to walk towards the kitchen. He was tired from tension and lack of sleep, and walked unsteadily over the slick ice. He stumbled over a carelessly placed wire, and grabbed at a high stack of crates in an attempt to steady himself. Without warning, they began to totter, and he hurled himself to one side just as the whole pile came crashing down, narrowly missing him. They were heavy, filled with canned food, and smashed open as they hit the ice, spilling tins that rolled in every direction.

He scrambled to his feet and gazed at the crates in bewilderment, not understanding why they should suddenly become unstable, but knowing he would have been killed had they landed on him. He gazed around wildly, but there was nothing to see. The door to the kitchen burst open and Julie rushed out, Hall and Senko on her heels. She gaped at the scattered cans in horror.

"What've you done? Surely you didn't expect to find one of your clues among those?"

"They fell," said Paxton lamely. "I'm getting paranoid. I was beginning to wonder whether someone tried to push them on top of me."

"Who?" demanded Hall. "We were in the kitchen, and the others've gone, remember? No one pushed them. You *are* paranoid!"

Julie went to the broken crates and inspected them carefully. "Someone put an empty box on the bottom that made the stack top-heavy. It was only a matter of time before it went."

"Coincidence," said Senko, patting Paxton on the shoulder. "Come inside. The last thing we need to do is start getting suspicious of each other."

"Right," agreed Hall. "We've got the Lake Vostok monster to contend with."

"Did you find anything?" asked Senko, ignoring Hall's comment as he followed Paxton into the kitchen. "Any clues as to what happened to the others?"

Paxton shook his head, not wanting to mention the hairs. Although he was convinced they were somehow important, he also thought that speculation would do them no good. Julie started to make some coffee.

"We're out of condensed milk," she said, waving an empty tin.

"Already?" asked Hall. "I opened a new can yesterday."

"I'll get another," offered Senko. "I saw one in the crates Paxton tipped over. I won't be a minute."

He left, closing the door behind him. Paxton watched him through the window. The Russian crouched down, and began poking among the spilled cans on the ground. Then there was a sudden loud pop that made Paxton almost leap out of his skin. Julie gave an apologetic grin.

"Sorry. It's the gas on the cooker. It does that sometimes."

"Not to me," said Hall, taking the matches from her and lighting the flame. "It only does that when you light it."

Paxton smiled, and then turned to look out of the window again. Senko was not there. With a growing fear, Paxton raced outside, his feet skidding on the slick ice. But the Russian, like the others, had disappeared.

"I was watching him!" Paxton yelled in angry frustration. "I saw him kneeling here, looking through the cans. How can he have disappeared?"

Julie glanced around her. "Perhaps there's something here that'll tell us what happened to him – drag marks or something."

"Drag marks?" asked Hall in a squeak. "What do you think's going on around here?"

"I don't know," snapped Julie. She took a deep breath to calm herself. "We thought everyone disappeared from inside the drill-house, but we were wrong – Paxton virtually saw Senko go, and he was out here."

Hall gazed about him fearfully, as if he imagined something might come barrelling out of the snow and bear him away to its air, while Paxton wondered what to do next. Absently, he picked up a tin and tossed it from hand to hand as he watched Hall and Julie prod among the spilled crates. Hall was using a pencil and Julie had her penknife. Paxton glanced at the can he held. It was the milk Senko had been searching for. He gazed down at it, wondering why the Russian hadn't found it immediately, when it had been lying on top of the pile. Then he inspected it more closely. The rim was damaged, as though something had hit it very hard, and a fibre of red wool clung to it. Senko had been wearing a red hat. Had he banged his head on the can as he had fallen? Or had someone hit him with it? If Senko had fallen, then he had done so very hard, because the dent was a deep one.

"I'm going back to the drill-house," he said, not knowing what else to do. "I think we'll find answers there, not here."

"I'm not going in there," whined Hall. "It's too dangerous."

"We'd better stay together," said Julie nervously. "And we should finish searching here first."

"I'll leave the door open," said Paxton. "We'll be able to see each other."

Hall and Julie exchanged a glance that suggested visual contact was not especially reassuring, given what had just happened to Senko. Paxton propped open the door to the drill-house and walked inside, crossing the ice floor to examine the drill itself.

He leaned his head against the cold metal, wondering what was happening to the team that had rubbed along so well for six months. They were all dedicated scientists, almost fanatical about the work they did, and there was a degree of rivalry. But it was usually friendly, and Senko and Hall were the only ones who ever had any serious arguments. Paxton glanced across at the American. Was he responsible for the mysterious disappearances? Paxton did not think so, and would have laid his money on the infinitely more cunning Senko as being the culprit.

He was about to resume his search, when he glimpsed a glitter of metal half buried in the snow at the foot of the drill. He reached down and picked it up, startled to find himself holding Bannikov's hip-flask. He inspected it carefully. It was dented, which it certainly had not been when in Bannikov's care. He unscrewed the top and sniffed at the contents. Whisky. His thick gloves made him clumsy, and the flask slipped out of his fingers. Swearing under his breath, he stopped to retrieve it – and then froze when he saw that the liquid that seeped from the flask was bright orange. It was, without doubt, the cadmium compound they used for lubricating the drill-bit.

Paxton was horrified. Is that what had given the contents of the hip-flask the bite that each of them had experienced once and would never try again? If so, it was a dangerous thing for Bannikov to do, because cadmium was a serious poison – even if its taste and smell could be masked by whisky. He recalled the last time the Russian had produced his flask – just before his disappearance, when he had gone with Morris to inspect the drill-house for a last look for Tanya.

Paxton was still staring at it when there was an agonized scream, full of fear and pain. Hall! He raced outside to see Julie running from the opposite direction. She grabbed Paxton's arm and gazed around her.

"Did you hear that?" she gasped. "It sounded like Hall."

"It was Hall," said Paxton. "Where is he?"

"I went to turn off the gas in the kitchen," said Julie. "We left it on when we rushed outside to look for Senko. I didn't want a burned camp to add to our problems, so I went to see to it."

"Hall would never let you leave him alone," said Paxton, snatching his arm away. "You saw how terrified he was. He'd have gone with you."

"Well, he didn't," said Julie angrily. "He stayed here, looking through the cans for the clues you seem so sure we'll find."

"I've got all the clues I need," said Paxton harshly. "It was you."

"Me?" asked Julie, startled. "What was me?"

Paxton pointed to a spray of tiny red spots that stained the cuff of her coat. "You've just done something dreadful to Hall. You've got a knife – I've seen it. Hall would never've allowed you to leave him alone while you went to the kitchen. You killed him. Where's his body?"

"This is nonsense," said Julie, starting to laugh uncertainly. "You've gone mad! The stress has finally got to you and you're losing your reason."

"No," said Paxton. "You killed Bannikov and Morris by poisoning them – there was cadmium in Bannikov's flask, and he doubtless offered a nip to Morris when they walked together to have one final look for Tanya in the drill-house."

Julie shook his head. "You're insane. How d'you imagine I could dispose of six bodies? And I was with you when Senko disappeared. How am I supposed to have killed him, when I was with you?"

Paxton gave a humourless smile. "Tanya's been helping you."

A soft footfall in the snow made Paxton spin around quickly. Tanya stood behind him, wearing her heavy outdoor gear. She was holding the plastic sample container filled with Lake Vostok water, cradling it carefully in both hands. Paxton gazed at her, wondering where she had been hiding when they had searched everywhere.

"You caught us," she said ruefully. "Not that it matters, since you're the last one."

"You killed them," said Paxton slowly. "You killed Senko with the can of milk he was looking for. I saw it on top of the pile, so he should've found it immediately, yet he spent some time rummaging for it. You'd moved it."

Julie and Tanya exchanged a glance that told him he was right. He continued.

"You hit him over the head with it – a strand of his hat caught in the rim. I was looking out of the window at the time, so Julie pulled that trick with the popping stove to distract me."

Julie nodded. "We had to take you one by one or you'd have been able to overpower us. After Tanya brained Senko, I stabbed Hall."

"But you managed Morris and Bannikov at the same time."

"Morris was a stroke of luck," said Tanya. "He took a swig from Bannikov's flask to give him courage when they went into the drill-house. The compound's got no taste or smell, so they only knew it was poisoned when it was too late."

"Senko heard Morris moaning," recalled Paxton. "Julie told us it was her."

"Bannikov died quickly," elaborated Tanya. "But Morris drank less and took longer. We tried to quieten him, but Senko heard anyway."

"Senko's death was carefully arranged, though," Paxton went on. "Julie claimed there was no milk, so he'd fetch some. But there was plenty of milk. Hall opened a new can yesterday."

Julie nodded. "If any of you'd had the sense to look in the can that Hall knew was virtually full, I'd have been caught in a lie."

"And Wilkes was strangled," said Paxton. "I found his necktie, twisted like it had been used as a garrotte."

"He was easy," said Julie. "He came alone to the drill-house, and I distracted him while Tanya slipped up behind."

"But why?" asked Paxton, bewildered. "I thought we were friends."

"We were," said Julie. "And a more congenial and pleasant team we couldn't have hoped for. But whoever analyzes that sample from Vostok will have a reputation for life. Why should we share? Hall was always boasting about how much money Americans have for science, and Bannikov and Senko have the backing of their government. Tanya and I wouldn't have stood a chance."

"But we will now," said Tanya. She glanced down at the container she held. "And we were lucky we *did* put our plan into action, given that you lot only managed to retrieve this one bottle. There isn't enough here for eight people to share."

"You killed five people just to promote your careers?" asked Paxton, aghast.

Julie nodded, unabashed. "There's a lot at stake here. Whoever publishes first will be famous."

"There may even be a Nobel Prize," suggested Tanya hopefully.

"But how can you expect to get away with this?" asked Paxton, horrified. "When the plane comes, you'll have to explain why all your colleagues are dead."

"That won't be a problem," said Julie smugly.

"Hall's radio messages," said Paxton, suddenly understanding why she had been so keen for McMurdo to be informed about the ludicrous notion that something from the lake was responsible for the disappearances. "You'll claim he went insane and killed everyone."

"Leaving only two frightened survivors," confirmed Julie. "Our only way out of here is on a plane sent from McMurdo, so we had to invent a story they'd believe. People go crazy on these remote polar bases all the time – why not here, with the added stress of being on the verge of a great scientific discovery? Anyone who knows Hall won't be surprised that he convinced himself some monster was on the loose. He watched too many videos altogether."

"How did you guess I was Julie's accomplice?" asked Tanya curiously.

Paxton sighed tiredly. "Because as soon as I knew Julie was the culprit, I also knew she couldn't have done it alone. You were the first to go, so it had to be you – using your disappearance to frighten the rest of us until you were ready to kill your first victim. I also found a scrap of wood with some of your hairs attached – caught when you struggled into your hiding place before anyone could see that you hadn't disappeared at all."

"And where was my hiding place? You searched the whole camp and didn't find me."

"The drill-house roof. You climbed up the drill and slipped between loose planks, which was why you were able to lock the door from the inside."

Tanya nodded.

"And you hid the bodies there, too," Paxton continued. "The snow on the roof is thick, and it'd be easy to hollow out coffin-shaped grooves that aren't visible from the ground. And a small ice cave would be an ideal hiding place for you – not too cold and out of the wind."

"But only for a short period of time," said Tanya. "That was why we had to act quickly."

"When I suggested we use the drill-house roof as a high point to scan the ice, Julie immediately volunteered to go because she said she was the lightest . . ."

"If you'd gone, you'd have seen our hollows," said Julie. "Not to mention the winch we assembled to haul the bodies out of sight quickly. Would you like to see them now?"

Paxton gazed at her. "So you can kill me and be saved the bother of taking my body up there?"

"You're the last," said Julie dismissively. "It doesn't matter whether we put you there or not. There's no one left to hide your body from."

Suddenly, her penknife was in her hand, and she was moving towards Paxton with grim determination. Tanya shoved the sample container in her pocket and darted behind him, dividing his attention. He realized he still held the heavy milk can that had killed Senko, and he hurled it as hard as he could. It hit Julie in the chest, knocking her from her feet so that the knife flew from her hand. Paxton was inclined to run, to escape the women who had murdered his colleagues, but there was nowhere to go. He would die on the ice just as surely as if Julie stabbed him.

He dived for the knife, aware that Tanya was close behind him. He skidded and lost his balance. Tanya was on him in an instant, clawing and scratching at him, and trying to prevent him from reaching the weapon. Meanwhile, Julie had recovered and was on her hands and knees, inching slowly towards the weapon.

In the distance, there was a dull growl that grew steadily louder. For a moment, Paxton thought it was something to do with the drill, but he glanced up and saw a tiny black speck in the sky.

"It's a plane!" he yelled, trying to scramble to his feet. "You made McMurdo so concerned by allowing Hall to broadcast his insane messages that they've braved the fog and sent help."

"But not soon enough to save you," said Tanya grimly. "Our plan will still work."

She lunged to one side, and Paxton felt his hood tightening around his neck. While he used both hands to try to loosen the choking grip, Julie finally reached the knife and climbed unsteadily to her feet. She staggered forward, the weapon poised for a swipe that would see her and Tanya the sole inheritors of the contents of Lake Vostok.

The plane droned nearer. Paxton was beginning to grow dizzy

from lack of air, and Julie's arm was already plunging downward. With the last of his strength, he twisted away. His feet slid on the ice and he fell, dragging Tanya with him. They landed on something that popped under their combined weight, and a gout of cold liquid burst across the ground. Tanya went limp.

"The sample!" screamed Julie, dropping to her knees and staring in horror at the pool of dirty water that ran in rivulets across the ice. "You fell on the container and broke it!"

"And you killed Tanya," said Paxton, struggling free of the inert body and watching blood mingle with the spilled water. The plane roared low overhead as it prepared to land, and Paxton could see people at the windows, gesticulating wildly at what he assumed they could see on the drill-house roof. "It's over, Julie."

Julie was white-faced as the last dribbles from the container seeped into the snow. "It was all for nothing! None of us'll be around by the time they agree to drill another borehole."

"You'll be serving a prison sentence for murder, anyway," said Paxton coldly. "You killed six of your colleagues."

"We almost did it," she said softly, still gazing at the pale stain. "We held it in our hands. But at least there's some justice in all this: you ruined our plan, but with the sample gone and the drill broken, at least it won't be *you* who'll be the first one to analyze Lake Vostok."

With a deafening roar, the plane landed a short distance away, and its passengers began to hurry towards them, pointing at the drill-house roof in horror and confusion. Julie's shoulders sagged in defeat. Paxton withdrew the small phial of Lake Vostok water he had secreted in his pocket when the others weren't looking, and showed it to her.

"I'd have been the first to publish the results anyway," he said softly. "All you've done is ensure that I'll succeed."

# THE MYSTERY OF THE TAXI-CAB

*Howel Evans*

*Now we step back in time again. I know little about Frank Howel Evans. He wrote several boys' books as Atherley Daunt at the turn of the last century, and it's probable that he was an actor or worked in the theatre in some capacity, as many of his stories involve the stage. He even wrote a Sexton Blake novel called* The Actor Detective *(1905). The following comes from a series of stories Evans wrote for* The Novel Magazine *in 1922 and which was reworked into the book* The Murder Club *(1924). The Murder Club is a collection of individuals who delight in solving bizarre crimes – such as the following.*

"Once more a humble person craves admission – NUMBER ONE."

Brinsley read this out from a slip of paper at the next meeting of the Murder Club.

White-haired, beaming, Number One, was admitted with Brinsley's butler carrying a large parcel, which he placed on a side table.

"Gentlemen," said the Chief of the Secret Service, "just a little memento. You will understand when you see it. Good night."

In a second the little silver-haired man of mystery had gone, and Brinsley, as President, drew the untied wrappings off the parcel and brought to light a magnificent chased gold cigar-box, on the lid of which was an inscription:

## TO THE MURDER CLUB
## FROM
## NUMBER ONE.

"And what's this?" Brinsley picked up a scrap of paper which lay at the bottom of the box and read aloud:

"I rather fancy the Murder Club and *The Wire* will be interested in the murder of Sir George Borgham. If the mystery is solved I shall be glad of any particulars that you may not care to give to the public. Secret please – NUMBER ONE."

Brinsley grabbed for an evening journal.

"The little man gets busy," he said. "It only happened this morning and Crimp's on it, that's why he's not here. I'll read the account, and then we shall have it in our minds clear and sharp."

And this was the account:

"Sir George Borgham appears to have left his house in Mayer Street, Sloane Square, at about twenty minutes to ten this morning. He was driven in his car by way of Piccadilly, making a call at a bookshop there, and arrived at the Law Courts at five minutes to ten. The policeman on duty outside the Courts, knowing the famous judge's car, opened the door as usual for Sir George to alight and make his way to the judge's entrance. But Sir George, instead of jumping out quickly as was his habit – he was a very active man for his sixty-eight years – remained seated in the near corner, with his head sunk on his chest. His silk hat was lying on the seat by his side, and in his right hand was the book which he had bought, closed, with his finger between the pages as if to keep the place. At first the policeman thought that he was asleep, so he said to him: 'You're at the Courts, my lord.' But receiving no answer, he put his head further inside the car, and instinct and experience then told him that he was looking at a dead man.

"The body of the judge was lifted out and carried into his own private room at the Law Courts.

"There is no mystery as to the cause of the death of Sir George

Borgham, for, embedded in the chest up to the hilt, piercing his heart, was found a long thin piece of steel, of the shape and size of an ordinary knitting needle, and as sharp as a stiletto, with a sort of handle at the end of it made from a piece of cork.

"That, brother members, seems as far as we have got up to the present with information as to this case."

Brinsley laid down the evening journal from which he had been reading, and looked at the members.

"It sounds like murder, doesn't it?" said Eustace Golbourne, the professor of mathematics from Scotland. "Surely a man couldn't kill himself by driving a thin piece of sharp steel into his heart?"

The president nodded.

"Yet men have done almost incredible things when determined to take their own lives," he said. "I'll ring up my office and see if anything further has come in from the police," and he reached for the telephone at his side. "If there's anything fresh Crimp will be at *The Wire* office by now."

Brinsley spoke through to his office, and after listening to the answer, replaced the receiver.

"The only further scrap of news is," he said, "that on the little finger of Sir George Borgham's left hand there was tied a small piece of red tape."

"The affair has a peculiar interest for me," put in a round jolly-faced man about fifty-eight or sixty, the Rev. Thomas Bowen, of Cornwall, the greatest living authority on the mental and moral out-look of the criminal. "A sad interest, indeed, for only last night I saw Sir George at the Athelonian Club, of which I'm a country member, and we had quite a long chat together."

"That's interesting, Mr Bowen!" said Brinsley. "Did you know him well?"

"Not very well," answered the clergyman. "Just well enough for us to be pleased to see each other when I happened to come into the club and find him there, and to enjoy a little chat together. A genial and a learned man was Sir George."

"Yes," agreed Brinsley. "Though I daresay, as a judge, he had a good many enemies. He has sent a lot of people to prison in his time, and hanged more than one. Revenge may have been the motive for the crime."

There came a gentle knock at the door, and Brinsley's manservant entered with a parcel, which the newspaper proprietor rapidly tore open.

"As I expected, gentlemen," he said, "here is the official photograph of the weapon with which the crime was committed. One, of course, has gone to every newspaper office in the kingdom, circulated by the police, and as a special favour, I asked Scotland Yard to let me have one here."

Just an ordinary plain, untouched photographic print showed a long strip of thin, flat steel, one end of which came to a sharp point, while the other was embedded in a long piece of cork.

"The steel is sharp at each edge," went on Brinsley. "The police have notified us of that. And with that sharp point it would go through the flesh like a knife through butter. And the long piece of cork would make a splendid handle, so that anybody could use it as a dagger."

There was silence for a few moments, while each member of the club in turn examined the photograph.

"And this is the latest news my men brought into the office," said Brinsley. "Sir George Borgham's chauffeur, Edward Morris, said that his master alighted from the car and stayed for a few minutes at Everton's bookshop in Piccadilly. He was inside about two minutes, and returned to the car, which the chauffeur drove to the Law Courts by way of Garrick Street and the Strand, to avoid the Covent Garden traffic in Long Acre. The outside limit of time that the journey took from Piccadilly to the Law Courts was five minutes, so, in that time Sir George Borgham met his death. And now, gentlemen, if you'll excuse me," Brinsley rose, "I've got to get back to *The Wire*. Don't forget that the resources of *The Wire* are at your disposal, and £500 is my offer for anyone who brings me exclusive news of the identity of Sir George Borgham's murderer."

"Come and have a look at Everton's, the bookshop," said Mr Bowen, the clergyman from Cornwall, to his friend Eustace

Golbourne, as they walked away from Brinsley's house. "It might give us something to think about. That £500 would be rather useful to send my godson, your boy, to college with, wouldn't it?"

Golbourne nodded, and they walked on to Everton's, in Piccadilly.

"Now," said Mr Bowen, "let's reconstruct the incident. Sir George leaves the shop, jumps into his car, presumably shuts the door himself, and arrives a few minutes later at the Law Courts with a piece of steel in his heart. Now, Sir George couldn't possibly have killed himself. The attitude in which he was found precludes all possibility of that. If he had stabbed himself, the body would have collapsed forward; it wouldn't have been leaning back."

"How do you know that?" put in Golbourne quickly.

"I was in the War, my friend," said Bowen a little sadly. "One learnt a good deal there. Very well then, let us assume that Sir George was murdered. Now, he was lying in the corner, nearest to the kerb. Suppose that he was stabbed through the window, by somebody leaning in and striking the blow."

"Impossible!" said Golbourne suddenly and firmly.

"Here's an empty taxi. I just want to try an experiment. Hi! Just a moment," he cried to the driver. "Stop still, will you? You'll get your fare just the same. I only want to get in and out of the cab."

Golbourne let down the window of the cab nearest the pavement, shut the door to again, and then, putting his hand and arm through the window, struck an imaginary blow, as if attempting to kill a man in the near-side corner. Then he opened the door, got inside the cab, and Bowen saw him, from various attitudes, bring his arm downwards, more than once, as if again endeavouring to strike a murderous blow.

"That's all right!" Golbourne jumped out and handed the astonished driver half-a-crown. "I don't want you any longer. Come on," and he took the clergyman's arm, "I've got an idea, a wild, freakish sort of idea, but I'm going to sleep on it and try an experiment in the morning. It's too late to-night, the shops aren't open."

After breakfast the next morning, Golbourne said to his friend at the hotel where they were staying:

"I'm going down to Guildford Street, Tom. I shan't be more than a few minutes. You wait here till I come back."

In less than a quarter of an hour Golbourne returned, and, placing a small, square cardboard box on the table, asked Mr Bowen to take off his coat and roll up his shirt sleeves.

"Don't look so surprised," said the professor, smiling, "for here's something else to make you still more puzzled. Hold out your arm, there's a good fellow."

From the cardboard box Golbourne took what at first sight appeared to be a wrist-watch, encased in the usual strap. This he proceeded to fasten round Bowen's forearm, just below the elbow.

"I'll tell you all about it in a minute," he said, settling himself in his chair.

"Now take a penholder, or pencil, or ruler, or anything you like, off that side-table over there, and then stand over me and stab downwards at my heart. You needn't dig the deadly weapon into me, let it just touch me, that's all. Just stab downwards and then check it."

Puzzled, Bowen did as he was directed. Then Golbourne got up and consulted the little round dial in the wrist-strap, and scribbled a figure or two on a scrap of paper.

"All right," he said. "And now, Tom, you can help me if you'll just go down to the hall and ring up *The Wire* office, and ask for Brinsley or Crimp if, with the influence of *The Wire*, they could communicate with Scotland Yard and ascertain the weight of that weapon which was found in Sir George's body. Also, I want the height of Sir George's car from the floor to the roof, and I should like to know whether all the windows in the car, which, I understand, was a large one, were open. Just a minute! What height are you, Tom?"

"Five foot eight and three-quarters."

"And your length of arm?"

"About two and a half feet, I suppose. I'm pretty long in the arm."

"Right! I'll get to work while you're at the 'phone. I think I'm just beginning to see a little bit of daylight. I should like to see Sir George's car, if possible, and measure it myself, but get *The Wire* people to communicate with Scotland Yard as soon as they can, will you? And ask them to ring us up here. Say that we'll be down at *The Wire* office to see Mr Brinsley later on."

While the clergyman was downstairs at the 'phone in the hall, Golbourne sat and figured away busily, covering sheet after sheet with figures and geometrical symbols, and was still busy with his calculations when Bowen returned.

"Just a moment, Tom," he said, without turning round. "Don't talk for a second or two. I'm in the middle of a most intricate bit of work."

"There, that's done for the present," said the professor a minute later, laying down his pencil with a sigh of relief. "Just let me get the weight and the length of that piece of steel, and things may begin to move. What's the news? Did you get on to *The Wire* all right?"

"Yes, I spoke to Crimp. He said Brinsley will be down there before twelve this morning, and he'll ring up as soon as possible and let us know about the weight and the length of that piece of steel, etc. As regards Sir George's car, he thinks there'll be no difficulty in our seeing it. Of course, the police have taken charge of it, but—"

"I suppose he wouldn't know whether all the windows were open or not?" asked Golbourne.

"No," answered Bowen, "but the police will be sure to keep it in exactly the same condition as when the body was found in it. Crimp tells me it's in the police station yard at Bow Street."

"Good! Then we can look in there on our way down to *The Wire* office. Ask Crimp whether that can't be arranged. Perhaps we may represent ourselves as belonging to *The Wire*, which, indeed, we do while we are investigating this case. Pop along now, Tom, and wait for the answer. Put the figures down carefully, won't you?"

Bowen returned in a few minutes with a scrap of paper in his hand.

"The length of the piece of steel, including the cork handle," he read from the paper, "is nine and a half inches, and the weight is exactly one ounce."

Golbourne turned to the table and again figured away busily.

"There's something wrong, something funny somewhere," he said at length.

"A piece of steel of the thinness and the evident suppleness of the weapon which killed Sir George couldn't possibly weigh an ounce; at least, I don't think so; but we'll see after we've been to Bow Street, and when we get to Scotland Yard, for that's where I want to go to see that steel. What about our seeing the car? Will that be all right?"

"Yes, they said at *The Wire* that the police would be only too glad to show it to us if we mentioned that we were working for the paper."

"Come along, then."

They hailed a taxi as soon as they got outside, and were soon being shown the motor-car of the late Sir George Borgham in the yard at Bow Street Police Station.

It was one of the very latest makes, with long sliding, lifting windows in front and at the sides. The two side windows were open; and the one at the left of the driver's seat was lowered also, the one in front of which the driver sat being closed.

"Is that exactly how it was found when the car arrived at the Law Courts?" asked Golbourne of the officer who was with them.

"Exactly," was the reply. "The old gentleman always liked plenty of fresh air, so his chauffeur said, and almost invariably had the windows open."

"If there's no objection to having one of the doors opened," said Golbourne, "I should like to take a measurement. I suppose there are no finger-marks on the door handles?"

"No, there are none. That's one of the first things we do – try for finger-prints," smiled the officer.

Golbourne produced a tape-measure, and with the assistance of Bowen took just one measurement – the height of the car from the floor to the roof. Then, after thanking the police for their courtesy, the two members of the Murder Club left.

"Tom," said Golbourne when they were outside, "there's a quiet little eating-house close by, which I believe boasts of excellent beer and sandwiches, both of which are things of delight. Let us go and lunch while I make certain observations."

At the little table to which their orders were brought, Golbourne again used his pencil and paper. At length he slipped them back into his breast pocket, and with an air of triumph, almost pointed a finger at Bowen.

"Tom," he said, "I think I've discovered how Sir George Borgham was killed!"

The Rev. Thomas Bowen drew in his breath with a gasp of surprise.

"But by whom," continued the professor, "and where, it's at present impossible to say. We'll go down to the office of *The Wire* now and get Brinsley to take us to Scotland Yard, where the inspector in charge of the case will, no doubt, allow us to examine the steel which was found in Sir George's heart."

"You've found out something!" was Brinsley's greeting when they arrived at *The Wire* office. "I'm sure, professor, I can see a glint of triumph in your eye. What have you to say?"

"With the powerful resources of *The Wire*, Mr Brinsley," said Golbourne, smiling pleasantly, "could you tell us at what rate the wind was blowing in the neighbourhood of the Strand, between twenty minutes and five minutes to ten on the morning of the day on which Sir George Borgham was killed? Do you think they would tell you at the Meteorological Offices in South Kensington?"

"Surely!" said Brinsley. "I'll get them on the 'phone myself at once . . . Hallo – hallo! Meteorological Society? . . . Yes, it's the editor of *The Wire* speaking. Could you tell me at what rate the wind was blowing in London at between twenty and five minutes to ten? . . . Thanks – just a minute, please . . . Here, professor, I think you'd better come. It's a bit too technical for me – something about pressure and weight and atmosphere, and all sorts of strange things."

Golbourne went to the telephone, listened, and jotted down some notes.

"Give me five minutes to myself," he said when he'd finished and put back the receiver, "and then I'll get you to take us to Scotland Yard, Mr Brinsley, if you will."

In a few minutes Golbourne looked up from his calculations.

"I think," he said, "that I've got at the way in which Sir George was killed. Shall we go to Scotland Yard now and see the weapon? Then I can tell better."

Inspector Mirch, who had charge of the case, received them with the usual courtesy extended by the police to the Press. The researches of the Murder Club were familiar, and, indeed, had been exceedingly useful, to the authorities, and the inspector willingly produced every exhibit in connection with this latest murder mystery looking with obvious curiosity at the silver-haired, white-moustached, elderly man who asked if he might be allowed to handle the deadly piece of steel.

"But a strip of steel of that length and width," said Golbourne, "wouldn't weigh an ounce, but about three-quarters of an ounce."

"How do you know that, sir?" asked the inspector.

"I should be a poor professor of mathematics if I couldn't measure and weigh things with my eye," smiled Golbourne. "Now let us see if the cork weighs the other quarter to make up the full ounce?"

Scientific appliances of every kind are in use at Scotland Yard, including delicate scales which will weigh a thread of silk or a woman's hair. And after experimenting the inspector said:

"Forty grains under a quarter of an ounce."

"Of course! I was wrong. I forgot the steel!" Golbourne spoke with excitement. "Gentlemen, I can now tell you how Sir George Borgham was killed!"

The silence in that large square room overlooking the Embankment was only broken for a second or two by the rumble of the traffic outside, and then Golbourne spoke again.

"I think, Mr Inspector," he said, "that if you cut open that cork, you'll find that it is weighted inside to make up the exact quarter of an ounce, minus the fraction of weight given by the steel inserted into it."

Mirch hesitated for a second, and then cut the cork across, severing it in two pieces. The inside proved to be slightly hollowed, and out rolled four or five little round shots of lead.

"Ah! I thought it was weighted," cried Golbourne triumphantly. "Put these in the scales and you will find that it is they which brought the cork up to a quarter of an ounce, an unusual weight for one of its size."

Further experiments proved that Golbourne's calculations were correct.

Then the professor took up one of the pieces of cork, and probed and pricked at it with a pocket knife, and gradually eased the pieces into two.

"You see," he said, taking up the other half and performing the same operation on it, "the cork was cut in two lengthways, the inside hollowed, the shot inserted, and the cork fastened together again with a strong adherent. It was cleverly done, too."

"What else have you to say about it, sir?" asked the inspector.

"This," Golbourne spoke solemnly. "Sir George Borgham was killed with this weapon from a distance of ten feet and a height of eight feet."

Silence, and again silence, broken after a few tense seconds by Inspector Mirch, who said, without any idea of sarcasm:

"Who was the murderer, then?"

"I don't know. At least, I'm not sure," answered Golbourne thoughtfully. "But could you, Inspector, obtain from the Admiralty the address of Sebastian Sanchez? He's a Spaniard by birth, a naturalized Englishman now. We might call on him. He came over from Brazil just before the War, and was employed at the Admiralty during hostilities. I worked with him there."

Scotland Yard can obtain any information it wants, and within a minute, over the 'phone, Inspector Mirch was answered.

"Forty-two Kentish Square, Camden Town, is where Mr Sanchez lives, or did live at any rate, during the time he was employed at the Admiralty."

"Right! Then we'll go and call on him, Inspector, if you can spare the time. But, first of all, I'd like to have a chat with Sir George's chauffeur. I suppose you know where he is?"

"Yes, we're keeping an eye on him, of course. I told him not to be far away from his garage. We'll go down there and see him."

"Good! Come along, Bowen, you'll see this through with me, won't you? We'll come back to *The Wire* office, Mr Brinsley, if we've any news for you."

At the garage near Sloane Square, Golbourne put a few searching questions to Edward Morris, the chauffeur.

"No, the car didn't stop anywhere during the journey from Piccadilly to the Law Courts," said the man. "There was just a little bit of a hold-up at Wellington Street, not enough to actually stop the car, but we had to go very slowly."

"Ah! Now, can you tell me what sort of a vehicle was exactly in front of you during that block?"

"Yes, sir; it was a van, a fruit van, full of empty orange-boxes. I've often seen that same van coming back from Covent Garden at just about the same time when I used to drive my master down. I've noticed it for a long time, because it was always so very badly driven and used to get in my way, like it did yesterday morning, when it nearly shaved my front off-wheel when it sneaked in just ahead of me, as it had no right to do."

"Oh! And was there any name on the car – a covered van I suppose it was, open at the back?"

"That's right, sir, and the name on it was Sanchez. I remember that quite well, because I vowed once that I'd write to Mr Sanchez and tell him about the nuisance his driver so often was."

"You didn't notice anything extraordinary during that little temporary slowdown, did you?"

"No, sir, nothing."

"Did you turn your head at all?"

The chauffeur considered for a minute.

"Well, I do remember turning round." Morris allowed himself a little smile. "Because I heard a mate – a pal of mine – toot his horn in a comic way he often does. I meet him most mornings, and I just looked round to give him a nod, but that was all."

That finished the interview with the chauffeur, and when Mr Bowen, the professor, and the inspector were in the cab again, Golbourne spoke very seriously.

"I'm going to take a risk with this man, Sanchez, Inspector," he said. "That's why I want you with me, in case there should be unpleasantness afterwards, or that I am mistaken. I'm only carrying out an idea of my own. Anyway, you'll keep your eye on the gentleman we're going to visit, won't you? I'm not much good at self-defence, or anything of that sort."

"All right, sir, I'll keep my eye on him."

Sebastian Sanchez, a tall, slim, swarthy man of about sixty-five years of age, received Golbourne with out-stretched hand and a smile, and bowed, with the courtesy of his race, to Inspector Mirch and Mr Bowen.

"And to what am I indebted for the pleasure of a visit from my old colleague, Professor Golbourne?" he asked in a smooth, even voice.

"Well, Sanchez, this is going to be a business talk, so why shouldn't we sit down?" began Golbourne affably. "Mr Sanchez and I," he said, turning to the others, "were working together at the Admiralty during the War. We were engaged on certain experiments."

"Yes," Sanchez smiled a little. "You, the professor of mathematics from the north of Scotland; I, by virtue of my experiments in the same line in Brazil, and as a naturalized Englishman. We worked well together, too, eh? But why—"

"Why am I here now?" Golbourne's foot went out and touched Mirch's, who imperceptibly edged his chair a little closer to the Spaniard's. "Well, I was thinking about that invention which was put before us concerning the discharge of missiles by means of compressed air. You remember it?"

Mirch moved a little in his chair and Bowen bit his under-lip.

"Yes." Sanchez's eyes narrowed and then turned to a corner by his desk where stood against the wall what looked like a long, black walking stick with a crutch handle. "Yes."

His hand stretched out a little as if to reach for the stick, but instinct and training impelled Mirch to snatch at it himself, and Sanchez rolled his eyes, the whites showing, tinged with yellow.

"These are strange proceedings in a gentleman's house!" he said at length. "I await your explanation, professor."

"In an interview such as this, Sanchez, witnesses are necessary. This is Inspector Mirch of Scotland Yard, and this is the Rev. Thomas Bowen, a very old friend of mine. Both are gentlemen of repute, whose evidence would be accepted in a court of law as to what took place at this interview."

Mirch placed the black stick on the floor between his own chair and Mr Bowen's. Then, leaning over, with professional dexterity, he patted Sanchez on the body from head to foot.

"That's all right," said the inspector, "no guns, or anything of that sort! Go on, Mr Golbourne."

"As I was going to say," continued the professor, "it occurred to me, Sanchez, that you might know something about the death of Sir George Borgham. In fact, I believe that it was you who killed him."

Sanchez looked at the carpet, then at the ceiling, then straight at Golbourne.

"Yes, I killed him!" he said very quickly, "and I will pay. So you found it out, I suppose, Professor, and considered it your duty to, well, as you English say, give away. I don't blame you." He shrugged his shoulders. "I took the risk. And perhaps you're justified in tracking out an old colleague, though I don't know whether I should have done it myself."

"Sir George Borgham was a great and a good man." Golbourne's face flushed a little. "And it was my duty to make use of such memory and such powers as I have."

"Quite right!" Sanchez seemed to be almost enjoying himself. "But Sir George Borgham was not a good man." Again the Spaniard's eyes narrowed. "But tell me, Professor, as one old colleague to another, how you found me out, for to me, as a scientific man, it would be interesting. Tell me that," he repeated, "and I will gladden the heart of our official friend here" – he looked towards Mirch – "and save him a lot of trouble by making a full confession."

"Shall I?" asked Golbourne, looking towards Mirch. The inspector nodded.

"Well, Sanchez," said Golbourne, after a moment's hesitation, "I came to the obvious conclusion that someone had killed Sir

George Borgham. I made experiments. I found that it was impossible for Sir George to have been killed by a man stabbing him through the car window, or even getting into the car. There are certain heights – my knowledge of mathematics tells me that – from which a blow must descend in order to ensure a death such as that suffered by Sir George Borgham, and in this case the raising of the arm to the necessary height would have been impossible, as it would have been stopped by the roof of the car, and the blow could not have descended with sufficient force. I proved that by means of an ingenious little instrument which measures the speed and strength of the slightest stroke, either downwards or upwards. I carried through the experiment with the aid of my friend here."

Mr Bowen nodded, remembering the little instrument which had been fastened to his forearm, which Golbourne had procured from a maker of scientific instruments in Guildford Street.

"And the blow was not delivered slantwise, but straight – absolutely straight, according to the evidence of witnesses who saw the dead body – therefore it must have been dealt from straight in front, and unless the murderer had sat in the car on the right side of Sir George, such a blow would have been impossible of delivery."

"It might have been dealt from the seat opposite Sir George, though, Professor," suggested Sanchez, coolly.

"No man could have got into that car and out again without being observed. Therefore the murder must have been committed by someone outside the car; that was my conclusion. Also, it was impossible that the blow could have been delivered by the chauffeur, or anybody sitting by his side. Therefore the weapon, that piece of steel, must have come in through the window in front on the left of the driver, which was open. I say 'come in,' by which I mean in some way projected in."

"That seems quite reasonable; indeed, quite clever, Professor!"

"To be propelled with sufficient force, then, I calculated that there must have been some tremendous power behind it, some power greater than would be possible if it were thrown by hand.

By the weight of it, one ounce including the cork loaded with shot
– clever that, Sanchez! – I decided that the missile must have
been, shall we say fired from a distance of not more and not less
than ten feet, to admit of the terrific force necessary to drive such
a light weapon into a man's body. I know that there is no gun in
the accepted sense of the word which could fire such a missile,
nor is there any explosive which could be used for such a purpose,
and memory at once took me back to my work at the Admiralty
with you, Sanchez, when there was placed before us – you and me
only, mind you, with the exception of the First Lord – a secret
idea for the discharge of projectiles of any kind by means of—"

"By means of compressed air," broke in Sanchez. "A wonderful idea, smokeless, noiseless, on an entirely different principle to
the famous Maxim noiseless gun! And it was claimed by the
inventor, now dead" – Golbourne nodded – "that it could be
adapted for use by any sized gun. Well, I worked at the idea in my
spare time, and at length I succeeded to my own satisfaction in
producing a serviceable weapon."

"And that's it, I suppose," said Golbourne, pointing to the
article resembling a black walking-stick, which still lay on the
floor by the inspector's chair.

"Yes, that's it." Sanchez drew his chair a little closer to his
desk in order to rest his elbow on it, watched all the time by the
inspector. "Quite an interesting little scientific chat, Mr Policeman, isn't it?" He smiled at Mirch. "I bear no grudge; at least,
not much of a one, towards the professor, who will doubtless now
proceed with his narrative."

"I worked it all out," went on Golbourne, "by the rules of
trajectory, velocity, weight, impetus, impact, and the effect, if
any, of the wind on the missile at the time of flight when it was
fired. These calculations told me that the weapon was dispatched
from a distance of ten feet and a height of eight."

"Quite correct," agreed Sanchez nodding. "And can you tell us
how it was actually discharged?"

"Yes, I think so. I believe that you, Sanchez, were in a fruit van
bearing your name. During that block in the traffic just close by
Wellington Street, Strand, yesterday, the body of the van was

about four feet, perhaps a little more, from the ground, and you were in a crouching position, with your walking-stick gun levelled over a box or two, or at any rate concealed in some way. That would bring the distance of the weapon from the ground to about eight feet. You had been awaiting an opportunity for two or three days to get in front of the judge's car, and there bide your time until you should be within reasonable distance, and the chauffeur's attention should be otherwise engaged. I take it, therefore, that you discharged your gun when the chauffeur's head was turned from the car."

"Yes, you're right in practically every detail," admitted Sanchez.

The two might have been discussing some subject of interesting mathematical concern, instead of a grim murder.

"I run an orange business at Covent Garden," he went on. "And I had carefully thought out the means which you have disclosed, Professor, of killing Sir George Borgham. Now I come to think of it, I ought to have used another van, but I thought it safer to be in my own, as I so often drive to and from the market in it, and I thought, therefore, that no suspicion would attach to my being in it at any time, of course, with a driver who was used to having me with him, and whose back was naturally turned to me while I sat inside the van, and – well, the rest you know."

"And why did you kill that good man?" at length asked the Inspector.

"Because he was a swine!" was the astounding answer. "Five years before the then Mr George Borgham returned to England to study for the Bar, he ran a rubber plantation in Brazil. My two brothers and I were peons then."

Mirch looked a bit puzzled, so Sanchez explained.

"A peon is a low-bred South American, a day labourer, sometimes, working off a debt by bondage. My brothers and I were in bondage – oh, yes, almost slaves! – on George Borgham's estate. He treated us more than brutally, he treated us vilely, and he killed my two brothers by his treatment of them. And there was a girl; she was of our class, too, and I loved her, and George Borgham took her from me – ah, you don't know what rubber plantations were like then – when I was sick with fever, and my brothers were dead. But I never forgot the girl, and I never forgot George Borgham. After George Borgham returned to England I was befriended by kind and good people, was educated, highly educated, and eventually worked my way to a professorship in mathematics."

Sanchez was speaking with his eyes fixed on the wall opposite, as if looking into the darkness of the dreadful past.

"As soon as I could I retired from my professorship and came to England. Here I embarked in business, the orange trade, and all the while I waited and watched Sir George. I meant to kill him in such a manner that no one should know how he came by his death. And you know, gentlemen, how the means and the opportunity came to me."

"I'm sorry. I wish I had known," murmured Golbourne, while Mirch fidgeted a little in his chair, and the clergyman put his hand to his face, for the situation was harrowing.

Suddenly, before Mirch could spring at him, Sanchez had pointed something at his forehead, and –

The three men turned sick as the body of Sebastian Sanchez, with the head a terrible bleeding mass, swayed and toppled to the floor.

The tale had to be told, and it was told exclusively to *The Wire*.

But when the members of the Murder Club met to dine a few days later, there was no feeling of triumph.

"A wonderful man was Sanchez, a wonderful man!" said Golbourne. "The pistol with which he blew his own head away was a marvellous adaptation of the rough idea which was originally set before the two of us. A clever idea originally, it required a genius, as Sanchez undoubtedly was, to bring it so such perfection. And by his will, found in his desk, he has left all particulars to the heirs of the original inventor."

"Yes, he was a clever man," said Brinsley. "Still, the law says 'Thou shalt not kill.' But hang it all," the newspaper man gave a little thump to the table, "if Sir George Borgham did what Sanchez said he'd done, he deserved all he got, and more. I've cabled over to my South American correspondents to trace back his career, and I'll print and publish every item of it. Professor, here's your cheque for £500 from *The Wire*."

"I couldn't take it," said Golbourne.

And Brinsley, like a wise man, didn't press the matter, but tore the cheque up, and after a pause the silence was broken by Crimp, the little journalist.

"What about that piece of red tape round Sir George's finger?" he said. "We've forgotten all about that."

"Oh," said Mr. Bowen, with a faint smile – the first that evening, "I can explain that! While I was chatting with him at the Athelonian Club the night before his death, he took it out of his pocket, and with a joke about red tape being appropriate for a lawyer, he tied it round his finger to remind him to buy a certain book he wanted for reference the next day. 'My memory's shockingly short for trifles,' he said. 'I shall go to bed with that on my finger, and wear it again in the morning, and I shall remember.'"

"Oh, so that was all!" said Crimp.

And at his disappointed tone a real laugh went round the table.

A few weeks later England was startled by the authentic and guaranteed story of the brutalities in early life of Sir George Borgham, which had lain hidden for so many years.

# HEARTSTOPPER

*Frank M. Robinson*

*Frank M. Robinson (b.1926) is probably best known today as the co-author (with Thomas Scortia) of* The Glass Inferno *(1974), one of the books from which the blockbuster film* The Towering Inferno *(1974) was made. Robinson's first novel was* The Power *(1956), about a malignant superman, which was filmed in 1967. Most of Robinson's work is either science fiction or technothriller, though he has also written more straightforward thrillers as with* Death of a Marionette *(1995), with Paul Hull. The following story was specially written for this anthology.*

Maxwell Harrison sat at his teakwood desk wearing a ratty cotton bathrobe, his scrawny hands hanging limply at his side. His head was face down on the leather-trimmed blotter, a loose strand of silver hair moving slightly in the breeze from an unseen air-conditioner. A morning newspaper had been opened to the financial section and was lying on top of the desk, carefully aligned to the left edge. A rolodex in a leather holder kept it company. The phone was carefully aligned on the right side of the desk. In the middle a tablet of ruled yellow paper served as a pillow for Harrison's head. So far as I could see, the tablet was blank.

There were no stab or bullet wounds – again, that I could see, no purple bruise marks on his throat, no pudding of matted hair, blood, and brains covering the back of his head.

Nevertheless, Harrison was quite dead.

O'Brien, the fat little coroner, fussed around the body, making absolutely sure of what was already obvious. He shifted the chair back slightly and tilted Harrison's torso so that his head lolled against the back of the chair.

We both stared.

Harrison had died with a smile on his face. Quite a broad one, as a matter of fact, with just a suggestion of having been startled. Death had caught him unaware.

"Let me guess," I said. "Heart attack."

"Probably," O'Brien said. "Maybe poison, but unlikely. Not with that smile." He stared a moment longer, then reached over and closed the eyes.

"He had a history," the secretary said casually. "He kept some pills in the top middle drawer – I had it refilled yesterday."

I reached around the body, located the small plastic bottle and passed it over to O'Brien without comment. The secretary and the chauffeur were standing by the huge mahogany entrance doors to the library, trying hard to hide their nervousness. The secretary's name was Sally – how long had it been since "Sally" was a popular name? – Fitzgerald. She was blondish, mid-thirties, just beginning to plump up though the formal cut of her suit hid it well. Not too much makeup, hair coiled at the back of her head. I guessed "Efficiency" was her middle name.

Mike Breall, the chauffeur, was in his mid-twenties, dark haired with a thin, handsome face. Cut his hair right and he might have modelled for Calvin Klein underwear, or maybe perfume. I guessed he didn't like being there, but then who would? I was there as insurance against rumours. San Joselito – little San Jose – is in the heart of Silicon Valley where there are more millionaires than plumbers. Somebody from homicide always teams up with the coroner to make sure "no signs of foul play" is prominent in news stories when somebody rich bites it.

Property values are very important in San Joselito.

"When did you find him, Miss Fitzgerald?"

"Around eleven, he usually gave me instructions for his brokers then. I called in Mike – Mr Breall – immediately. Then we phoned you people." She hesitated. "Mr Harrison was . . . just like that."

"Neither of you touched him?"

They shook their heads in unison.

"You didn't see him earlier?"

"Matty – she's the cook – brought him his orange juice and toast at nine and I came in with her to get the servant assignments for the day. Mr Breall usually goes out to the driveway to pick up the morning paper and he came in about the same time."

I couldn't get over the smile.

"And between nine and eleven?"

"We met in the kitchen right after nine and had a little brunch and I passed out the assignments for the day."

"And all of the servants were there?"

She nodded, only slightly curious.

"So nobody else came in between nine and eleven?"

"I don't see how they could have. All the servants were in the kitchen and there are dogs on the grounds. We would have known if anybody had come to the door . . . or if there were prowlers."

"I should send in the crew," O'Brien said. "You through?" I nodded. Miss Harrison and Breall started for the door and I said, "Please don't leave – wait for me in the living room. And tell the cook to wait as well. It won't take long."

I paused at the door for one last look before the coroner's men with the gurney showed up. Maxwell Harrison was an anomaly in town. Early eighties – far older than the young computer mavens who had struck it rich and settled there. Harrison was the Old Money in town and could probably have bought and sold any two or three of the youngsters. Wife had died years before; he lived alone except for the servants. So far as anybody knew, he kept busy clipping coupons and watching over his investments – and there were a lot of them.

I walked back to the desk and took another look at the broad smile on his face. Smiles have classifications and the one I would have compared his to was the smile on a football coach when his team has just made it to one of the bowl games. Or that of a stockbroker who just sold short and made another million or two.

It was a fleck of white that caught my eye, something I had missed the first time. I pried the small piece of folded paper from his stiffening fingers, glanced at it and slipped it in my pocket. No help there, just a scrawled bunch of numbers. Then I picked up the newspaper and stuck it under my arm – save the trouble of buying one on the way home.

It turned out they were all the evidence there was. And all the evidence that was needed. At least for justice, if not for law.

The cook was in her sixties, slightly deaf, and had worked for Harrison less than six months. Yes, all the servants had met in the kitchen after nine and yes, it had turned into something of a kaffeklatsch that had lasted until eleven. Had she liked Mr Harrison as an employer? She shrugged and I gathered he was no better nor worse than a dozen others she'd worked for. I took down her address and phone number, asked her to keep in touch and to let the department know if she moved from the area.

Sally Fitzgerald was hardly more informative.

"You've worked for Mr Harrison for how long?" Slog work – no smart questions, no special insights, simple $Q$ and $A$.

"Fifteen years—" A moment of thought. "Closer to sixteen."

"And you're—?"

A flash of . . . what?

"Thirty-eight."

Which made her twenty-two when she started. Not impossible but . . . a little young for a secretary. Maybe she'd been hired as something else. "Paid companion" as the tabloids might say. Harrison would have been in his late sixties, just becoming aware that life and love and lust were passing him by. By the time the arrangement had devolved to the hand-holding stage, she had become his secretary. On-the-job training.

And I could be doing her a deep injustice and have it all wrong. She was smart for her years, she'd gone to secretarial school, he was in the middle of acquisitions and mergers and she was just what the entrepreneur in him had ordered.

Curse me for being a dirty-minded, middle-aged man.

"He was a generous employer?"

"I never had any complaints." Very cool.

"He was a fucking old miser," Breall broke in, angry.

Sally glanced at him with just a trace of contempt. Very, very cool.

I raised an eyebrow and Breall said, "He only cared about money. It's all the old bastard ever talked about."

"What should he have talked about?"

Breall wasn't about to forget his grudge. "I once asked him for an advance. My folks needed a loan, hospital stuff. He wouldn't even listen to me."

"And you'd worked for him for how long?"

Sally answered for him, a little acidly. "Six months."

I kept my eyes on Breall. "I take it Mr Harrison wasn't much of a sportsman – never talked about baseball or world soccer or anything like that."

He gave me a fishy look – I was putting him on – then shrugged. I could have told him that the only game left for Harrison in his old age had been stocks and bonds and buyouts and they're not something you can chat about with twenty-five-year-old chauffeurs. But the antagonism was pretty standard. Harrison had a lot of money and Breall had very little, if any.

Unfair.

I asked a few more questions, then gave them the same instructions I'd given the cook. Stay in touch and stick around.

What was important was not what they'd said but what they hadn't. Breall was probably right. All Harrison had cared about was money. No hobbies had been mentioned, no parties, no guests, no friends, no relatives dropping by. An old man counting his coins and hoping he got to God knows how many millions before life foreclosed on him.

As for Sally, she had shed no tears, had looked neither bereaved nor distraught nor even unhappy at the loss of her employer of almost sixteen years.

I started for the door and Breall pointed to the couch. "You forgot your paper."

I said "Thanks," retrieved it and watched them as they walked out the door and down the walk. They weren't holding hands but it almost seemed as if they were in lockstep. I stared until they disappeared around the corner of the house and wondered if they were going to his rooms or hers.

O'Brien had been waiting by his car. He was staring after them, too. "Quite a pair, aren't they?"

"Why do you say 'pair'?"

"For the same reasons you're thinking," he wheezed. "And I think we're both wrong. No knives, no guns, no struggle and I'll bet you dollars to doughnuts Harrison didn't eat anything that fatally disagreed with him. Somewhere between nine and eleven he bought the Big One."

He suddenly frowned. "Look, Sam, trust me. He was alone that morning, nobody else was around, and there are no signs anybody hit him, stabbed him, shot him or strangled him. He died of old age – some people do, you know."

"They pay me to be suspicious," I said. "You find out anything different, you let me know."

"You'll be the first, Sam." Then, curious: "What are you going to do?"

"Wait until they leave, then take out the garbage."

It was an hour until Breall left in his Honda, Sally beside him. I'd spent the time sitting in my own car around the corner, reading the paper.

I was going to have to buy one, after all. The Local News section was missing.

Bummer.

I saw O'Brien three days later in his office. He had his feet up, his hands across his paunch, staring out the window at a pleasantly green and sunny spring day. His eyes were at half mast; I'd interrupted the start of his afternoon siesta.

"On your way out, tell Coral not to let you back in without notifying me first."

"It's always nice to feel welcome," I said. I helped myself to a cup of lukewarm coffee from the Mr Coffee on the filing cabinet, then made myself comfortable in the battered easy chair facing his desk.

"I thought you were going to let me know all about Harrison, from his broken heart to the tattoo on his heinie."

He yawned and opened his eyes wide for a moment, then swivelled around to face me.

"No tattoo and nothing to tell you about his heart that you don't already know."

"I made a guess," I said. "I didn't say I knew for a fact."

"Sudden heart failure, Sam – I'll send over an official report in the morning. Somewhere around ten in the morning the old pump decided to give up the ghost and it was all over in a second or two. Don't think he felt a thing. Maybe a brief warning and *ping*, that was it. Doc Sturdevant was surprised he lasted as long as he did. Didn't eat right, never got out, pressure of business . . . After eighty or so, it's all borrowed time anyway. He lived life the way we all do, which is never the right way. Hell, when I was in private practice I never followed the advice I gave my patients. You might live longer but who the hell would want to?"

I picked a newspaper out of his wastebasket and started leafing through it professionally, starting with the comics first.

O'Brien looked at me over the top of his glasses. "Don't you have an office of your own you can waste time in? Or did you drop by to tell me something?"

I hesitated, struck by a headline, but not exactly sure of why I had hesitated.

"The saga of the secretary and the chauffeur," I said. "Or, to be more accurate, the tale of the secretary – no pun intended."

O'Brien leaned forward, suddenly interested.

"And?"

"Harrison had no relatives, no deep philanthropic interests, he hadn't contributed a dime to his Alma Mater in years so it was unlikely he remembered it in his will. And as a matter of fact, he didn't. Guess who his 'great and good friend' was who inherits?"

"Our gal Sal."

I nodded.

"Very sharp; those afternoon naps help. His attorney let me see his Living Trust. Sally doesn't have to wait for probate, she can cash in right away."

"What happened to attorney – client privilege?"

I yawned; the chair was too damned comfortable. "Come on,

it's a small town, everybody knows where the bodies are buried and besides, he owed me a favour."

O'Brien looked thoughtful.

"So she had motive."

"She didn't seem heartbroken that Harrison had shuffled off." I looked expectant. "I was hoping you could tell me how."

"How she did it? She didn't. Nobody did. God pulled the rug out from under him and that was that. Judging from the smile on his face, it wasn't all that bad."

I stood up and started to drop the newspaper back in the basket beneath his desk, then stopped and stared at the headlines. Damn. Our modern society. If they recycled the news every few days, nobody would ever notice. I'd been hitting on three-day-old headlines.

Then I remembered where I had seen them before and sat back down.

"You got the rest of this?"

"In the trash basket, help yourself. Coral's on a work slow-down, she only empties it once a week."

I pawed through the papers and found the missing news section for the paper on Harrison's desk. I had to leaf through it twice before I realized what I was looking for.

Then I figured I knew how. I also doubted there was any jury on God's green earth that would send Sally Fitzgerald or Mike Breall to the slammer.

I went back to the Harrison mansion the next day, along with O'Brien – I hadn't told him much and he was dying of curiosity – and a couple of uniforms just in case.

Sally had let her hair down – a nice cascade of blonde – and changed out of her suit-like uniform into something looser and more appealing. For mid-thirties, she was doing very nicely. Breall had ditched his chauffeur uniform and looked more like an ageing delinquent than he had the day before. His personality fit his appearance – surly, apprehensive, defiant and if he had been any younger, I would have called him snotty.

I looked at Sally and said how sorry I was she had lost such a good friend and employer.

"I'll live," she said.

She was handling her grief real well, I thought.

"Mr Harrison died of natural causes," I said.

That cheered them both up, though Sally still looked uneasily at the two uniforms by the door. I stared at Breall.

"How badly did you hate Mr Harrison?"

"I told you I thought—" He caught the warning look from Sally and shot a quick glance at the uniforms. "Not that badly." Then, blurting: "I thought you said he died of natural causes?"

"Falling down a flight of stairs can be an accident," I said. "Unless somebody pushes you. And for a guy with a bad heart, walking up behind him and yelling 'boo!' might qualify you for a homicide rap."

A frown. "I didn't—" And then he caught another look from Sally and shut up. He could drive a limo and he must have been good in bed, otherwise I couldn't understand why Sally put up with him. But then, she hadn't planned to for very long.

I took the piece of crumpled paper out of my pocket and pushed the yellow tablet to the front of the desk. I crooked my finger toward Breall and he reluctantly walked over.

"Do me a favour, Mike, and write the following numbers on the paper." He hesitated, then picked up the pencil. "Thirty-six," I said. "Fifty-four, twelve, eleven, forty-five and twenty-two."

He slowly printed them out and I compared them to the figures on the paper. The handwriting experts could probably prove they matched up.

Now it was Sally's turn.

"Would you call Mr Harrison a gambler?"

She shook her head. Cool but wary.

"Not at all. He was very shrewd in making investments—"

"But it amused him to play the state lottery, didn't it?"

She froze. "I . . . really don't know."

"Oh, I'm sure you do," I said. "He never left the house so you would've had to buy the lottery tickets for him. You or Mike. There were a lot of discarded tickets in the trash."

Her face was a mask.

"I bought him anything he wanted. I might have bought him some tickets."

I wasn't paying much attention to either she or Breall – that was the uniforms' job. I opened up the drawer where Harrison had kept his pills. Three tickets; I had spotted them when I'd first checked for his pills but hadn't thought anything of them. One of them had all the numbers that Breall had written down.

I sighed and leaned back in the chair, fanning the tickets between my fingers, then opened the three-day old section of newspaper that I'd found in O'Brien's office.

"When Harrison found that the Local News section was missing from his newspaper – the section that always prints the lottery results, the section you removed before giving him the paper, Mike – he asked you to find out the winning numbers. Sally knew the numbers on his tickets – she had seen them when she refilled his prescription. She gave you a set of six, you copied them down and gave them to Harrison. What was the jackpot? Fifty-five million? Harrison was a businessman so he always went through the financial pages first, before he indulged himself and checked the numbers you gave him against his lottery tickets. Of course, he didn't have the winning numbers. He just thought he did."

I looked up at the now-pale Breall. "Harrison thought he'd finally hit the Big One and the excitement was too much for his heart."

Sally was acid.

"That's not much of a case."

"You were with him for sixteen years, Sally, you probably knew his medical condition better than he did. For a heart patient, good news can be as bad as bad news. Harrison had to avoid stress – and you hit him with a ton of it."

"The old bastard died happy," Breall chimed in, bitter.

"Shut up," Sally said dully. "They can't hold us."

I nodded to the uniforms. "Not for me to judge," I said. "But I think you'll have to delay that trip to the Bahamas."

Breall was a quicker study than I thought. He whirled on Sally. "What trip?"

I played it innocent.

"Lois at the travel agency said that you would be gone for a month, right, Sally? A real gossip, Lois. She couldn't understand why you'd be going by yourself."

The uniforms grabbed Breall just as he lunged at her.

"That was dirty pool," O'Brien said. We were at the local McDonald's and O'Brien was on his second Big Mac and fries.

I'd ordered coffee and was nibbling on some of the fries out of his basket.

"Murder's murder, whether Harrison was cheated out of two more days or another decade. Sally got impatient – she could see the best years of her life slipping by. Breall was a wild card. He was a recent hire and as the chauffeur probably had as much face time with Harrison as she did. She had a foolproof plan and enlisted Mike to cover all bases just in case."

"Flimsy stuff," O'Brien said around his hamburger. "It won't stand up."

I shrugged. "A lot of murder cases are made of flimsy stuff. But if they get off, they still won't be a pair of happy campers. I suspect by now that love has turned pretty sour."

O'Brien blinked owlishly at me.

"They'll be at each other's throats."

I sprayed one of his fries with catsup.

"Ain't that a shame," I said.

# BLIND EYES

## Edward Marston

*Edward Marston is the best known pseudonym of author and playwright Keith Miles (b.1940). A former lecturer in modern history, Miles has written over forty original plays for radio, television and the theatre, plus some six hundred episodes of radio and television drama series. He has also written over twenty-five novels. These include a series featuring Nicholas Bracewell and his company of Elizabethan actors, which began with* The Queen's Head *(1988), plus a series featuring Ralph Delchard and Gervase Bret, who resolve crimes as they travel the country helping compile the Domesday Book in 1086. That series began with* The Wolves of Savernake *(1993). For a change, however, the following story is not historical.*

The first explosion came at midnight. No warning was given. Oxford Street was surprisingly busy at that time on a Saturday. People waited for buses, hovered for taxis, searched for somewhere to eat, headed for nightclubs or simply walked aimlessly along. Drunks relieved themselves in dark corners. A man with an accordion played evergreen favourites with fitful enthusiasm. A group of young women, fresh from a hen party, laughed and joked their way boisterously along the pavement. Curled up in sleeping bags, self-appointed tenants of the various shop doorways had already counted the day's takings and turned in for the night. Two burly uniformed policemen studied the suits on display in *Next* and shared their misgivings about the prices. A lone cyclist headed towards Marble Arch.

The explosion sounded far louder than it really was. It came from a card shop near Oxford Circus and terrified everyone within earshot. The plate glass window became a thousand deadly missiles that shot across the road. Cards were scattered everywhere. Those in the "Get Well Soon" rack were the first to ignite. Women screamed, men yelled, residents lifted bedroom windows or came dashing out of front doors. The two constables abandoned their shopping and ran towards the scene of the blast, one of them raising the alarm on his mobile while the other warned bystanders to keep well clear of the danger area. It seemed only minutes before police cars converged on Oxford Circus to investigate the crime and to control the gathering crowd. A fire engine arrived soon afterwards with an ambulance on its tail. The noise was deafening.

It was a scene that was repeated elsewhere in the city. A second bomb went off in the Euston Road, a third near Victoria Station and a fourth in Baker Street. No sooner had the emergency services reached one devastated area than another explosion was heard. Nor were the bombs confined to central London. Blackfriars, Belvedere, Chingford, Whitechapel, Pentonville, Clapham Common, Greenwich and other sites were targeted. The Metropolitan Police were at full stretch, the Fire Service pushed to the limit. Chaos reigned for hour after hour. The one consolation was that there seemed to be very few casualties.

At the height of the crisis, the biggest explosion of all went off in an electricity sub-station and the whole of the West End was suddenly blacked out. Panic spread uncontrollably. Older inhabitants were reminded all too vividly of the Blitz, younger people were convulsed with fear. Everyone rushed around wildly, wondering what was happening. A foreign invasion? A bombing campaign by Irish dissidents? A visit by aliens? The end of the world? It was only when dawn finally lifted the blanket of night that another crime was uncovered, a theft so shocking that it was totally impossible to believe even though the evidence was there for all to see.

Lord Nelson had been stolen from atop his column in Trafalgar Square. In his place, usurping his position of honour, gazing down Whitehall with a smile of triumph and outraging every true English patriot, was a huge statue of Napoleon Bonaparte.

Fluttering at his boots was a self-explanatory banner.

VIVE LA FRANCE!

Commander Richard Milton was not pleased to be hauled back from his holiday. His week in Cornwall had been curtailed before it had even begun and he was determined to make someone pay for his loss. With his wife's complaints still ringing in his ears, he was flown back swiftly to London to take charge of an inquiry that was dominating the media like the outbreak of the Third World War. A tall, thin, angular man with a face like a Victorian poisoner, Dick Milton had the experience, the guile and the stamina to lead a large team of detectives in the investigation of what appeared to be a series of interrelated crimes. He got results. That was why he was chosen. When he worked in harness with his old friend, Detective Inspector Kenneth Hurrell, results tended to come quickly.

An incident room was set up in Scotland Yard. By the time that Milton came charging in, Hurrell had already been busy for hours.

"What the hell is going on, Ken?" demanded Milton.

"I wish I knew," sighed Hurrell. "A series of bombs went off all over London last night. Soft targets. Extensive damage to property. Minor injuries but no fatalities. And then – this other bombshell!"

"Nelson can't have *disappeared*!"

"He has, Commander."

"How?"

"That's the bit we haven't worked out."

"And is it true that someone else is up there?"

"Napoleon Bonaparte."

"Bloody hell!"

"The media are calling it a national scandal."

"And that's exactly what it is, Ken!" said Milton vengefully. "My holiday's been ruined. Nothing could be more scandalous than that. I had strips torn off me when I left St Ives. You try telling your wife that she'll have to manage without you while you go off in search of Nelson."

"I'm not married, sir."

"Be grateful. At times like this, celibacy is a blessing."

"I didn't say I was celibate."

Kenneth Hurrell grinned. He was a wiry man of medium height with wavy black hair that was the envy of his colleagues. His immaculate suit made Minton's tweed jacket look positively shabby. The Commander became businesslike. He snapped his fingers.

"How far have you got?"

"This far," said Hurrell, moving to the large wall map. "The pins indicate the locations of the bombs. Twenty-one in all."

"Twenty-one! What did they think it was – Bonfire Night?"

"Oh, no. They were very precise about the date."

"What do you mean?"

"It's October 21st."

"So?"

"The date of the Battle of Trafalgar."

"But that was years ago, Ken."

"A hundred and ninety-five years. October 21st, 1805."

"Is that relevant?"

"Extremely, sir. Some people obviously have long memories. The pattern of bombing proves that." He jabbed a finger at the map. "At first, I thought they were just random explosions to create a diversion and move every available officer well away from the vicinity of Nelson's Column."

"And they're not?"

"No," said Hurrell. "Take this one here, for instance," he continued, touching one of the pins. "Old Bethnal Green Road. The bomb was very close to Nelson Gardens. Then there's this one, sir." He indicated another pin. "On the site of Greenwich Market. Close to Nelson Road."

"Could just be a coincidence."

"Not when it happens in every case," argued Hurrell. "There was a bomb near Nelson Walk in Limehouse, another on Morden Road, close to the Nelson Industrial Estate and a third in Nelson Yard, off Mornington Crescent. So it goes on."

"What about Oxford Street and Victoria Station?" asked Minton. "I don't recall any Nelson Roads in those areas."

"There aren't any."

"So the pattern is incomplete."

"Far from it, Commander. The explosion in Oxford Street was less than forty yards from the 'Admiral Nelson' pub. The one in Victoria Station was directly opposite 'The Trafalgar'. No question about it, I'm afraid. We're dealing with a case of aggravated revenge."

"Some militant Frogs?"

"All the signs point that way."

"So it seems."

"You can't fault their timing."

"Timing?"

"Yes, sir. Until last week, workmen were at the top of the column to give Nelson his habitual clean-up. The thieves didn't just get away with the most famous statue in London. They waited until all the bird shit had been scraped off it. We're up against pros."

"No phone calls from them?"

"Just one, sir. In French."

"What was the message?"

"Short and sweet. We were ordered to leave him where he is."

"Who?"

"The Emperor Napoleon."

"Ruling the roost in Trafalgar Square!" exclaimed Milton with an upsurge of patriotism. "We'll see about that! Nobody gives me orders, especially in Frogtalk. Come on, Ken. Clap on full sail. We're going straight over to Trafalgar Square. You can fill me in on the way. Leave him there indeed!" He gave a snort of defiance. "We'll have the bugger down off that column before he can say 'Not tonight, Josephine.'"

Napoleon Bonaparte had drawn a vast audience. Though the police had cordoned off Trafalgar Square itself, all the approach roads were heaving with sightseers. Every window which overlooked the column had its own private audience. Television cameras had prime positions and sent their pictures to the watching millions. Driven to the scene of the crime, Dick Milton was furious when he caught sight of a French television crew.

"What are *they* doing here?" he growled.

"Somebody must have tipped them off," said Hurrell.

"They're in on the conspiracy."

"If that's what it is, sir."

When they got out of the car, Milton took his first proper look at the statue which had displaced Nelson. He craned his neck to get a good view, realizing how rarely he even noticed the usual occupant of the fluted Corinthian column. Nelson was such an essential part of the fabric of London that he could be taken for granted. Like St Paul's Cathedral or Westminster Abbey. In a sense, it was a compliment not to look at him, an acknowledgment of his status and permanence. Only foreign tourists actually stared at the column. Everyone was staring now. The new arrival compelled attention. Napoleon looked bigger, bolder, more authoritative. There was a mutinous rumble among the spectators.

Dick Milton shared their disgust. His faced reddened angrily.

"What, in God's name, is he doing up there?"

"Making a statement, sir."

"I'll make a bloody statement myself in a minute."

"Not when there are so many microphones about," warned Hurrell. "We have to be diplomatic. Keep our own opinions private."

"Well, *he's* not keeping his opinion private, is he?" said Milton, looking up at the banner. "VIVE LA FRANCE! That doesn't leave much to the imagination, does it?"

"No, sir." Hurrell gave a signal and a detective walked briskly across to them. "Let's see if we have any more leads. DS Williams was in charge of taking statements from witnesses."

"Good." He appraised the newcomer. "Well?"

"They all say the same, sir," explained Williams, referring to his notebook. "There were over a dozen of them, sleeping here last night or sharing bottles of cheap booze. They saw very little."

"They must have, man!"

"There was a total blackout, Commander."

"Winos are nocturnal. They can see in the dark."

"Not when they're pissed out of their minds," said Hurrell before turning back to Williams. "Sorry, Jim. Do go on."

The Detective Sergeant nodded and ran a tongue nervously across his lips. Knowing all about Dick Milton's hot temper, he had no wish to be on the receiving end of it. He consulted his notebook.

"They saw little but heard a lot," he resumed. "The one thing they all agree on is the balloon. Not a hot-air balloon. The other kind. You know, like a Zeppelin."

"A dirigible," said Milton.

"They all called it a balloon."

"Technically, it's an airship. What else did they hear?"

"A strange noise."

"Noise?"

"A sort of loud grinding," said Williams, stooping to pick up a handful of chippings. "Stonecutter, I reckon. You see, sir? These are pieces of Craigleith stone from the statue of Nelson. My theory is that they had to cut through its base before they could detach it from the column and carry it away."

"By the dirigible?"

"How else?"

"But it must have been a hell of a weight.

"Several tons, sir."

"How tall was the statue?"

"Seventeen feet," said Williams. "And the column is a hundred and forty-five. Devonshire granite from Foggin Tor. It supports a bronze capital cast from old guns from Woolwich Arsenal."

"You've done your homework. Good man."

"Thank you, sir."

"A hot air balloon couldn't have winched it up," said Hurrell, "but a large airship might have. Several sightings of a flying object were reported. People couldn't pick it out clearly but they thought they saw something dangling from it. They didn't realize that it was a priceless chunk of English history."

"No," grumbled Milton. "Anything else, Williams?"

The detective rattled off the other information he had gleaned before being sent back to interrogate the witnesses for a second time. They were a motley crew: tramps, winos and homeless students. There was one old woman among them, singing hymns at the top of her voice. Milton ran a jaundiced eye over them. None would be at all reliable in a witness box. He turned to face Hurrell.

"This was a well-planned operation, Ken."

"Yes, sir. Involving several people."

"Do we know any French extremists capable of this?"

"Not really, sir," said the other, "though I was surprised to find out just how many different political groups there are. Apart from the usual anarchists, nihilists and assorted nutcases, that is. There's a Pro-Euro Ginger Group, a Friends of General de Gaulle Society, a Jacobin Club, a League of French Imperialists, a Marquis de Sade Brotherhood and heaven knows what else. I'm told there are some pretty dodgy characters in the Gerard Depardieu Fan Club as well. France is steeped in revolution. It's in their blood. When something rouses them, they act. One thing is certain about this lot."

"What's that?"

"They mean business."

"Yes, they stole one of our great national heroes," said Milton bitterly. "And what they they give us in return? Those tasteless Golden Delicious apples and seventeen feet of Napoleon Bonaparte."

"Amazing, really. You've got to admire them."

The Commander was appalled. "Admire those thieving Frogs!"

"They whisked Nelson off into the sky."

"They did more than that, Ken. Apart from insulting a naval man by flying him out, they achieved an even greater feat." He glanced up at the statue. "They stuck that monstrosity up there at the same time. How? One dirigible, two national heroes. How on earth did they remove one and replace him with another in such a short space of time?"

"The blackout lasted for a few hours."

"That means they were working in the dark."

"Maybe they had a second dirigible."

"None of the winos mentioned it and they're used to seeing double."

"I don't think we can trust their word," said Hurrell with a sad smile. "They were either too drunk to notice much or too frightened to remember what they did see and hear. The other reports are the ones to trust. Something moving silently across the sky with an object dangling from it. There were a number of sightings."

"It must have made two journeys," decided Milton. "Nelson was spirited away to a nearby hiding place then Napoleon was brought back in his stead." He took out his mobile phone. "Let's knock old Nappy off his perch, anyway. Who were those people who cleaned the statue recently?"

"Gostelow and Crabtree."

"Sounds like a firm of corrupt solicitors."

"Are there any other kind?"

They traded a professional laugh. Hurrell gave him the phone number and the Commander dialled it. After barking a few orders, the latter switched off his mobile and put it in his pocket.

"They're on their way."

"How will they get up there?"

"Scaffolding."

"Then what?"

"Well," said Milton firmly, "the first thing they can do is to get that VIVE LA FRANCE banner down. It's making my stomach heave." He looked across at the massed ranks of cameramen and journalists. "I suppose that I ought to throw them a bone. Give them the idea that we have everything under control. Ho, ho! You wait here, Ken. I'll go and make a non-committal statement to the media or they'll be hounding us all day." He gazed up at Napoleon again. "By the way, what's French for 'We're coming to get you, you mad bastard'?"

Emblazoned with the name of "Gostelow and Crabtree", the lorry arrived within half-an-hour. In the rear was a large tarpaulin and an endless number of scaffolding poles. The lorry was closely followed by a huge mobile crane. Fresh interest was stirred up in the crowd and the cameras recorded every moment for the television audience. While waiting for the men to arrive, Commander Milton had pacified the media, given his statement, and spoken to some of the denizens of Trafalgar Square to hear first-hand their reminiscences of a night to remember. Two of them came out of their drunken stupor to claim that they had seen a balloon in the sky with something dangling from it.

Milton went across to introduce himself and Kenneth Hurrell to the newcomers. They treated him with muted respect.

"Who's in charge?" he asked.

"I am," said a hefty man in his thirties.

"Who are you? Gostelow or Crabtree?"

"Neither, sir. Mr Gostelow died years ago."

"What about Crabtree?"

"On holiday."

"Lucky devil! So was I until this little caper."

"My name's Pete Sylvester," said the foreman, extending a gnarled hand. "I was in charge of cleaning Nelson, so I have a real stake in getting him back. You grow to like a man when you've been chiselling away at him for as long as we did."

"I thought you just gave him a wash and brush-up."

"I wish it was that easy, sir. But we're not just cleaners. We're trained sculptors. We actually have to re-carve bits from time to time. Freshen up the contours. It's skilled work. We've sculpted bits of half the churches in London before now."

"What about taking a statue down?"

"That's more difficult."

"But you have done it before?"

"A few times. We'll manage somehow. Leave it to us."

Peter Sylvester's craggy face split into a grin. He had a reassuring jauntiness about him. While he was chatting to the detectives, his men were already starting to build the scaffold around the column. In the background, another crew was assembling the crane.

"Listen, Pete," said Hurrell familiarly, "when you were working on the Admiral, did you see anything?"

"We saw everything, mate. Best view in London."

"I meant, did you see anything unusual?"

"Unusual?"

"People taking a close interest in what you were doing."

"There were dozens of those. Real nuisance at times."

"Were any of them French?" asked Milton.

"Yeah, couple of girls. They took our picture."

"Nobody else?"

"Not that I recall. When you climb all the way up there, you can't chat to anyone down here. Some people watched us for hours. We felt a bit like performing monkeys."

"Did anyone else come up after you?"

"Oh, no! We wouldn't stand for that."

"What happened overnight?" wondered Hurrell. "Presumably, the scaffolding was left in place. Did you ever arrive in the morning and get the feeling that someone had been up there?" Sylvester shook his head. "How can you be so sure?"

"Because we had a nightwatchman on duty. If you don't guard them, scaffolding poles have a nasty habit of walking off in the dark. Besides," said the other, "we didn't want idiots climbing all over the column. It's bad enough when they get on the lions' backs. Admiral Nelson deserves to be protected."

Pete Sylvester was a man who clearly liked his work but he was unable to help them with their enquiries. When they released him, he went off to supervize the erection of the scaffolding. It was a long but methodical process. The column was slowly encased in an aluminium square which rose steadily upwards. Hurrell was impressed.

"It must have taken much longer with timber," he observed.

"Timber?" echoed Milton.

"Yes, sir. When they first put up the column, a hundred and fifty years ago, they used wooden scaffolding. The statue itself was raised in 1843 by means of a winch. It must have been a wonderful sight."

"Someone else has been doing his homework, I see."

"I like to be thorough."

"It's the only way, Ken."

Pete Sylvester eventually drifted back across to them.

"I'd suggest that you clear the square completely," he said. "I'm fairly sure we won't drop him but it's better to be safe than sorry. It's a long way to fall."

Milton gave a command and everyone was moved away.

"When you get him down," he said, "our forensic boys will want to give him the once-over. Only not here in the glare of publicity."

"We'll take him back to the warehouse, sir. More private there."

"Good."

"One favour."

"What's that?"

"Could you keep the press off our backs? We don't want them clambering all over our lorry to get exclusive pictures."

"They won't get a chance, Mr Sylvester."

"Thanks."

When the scaffolding finally reached the capital, Sylvester swarmed up it so that he had the privilege of tearing down the banner. To the cheers of the crowd, he hurled it to the ground. A policeman retrieved it then scurried back out of the way. Dick Milton and Kenneth Hurrell watched with admiration from the safety of the steps of the National Gallery. Pete Sylvester was efficient. Using a small pickaxe, he chipped away at what appeared to be fresh concrete at the base of the statue, then exchanged the implement for a stonecutter. Its whine soon rang across the square and the noise intensified as it cut into solid stone.

One eye on developments, Milton gave his orders.

"Check out all of these fringe groups," he said.

"Even the loony ones, sir?"

"Especially those. Leave no stone unturned, Ken. If someone so much as asked for Eric Cantona's autograph, I want him checked out for Gallic sympathies. We're supposed to be fellow-Europeans now but that message obviously hasn't got through to the Froggy mentality. Out there somewhere is a sawn-off Napoleon with delusions of grandeur."

"We'll find him, sir."

"And soon."

Hurrell was about to depart when his colleague's mobile phone rang. The Commander snatched it from his pocket and turned it on.

"Yes?"

"Commander Milton?" said a heavily-accented voice.

"Who's this?"

"I told you not to take the Emperor down!"

"It's him!" said Milton, cupping a hand over the mouthpiece. "The anonymous Frog. He's watching us."

"Can you hear me?" said the voice.

"I hear you, *mon ami*," replied the other with polite contempt. "And I don't care two hoots for your orders. Napoleon comes down."

"In that case, we double the price."

"What price?"

"For Nelson."

Milton rid himself of a few expletives but the line went dead.

"They're holding him to ransom," he told Hurrell."

"Where?"

"He forgot to tell me."

"How much do they want?"

"A lot, by the sound of it." He put the mobile away. "Well, let's get rid of one statue before we try to reclaim the other. Meanwhile, you do what I said, Ken. Get your men on the case, chasing down every weird group of French sympathizers they can find. Join me when it's time to take the Emperor for a ride."

Hurrell moved swiftly away to pass on the orders to a small squad of detectives. Milton turned his gaze back to the statue. Pete Sylvester seemed to have cut through the base of the statue and was ready to have it removed. Using thick ropes with great dexterity, he lassoed the statue at various points. He was quite fearless, even climbing part of the way up the solid stone to secure the ropes more tightly. When he'd finished, he waved to the crane driver and the massive hook swung slowly towards him. Sylvester waited until it had stopped swinging before he began to loop the ropes around it. After tying them off with great care, he and his men descended the scaffolding at speed, then stood back to watch.

The crane applied pressure but the statue refused to move at first. A yell of encouragement went up from the crowd. When the driver put extra power into the tug, the statue was suddenly lifted clear of its base, sending rubble hurtling to the ground. Shorn of his majesty, the deposed Emperor made a slow descent until he rested horizontally in the back of the lorry. Sylvester and his men swiftly covered him with their tarpaulin. As the lorry drove away with its foreign cargo, it was greeted with the kind of ovation that only a winning English goal in the final of a World Cup could have evoked. Even Commander Milton applauded.

Before he could get away, he was obliged to make another statement to the media and hinted that he was already in contact with the kidnappers. Hope was firmly planted. Nelson had not been abducted in order to be destroyed. A ransom demand presupposed that no harm had come to him. If the money was paid, he might return unscathed. ,

"Is this a French conspiracy?" asked an interviewer.

"I'll tell you when I find out."

"What else can you tell us?"

"Nothing at this stage."

Milton excused himself and elbowed his way to a waiting car. He and Hurrell were soon being driven after the lorry. Having discharged his orders, the Detective Inspector had grown pensive.

"Do you know much about the Battle of Trafalgar?" he asked.

"I know the only thing that matters, Ken. We won."

"But do you know how, sir?"

"Our sailors were better than theirs."

"And our commander. Villeneuve was no match for Nelson."

"Who?"

"Villeneuve. The French Admiral."

"I was forgetting," said Milton, running a hand across his lantern jaw. "Napoleon was a landlubber, wasn't he? The Emperor didn't fight any sea battles." He glanced over his shoulder. "Why did they put him up there instead of the French Admiral?"

\*    \*    \*

Pete Sylvester and his men had been remarkably efficient. By the time the detectives arrived at the warehouse, the rear of the lorry had been tipped hydraulically and the statue had been eased gently out on to a bed of sand. Sylvester waved the lorry off then turned to welcome Milton and Hurrell. Other detectives emerged from a second car.

"He's all yours, Commander," said Sylvester, gesturing.

"Thanks to you."

"It was much easier than I thought."

"Why?"

"Because he's not made of solid stone." The foreman kicked the base of the statue. "This part is, as you can see. But I think your men will find that Napoleon Bonaparte is largely made up of plaster."

"So he could have been carried by a balloon!" said Hurrell.

"Balloon?"

"Nothing, Mr Sylvester," said Milton, taking him by the shoulder to usher him away. "Thank you for all you've done. We won't detain you any further. As long as you're on stand-by for the important part of the operation." Sylvester looked puzzled. "Putting Nelson back up again."

The foreman chuckled. "I can't wait, sir. That's why we left the scaffolding in position. We're so confident that we'll get him back."

"You have my word on that."

Peter Sylvester went out and Milton motioned his men into action. They put down their cases and began an examination of the statue. The base was indeed made of solid stone but there was a hollow sound when they tapped the head and the shoulders. Dick Milton was merciless. He had no qualms about giving the order for execution. With a well-judged kick, one of the men struck the Emperor's head from his shoulders. The Commander peered inside the torso. He could see all the way down to the knees. He gave a grim smile.

"I bet he's got feet of clay as well!"

A uniformed constable entered with a large brown envelope.

"This is for you, Commander," he said, handing it over.

"Where did you get it?"

"Someone in the crowd thrust it at me."

"Didn't you get his name, man?"

"I had no time, sir. He said something in French and ran off."

"In French?" Milton looked at the envelope. "A ransom note."
He tore it open and quailed. Hurrell looked over his shoulder.

"Five million pounds!" he said with a whistle.

"Payable in unmarked notes of specific denominations."

"Is that the going rate for a stolen statue?"

"Look at the signature, Ken."

"I can see it, sir."

"Villeneuve."

It was over three hours before the call came. In the interim, Dick
Milton and Kenneth Hurrell left their colleagues to continue
their work at the warehouse and returned to Scotland Yard. The
first thing which the Commander had to endure was a searching
interrogation by the Commissioner. He limped back to the
security of his own office.

"He made it sound as if I'd stolen the bloody statue!"

Hurrell looked up from the book he'd been reading.

"What about the ransom?"

"He thinks we should pay it, Ken. If all else fails."

"Never!"

"That was my feeling. The Commissioner's argument was that
we're talking about a national treasure. In emotional terms, it's
worth far more than five million. He even had some crazy idea
about opening a public fund. A quid a head from five million
people. I ask you!" sighed Milton. "All I'm interested in is
nailing this gang."

"Me, too."

"No word from the lads while I was out?"

"Not a peep, sir. Somehow I don't think Napoleon is going to
yield up many clues. Seems to have been made out of the sort of
materials you could buy almost anywhere."

"In that case, we must concentrate on the dirigible. There can't
be all that many in existence. See if any were reported stolen. And

chase up the bomb squad. They should have analyzed those devices by now. My guess is that they were made by someone with Army training."

"With a friend who can fly an airship."

"Yes," said Milton, pacing the room. "The dirigible took Nelson away and brought Napoleon in. Or did it? Something's been bothering me, Ken. Remember when the statue was lowered from that column? The crane had to make a real effort to shift it."

"The weight made the ropes tighten."

"Yet Napoleon was as hollow as an Easter egg."

"It doesn't make sense."

The telephone rang to interrupt their cogitations. Milton put the receiver to his ear. He had no need to speak. A continuous stream of information gushed down the line and put a look of utter amazement on his face. Milton eventually asked a few questions, recoiling from the answers. When he put the phone down, he was in a daze. He lowered himself into a chair. Hurrell stood over him.

"Who was that?"

"Mr Crabtree of 'Gostelow and Crabtree'."

"I thought he was on holiday."

"He was. Tied up for two days in his own warehouse. And he wasn't the only one. His wife was there with him so that she couldn't raise the alarm. The pair of them have just been released."

"But we were in the warehouse ourselves."

"No, Ken. That wasn't Crabtree's place."

"Then why did Pete Sylvester take us there?"

"It was all part of the ruse," said Milton, thinking it through. "He pulled the wool well and truly over our eyes. I know that my namesake was blind but I don't think he could have blind as the pair of us."

"What do you mean, sir."

"Crabtree had never heard of Pete Sylvester."

Hurrell gulped. "I'm beginning to guess what happened."

"So am I, Ken. And I certainly don't relish the idea of telling the Commissioner. Peter Sylvester – or whoever he really is – has duped us good and proper. He pulled off the most astonishing trick in front of millions of viewers. And nobody saw it happening." He punched a fist into the palm of his other hand. "Where is the sod?" he said through gritted teeth. "More to the point, who is he?"

"I can tell you where he got his name from, sir."

"Can you?"

"Yes, sir," said Hurrell, opening the book he'd been studying. "While you were out, I read up on the Battle of Trafalgar."

"What's that got to do with it?"

"Everything. He's playing games with us. Do you recall the name of the French Admiral in the battle?"

"Yes. Villeneuve."

"But do you know what his Christian names were?"

"Who cares?"

"We ought to, sir," said Hurrell, putting the book in front of him. "Look at the name under that portrait of Villeneuve. Pierre-Charles-Jean-Baptiste-Silvestre Villeneuve. Do you see now? Pierre Sylvestre."

Milton grimaced. "Pete Sylvester!"


When the cargo had been unloaded on to a bed of sand, the lorry was taken away to be disposed of with its false number plates. The gang congratulated themselves on the success of their plan and celebrated with bottles of beer. There were ten of them in all, each of them due to pocket a half a million pounds when the ransom was paid. In the meantime, everything had been laid on at the warehouse. Food, drink, comfortable chairs, beds and two television sets had been installed. There was even a stolen microwave.

The preparation had been faultless. It was time to relax.

"We should have asked for more than five mill," said one man.

"We will," promised their leader. "Let them sweat it out first."

"What did old Crabtree say when you released him?"

"Swore like a trooper. Couldn't believe a trusted employee like me would turn on him and his wife." He glanced at his watch. "I expect he's told his tale of woe to the coppers by now and discovered why we nicked his lorry and scaffolding. Crabtree will have given them the name I used when I worked for him. While the boys in blue are scouring London for John French, I'm living it up here with my mates in Milton Keynes." He gave a harsh laugh. "Know the bit I enjoyed most? Having that detective call me 'Mr Sylvester'. I really fooled him and his sidekick."

They savoured the details of their crime and the hours oozed past with ease. Hamburgers were heated in the microwave. More beer flowed. A card game started. They lost all purchase on time and all sense of danger. When the police eventually burst in, the whole gang was taken by surprise. They fought hard but they were hopelessly outnumbered. All but their leader were dragged off to the waiting police vans.

Dick Milton and Kenneth Hurrell watched as their man was handcuffed before they questioned him. They looked him up and down.

"Did you really think you could get away with it?" asked Milton.

"I did get away with it!" insisted the other. "Nobody rumbled us."

"Until now, Mr Sylvester. Oh, I'm sorry, that's not your real name, is it? Nor is John French, the alias you used when you worked for Gostelow and Crabtree. No, your real name is Charles Villeneuve. Or, in plain English, good old Charlie Newton. Late of Her Majesty's armed forces. It takes a lot to get a dishonourable discharge, Charlie. Your service record makes colourful reading.

"How did you get on to me?" snarled the captive.

"Ken must take the credit for that, explained Milton with a nod at his companion. 'When you threw all those clues at him, he read up on the Battle of Trafalgar and learned about your namesake, Admiral Villeneuve, Pierre-Charles-Jean-Baptiste-Silvestre de Villeneuve. You were clearly obsessed with him. From his one name, you got three. Charlie Newton, your baptismal name, Pete Sylvester and John French, or, as you probably saw it, French Jean. I must confess, you used some cunning diversionary tactics.

Had us believing this whole business was planned and executed by some French extremists. Whereas you're really as English as boiled beef and carrots."

"There were other clues," said Hurrell. "A series of bombs, the use of an airship, the removal of a statue in broad daylight. All the hallmarks of a military operation. That's where we started looking for you, Charlie. Among the Army's drop-outs."

"It deserved to work!" protested Newton. "It did work."

"Only up to a point," said Milton, strolling across to the statue of Napoleon that lay on the sand. "Your stage management was superb. Worthy of Shaftesbury Avenue. Only instead of giving them live theatre, you blacked out the West End and offered them a radio play. They all thought a statue of Nelson was being hoisted away by an airship with one of Napoleon taking its place. But the simple truth is that old Horatio didn't move one inch during the night."

"No," added Hurrell, bending down to pull away the Emperor's fibreglass hat. "Now, then, what do we have here?" he asked in mock surprise. "I do believe's it's Lord Nelson's hat hidden underneath." He tapped it with his knuckles. "Solid stone. That won't come off."

"You didn't steal him from the column," said Milton with a grudging admiration. "You disguised him as Napoleon so that you could take him down legitimately – or so it appeared – today. No wonder you came so quickly when I called the office number of 'Gostelow and Crabtree'. You were ready and waiting. Now I see why you wanted us to keep the media off your back when you took the statue away. You didn't want them around when you made the switch. The fake Napoleon was already under the tarpaulin when you laid Lord Nelson beside him. All you had to do was to unload the plaster version and send your men off with the real statue. Ingenious."

Newton was sullen. "We could never have stolen it in the pitch dark. Too complicated. So I got myself a job with Crabtree because I knew he had the contract for cleaning Lord Nelson. While I was up there, I took exact measurements of the statue. I paid a sculptor to create a fibreglass Napoleon which would fit

Nelson like a glove. Nobody could tell the difference from down below."

"You covered every option," said Milton. "But made one mistake."

"Yes," agreed Hurrell. "You tried to be too clever. You played the Nelson game to the hilt and it was your undoing. You couldn't resist one final trick on that name. Villeneuve. New Town. You were taunting us, Charlie. Telling us exactly where you were hiding."

"There weren't all that many new towns to choose from," said the Commander. "Milton Keynes was the most obvious. We got the local police to check the footage on their motorway cameras and there you were. You'd painted out the name of 'Gostelow and Crabtree' on the lorry but you couldn't disguise a seventeen foot statue under a green tarpaulin. It showed up clearly, taking the exit for Milton Keynes. All we had to do was to check up on warehouse space that had been recently let and we had you. Caught in here like standing statues."

"You lost the battle," said Hurrell. "Just like Admiral Villeneuve."

They took him by the arms and marched him out. As they headed towards the police van, the Commander gave a ripe chuckle.

"It wasn't all a case of brilliant deduction," he admitted frankly. "Luck came into it. But, then, I've been due a bit of good fortune for some time and this was it. You were so busy playing games with your own name that you never thought to consider mine."

"Yours?" said Newton.

"Dick Milton. Poet by name and policeman by nature. And where did you decide to hole up and toast your success? The whole of Britain was at your mercy but you picked Milton Keynes. There's a poetic justice in that, Charlie. Thank you."

He shoved the prisoner hard into the rear of the police van.

"Any room in there for Lord Nelson?" he asked.

# THE AMOROUS CORPSE

*Peter Lovesey*

*Peter Lovesey (b.1936) rapidly established himself with his first novel about the Victorian detective Sergeant Cribb,* Wobble to Death *(1970). Apart from the Cribb series he has also written novels featuring the Prince of Wales (the future Edward VII) as detective in* Bertie and the Tinman *(1987),* Bertie and the Seven Bodies *(1990) and* Bertie and the Crime of Passion *(1993). He won the Crime Writers' Association Gold Dagger Award for the year's best novel with* The False Inspector Drew *(1982) set aboard the* S.S. Mauretania *in 1921. The following story, however, has a modern-day setting, and was specially written for this anthology.*

I'd been in CID six months when the case of the amorous corpse came up. What a break for a young detective constable: the "impossible" evidence of a near-perfect murder. You've probably heard of that Sherlock Holmes story about the dog that didn't bark in the night-time. Well, this was the corpse that made love in the morning, and I was the super sleuth on the case. I don't have a Dr Watson to tell it for me, so excuse me for blowing my own trumpet. There's no other way I can do it.

It began with a 999 call switched through to Salisbury nick at 9.25 one Monday morning. I was in the office waking myself up with a large espresso. My boss, a deadbeat DI called Johnny Horgan, never appeared before 10, so it was up to me to take some action. An incident had just occurred at a sub-post office in a village called Five Lanes, a short drive out of the city. The call from the sub-postmistress was taped, and is quite a classic in its way:

"Police, please . . . Hello, this is Miss Marshall, the sub-postmistress at Five Lanes. Can you kindly send someone over?"

"What's the emergency, Miss Marshall?"

"Well, I've got a gentleman with a gun here. He asked me to hand over all the money, and I refused. I don't care for that sort of behaviour."

"He's with you now?"

"Yes."

"Threatening you with a gun?"

"At this minute? Don't be silly. I wouldn't be phoning you, would I?"

"He's gone, then?"

"No. He's still here as far as I know."

"In the post office?"

"On the floor, I believe. I can't see him from where I'm speaking."

"Are you injured, Miss Marshall?"

"No. I'm perfectly all right, but you'd better send an ambulance for the man."

I decided CID should be involved from the beginning. Having told the switchboard to inform DI Horgan, I jumped into my Escort and burned rubber all the way to Five Lanes. I'm proud to say I got there two minutes before uniform showed up.

The crime scene was bizarre. The post office door was open. A man lay on the floor in front of the counter with a gun beside him. He was ominously still. *And two old women were buying stamps.* They must have walked around the body to reach the counter. The doughty Miss Marshall was serving them. Crazy, but I suppose they remembered doing things like that in the war. Business as usual.

We put tapes across the entrance to stop a queue forming for stamps and I took a deep breath and had a closer look at the git-em-up-guy. He was wearing a mask – not one of those Lone Ranger jobs, but a plastic President Nixon. I eased it away from his face and didn't care much for what I saw. I can't handle death scenes. I felt for a pulse. Nothing.

My boss, Johnny Horgan, arrived soon after and took over. He was supposed to be the rising star of Salisbury CID, an inspector at thirty-one, one of those fast-track clever dicks, only two years older than me. "Did you call the hospital?"

"I just got here, guv."

"The man is obviously dead. What's the ambulance outside for?"

The sub-postmistress spoke up. "I sent for that."

DI Horgan phoned for the meat wagon and a pathologist. Meanwhile, we got the full version of the hold-up from Miss Marshall:

"No one was here at the time. The man walked in wearing some kind of mask that made him look very peculiar."

"Nixon."

"I beg your pardon."

"Nixon, the ex-President of America."

"He didn't sound like an American. Whoever he is, we don't walk about wearing masks in Five Lanes, so I was suspicious. He pointed a gun and said, 'This is a gun.' I said, 'I can see that.' He said, 'Give us it, then.'"

"How did you respond?"

"I told him not to be ridiculous, to which he replied, 'Hey, come on. I'll blow your frigging head off.'"

"He actually said 'frigging'?"

"I may be unmarried, but I'm not mealy-mouthed, inspector. If he'd said something stronger, I'd tell you."

"So what did you say to that?"

"I said, 'Go on. Pull the trigger. You won't get the money if you do. I'm all locked in. And don't even think of trying to smash the glass.' He said, 'Lady, who do you think you are? It's not your dosh.' I said, 'It's not yours, either. You're not having it.' To which he replied, 'Jesus, are you simple? This is a stick-up.'"

"What happened then?"

"I led him to believe that I'd pressed an emergency button and the police were already on their way. He said, 'Frigging hell.' He took a step back from the counter and I thought for a moment he was about to give up and go away. Then he said, 'I'm not quitting. I'm not a quitter.'"

"Just like Nixon," I remarked.

My boss glared at me.

Miss Marshall continued, "He lurched forward again, and I wondered if he was the worse for drink, because he reached for the glass wall of my serving area, as if for support. Then he lowered the gun, I think, and said, 'Oh, shit.'" She gave Johnny Horgan a look that said how about that for a maiden lady.

"You hadn't touched him?"

"What are you suggesting? That I assaulted him? I was shut in here."

"And nobody else was in the shop?"

"Nobody except him and me. To my amazement, he swayed a little and started to sink down, as if his knees had given way. It was like watching a lift go down. He disappeared from view. The last thing I saw was the hand pressed against the glass. I expect there are fingerprints if you look."

"And then?"

"I looked at the clock. It was twenty past nine. Sitting on my stool here I had the same view I always do, of those notices about ParcelForce and the postage rates. The man had disappeared from sight. To tell you the truth, I half believed I'd imagined it all. It's a fear you live with when you run a post office, having to deal with an armed robber. I was tempted to unlock my door and have a look, but what if he was bluffing? So I stayed here and called 999."

"Good move."

The local pathologist, Dr Leggatt, arrived and didn't take long with the stethoscope. "Calling the ambulance was optimistic," he told us.

"Wasn't me," said Johnny Horgan. "I knew he'd croaked as soon as I saw him."

"You can't tell by looking."

I said, "I checked for a pulse."

"We all agree, then," said the pathologist with just a hint of sarcasm. "This is a dead man."

"But what of?" said Johnny Horgan.

Dr Leggatt answered curtly, "I'm a pathologist, inspector, not a psychic."

"Heart?"

"Weren't you listening?"

"He's not a young man."

"Do you know him, then?"

Fat chance. Johnny didn't know anyone in the county. He was fresh from Sussex, or Suffolk, or somewhere. He turned to me. I'm the local guy. But I was trying not to look at the body. Green in more senses than one, I was.

I saw my boss wink at the pathologist as he said, "His first one." His eyes returned to the corpse. "Fancy dropping dead in the middle of a hold-up."

"It could happen to anyone." Like most people in his line of work, Dr Leggatt had a fatalistic streak.

"Anyone stupid enough to hold up a post office."

"Anyone under stress," said Leggatt – and then asked Johnny with a deadpan look, "Do you sleep well?"

The DI didn't respond.

The doctor must have felt he had the high ground now, because he put some sharp questions to us about the conduct of the case. "Have the scene of crime lads finished?"

"All done," said Johnny.

"Pockets?"

"He wasn't carrying his calling card, if that's what you mean."

"What's the gun?"

"Gun? That's no gun," said Johnny, glad of the chance to get one back. "It's a toy. A plastic replica." He turned to the postmistress, who up to now had preferred to remain on her side of the counter. "Did you know the man, Miss Marshall?"

"I haven't seen him."

"But you told us—"

"Without the mask, I mean."

"You'd better come round here and look."

Miss Marshall unlocked, emerged from the serving area and took a long squint at the body. She was less troubled by the sight of death than me. "He's a stranger to me. And I didn't know it was a toy gun, either."

"You were very brave," Johnny told her, and muttered in an aside to Dr Leggatt and me, "Silly old cow."

He went on to say more loudly that he'd like her to come to the police station and make a statement.

"What did you call her?" Leggatt asked, after she had been escorted to the police car.

"I meant it," said Johnny. "She might have had her stupid head blown away for the sake of Post Office Counters Limited."

Leggatt gave Johnny a look that was not too admiring. "What happened to good citizenship, then? Some of you coppers are born cynics. You've no idea what it takes for a woman to stand up to a gunman."

"Have you?" Johnny chanced it.

"As it happens, yes. My sister stood up to one – and didn't get much thanks from you people. You don't know how often Miss Marshall will wake up screaming, reliving what happened this morning."

"Hold on, doc," said Johnny. "I said she was brave."

The pathologist didn't prolong it. "If you don't mind, I'd like to get this body to the mortuary."

"Yes, and we've got to find his next of kin," said Johnny.

When he said "we", he meant me. He'd already decided there wasn't anything in it for him.

I may be squeamish with dead bodies, but I'm fearless with the living, especially blondes. It was the day after the hold-up and I'd come to a flat in Salisbury, the home of a recently released prisoner. Jack Soames had served four years in Portland for armed robbery of a building society. Check your form runners first.

The chick at the door said he wasn't in.

"Any idea where he is?"

"Couldn't tell you."

"When did you last see him?"

"Yesterday morning. What's up?"

Bra-less and quivering under a thin T-shirt, she looked far too tasty to be shacking up with a middle-aged robber. But I kept my thoughts to myself.

"Are you a close friend of his, miss?"

She made a little sound of impatience. "What do you think?"

"What's your name?"

"Zara."

"And you spent last night alone, Zara?"

"That's my business."

"Jack wasn't here?"

She nodded.

"When he went out yesterday morning, did he say where he was going?"

"I'm his crumpet, not his ma."

I smiled at that. "He could still treat you like a human being."

"Jack's all right," said Zara. "I've got no complaints."

Don't count on it, I thought, sleeping with an ex-con.

Zara said anxiously, "He hasn't had an accident, has he?"

"Does he carry a gun?"

"What?"

"Don't act the innocent, love. We both know his form. Was he armed when he left here?"

"Course he wasn't. He's going straight since he got out."

It was time to get real. "There was an armed raid at a sub-post office yesterday and a man died."

"The postmaster?"

"No, the robber. It's just possible he was Jack Soames. We're checking on everyone we know."

"Oh, my God!"

"Would you be willing to come to the hospital and tell us if it's him?"

Zara looked, squeezed her eyes shut, and looked again. I watched her. She was easier to look at than the corpse.

"That's him, poor lamb."

"Jack Soames? You're certain?"

"Positive."

I nodded to the mortuary assistant, who covered the dead face again.

Outside, I thanked Zara and asked her where she wanted me to drive her.

She asked, "Will I have to move out of Jack's place?"

"Who paid the rent?"

"He did."

"Then I reckon you will."

"I can go to me Mum's place. What killed him?"

"We'll find out this afternoon, when they do the PM."

In her grief, she got a bit sentimental. "I used to call him Jack the Robber. Like . . ." Her voice trailed off.

I nodded. "So you knew he was an ex-con?"

"That was only through the toffee-nosed bitch he married." Zara twisted her mouth into the shape of a cherry-stone. "Felicity. She claimed she didn't know she was married to a bank robber. Where did she think the folding stuff was coming from? She was supposed to give him an alibi and she ratted on him. He done four years through her."

"And when he came out he met you."

"Worse luck."

"I wouldn't say that," I tried to console her. "It's not your fault he went back to crime, is it?"

She didn't answer, so I decided not to go up that avenue.

She said, "What did he want to do a piddling post office for?"

I shrugged.

"Where did you say it was?"

"Five Lanes."

"Never heard of it. He told me he was going up the Benefits Office."

"It's a village three miles out. That's where he was at nine-fifteen yesterday."

"Get away," said Zara, pulling a face. "He was still in bed with me at nine-fifteen."

"That can't be true, Zara."

She was outraged. "You accusing me of lying?"

"Maybe you were asleep. You just thought he was beside you."

"Asleep? We was at it like knives. He was something else after a good night's sleep, was Jack." The gleam in her big blue eyes carried total conviction. "It must have been all of ten o'clock before he left the house."

"*Ten*? But he was dead by then."

"No way."

"How do you know?"

"Me watch."

"It must be wrong."

She looked down at her wrist. "How come it's showing the same time as the clock in your car?"

My boss was unimpressed. "Why is she lying?"

"I'm not sure she is," I told him.

"How can you believe her, dickhead, when you saw the body yourself at just after nine-twenty-five?"

"She's got nothing to gain from telling lies."

"She's muddled about the time. She was in no state to check if they were humping each other."

"She's very clear about it, guv."

"Get this in your brain, will you? Jack Soames was dead by nine-twenty."

"Would you like to talk to her yourself?"

"No, I bloody wouldn't. You say she identified the body?"

"Yes."

"Well, then."

I had to agree. Something was wrong with Zara's memory.

Horgan made the first constructive suggestion I'd heard from him. "Find the wife. She's the next of kin. She'll need to identify him."

I didn't fancy visiting that mortuary again, but he was right. I traced Felicity Soames routinely through the register of electors, a slight, tired-looking woman in her fifties, who lived alone in a semi on the outskirts of Salisbury and worked as a civil servant. She was not much like the vindictive creature Zara had portrayed.

"I don't want any more to do with him," she said at first. "We separated."

"But you're not divorced?"

"Not yet."

"Then you're still the next of kin."

For the second time that morning, I stood well back while the mortuary assistant went through the formalities.

Felicity confirmed that the body was her husband's.

Zara's steamy sex with Jack that Monday morning was beginning to look like a fantasy, but I couldn't forget the sparkle in her eyes as she spoke of it.

"Right, son," said Johnny Horgan when I told him I had lingering doubts. "There's one final check you can make. The post-mortem is at two. I'm not going to make it myself. Frankly, it's not high priority any more, one old robber who dropped dead."

My knees went weak. "You want me to . . . ?"

He grinned. "There's a first time for everything. Have an early lunch. I wouldn't eat too much, though."

"I'm sure the body is Jack Soames," I said. "I don't really need to be there."

"You do, lad. You're standing in for me. Oh, and make sure they take a set of fingerprints."

My hand shook as I held my mug of tea in the mortuary office, and that was *before*.

"So you're the police presence?" Dr Leggatt, the pathologist, said with a dubious look at me.

I nodded. This was a low-key autopsy. The man had died in furtherance of a crime, but there was nothing suspicious about the death, so instead of senior detectives, SOCOs, forensic scientists and photographers, there was just me to represent law and order.

Cosy.

"I'm supposed to go back with a set of fingerprints."

"No problem," said Dr Leggatt. "We'll start with that. You can help Norman if you like."

Norman was his assistant.

"I'd rather keep my distance."

"Fair enough. Shall we go in, then?"

I fixed my gaze on the wall opposite while the fingerprints were taken. Norman brought them over to me and said I could stand closer if I wished.

I nodded and stayed where I was. They were still examining the body for external signs when I started to feel wobbly. I found a chair.

"Can you see from there?" the pathologist called across.

"As much as I want to."

"Stand on the chair if you wish."

"Coronary," said Dr Leggatt when he finally removed his latex gloves.

"Natural causes, then?"

He smiled at the phrase. "Any middle-aged bloke who holds up post offices lays himself open to a fatal adrenaline response and sudden death. I'd call it an occupational hazard."

Some people call me cussed, others pig-headed. I don't particularly mind. These are qualities you need in police work. I refused to draw a line under the case.

Everything checked except Zara's statement. The fingerprints taken at the autopsy matched the prints we had from Soames's file at the National Identification Service. His mugshot was exactly like the man his wife and girlfriend had identified and the pathologist had dissected.

I tried discussing it with my boss, but Johnny was relentless. "Constable, you're making a horse's arse of yourself. Soames is dead. You attended the autopsy. What other proof do you want?"

"If he had a twin, or a double—"

"We'd have heard. Drop it, lad. Zara may be a charmer, but she's an unreliable witness."

"I know it sounds impossible—"

"So leave it out."

I was forced to press on without official back-up. I won't bore you with all the theories I concocted and dismissed. In the end it came down to whether Zara could be believed. And after hours of wrestling with the problem I thought of a way of checking her statement. She'd told me Soames had said he was going to the Benefits Office after he left her. If *they* had a record of his visit – *after he'd died* – Zara would be vindicated.

I called the Benefits people and got a helpful woman who offered to check their records of Monday's interviews.

She called back within the hour. Zilch.

I was down, down there with the *Titanic*.

Then something triggered in my brain. I asked the woman, "Do you have security cameras?"

"Sure."

"Inside the office?"

"Yes."

I drove down there and started watching videotapes.


"Guv, I'd like you to look at this."

"What is it?"

"Pretty sensational I'd call it."

I ran the video. Two sergeants from CID who remembered Soames from before he went to prison came in to look. The screen showed tedious views of people waiting their turn to speak to the staff. I pressed "Fast Forward", then slowed it to "Play".

"Look behind the rows of seats."

A slight man with straight, silver-streaked hair came into shot and hesitated. He stared at one of the desks where a young woman was being interviewed, partially screened from the rest of the room. He took a step to the right, apparently to get a better view of what was going on.

I touched the "Freeze Frame" and held a mugshot of Soames against the screen. "How about that, guys?"

"My God, it could be him."

"No question," said one of the sergeants. "The face, the way he moves, everything."

"And look at the time."

The digits at the bottom right of the screen were frozen at 10:32.

"All right. Joke over," said Johnny. "How did you fix it?"

"I didn't. This is on the level."

"Run it again."

White-faced and muttering, my boss continued to stare at the screen until the figure of Soames turned away and walked out of shot.

"That man died at 9.20. It can't be."

"It must be."

We spent the next half-hour debating the matter. Johnny Horgan, desperate to make sense of the impossible, dredged up a theory involving false identification. Zara had lied when she came to view the body: Soames had put her up to it, seeing an opportunity to "die" and get a new name, and maybe plastic surgery, before resuming his criminal career. She, the dumb blonde, had stupidly blown his cover when I called on her.

It was a daft theory. How had he persuaded his wife Felicity, who had shopped him, to join in the deception? And why would he be so foolish as to parade in front of cameras in the Benefits Office?

"Anyroad," Johnny said when his theory was dead in the water, "we can't waste time on it. The post office job was the crime. Attempted robbery. There's no argument that the robber died of a coronary, whether he was Jack Soames or bloody Bill Sikes. The case is closed."

For me, it was still wide open. While the arguments were being tossed around, my mind was on a different tack. What had Soames been up to in the Benefits Office? He hadn't been interviewed, so he didn't collect a payout.

When the others had left the room, I ran the video again and made a stunning discovery. There *had* been a crime, and it was far more serious than a botched hold-up. Zara hadn't lied to me; hadn't even made a mistake. Impossible, it had seemed, because none of us made the connection. I slipped out of the building.

I found Felicity Soames in her place of work – at one of the desks in the Benefits Office. "It took a while for the penny to drop," I told her. "I was in here this morning to examine the security videos and I didn't spot you."

"Were you expecting me to be here?"

"To be honest, no. You told me you were a civil servant, but I didn't link it with this. You must have had a shock like a million volts when your husband walked in here on Monday."

She flinched at the memory. "I was terrified. He stood staring at me, putting the fear of God in me."

"We have it on tape. I watched it five times before I saw you behind your desk. We were all so gobsmacked at seeing him alive that we didn't give anyone else a look."

"He wasn't there for an interview. He just came in to check on me."

"To let you know he was out."

"Yes, I've lived in terror of him for four years. I put him away, you know. My evidence did it."

"And you're all alone in the world?"

"Yes."

"No, you're not, love. You've got a big brother. And you called him and poured out your troubles."


At the mortuary, I asked to see the body of the post office robber.

"I had the impression you'd seen enough of him already," said Dr Leggatt, smiling.

"Would you get him out, please?"

The pathologist sighed and called to his assistant. "Norman, fetch out number seven, the late Mr Soames, would you?"

I said mildly, "Jack Soames isn't the post office robber."

The doctor hesitated. "How do you work that out?"

"But I'd like to see his body, just the same."

Leggatt exchanged a world-weary look with Norman, who went to one of the chilled cabinets and pulled out the drawer.

It was empty.

Leggatt snapped his fingers. "Of course. He's gone."

"Not here?"

"Storage problems. I asked the undertaker to collect him."

"Along with the real post office robber, I suppose?"

Leggatt said, "You're way ahead of me."

"I don't think so, doctor. The man who held up the post office probably died of a heart attack triggered by stress, just as you suggested."

"What a relief!" Leggatt said with irony. But he wasn't looking as comfortable as he intended.

"You came out to Five Lanes and collected him. On the same day, Jack Soames, recently released from prison, decided to let his wife know he was at liberty. After a passionate lie-in with his girlfriend, he made his way to the Benefits Office where Felicity worked. She was terrified, just as he wished her to be. He had a four-year score to settle. When he'd gone, she phoned you."

"Me? Why me?" said Leggatt in high-pitched surprise that didn't throw me in the least.

"Because she's your sister, doctor. She's really suffered for blowing the whistle on her husband. Waking up screaming, night after night, all because she stood up to him. You told us about that after DI Horgan made his insensitive remark about the sub-postmistress."

"Idiot," said Leggatt, but he was talking about himself. "Yes, that comment angered me at the time. I'd forgotten. So much has happened since. And you made the connection?"

He'd virtually put up his hand to the crime. Elated, I held myself in check. "I think you saw an opportunity and seized it. You'd already taken in the body of the post office robber, a middle-aged man with greying hair, not totally unlike your brother-in-law. No one seemed to know who he was, so he was heaven-sent. You had a marvellous chance to kill Soames and end your sister's suffering without anyone knowing. You're a pathologist. You know enough to kill a man swiftly and without any obvious signs. An injection, perhaps? I think you believed your sister was in real danger."

"She was."

"Maybe," I said.

Leggatt shook his head. "There was no 'maybe' about it. He was waiting outside the Benefits Office for her. He wasn't there to make a scene. He intended violence."

"And you approached him, invited him into your car, killed him and drove him here. You chose a time when Norman was out of the mortuary – possibly at night – to unload the body into a drawer, the drawer supposedly holding the bank robber. You changed the tag on the toe."

"You watch too much television," Leggatt commented.

"When I came here with Zara, you wheeled Soames out. You knew I wasn't likely to take a close look at the face, seeing that I'd been so troubled by the sight of death. Anyway, I hadn't taken a proper look at the real robber."

"Your inspector did."

"Yes, but he delegated everything to me. He's new to our patch. He didn't know Soames, except from mugshots, so when he saw the security video from the Benefits Office he had Soames imprinted on his memory."

"You've got Soames on video? Thank God for that."

I nodded. "I expect your defence will make good use of it. Extenuating circumstances – is that the phrase?"

"Professional misconduct is another," said Leggatt. "Doctors who kill don't get much leniency from the courts."

"You carried out the autopsy on Soames, deciding, of course, that he died of a coronary, and it wouldn't be necessary to send any of the organs for forensic examination. But what did you plan to do with the other body – the poor old codger who dropped dead when the sub-postmistress looked him in the eye?"

"Not a serious problem," said Leggatt. "This is a teaching hospital and bodies are donated for medical research. We keep them here in the mortuary. It could all be fixed with paperwork."

"I wonder if we'll ever discover who he was," I said, little realizing that it would become my job for the next six weeks. A DC who solves an impossible crime doesn't get much thanks from his superior. The reverse, I discovered. I'm still looking for promotion.

# AFTERWORD

## Impossible Crimes: A Quick History

### Mike Ashley

The impossible crime story has been around as long as the mystery story has existed. The gothic mystery, so popular in the late eighteenth century, abounded in stories of purportedly haunted rooms, though the solution usually related to a secret passage. Such was the case in Ann Radcliffe's *The Mysteries of Udolpho* (1794) and even E.T.A. Hoffmann's "Mademoiselle de Scudari" (1819), even though the latter gives some pretext to being a genuine locked-room murder.

The first real locked-room mystery that did not rely on a secret passage – despite its title – was "A Passage in the Secret History of an Irish Countess" by Joseph Sheridan Le Fanu published in *The Dublin University Magazine* for November 1838. Le Fanu is best remembered today for his macabre novels like *Uncle Silas* (1864), which also includes a variant on his locked-room idea, and the vampire story "Carmilla" (1872). The only feature that Le Fanu's story lacks is that of a detective intent on solving the mystery. That was soon provided by Edgar Allan Poe who, in "The Murders in the Rue Morgue" (*Graham's Magazine*, April 1841), provided the firm footing for the detective story. Needless to say Poe's story is grotesque and bizarre, but it is a *bona fide* locked-room mystery.

A few other locked-room stories appeared during the mid-nineteenth century, perhaps the best known being "A Terribly Strange Bed" by Wilkie Collins (*Household Words*, 24 April 1852). The story was published by Charles Dickens, and I'm a little surprised that Dickens did not turn his hand to the impossible crime story as he would certainly have brought considerable ingenuity to it. By and large the mid-Victorian impossible crime story retains too many trappings of the gothic era and, though original at the time, today seem a little too trite. That's the main reason I have not reprinted them – beyond the fact that most are easily available in the authors' collected stories. The only one I have selected is from *Out of His Head* (1862) by Thomas Bailey Aldrich, which is both original and feels far more modern than its contemporaries.

The real explosion in the impossible crime story came in 1892 as a result of two significant publications. The first was a novel, *The Big Bow Mystery* by Israel Zangwill, serialized in the London evening paper *The Star*. This is the first full-length novel written solely round a murder in a locked room. Zangwill had thought about the problem for several years before he wrote the novel and his creativity and originality shows. Gone are the secret passages and other devices. Here was a novel where the crime had been committed with incredible ingenuity and had to be solved with equal skill and deduction. Needless to say during its serialization readers of *The Star* wrote in suggesting their own solutions – none of which was right – and the thrill and enticement of the locked-room mystery became only too evident.

The other publication was a Sherlock Holmes story, "The Adventure of the Speckled Band" (*The Strand Magazine*, February 1892). The immediate success of the Holmes stories in *The Strand* is well known. Arthur Conan Doyle was fascinated with the idea of unusual crimes, and what makes the Holmes stories stand out is that all of the crimes are bizarre, a real test for Holmes's deductive powers. Holmes had no interest in the run-of-the-mill crime. Perhaps, because of that, it is surprising that there are not more impossible crimes amongst the Holmes canon. Strictly there are only two, the other being "The Problem of Thor Bridge" (*The Strand Magazine*, February 1922) where a murder is committed but no visible weapon.

The *Big Bow* and "Speckled Band", coming together just at the time when the popular fiction magazine was blossoming, opened the door for the impossible crime story. The late Victorian and Edwardian writers loved them. Conan Doyle wrote one further example, "The Story of the Lost Special" (*The Strand Magazine*, August 1898) where a train vanishes from a stretch of rail. L.T. Meade produced ever more bizarre solutions to her crimes, especially those collected in *A Master of Mysteries* (1898).

The next major breakthrough, however, came in 1905. In America the author Jacques Futrelle published "The Problem of Cell 13" as a serial in *The Boston American* (30 October – 5 November 1905), challenging the newspaper's readers to solve the story. It introduced Futrelle's character Professor S.F.X. Van Dusen, known as the Thinking Machine, who has such a power of deduction that he is able to resolve any problem, no matter how impossible it seems. In this first story he set himself the challenge of escaping from a locked cell in a high-security prison, kept constantly under watch. How he did it remains one of the most remarkable stories ever written. Over the next six years Futrelle wrote several dozen Thinking Machine stories, not all of which appeared in book-form. They included stories in which things disappear from guarded rooms, a car vanishes from a stretch of road, and even an entire house disappears. It was such a tragedy that Futrelle was killed when the *Titanic* sank in 1912.

It was also in 1905 that Edgar Wallace published *The Four Just Men*, along with much publicity and gimmickry. Wallace had published the book himself and deliberately left the ending open, offering a prize to the reader who could solve the baffling murder of a man in broad daylight surrounded (but not touched) by policemen in a locked room. Needless to say the redoubtable Edgar Wallace employed the locked-room idea many times in his books and stories, with perhaps the most ingenious being in *The Crimson Circle* (1922), where a man is found gassed in a locked room.

Soon after *The Four Just Men* came one of the most popular of all locked-room mysteries, *The Mystery of the Yellow Room* (1908). The author was Gaston Leroux, best known for *The Phantom of the Opera* (1911). The novel, which is still in print, is one of the best developed of all locked-room deaths, and is all the more fun because of the rivalry between the detective, Frederick

Larson, and the newspaper reporter, Joseph Rouletabille, to solve the crime.

If the impossible crime story needed any final seal of approval it came in 1911 with the publication of *The Innocence of Father Brown* by G.K. Chesterton. The stories had already caused a sensation in *The Story-Teller*, where they had started to appear from the September 1910 issue. The editor of *The Story-Teller*, Arthur Spurgeon, was so impressed by the stories that he announced them with the proclamation that: "the plots are so amazing and so cleverly worked out that I believe they will prove to be the best detective stories of our time." There were in total five volumes of Father Brown stories, many of them falling into the category of the impossible crime, especially those in *The Incredulity of Father Brown* (1926).

By another remarkable instance of synchronicity, at the same time as Father Brown appeared so did Melville Davisson Post's Uncle Abner. Although the first collection, *Uncle Abner, Master of Mysteries*, did not appear until 1918, the stories were being run in *The Saturday Evening Post* and other magazines from 1911 on. Alas, all too few of them are miracle murders, though the best, "The Doomdorf Mystery", which David Renwick refers to and which is reprinted in this anthology, most certainly was.

Chesterton and Post provide the link across the Great War and into the 1920s. There were less impossible crime stories written during this period than one might expect, though the form was well enough established for P.G. Wodehouse to spoof it in the perfectly acceptable "The Education of Detective Oakes" (*Pearson's Magazine*, December 1914), where a man in a locked room appears to have been killed by snake venom.

S.S. van Dine, the creator of Philo Vance, gave it a good stab in *The Canary Murder Case* (1927) and later novels. Agatha Christie also turned her mercurial mind to the matter. Several of the stories in *The Thirteen Problems* (1932), such as "The Blue Geranium" (*The Story-Teller*, December 1929) are seemingly impossible crimes which Miss Marple is able to solve simply by applying her mind.

It was now, though, that the real doyen of the impossible crime story emerged onto the scene – John Dickson Carr. Carr had started writing when he was at Haverford College, Pennsylvania, placing stories in the college magazine, *The Haverfordian*. His third story, "The Shadow of the Goat" (November–December 1926) was his first locked-room murder and also introduced his detective Henri Bencolin. It's an ingenious crime involving both a disappearance from a locked room and a murder in a house both locked and guarded. Carr was perfecting his craft from an early age – he was only twenty when these appeared. A later Bencolin serial, "Grand Guignol" (*The Haverfordian*, March–April 1929) was expanded into Carr's first novel, *It Walks By Night* (1930).

Over the next forty years Carr was to write over fifty novels featuring impossible crimes, plus numerous short stories. It is impossible to list them all here, but I must single out a few. Probably the classic of them all is *The Hollow Man* (1935), also published under the title *The Three Coffins*. When, in 1980, Edward Hoch conducted a poll amongst a panel of seventeen experts on mystery fiction, this novel came out head-and-shoulders above the rest. It involves two impossible murders – a death in a locked and guarded room and a death in a snow-covered street with no footprints. The book features Carr's best known detective, Dr Gideon Fell, and is notorious for the fact that Carr stops the action at a crucial point to allow Fell to deliver a lecture about the locked-room crime and the various ways in which it can be achieved. The book – and the lecture – remain models of their kind.

There were three other Carr novels in the experts' top ten. *The Crooked Hinge* (1938), another Gideon Fell novel, came in fourth. This provides a slightly less satisfying but nevertheless intriguing solution to a murder in the sand with none but the victim's footprints. *The Judas Window* (1938), published under his Carter Dickson alias, and mentioned by David Renwick in his Fore-word, was voted fifth. I personally rate this as Carr's best constructed novel – ingenious, surprisingly plausible, and rivet-ing. It features Carr's detective Henry Merrivale, as does *The Ten Teacups* (1937), also known as *The Peacock Feather Murders*, and tenth on the experts' list. In fact the Henry Merrivale mysteries include some of the most unusual impossible murders such as those in *The Plague Court Murders* (1934), *The Unicorn Murders* (1935) and *The Red Widow Murders* (1935).

Carr also used the impossible crime idea in many short stories. Some of the best are found in the collection *The Department of Queer Complaints* (1940) featuring a new detective, Colonel March. It is one of the those stories, "The Silver Curtain", that I have reprinted here. Perhaps one of the best examples of misdirection in misleading the reader arises in the novella *The Third Bullet* (1937) in which three bullets are fired in a locked room, each from a different gun, and yet the only other person in the room did not have the murder weapon.

You would think that with the amount of books Carr produced, and with his profundity of ideas, no one else would attempt an impossible crime story in his shadow. But the reverse happened. Rather than cornering the market, Carr stimulated it. The 1930s was a golden era for the miracle crime. Ellery Queen, which was both the name of the detective and of the authors (the pseudonym adopted by cousins Frederic Dannay and Manfred Lee) produced two remarkable locked-room mysteries: *The Chinese Orange Mystery* (1934) and *The Door Between* (1937). The magician Clayton Rawson, creator of the character The Great Merlini, specialized in impossible crimes and produced some of the best, starting with *Death From a Top Hat* (1938) in which a whole bunch of magicians are involved. His other novels are *The Footprints on the Ceiling* (1939), *The Headless Lady* (1940) – which involves an escape from an electrically controlled, double-locked room, and *No Coffin for the Corpse* (1942). Rawson, Dannay and Carr often used to challenge each other to come up with the most impossible situations for an impossible crime. On one occasion Carr challenged Rawson to explain how a man could enter a telephone booth and disappear. That story, "From Off the Face of the Earth", is the one I've selected for this anthology.

Another of the Ellery Queen circle, Anthony Boucher, did not write anywhere near enough locked-room mysteries as he would have liked, though both *Nine Times Nine* (1940), as H.H. Holmes, and *The Case of the Solid Key* (1941) are competent and ingenious. For ingenuity, though, and barefaced bravado, it was difficult to beat the pseudonymous Hake Talbot. In the early 1940s he produced two novels on a par with the skilled plotting of Carr and the audaciousness of Rawson. Both *The Hangman's Handyman* (1942) and especially *Rim of the Pit* (1944) confuse the reader with all manner of apparent supernatural paraphernalia before the real solutions to the impossible murders are revealed. If I tell you that in one book a man is cursed and his body immediately decomposes, whilst in another an apparent, wind-walker (Wendigo) menaces a snowbound house, you'll have some idea of the thrill of these novels. Professor Douglas Greene, a noted expert in the history of crime fiction, has called *Rim of the Pit* "one of the most extraordinary tales of mystery ever written."

Ethel Lina White produced a minor masterpiece in *The Wheel Spins* (1936), in which a woman disappears from a moving train. The book is probably better remembered as the film *The Lady Vanishes*, made in 1938.

Unfairly forgotten today, though thankfully his works are gradually being rediscovered, is Clyde B. Clason who wrote a series of novels featuring the historian and amateur sleuth, Professor Theocritus Westborough. Seven of these novels feature impossible crimes of which the best is *The Man From Tibet* (1938) in which a man, locked inside a room full of Tibetan exhibits, apparently dies from a heart attack.

The British composer Bruce Montgomery also wrote mysteries as Edmund Crispin. He was the creator of the amateur sleuth Gervase Fen, who is an Oxford don and a literary critic. The first of his investigations, *The Case of the Gilded Fly* (1944), involved a murder in a room under constant observation. Perhaps his most audacious is *The Moving Toyshop* (1946), in which an entire shop disappears.

Author and lawyer Michael Gilbert who, amongst other things, was involved in drawing up the will of Raymond Chandler, began his writing career with an impossible murder, *Close Quarters* (1947), the first of his Inspector Hazelrigg novels. Soon after the brothers Peter and Antony Shaffer, writing as Peter Antony, produced a delightful locked-room mystery with *The*

*Woman in the Wardrobe* (1951). By and large, though, the locked-room mystery seemed to fall from favour in the fifties, and it only began to re-emerge in the sixties and seventies.

Much of the modern delight in the art can be ascribed to two writers – Bill Pronzini and Edward D. Hoch. Pronzini is a highly versatile writer producing novels and stories in several fields (science fiction, mystery fiction, westerns, horror) but he is probably best known for his books featuring the Nameless Detective. Several of these involve locked-room murders, starting with *Hoodwink* (1981), which won the Shamus Award of the Private Eye Writers of America. In fact it includes two locked-room murders, of which the victim killed by an axe in a locked shed has the most ingenious solution. *Scattershot* (1982) goes one better and has three impossible crimes – a stabbing in a locked car, a shooting in a cottage under observation and the theft of a ring from a guarded room!

Although Edward Hoch has written novels, he is the master of the short story, having written over 800 since his first in 1955; and a large number of these are impossible crimes. In fact he has written one long series devoted to nothing but impossible crimes. These are the stories narrated by his New England doctor, Sam Hawthorne, who reminisces back to his early days in the twenties and thirties, where an impossible crime seemed to happen three or four times a year! The series is still running in *Ellery Queen's Mystery Magazine* (*EQMM*). The early stories have been collected as *Diagnosis: Impossible* (1996) and I have reprinted a more recent one in this book.

However Hoch does not confine his impossible murders to just one series. He has several series on the go at once and a miracle crime is as likely to crop up in several of them. This happened from the start with his first series character Simon Ark. In "The Man From Nowhere" (*Famous Detective Stories*, June 1956) a man is found stabbed to death in the snow with no footprints around him. In the Inspector Rand story "The Spy Who Walked Through Walls" (*EQMM*, November 1966), top-secret blueprints disappear from a guarded office. There's the Nick Velvet story, "The Theft of the Bermuda Penny" (*EQMM*, June 1975), where a man vanishes from a speeding car, even though his seat belt is still fastened! There's the Captain Leopold story, "Captain Leopold and the Impossible Murder" (*EQMM*, December 1976), where the man driving alone in the car in front in a traffic jam turns out to be strangled. The title of the Ben Snow story "The Vanished Steamboat" (*EQMM*, May 1984) tells it all. And then there's the non-series story "The Impossible 'Impossible Crime'" (*EQMM*, April 1968), where a man is shot in a snow-bound hut, with no one else around for hundreds of miles except for one other who was asleep at the time. Hoch's versatility seems boundless and I have no doubt he will create plenty more impossible crimes in the years to come.

In addition to Pronzini and Hoch there are plenty of writers prepared to turn a hand to the impossible crime. Michael Innes dabbled with it, with a murder in the library in *Appleby and Honeybath* (1983). Kate Wilhelm defied computer security for her suffocation in a lift and drowning in a jacuzzi in *Smart House* (1989). Michael Dibdin pits Inspector Zen's wits in *Vendetta* (1990) where a murder takes place in a high security fortress with video cameras everywhere. Whilst that doyen of the historical mystery, Paul Doherty, has shown the influence of John Dickson Carr in a number of his novels. There's a murder in a locked church in *Satan in St Mary's* (1986); a murder in full view of a crowd with no visible agency in *The Angel of Death* (1989); a murder in a locked room in the Tower of London in *The White Rose Murders* (1991) written as Michael Clynes; and the magnificent disappearance of an entire ship's watch in *By Murder's Bright Light* (1994), written as Paul Harding.

And we must not forget David Renwick's "Jonathan Creek" who solves some of the most bizarre and idiosyncratic crimes on television.

There is no doubt that the future of the impossible crime story is in safe hands as I hope the stories in this anthology have shown. If this anthology has intrigued you I strongly urge you to seek out *Locked Room Murders and Other Impossible Crimes* by Robert Adey (Minneapolis' Crossover Press, 1991), which is a remarkably detailed survey and bibliography of the field. You may also want to track down other anthologies, alas all out of print, but which give a flavouring of impossible crimes: *The Locked Room Reader* edited by Hans Stefan Santesson (New York: Random House, 1968); *Tantalizing Locked Room Murders* edited by Isaac Asimov, Charles G. Waugh and Martin Harry Greenberg (New York: Walker, 1982); *All But Impossible!* edited by Edward D. Hoch (New Haven: Ticknor & Fields, 1981); *Locked Room Puzzles* edited by Martin H. Greenberg and Bill Pronzini (Chicago, Academy Chicago, 1986); *Death Locked In* edited by Douglas Greene and Robert Adey (IPL, 1987) and *The Art of the Impossible* edited by Jack Adrian and Robert Adey (London: Xanadu, 1990). I have tried to avoid duplicating too many stories from these books, although as they are all out of print, there are some gems that beg to be reprinted again. I hope your quest is not impossible.

# COPYRIGHT AND ACKNOWLEDGMENTS

My thanks to Ken Cowley, Richard Lupoff, Bill Pronzini, Edward Hoch and Peter Tremayne for their help and support through this project. My thanks also to David Renwick for his Foreword. And a special thanks to Robert Adey for his invaluable book *Locked Room Murders and Other Impossible Crimes* (Minneapolis: Crossover Press, 1991), which was an ever trusty guide through the minefield of the impossible crime.